THE MAN WHO WALKED OUT OF ISABELLE

J. C. Bourg

ISBN-13: 9780991007608
ISBN-10: 0991007603
Library of Congress Control Number: 2013953386
CreateSpace Independent Publishing Platform
North Charleston, South Carolina

1954 Indochinese Peninsula

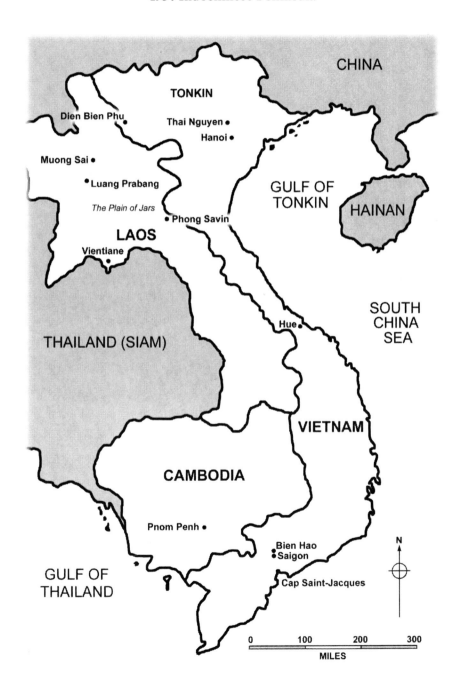

For Sharon.

Preface

Isabelle is a historic novel. I've attempted to portray an accurate but fictional account of the multi-cultural players that flowed through the chaotic times and battlefields of various Indochina wars. The cast is fictitious. I've extrapolated their imaginary stories from events that did occur or possibly might have. Ngo Dinh Diem, his younger brother Nhu and Nhu's wife, Madame Nhu are historic characters, their dramatized portrayal imagined.

I used the term Hmong, *Montagnards*, Meo, Moi, and Tai to identify the independent Asian ethnic group of the mountainous regions of Vietnam and Laos. In Book Three I note that Meo is a dated term and highly offensive to the Hmong people. Its early use intended for historic accuracy, no offense was intended.

Book One

Transition

*"Legionnaires, you became soldiers in order to die,
and I shall send you where one dies."*
- General de Négrier - December1883
Addressing French Foreign Legion troops
departing for Tonkin, (northern Vietnam).

CHAPTER ONE

It was an unusually warm Saigon summer's night in 1955. In the depths of a dark opium den, a telephone rang. The small room's only occupant lay in a drug induced state of euphoria bordering on comatose. The smell of burnt caramel still lingered in the air from the last bowl smoked. To the rapid high-pitched ringtone, the addict floated above sweaty sheets. The steady clang became annoying. Blindly a boney hand searched for the receiver. Skeletal fingers toppled a cadre of empty longneck beer bottles. Two escaping bottles hit the warped wood floor. Shards of amber glass exploded. Locating the phone, the addict triumphantly terminated the irritating chime.

"Hello," he mumbled.

"Petru Rossi?"

"Yes," Petru answered.

"This is Francoise at the Continental Hotel. Sir, we have been trying to reach you all night." Uncomfortable static crackled. Seconds ticked by. "Mister Rossi?" Francoise questioned.

"What is it?" mumbled Petru.

"The German and the tribesman were in the Lobby bar this evening," Francoise responded.

"Were they looking for me?" Petru asked.

"I don't believe so, sir," Francoise replied. "They left with a high priced whore. The tribesman called her Mei."

"Thank you for the information," Petru said dropping the receiver on a rattan nightstand littered with surviving beer bottles.

Melting back into the dream session, he felt the comfortable pulse of life in his frail frame. Usually any mention of Max and Loc caused the

1

Unione Corse hit man to feel the pain of the bullet lodged in his back. He didn't feel any physical discomfort now; just his inbreed desire for vendetta. Looking up, he watched the creaking ceiling fan slowly rotate. The revolving blades cast pulsating shadows across the dimly lit room. From the fan's rusted base plate, a chitchat emerged. The small tailless gecko clung to the cracked plaster ceiling. Over the spinning blades, the lizard calmly waited for an insect meal. A slow satisfying grin emerged across Petru's numb face. He remembered an old Corsican proverb; *if you want revenge and act within twenty years, you're acting in haste.* German military discipline my ass, he thought, Corsican patience will always prevail. I'll slowly bleed the German and his milkshake drinking subordinate before restoring my honor.

CHAPTER TWO

It was February 1954. In the Tonkin region of Vietnam, the local population recently celebrated Tết. The Vietnamese lunar New Year marked the arrival of spring and the year of the horse.

A tropical sun hung high in a cloudless sky. A series of flooded fields descended across the fertile rolling hills. Little dikes, trees and clusters of bamboo framed a rich green patchwork. Bright sunlight reflected off the terraced sheets of liquid glass. In the shallow paddy water, the helmeted heads of French Legionnaires bobbed along a muddy embankment.

Max, a German in the unit comprised of foreign nationals reclined comfortably in the warm water. He peered at a large cluster of bamboo a hundred yards away. Focusing his gaze, he concentrated on a small piece of foliage. The tiny shrub slowly moved against the wind. Lowering his head, he looked back across the elevated rice paddies. Spotting the tall lanky French Lieutenant securely planted in the mud, Max waved two fingers. Indifferently the Frenchman shrugged. Fucking amateur, Max thought returning to gaze down the barrel of his rifle. With a moist trigger finger, he searched for the elusive twig. There it is. It moved again. To compensate for the rifles inaccurate sights, he aimed a little left of the target. Taking a satisfying breath of humid air, he squeezed the trigger. The rifle barked. The target erupted into a wet crimson plume. A barrage of Communist automatic weapons fire answered the single shot. Max rolled deeper into the comfortable water. His fellow legionnaires hugged the mud base shelter. Communist bullets buzzed overhead. Wanting to enjoy the cooling effects of the murky bath, he laid back. A self-satisfying grin spread across his face. Rippled pond water lapped at his chin. His heart pounded. It always did under fire. Taking a deep breath, he slowly looked over the muddy embankment. The fading Vietminh gun-fire became sporadic. Legionnaires blindly fired into the brush. A waste of ammunition, Max realized. You'll learn soon enough, he thought. The Communist only come out to play, when they have an advantage. Our deceptive hit and run adversaries are long gone.

Soaking wet and covered in mud, Max stood in the knee-deep water. The heavy fabric of camouflaged fatigues clung to his muscular frame. Chilled by a warm breeze, he realized the sensation would be brief. It's going to be a long uncomfortable day of trekking in wet clothes.

The slow rising Lieutenant blew into a metallic pea whistle. The one-hundred-and-fifty men under his command sloshed forward crippling the regions rice harvest.

A legionnaire on the adjoining terrace cried out. Max jerked violently to investigate. A traumatized soldier frantically splashed in the shallow pond. Two soldiers came to his aid. Lifting the wailing man revealed a studded wooden plank attached to a bloody boot. A barb must have gone right through his foot, Max concluded. Squinted into the reflecting spark-ing light, he attempted to identify the victim. Nobody I know, he realized. Poor bastard, he thought. Infection guaranteed. The legionnaire will be walking with a limp for the rest of his days.

Stepping out of the submerged field, Max stomped the ground several times. Flexing broad shoulders, he strutted to examine his kill. In the cool shade of tall bamboo lay the body of a young Vietminh soldier. The top of the victims head was missing. Buzzing flies disrespected the corpse. Skull fragments and brain tissue clung to the surrounding plants. Reaching down, Max picked up the remnants of the victim's helmet. Smiling he flicked the tell tale piece of foliage in the camouflage netting. This is what I do, Max thought and I do it well. After confirming the kill, he tossed the bloodstained target aside. Several other legionnaires stood around admiring the single fatality of the small victory. With the callousness of a professional soldier, Max glanced into the empty brown eyes of the dead boy. Better you than me, he thought. Focusing on the corpse's quilted mountain uniform he flinched. This is not a guerrilla partisan, he questioned. What is a regular soldier in the People's

Army doing in the Tonkin region? Shaking his head he mumbled, "What are those devious Communist planning?"

The approaching Lieutenant looking at Max said, "Nice shooting legionnaire."

Puffing out his chest, Max removed his helmet. Running damp fingers through his sweaty blond hair, he acknowledged the praise with a slight nod.

"Where did you learn to shoot like that?" The Lieutenant asked dispersing the other loitering soldiers with a wave.

Standing stone-faced, Max looked dumfounded at the officer. No need to reveal my French linguistic skill, he thought. The Lieutenant pantomimed out the inquiry and slowly repeated the question.

Biting his bottom lip, Max suppressed the urge to laugh. Concluding the charade, he responded in broken French, "Hitler Youth." Lifting up his shirt collar, he exposed a tarnished circle, one inch in diameter, a shooting proficiency badge. The pin displayed cross rifles over a target. In the center, a diamond in white and red accented a black swastika.

The Frenchman responded to the swastika visual with a sour face.

Grinning Max dropped his collar. The arrogant French sure do not like any reminders about their crushing defeat to Germany, he delightfully concluded.

A loose column of legionnaires plodded along a narrow rural pathway. Towards the back of the pack, Max tugged the harsh damp fabric chaffing his crotch. Jesus, why did I reenlist for a second tour of duty, he wondered. What else could I have done? He thought. The perils of combat seem a better alternative than the life of an unskilled laborer. He studied the stoic expressions of his fellow legionnaires. Smirking, he took solace in the fact that his comrades in arms were mostly *Wehrmacht* veterans. They undoubtedly had come to the same conclusion, he realized. Germany trained us to be soldiers, and that is what we are. Inhaling deeply, he stuck out his chest. Ignoring the coarse fabric tormenting his crotch, he reflected back to another war.

It was a warm day in the summer of 1944. The boy soldiers of the 12th SS Panzer Division *Hitlerjugend* incurred heavy losses. Seeking shelter in a bombed out cafe in Northern France, a teenage Max choked back tears. To the crunching sound of glass, he glanced up and with watery eyes. Sergeant Franz stepped into the fire-gutted structure. The battle hardened thirty-year-old veteran covered in soot. The wrinkles of his blackened face showed fatigue. The fire in his brown eyes burned with determination.

"Are you alright Maximilian?" Franz asked dipping a shoulder to remove his pack.

Max nodded quickly cloaking emotions.

Placing a hand on the boy's shoulder, Franz said, "Max we are German soldiers. We follow orders unconditionally; however stay disciplined and true to the profession." Pausing his sooty face softened. "Remember my sharpshooting *kamerad*, we are soldiers in the finest fighting force to march across the face of this planet not fanatics. When we meet our maker, we do it with pride."

The penetrating high-pitched wail of the French Lieutenant's pea whistle caused Max to refocus. They had reached the village objective. A simple stone archway framed a small community of pitched palm frond huts. Under the sun-bleached sky, a soft wind escorted a twirling column of dust through the village square. The dust devil floated past empty livestock pens before dissipated over the stone communal well. Laundry flapped in the breeze. The patrol spread out. To greet the legionnaires, the entire population of this small rural community spilled out of the **đình làng** (communal house). Into the town square flowed old men, women and children. A slouching old man wearing the familiar soiled peasant black pajamas led the procession. A cloth strap across his neck secured a pointed straw paddy hat on his back. His stringy gray hair flickered in the soft wind. The French Lieutenant approached the apparent village chief.

"Have you seen any Communist?" the lieutenant asked the village representative.

The timid old man shook his head.

"Has your village made a contribution to the Vietminh rice tax?" the lieutenant continued.

Once again, the submissive old man shook his head.

"Where are all your young men?" The lieutenant probed motioning towards the assembled population of women, children and seniors.

After a challenging silence, the old man mumbled, "They are working in the fields."

Two actors in a very bad play, Max thought, repeating the same lines over and over to an unappreciative audience. For the last five years, I've heard the same dialogue. The lieutenant concluded the performance by blowing his whistle. This was Max's cue in the tragic theatrical production. It was time to enhance his evening meal.

Passing by the assemblage of one hundred civilians, Max viewed them as expendable extras. The adults timidly stood in a close formation wearing the familiar black peasant garb. Their obvious contempt for this intrusion shielded with bowed heads and conical hats. The only faces visible were the malnourished half-naked children clinging to their mothers' baggy pants. Ignoring the deprived children's hollow gaze, Max quickened his pace. The competition to loot the village's limited supplies had begun. Unfortunate peasants, he thought. They undoubtedly pay both the government tax collector and the Vietminh's rice tax. Casualties of war, he rationalized. The allied bombing of Nuremberg terminated my parents, he reflected.

Kicking in the driftwood planked door with a mud covered boot, Max barged into a single room residence. The wood floor creaked under his weight. He stomped around clearing the shelves with the barrel of his rifle. Broken glass and the clamor of metal cookware resonated in the hut. He began flipping over furniture. Tossing the bed across the room, he grinned. "Oh yeah," he mumbled at two scrawny chickens in a small bamboo cage and a twenty-pound gunnysack of rice. Suddenly his stomach felt empty. He licked his lips. No need to figure out how to free the birds, he thought punching a hole in the cage. Quickly snapping the necks of the skinny chickens, he hastily stuffed the poultry prize into his daypack. Tossing the rough cloth bag of rice over his shoulder, he paused. Visualizing the submissive herd of farmers in the village square, he mumbled, "Ah shit." Reaching into the bag, he stuffed several handfuls of the loose grains into the moist leg pocket of his fatigues. No need to accelerate their demise, he thought leaving the bulk of the rice in the debris-cluttered shack. To the sound of other legionnaires approaching, he began tapping the floorboards with his rifle. Insincerely he searched for a hidden weapons chamber knowing the quest futile.

CHAPTER THREE

A C-47 military transport's twin engines hummed. The monotonous buzz echoed throughout the crowded cargo plane. Along one side of the cabin, Mei sat quietly with six other Vietnamese working girls and a Madame. She folded her arms in an attempt to stay warm. Across from her in brightly colored North African robes, eleven Algerian prostitutes cackled. Mei smiled. The black courtesans from the Oulad-Nail tribe chose this vocation, she realized. For them it is an honorable occupation to earn a wedding dowry. If they can retire and find a man that loves them, why can't I, she wondered.

Rubbing the course material of green fatigues, Mei combated the chill. She readjusted the military issued sun cover that corralled long silky black hair. Glancing around the noisy cabin, she estimated her uniformed Vietnamese companion's ages were close to her nineteen years. We are part of the war effort she rationalized. Soldiers don't like to kill and we don't like to service an inexhaustible line of customers. We all have to make sacrifices. I am not a whore, she concluded. I'm a conscript in the *Bordels Mobile de Campagne,* serving my country.

Closing her eyes, the noise of the aircraft lulled her towards sleep. For the first time in years, she recalled the rural village where the brothel journey began.

The cloudless sky was a deep blue on this mild summer day. Barefooted Mei walked along the tomato plants beginning to bear fruit in her small garden. Callus feet sunk into the moist soil. She beamed. I'm contributing to our dinner table, she thought. A flirtatious whistle caused her to flinch. In front of her family's modest residence, Hien and another village boy stood snickering. Hien repeated the catcall. Shielding a big smile, Mei focused on gardening. Silly boys, she thought. Placing both hands in the small of her back, she stuck out her chest and stretched. I hope Hien is enjoying the visual, she thought showing off a shapely fifteen-year-old figure. Glancing over in her admirer's direction, Mei jerked into a submissive pose. Her father approached with a well-dressed stranger. Timidly looking down, she focused on the man's glossy shoes. Who is this man? She wondered. His patent leather footwear sparkled. Her father stood nervously fidgeting with his coolie hat. The mysterious man looked Mei up and down. Her heart pounded. He walked around her. Breathing heavy Mei gasp as he firmly grabbed her chin. He looked deep into her eyes.

"She will do," the inspector casually informed wiping his hand with a handkerchief.

"Thank you, she will be a good girl," her father muttered.

"Have her clean up. We'll leave in an hour." The stranger said gruffly. Gingerly he pranced out of the garden in his shiny shoes.

Choking back tears, Mei questioned, "Father?"

"He has work for you in the city. It will be good for you and good for the family. You work hard and do as he says," her father stated in a firm tone.

Looking up, Mei saw her mother weeping in the distance.

Mei followed behind the arrogantly strutting man with the shiny shoes. They walked past the terraced rice paddies of her small community. What kind of work does he have for me? She wondered. Was he married? Does he have children? That is probably it, she concluded. I'll take care of his children. I'm going to be his amah, she rationalization. I'm going to be a good amah, she concluded.

At the end of the narrow village pathway, a dusty automobile sat under the shade of a large tree. I'm going to ride in a car for the first time, Mei realized. My new master must be wealthy, she concluded. A large pot-bellied man sleeping in the car awoke. Stepping out of the vehicle, he greeted his companion. Mei stood toying with the ends of her long hair unable to comprehend the dialogue.

Shiny-shoes lit a cigarette. Calmly he inhaled the smoke. Looking at Mei, he exhaled through a wicked grin. Chubby firmly grabbed Mei's wrist. Forcibly he pushed her to the back seat of the car. Why was he doing this? She wondered. Climbing on top of her, he began rubbing the palm of a flabby hand across her chest. Breathing heavy Mei gasp for air. She tried to speak but could not find a voice. Finally, "Please don't," rolled out of her dry mouth. Her timid hands tried to push away his groping advance. Snickering, he easily brushed aside the attempted resistance and grabbed a breast. Shiny-shoes peered through a car window. His demented gaze offered no hope of rescue. Releasing the painful grasp of her bosom, the assailant, pulled down her pants. Attempts to cover-up allowed free hands to explore. A probing finger detected her innocence. Grunting he celebrated the discovery. Weeping quietly, she surrendered under his sweaty weight. She stared at the stained and torn automobile headliner. Potbelly continued thrusting unimpeded. Did her parents know about these men, she wondered. They must have known. Why else would my mother have wept?

The assailant sat up. Inhaling deeply, he ran fingers through his sweat soaked hair. Exiting the vehicle, he slammed the door shut. Mei lay naked in the back seat of the hot car. A small burgundy stain on the vehicle's upholstery marked the loss of innocence. Exposed she breathed the trapped stale air. It reeked of the rapist foul odor. Is that it? She wondered. Can I go? Cautiously she reached for her clothes. The car door metallically creaked open. Stagnant air escaped. The doorway framed Shiny-shoes. A cigarette smoldered between his lips. Grinning he pulled down his slacks. "No," Mei said. He climbed on top of her. "Please, no," she begged.

Bright red rugs covered the floor. Mei stood trembling. The large crowded house buzzed. Focused on the floral pattern at her feet, she swallowed with a dry mouth. I have not spoken since leaving my home three days ago, she realized. I wonder if I'll ever talk again, she thought. Gigantic uniformed white men conversed in a disgusting incomprehensible language. Painted young girls lingered amongst the large foreigners. Mei closed her eyes. I wish I could feel the moist earth of the vegetable garden between my toes, she thought.

A nudge from Shiny-shoes jostled Mei. A short, fat elderly woman wearing a colorful silk dress lifted Mei's chin with a folded fan. The painted women flicked her wrist. The fan opened. Stirring the air the Madame cooled herself. Her free hand examined Mei's breast. Pleased with the inspection, the old women smiled wide. Crooked yellow teeth appeared between liquid red lips. Collapsing the fan, she lifted an arm and snapped her fingers. A skinny Asian in a wrinkled black suit paid Shiny-shoes.

"Come with me," The painted Madame said to a confused Mei. "Come, come," the old woman said again. "We will get you something to eat, before you start work."

Mei stood naked in the small room. The white man casually opened the second floor window. Urban noise of the evil city resonated against the walls. The tall lanky man, with piercing dark eyes methodically placed a wallet, watch and pistol on a chair. Inhaling the intense scent of fragrant flowers, Mei thought how peculiar he smelled. Removing his trousers, he carefully folded them. Neatly he draped his clothing over the chair. He walked over to Mei. Raising his arm, he slapped her hard. The blow sent her to the floor. Tears welled up in her stunned eyes. Grinning from ear to ear, he stroked himself. Pulling her up by the hair, he struck her with the back of his hand. Her lip split wide open. At the sight of blood, he began to moan. After several more blows, he mounted her. Randomly he slapped her throughout the coupling.

After finishing his business, the wiry man rose. He used Mei's gown to wipe off the blood splatter from his sweaty torso. Meticulously he began to dress. After straitening the lapels of his white suit jacket, he dragged a pocket comb through greasy black hair. Approaching the battered and weeping Mei, he flexed brandishing the back of a hand. She cringed. Turning with a lingering chuckle, he opened the door.

Standing in the doorway the pimp mama greeted him. "Mr. Rossi was the new girl to your liking?" She asked peering around his tall frame.

"No fight in that one," he said with a slight shrug.

"We have new girls arriving next week. I make special effort to find one that resist," she offered.

"I'll look forward to it," he politely said exiting.

The mama quickly entered the room to assess the damage. Picking up the bloodstained gown, she wiped the blood from Mei's face. She grinned, having seen far worse. "Petru Rossi is an important man, French gangster. He likes the new girls, but only once," she informed. "It is good you did not fight back." Looking into Mei's bruised face, she added, "You are pretty girl, you will do well here. You should use your mouth as often as you can. There is less risk of contamination."

It was a hot muggy afternoon. Kneeling before an acne faced soldier, Mei serviced him with the oral skill she had perfected. Through an open window flowed the sound of working girls mimicking that disgusting foreign tongue. How pleasant it would be to spend a portion of the day in the sun, Mei thought. The satisfied customer pulled up his trousers. As he opened the door to exit, another anxious serviceman rushed in. Other impatient soldiers peered through the doorway.

Exhausted a naked Mei slowly rose. She used a chair to stabilize her wobbly legs. Preparing for the next client, she stood in front of a washbasin. Inhaling deeply, she looked at her reflection in the water-stained mirror above the sink. Strong cheek and jaw muscles now accentuated her facial features. I can do this she rationalized. At least I won't have to endure another session with the Corsican Rossi. He nearly killed a new girl last week. Feeling light headed, she splashed handfuls of water on her bare chest and shoulders. A hairy customer lay in waiting. Proceeding to fulfill his needs, Mei felt the bright sunlit room spinning. Everything turned to black.

Metallic white blades slowly rotated. Comfortably reclining between clean sheets Mei inhaled an antiseptic aroma. Where am I, she wondered studying the painted white metal bed frame. A soft-spoken foreigner with a white coat over his uniform stood bedside. He spoke to her in a musical tone. Blinking to adjust to the brightly lit sanitized environment, she reached for his hand. Grasping his clean soft palm, she mumbled, "Thank you," with a dry mouth.

"I can see my top producer is recovering," said the pimp mama.

Startled Mei's stomach churned. Her yellow-toothed handler stood beside the doctor.

"The doctor has determined that after two days rest you will be able to return to the House of Butterflies," The mama said quietly, "And that we should limit your customers for the next couple of weeks."

Immediately Mei released the doctor's hand. She squinted into his alien face with a scowl. I mistook your care for kindness, she thought. I'll never make that mistake again.

The C-47 Dakota military transport ran into turbulence. Glancing around the noisy aircraft cabin, Mei made eye contact with Lan and smiled. At seventeen Lan, a child of the Saigon streets was the youngest of the working girls. Short and round-faced, Lan resembled a pudgy boy in army fatigues.

To compensate for the aircraft noise, Lan leaned forward and asked, "Have you worked in a combat zone before?"

"Yes," Mei replied, "I like working at the front lines or in the isolated outpost. The danger proves just how important our services are to the war effort. These fighting men need our aid and comfort."

Tilting her head to the side, Lan asked, "What do you mean, aid and comfort?"

"You know," Mei responded, "Under the supervision of Army Medical the sex is official. We are like soldiers."

"This is my first front line assignment," Lan informed. "I'm hoping to see a tiger."

Grinning Mei replied, "I've never seen one, but maybe we both will this time. We are heading to a remote jungle valley called Dien Bien Phu."

CHAPTER FOUR

S unlight faded over the harsh mountainous landscape. A remote crevice sparkled with glowing campfires. In the center of the isolated French forces bivouac, Max stood amongst five other mud-covered soldiers. The cadre stared at a pot of boiling broth suspended over a small cooking fire. Tiny flames licked at the bottom of the cast iron container. A plucked chicken surfaced in the bubbling sauce. The audience sighed.

Looking down at the wet ground, Max shifted his boots in the gummy muck. The real estate we've been delegated to fortify would always have a mud floor, he realized. The only variation for the moist base will be differing degrees of consistency. "What do they call this swamp?" he asked his fellow German speaking legionnaires. No one responded. The flickering light revealed focused men salivating in anticipation.

A husky voice with a slight Bavarian accent broke the silence. "Isabelle," Muller responded.

Puzzled, Max looked over at the bald, wide necked Bavarian. Muller's clean-shaven head and neck rested on broad shoulders as a single unit. "Isabelle?" Max questioned.

"Leave it to the French," Muller responded smirking. "The French commander chose to name the seven positions at Dien Bien Phu after his former mistresses." Lifting up a mud-encrusted jungle boot, he added, "Judging from the conditions at Isabelle, she must have given him the clap."

Smiling, Max pulled several handfuls of rice from his moist leg pocket. He tossed the grains into the pot. Muller is not a bad fellow, Max thought; even though he claims to be Swiss. Studying the thirty-five year legionnaire in the fire's soft light, Max snickered. Give his age and accent most likely a former Nazi. "Why here of all places?" Max asked.

"Bait, my marksman friend," Muller responded. "We need to give these wily Communist revolutionaries some sense of a tactical advantage to lure them onto the battlefield. Those sandaled peasants can have the high ground. We have artillery, armor and the skies."

Nodding Max said, "If having us stand in mud at the basin of this valley is suppose to entice those monkeys into combat, they can at least feed us better. I don't think I could have tolerated another night on those British surplus rations. How *Tommy* won the war eating that bland tinned meat and vegetables, is beyond me."

"Don't you think the age has something to do with the lack of taste? I haven't been issued a ration that wasn't at least ten years old," Muller said spitting at the bitter recollection.

"Enough talk about bad rations. We will dine well tonight. Tomorrow we can complain about the food." The fair-skinned Gregor interjected. Distancing his sun burnt complexion from the small fire, he asked from the shadows, "How much longer Max?"

"Not soon enough," Max responded winking. "I'm afraid the smell may attract some French flies."

"Don't look now but those bison boys are looking this way," Muller said flicking his large head.

In unison, Max and his dinner party all rotated to investigate the adjoining campfire of French tank crewmembers.

"I said not to look," Muller reminded sarcastically.

Tending the fire, Max realized that one of the bison boys interpreted his glance as an invitation. A portly Frenchman breaching the informal camp etiquette of cultural segregation approached the German campfire. He had a slight paunch on a hefty frame. A round face sported a scraggly mustache. His head seemed too large for his cap and his fatigues too small for his physique. Probably in his late thirties, Max estimated, likely a French veteran of World War II.

"Smells good," the uninvited Frenchman announced in German.

The Germans stood silent. Muller flexed his wide back clenching his fist. The Frenchman reached into one of the pockets of his baggy camouflaged uniform and produced a flask. Taking a sip, the French intruder handed the container to a squatting pot stirring Max. Sniffing the small flat container, Max inhaled the sharp antiseptic aroma of alcohol. Mimicking an impromptu toast, he partook. Warm rum rolled down the back of his throat. A spontaneous soothing calm flowed through his veins. Graciously he nodded at the Frenchman and handed the container to the aggressively postured Muller. One shot of alcohol deflated the former Nazi's taut posture. Mueller heartily patted the Frenchman on the back before handing off the rum. The libation slowly orbited the German campfire.

"Would you like to join us for some chicken soup?" Max asked slowly in German.

In very good German, the Frenchman replied, "If you insist."

The German-speaking clique chuckled.

"My name is Jean Paul, but everyone calls me JP." Jean Paul said retrieving the empty flask. Placing the container in a pant pocket, he added with a crooked grin, "Now that the tanks and artillery have arrived, it looks like they will be bringing in the final component for our defenses. Women."

"What?" questioned a confused Max.

"Not really women," Jean Paul said casually waving. "The additional support will come in the form of young girls, shapely teenagers. The *Bordel Mobile de Campagne* will be arriving shortly."

Slight smiles replaced confused expressions. Stirring the pot, Max recalled his last BMC sexual encounter. The sweaty petite teenage whore was insatiable.

"I remember," Muller spoke up. "We were in an isolated outpost in Tsinh-Ho. Two of the BMC girls made the two-day jungle trek into the Communist occupied territory. They came in under commando escort wearing jungle boots and fatigues. I never saw anything look so enticing in a uniform. When I finally had my turn, I had the young girl take off her silk robe and put back on the jungle fatigues. I still think about that afternoon."

"Of course the girls that they will be sending to Isabelle will be missing teeth and more than likely be contaminated," Jean Paul commented.

"I could live with that," Muller chuckled, "Just as long as I can get her to put on a uniform."

Stirring the pot one last time, Max sampled the stew. Closing his eyes, he savored the poultry rich broth rolling across his tongue. His broad smile acknowledged mealtime. Carefully, he ladled out equal portions under the scrutinizing stares of the dinner party. On the moist ground, the small group sat around the fire. Quietly they enjoyed the hot chicken and rice concoction.

Feeling relaxed by the rum and a warm meal, Max pulled out his poncho. He laid it out next to the small fire. Reclining in his soiled damp clothes, he looked up at the star covered sky. The fire crackled. The muffled German campfire dialogue faded. They are like the brothers I never had, he thought. Uncomfortably he reflected scolding his mother for not producing children for the Reich. I was only ten, he recalled, an only child. I stood proudly in my *Jungvolk* uniform waving a finger in the face of my terrified and weeping mother. With a quick snort, he erased the disturbing recollection. A falling star streaked across night sky. "It looks like it is going to be another cold night in the highlands," he said to no one in particular. "More than likely we'll awaken to that jungle haze, *crachin*, to start the day."

"That thick fog always reminds me of that communist frontal assault in the Red River Delta," Muller said. Glancing over at the cigarette smoking Jean Paul, he explained, "The Vietminh start the show by sending these Volunteers of Death, blowing up themselves and a breach in our outer wall. Then out of the fog comes wave upon wave of Communist infantry throwing themselves against our dug-in positions." Muller focusing on the horizontal Max continued, "Max, I never saw anyone work a bolt action rifle like you did that day," he turned to the group. "He would empty and reload that five round clip, sweeping left to right then back, right to left never missing a shot."

Gazing at the sparkling sky Max said, "I missed more than a few shots that day," Recalling it had taken him several shots to adjust his aim at that distance. A smile spread across his face. He remembered the sense of accomplishment once he got into a rhythm.

"Those fanatic Communists just kept coming. As they got closer, most of them appeared to be children. It is difficult to tell in this country. Everyone looks either fifteen or one hundred and five." Muller said to an audience more interested with the last cigarette of the day than the rant. "Max," Muller exclaimed, "You were a boy soldier. How old were you when you fought in France?"

Flinching in his comfortable repose, Max felt embarrassed for Muller. His fireside companion had violated the professional soldiers' first rule of etiquette. You never ask about a man's past. To compound the infraction, the French war veteran Jean Paul was present. Apparently unaware of his error, Muller's silence solicited a response. Did I discuss my military history with this former Nazi who claimed to be Swiss? Max wondered. It really does not matter he concluded, I do not want to discuss it now. Propping himself up on an elbow, Max examined the men sitting and standing in the glow of the small fire. Their bowed heads and roaming glances acknowledged Muller's breach of protocol. Max answered Muller's anticipating gaze with a somber expression. Realizing the error Muller looked away. Mustering compassion for his friend, Max answered, "Seventeen. I was seventeen when I was captured at Caen."

CHAPTER FIVE

The transport skidded to a bumpy termination. Mei jerked hard against the harness restraints. The madam took charge. Unbuckling the pimp mama pushed through the precious female cargo to the rear of the aircraft. Through an open hatch, sun light poured into the fuselage. Tropical heat engulfed the compartment.

Shuffling behind the other girls, Mei moved towards the exit. Framed by the cargo door she gazed out. Thousands of shirtless men toiled in a confusing spectacle. Trucks and heavy equipment raced back and forth across the dusty runway. The pulse of commotion slowed. Laborers paused to get a glimpse of a female form. Soldiers flanked the short gangway offering unloading assistance. Mei chuckled at the magnetic power of her presence. As she descended the narrow walkway, the male audience broke into applause.

The madam conversed in guttural French with a young medical officer of the 2nd Foreign Legion Infantry Regiment. The dialogue hindered by the deafening sounds of aircraft. Mei and the six other Vietnamese girls stood off to the side in a small group. The more boisterous North Africans solicited all the attention. The black courtesans shouted and waived at future customers.

A sweaty Xiong gazed at the commotion on the runway. Loc handed him another wooden box of supplies. A large 'I' branded the neatly stacked crates headed for Isabelle.

"What is it?" asked the French warrant officer in charge.

"Women," said Xiong, "Colorful black women dancing on the runway."

"Carry on," instructed the officer. "I'll go investigate." Placing his clipboard on the stack of unloaded supplies, he joined the migration to admire the seductive cargo.

Knowingly smiling at the other Tais, Loc squatted down on his haunches in the shade of a supply truck. The other tribesman joined him. Loc pulled out a full pack of cigarettes and lit up. Closing his eyes, he puffed away satisfying his smoking addiction. This is my last pack of smokes, he realized. How am I going to appease my craving until the next allotment? He pondered. Opening an eye, he studied the smoldering canister between his nicotine stained fingers. I'll worry about that tomorrow, he concluded. Placing the wrapped tobacco between his lips, he inhaled deeply.

In a hushed tone, Xiong appealed to the group in their native dialect, "I'm sick of the food here. It is only going to get worse. I'm tired of digging trenches. I don't mind killing Communists but not like this. We should be fighting the Vietminh in our highlands. The reason why we dig in and wait is that the French can't survive in the jungle. I'm leaving in the morning."

No one responded. Loc took several satisfying puffs. Desertions from the Tai battalion were a daily occurrence. I don't blame you for your chancy rhetoric my Black Tai brother, Loc thought. Exhaling he mumbled, "Where are you going to go?"

"I'm going home!" Xiong responded.

"I have no home," Loc stated with a shrug. "The Communists burned my village for siding with the French. So I'm staying to fight."

"Loc if you want to fight, do it in our highlands, not here in the open," Xiong said glancing around the valley. "I'm slipping under the wire tonight. Most of my people have relocated to Laos. That is where I'm going. Allying with the French was our mistake. If my people stayed neutral, I'd be going home."

Nodding his understanding Loc terminated the conversation. Inhaling another relaxing dose of nicotine vapors, he looked over at the dancing North African whores. Surrounded by military personnel, the girls teased and flirted. A dusty wind blasted the spectators. A green sun-cover shot up into the air. Below the floating hat, long black silky locks rippled. A Vietnamese girl in jungle fatigues, Loc realized. Encouraged by the wind, the jungle hat hit the ground and accelerated across the runway. Tossing his cigarette-butt aside, he ran over and scooped up the escaping head-gear. Walking across the runway, he handed the hat to the smiling girl. Her unrestricted long black hair floated in the sultry breeze. At a little over five feet, she was about his height. Grinning nervously, he admired her deep dark eyes and angelic features. Speechless, he realized his mouth was open. What is your name? He wanted to ask. Should I say it in French, he wondered. Would that impress her? Should I offer her a cigarette? His heart pounded. I need to do something, he realized.

"Come here girl!" called out an elderly woman standing next to an officer.

Unable to move or speak, Loc watched the young vision graciously nod and walk away.

"Mei, come here girl," the madam called out a second time.

Strolling towards the madam, Mei tucked her long hair into the sun-cover. Glancing over her shoulder, she got a second look at the chivalrous transfixed tribesman. She giggled.

Standing in front of the officer and madam, Mei could not comprehend the French conversation. She did recognize her name in the dialogue. The tall and thin Frenchman looked at her through dark sunglasses. The shirtsleeves of his wrinkled uniform rolled up above his elbows. An insignia displayed on shoulder patches identified his officer designation. His closely cropped black hair was uncovered. Approvingly, he nodded towards the madam.

The madam turned to Mei and said, "Henri is most important man. He will be in charge of the Mobile Field Brothel here at Claudine. He is looking for oral pleasure, nothing else."

Claudine? Mei questioned. Why would they name a place Claudine?

The madam walked away leaving Mei alone with the young officer. Reaching for her hand, he escorted her towards a wall of stacked wooden crates. She followed him through the twelve-foot high maze of supplies. They stopped at a secluded spot within the labyrinth. Instinctively Mei dropped to her knees. Contributing to the war effort, she comforted the officer with her oral talents.

CHAPTER SIX

A morning breeze rippled across the surface of the grassy savannah. The rising sun slowly illuminated the rolling sea of dark green growth. Concealed in the depths of the tall razor sharp elephant grass, a long single file procession of committed communist advanced. Division 308 of the People's Army was on the move. Vuong Cam a Vietminh soldier marched at the uncomfortably brisk pace. I can do this, he thought. The sunlight gave him a clearer sense of direction. No need to high-step in the dark, he realized shuffling blistered sandaled feet.

Without warning, the soldier in front of him dropped to the ground. Cam got a brief glimpse of other combatants hugging the narrow trampled grass pathway. Following in unison, he fell upon the moist earth. Sweating profusely, he lay motionless. Hearing the distant drone of an aircraft, his heart began to race. Cowards, he thought. Involuntary he stroked the scar tissue blanketing the left side of face. The deformity a reminder of the napalm attack he survived in his teens. His fingers investigated the jagged stump that replaced his ear and lack of hair. A small contribution for the cause of my people, he concluded. The buzz of the aircraft intensified. Cam gulped for air. Closing his eyes, he recalled the fire that fell from the French controlled sky. His disfigured face throbbed with the memory of the intense burn. "Foreign devils," he mumbled under his breath. We will be victorious in driving you from our shores, he vowed. The people will once again own the land. That is the way it is supposed to be. If I have to die to achieve that goal, so be it, he thought. I just hope I don't perish before I get to the valley.

The aircraft faded over the horizon. Cam felt a sense of relief. Tired bones and aching feet slowly rose. Hastily he checked the elephant grass attached to webbing of his saucer shaped helmet. The man to his rear checked the camouflage attached to the wire mesh of Cam's pack. Cam performed the same task to the soldier in front of him. The forced march resumed.

In the tall grass labyrinth, Cam high stepped over the ant-covered corpse of a fellow soldier. Glancing down he could tell his passing comrades had already picked clean the shoeless uniformed teenage casualty. Snakebite, Cam wondered, fatigue? We all have to make sacrifices to insure a better life for all.

Entering tropical forested highlands the procession stopped. The Vietminh replaced savannah camouflage with jungle foliage. Cam secured new shrubbery on his palm fiber helmet. Scanning the dense rain forest, his stomach dropped. This is going to be different than fighting around the towns and villages of the Delta flatlands, he concluded. If I have to endure the hostile environment to get to the French, so be it, he thought.

In the bowels of the rain forest, a handicapped smile appeared on Cam's disfigured face. Division 308 flowed into a stream of freedom fighters headed to the valley. Thousands of coolies, both men and women, carried bags of rice, disassembled artillery pieces and crates of munitions. Lashed together treetops created a veiled tunnel of green. Looking up Cam grinned. In front of him, Division 308 walked across the surface of a small river. At the water's edge, he discovered a log bridge concealed just below the surface.

"Everything for the front, everything for victory," a political commissar called out from the riverbank.

"Everything for the front, everything for victory," Cam mumbled. The rally cry became his mantra. I'm in pain, but I will endure, he convinced himself marching to a new rhythm. My left foot will get me closer to the front. My right foot that much closer to victory. The French can harass us from the air, he thought, but they will never stop us. Our enemy may force us to change our route, but we march on.

On a cool morning, thick fog provided cover. The ten day journey was about to end. Shielded by the heavy mist, Cam could hear his comrades breaking out in song. Hearing *The Call to Youth* lifted his spirits.

Proudly he sang out with a dry throat. *"Youth of Vietnam, arise! And at our country's call, single in heart let us open the way..."* Ascending the steep grade of a narrow mountain pass, he no longer felt the aches and pains of his mortal shell. The convoy and the patriotic song came to an abrupt end. Peering around the man in front of him, Cam saw two porters laying on the narrow mountain trail. A running political officer pushed Cam back into formation. The officer rushed past the stalled procession to investigate.

Examining the fallen workers, the political officer frowned. Waving an arm over his head, he cried out, "Keep moving! Keep moving."

Briefly surging forward, Cam abruptly stopped. The soldiers in front of him hesitated treading over the fatigued laborers.

"I said to keep moving!" the officer commanded. "These men are expendable. They have made their contribution."

Proceeding Cam heard one of the lifeless forms under his sandaled feet moan. Grimacing, Cam closed his eyes contemplating his own expendability. "We all have to make sacrifices," he mumbled.

Treading on a well-traveled pathway, Cam threw his shoulders back. Crates of munitions and large stacked piles of rice sacks flanked the trail. Proudly he marched the final steps into the hidden encampment overlooking the remote valley.

"Brothers," the political officer of Division 308 called out to the assemblage of exhausted men. "Congratulations on completing your long journey in such a short amount of time. I am here to inform you that as a combat soldier you are required to follow a strict order of hygiene as preparation for battle. You will wash your feet daily in warm water with salt. Your daily rations will consist of hot rice with a meat and vegetable garnish. Victory is within our grasp. Once we defeat the French Imperialist at the bottom of this narrow valley, we will do away with landlords and tax collectors, and redistribute the land back to the people."

On the moist ground in the shade of the dense forest, Cam reclined. Looking up into sunlight filtering through the jungle canopy he sang quietly, *"Youth of Vietnam, to the very end! This we resolve. To give ourselves completely, this we vow. Forward together for a glorious life..."*

CHAPTER SEVEN

H enri quickly made his way across the garrison towards the Field
Brothel. Damn foreign press, the young Medical Officer thought,
especially those Americans. It has been two weeks since the girls had arrived without an incident. Now I have to contend with this. "So I get to
shut it down until the reporters leave," he grumbled. "Hell, who are the
Americans to tell us what is proper. The BMC has a long tradition with the
French military."

Seeing a short line of soldiers lingering outside the plywood brothel,
Henri grinned. At least I won't be disappointing too many men, he
concluded.

"Sorry, Gentlemen," he said. "We are shutting down the BMC under
strict orders."

The thirty servicemen standing in line let out a simultaneous groan.

"Sir," a baby faced soldier said. "I am back on patrol tomorrow. This
is the only chance I'll have."

"Sorry son," Henri said. "Orders are orders."

At the entrance, Henri defiantly stood with folded arms. Thwarted
customers slowly dispersed. Entering the facility, Henri let out a comforting sigh.

"What is it?" the madam asked.

"Reporters and dignitaries are arriving this afternoon. The high command does not want to initiate a debate with the Americans about the
advantages of legalized prostitution." Henri explained.

The madam turned her head sideways and responded, "I don't
understand."

"You don't have to," Henri abruptly answered. "Just keep your girls inside. I'll let you know when you can resume business."

"I understand," she said bobbing her head.

Checking his watch, Henri asked, "Tell me. Is that long haired beauty available for a quick oral session?"

"I see you like my recommendation. She very skilled girl. She also very busy. You wait here. I'll go check," the madam said.

The lucky few servicemen engaged during the shutdown exited. How many of them would eventually catch the sickness of Venus, Henri wondered. Hell, venereal disease is chalking up more casualties than the Vietminh. The working women fair far worse than the troops, he realized. Visualizing the last infected whore he discarded, he shuttered. Poor girl suffered a deadly occupational hazard.

Reappearing in the hallway, the madam summoned him with a waving finger. Checking his watch again, he proceeded down the tight corridor. Entering the small room, he dropped his trousers. Looking down at the top of the young girl's silky black hair, he moaned. A very satisfying compromise to the risk of contamination, he concluded. There was no better military assignment, Henri realized, then being in charge of *la boîte à bonbons* (the candy box).

CHAPTER EIGHT

I t was a cool spring morning. Mei held Lan's hand. They calmly strolled through the chaotic French garrison. The sun shined down on the girls in their baggy field wear. Mei playfully swung their embraced palms back and forth. Lan is like my little sister, Mei thought. We have the same female cycle and can enjoy our holidays together. Inhaling the crisp air spiked with diesel fumes, Mei ignored the slight cramping. She concluded the periodic discomfort well worth the time off.

An empty supply truck skidded to a dusty stop beside the girls. Startled Mei put a protective arm around Lan's shoulder. The passenger door swung open. Grinning, the driver spoke incomprehensible French. With a shrug, he extended a hand over the empty seat.

"We are going to village outside of the garrison to buy fruit," Mei said in Vietnamese.

The driver shook his head with a friendly frown.

"Ban Co My," Mei informed the name of their village destination.

The soldier nodded.

Glancing down at Lan, Mei smiled and climbed into the truck. She slid over on the cracked vinyl bench. Lan followed. It will be good to get off the dusty road, Mei thought. Lan slammed the door shut. The driver popped the clutch. The vehicle slowly rolled forward. We could have walked faster, Mei thought. The driver placed a sweaty palm on Mei's knee. Trying not to chuckle, Mei reciprocated by placing her hand on his leg. He no doubt wants to extend the journey, she concluded. They drove slowly in silence. At the garrison's exiting checkpoint the truck rolled to a soft termination. Mei squeezed the young man's leg. He flinched. Breathing heavy through an open mouth, he attempted to speak. Graciously the shy driver gave Mei a nervous smile. The girls giggled as they climbed out of the transport. Looking back at the timid driver, Mei flashed a seductive smirk and winked.

Scattered along the base of the foothills was the small rural community of Ban Co My. Local tribesmen still used this partially evacuated frontier town for commerce. Hand in hand, Mei and Lan slowly walked down the main thoroughfare. Hawker stalls flanked the dirt road. French soldiers bartered with civilians. Yanking Lan by the hand, Mei pushed her way through the crowd of a produce stall. Bundles of dark red *chôm chôm* jumped out of the displayed fruits and vegetables. Mei swallowed back salivating anticipation as she bought two bundles of the soft fleshy haired tiny apples.

Sitting in the shade of a deserted building, Mei and Lan peeled the thick-skinned fruit. Sucking on the sweet large grape like center, they began to laugh. Spitting out the almond sized seed became a competition. Laughing hysterically, the girls plucked a *chôm chôm* from the bundle, peeled, popped and spit for distance. Snickering Mei wiped fruity syrup from her chin. An intruding middle-aged local disrupted the contest. The girls hastily stood.

"Why do you children sell your bodies for the French?" He asked in a pleasant tone.

"We are paid in the service for our country," Mei answered defiantly.

The man smiled. "It is not their country. It is not a French country. It is our country, yours and mine."

Looking at Lan, Mei frowned. What is he talking about? She wondered.

"You children should leave this place and work towards complete independence from the French devils," he said with a harsh tone. "We can create a workers society where there is equality between men and women. You would not have to sell yourselves for the lustful pleasure of foreigners."

Scowling, Mei glared at the man. Who are you to remind me that I'm a whore? She thought. Why should you care? Grabbing Lan's sticky hand, Mei pulled her little sister towards the security of the open market.

"What did he mean that men and women are equal?" Lan asked.

"I don't know," Mei replied, "He was talking crazy."

The communist infiltrator watched the two exploited young girls scurry away. They have no idea about the events that are about to unfold, he thought. Not being able to comprehend my simple message will cost them their lives.

CHAPTER NINE

Pacing back and forth down the narrow plywood corridor of the mobile field brothel, the madam clapped her hands. "Come, come," she called out.

A sleepy Lan rubbing her pudgy face mumbled. "What is it?"

"Some emergency at the hospital," Mei said lacing up her jungle boots.

"What time is it?" Lan yawned.

"Time for us to go, little sister," Mei said. Tucking her long black locks under a jungle hat, she rushed out the door.

The sun was bright. The air was cold. Mei, the madam and several other prostitutes raced towards the infirmary. The base buzzed with activity. Focused soldiers ran in all directions. Approaching the small field hospital, Mei stopped dead in her tracks. Laid out on the blood soaked ground lay hundreds of wounded men. The casualties sang out in a chorus of pain and suffering. Who are these men? Mei wondered. Surveying the rippling mass of the dead and dying, she wiped her face with a sweaty palm. A morning breeze engulfed her senses with the stench of death. Her stomach churned. She choked back surfacing vomit. How could this be, she thought? The large foreigners were invincible.

A medic squatting down beside a writhing casualty frantically waved at Mei. His other hand tried to ebb the flow of blood from a shattered leg. She ran to his aid. Dropping to her knees, she held the dark red soaked wade of gauze in place. The doctor injected the man with morphine.

"Ahhh!" Mei cried out. From behind a reclining soldier latched onto her calf. Boney fingers squeezed into her tender flesh. Over her shoulder, she saw a scared man trembling in the tropical sun. His fair hair soaking wet. Disconnected eyes danced on his twitching sweat covered face.

Enduring the vice grip, she continued to apply pressure on the pulsing saturated rag. The patient slowly drifted out of reality. The medic dismissed Mei with a quick nod. She wiped bloodstained hands across her chest and turned around. The soldier latching onto her leg released his grasp. Kneeling in the dirt beside him, she gently stroked his moist hair. He stopped twitching. Death claimed him. Mei stood. Tears welled up blurring her vision. Gasping for air, she spun around. Chilled by a pocket of cold air, she knew death walked amongst the wounded. What can I do? She wondered. Casualties howled, screamed and barked in French. *"De l'eau,"* kept surfacing in the desperate refrain. Mei ran to fetch water.

In the open-air field hospital, a blue-eyed soldier tilted forward. He winced. Mei slowly poured water past his parched lips. After taking several large gulps, he smiled graciously. Glancing up, she spotted a recipient of her oral services. The focused medical officer sewed up the leg on an incoherent patient. Hastily he completed the task and nodded to stretcher-bearers. They quickly replaced the victim with another. What is his name? Mei wondered. He is a person, she realized, a healer.

"Water! Water!" the wounded began to cry out.

With a dozen canteens slung across her shoulders, Mei fulfilled the request.

It had been a long bloody day. Dark red splotches stained Mei's fatigues. She strolled amongst the last group of wounded awaiting air transport. The tender touch of her hand or a reassuring smile comforted the reclining men. Looking down at yet another victim, she saw the shy Ban Co My driver. It was just two days ago, he offered Lan and me a ride, she realized. That seems like an eternity. The soldier gazed skyward with heavy eyes. A content grin lay across his face. I rarely remember customers, she thought. I wonder why I recognized him. Reaching down she squeezed his leg. The young man methodically looked at her grasping hand. He smiled at her from a morphine-induced trance. Gazing into his sleepy eyes, Mei ignored the blood soaked bandage on the stump below his shoulder. Opening his mouth, he attempted to speak. Stretcher-bearers arrived. He smiled at Mei as they carried him away. Teary eyed, she smiled back. How terrible life would be with only one arm, she thought. Using a bloodstained sleeve, she wiped her runny nose.

The sun began to set. Mei saw her medical officer customer sitting against a wall of sand bags. He waved her over with a tired arm. Sitting down next to him, she realized how much her feet hurt. Leaning into the sand bags added to the comfort.

In broken Vietnamese he asked, "What is your name?"

Chuckling at his attempt, she responded, "Mei."

"Mei," he repeated. Pointing a finger at his chest, he said, "Henri."

"On nee," she repeated.

"Close enough," Henri replied. Pulling out a pack of cigarettes, he asked, "Cigarette, Mei?"

Nodding she accepted the offer. She leaned forward and he lit it behind a cupped hand. They both took several puffs. The sunlight slowly faded over the valley. Henri placed his arm around her shoulders. She rested her head on his chest. The setting sun ignited the sky.

CHAPTER TEN

S lowly waking, Mei gazed up at the wood and sandbag bunker ceiling. A content smile spread across her face. Squeezing the pillow behind her head, she inhaled the cool early morning air. Twisting she stretched sore muscles. It's been how long now, she wondered, three weeks since my last sexual encounter? It really doesn't matter, she concluded. I am no longer a whore. No need to fool myself, she thought. I am really part of the war effort now. "I am a nurse," she mumbled rolling on her side. Scanning the small shelter, she saw the empty cots of her brothel companions. My fellow nurses allowed me to sleep in, she playfully concluded.

Rising from the folding bed, Mei picked up blood stained garments. She gave the dusty clothes a quick shake and dressed. After washing her face in a fairly clean pot of water, she tied her long black hair into a pony-tail. Exiting the shelter, she held her head high and began the short walk towards the infirmary.

Three paratroopers in full battle gear looked into the sky. Mei followed their gaze. A faint high-pitch escalated into a shrill whistle. The paratroopers sprinted for cover. Mei covered her ears. An incoming round shook the ground with a deafening blast. The command bunker erupted. Splintered wood and debris spewed into the atmosphere. Like a sudden tropical downpour, bomb after bomb rained down. Transfixed, Mei stood. Her guts vibrated. All around her, the hailstorm annihilated buildings and bunkers. Planes smoldered on the runway. A transport attempted to take off. The aircraft burst into flames. Survivors staggered out of the wreckage ablaze. A rescue crew racing across the tarmac vanished. Blood splattered remains reappeared.

Dropping to her knees, Mei threw up. Focused on the regurgitated meal in the powdery earth, she felt the cold breathe of death. Swirling dust engulfed her. She stumbled forward. In the dirty haze, she fell. Getting up she ran a few steps before kissing the hard ground again. Conceding she crawled on all fours.

Covered in fine dry filth, Mei scurried into the infirmary. Standing in the small sandbagged framed entrance, she looked into eyes of shocked and bewildered men seeking refuge from the storm. The ground pulsed. Sand trickled down. Mei pushed her way into the crowd. In the limited light, she spotted Lan. The two girls embraced under a creaking support beam. The earth below them shook.

CHAPTER ELEVEN

Days of intermittent shelling succeeded days. The downpour drove the inhabitants of Claudine underground.

Lan popped her head out of the crowded hospital bunker into the mid-day sunlight. She squinted in the bright light. Burnt out vehicles and piles of debris littered the landscape. Swirling dust floated across the wasteland. Closing her eyes, she basked in the warm air. Behind her, a chorus of misery crooned. Taking a deep breath, she slowly opened her eyes. She realized that without morphine, the volume of suffering had intensified. With a confident smirk, she mumbling, "The time is right."

Preparing for her daily errand, Lan grabbed a small canvas satchel. Slinging the cloth bag over her shoulder, she peered back into the shelter. The invading afternoon light illuminated the glistening sweat of half-naked medics. In the foul stagnant bunker, doctors stitched torn flesh, splinted fractures and removed appendages. To complete my exiting ritual I need to say goodbye to Mei, Lan thought. Assisting an amputating physician, a surgically masked Mei looked up. Her dark eyes showed concern. A soft nod said farewell.

Smiling, Lan waved and mouthed, "I'll be back."

Why does Mei always look sad when I leave? Lan wondered. Adjusting the satchel strap, she walked out of the sanctuary. If death wants to find me in the valley, he will. It doesn't matter if you are hiding in a bunker or strolling out in the open.

Under the bright tropical sun, Lan took a deep breath. Exhaling she cleansed her lungs of stagnant underground air. A blast erupted on the deserted tarmac. It's strange, she thought, that the Communist continued to shell the runway. There had been no evacuations or incoming flights for weeks. She quickened her pace. Fresh craters scarred the path. Altering her course, she passed the remains of the mobile brothel. A pile of sticks stuck out of the ground. Trapped in the rubble, the frayed remnants of an African girl's colorful robe flapped in the wind. An appropriate marker, she thought. Bowing she paid her respects for the four Algerian courtesans entombed in the mound. Getting a whiff of the dead, she resumed her journey. They might have been fortunate, she concluded. Their fate had been determined.

At an enclosure dug into a mound of sand bags, Lan squatted down on her haunches. She snorted at the stench emanating out of the cavern. Turning her head, she pulled out a small tin of canned meat from her pack. After opening the can, she crawled into the hole. A French officer curled up in the corner greeted her with a shy smile. Propping his head out of the fetal position, she gave him some water from a canteen. After quenching his thirst, she spoon-fed the man-child canned meat. Now comes the difficult part, she realized. It's time for me to go. The man began to weep. Running her fingers through his oily hair, she calmed him down. Smiling into his confused expression, she slowly retreated into the sunlight.

Approaching the hospital bunker, Lan grinned. Another successful errand, she concluded. A crate tethered to a parachute hit the parched earth beside her. She jumped. White silk danced above the wooden box. Across the blue-sky, specs of cargo harnessed to white canopies slowly descended. Crates drifted into the Communist controlled hills. Other supplies joined previous drops in the no-man's-land of barbed wire and land mines. Having seen this play before, Lan sprinted towards the hospital. Emerging from the barren landscape, the underground residents ran towards the supplies. The Communist initiated another bombardment of the valley floor.

CHAPTER TWELVE

A good three-and-a-half miles south of the battered garrison Claudine, was Isabelle. The isolated fortified position cut off from the other French forces. Having exhausted her water supply and low on ammunition, Isabelle lay dying. It was a dark night. The fading light of a parachute flare sparked the black sky. Man made thunder echoed off the surrounding hills.

In a miserably cramped sand bag bunker, Max prepared his field gear. Taking another large spoonful of canned meat, he chomped down the bland substance. Attempting to quench his thirst, he slowly chewed the fibered glob with back teeth. Sucking out the moisture, he cleaned his MAS-49 rifle. After loading the ten round magazine, he shuffled through his horded rations. He opened another tin of meat. I'd rather carry this in my belly, than over my shoulder, he thought. Swallowing a wad of protein, he felt a renewed sense of energy. His lack of sleep faded. The lighter the load the better my chances, he concluded. He picked up a German Luftwaffe energy bar. Holding the small packet to his nose, he inhaled the sweet coconut fragrance the ten-year-old ration still emitted. Tucking three bars into a pant pocket, he decided this would be the only food he would carry. Shaking his half-full canteen next to his head, he heard the sloshing of the most precious commodity in Isabelle. What the hell, he thought. Unscrewing the metal flask, he downed the warm water with several satisfying gulps.

"What are you going to do for water once we escape the valley?" Muller inquired.

Shaking the last drop onto his extended tongue, Max turned to his friend and replied, "Do you really think we are going to make it that far?"

Muller smiling darkly said, "Some of us will make it. That is the point of the exercise." Chuckling he added, "Besides the one thing the French are good at is fleeing the battlefield."

"Spoken like a true German," Max said.

"Max you know I'm German?" Muller asked tilting his large baldhead.

Max nodded. Everyone knew.

"I changed my name and said I was Swiss to hide from the war crimes committed in my former life. I was a member of the *Waffen- SS*." The shirtless Muller informed. Lifting his left arm, he displayed a large distinctive scar on the underside.

Examining the incriminating evidence, Max nodded. He was familiar with the military wing of the Nazi party. Members of the *Waffen-SS* had their blood type tattooed under their arms. The distinctive marking assisted the allies searching for war criminals. Squinting Max said, "Muller you have been a good friend and companion. You do not need to confess your sins to me. We all joined the Legion to erase the past." Grinning he added, "You will always be Muller to me. There is nothing more to be said."

"I know the way it is supposed to work tonight. We all charge out of here, hoping that you are the one that makes it to the tree line. Those are long odds," Muller said. "I just needed someone to know if I die tonight, I die as a German. That is important."

"Muller, if I die tonight, I don't want to die thirsty. That's why I drank my water ration. Now enough talk about death. Let's get the fuck out of here." Max said shouldering his pack. Slapping Muller hard on his bare back, he climbed out of the humid bunker.

Once in the open, Max scanned the remnants of Isabelle. The southern outpost battered beyond recognition. Small fires burned. Flickering light reflected off the shiny mud. A swirling wind circulated foul plumes of smoke. Patiently Max waited for exiting order: the *Percee de Sang*: the "blood breakout." Studying the barbwire and a maze of trenches, he tried to formulize a strategy for the desperation sortie. Beyond no-man's land, he visualized the flat rice paddies, the steep ascent out of the valley and finally the security of the rainforest. Contemplating the escape route, he caught a whiff of Isabelle's dying stench. It had been over a month since the inhabitants buried their dead. Imagining fresh air beyond the valley, he grinned. Inhaling a cleansing breath in the rainforest is my objective for tonight, he decided.

Reaching into his breast pocket, he pulled out the stub of his last cigar. Delicately holding the last few puffs of enjoyment between his thumb and forefinger, he lit the stogie. The smoke shielded some of the environments foul smells. There was no sense of order. Anxious men abandoned their posts fading into the darkness. Taking one last toke of the cigar butt, he tossed the smoldering remains into the mud. It's now or never, he thought. On his belly, he crawled into the soupy soil under the barbwire.

Wriggling through the muck in the dark, Max heard the movement of other desperate men. Stray explosions added a flash of light. A burst outlined Vietminh troops infiltrating the barb wired obstacle. Max rolled into a rancid smelling trench. What is it? He wondered choking on a lump of resurfacing canned meat. Reaching out in the darkness, he felt the bloated maggot ridden remains of a Tai mountain pony. Nuzzling up against the carcass, he heard hundreds of hurried sandaled feet pass by. I need to piss, he realized. Maybe I shouldn't have chugged my water ration. Random gunfire rang out in the distance. He climbed out of the ditch. Three silhouettes turned to observe his exit.

Without hesitation, Max lightened his load up the hill by half a dozen rounds. The gun-barrel flash illuminated the shocked expressions of three boys falling backwards. Amateurs, Max concluded, running past the dead Vietminh. You never hesitate.

Jogging up-hill, Max's head jerked back and forth. Aided by the burst of gunfire, he could make out men on both sides running in all direction. Small arms' fire blanketed the hillside. Legionnaires and Vietminh shot at friend and foe. My best chance of success is as a loner, he concluded. He dropped to the ground, a wave of men rolled by. Hugging the moist earth, a loud explosion caused the hillside to shake. A rapidly expanding column of fire rose above Isabelle. There goes the ammunition dumps, Max thought. Whether hit or intentionally destroyed it doesn't matter. Isabelle is dead.

The eerie glow of Isabelle's last breath slowly faded over the battle-field. Max got a glimpse of a Tai soldier trying to claw his way out of waist deep mud. Crawling over, Max reclined on the slippery slope. He reached for the tribesman. Locking forearms, Max used what little reserves he had left and pulled the young Tai from the mud's grasp.

"*Merci*," the Tai whispered.

Ignoring the gratitude, Max started to slither away. The tribesman grabbed the German's pant leg. Looking over his shoulder, Max scowled. The Tai shook his head and pointed up the corpse-strewn hillside. A second wave of Communists emerged from the shadows.

On his belly, Max laid motionless. Holding his breath, the damp earth caressed his cheek. He closed his eyes. The rhythmic pounding of the advancing troops tempting him with sleep. To the fading sound of the Communist stampede, he slowly opened an eye. The backs of straggling Vietminh raced downhill towards Isabelle. The mud covered Tai soldier raised his head amongst the recently harvested dead. A French-speaking tribesman, Max thought. He'll know the jungle. I need to stay close. "What is your name?" Max whispered to the potential guide.

"Loc," the tribesman replied.

"Good luck Loc," Max said.

The German and tribesman crawled into the cover of tall grass. The knee-deep field of green ended. Max parted the blades. Terraced sheets of glass reflected the night sky. On a small dike separating the rice paddies three helmeted survivors of Isabelle ran. Looking at his new companion, Max winked. Rising from the grass, he slung his rifle over his shoulder and joined the sprint to the tree line. Starlight sparkled off the smooth surface that fringed the raised berm. Max's heavy boots pounded down on the slick surface. Huffing and puffing, he pumped his arms trying to maintain balance. The dark security of his destination continued to grow. Motivated he ignored his chest palpitations and lack of oxygen. In a cluster of bamboo at the edge of the paddy fields, he dropped to his knees. Sucking in the sweet clean air, he rolled onto his back and smiled at the dark sky. Loc collapsed beside him.

"We need to keep moving," a familiar voice said from the shadows.

With a heavy head, Max looked up. Jean Paul stepped out of the brush with two other tank crewmembers. The old veteran JP made it out, Max thought. Using his rifle, he lifted his tired bones. Behind Jean Paul, five Tai auxiliary troops got rid of their uniforms. The tribesmen French allies put on the black pants and smock tops of the hill tribe people. No surprise, Max thought. I wish I had the option of blending in with the local population. Loc joined his countrymen's costume change.

"I count ten," Max whispered to Jean Paul.

"Eleven," Jean Paul responded pointing down into the surrounding brush.

Waddling over with cramped legs, Max gazed over the jungle hedge. A German Legionnaire reclined. One of his pants legs ripped and bloody. "Wagner?" Max whispered at the soiled faced soldier. "We're moving out."

Slowly rising Wagner winced in pain. Catching Max gawking at the crimson gash exposed by torn pants, Wagner grumbled, "Fucking barbwire."

Eleven exhausted and fatigued former defenders of Isabelle moved through the cover of early morning darkness. Random distant gunfire faded. The morning sky glowed in anticipation of the suns arrival. The sun peeked over the horizon. The procession stopped. Wagner collapsed. The injured German fell asleep as he hit the ground. With a heavy rifle, Max poked a patch of knee-deep grass. The vermin that inhabit the jungle floor are the least of my concerns, he realized. Lying down in the deep brush, he surrendered to the comforting sleep. Relaxing darkness closed in.

A leaking faucet, Max visualized. Shiny and clean, dripping fresh water. Licking dry lips, he thought of opening his mouth under the spout and turning the spigot. Slowly he awoke. His fatigues soaking wet. The surrounding jungle foliage shook of the remnants of a recent down pour. He started sucking the moisture from his damp shirtsleeve. Wagner snored open-mouthed. Squatting in a tight circle the six Tais whispered amongst themselves.

Standing and stretching a drowsy Max approached the Tais' inner circle and asked, "What is it?"

Rising Loc translated, "The hills are infested with Vietminh in search of French stragglers. Our only hope is to find a friendly tribe before the

Communist find us. We need to stick together and head west through the forest avoiding jungle trails."

"Sounds like a good plan," Max said, taking off his helmet and scratching his blond crew cut.

"Max," Loc said looking into the German's eyes, "The Vietminh are not taking prisoners."

"How do you know?" Max asked with a squint.

"We saw the spiked heads of Legionnaires on a jungle trail earlier today," Loc responded.

.

CHAPTER THIRTEEN

The morning sunlight crept across the rough terrain that surrounded the valley of death. The hills around Isabelle's corpse pulsed. Waves of foliage adorned Vietminh launched their final assault. Peering out of a crowded trench, Muller loaded his last clip of ammunition. He paced his final shots at the rippling horde. Squeezing the trigger several times with no response, he felt his stomach churn. Around him, the gunfire from his fellow Legionnaires became sporadic. Squatting down, he removed the bayonet mounted in a tube underneath the barrel of his rifle. Dropping the blade into the soupy mud at his feet, he retrieved it from the water, dirt and blood soaked mixture. His hand shook. This is it, he thought. Death has found me. He fixed his bayonet for a suicide charge. Preparing for the inevitable Legionnaires spoke to their maker. Several made the Catholic sign of the cross. If there is a God, Muller thought. He wants nothing to do with me. Taking a deep breath, he realized the only thing he truly believed in was the racial ideology of the National Socialist Party. I'm a pure Aryan of the master race, he concluded. I am a direct decadent of the noble warrior culture that flourished on the northern plains of Germany in prehistoric times. If an unmarked grave is my destiny, he pondered, I don't want there to be any doubt about my nationality. Looking at his German comrades, he said in a gruff confident tone, "Gentlemen it's been a pleasure. Now let's show these fucking monkeys how real soldiers...no how Germans launch an attack."

The start of the new day glowed across the horizon. Several hundred Legionnaires with fixed bayonets flew out of the trench. They charged into a swarm of ten thousand soldiers of the People's Army.

Proudly puffing out his chest, Muller cried out defiantly, *"Deutschland ubera alles,"* (Germany above all). Ignoring the Communist bullet that tore through his shoulder, he planted his feet and thrust a cold steel spike into the enemy. Pulling back the close-quarters weapon, automatic weapons fire riddled his torso. Dropping to his knees, he slouched forward. Smiling he stained the battlefield with pure Nordic blood.

CHAPTER FOURTEEN

The last two months of constant shelling churned the valley floor into a fine powder. All was quiet. The French conceded the battle of Dien Bien Phu to a victorious guerilla army. Emerging from the hospital bunker, Mei blinked at the bright sunlight. She closed her sensitive eyes. Tilting her head back, she bathed her soiled face in comforting warmth. Cautiously she peeked into the rich blue sky and smiled. I'm still alive, she thought inhaling the summer air. Feeling the tender grasp of her hand, Mei interlocked fingers with Lan. They shared this joyful moment. Glancing at Lan, Mei hardly recognized her little sister. Lan's pudgy round face seemed out of place atop a an oversized shirt and baggy pants. The loose fitting attire secured by a canvas belt cinched tight around a thin waist. Lan scratched at the oily black hair matted on the back of her head. I wonder what I must look like, Mei thought glancing down at her blood stained fatigues.

The wasteland of Claudine came to life. Out of the ruble and holes in the ground, the defeated occupants eerily emerged. Small arms fire popped. Mei and Lan flinched. Around a muddy puddle, soldiers fired their weapons' last round into the muck. The revving sound of oil-drained vehicles raced to freezing. Larger guns detonated to ruin. Mei squinted at an approaching low-lying dirt cloud on the horizon. Oh my god, she thought. Thousands of fatigued and bewildered French troops staggered under the dust plume.

Feeling a hand on her shoulder, Mei turned.

"Put these on," Henri said handing the girls Red Cross armbands. "The Communists are coming."

"Merci," replied a beaming Mei. We made it Henri, she thought. The siege has ended.

He returned her pleasant gaze with down cast eyes. Shaking his head, he walked away.

Mei felt queasy, something was wrong. With a dry mouth, she swallowed and assisted Lan with the armband. The hospital staff changed into medical apparel. Their French faces flush with concern. Mei tugged at her white armlet displaying a red cross. Is this going to save me, she wondered? It should. I'm part of the medical staff, she reasoned. Henri would protect me, she concluded. He is a doctor. He is a good man.

In the stagnant hospital bunker, Mei assisted Henri. The medical staff's sweaty new costumes clung to the defeated caregivers. In the sandbag-framed doorway two Vietminh soldiers appeared. The Communists had arrived. The invaders were barely over five feet tall. Flat helmets covered with branches adorned their heads. They brandished submachine guns with distinctive curved banana box magazines. In the limited light, Mei gasped. One of the soldiers had half a face. Severely scarred and missing an ear, he squinted at Mei. How could this be the enemy? She wondered. How could these young boys inflict so much death and destruction?

The victorious soldiers stood in silence. The apprehensive French medics focused on the intruders. The moans of the wounded interrupted the stalemate. The medics returned to their duties. Scar face looking at his companion shrugged. The Vietminh quietly exited. Gazing at the empty doorframe, Mei felt relived. A humane gesture, she thought. A surgically masked Henri comforted her with a gentle nod.

Late in the afternoon, a curious Mei peered out of the underground sanctuary. A small contingent of Vietminh stood triumphantly atop a French bunker. A victor waved a large red flag fastened to a long pole back and forth. His comrades cheered. Hundreds of exhausted French troops lay on the ground in front of the hospital. The much smaller Vietminh randomly pulled out Europeans from the assemblage. The selected prisoners forced to join an organized march out of the valley. In the distance, the Communists systematically dismantled the French base.

A Communist officer strutted towards the field hospital. Four Vietminh kept pace with the officer's brisk stride. "Out of my way, French whore," the officer barked at a startled Mei. Brazenly he pushed her aside. The officer and the four soldiers entered the infirmary.

Why would he say such a thing? Mei wondered. She checked her Red Cross armband. Did he not see that I am a nurse? Mei jumped. Angry voices flowed out of the bunker. The argument ended. Carrying the infirmary's limited medical supplies, the Communists exited the hospital.

"Mei," Lan called out. "We need your assistance. The Vietminh want us to relocate the wounded."

Grabbing a handle of a stretcher, Mei and three other former working girls began the task of moving the wounded. Late in the afternoon, on the dusty ground laid hundreds of French casualties. Parachute canopies provided shade. The overhead white silk flapped in the dusty wind. In the background, the steady march of prisoners of war. A Communist political commissar waded through the sea of casualties. The Vietminh officer performed racial triage. Vietnamese soldiers fighting for the French received medical care. European officers did not.

Mei knelt down beside a bloodstained cot. Smiling in the face of a French officer left to die, she asked, "Cigarette?"

Slowly he nodded.

Placing the precious wrapped tobacco in his quivering lips, Mei attempted to light it. In the soft afternoon breeze, several attempts failed. She removed it. Successfully she lit it on her own. After taking several large puffs, she gently placed the smoldering cigarette into his mouth. Secured by saliva, it just hung on his lower lip. The Frenchman stared into space. Placing two fingers on his oily neck, she determined his passing. Retrieving the cigarette, she took several puffs for the benefit of the deceased. Gently she closed his eyes and tossed the cigarette onto the blood stained ground.

A Vietminh cadre of five female combatants in black peasant garb marched into the open-air infirmary. Fashionably drooping black berets with a red star insignia adorned their heads. The petite soldiers walked tall. Bolt-action rifles slung over their shoulders. The smallest of the female fighters led the procession. She approached the political commissar. Respectfully she handed him a folded page. After a quick glance at the document, he gave a knowing nod. Slowly turning, he began pointing out the BMC girls. Looking down the finger of his extended arm, Mei froze. Her heart sank with the familiar hollow sensation of a whore in a brothel line-up. This is it, she thought. Death has chosen me for his pleasure.

The expressionless female militia quickly rounded up the Vietnamese prostitutes. Standing in a terrified cluster, Mei hugged the trembling Lan. "Be brave little sister," Mei whispering. A handler broke the embrace.

The female guards pushed and shoved the girls into a single file line behind their madam. The Medical staff and surviving Algerian prostitutes watched. The guards walked down the line tearing off the Red Cross armlets.

A guard tugged at Mei's band. She looked over at her medical officer mentor. "On nee?" she whispered.

Henri looked embarrassed. He shrugged and returned to the safety of humanitarian labor. Coward, Mei thought. A guard shoved her forward. He was just another customer, she realized. She never looked back.

Feeling light-headed, Mei stayed in step with the quick pace. They are going to shoot us, she concluded. I don't want to see Lan die, she feared. Holding back tears, she marched across the pockmarked runway. The petite communists herded the whores to the sunny side of a large antique truck. The rusty transport rode high on bald mud tires. A dark green canvas canopy shrouded the wood paneled truck bed.

The tiny beret-wearing leader brandishing a pistol shouted. "Turn around and lean against the transport."

The female communist randomly patted down the whimpering BMC girls. The guards kept the spoils of cigarettes and jewelry. The harsh handlers amused themselves discarding tubes of lipstick and mirrored compacts.

The pistol-toting leader placed her sandaled foot next to Mei's boot. "Take them off," she commanded.

Obliging, Mei removed her footwear.

Confiscating the boots the handler barked, "This is so you French collaborators won't run away. Now get into the truck!'"

Mei climbed barefoot over the tailgate. Pulling back the flap of the canvas tarp, she glanced over her shoulder. Sitting in the shade, the Communist bitch put on her boots. It appeared to be a good fit. Common thief, Mei concluded. The other BMC girls followed Mei into the hot stagnant cargo hold. Sitting beside Lan on the splintered wood truck bed, Mei hugged her knees. The madam wept. No one spoke. An empty supply tin flew through the canvas flap. The girls flinched. A long faced woman peered in over the tailgate. A crooked grin spread across her hard features. Pointed at the empty metal container, she delightfully informed, "This is for your waste. We wouldn't want you French whores soiling yourselves on the long journey."

Mei chuckled. You arrogant bitch, she thought. We have been burying our own feces in the corner of a crowded bunker for the last two months. The supply tin is a luxury.

The truck coughed to life and lunged forward. The female prisoners bounced around in silence. A beam of light flowed through a hole in the canvas tarp. The penetrating ray danced across the female prisoners. The light faded at dusk. In darkness, Lan poked Mei. Opening Mei's hand, Lan placed an ivory comb that their captors missed. Feeling the small victory in the palm of her hand, Mei grinned.

CHAPTER FIFTEEN

Was it yesterday? I finished my last energy bar or this morning, Max thought. Must have been yesterday, he concluded. It's been four days since the death of Isabelle. Max's moist boots shuffled on decomposing vegetation. Using a straight arm, he shoved the shirtless injured Wagner. Assisted by a moss-covered branch crutch, Wagner moaned wobbling forward. A wadded up shirt cushioned, Wagner's armpit. We are down to three steps today, Max realized. One, two, three, shove, he calculated hearing Wagner's grating groan. Jesus, does he have to make that sound, Max thought scowling at the sweat covered bare back. Up ahead through the dense growth, bobbed the helmeted heads of Jean Paul, Felix and Augustin. The tank crewmembers, are not a bad lot, Max concluded. Considering they are French, he chuckled. Pacing himself behind Wagner, Max realized the jungle's occupancy fee escalated with each step.

Max pushed Wagner past a squatting Felix. Flies buzzed around the Frenchman relieving himself. The grotesque sounds of Felix's dehydration competed with insect clamor. The dazed Wagner snorted at the stench. We are spiraling out of control, Max thought. We escaped Isabelle to die at the hands of diarrhea.

The moaning Wagner came to an abrupt stop.

"What is it?" Max growled peering over the cripple's shoulder.

Wagner mustered up a grunt attempting to point.

A winded Loc came out of the brush. Jean Paul and Augustin followed.

"About twenty Vietminh approaching," Loc said gulping for air.

Checking his rifle, a composed Max prepared for battle. Training and discipline took charge. "What do the Tais want to do?" Max asked.

"The Tais can run," Loc informed. "Hopefully elude them." Glancing at the teetering Wagner, he asked, "What do you Europeans want to do?"

Max studied the scared schoolchildren expressions on the Frenchman's faces. Glancing around at the deep sea of green, Max said to Loc on behalf of the Europeans, "We're going to hide."

Nodding Loc disappeared. The Europeans rolled into the thick foliage.

Lying down in underbrush, Max nuzzled up next to a fallen tree. A very large and colorful centipede traversed down the decomposing log. The rotting timber's parasite population hummed. Motionless in the intimidating bed of green, he grimaced. A needlepoint pricked his lower back. The fungal rash on his groin beckoned him to scratch. The tall grass beside him began to move. Could it be a snake, a rat or just a lizard? Whatever it was, it's large. Slowly inhaling the clammy air, he felt another insect piercing. Flinching, he delicately ground his back into the rotting undergrowth.

Lying silent for the unexpected, he reflected to the nightly ordeal in the Hitler Youth evacuation camp. Uprooted to escape the allied bombing of cities, the youth of Germany found themselves in harsh National Socialist institutions. In the dark to the sounds of whimpering boys, the Nazi squad leader paced the dormitory's hard wood floor. Periodically the youth leader chose a vulnerable boy for his pleasure. To the sound of heavy boots, Max lay in the upper bunk thinking of his mother. She was a well-proportioned Bavarian beauty. Her best feature, long thick blonde locks braided into a crown. When he was very young, they were close. He remembered hugging her in the dark green apron. Her kitchen always smelled of fresh baking bread. Their relationship deteriorated under National Socialism. At first, he would share with her the lessons of his Nazi mentors. Those sessions turned to lectures. When he was ten, she feared him. And well she should. He would have turned both of his parents in if they opposed the Reich. At the Nuremberg train station, she told him he would always be in her prayers. It made him sad to think he snickered at her Catholic devotion. She didn't understand there was no god. If there was a god, he certainly wouldn't have a Jewish son. The rhythmic sound of heavy boots on the creaking floorboards terminated at Max's bunk. Clutching his pillow, Max wished it was his mother's green apron. I hope your prayers protect me, he thought. That night the squad leader selected the boy in the lower bunk.

A snapping twig ended Max's reflection. Peering through the dense brush, he got a glimpse of a Vietminh soldier. Holding his breath, he placed an anxious finger on the trigger. If these bastards are planning to spike my head, it's going to be expensive. I'll take a few of these monkeys with me, he thought. Focused on killing Communist, a collected Max squinted in the direction of the advancing predators. The rustling of advancing troops intensified. Just as quickly, it faded. Looks like my head will remain attached to endure another day in the jungle, he thought. Repositioning provided relief to his sensitive crotch. Staring up into the filtered sunlight, he visualized his mother at the Nuremberg train station. That was the last time he saw her.

CHAPTER SIXTEEN

Max pushed Wagner into the encampment. Ethnical segregation still prevailed. The encircled Tais held court in a squatting repose. The three Frenchmen reclined in a patch of elephant grass scratching at infected leech bites. Assisting Wagner to the moist ground, Max got a whiff of the Legionnaire's infected leg. Closing one eye, he peeked at the swollen blue limb. Wagner's days are numbered, he realized. He covered his shivering countryman with a blanket.

Removing his tattered boots, Max glanced over at the whispering Tais. The soft tribal dialogue evolved into a heated discussion. Rising from the conference, Loc tossed some meager corncobs and manic roots at the French. Walking over the tribesman handed Max a helping of scrounged rations.

Gnawing on the tiny unripe ear of corn, Max asked the departing Loc, "What was that all about?"

Turning, Loc responded over his shoulder, "We did not want to waste our food on the whites."

The next morning, Max slowly rose. His aching frame made it difficult to stand. Jean Paul sat on the moist ground poking at fresh mosquito bites. The other Frenchmen lay on their backs. Sleepy eyed they blinked at the morning sky. Empty matted grass the only trace of the Tais.

"Where are our guides?" Max asked.

"They were increasing their odds of survival, by abandoning their European load." Jean Paul informed. "They left before dawn."

"You can't blame them," Max said with a shrug. "At least they fed us last night." Realizing what little hope they had departed with the tribesmen, his empty stomach churned. Seeing Loc walk into view, he flinched. "What are you doing here?" He exclaimed.

A stoic Loc answered, "You pulled me from mud."

Grinning with blistered lips, Max gave a respectful nod. It was a bad decision to stay but an honorable one. "I'm impressed with your commitment...my friend," he said.

"What should we do about Wagner?" Jean Paul asked. The group all turned to look at the sleeping legionnaire.

"We can't leave him," mumbled Augustin. Removing his shirt, he exposed the infected rash under his arms and belly. "He would be covered with ants by day's end."

"Does anyone have any morphine for an overdose exit?" Felix inquired. "Does anyone want to assist in his...termination?"

"I have a couple of morphine ampoules, I was saving for myself." Jean Paul confessed.

"Belly shot, head shot - it's an overdose job," Max mumbled under his breath. The German expression summed up the solution of injecting a wounded colleague to hasten death's journey.

"Let's hold council tomorrow. I think we can assist him for another day," Jean Paul announced. "In the meantime, I say we piss on him. The fluid that I've been leaking can kill any infection."

The Isabelle alumni encircled the sleeping legionnaire. Holding their manhood, the group stood prepared. Max pulled back Wagner's blanket revealing the blotted dark blue limb.

A disoriented Wagner awoke. Blinking at urine showering his wound, he grumbled, "What? What's going on?"

"Be grateful," Jean Paul told the sleepy German, "That our aim is better than our artilleries."

CHAPTER SEVENTEEN

The communist vehicle skidded to an abrupt stop. In the putrid cargo hold, the BMC girls rolled forward. Lan flexed a leg. Her combat boot pinned the sloshing waste container against the tailgate. It had spilled over twice during the two-day journey. She was determined not to allow any more shit into their tight quarters.

A Vietminh soldier with a saucer shaped helmet pulled back the shielding tarp. He peered in at the girls. His face immediately puckered at the stench. Waiving an automatic weapon, he signaled for them to exit. Mei and the girls hopped out of the truck. Mei's bare feet sank into soft mud. She blinked at the setting sun. A cluster of straw huts cast long shadows across a rain soaked jungle clearing. There were no guard towers or barbwire. Rippling foliage, tall trees and an endless sea of green surrounded the isolated outpost. The engulfing rainforest spoke in the muffled tone of birdcalls, howling monkeys and insect clamor. A work party of thin broken prisoners toiled in a terraced vegetable garden. The existing inmates paid no attention to the new arrivals. The camp's few guards strutted over to investigate. In front of a curious audience, a sentry ordered the girls to strip. They stood naked. The guards salvaged belts and boots from the discarded uniforms. The pile of blood stained clothing set ablaze. A disconnected inmate handed the French collaborators black pants and smock tops. Sliding her muddy feet into peasant sandals, Mei caught the guards gawking. The prison attire did little to hide her shapely frame.

A sentry ushered the former courtesans to an open-air thatched roof facility. In the large empty room, a set table of hot food and fruit awaited the eight girls. Mei and her companions enjoyed a warm meal of rice and fish. Having existed on limited rations during the siege at Dien Bien Phu, this was the best meal Mei had eaten for several months. The portions were ample and included bananas and tea. Taking her time, Mei pealed a small green banana. Her juices flowed in anticipation. She had a hard time recalling anything that tasted so good. A guard instructed the girls to rise. The camp commissar entered the room. He wore a clean but frayed uniform. The tightly buttoned collar appeared uncomfortable. A hard life etched in the wrinkles of his weathered lean face.

"Welcome ladies to Learning and Transformation Camp Number 17. I am Commissar Nguyen Dai Thein. Please be seated." He said in a clear and pleasant tone.

Is this the enemy? Mei questioned. I don't understand the pleasant introduction and fine meal. Taking a seat, Mei shot a suspicious glance at a bewildered Lan.

"I am happy to inform you that you will no longer have to face further oppression from the French imperialists. Due to Uncle Ho's great mercy, you will no longer have to sell your bodies for the pleasures and profits of others. You will come to understand simplicity and purity are what defines a woman's beauty. That through hard work, sacrifice, and education you will be able to re-enter our new society as productive citizens. We have suffered greatly during this struggle for independence. You must realize how your comrades have labored. Hard work will help you find truth. We will start early tomorrow. It will be good for you to experience the worker's joy of harvesting, gathering firewood, carrying water, and sewing. Tomorrow will be your first step towards enlightenment."

The Commissar finished his remarks. The guards instructed the girls to rise. Standing Mei looked down at the wooden floor, perplexed. The commissar was articulate, and spoke as an educated man. What does enlightenment mean? She wondered. Glancing up at the commissar, she caught him examining her body. His gaze was familiar. She attracted the same lustful stare from so many potential customers. She refocused her attention back down at the floor.

The girls occupied a single hut. The sleeping accommodations consisted of individual workers' woven grass mats on the floor. Mei stared up at the thatched roof ceiling. I don't want to a citizen in a Communist society, she thought. I am a nurse for the French Forces. I performed admirably in the valley, she reasoned. I saved lives. I stayed with dying men until the end. I was not a whore. I was a nurse. Rolling over on the hard floor, she realized it didn't matter what she wanted. It never did. Slowly drifting off to sleep, she knew her destiny would always be in the hands of others.

The next day began at dawn. In the center of the compound, the former prostitutes stood with ten other female inmates. The other women wobbled on thin legs. Stoned faced they glared at their keeper. A subtle hand gesture from the guard triggered the assembly to move. Sandaled feet sloshed through the mud. The inmates marched past the camps cluster of thatched roof buildings and entered the jungle. The trail was slick and narrow. It was difficult to keep pace. Where are we going? Mei wondered. How far is it? A glance at a fellow prisoner offered no clues. The detached female just trudged ahead.

An hour later, the small contingent had reached a clearing in the rain forest. The guard climbed atop one of several large piles of wood. He lit a cigarette and said, "Ladies." He paused to take a satisfying puff. "The task is simple. Each of you is required to carry one of these piles of fire wood back to the camp. Take as many trips as you need. If you complete the task, you will eat. If not, you will have the opportunity to finish today's quota along with tomorrow's load." Leaning back, the guard enjoyed his smoke.

The ten veteran prisoners immediately claimed the woodpiles closest to the trail. They began tying the rough timber into bundles. The former prostitutes stared at each other in disbelief.

"We can do this." Mei whispered to Lan.

The veteran inmates headed back down the trail with loads strapped on their backs. Mei remembered using a *mau len* as a child to carry large quantities of rice. Utilizing a bamboo yoke, she balanced a very heavy load across her shoulders. Taking small steps, she set a comfortable pace. Returning for her second load, she passed the former madam. Under a small load, the exhausted middle-aged brothel proprietor gulped for air.

"Be strong," Mei counseled.

It was late in the day. Mei completed her task before assisting with Lan's last load. Mei and her little sister would eat that night. The madam would not.

That night a hundred fatigued prisoners sat on the floor. The commissar had been lecturing for over an hour. Mei sat uncomfortably. She wanted to lie down. The day's hard labor required sleep. The commissar continued with his meaningless rant. What are Marx-Leninist teachings, Mei wondered? She glanced at Lan. Tomorrow I'll show my little sister how to use the bamboo yoke, She decided. That should insure us continuous meals. Searching the inmates, Mei sought out her former madam. The middle-aged woman desperately tried to stay awake. Poor thing, Mei thought, she is not going to last long. Listening again to the relentless drone of Communist rhetoric, Mei wondered, when will it end?

Two hours later, the girls returned to the Spartan accommodations. Lying beside Lan, Mei whispered. "Little sister, do you still have the ivory comb?"

Lan retrieved the treasure from under her mat. She handed Mei the only item that remained from their former lives.

Mei ran the comb several times through her snarled hair. She thought about the sense of satisfaction she'd received, comforting the wounded men under her care. After bringing a sense of order to her long black hair, she curled up. Holding the comb next to her cheek, she quickly joined her snoring roommates in a deep sleep.

CHAPTER EIGHTEEN

"**D**o you think he's coming back?" Jean Paul asked.

Max peered through brush. Plumes of smoke rose from the valley below. "He'll be back," Max responded, "Loc is a man of his word."

"I still think we all should have gone down there," Jean Paul said, "I'd be finishing my second bowl of hot rice by now."

Rolling his eyes at the Frenchman, Max said, "Yes, and I'd be on my third cold beer." Spotting Loc scurrying up the hillside, Max shook his head, "He's alone, and in a hurry. This doesn't look good."

Loc crashed through the brush. Placing his hands on his knees, he took large gulps of air. Between breaths, he informed, "Not friendly...these villagers looking for French stragglers to get Communist reward...Vietminh pay hefty bounty...make tribesman wealthy for life."

Max placed a hand on Loc's shoulder, and said, "Good job." He paused as Loc caught his breath. "Which way do we go?" He asked.

Still bent over, Loc pointed straight up to the saw-toothed crested summit. "Only hope for rescue is higher ground and the friendly ridge-running Meos."

Max leaned into Jean Paul and whispered, "Wagner's fate has just been determined with this course change."

A grim looking Jean Paul nodded. "I'll do it."

From a distance Max watched. A solemn Jean Paul injected the comatose Wagner in the buttocks with several morphine ampoules. The Frenchman rolled the legionnaire onto his back. The young German reclined peacefully gazing skyward with a drug-induced smile. Picking up Wagner's pack, Jean Paul returned to the group.

"Is it done?" Max questioned.

"Yes," Jean Paul said, "It's done. Now let's see if there is anything he has left us to eat." The Frenchman pulled out and dropped a poncho and a blanket. Looking into the almost empty satchel he mumbled, "Son of a bitch."

"What is it?" Augustin asked licking his lips.

Jean Paul pulled out a large bundle of currency to disappointed expressions. He fanned the large denomination bank notes with his thumb "There must be one-hundred-thousand piastres, ($1,200 US), here," He estimated. "How did he get this?"

"I didn't know Wagner that well." Max answered. "I know he liked to gamble. I heard he was lucky with the cards."

Jean Paul squinted in the direction of the corpse. Wagner's shredded boots poked out of the thick brush. "He wasn't that lucky." Jean Paul commented. Holding up the wad of bills, he asked. "What should I do with this?"

"You can carry it if you like," Max said, "It's useless."

"So, I can have it?" Jean Paul questioned.

"No," Max said, "You can carry it. We'll all expect a share when we get to a place it has value."

With a shrug, Jean Paul placed the money in his pack.

Loc motioned the men to follow him up the slippery hillside. The Europeans slowly ascended. On all fours, they crawled up the steep muddy incline. Felix brought up the rear climbing barefooted. The Frenchman's swollen feet no longer fit into his boots.

CHAPTER NINETEEN

It had been a long week transporting firewood. Mei watched as the wood gathering work party plodded into the jungle. Uneasy about the labor reprieve, her heart pounded. A guard escorted her across the compound. What does the commissar want? She wondered. Ascending the three small steps to the commandant's hut, she took a deep breath. Removing her sandals, she entered the office barefooted. The commissar sat behind a large desk writing feverously. Briefly, he glanced up acknowledging her presence and returned to the industrious correspondence. Mei stood submissively. The large desk dominated the small office. A pleasant cross breeze flowed between open windows. On the back wall, in a cracked frame, hung a faded black and white photo of 'Uncle Ho'. On the corner of the cluttered desktop, a large bowl overflowed with ripe fruit. Mei focused on the bananas within her grasp. Her stomached turned. Swallowing back anticipation, she looked away.

A half hour later, the commissar put down his pen. After corralling scattered papers, he placed them in a neat pile. Acknowledging Mei, he said, "Please be seated." With a friendly hand, he identified a small stool.

"Are you from the city or a village?" he asked.

Trying to maintain balance on the wobbly stool, Mei responded softly, "A small village, commissar."

"So, then tell me how you became a whore for the French Imperialist."

Mei felt her mouth drop. Swallowing she responded, "My father could not afford to pay his debts, so I was sent away."

"What was your life like before your father's debts?" he asked.

Looking up, Mei made eye contact. "We were rice farmers producing two crops every year. The planting and harvesting required long days, but for the rest of the year life was simple. We had a vegetable garden that I maintained as the eldest. My younger brothers took care of the chickens and pigs. My father always enjoyed the rewards of his daily fishing trips." Mei paused. Reflecting she visualized her father standing in the open doorway of their modest home. He proudly displayed a dozen large fish tethered to a line. I forgot, I once loved the man who sold me, she realized.

"Do you recall what disrupted your simple life?" The commissar asked.

Slowly nodding she responded, "The village began to trade with the outside world through Chinese merchants. My father enjoyed the initial tools and goods he bartered for with his harvest. The family had always paid a tribute to the government, but it escalated to an unrealistic amount. The entire community toiled to pay taxes. My father became a common laborer. We worked the fields we once owned. Outsiders claimed more and more of the harvest."

"Mei, what 'Uncle Ho' is going to achieve is that all of Vietnam will be like your village was before the French capitalist. We all work together. No one goes hungry. We will abolish unjust taxes. The taxes are why your father went into debt, lost his farm, and sold you. Under communism, we will take back the plantations and redistribute the land to the poor villagers in the rural communities. Like the one you came from."

Is that communism? Mei pondered. It is so simple and morally just, she realized.

"So what do you think of your father now?" he continued.

"He was a victim of the French and forced to sell his daughter," Mei answered.

The commissar grinned. "He was made weak by external forces. The state should raise and educate children. The state would never sell its children into prostitution. You were devoted to your family, and your family sold you. If you were devoted to our cause, we would educate you. You would become a productive member in a workers society. Under communism men and women contribute equally."

As he spoke, Mei began to reflect. Colonialism disrupted her child-hood. She should have been in school at sixteen not a brothel. The medical care she received was so she would not pollute the foreign troops. The French solution for a contaminated BMC girl was abandonment and a diseased death. 'Uncle Ho' was a just and merciful leader to give her this chance at redemption. Tears formed in her dark gemstone eyes. Lowering her head, she wept.

"Mei," he said. "You are also a victim of French Colonialism, not a collaborator. You have paid the price with lost innocence. I will personally educate you. With our glorious victory over the French, you will need to be prepared to contribute to our Communist society. All of us need to work for a unified Vietnam."

"Thank you commissar," she said a sobbing. "Thank you."

Leaving his office an elated, Mei wanted to learn more about the Communist philosophy. The Commissar is a wise man, she thought. I am privileged. He personally is going to instruct me. Running back to her quarters, she entered the empty hut with a single purpose. Lifting up Lan's woven grass mat, she retrieved the ivory comb. Lan will understand, Mei concluded. I'll explain it to her. Exiting the premises, she approached the nearest guard. Extending her arm, she offered the frivolous grooming accessory. The sentry took the possession. After looking from side to side, he pocketed the comb. The guard's reaction puzzled Mei. I anticipated a more dramatic acknowledgement, she thought.

In the cool night air, Mei walked unescorted towards the Commissar's hut. I wonder why he summoned me for an evening session, she thought. Today's lengthy discussion about a classless society was powerful, she reflected. Why doesn't Lan comprehend the simple philosophy? She wondered. The ivory comb was a symbol of our past. We all need to focus on the future. Ascending the steps to the Commissars office, Mei realized, Lan may never understand.

After removing her sandals, Mei entered the small room. The commissar stood with his back to the door. His focus was the picture of Ho Chi Minh. Glancing over his shoulder, he slightly smiled at Mei. Turning back, he continued admiring the black-and-white photo. A bottle of liquor sat atop the cluttered desk. The Commissar held a half-full glass of white whiskey.

"Have a seat Mei," he said staring at the picture. "Help yourself to some fruit if you like."

Mei flinched. The commissar had never offered her food before. "Thank you," she said reaching for the tempting produce. Since their first session, it took great effort to ignore the heaping bowl of fruit. She plucked the largest banana. After a hasty peeling, she shoved the curved creamy softness into her mouth. It tasted so good. Looking at his back, she greedily took another banana.

"Uncle Ho is a great man," the Commissar said admiring the portrait.

Mei gulped down banana chunks.

"He is an educated man, like me." The Commissar continued. "In our new society we will accept all types, farmers, soldiers, peasants, philosophers." Turning to face her, he took a sip of whisky, and added, "And beautiful women like you."

Mei did not fully understand Marx-Leninist teachings. An extensive brothel education schooled her in the desires of men. Standing up, she walked around the large desk. The Commissar took his seat. She knelt down on the wooden floor in front of him. Under the photo of "Ho the Enlightened," she thanked him for the two bananas with an oral talent perfected under capitalism.

CHAPTER TWENTY

Methodically, Max placed one foot in front of the other. Snarled twisted brush clawed at his passing. With a blistered palm, he swung a bayonet at the dense growth. Glancing over his shoulder, he scowled at the trailing Frenchmen. Would it kill one of them to take point, he thought. Grinning darkly, he realized it probably would. Strokes of the long thin blade scratched at the endless jungle. Foliage fell. Max moved forward. He felt a hand on his shoulder. Loc took the lead. Max handed the tribesman the heavy bayonet. Loc took his turn hacking at the emerald wall. Flexing his sore hand several times, Max allowed Loc to find the rhythm. After blazing a twenty-yard trail, Loc broke through the vegetation barrier. The tribesman dropped the knife in the center of a Meo mountain path. Looking back at Max, a stone faced Loc removed his pack and staggered in the direction of barking dogs. Following Loc, Max's pack rolled off his shoulders. I don't care if they are friend or foe, Max thought. I'm done stumbling through this fucking forest.

Tethered dogs howled. Chickens roamed under stilted huts. Pitched palm frond roofs flowed down the steep hillside. A Meo women staring at the two intruders herded a gaggle of children to safety. From the shadow of a dwelling, three tribesmen emerged. Wearing black smock tops, baggy trousers, and sporting colorful blue headbands, the Meo sentries brandished surplus firearms. On wobbly legs, Max and Loc stood in front of the greeting party. The tribesmen scrutinized the trespassers with sympathetic expressions of concern. Thank god, Max thought. Tilting his head back, he closed his eyes. These Meo partisans are French allies.

Cool water, Max thought. His tongue moistened parched lips. Through the slits of heavy eyes, he saw a round faced Meo angel. She slowly poured the clean clear liquid into his mouth. After several satisfying gulps, he yanked the clay jug from her grasp. She jumped back. More, I need more he selfishly rationalized. Elevating the container, he dowsed his open-mouthed face. Cool water flowed down his neck and chest. The wasteful-ness added to the refreshing sensation. I'm alive, he realized. Setting the jug down, Max looked over at Loc. The German winked with a big grin. I could not have done it without you, my little brown guide, he thought.

The standing audience of curious Meos parted. Jean Paul and Augustin collapsed in the comforting shade. Propped up by his elbows, a reclin-ing Max watched the two possessed Frenchmen hydrate. After a few large gulps, Augustin dropped the water jug. Placing his face in his hands the Frenchman wept.

A Meo sentry squatted down. Extending a hand, he offered cigarettes from a wrinkled pack. Loc hastily accepted the offer. Leaning back, he greedily sucked down the addictive vapors.

With more poise, Max delicately pulled an encased cigarette from the paper box. After igniting the tobacco, he took several strong puffs. Lifting a pants leg, he placed the glowing red tip on a very fat black leech. "How does that feel bloodsucker?" he mumbled. Sadistically he twisted the ciga-rette between thumb and forefinger. The sizzling parasite squirmed.

Barking dogs distracted Max's leech hunt. He glanced up along with the Meo audience. A shirtless and barefooted Felix stumbled down the dusty village thoroughfare. The young Frenchman covered with festered sores. Guided by tombstone eyes, he staggered past his companions.

"Felix!" Jean Paul cried out.

Slowly turning, Felix collapsed.

Soothing petite hands caressed Max out of a deep slumber. If I'm dreaming, I hope I never wake, he thought. Tall and graceful Meo women washed out his wounds. They whispered amongst themselves in a musical tone. In long tightly draped black skirts and blouses they cleansed Max's naked battered frame. The warm water and soap massage lulled him back towards sleep. I've heard tales of the insatiable sexual appetite of these vil-lage girls, Max thought. Closing his eyes, he realized no sexual release can compare to what I'm feeling now.

CHAPTER TWENTY ONE

It was warm. Sunlight spread across the interior of the wood shelter. Max rubbed waking eyes. It's late afternoon he concluded. A young partisan squatted amongst the awakening Isabelle survivors. With a toothless smile, the partisan thrust a wicker-encased bottle in Max's face.

"*Nam lu*," he said in a friendly tone.

"He says; let's get drunk," Loc translated stretching from the deep slumber. "It is the universal greeting of the highland people to welcome strangers."

Max nodded at the toothless host. Accepting the libation, he took a healthy swig of Meo moonshine. "Whoa," he exclaimed exhaling toxic fumes. "God, how I needed that," he declared passing off the bottle.

Taking two large gulps, Jean Paul let out a quiet sigh. Loc had a taste and assisted the reclining Augustin.

"Thank you," Augustin whispered.

Everyone glanced over at Felix. The young Frenchman remained in a deep sleep. Covered in sweat, his body fought to heal. Infected and swollen feet poked out of the bedding. Loc shrugged, took another swig and re-started the bottle's rotation.

"It is good to be off the ground," Max slurred slightly.

"I can't wait to dry out my crotch," Jean Paul said evoking laughter. Even the Meo partisan chuckled.

The bottle quickly emptied. The host motioned towards a basket of freshly laundered and mended jungle fatigues. It took some time for the stiff, sore and inebriated Loc, Max and Jean Paul to rise. They dressed slowly. Felix remained unconscious. Curling up in a fetal position a mumbling Augustin pulled a blanket over his head.

Following behind their Meo drinking companion, Loc, Jean Paul and Max limped through the village. The guide pointed up the wooden stairway of a raised long house. The crowded hut buzzed. Gingerly on blistered feet, Max led the way up the creaking steps. He paused in the open doorway. Squatting and seated Meos blanketed the floor. Max flinched. A tall bearded European sat cross-legged amongst the tribesmen. A blue headband knotted on the side, held long black hair in place. The leathery-skinned European wore a tattered, frayed commando uniform. On the shirtsleeves, the three stripe markings of a *sergent-chef*. The commando cackled with the locals in their native tongue.

Spotting Max, the bearded man leapt to his feet. "Welcome gentlemen." He exclaimed. Approaching the three survivors, he offered a firm handshake. "I am Sergeant Jean Guillian of the Composite Airborne Command Group. Please join us," he said motioning an open hand to vacated floor space. "We will eat, drink, and talk about your rescue options." The rapidly talking Guillian continued, "Forgive my excitement, it's been awhile since I spoke French."

"We understand," Jean Paul responded slowly seating himself on the hard wood floor.

"Congratulations on making it this far," Guillian said taking a seat. "I know why you are here. Bad news travels fast."

Getting a whiff of hot food, Max salivated. Several Meo women dished steaming rice into wooden bowls. Focused on the serving process, he calculated his turn. Licking his lips, he painfully waited. A young girl with a round face, sporting a nervous smile handed Max a meal. He immediately grabbed a handful of rice and shoved it into his mouth. Pork fat, Max questioned while he chewed on the seasoned rice. Chomping with an open mouth, he continued to feed his face. Beside him resonated the gluttonous sounds of Loc and Jean Paul.

"How are the other two men?" Guillian asked his ravenous guest.

Through a mouthful of sticky rice, Jean Paul replied. "The jungle has broken one physically and may have broken the other one mentally."

"We have all seen that before," Guillian stated.

"Are there any other commandos in this region?" Max asked wiping greasy lips with a clean shirtsleeve.

"There were originally three of us assigned to organize the hill tribe resistance in this region. The group leader died well over a year ago from battle wounds. The jungle took the other NCO about six months ago. Whether it was a snakebite or tropical disease, no one knows."

"So you are alone?" Max asked as a young server handed him a wine filled bamboo stock flagon.

"Not at all, I have a wife and a child on the way. And this...." Guillian motioned towards the seated Meos "...is my family."

"I'll drink to that," Max said taking gulping potent rice wine.

Ignoring Max's gesture, Guillian continued, "We heard of the big defeat from another mountain village. The bad news initially came from Laotian deserters out of Muong Sai. One defeat and the Laotians show their true loyalty." Guillian informed. He translated the dialogue insulting the low land deserters for the locals. The tribal audience snickered. In French he continued, "Muong Sai is still French and your best course for a safe haven. Or you can stay here with us."

"I don't think we are going anywhere for awhile," Jean Paul responded. Max and Loc nodded.

"Fine, then let's get drunk," Guillian proclaimed lifting up a bamboo stock mug.

CHAPTER TWENTY TWO

It was early morning. Max stood barefoot on the veranda of a Meo hut. Dressed only in a pair of pants, he enjoyed the crisp mountain air on his naked torso. Lifting up his elbow, he examined the receding fungal rash. Smiling at the progress, he turned to enjoy the vista. The coming dawn glowed behind the jagged horizon. Small plumes of smoke rose from neighboring huts. A cadre of gossiping women strolled towards terraced fields. "These are good people," Max mumbled. Hospitably they brought back to life a group of foreign strangers. They feed us. They bath us. They get us drunk. Moreover, they ask for nothing in return. I can see why Guillian has chosen to call this remote corner of the world home. The French commando found paradise in the highlands. The National Socialist classified these people as *Untermenschen*, Max reflected, something less than human. The Vietnamese refer to them as savages, how far from reality these labels are, he realized. The *montagnards*, the mountain people, are a noble race.

At a brisk pace, the tall lanky Guillian strutted through the waking village. Jogging he ascended the stairs of the Isabelle survivors longhouse.

"Good morning, Guillian," Max exclaimed buttoning up his shirt.

The commando nodded in response to the German's greeting. Focused on the dressing Jean Paul, Guillian said, "JP, I'd like to have a word with you. Would you care to join me for a walk?"

Looking at Loc, Max squinted at the exclusion. Must be a French thing, he thought.

"Sure Guillian," Jean Paul replied lacing up his boots. Standing the Frenchman stomped his feet securing the fit. Turning towards the German, he asked, "Max, why don't you join us?"

Guillian frowned at the German inclusion. Hastily he exited. A pursuing Jean Paul followed.

Glancing at Loc, Max shrugged and said, "Let find out what's going on."

Plodding up the steep grade of the village thoroughfare, Jean Paul caught up to the commando. "I hope you don't mind that I asked Max to join us," said a winded Jean Paul.

Looking over his shoulder at the lingering Max and Loc, Guillian turned back to Jean Paul and whispered, "I'm Jewish. Our family owned a department store in Paris. You may have considered us wealthy at the time. When Max's countrymen occupied France, the only thing our wealth bought was deportation to a labor camp rather than a death camp. My mother and I are the only family members who survived. When I say my mother survived, I mean physically. Mentally she will never be the same. If I'm a little crass to your German companion, that's why."

Jean Paul nodded. He did not like dwelling on his own family's wartime loss. Even more, he disliked hearing about someone else's. "I understand," he responded.

The two Frenchmen stopped in the shade an A-framed bamboo shed. Palm branches covered the steep angle pitched roof. A large open doorframe exposed neatly stacked bundles of opium. The cash crop filled the jungle warehouse.

"It has been some time since we have come into contact with the outside." Guillian informed.

Max and Loc lingered into the conversation.

Guillian continued, "Even this spring the Chinese merchants that barter for our opium harvest did not arrive. I fear that our government is about to abandon the highlands to the Communists. We will fight on with or without outside assistance. We have no choice. We would however be able to last a little longer with some support. With the loss of French Airborne Weapon drops, this..." Guillian waved a sweeping hand at the packaged opium, "is our only currency for resupply."

"Guillian, with your knowledge of the highlands and the mountain tribes, why do you need us?" Jean Paul asked.

"Because I'm not going back, I'm never going back!" Guillian stated emphatically. "This is my home. I will never abandon these people!"

Jean Paul flinched at Guillian's outburst. Raising his brows, he solicited Max's assistance.

Breaking the awkward silence, Max said, "Guillian, we owe you and your people a debt of gratitude. How can we help?"

Looking back and forth between Jean Paul and the German, Guillian's pivoting head focused on Max. "I need you to notify the right players that the hill tribes are warehousing last year's harvest. The objective is a weapons-for-opium transaction. The greed of opium merchants should do the rest."

"Guillian, we are common soldiers," Jean Paul said. "I just want to go home." Raising his shoulders, he confessed, "I wouldn't know who to notify."

Placing his hand on Jean Paul's shoulder, Max addressed Guillian, "I don't know who to talk to either. However, I will try to find out. Your message will get delivered."

"Thank you, that is all I can ask," Guillian said.

"I just don't think we are ready to deliver your notification today," Max said smiling.

"As I said before stay as long as you like," Guillian replied. "When the time is right, we will escort you to the outskirts of our territory,"

CHAPTER TWENTY THREE

Max placed a leather patch inside a tattered boot. This is it, he thought. After two weeks of *montagnards'* hospitality, our westward march resumes. Standing up, he stretched his stocky frame. Taking a deep breath of the cool air, he glanced around the thatched roof hut. Jean Paul dressed a mumbling Augustin. That's going to be trouble, Max concluded examining the fragile Augustin. The jungle broke the Frenchman once, he realized, he might never recover. Gazing at the reclining Felix, Max said grinning, "You're the lucky one. While we spend the next week trekking towards the Muong Sai airstrip, you'll be having Meo girls washing you daily."

"Just don't forget about me Max," Felix mumbled between short breaths.

Squatting down next to Felix, Max said "I won't forget about you," then glanced over his shoulder at Jean Paul and Augustin added, "They won't let me. Adieu, my friend."

Shouldering his pack, Max exited the hut. The three Frenchmen said their farewells. A light morning fog clung to the terraced hillside community. In the cool mist, Loc stood amongst Guillian and a dozen Meo warriors. This may not be that bad, Max thought admiring the heavily armed escort. Departing Max exclaimed in a humorous tone, *"Marche our Creve"*.

Guillian translated for the Meos the unofficial motto of the French Foreign Legion, "March or Die."

Three days later, a light rain began to fall. Great, just fucking great Max thought. He trudged forward maintaining a visual with the Meo escort. "Nothing like a little moisture to accelerate my fungal rash," he grumbled.

The trail dead-ended. Cascading boulders draped in growth rose into the clouds. Across the steep grade, the Meos traversed skyward.

Looking up at the spectacle, Jean Paul exclaimed, "You've got to be kidding me."

Max smiled at the Frenchman and shouldered his rifle. Grabbing hold of a crevice in the moss covered wet wall he started his ascent. The air was thin. His heart pounded. Max clawed at the rock surface with soiled hands. His muddy boots blindly searched toeholds.

"Do you need any help?" Guillian asked.

Max flinched. Where did he come from? He questioned. Catching his breath, he responded by shaking his head.

"Good, I'm going to check on the Frenchmen," Guillian informed.

Max clung to the mountain face. The lanky Guillian nimbly descended with the agility of a jungle cat.

Exhausted Max reached flat terrain. Sunlight broke through retreating storm clouds. In the shade of a banyan tree, Loc and the Meo escorts squatted in a loose circle. A cloud of cigarette smoke hung over the encircled tribesmen. Lying down on the wet ground, Max caught his breath. The agile Guillian suddenly appeared carrying an extra pack and the Frenchmen's rifles. The commando dropped his arduous cargo and squatted down amongst the Meo.

Max studied Guillian resting on his haunches. Jesus the commando is hardly winded, he thought. What an amazing specimen. Jean Paul's head popped up above the ridge. Max's tired bones groaned. It's time to move on, he realized. The procession resumed.

Sunlight faded over the horizon. Guillian made his way back to the sluggish Isabelle cluster. Leaning into the exhausted cadre, he whispered, "Communist patrol headed in our direction, about ten to twenty. It looks like they are escorting a small work party. Follow our lead."

Max nodded.

Guillian crawled into the brush.

Dropping his pack, Max prepared for battle. Loc did the same.

"We hide?" Jean Paul questioned in a high-pitched scratchy voice.

Max scowled at the Frenchman. Not this time *Crêpe Suzette*, he thought. My days of hiding are over. I'm about to payback those Commie bastards with interest.

Wobbling in place an opened mouth Augustin dropped his rifle. He started to wander off. Jean Paul tackled the disoriented Augustin. The two Frenchmen rolled under the covers of the blanketing growth.

Max pulled back the thick brush. Through clenched teeth, he growled, "Just keep him quiet."

On his back, Jean Paul wrapped his legs around his companion. Muffled sounds emanated from JP's cupped hand across Augustin's mouth. Looking over the shoulder of the confined Frenchman, Jean Paul acknowledged the German's order with a nod.

Max hugged the moist earth. All was quiet. A twig snapped. Distant brush crackled. The rustling jungle pulsed. Ten? Twenty? Max thought trying to confirm Guillian's Vietminh estimate. In the fading light, an armed Communist escort and common laborers waded through the waist high brush. Max took a shallow breath awaiting the Meo's lead. He calculated a shooting sequence. Potential targets came in and out of view. An anxious trigger finger focused on a head shot. The Meos opened fire shredding Max's intended target. The precision firepower of the tribesmen eliminated his second and third objectives. Max's rifle barked once. A fleeing unarmed collie collapsed.

Smoke hung over the kill zone. The Meos emerged from the brush. Merciful bullets silenced the moans of the wounded. Max approached a young soldier of the People's Army. The victim squinted hard at the German. Pumping blood flowed from the boy's thigh. His black pants glistened. The hostile took short breath. His existence faded. Max confiscated the dying man's pack. Ignoring the moaning owner, Max pilfered a pack of *Gauloise Bleue* cigarettes and an engraved Zippo lighter. He rubbed his thumb across the etched inscription; *3e Bataillon / 13e Demi-Brigade de la Legion Etrangere*, (the 3rd Battalion /13th Foreign Legion Half-Brigade). "This was my unit," he mumbled to the communist thief. The dying boy's gaze pinched with fear. Focused on the enemy Max lit up a smoke. Exhaling a victorious plume, he mumbled the brands slogan, "Freedom Forever."

"Leeches?" Loc asked.

"No, just this leech here," Max motioned towards the dying hostile. "Blood suckers, with their artillery, shelling us day and night, slowly sapping the life out of us."

Flicking the soft pack of *Gauloise* in Loc's direction, Max offered a smoke. Loc accepted. The tribesman and German puffed away. The dark tobacco produced a strong rich aroma. Observing the smoking ritual, Jean Paul joined his Isabelle alumni.

Max blew a cloud of smoke. As the dancing vapors dissipated, he reflected on his eight-week affair with Isabelle. How could men of such commitment and honor be so soundly defeated? "I took the water off wounded Legionaries to survive in the valley," He confessed. "I didn't think I would make it this far."

"Where are we?" Jean Paul replied glancing around. "We haven't made it anywhere."

"You're right," Max agreed, sucking in the acrid fumes. "When they..." He nodded to the victim at his feet, "started that precision bombardment, I thought that was it. I'd have coffee in the morning with a *komerad* and by afternoon all that would be left of him was a bloody foot."

"Who are you talking about?" Jean Paul questioned.

"There are so many examples, but the one I refer to was Gregor. You remember we drank your rum with him one night." Max responded.

"Beside his foot, that was his arm in the wire," Jean Paul informed.

"Was that his?" Max questioned.

"I'm pretty sure," Jean Paul said looking at Loc for verification.

Loc responded with a polite but confused nod.

"God I hated seeing that arm every day," Max said taking a long drag on the cigarette. "What do you think happened in the valley after our departure?"

"I don't like to think about it," Jean Paul answered softly tossing and catching the engraved lighter, "but this is not a good sign."

Looking down into the soiled twitching face of the dying boy, Max visualized him picking through the remains of dead Legionnaires. Taking another puff on the cigarette, he thought of the military bureaucracy that placed him at the bottom of the valley. "Fuck them," he mumbled flicking the smoldering butt. It's all just a game moving expendable pawns around the battlefield, he concluded. Dien Bien Phu was a fool's errand. It's not the first time I've been duped, he realized. Blinded by military discipline and loyalty, I've paid for the mistakes of others. The battle of Caen was no different, he thought. Superior British and Canadian forces slaughtered the boy soldiers of the 12th SS Panzer Division *Hitlerjugend*. Gazing into the face of the dying Communist, he saw the hopeless expression of *gefallene kameraden* (fallen comrades). There was no honor in unconditional loyalty, only death. Reaching under his collar, he tore out the Hitler Youth shooting proficiency badge. Rolling the small token in his hand, he recalled the sacrifices he made to keep the memento. It had been with him through the war, the prison camp, and here in Indochina. Letting out a satisfying sigh, he tossed the tiny disc on the jungle floor.

A pistol popped. Max jumped. A Meo accelerated the dying boy's afterlife journey. Lifeless eyes gazed into the jungle canopy. The peaceful expression distorted by a gapping blood splattered bullet hole. The compassionate Meo smiled wide. Displaying a mouth empty of teeth, the shooter gestured for a cigarette. Max obliged.

"Next time let's kill one that smokes cigars." Jean Paul said.

Chuckling at the black humor, Max pivoted around. Victorious Meos robbed the dead. Other tribesman dragged the fallen into the brush. Realizing the smoking ritual wasted valuable time; Max grabbed the corpse at his feet and assisted with the clean up.

Turning over a Vietminh body, Max stared at the victim's feet. Like a circus clown in oversized shoes, the small corpse looked comical in a pair of large Legionnaire boots. Snickering Max pulled off the boots. Tying the laces together, he tossed them over his shoulder. Extracting the dead man's pistol, Max grinned. He stood to examine the remarkable weapon in the jungle's filtered sunlight. A TT-30 Tokarev, he realized enjoying the grip of the Soviet handgun. Turning his hand back and forth, he recalled the *Wehrmacht* cherished this captured weapon during World War II. Glancing around, he brandished his prize. The toothless Meo responded to Max's enthusiastic handgun display by holding up a handful of European watches.

"We're heading back in the morning," Guillian said to Max as they exited the cleanly picked battlefield.

"Understood," Max said.

"We will eat well tonight on the food provided by the People's Army," Guillian said grinning.

Around a small campfire, the group ate, smoked and enjoyed some rice wine on their last night together. In the shadows at the edge of the fire, Jean Paul held onto a broken Augustin. The young Frenchman had been mumbling incoherently since the ambush.

In the morning over a smoldering fire, the Isabelle survivors said farewell. Grabbing hold of Max's shirtsleeve, Guillian pulled him aside and said, "We are counting on your assistance to find us an opium broker."

"Don't worry, Guillian," Max said patting the commando's shoulder, "If I can't find you a sponsor, I'll procure munitions for you on my own. It's the least I can do to repay your people for their hospitality."

Squinting at the German, Guillian asked, "Will you be able to find us?"

"No," Max said, then pointing at Loc added, "but he will."

The rotors of the French Air force H-19 helicopter cut through the humid air above the jungle canopy. Blurred terrain passed beneath the aircraft. The pilot had little hope of spotting any survivors. It had been a month since the defeat at Dien Bien Phu. The odds of trekking over a hundred miles in this environment were long, especially for Europeans. The tropical sun began to set over the horizon. The pilot gave a slight shrug to his co-pilot and started a slow sweeping turn towards the French outpost of Muong Sai.

"Wait!" the co-pilot called out. A flickering spark reflected the setting sunlight.

Changing course, the pilot hovered in the direction of the twinkling signal. Peering through binoculars, the co-pilot spotted four men waving their arms frantically. One held a tiny mirror above his head.

"My god," exclaimed the co-pilot, "three of them are white."

CHAPTER TWENTY FOUR

The rain continued to fall. It was midday. The skies over Transformation Camp Number 17 were black. Soaking wet and standing ankle deep in mud, Mei assisted by Lan dug a shallow grave. Awaiting internment, the wet corpse of their former madam lay peacefully next to the three-foot deep hole. The brothel executive died from a combination of starvation and fatigue. Mei felt some comfort in knowing that her former employer would no longer have to suffer. What was the Communist lesson in working a woman to death? Mei wondered. She deposited another shovel full of soupy mud next to the corpse. The commissar stood on the porch of his hut observing her labor. He will undoubtedly want me for another session tonight, she thought. I hope we can get the sexual business over with quickly. I don't mind reciting Communist gibberish during the day, she realized. It is a better alternative than hard labor. However, at night all the talk about a workers' society as a prelude to sex is a waste of precious sleep time. I'm still a whore, she concluded, just servicing one client to stay alive.

Lan's black prisoner attire speckled with splattered mud. She mechanically shoveled small handfuls of muck from the hole. Stone faced, with sunken eyes and sharp cheekbones, she made the meager grave digging contribution. Mei was tired, but healthy. After sex, the Commissar would pay for her talent with fruit or the left over remains of his meals. She knew better than to ask for permission to take any food back to the prison population. The strict rules forbid it.

The feisty Lan, had become another lifeless inhabitant of the camp, Mei realized. When was the last time my little sister smiled, she wondered. It must have been when we would use the ivory comb on each other's hair at night. Why did I steal her treasured comb? I was a fool, she concluded.

The steady rain accelerated. The commissar abandoned his observation post for the dry protection of his office. A barefoot Mei climbed out of the grave. In the torrential downpour, she spun around. There were no guards. Under the cover of the rainstorm, she pulled Lan out of the hole. She assisted her frail little sister to the shielding protection of a nearby tree. Leaning against the trunk a shivering Lan hugged her knees.

Searching the saturated ground, Mei picked up a small twig and broke it in half. This will have to do as chopsticks, she thought rubbing the sticks together. Coins, she remembered. I need three small coins. Kneeling down she sifted through the mud and retrieved three small stones. Hastily she cleaned the pebbles on a wet sleeve. Returning to the gravesite, she rolled the dead body of her former madam into the watery grave. Soupy mud engulfed the corpse. Mei knelt on the madam's chest. The three stones coins went into the deceased's mouth. The crude chopsticks placed between the madam's teeth. "You can now leave this world without want or hunger," Mei whispered.

Entombing the madam in heavy mud took time. Mei patted the grave with the crude spade. Dropping the shovel, she joined her little sister. A whipping wind blew the cascading rain across the deserted graveyard.

"I am so sorry Lan," Mei said embracing her trembling friend. "I never should have stolen your comb."

Lan looked at Mei, with hollow eyes. She said nothing. Lowering her head, she snuggled against Mei's bosom. Concealed by the storm, Mei held her broken companion.

CHAPTER TWENTY FIVE

The late afternoon sun hung in the clear blue sky. After two days in the infirmary, Max blinked at the bright sunlight. Flanked by Jean Paul and Loc, he strolled down the dusty path towards the garrison's exiting checkpoint. The rolled up sleeves of new fatigues revealed his tan and scratch-marked forearms. The unbuttoned shirt exposed his muscular chest. The shoulder holster strapped to his torso displayed a confiscated Soviet pistol. He walked in a pair of new boots. With each step, he enjoyed the sensation of dry feet. Seeing the highland village below the airstrip, he licked his lips anticipating a cold beer.

Jean Paul kept pace. A large puffy shirt emphasized the Frenchman's weight loss. A tightly cinched belt held up a pair of baggy khaki slacks.

Loc tagged along in the green military fatigues of a Tai solider. The long sleeved uniform had two large breast pockets and additional storage pouches on the sides of the pants.

Upon exiting the garrison, a tiny old man blocked their advance. He removed his pointed coolie hat. Looking submissively at the ground, he mumbled, "Laundry?"

Shaking his head, Max sidestepped the solicitor.

A teenage boy wearing a white singlet draped over a bony frame ran up to Max. He pulled a cigarette from behind the ear of his close-cropped head and asked, "Soldier, you got light?"

Stopping, Max flicked his lighter obliging the request. After taking several puffs the skinny kid asked, "Soldier, you want young girl to suck you?" With the smoldering cigarette, he pointed in the direction of a smiling soiled faced teenage girl. In the familiar peasant black attire, she waived at the potential client. Glancing at the merchandise, Max shook his head and continued towards the cold beer objective.

"Soldier, maybe you want opium?" The teenage pimp called out.

Ignoring the proposal, Max turned to Jean Paul and asked, "How is Augustin doing?"

"Not good," Jean Paul said. "He slept under the hospital bed again last night. When I asked him why, he said in a matter of fact tone, that he was hiding from Communist patrols."

"I've seen strong men break before. It is never a good thing," Max responded.

"At least he stopped that irritating mumbling," Jean Paul said.

"So tell me JP, do you have Wagner's money?" Max asked.

"Sure do. He would have wanted us to enjoy it," Jean Paul responded.

"Since the drinks are on Wagner, let's drink to him first." Max said.

"Agreed," Jean Paul answered.

Max and Jean Paul looked at Loc for his confirmation.

After a short pause, Loc mumbled, "Agreed."

Entering an open-air bar under a thatched roof, Max felt the temperature drop. The air circulating under the palm frond ceiling provided a comfortable shaded atmosphere. The saloon's dirt floor showed the blemishes of many a spilled drink. An assortment of French military personnel and prostitutes occupied the tavern. The bar girls far outnumbered the servicemen. A skinny chicken roamed around the earthen floor in search of food. The drinking counter consisted of a large wood plank resting on several oil drums. Behind the bar, two flat-nosed Laotian girls in white cotton dresses served up bottles of cold brew from an ice filled galvanized tub.

A small elderly Laotian woman greeted the trio with basic French, "Welcome, brave men, what please you?"

"We are looking for cold beer," Max informed.

"You come to right place. I have cold beer fresh from Hanoi. You want girl?"

"No, just beer," Max insisted.

"Maybe girl later then." she persisted. "We have many very clean young girls for you to choose from."

The seating consisted of a combination of wood stools, benches and chairs around and wooden tables of various shapes and sizes. The three jungle survivors selected a wobbly table and confiscated three chairs. A petite, round-faced teenage girl brought three glistening bottles of beer. Grabbing a cold bottle out of her hand, Max lifted it up and said, "To Wagner." Tilting his head back, he poured the cool carbonated refreshment down his throat. After only a few large gulps, he drained the glass container and slammed the empty bottle on the table. Wiping his moist lips with the back of his hand, he concluded that beer is a good thing.

The round faced bar girl brought over a replacement bottle. Max grabbed hold of her wrist and spun her onto his lap. Touching bottles with his drinking companions, he took another swig of cold brew. The teenage girl snuggled up to his bare chest. Looking up into the bamboo rafters, Max blindly called out to the proprietor, "Mama, some smokes please, cigars and cigarettes!"

A carton of Lucky Strikes and a handful of cigars joined the empty beer bottles cluttering the unbalanced tabletop. Max lit the large stogie, with the legionnaire engraved lighter. Acknowledging the clinging bar maid, he politely exhaled out of the side of his mouth.

"At least we did not have to kill anybody for the smokes this time," Jean Paul said biting the tip off a cigar.

"At least not yet," Max commented grinning.

With the cigar smoldering between clenched teeth, Max closed his eyes. His callused hand comforted by the grasp of a cold bottle. Dry feet, cold beer, a young girl and pleasant smoke, he thought. The payoff he realized for cheating death once again. This moment is all that matters. Placing the chilled bottle to his lips, he took another taste of reality.

Max investigated a tug on his shirtsleeve. Loc pointed to a group of Tai Auxiliary troops entering the bar. Son-of-a-bitch, Max thought. "Excuse me darling," he said lifting the girl from his lap. She elegantly stood beside his chair as Max, Loc and Jean Paul focused on the new arrivals.

The five Tais procured a table. The table of three stood up. Loc proclaimed loudly, "*Nam Lu*" raising a beer to his countrymen.

"Mama!" Max roared, "Beers for my brown brothers." They made it, Max thought. They did not abandon us. They carried us for a week.

The startled Tais stood sporting wide smiles. They embraced their fellow Dien Bien Phu survivors. Dust kicked up from the reception. The two groups made it a point to hug one another.

"Loc," Max said, "Tell our brothers the drinks and anything else they want is on us." A token payback, Max realized for a shriveled unripe ear of corn.

Loc pulled up a stool to join his countrymen. Max made eye contact with Jean Paul and titled his head in the direction of their vacated table. No need to complicate the reunion, with language issues, he thought.

Relighting his cigar, Max leaned forward across the table and asked, "What do you want to do about Felix and Guillian's request?"

"I'm going to do nothing," Jean Paul responded with a sour face. Leaning back in his chair, he added, "They'll probably send a rescue mission for Felix. Guillian should just come home then."

"Guillian is not coming home," Max responded. "He asked for our help after saving our lives, we owe him," Accepting two fresh bottles of beer, he dismissed the barmaid with a wave.

"Max, did you know Guillian is a Jew?" Jean Paul said taking a sip of beer. "The commando lost most of his family due to German incarceration."

Flinching back, Max responded, "I had no idea."

"You seem surprised."

"I am surprised," Max said with a wrinkled brow. "So much of my education evolved around trying to identify Jews. It was all part of the National Socialist agenda. They would even bring Jews into the classroom. The poor bastard would stand at attention, the teacher would use a pointer to identify his inferior facial characteristics. I have to tell you JP, I never would have guessed that Guillian was a Jew. He looks more like a Meo, than a European."

"So do you still feel a sense of obligation towards Guillian?" Jean Paul questioned.

"You think because he is a Jew, I'm going to change my mind. I will admit it makes it awkward. I do not like the reminder of the anti-Semitic behavior of my youth. But the fact that he is a Jew doesn't change my commitment," Max said.

"Max, we are soldiers. We follow orders. Let somebody else pay him back. This is not our responsibility," Jean Paul lectured.

Sitting up Max responded in a harsh tone, "I've always been a soldier, since I was a boy. The Hitler Youth taught me to obey all orders unconditionally. The Nazis taught me to shoot, to hate Jews, and to fight back if I did not want the older boys to sodomize me. The last order I followed unconditionally placed me at the bottom of a valley to endure. I have more than paid my debt to the Legion. I endured." Taking a deep breath, his speech softened. "We have all been broken down differently, Augustin mentally, Felix physically and my sense of loyalty has been shot to pieces. I am no longer going to have someone else decide my battles. Whether it was the *Wehrmacht* or the French Expeditionary Forces, I have been loyal to two losers and two lost causes. From now on, I am going to pick my own battles and my own causes. If they are the wrong ones, then I am to blame. My blind loyalty has brought me to the edge of the abyss many times. I told Guillian, I would try to pay him back and that is what I am going to do. The fact that he is a Jew is irrelevant. Nobody is ordering me to do this. For the first time in my life, the only person I'm going to be loyal to is Max Kohl."

"Are you going to walk out on your Legionnaire commitment?" Asked a squinting Jean Paul.

"I abandoned that obligation with the first step I took out of Isabelle. I just didn't know it at the time," Max responded with a crooked smile.

"What are you going to do after you fulfill your sense of responsibility to Guillian?" Jean Paul asked.

Taking a puff on his cigar, Max glanced around at the tropical bar. Focused directly at Jean Paul, he answered, "I'm going to do the same thing I've done since I was a boy. I'm going to survive one day at a time."

"Max, I hate to see you throw your life away in this god-forsaken country," Jean Paul pleaded.

"If it is any consolation my French friend, I should have died long ago," Max said grinning.

"Well since I'm not going to talk you out of it. Is there anything I can do for you, my *Boche* brother?" Jean Paul asked.

"You can give me a share of Wagner's money," Max replied.

"I'll give you all of Wagner's money," Jean Paul answered. "That is if there is anything left after tonight"

"Thanks JP."

"No thank you Max."

The two men touched bottles. "March or die," Max toasted.

"March or die," Jean Paul echoed.

CHAPTER TWENTY SIX

The ceiling fan creaked. The swirling metal blades feebly circulated the humid stagnant air in Petru Rossi's second floor flat. Cigarette smoke had stained the white plaster walls a murky yellow. A chitchat scurried across the tainted plaster. The gecko took refuge behind a non-descript painting hanging at a slight angle. The urban clamor and pungent aroma of downtown Saigon flowed through open windows.

Waking to the barking morning rush hour, Petru rose from sweat-moistened sheets. He sat on the edge of the bed with a heavy head. Motionless he contemplated his next move. No sudden movements, he concluded.

"Shit," he grumbled rubbing his throbbing noggin. Six, maybe six and half hours of sleep, he calculated. Is it Tuesday? He questioned. Damn, today is a travel day, he realized. Because of the French defeat, I have to fly into Laos to assess the effect on the opium trade. It had better be good news, he thought. The heroin laboratories of Marseilles depend on Indochina opium.

Standing on the wood-planked floor, he stretched his tall lean physique. His bare feet shuffled towards the water closet. In a wobbly stance, he took a healthy piss. Turning on a calcium-encrusted facet, he braced for the sobering cold. Holding his breath, he doused his face with cupped hands of cold water. Between the third and fourth handfuls, he diluted the hangover. In the water spotted mirror, he studied his reflection. Guided by the image, he investigated fresh scratches on a left cheek. The shallow cuts tender to the touch. Stroking his cheek, he recalled his satisfying late night exploits at the House of Butterflies. That little China doll was feisty, he thought. She was louder than most and unwilling to submit. She surrendered. They always do.

Using a straight razor, he began to remove thick stubble. The sensitive cheek required extra care. After shaving, he massaged hair tonic into his scalp. The thick black greasy locks combed straight back. To compensate for the humidity, he drenched his chest with cologne.

Buttoning up a starched white shirt, Petru's heart raced. God how I hate to fly, he thought. Large planes are bad enough, he concluded. But these northern junkets require a small single engine aircraft. The journey always ends on a dirt runway next to some isolated Laotian village whose name I can't pronounce.

He tossed a paper wrapped package of clean laundry into a soft leather satchel. I don't to confirm its contents, he realized. The cleaners know who I am. They would not make a mistake. After zipping up his travel bag, he checked his French MAB Model C pistol. The "pocket pistol" was his weapon of choice. He always did business at close quarters.

Carefully Petru wrapped a shriveled clove of garlic in a handkerchief and placed it in his pants pocket. The garlic an ingredient for Petru's chosen profession. Petru Rossi was in the *milieu*, an accepted gangster in *Unione Corse*. The secretive criminal organization rooted in the traditional social codes of the arid, mountainous island of Corsica. Adhering to custom, Petru initiated bloody vendettas to defend uncompromising family pride and loyalty. The seasoned hit-man sought vengeance by rubbing garlic on the barrel of his gun. The ritual assured painful bullets.

The small single engine plane hummed. The rear seats removed to facilitate cargo. The destination was Phong Savin, on the Plain of Jars in Northern Laos. A former French air force officer Rene Bergot piloted the aircraft, Petru the only passenger. Rene was as tall as Petru and at the age of thirty, a few years younger. Although not good looking, Rene had a pilot's confident attitude and a natural charm that made him extremely likeable.

Glancing over his shoulder at the tightly packed cargo, Petru shouted over the engine drone, "What are you hauling?"

"Liquor and cigarettes," Rene responded. "They always seem to be in short supply in the north, and always good for bartering purposes. I had the seats and parachutes removed to allow for the full load."

"Parachutes?" Petru asked.

"Don't worry Petru. When I flew military missions over the rain forest, I, like most pilots, deliberately left the parachutes behind. There was no need to survive a crash only to prolong your misery by a slow death in the jungle."

Reaching down, Petru firmly grabbed the underside of his seat. He focused on the horizon. God how I hate this, he thought.

"I know someone you should meet once we get to the hotel," Rene said. "He's a German, survived the big defeat by walking out of Isabelle."

"Isabelle?" Petru asked.

"Dien Bien Phu, Isabelle was the southernmost garrison," Rene answered. "Well, the German and a handful of other survivors marched out on the last day of the battle one-hundred-and- twenty-five miles to safety."

Turbulence jostled the tiny plane. Petru closed his eyes. Sweaty palms clutched the underside of the flimsy seat.

Rene continued. "So the German tells me he owes gratitude to the mountain tribe that assisted him on his journey. He gets me to fly him and a cargo of small arms to a remote airstrip. It was the saddest collection of munitions I have ever seen. He still has a couple of day's journey left. I watched him bury the cargo and then disappear into the brush."

"Was he by himself?" Petru asked.

"No, he is always with this young Tai. The Tai walked out of Isabelle with him. The two are inseparable. So the German asked me to pick him up in two weeks. I buzz the dirt runway two weeks later out of curiosity. The German and Tai were waiting for me. But get this. They have twenty-five kilos of pure opium and another passenger. Apparently the German left this kid from one of the Tank crews behind and went back to get him. I fly them all back to the Plain of Jars. They sell the opium below market. The German gives me a nice tip to fly the young soldier back to Saigon."

The chattering pilot may be on to something, Petru thought. This German may have a unique insight on the flow of opium from the grower's perspective. "What is his name?" He asked.

"Max," Rene responded, "He'll be easy to find. He stands out. As I said, he is German, blond hair, firm jaw, broad shoulders. Looks like an Aryan model off a Nazi propaganda poster. He and his tribal partner Loc are regulars at the King Cobra."

The small aircraft bounced along the red clay tarmac of the Phong Savin airport. Petru let out a soft sigh. As the plane taxied off the runway, he dried wet palms on the front of his pants. Emerging from the aircraft, Petru stepped down onto the red soil. Taking a calming breath of mountain air, he resumed his cool calculating mobster persona.

While Rene negotiated with locals to unload the cargo, Petru helped himself to a bottle of scotch and a carton of cigarettes. Rene gave him a slight nod of acceptance. Petru nodded back and placed the liquor and smokes in his under packed satchel. Slinging the bag over his shoulder, he headed off to the King Cobra Lodge.

The dirt road glistened from a recent rain. The air was crisp and clean. Strolling through the frontier town of Phong Savin, Petru was happy to be back on the ground. He took extra caution to avoid puddles. In the distance, hollowed-out boulders of various sizes littered the grass-covered hills. The Corsican had no interest in the historical significance and unsolved mystery of these two thousand year old stone jars.

Thatch-roofed storefronts flanked the thoroughfare. Petru felt the glare of the Chinese merchants observing his passing. Defiantly he stared back. Opium intermediaries, he thought. They carved out a very profitable niche for themselves in these highlands. Their basis was nothing, he concluded. They traded cloth, salt and worthless manufactured goods for bundles of opium from the tribal farmers. Transportation was really all they provide, he surmised. They moved their insignificant barter goods into the mountains and retrieving opium on pack animals. There should be a cost effective way to remove them from the equation. Contemplating the possibilities, he stepped into a deep wet puddle. To the sucking sound of thick mud, he pulled a muck-covered shoe from the murky hole. Immediately he spun around to gauge the reaction of the storefront spectators. His menacing gaze caused the viewers to retreat to the sanctuary of their shops. Without an audience, Petru shook his soiled incrusted shoe. "Goddamn it," he mumbled stomping the ground. "Fuck it," he said between clenched teeth. He advanced. Every other step produced a sloshing squirt.

In the fading sunlight, the King Cobra Lodge glowed. Kerosene lanterns strung along the raised porch flickered. An architectural misfit, the hunting lodge designed hotel looked out of place among the thatch-roofed Laotian structures.

Petru clomped up the wooden stairs into the hotel lobby. A short Laotian clerk peered down over the front desk. Open mouthed, he examined the arriving guest's mud encased shoe. "Did you have an accident, Sir?" he asked.

"What the fuck do you think?" Petru grumbled.

Timidly looking away, the clerk produced a room key attached to a small lacquered piece of bamboo. Petru snatched the key from the boy's grasp. Plopping his satchel on the front desk, the Corsican extracted the bottle of scotch and carton of cigarettes.

Rushing in from the back office, the hotel manger threw on a black suit coat. Adjusted a thin tie, he extended his hand saying, "Mister Rossi, welcome back to the King Cobra, always good to see you."

Zipping up his travel bag, Petru turned and placed the satchel in the manager's extended hand. He headed straight for the adjoining bar. The sign over the doorway read, 'NO OPIUM SMOKING IN LOBBY'.

It was a pleasant summer's eve. Cool air flowed through the open-air bar. Petru plunged into the crowded room. The volume of the boisterous patrons diminished. Petru acknowledged other Corsican mobsters with a glance. Meo tribesman, clad in red and blue turbans, black pants and tunics, drank alongside armed mercenaries of various nationalities. A significant number of young bar girls worked the crowd. The newly employed whores no doubt, a result of the growing refugee population, Petru concluded. Smirking, he realized, a young refugee seeking employment could always find work in the world's oldest profession. In a dark corner, a seated patron grinned into the smoke filled rafters. Under his table, a barmaid performed the oral services of her trade. Business before pleasure, Petru thought, envying the recipient.

Petru paused. He glared at the back of a white man in a Hawaiian shirt engaged in a deep conversation with local merchants. The Americans have arrived, Petru thought. The hip Yank seemed out of place in the den of opium opportunists. The colorful dressed American turned around. He was mid thirties, clean-shaven with short salt-and-pepper hair and sporting aviator glasses. Petru stared at his reflection in the dark green sunglasses. No doubt, a CIA operative, Petru concluded. The American turned away and resumed his conversation. Petru cleared his throat before departing.

Looking around, Petru spotted the stocky blond German and a tribesman sitting at a corner table with a young bargirl. The German puffed away on a large cigar. A cigarette dangled from the side of the tribesman's mouth. Beer bottles cluttered the table. The German's unbuttoned starched shirt revealed a muscular tan chest. His bleached white hair cropped short. A shoulder holster displayed a Soviet TT-30 firearm.

Petru snapped a finger at the happy Buddha looking bartender. The chubby server stopped in the middle of processing a tab to accommodate the Corsican. Holding up the bottle of scotch, Petru motioned at the German's table. The bartender nodded, grabbed three glasses and followed Petru to the corner table. Petru placed the scotch and cigarettes on the table just ahead of the bartender's fairly clean glasses.

Glancing up through a cloud of cigar smoke, Max saw a greasy Corsican. Definitely Corsican, Max realized, having encountered the criminal element that used the Legion for refuge. This one is ripe, he thought snorting at the strong cologne stench.

"Can I join you?" the Corsican asked.

Max nodded pointing at an empty chair.

The Corsican extended his hand and said, "Petru Rossi, it is a pleasure to meet you. I heard you walked out of Isabelle."

Max shook the oily hand with a firm grip. "Max Kohl, and this is Loc. We both walked out of the valley." He smiled at Loc. Their embellished Isabelle exploits initiated many bar room conversation.

"I also heard you recently went back into the jungle and retrieved twenty-five kilos of opium," Petru said.

Well that confirms Guillian's theory, Max thought. A twenty-five kilo notification would produce a greedy opium merchant. In anticipation of the Corsican's proposition, Max leaned back in his chair.

"I ask only for business, friend," Petru said pouring three glasses of Scotch.

Not a big fan of the harder spirits, Max slid the glass of caramel liquid over to the seated bar girl. "I prefer beer," he said.

Petru picked up an empty beer bottle from the tabletop. He waved it in the direction of the pudgy bartender. The server snapped at the request.

This is no bit player, Max realized. When the beer arrived, bar etiquette prevailed. Max toasted his host with the fresh bottle.

"Can we talk?" Petru asked sipping scotch.

"Proceed," Max responded. He focused on Petru's dark eyes.

"I need to know what is going on with the highlands. If you have contacts with the tribes, and if it is of value to me, I can compensate you. The defeat has made everybody very nervous, and is bringing in new competition." Petru said glancing in the direction of a Hawaiian shirted patron. "Can you assist me?"

"I owed a favor to a friend that helped us on our journey," Max answered. "He asked for weapons, which I gave him as gratitude for saving our lives. He gave me the twenty-five kilos of jam as a gift."

"Who is your friend, a tribesman?" Petru asked.

"No, French commando," Max responded.

Petru grinned at this revelation. Leaning forward, he asked, "Do you know how much jam he controls?"

"With all the disruption in the hills, most of this year's crop never made it to market. He gave us a taste. They want weapons and ammunition to continue the fight," Max said.

"So, your friend, the commando, is in it for the long haul?" Petru asked.

"No, he is in it to the end," Max said puffing on the red tipped stogie.

Breaking open the carton of cigarettes, Petru retrieved a smoke. He tossed an open pack onto the community tabletop. After lighting his cigarette, he took a deep draw. Exhaling he asked, "How much opium does your friend want to barter with?"

"I'm talking initially about two hundred kilos of pure opium, and this is the desired list of munitions." Max answered pulling a folded piece of paper from his shirt pocket. After unfolding the laundry list of weapons, he handed it to the Corsican.

Max watched Petru's empty eyes scanning the detailed list. The Corsican has no idea what he was looking at, Max concluded.

After the charade assessment, Petru glanced up for page and said, "This will not be a problem."

"He also wants rice." Max added. "Producing opium and fighting does not give the tribes any time to grow edible crops."

"I can obtain Red Cross relief supplies at no cost. Consider the provisions my donation to your friend's struggle," Petru said.

This gangster is too accommodating, Max thought staring unblinking at Petru. The Corsican obviously doesn't know anything about munitions, but then again I have no idea what the opium is worth.

Breaking away from Max's gaze, Petru took a sip of scotch. Placing the glass back on the table, he refocused and said, "Here is my proposition. I'll get the weapons, fresh off the boat; supply the transport, same pilot as your last run, same drop site. I'll pay you one-thousand piastres, ($12 US), commission per kilo once it is delivered to me here, or if you prefer I can pay you in Francs, one-hundred per kilo."

"Make it two-thousand piastres per kilo and we have a deal," Max said.

"Rather than dance back and forth, let's agree on eighteen-hundred piastres per kilo?" Petru responded.

Max nodded. "The commission is acceptable. However before we agree to a deal," Max said taking a long puff on his cigar, "I examine the weapons." I owe it to Guillian, he thought. I need to make sure the munitions are right off the boat and not just World War II surplus firearms or battlefield pillaged French and Communist arms.

"The weapons are in Saigon, we can leave tomorrow," Petru said emptying his glass of scotch with a gulp.

Rene joined the group announcing, "So I see you found each other." He touched the seated Max on the shoulder. The German reached up and patted Rene's hand. The pilot acknowledged Loc with a nod while confiscating an unoccupied chair.

"Max will be joining us on the return flight," Petru announced.

"Do you have room for another passenger?" Max asked looking at Rene and motioning towards Loc.

Scratching his chin, Rene looked at the Corsican for guidance. With a slight glance, Petru approved. Rene exclaimed, "Always room for one more."

"We can leave in the morning after breakfast. I'll meet all of you on the runway at ten?" Rene asked seeking Petru's guidance.

Petru nodded refilling the glasses with scotch. He removed three packs of cigarettes from the carton and placed them in front of Loc. "Until tomorrow," he said raising his glass and himself from the table. Downing the whisky, he set the empty glass on the table. Grabbing the neck of the scotch bottle and the balance of the cigarettes, he disappeared into the ruckus crowd.

Rene warned, "Be careful Max, he is dangerous."

Relighting his cigar stub with the Legionnaire liter he took off the dying communist, Max took a few puffs and said, "I appreciate the advice, but remember I'm the one who walked out of Isabelle." Taking another puff, he added, "If I can get my commando friend MAT-49 submachine guns right off the boat, it will be worth the risk in dealing with a Corsican."

CHAPTER TWENTY SEVEN

Acool morning breeze blew wisps of crimson dust across the red clay tarmac. Early for the ten AM departure, Max and Loc stood beside a corrugated tin hanger. Their light colored civilian suits flapped in the wind. Flexing his broad shoulders in the snug fitting suit, Max felt uncomfortable in the business attire. At least the jacket conceals my shoulder holster, he thought. Looking at Loc, Max grinned at the enthusiastic tribesman. Like a boy playing dress-up, Loc kept smiling nervously in the oversized European apparel.

"First time to a big city?" Max asked.

"Yes," Loc replied with a wide smile. "I have seen films of cities with flat roads and cars, but I have never been beyond the highlands."

"Just remember that Saigon is as deadly as it is beautiful," Max said.

From the front pocket of his baggy trousers, Loc pulled out his military issue MAB Model D pistol. Brandishing the weapon, he said, "I'm prepared."

Rene strolled across the tarmac. "The plane is just about ready," he said. "I'm having the back seats installed."

"Where is Petru?" Max asked.

"He will probably be late, he usually is." Rene informed. "Let me warn you, he is a nervous flyer. It would be to all our benefit if you don't mention it."

The haughty gangster has a fear of flying, Max thought snickering. "Speak of the devil," he said. The Corsican casually approached. Petru's slicked-back black hair remaining motionless on the windy runway.

"Good morning Petru, rough night?" Max asked getting a whiff of alcohol and the Corsican's signature cologne.

A sour faced Petru grumbled, "The bitch bit me." On a swollen hand, he displayed the scabbed impression of arced teeth.

Glancing at the wound and Petru's bruised knuckles, Max had no further interest in discussing the Corsican's nocturnal activities.

They flew south with Max and Loc in the back of the plane, the pilot and Corsican up front. At the sight of his friend taking in the surrounding countryside with such delight, Max decided that, if they had time, he would show the naive tribesman the city.

It was late afternoon when they arrived at Cap Saint Jacques about sixty miles from Saigon. After a quick bathroom break, a car and driver took Max, Loc and Petru to downtown Saigon. The drive into the capital captivated Loc. His windblown head stuck out of the rear window. He focused on the bikes, cars and people that flew by. In the city center, he gazed up in awe at the large French colonial buildings. Passing Saigon's Notre Dame Cathedral, he turned to Max and asked, "Did you see that?" Before Max could answer, he returned to his windy perch. Max chuckled. Petru rolled his eyes.

The car stopped in front of the Continental Hotel. Max and Loc followed Petru into the lobby.

"Wait here," Petru said. "I'll handle your check-in. The owner is an associate of mine."

In the opulent lobby, a large floral arrangement sat on a round lacquer table in the center of the room. The marble floor sparkled. French designed furniture lined the windowed walls. Well-dressed Europeans and a few Vietnamese enjoyed an evening cocktail. Hotel staff in white tuxedo jackets buzzed about. Open-mouthed, Loc slowly spin around on the polished flooring.

"What do you think?" Max probed chuckling.

"I have never seen anything so clean." Loc replied.

"Neither have I," Max mumbled.

"Look at the flowers," Loc exclaimed taking a deep breath. The lobby's floral centerpiece of colorful lilies, orchids and roses exploding out of a three-foot blue and white ceramic vase. The blossoming creation reached into the ceiling. Loc closed his eyes and inhaled the sweet fragrance of nature's art.

Max smiled. It really is quite beautiful, he concluded. Whispers replaced the lobby's lighthearted cocktail chatter. Glancing around the room, Max discovered the muted dialogue focused on Loc. The words savage, jungle man, vagabond surfaced out the lobby buzz. Oblivious a beaming Loc admired the flowers with childish appreciation. Placing a hand on Loc's shoulder, Max thought, you helped me navigate through your jungle my brown friend. I'll protect you in mine. Gazing around the lobby at the gawking employees and patrons, Max calculated a shooting sequence. Wearing the mask of death, he watched the employees dissipate. Nervous patrons gulped down their overpriced drinks.

"You are all set, everything is taken care of," Petru said interrupting Max's defiant persona. "This is your room. I have some arrangements I need to make. I'll meet you back here in the lobby bar at dusk tomorrow. You can examine the munitions tomorrow night."

Max took the key slowly nodding.

Petru exited the lobby with a self-assured stride. He handed a few bills to a white gloved doorman and then hopped into the waiting car.

Looking at Loc, Max said, "I'm glad we do not have to see him until tomorrow. Now let's eat before we get drunk."

In the hotel restaurant, Max studied the symmetrically placed array of plates and eating utensils on the white linen tablecloth. Glancing up at Loc, he shrugged. "I don't know about you, but I'm just going to use a fork and knife."

Loc pointed at the largest of the three forks lined up in front of him.

"That's the one I'm going to use," Max said winking.

I've got a pocket full of money, Max thought. I've cheated death to many times to worry about tomorrow. As for today, my brown brother and I will enjoy the excesses this city has to offer.

The survivors of the valley of death dined on green salad, sirloin steak and fried potatoes. They washed down the expensive meal with red wine.

Loc struggled with the heavy western cuisine. After the main course, Max ordered himself black coffee and cake, and tea and ice cream for his friend.

"What is this?" Loc asked sucking on a spoonful of frozen dessert. He smiled wider than Max had seen yet.

"Its vanilla ice cream," Max answered trying not to laugh.

"It's so... cold and... sweet," Loc struggled to find the French words.

"Yes it is," Max replied.

"Can we get more?"

"Sure, would you like another flavor?" Max asked.

"What do you mean flavor?"

"Ice cream with a different taste," Max said summoning the very attentive waiter. "Chocolate ice cream for my friend," he ordered.

A short time later, a much larger portion of dessert appeared to the Tai's delight. "This is just as good."

"I'm glad you like it, now we can get drunk. Tomorrow I'll get you a milkshake. It's like ice cream, only better," Max informed.

Loc smiled widely.

It was late morning. Under a circulating ceiling fan in the Continental Hotel restaurant, Max and Loc enjoyed breakfast *a la Francaise*. On a linen tablecloth, an assortment of jams surrounded a wicker basket overflowing with a variety of fresh baked breads. Max took a sip on strong coffee from a porcelain cup. I can get use to this, he thought. Closing his eyes, he recalled the expensive girl he bedded the night before. I sure couldn't have afforded her services on a Legionnaire's salary, he realized. She was worth the premium, taking her time, more interested in the quality of the session, then the quantity of customers. Sporting a satisfied smirk, he peered over the misting saucer. "Did you have a good time last night?" Max asked the tribesman.

"I loved the ice cream," Loc replied, "And the hotel bath this morning. The hot water was nice."

"Loc," Max teased. "We had the most expensive dinner of my life. I buy you a night with a high-priced whore, and all you remember is the ice cream and hot shower?"

"I liked the vanilla ice cream better than the chocolate," Loc responded.

"How about the girl you bedded?" Max asked.

"She was pretty and nice." Loc answered. "But there was this girl stationed at Claudine I wish I could have been with."

"You mean one of the BMC girls?" Max asked.

"Yes, she had the face of an angel," Loc answered looking skyward. "Her silky long black hair danced in the wind." Squinting he asked, "What do you think happened to her?"

"I hate to say it but she is probably dead," Max shrugged.

"That is too bad, she was so beautiful," Loc said lighting the first cigarette of the day. "Is our business here dangerous?"

"We need to be cautious dealing with weapons, opium and Corsicans," Max said exposing his shoulder holstered weapon. Grinning he added, "This will still be a lot safer than walking through your highlands."

.

CHAPTER TWENTY EIGHT

The late afternoon drinking crowd punched in at the Continental Hotel's lobby bar. Beside a high-arched window under the raised ceiling, Petru and Captain Ghjuvan Casta eyed the arriving patrons. Casta was an officer in France's military intelligence agency; the *Deuxième Bureau*. Like Petru, Casta hailed from the Mediterranean island of Corsica. In clammy Saigon, he looked cool and collected in a lightweight double-breasted gray suit. Puffing on a cigarette, the thin Casta appeared younger than his thirty-five years. His receding dark hair cropped short. A thin mustache his distinguishing trademark.

In cushioned rattan chairs, the two Corsicans awaited the dusk rendezvous with the German. A slow rotating ceiling fan provided a pleasant draft. Petru enjoyed a scotch. Casta nursed a red wine.

"It does not look good," Casta said fidgeted in the cane chair. "The Americans are posturing for control. They handpicked this anti-French Prime Minister to take over. With his promise of sweeping reforms, he will close the opium dens. The brothels won't be far behind. That is the bulk of our cash flow. No cash, means no influence. No influence means the show is over."

"Casta, please," Petru said frowning. "We still have our alliance with the Binh Xuyen. Those river pirates are not going to hand over Saigon. It is their city. They control the police. They control all the rackets. Moreover, the French still control the military and banking. I appreciate your concern. I've worked with the CIA before in Marseille. *Unione Corse* aligned with the American intelligence agency to topple the French Communist Party. The CIA would be a formidable foe. They may disrupt operations even erode our power base. But they are never going to seize control of Saigon."

"What do you know about the opium in Laos?" Casta asked.

"I spotted an American operative snooping around Phong Savin. No doubt the Yanks are posturing with the supply side of the opium trade," Petru answered.

"We cannot let it happen. We need cash and lots of it if we are to deal with the CIA. The Americans have unlimited resources." Casta said flicking cigarette ash into a potted plant.

"The thing I like about this deal with the German is the Americans paid for the weapons. We trade American donated munitions for opium. The profit used to confront the CIA. It is poetic." Petru concluded.

"So tell me about this German?" Casta asked.

"What is there to say? He's a German soldier. Which means he's as disciplined and loyal as a blind dog, very controllable," Petru responded.

Max and Loc entered the lobby bar. Max perused the clientele. Amongst the wealthier French businessmen, foreign journalist and a few well dressed Vietnamese, he spotted the fragrant Petru beside a well-tailored companion. Followed by Loc, he wove through the maze of occupied tables. Petru and his double-breasted companion rose.

"Max this is Captain Casta of the *Deuxième Bureau*, Ghjuvan this is Max." Petru announced. The two men shook hands. The Corsicans returned to their seats. Max and Loc pulled out the table's remaining chairs.

"This is Loc." Max informed.

The Corsicans politely nodded in the tribesman's direction.

"Max, I'm aware you have relinquished your association with the Foreign Legion. It is of no concern to me, nor the French government." Casta conceded. "My concern is making the successful transfer of weapons, so badly needed in the highlands, for one-hundred-and-fifty kilos of jam."

At the mention of the one-hundred-and-fifty kilos, Max shot a side-glance at Petru. You slick bastard, he thought. You are skimming fifty kilos off the top. I shouldn't be surprised, he realized. Corsica is part of France. And the French are nothing more than butterfingered soldiers. Those *parlez-vous* could not hold onto their weapons any longer than the six weeks it took the W*ehrmacht* to overrun them. Go ahead and deceive your country-man, Max concluded. You are not going to cheat me.

"Let's drink to a successful transaction," Petru said, waving at a tuxedo clad waiter. The waiter approached holding a small pad an anxious pen. "I'll have another scotch," he said. "Another wine?" he asked Casta, who held his hand over his half full wine glass to decline. "Max what is your pleasure?"

"I'll have a beer," Max replied.

Loc leaned into Max and whispered.

Grinning Max declared, "My friend would like a milkshake." Looking back at Loc, he questioned, "Vanilla?"

Loc responded with a smile.

The drinks and milkshake arrived. Petru raised his refreshed glass of scotch toasting, "To the first of many successful transactions."

Touching his beer mug against Loc's fluted fountain glass, Max winked at his friend. I'll go along with the charade, Max thought clinking Corsican glass. The deal has a higher chance of success, if perceived as the first of many more to come. But I don't trust you. Moreover, after this transaction, I hope our paths never cross again.

"So tell me about your commando contact in the highlands," Casta said.

"There is not much to say," Max shrugged. "He was with the Composite Airborne Command Group, and is going to fight to the end."

"Does he have a name?" Casta questioned. "I have a list of unaccounted commandos. We would like to make contact. We might be able to aid in his resistance."

"He wishes to remain anonymous," Max replied taking a swig of beer.

"Are you protecting your opium source?" Casta probed.

"No," Max nonchalantly responded. "I'm abiding by the wishes of a friend."

"I'll respect that," Casta nodded. "In addition to the weapons, I've included a radio for you to deliver. In case the mystery commando changes his mind and would like to make contact. The added communication would also help expedite future transactions."

"I have no objections," Max said downing his beer. "Now tell me about the munitions."

Petru took this as his cue, "As promised, we have the crates of MAT-49 submachine guns you requested, with the specified ammunition. Max, these are fresh off the boat and never been fired. Also, the American grenades, I think they're MKII or something like that. We have two crates of MAS 36 Bolt-Action rifles, we are throwing into the deal as a sign of good faith." Petru paused looking for a reaction. When he did not see one, he continued, "We finish our drinks, head down to a warehouse in the harbor district, where you can examine the weapons. We control the docks, so it is a secure environment. If you are satisfied with your inspection, we will return at four in the morning to collect the weapons. I'll personally pick you up at the hotel with truck and porters ready to go. Once loaded, we head back to the airport, Rene will fly you back to the Plain of Jars. The toughest part will be getting up in the morning."

CHAPTER TWENTY NINE

In front of the Continental's lighted entryway, Max paced back and forth. It had rained during the night. Humidity thickened the pre-dawn air. Out of the dark, a lone cyclist passed on the slick surface. Leaning up against one of the deserted hotel's French colonial columns, Loc enjoyed a cigarette. In the distance, a pair of headlights appeared. The twin beams reflective off the wet road. The headlamps brightened. A coughing truck engine rumbled down the still street. Loc tossed the glowing remnants of his smoke into the gutter, and joined Max curbside. A screeching lorry skidded to an abrupt stop. The piercing termination undoubtedly woke up a few hotel guests. Leaning out of the passenger window, a sleepy Petru greeted the German with a nod. The Corsican grunted opening the creaking door. Wearing the same white suit from the night before, Petru slid next to the chubby driver. Climbing into the cab, Max glanced into the metal truck bed. A half a dozen curled up porters attempted sleep. The passenger compartment reeked of petrol. Getting a whiff of Petru's sharp perfume, Max snorted. Jesus, he thought. I don't know what smells worse, diesel fumes or the fragrant Corsican. Crawling into the crowed toxic compartment, Loc slammed the door shut. The driver popped the clutch. The noisy truck plunged into the early morning darkness of Saigon.

Looking through the insect splattered windshield, a round-shouldered Max said, "Just so we are in agreement, my commission is on two-hundred kilos not one-fifty."

"Agreed," Petru muttered.

Firmly grabbing Petru's boney elbow, Max said, "That did not sound very convincing. Are we in agreement?"

Shaking loose, Petru growled through clenched teeth, "Yes, I said yes, don't ask me again."

In front of the warehouse, the truck stopped with a high-pitched squeal. Stepping onto moist concrete, Max inhaled the aroma of stagnant water. Surveying the empty docks, he instructed Loc, "Stay with the truck, be alert."

Loc nodded, pulling out his pistol.

Petru rolled his eyes.

"What is it?" Max asked frowning.

"Max," Petru said shaking his head. "These are my docks. Nothing is going to happen here."

"Just indulge my military background," Max said, "I've been trained to prepare for the unexpected. And with regard to that, I want to examine the weapons a second time."

Staring in disbelief, at the focused German, Petru took a deep breath. Letting out a sigh, he mumbled, "Agreed."

Loc and the driver stayed with the vehicle. Max and Petru entered the warehouse with the laborers. Satisfied with the confirming inspection, they resealed the crates. A cautious Max led the procession of grunting munitions totting collies and a trolling Petru back to the truck.

Exiting the warehouse, Max could not see the driver or Loc. Something is not right, he thought. Un-holstering his pistol, he placed it in a front coat pocket, a finger on the trigger. The porters began loading the cargo. Max scanned the dark and quiet surroundings. Nonchalantly, Petru strutted over to the truck cab and opened the door. The bloody carcass of the driver tumbled out of the vehicle. The chubby corpse lay face up. Disconnected eyes gazed skyward. A surgical gash traversed across the victim's flabby throat.

The discovery prompted a work stoppage. Perplexed, the porters stared at the corpse. Out of the shadows, three armed Asian thugs emerged. Dressed in black, they targeted their prey with French revolvers clenched in extended arms. Waving a pistol, the thinnest hijacker instructed the workers to continue loading. He followed the laborers to the back of the truck to supervise. His companions detained the Europeans. A thick-necked thug looking down the barrel of his targeting weapon at Max and Petru grunted, "Hands."

Gripping the concealed weapon, Max calculated a shooting sequence. The equation was unsolvable. One hip shot is all I would get off, he realized. Releasing his grip on the pocketed weapon, he showed the gunmen moist palms. Petru did the same. These are not amateurs; Max concluded reading the two assailants' unemotional and patient expressions. They are going to kill us once the truck is loaded. It's up to Loc, he thought. There is no way, they could have got the drop on the tribesman. Petru flinched as a wooden crate scraped across the metal truck bed. The other participants in the one sided standoff remained stoic. Concentrating on the assassins, Max detected movement under the lorry. I'm looking at dead men, he realized. Loc emerged from under the transport. Behind the two thugs, the tribesman rose undetected. The first gunman's forehead exploded from a point blank shot to the back of the head. Crimson splatter sprayed Max and Petru. Instinctively Max turned to the side avoiding the warm shower. He ripped his pistol from his coat pocket. Loc fired a second shot into the temple of the other gunman. A thick stream of blood spouted out from the side of the thug's head. The target collapsed where he stood. Extending his arm, Max aimed at the back of the truck. The third hijacker peered around the truck's tailgate. Max shot him in the chest. Adjusting for the weapon's recoil and anticipating the falling victim, Max fired again. The second bullet sent the lifeless body crashing backwards. The deceased hit the moist rubbish strewn concrete. A plump wharf rat scurried out of the disturbed trash. The porters followed the rat's lead and ran.

Max's chest pounded. "What the fuck was that?" He asked in a harsh tone.

Examining the battlefield, Petru's head twitched. "I have no idea who they were," he replied.

"These are your docks? Nothing is going to happen here," Max shouted wiping the moist hijacker blood from his face.

"Max, I don't know what happened. Nevertheless, I'm going to find out. Whoever betrayed me will pay," Petru said. Pulling out his pimp pistol, he examined the victim missing a forehead.

For Petru's benefit, Max said, "Loc, while Petru plays detective, let's finish loading. We need get off his docks, before someone else tries to hijack the load."

Breathing heavy, Max tossed the smaller boxes of munitions into the back of the truck. With a nod, he instructed Loc to assist with a large crate. The small framed Loc easily handled the arduous cargo. What an amazing specimen, Max thought, quiet as a cat and strong as an ox.

"Let's go Petru!" Max shouted slamming the tailgate shut.

Behind the wheel, Petru turned the ignition key with a shaking hand. The sleepy engine sputtered to life. The Corsican revved the vehicle and dropped the clutch. The truck lunged forward and stalled. Looking at Loc, Max rolled his eyes shaking his head. On the second attempt, Petru succeeded in launching the vehicle. In the quiet streets of pre-dawn Saigon, Petru learned to shift gears.

Max looked out the open passenger window. The heavy air brushed his cheek. Saigon slowly awoke. It's that overconfident Corsican's fault, Max thought. If Petru wasn't so cocky about his docks, I wouldn't have been sprayed with hijacker blood. Thank god for Loc, he concluded. Jesus, he realized. The tribesman saved my life.

"Good job partner," Max said patting Loc's knee.

Loc responded with a childlike grin.

CHAPTER THIRTY

It was early morning. Petru checked himself into a luxurious corner room on the fourth floor of the Continental Hotel. I need answers he grumbled entering the suite. His white linen suit speckled crimson from the failed hijacking. I won't be returning to my flat, until I know who breeched the security of my docks. He placed his wallet, room key, and the small clove of wrapped garlic, next to the rotary phone on the entry table. Picking up the receiver, he harshly dialed a familiar number.

The line rang several times. A sleepy, "Yes?" answered.

"Casta its Petru," he barked.

"Petru? What is it Petru? Problems with the pick up?" Casta asked.

"There are four dead men at the warehouse," Petru growled. "One was my driver. I need to know who the other three were, and who they were working for."

"Are you alright?"

"No I am not alright!" Petru shouted. "If it wasn't for that milkshake drinking savage, I'd be dead. He killed two of the hijackers. The Nazi killed the third."

"How about the pick up?" Casta asked.

"Don't worry Casta, the weapons are heading toward Laos. You'll get your one-hundred-and-fifty kilo package. Someone on your end tipped off the hijackers. I need answers. I want to know who the informant is and who the three dead men were working for."

"Understood Petru, give me some time," Casta responded.

"Three o'clock this afternoon; Continental Hotel," Petru said terminating the connection.

Calling the front desk, Petru demanded, "Send up a bottle of scotch and I have laundry for pick up."

Petru placed the receiver back in its cradle. God, I can't stand that obnoxious German, he thought. Who is that common soldier to lecture me about my docks? Tapping resonated from the glossy white door. He pulled out his pistol. Cautiously he answered the knock. Peering through a narrow crease in doorway, he discovered a smiling tuxedo clad attendant. The cheery bellhop in a pillbox hat stood at attention. A bucket of ice and a bottle of Johnnie Walker displayed on a wicker tray. Frowning at the servant's pleasant demeanor, Petru sheathed his weapon. In the open doorway, he took off his bloodstained suite coat and pants. Dropping the laundry at the employee's feet, he grabbed the bottle of liquor. Without leaving a tip, he slammed the door on the efficient employee and the bucket of ice. Downing a healthy glass of warm scotch, he placed his pistol under the pillow, and crawled into bed. Someone will die, he thought looking up at the ceiling.

It was mid afternoon. At the curbside cafe in front of the Continental Hotel, Petru sipped strong black coffee to start his day. A slight breeze pushed humid air across the shaded linen tablecloth. A stream of pedestrian flowed by the sidewalk table. The Corsican fidgeted in a wrinkled shirt. I should have had everything laundered, he conceded. Lighting a cigarette, he leaned back in the wobbly chair. Who had the audacity to steal from him? He thought sucking in nicotine vapors. I'll find out and kill them, he concluded. They will know why they are about to die, before I kill them, he clarified. A Corsican message is required. You steal from me you die. Exhaling a satisfying plume, he grinned. Through the dissipating smoke, he spotted Casta exiting a blue and white Renault taxicab. Glancing at his watch, he verified Casta's punctual arrival.

Casta pulled out a chair to sit down.

"What have you found out?" Petru snapped.

"Good afternoon Petru," Casta said taking his seat and motioning to the waiter for a cup of coffee.

"Who was it?" Petru persisted.

Casta took a sip of coffee and said, "It was that fanatical Buddhist sect the Hoa Hao who attempted the hijacking. I'm assuming they were arming themselves for a potential coup against the American's puppet prime minister."

"Do you have names?" Petru asked.

"Petru listen, it is not that simple," Casta informed. "We need to maintain a relationship with these religious extremist. They are good allies in opposing the Americans' agenda."

"I need names," repeated Petru.

"Here is what I have," Casta said. "The Hoa Hao were tipped off by a Binh Xuyen soldier that works the docks. The Binh Xuyen will deal with him and I can give you a piece of an arms deal with the Hoa Hao. No new munitions, we need to distance ourselves for appearances. It has to be surplus weapons from the north."

Petru grinned. I will not only have my revenge but monetarily compensated, he thought. "I'll take care of the informant," he said. "I want the organizers of the hijacking present when I do, and I want the entire arms deal. I have contacts in the north."

"I'll see what I can do," Casta said. "As far as the organizers of the hijacking, you left three of them dead at the warehouse."

"It was the German and his sidekick who took care of those three. I've never seen anyone move as quietly as that little brown savage. Two of the hijackers never knew what killed them. I have a hard time tolerating Max, but that Fritz can shoot. We must not underestimate our *Boche* errand boy," Petru said.

"The German may be a resource. We can use him in assessing the flow of opium from the highlands. He may also assist in the re-establishing of a hill tribe mercenary operation. He knows of one rogue French commando, we have over four-hundred French officers still in the highlands. The only thing we lack is capital." Casta pulled out a pack of *Gauloise* and lit one of the cigarettes. "The real issue here is the Americans, with their resources and influence. It is only a matter of time before they take control. We all have a lot at stake."

"We need," Petru paused, searching for the appropriate words, "to send the Americans a Corsican message before it is too late. It may just delay the inevitable. However, it would extend the substantial opportunities for profit in the short term. The proper message may just derail their aspirations for total control."

"Petru, I need to be careful here. I am an employee of the French government. On the surface, the debate over the fate of Vietnam between the United States and France must remain as cordial policy disagreements. I cannot cross that line. However, the *Deuxième Bureau* has full authority to use its covert resources, to enhance our position for a unified Vietnam. We all have a vested interest in maintaining our various Vietnamese business enterprises. I think the timing is appropriate for a proper message." Casta leaned across the table and continued quietly, "The CIA has started an investigation into our financial dealings with the Binh Xuyen, more importantly, our opium dealings with the Binh Xuyen. They are receiving assistance from a Chinese Banker here in Saigon, Tan Sek Ng. You and your associates may have used him."

"I don't know him well, but I know who he is," Petru said.

"I think it would be in all our best interest, if he was to stop his investigation. It would also inform the CIA, whom they are dealing with. Will you be able to assist?" Casta asked sipping coffee.

"If I have the arms deal with the Hoa Hao, I think I can handle terminating the financial investigation," Petru replied.

"I think we are in agreement," Casta said.

CHAPTER THIRTY ONE

The Cholon district was one of the seedier sections of Saigon. In the back office of a brothel, two Binh Xuyen soldiers sipped whisky and puffed away on cheap cigarettes. A single bulb dangled over their nicked and splintered table. Smoke danced around the bright light. In a corner neatly stacked cases of brand liquor. Empty bottles stored in another. A gangly overdressed teenager stood attentively against the wall.

Leaning back in his chair one of the gangsters addressed the boy, "Be alert tonight Han. I want you to accompany three businessmen to a meeting they have here in Cholon. When you return, we will get you something to eat and I'll show you to your new quarters."

"Thank you sir," Han said relishing his good fortune.

In an attempt to suppress a smile, Han scowled. I need to show my handler, I'm up to the task, he thought. Han grew up on these mean streets. He evolved from child beggar to thief. Lately, he had become more brazen, robbing his victims with a knife. The request of a local gangster to act as bodyguard that night surprised him. He had always sought recognition from the Binh Xuyen criminal organization. My luck has changed for the better, he thought. I no longer will have to sleep under the bridge. The palm of his callus hand stroked the clean fabric of his new suit coat. I never imagined, I would wear such fine clothes, he thought. He looked down at the first pair of shoes he had ever worn. These sure are uncomfortable, he thought fidgeting in the restraining footwear.

Three well-groomed Asians entered the room. Han stood at attention. One was small in stature wearing a gray suit. His much larger, broad shouldered companions wore darker sports jackets and slacks. The small man conversed in French with Han's sponsor. Throughout the incomprehensible dialogue, they shot glances in Hans's direction.

"Show us your knife," Han's mentor asked.

Proudly Han pulled the four-inch blade from his pants pocket. Gripping the wooden handle, he exhibited it with a twist. His audience grinned. They are impressed, he concluded.

It was late night. Rush hour for the vices Cholon offered. Han followed the three well-dressed Asians weaving through the crowded streets. Recent rain had showered the district. The wet boulevard reflected the colorful soliciting lights of bars and brothels. The air was thick. It reeked of saturated garbage. Street hawkers crowded the sidewalks selling low budget cuisine. Working girls stood in doorways and on overhead balconies purring at potential customers. Intoxicated men of various nationalities staggered in the migrating herd. The three men bullied forward. Han trailed in their parting wedge. Passing a gaggle of begging street children, Han stuck out his chest. Those days are all behind me, he thought.

Leaving the crowded main strip, the three men headed down a dark side street. They stopped under the lighted doorway of an opium den. The gray-suited leader looked back at the trailing Han. Impatiently he tapped his foot. Han accelerated in the uncomfortable stiff leather shoes. Approaching the irritated man, Han bowed. A sour expression answered the apology. Gray-suit motioned for Han to open the door. Han nodded and took the lead. Entering the facility, he stood in the silent foyer peering into darkness. The three men crowed in behind him. Han's eyes adjusted to the gloomy atmosphere. A long hallway extended into obscurity. A female opium-dispensing cashier sat behind a caged window. The stone-faced cashier stuck a thin arm through the bars. A bony finger pointed down the corridor. Leading the procession, Han inhaled the familiar and distinctive smell of burnt sugar. The charred aroma singed his nostrils and scorched the back of his throat. The men piloted their way through a maze of corridors. They passed several small dark rooms. The unnatural glow of dim lamps identified the addicted patrons. Spread out like corpses, motionless men occupied every conceivable space in the crowded rooms. The only sound the gurgling of water in an active pipe.

Entering a brightly lit smoked filled back room, Han blinked. Around the room, several men stood watch. A tall thin white man with slicked back black hair sat at a table with three locals. A bottle of liquor, shot glasses, overflowing ashtrays and a pistol cluttered the tabletop.

Han's stoic companions flexed. Han reached into his pocket grasping his blade. His mentor told him to be alert. The white man in his light colored suit greeted them in French. The seated locals vacated the table. Han's companions sat down.

The white man spoke calmly. He picked up the pistol. Methodically he rubbed the barrel of the gun with a garlic clove.

How strange, Han thought. The white man's foreign tongue took on a musical tone. What a beautiful language, Han concluded. He released the knife. Joining the standing observers against the wall, he stroked his new suit. It felt so clean and soft. The white man rose from the table smiling. He approached Han. The man pointed the barrel of the shiny pistol at his head. Han thought...

Petru shot the standing punk in the forehead. The crack of the pistol transformed the wide-eyed expression on the young hooligan's face, to the blank stare of death. Like a sack of potatoes, the lifeless body in the oversized cheap suit, hit the floor.

That's refreshing, Petru thought. He took a victorious deep breath of musky back office stench. Grinning at the corpse, he conjured up a mouthful of saliva and spat. Examining the kill, he noticed the victim not wearing socks. This is no Binh Xuyen informant, he realized. Does it really matter? He questioned. It felt good. A vendetta was due, and somebody had to pay. Shrugging he took his seat. Blood flowed from the dead man's head. The burgundy puddle slowly migrated across the dirty wood floor.

"Now that the unpleasant business is taken care of, let's discuss your munitions needs," Petru announced. Pulling out a folded piece of paper from his inside coat pocket, he laid it out on the table. A confident finger slid it in front of the Hoa Hao representative. "This is the list of weapons proposed, and the pricing." Petru took a sip of scotch, and added, "My terms are not negotiable."

The envoy examined the overpriced list of poor quality weapons. The page twitched in his nervous grip.

Petru snickered. Try to steal from me, he thought. It's going to cost you.

"Agreed," the representative, conceded with a scratchy throat.

"It is a pleasure doing business with you," Petru said smirking.

The Hoa Hao representatives exited the premises, avoiding the slick puddle staining the floor.

Scooting his chair over slightly, Petru leaned back and rested his feet on the corpse. Sipping on scotch, he fumbled with the garlic clove. Some die and others bloom, he reflected. I was ten, when a neighbor killed my uncle over the rights to a chestnut tree. During the funeral procession, I mournfully marched. The rival clan laughed, calling my family lice infested vermin. Returning from the cemetery, my family did not hesitate in killing three and wounding four of the other family. As a boy, I had never felt so proud. The family honor defended.

I should go over to the House of Butterflies, he thought. Breaking in a new girl would be a good way to celebrate my good fortune. Maybe latter, I need to stay focused on the threats to my chestnut tree, he realized. Saigon belongs to me. The Americans and their nosy Chinese banker will pay for their infringement. Per the terms of my agreement with Casta, I'll kill the banker, he thought. As a bonus, I'll kill an American agent. After I deliver these Corsican messages, he concluded taking a sip of scotch. I'll go to the brothel to enjoy the excesses my wonderful city has to offer.

CHAPTER THIRTY TWO

It was an especially dark night. Mei walked back to her small hut after a long indoctrination session with the commissar. The rain stopped during their coupling. The wet ground reflected the kerosene lighting from the compound's cluster of buildings. The towering trees of the surrounding jungle rippled under a slight wind. Standing in front of the limited shelter, Mei looked up into the black sky. When will it end, she wondered about her incarceration. Shaking her head, she realized her future consisted of the next day. Looking beyond that would be futile.

Stepping onto the rotting wooden porch of the grass-roofed barracks, Mei paused in the open doorway. Underfeed, overworked prisoners blanketed the floor. So many landowners, she thought, reflecting on the crime of new inmates. The commissar boasted about the sweeping land reform of the victorious Vietminh, she realized. However, could there really be this many property-owners.

Carefully traversing through the obstacle of frail bodies, Mei searched for an opening. Spotting Lan snoring with an open mouth, she hoped her little sister had escaped Camp Number 17 in her dreams. Walking past Lan, she saw a vacancy beside a squatting elderly woman. The old women had removed her black pants. With teeth and hands, the recently incarcerated senior tore the black material into strips of cloth. Mei reclined next to the industrious woman.

"What are you doing Comrade?" Mei whispered.

"We were hard working farmers," the women said, raising her voice above a whisper. "We paid a tribute to the Vietminh with a percentage of our harvest. We supported the revolution, housed, and fed its brave fighting men. We celebrated the victory. Shortly after the celebration, the Land Reform cadre arrested my husband for being in possession of one acre of land and owning a water buffalo. They said we were rich. They said we were evil. With his hands tied behind his back, they beat my husband and forced him to prostrate himself before the judge. My children and I watched. Our neighbors shouted lies. The judge instructed the crowd to accuse him one at a time. They each approached my poor husband and taunted him. Some spat on him and some hit him." The rambling women started to cry.

"Comrade you should not talk of such things." Mei said trying to calm the broken inmate.

The woman turned and looked at Mei. "What will they do?" she asked. "Shoot my husband? They did that; he is dead. Take all our processions and give them to the crowd that condemned the father of my children? They did that. Starve me? I have not eaten in three days. What will happen to my banished children? I do not know how they will survive. What more will they do to punish me?"

"If you are not quiet, they will punish us all. That is what they will do." Mei pleaded. My little sister is so weak, she realized. Surely, Lan will die if they cut the rations because of this crazy woman. "Please go to sleep." Mei counseled.

The woman quietly continued shredding her pants.

To the rip of fabric, Mei drifted into a deep sleep.

The early morning light crept through the open windows of the prison barracks. A playful shadow danced back and forth across Mei's sunlit face. To the creaking of wood, Mei awoke under a pant-less woman hanging from the rafters. With a tilted head, the body of the female property owner swayed at the end of a braided cloth noose. Standing Mei bowed respectfully at the dangling corpse. She whispered, "Sleep peacefully *bà cụ* (grandmother), there is nothing more the Land Reform Committee can do to punish you."

Under a gray morning sky, Mei stood in the center of the compound. Around her wobbled thirty hunched broken women. The haunting pale-skinned female creatures shivered under a slight drizzle.

"Lean on me, little sister," Mei said to Lan.

Slowly Lan's head elevated. Disconnected eyes, housed in dark sunken cavities, attempted to register the offer.

A guard in a saucer shaped palm fiber helmet casually blew into a metallic whistle. To the shrill sound, the female wood gathers shuffled forward to gather the strict quota. After only a few steps, a tall boney prisoner collapsed in the mud. The procession sloshed forward. The rules were simple. You worked. You ate. You didn't work. You died.

It's the randomness, that I don't understand, Mei thought passing the growing cemetery that flowed up the hillside. Sometimes we get extra rations and a work reprieve, other days harsh discipline. Why am I working firewood today? She wondered. Is the commissar tired of my role as attentive student and willing concubine? Or is this just another lesson. One day at a time, she rationalized. Thanks to the extra food for my sexual services, I have the strength today to insure another meal for me and my little sister, and another day's existence.

On the wet march down the narrow jungle path, Mei whispered to Lan, "Don't worry, once I fill my quota I'll help you."

The expressionless Lan, did not react. Just as well, Mei thought, save your strength.

It was approaching dusk. The setting sun made an appearance through the dark clouds over Learning and Transformation Camp Number 17. Behind the oversized desk in the small administration shack, the commissar sipped tea while reviewing the list of new prisoners. To the sound of a vehicle sloshing through the muddy compound, he shook his head. Please, no more landowners, he thought. Well I'm in no hurry, he realized enjoying his tea. Squinting he looked over the cluttered desk and through the open doorway. A dozen militiamen tromped through the mud. Two shabby men in dirty ill fitting communist uniforms led the civilian soldiers. The military aides had bolt-action rifles slung over their shoulders. The raggedy pair stomped into the commissar's small office. The armed escort circled the hut.

"What is the meaning of this?" The camp commander demanded in the crowded room.

Running a hand through greasy hair, an unshaven communist representative chuckled. Out of the side of his mouth, he said, "Nguyen Dai Thein you are under arrest by the authority of the Central Land Reform Committee for owning four acres of land in Thai Nguyen province. We are here to transport you back to the Dai Tu district to stand trial as a Rich Peasant. You are relieved of..."

The commissar cut off the messenger in mid sentence. "This is outrageous, get out of my office now!" he demanded.

The messenger stepped aside. Snickering he nodded to the other member of the Land Reform Team. Taking his cue, the representative stepped forward with a very sturdy bamboo cane concealed against a pants leg. Methodically he raised the cane over his head. With his full force, he stuck the camp commander on the head. The commissar toppled to the floor.

"Again!" ordered the messenger.

The smirking henchman smacked the commissar a second time, splintering the bamboo stock.

The messenger stepped forward. He continued, "You are relived of all of your duties. You will remain in our custody for transportation to Dai Tu."

The slumping commissar used a shaky hand to investigate the bleeding lumps on his head. "I am a high ranking party member." He mumbled. "You will pay for this outrage." Pausing to gain strength, he shouted, "Guards! Guards!"

The Central Land Reform representatives and their armed escorts found the commissars' plea amusing. Chuckling they administered several more blows with the shattered cane.

The setting sun glowed somewhere behind the towering trees of the rain forest. Exhausted Mei shuffled along with the other wood gathers on the slick muddy path. The long hard day was ending. Walking past the camp's burial ground, Mei saw six fresh bodies waiting interment. Apparently, the deceased could not comprehend the communist lesson of seeking truth through sacrifice, she thought shaking her head. It doesn't matter, she realized my little sister and I will eat tonight as for tomorrow...I'll worry about that then.

Entering the compound, the woman in front of Mei mumbled, "It's the commissar."

Peering forward, Mei saw her strict mentor kneeling in the mud in the middle of the camp. His hands tied behind his back. The left side of his face covered in blood. His right eye swollen shut. Hanging from his neck by a piece of wire, a crude sign read *'phú nông'* (rich peasant). A wicker basket filled with large stones balanced on top of his head. Two grubby men in dirty uniforms playfully poked him with bamboo rods. The women's procession joined the other inmates that encircled the sadistic ritual. To the delight of the tormenters, the basket of rocks toppled to the ground. Slumping forward the Commissar received a whack across his back. A guard collected the stones and added another rock to the basket. The heavier load repositioned atop the *rich peasant's* head. Determined to balance the burden, the Commissar straightened his back. Strained neck muscles pulsed under the weight.

How can this be? Mei wondered observing her keeper suffer. Slight smirks surfaced on her fellow inmates. She glanced at Lan. For the first time in months, a smile appeared on Lan's emotionless face. The expression of joy seemed out of place under her little sisters sunken eyes.

To the tortured moans of her communist mentor, Mei realized, without out the food she received from her only customer, she would join the rest of the prison population's slow and painful journey to a shallow muddy grave. Weak-kneed and short of breath, she watched her broken client struggling to balance the basket of stones.

The commissar collapsed face down in the mud. Several attempts to revive him failed. The militiamen dragged the broken body through the compound before tossing it into the back of a waiting truck. Whatever hope Mei had clung to in this retched place vanished. She knew death would find her.

CHAPTER THIRTY THREE

Leaning back, his chair resting against the back wall at the King Cobra Bar, Max puffed away on a fresh cigar. His favorite barmaid snuggled up under his protective arm. My last night of cold beers and the comforts of clean sheets, he thought. I'm actually looking forward to the challenges of a jungle trek, he realized. He shot a side glance at the chain-smoking Loc. My tribal compass, he reflected. At least I won't get lost.

Entering the crowded saloon, Rene grabbed a beer at the bar. The pilot headed straight for his two passengers. Pulling out a chair, he gave the update, "We are loaded and ready to go at first light. You probably heard that the armistice was signed in Geneva." He informed, tossing back the cold bottle. "The war is officially over. As part of that agreement, we have to be careful. Light aircraft is prohibited from flying over the north."

"There is also talk that there is a cease-fire," Max injected. "But fighting continues in the tribal regions. The same politicians that placed me at Isabelle signed the agreement. If they want to come out here and enforce it, I'm willing to negotiate my own terms."

"Max, all I'm saying is, we have to be careful. We are smuggling munitions into a no-fly zone. I'll be flying very low tomorrow," Rene said.

"Understood, did you get the rice?" Max asked.

Rene nodded adding, "I'm very concerned about payload."

"Relax Rene," Max said grinning. "If we have to lighten the load in the morning, you can make it up when you return to pick us up. I have to tell you, the munitions we received far exceeded my expectations." After a reflective pause, he added, "Please don't disclose that fact to your Corsican friend."

"Max, let's make one thing clear," Rene snapped. "Petru is a business associate of mine, not a friend."

Slowly nodding, Max concurred. "Dealing with Corsicans is an unfortunate cost of doing business in Indochina."

Sunlight peeked over the horizon. Dawns first light reflected off a prop plane skimming across the rain forest. High above the gray sky turned azure blue. From the cramped cockpit, Max saw the highlands come to life. A large canopy of green unfolded beneath the low-flying aircraft. The jungle ocean lapped at the base of foliaged draped mountain ranges. Random Meo smoke trails danced across the rippling surface. So beautiful, Max thought and so deadly.

The short flight landed hard on a small sliver of real estate. The narrow red clay strip scarred by the encroaching jungle. Rene taxied over sprouting growth. In the shade of the tree line, he pivoted the aircraft for a quick exit. Prop wash blasted the surrounding forest. Armed with one of the new submachine guns, Max hopped down onto the moist ground. Loc followed. The German and tribesman disappeared on opposite sides of the jungle tarmac. A nervous Rene revved the aircraft engine. A long twenty minutes passed. Max and Loc re-emerged a hundred yards up the runway. Loc gave a thumps up sign to Max. Max gestured to the anxious pilot, with a flat hand across his throat. Rene cut the engine, silencing the deafening drone. A chirping flock of colorful birds passed overhead. From the dense growth, monkeys howled. The clamor of tropical insects escalated.

Returning to the plane, Max and Loc found Rene unloading the cargo. "I want to get back in the air as soon as possible," he said, craning his neck behind him as though someone might be approaching.

Laying his weapon on top of an unloaded crate, Loc joined the industrious pilot. Pulling his backpack out of the aircraft, Max retrieved a machete. He gave a slight nod to Loc and hacked his way into the jungle. About twenty yards into the brush, he examined the surrounding palm trees. A satisfying smile spread across his face. A distinguishing cut 'V' marked a tree trunk. Just below the symbol, he removed dry palm fronds concealing the Meo bunker. Peering inside the underground storage, hot stagnant air slapped his face. Recent rains had left a wet muddy base in the hole.

Returning to the plane, Max swung the broad bladed back and forth. Severed growth fell. At the end of the fresh pathway, the unloaded supplies awaited interment.

"You find it?" Rene asked sitting on a wooden box.

"Yes, a little worse from the elements. I'm glad we brought the extra tarps," Max answered.

"Are you going to need help getting this into the bunker?" Rene asked.

Max grinned. Sweat rolled down his face. I appreciate the gesture, he thought. But I know you want to get back into the sky. "No, we can handle it." He responded. "Good luck getting back."

Rene sprang to his feet. Dusting off his bottom, he said, "You have a radio now. Call me for pick up. If for some reason you cannot radio me, I will be here in ten days with the second load, late morning. I don't want to take the chance there may be early morning fog. If you are waiting, leave a sign on the runway. I won't land without a signal. Also, have your Meo friends clear the brush off the strip, we got lucky this morning."

"Got it," Max said, patting Rene on the shoulder. "One more thing, if you don't pick us up with the jam, nobody gets paid."

"Thanks for the reminder Max," Rene said raising a brow. Looking at Loc, he added, "Keep an eye on the German for me. We all want to get paid." With a playful salute, he concluded, "Good luck boys, see you no later than in ten days time."

CHAPTER THIRTY FOUR

O ut of the jungle, a towering limestone pinnacle covered with trees and brush stood defiantly. There it is, Max thought. The shrouded spire signified the outskirts of the Meo's realm. Chuckling under his breath, he mumbled, "at least we are heading in the right direction." Now where is Loc he wondered? He peered forward through the dense brush. The tribesman stood transfixed in the narrow path. Max approached his faster paced companion. Standing next to Loc, Max followed his partner's gaze. Symmetrically spaced five-foot high bamboo poles stretched out on the face of the sloping terrain. A spiked communist head capped the top of each post. Some looked like recent kills, others unrecognizable as human remains. Flat camouflaged helmets adorned the trophies. The ghastly exhibit faded into the dense brush. A trail of ants traversed up and down a blood stained pole. The insects feasted on the speared remains. The infested decapitated head stared at the intruders through hollow eye sockets.

A soft breeze brushed Max's face with the rancid aroma of decay. He snorted. It brought back memories of the unburied of Isabelle during her last days. He reflected to the slaughter at the battle Caen when he was seventeen. You never forget the foul lingering odor of your decomposing friends.

"This is not good," Loc said.

"No it's not. You kill your enemies, you shouldn't put them on exhibit," Max muttered. "Let's move on, this means we are getting close."

Loc nudged Max, out of a shallow sleep. A chill floated through the humid morning air. Through tired eyes, the German saw sandaled feet milling around the campsite. The rising sunlight cast the long shadows of armed men. Max propped himself up on his elbows. He offered a sleepy grin to thirty heavily armed partisans. The Meo patrol brandished captured Chinese burp-guns, Legionnaire bolt-action rifles and World War II British surplus weapons. A weathered warrior in a blue turban squatted beside Max. The Meo's hard features softened, he flashed a toothless smile.

"Good morning Chue," Max said.

Chue spoke to Loc who translated. "He said they had been looking for us for some time, and wondered if we would return."

"Tell them a deal is a deal, we got their weapons." Max said slowly raising his stiff frame.

Loc translated.

Max held a virgin submachine gun over his head.

The tribal audience sighed. The toothless Chue pushed his companions aside to get a closer look. Obliging the zealous tribesman, Max handed him the weapon.

"Tell Chue he can have this one," Max said.

Beaming with delight, Chue released the bolt-action carbine slung over his shoulder. Proudly he showed off his new possession to his comrades.

After a brief tribal discussion, Chue spoke to Loc, who translated, "We can make the village by nightfall. It looks like five will escort us back to the village. Chue and the rest are going to start retrieving the munitions."

A snickering Chue spoke to Loc.

Loc chuckled and translated, "Chue has invited us to a celebration upon his return. He wants to get drunk with his large white brother."

Max laughed and said, "Tell him it is a deal, *Nam lu* (Let's get drunk)."

At dusk, to the yelping of dogs, Max's small group entered the mountain village. The procession headed for the main long house. Looking up from the base of the stairs, Max saw the lanky Guillian standing above him. A noble warrior, Max thought. The French Commando abandoned the responsibilities imposed by others to follow his moral compass. Guillian is not the Jew I was indoctrinated to despise, Max reflected. A shard of angst poked the German's gut. Why did I allow myself to be swept up in the Nazi's anti-Semitic fervor? I was young? It was mandatory? Those excuses don't hold water, he realized. Rather justify my past sins, he concluded. I just won't think about it. Guillian is my friend and that's all that matters.

"Welcome back boys," Guillian called out waving. "It is good to see you."

"Guillian, always a pleasure," Max responded.

Max ascended the stairs. He and Guillian embraced. Entering the raised structure, they sat down with about ten locals.

Taking his seat on the hard wood floor, Max asked, "Do you mind if I take off my boots. I need to unleash a pair of barking dogs."

"Please, go right ahead, my friend," Guillian responded. Leaning over he whispered something to a tribesman. The man got up and exited. Max unsheathed his tender feet. The tribesman returned with a teen-age girl, carrying a bucket of water. The tall girl had a round face and flat nose. She wore a white blouse and tight fitting long black skirt. The sarong accentuated a very shapely bottom. The young girl with penetrating dark eyes smiled as she knelt in front of Max. She began to wash his blistered feet.

"Thank you," Max mumbled to the sensation of warm water and soft caressing hands. He let out an involuntary sigh. Tilting his head back, he declared. "This is better than oral sex in Saigon."

Guillian translated for the group. The locals broke out in laughter. The foot maiden blushed with a mischievous grin.

"I know you're tired but we have been waiting for your return," Guillian said, picking up a wicker-encased bottle of liquor. "If you don't mind, let's get drunk and you can tell us about the munitions."

Holding Loc's submachine gun, Max said, "We have three hundred MAT-49 submachine guns with ninety-thousand rounds of ammunition. These are new, right off the boat and never been fired." Passing the weapon to Guillian, he continued. "We also brought one hundred MAB pistols with ten-thousand rounds of ammunition, and five hundred American MKII grenades. We were limited because of weight, so split the cargo. The submachine guns were included in the first delivery. The second load will have two crates of bolt-action rifles and ammunition. To coordinate the second drop we brought a radio."

Guillian translated as the submachine gun joined the bottle of liquor circulating the room.

"Max, this is excellent, did you have any trouble acquiring the weapons?" Guillian asked.

"No problem, thanks to Loc. He left two attempted hijackers dead on the docks," Max replied.

Adding a little embellishment, Guillian translated Loc's heroics for the group. Loc could not contain a nervous smile from the acknowledgement. The Meos in the room nodded respectfully.

CHAPTER THIRTY FIVE

Max awoke in a raised long house. His head throbbed. Through heavy eyelids, he stared up at the pitched palm frond ceiling. Beside him, Loc rolled over with an uncomfortable groan. I need to stick to beer, Max thought. That local white whiskey packs a heavy punch. Crisp mountain air flowed through an open window. Max took a deep breath of the pleasant atmosphere. That's not a cure for nausea, he realized. But it helps.

Max rose. He braced himself against the matted wall. The room appeared to sway. The foot maiden entered through the open doorway. She cradled in her arms a steaming hat shaped bamboo basket of gluey rice.

Max mustered up a groggy smile for room service. Turning to Loc, he grumbled, "Wake up partner."

Loc stirred. With closed eyes, he blindly responded, "What is it Max?"

"I need a counter-beer," Max informed. "'Can you translate for this maiden."

"You need a what?" Loc questioned.

"It a German expression," Max informed. "I need some alcohol to dilute the effects of my hangover."

"That is a good idea," Loc mumbled before translating the request.

The young girl giggled.

A few medicinal swigs of liquor, a warm meal, and dry clothes, Max felt better. Stretching his stiff frame on the raised deck, he began to envy Guillian. This is a good life, he thought. These are good people.

In search of Guillian, Max and Loc exited the raised shelter. They walked through the sun-lit streets of the village. Warm smiles and respectful bows greeted them. Enjoying his celebrity status, Max responded to the friendly gestures with a nod. At the base of Guillian's hut, Max and Loc looked up at the Frenchman.

In a blue turban, black tunic and pants Guillian leaned over the bamboo railing of a raised deck. "Decided to sleep in?" He questioned chuckling.

"We are a little slow this morning," Max responded. "The white whisky left a little hammering man in my head."

Guillian laughed. "Come on up. There is someone I want you to meet," he invited waving a welcoming arm.

Max and Loc ascended the creaking wooden stairway. Guillian placed a finger over his lips. Gingerly the commando led the German and tribesman into a back room. In the corner, a young village girl sat cradling a baby. In colorful Meo attire, she gently rocked back and forth. A bright bandana dominated by red covered her head. Large silver looped earrings dangled from pierced lobes. Based on her taunt radiant complexion, Max guessed her age at fifteen. However, given the youthful looks of the mountain people, she could be twenty-five. Delicately she handed Guillian the indigo wrapped infant.

"This is my son, Etienne," Guillian whispered looking down at God's gift. "I named him after my father."

A speechless Max peered into the small package. The baby softly yawned. A miniature hand grasped at nothing with tiny fingers. Involuntarily Max grinned. The noble warrior is a father? Max pondered. I never pictured the Commando with a family. He glanced at the proud father. Guillian glowed. "He is ... beautiful," Max muttered.

Loc pulled back the indigo cloth to peek. "Your son is beautiful," he concurred.

"Yes he is," Guillian agreed handing the infant to its mother. "This is my wife, H'Liana, she had the baby a week ago. We are both very happy." As she took the child, Guillian planted a softy kiss on her forehead. The young mother blushed. Addressing his guest, Guillian suggested, "Let's take a walk to discuss the timing of your departure. I want to let H'Liana and Etienne rest."

Max smiled at H'Liana. The defiant commando not only found sanctuary amongst the Meos, he realized. Guillian had found a home.

A heavy summer sun shone brightly in the blue sky. Raised wooden residences clung to the side of the mountain. Connecting the hillside community, a dirt trail twisted between the stilted structures. Max, Guillian and Loc strolled down the path. Dust danced at their feet. Dogs barked. Guillian acknowledged passing neighbors.

"The patrol should be back late tomorrow with the first load," Guillian informed. "Then we can leave the next day with your opium. Does that work for you?"

"That'll work," Max said.

Loc nodded and paused to light a cigarette.

The German and Frenchman ambled forward.

"Max, any idea what will become of the mountain tribes?" Guillian inquired.

"No, there is a lot of confusion. The war is officially over. A cease-fire is in place. Were you aware of that?" Max asked.

"Yes, we still get some news up here, word of mouth, from tribe to tribe. Did you come across our answer to the cease fire?" Guillian asked.

"If you are referring to the spiked heads, yes I did," Max said.

"Max, these people do not understand Communism. Look around you. Common ownership of production, a classless society and workers utopia are tough sells. There are no landlords to vilify. The Vietminh will never indoctrinate them. Because of their French alliance, the Communists will annihilate the hill tribes. I fear the French are going to abandon them. It would not surprise me. I have experience with French betrayal as a Parisian Jew." Guillian stopped in the middle of the trail. "I will not forsake my wife and child or these people. We notified the communist of our intent, by spiking a message across the border." Guillian glanced around at the terraced community and smiled. "We got the inspiration for the spiked head display from the Vietminh. We are answering our enemy in his dialect."

Max turned and looked into Guillian's eyes. "Guillian, I came back up here the first time because I owed you. I came back this time for profit. You are and will always be my *copain*. I will help you any way I can. However, it does not look good. Your lands are on the wrong side of a divided country. The radio we brought could facilitate parachute drops of food and munitions. French Intelligence seemed interested in continuing your fight. However, the French forces are heading to Algeria for another war. I'll talk to the *Deuxième Bureau* on your behalf. Then there are the Americans. I don't think they are going anywhere. The Yanks just got here. A Hawaiian-shirted American has been snooping around the Plain of Jars. Maybe he can point me in the right direction. Don't give up hope *ami*." Max said placing his hand on Guillian's shoulder.

"Thanks Max, I...we appreciate it," Guillian said patting Max's hand.

"Good Guillian, now can you ask that young girl with the nice ass to wash my feet again." Max chuckled.

Guillian grinned. "I can get her to wash more than just your feet."

A gap in the jungle canopy framed the familiar limestone butte. Max glanced up at the towering spire. We are making good time, he concluded. A heavily armed Meo escort blazed the trail. Opium bearing porters brought up the rear. The procession stopped. Max got a whiff of death. The wall of heads appeared out of the brush. A porter dumped seven new trophies out a blood soaked gunnysack. The morbid cargo hit the moist jungle floor. Attempting to escape the disrespectful fate, the severed heads rolled for cover. The tribesmen began cutting bamboo into spikes. The head totting porter rounded up the reluctant remains.

Max moved upwind of the defiant exhibit. I don't need another pungent reminder of the brutality of war, he thought. Joining him, Loc lit up a cigarette. Max welcomed the smoke. It diluted the stench. He focused his gaze on the horizon.

"You don't approve?" Guillian asked.

"No, it is not that. I understand you need to make your statement," Max responded.

"Max, most of the heads came off dead men. Very few of the Vietminh were decapitated alive." Guillian explained.

"Guillian, it's the smell." Max clarified. "It reminds me of places I'd like to forget."

"I understand. A soldier's past is filled with unpleasant memories," Guillian conceded.

Chue spiked the burn-scarred head of a one-eared young combatant. The Vietminh soldier in Division 308 of the People's Army had survived a napalm attack in his youth.

Standing next to Guillian, Max watched the final bundle of opium loaded into the prop plane. Rene climbed into the cockpit and fired up the aircraft.

Guillian placed his hand on Max's shoulder. Leaning in, he shouted over the growling Cessna, "I hope you can find us a sponsor. We won't last long on our own."

Max smiled. "You're not alone, my Jewish friend. Even if I can't find you a backer, you will always have Loc and me for support."

Rene revved the aircraft.

"It appears your pilot is growing impatient," Guillian shouted.

Max nodded. "Goodbye Guillian," he said embracing the commando.

CHAPTER THIRTY SIX

Refreshing cold carbonated beer flowed across Max's tongue and down the back of his throat. It is good to be back to civilization, he thought wiping moist lips. Leaning back, he propped his chair against the wall and placed the chilled bottle next to his head. Beside the German, Loc in western attire puffed away on an American cigarette. Rene sipped chilled scotch. The King Cobra Lodge barroom hummed. Chinese opium merchants haggled with tribesmen. Mingling prostitutes solicited customers. Former Legionnaires embellished exploits. Boisterous English dialogue from the recently arrived American opportunists pierced the multilingual clamor. Studying the colorful patrons, Max lit a cigar. A good venue to finalize the opium transaction with the Corsican, he surmised.

"Rene, do you know the French Intelligence Officer Casta?" Max asked.

"Yes I do, I know him well. He has used my transportation services," Rene replied.

"Could you set up a meeting with him for me? I told Guillian I'd plead his case for additional munitions." Max asked.

"Sure Max. I can set it up." Rene said.

"Thanks, I owe those Meos my life and will assist them any way I can," Max said.

Taking a puff on his cigar, Max looked up through the cloud of smoke. His favorite barmaid stood sheepishly. He smiled. Cold beer, a good cigar and my favorite whore what more do I need, he thought. The usually playful Chimmy slouched forward. Long black hair shielded her face. Max rose and pulled out an empty chair. Sitting down, Chimmy winced.

"What is it?" Max asked softly. Gently he brushed back her silky long black veiling hair. Startled by her purple blackened eye and bloated split lips, he jerked back. Chimmy covered her face attempting to leave. "No, my precious, please stay," Max consoled. Pulling back her hair, he smiled into her broken face. Looking up at Max through blood red eyes, she mustered a missing tooth smile. He stroked the back of her head. She rested her hand on his leg. "Who did this?" he asked.

"Bad white customer," Chimmy muttered.

"I'm sorry," Max said. It's sad to see the bubbly Chimmy like this he thought. I've always enjoyed her company. In the bedroom and as a drinking companion, I've never been disappointed. He focused on her injuries. She will heal, he hoped. It is a job related risk for the timeless profession, he reasoned. Nevertheless, it still did not make it right. Nobody should beat up a whore he thought, especially if she is my whore.

Looking at his watch, Max asked Rene, "Where is your Corsican friend?"

"I told you he is always late," Rene said and with a sour face added. "And I told you, we are business associates, not friends."

"Understood, now when he gets here I would like you to move over to the bar counter," Max informed.

"Why?" Rene questioned.

"Because I'm afraid your Corsican business associate is going to try and cheat me." Max replied, "and if he does, it will get...messy."

"Max, the opium has been paid for. We are only talking about your commission," Rene said.

"Rene, I know the type. It is not about the money. It is about power and control. I may be wrong, but he is skimming fifty kilos from French Intelligence. If he comes in with back up, he's going strong arm me." Max looked up at the parting crowd. He grinned. Flanked by two large Binh Xuyen thugs, Petru strutted towards the table. The wide heavy Asian gunmen wore taut gray suits, the lanky Corsican a white linen sport coat.

Rene gave a slight nod to Max and relocated over by the bar.

The Corsican took the vacated seat across from Max. The two thugs stood guard behind Petru. The bodyguards defiant posture a declaration of war. Loc glanced up at the towering beef twins and grinned. Sucking on a fresh cigarette, the tribesman exhaled into the goons' hostile pose.

Petru scowled at the defiant Loc, before ignoring the tribesman. Spotting the battered Chimmy, the Corsican lit up with a big smile and mumbled, "good evening sweetheart."

Chimmy cringed.

Max placed a protective arm across the girl's shoulders. Staring into Petru's dark eyes, he gave her a reassuring hug. The arrogant Corsican beat *my* whore, he realized. His heartbeat accelerated. "Do you have my commission?" He asked slowly puffing on his cigar.

Taking out a stack of large denomination piastres, Petru placed the currency it in the middle of the table. "Here is one-hundred-and-fifty-thousand piastres, ($1,800 US)," he declared. "I had some additional expenses, so we," he glanced over each shoulder at his granite faced escorts, "are not able to pay the full commission."

"The deal was eighteen-hundred piastres per kilo, with two hundred kilos that three-hundred-and-sixty-thousand piastres. No commission, no opium," Max responded.

"Max, I can just take the opium and pay you nothing. It is your decision." Petru said playfully waving his hand over the table.

"You need to know where the opium is before you can take it," Max said grinning.

Raising an eyebrow, Petru turned around, eventually spotting Rene at the bar. Glaring at the pilot, he sought confirmation. Rene simply shook his head and threw up his hands. The Corsican pulled out his gun. His bodyguards unsheathed holstered pistols.

"You can tell me where the opium is, or I'll kill you," Petru snorted brandishing the small sidearm.

The hardened clientele of the King Cobra Bar ducked or stampeded out the door. The pudgy bartender squatted behind the counter. Rene shielded himself behind a wooden column. Working girls crawled under empty tables. A curious crowd peered through the establishment's open doorway. Ten tribesmen stayed. Standing amongst overturned chairs and cowering barmaids the tribesmen targeted Petru's gunmen with automatic weapons.

Petru's bodyguards placed their firearms on the table. Blocked by his men, a confused Petru looked around. Ten focused gun barrels stared back. Reluctantly the Corsican surrendered his weapon.

"Let me see your wallet!" Max demanded.

Petru hesitated.

Loc pulled out his gun. He placed the barrel against Petru's temple. Flexing his arm, the tribesman twisted the weapon into the Corsican greasy scalp.

"I'm not going to ask again," Max stated.

From an inside coat pocket, Petru slowly pulled out his billfold. He tossed the alligator skin folder on the table.

Loc lowered his weapon.

Picking up the wallet, Max pulled out a wad of money. Quietly and calmly, he counted it. A little more than one-hundred-thousand piastres, he calculated. "You're still short," he informed. "I'll take this and give you the one-hundred-and-fifty kilos you negotiated with Casta. I'm keeping fifty kilos as your penance for sort changing me. As a good Catholic, you know all about paying penance for your misdeeds."

Picking up Petru's gun from the table, Max slowly unloaded it. One at a time, the bullets hit the floor. Clinking metal bounced off wood. Placing the empty gun on the table, he growled, "Now pick up your pimp pistol and get the fuck out of here."

Snarling Petru reached for the gun. As the Corsican glanced down, Max grabbed the back of Petru's greasy noggin. Firmly grasping a handful of oily hair, Max elevated the head. The full force of a massive German forearm slammed Petru's face into the table. Listening for it, Max heard the victorious crack of a nose breaking. Beer bottles flew. The escaping glass shattered. The audience jumped. An explosion of blood stained the tabletop.

"That...," Max barked wiping his oily palm on Petru's sport coat, "Is for beating my whore."

Petru slumped into his chair. His face smeared with blood. Hyperventilating he sprayed the crimson fluid flowing out of a broken nose. The splatter glistened across his white suit. "I'm...going...to...kill... you!" Petru gurgled.

"Do you think I'm scared of dying?" Max hollered standing up to his full height. "I stared death in the face when I walked out of Isabelle, and watched the bastard blink. The threat from a woman-beating Corsican means nothing to me. The only reason you are alive, is to be a delivery boy for the French Intelligence's opium. Now if you want to try to kill me, please do. If not, get the fuck out of here, you're bleeding all over the floor."

Snorting blood, Petru glared up at Max. His bodyguards cautiously assisted him to his feet.

"Get this gawking errand boy out of here!" Max yelled pulling out his pistol.

The two Binh Xuyen henchmen supported a weak-kneed Petru out of the bar.

Max summoned Rene with a hand motion. Pulling out a folded piece of paper from his front shirt pocket, he handed it to Rene. "Here are the directions to the location of the one hundred and fifty kilos of jam. Get it to the Corsican. I want to make sure Casta gets his opium," Max instructed. "Also, if he shorts you, let me know. I'll make up the difference. I did much better on this transaction than originally projected."

"Max, he is going to come after you," Rene warned.

"Once he delivers the opium, I hope he does. Remind him that is the only thing keeping him alive. If I see him after that, I will kill him. In the meantime, I'll be staying with my Tai friends," Max said motioning to the group of heavily armed tribesman.

Max said to Loc, "Tell your Tai brothers job well done. They earned their wages tonight." Then holding up the commission money he added, "now that that is over with, let's find a quiet bar near the refugee camp and get drunk."

Loc translated for his countrymen. The blue turbaned reserves accepted the invitation by brandishing their firearms over their heads with a victory howl.

Chimmy affectionately hugged the German. Holding her innocent bruised face in his hand, Max smiled. Looking into her brown eyes, he winked. "*Es machts nichts,*" he mumbled.

CHAPTER THIRTY SEVEN

Mei struggled down the narrow jungle pathway. A bundle of Lan's wood balanced on the bamboo yoke across her back. Trudging through a pocket of heavy stagnant air, she scowled at Lan. I cannot continue to fill my quota and hers, she thought. We are both going to die. It is just a matter of time. I hope Lan enjoys the meal I'm providing for her tonight, it may be her last. Mei sighed. I have no choice she realized choking back tears. I have to abandon my little sister. Tears rolled down her soiled face. She focused on her sandaled feet shuffling along the slick surface. Each step gets me closer to the end of the long day, she realized. I was a whore, she reflected. I always hoped the large white man entering my room was the last in line. In the bunker at Claudine, I prayed for silence after each explosion. Even here at the camp of learning, I truly believed I would enter a workers society as a productive member. Dropping the arduous load of wood on Lan's pile, she glanced at her friend. The emotionless Lan wobbled on frail limbs. Mei's tears returned. The only thing I desire now, she realized. Is a quick death for my little sister.

Slouched over from the day's toil, Mei and Lan walked amongst the wood gathers towards the compound. At least my little sister will eat tonight, Mei thought. She rubbed a dirty sleeve across her sniveling nose. The procession stopped. New prisoners clogged the courtyard. In the distance, new inmates flowed out of six Russian Molotova trucks. The irate commandant stomped around like a spoiled child in front of the caravan's military escort. The newcomers in civilian clothes stood in silence.

Mei's approaching work party in their black prison attire, interrupted the red-faced warden's tirade. The commandant walked over towards the firewood detail. Standing in front of Mei, the confused commissar examined the laborers. He glanced back over his shoulder at the trucks. An enlightened expression flashed across the simpleton commandant's face. Addressing the fifty wood gatherers, he said. "Comrades, due to Uncle Ho's great mercy, you are free to go." He then gestured with a sweeping hand motion towards the line of transports.

Is this a cruel joke, Mei wondered, or is this ignorant man attempting to make room for new prisoners. This is not the time to hesitate, she realized. She grabbed Lan's hand and dragged her little sister towards the lead vehicle. After climbing over the tailgate, she reached down and pulled Lan into the truck bed. Confused and bewildered wood gathers followed. The passengers sat quietly.

"You can't do this!" the military representative protested.

With her eyes shut tight, Mei held onto Lan. Please, oh please, let us go, she prayed.

"Can't do what?" the commandant responded. "These were not my prisoners. I am here to punish landowners. Who knows what these peoples crimes were, and who cares. Just get them out of my compound."

"Where do you expect me to take them?" The military man questioned.

"I just said I don't care."

The debate abruptly ended, Mei did not want to open her eyes. An eternity later, the vehicle's door slammed. The truck's engine coughed to life. The transport jerked forward. Taking a calming breath Mei looked around. Hopeful expressions blossomed on the stoic faces of the oppressed. Peering over the trucks tailgate, Mei grinned. Learning and Transformation Camp Number 17 faded into the distance.

CHAPTER THIRTY EIGHT

Sipping on a glass of warm bourbon at the Imperial Hotel Bar in downtown Saigon, Tom Roche forgot what a precious commodity ice is. If you didn't specifically request it with your drink order, you did without. Having spent the last month at the Plain of Jars, he traded the cooler temperatures of the Laotian highlands for the comforts offered by Saigon. However, drinking warm whisky in a muggy hotel bar did not seem very luxurious. He scrutinized the accommodations his limited government per diem allowed. The Imperial was a small clean hotel with about thirty rooms. The lobby bar's raised ceiling rested on stoic French columns. Several light bulbs hanging down on frayed and dusty electrical cords brightly lit the room. The bar was quiet. Three local businessmen enjoyed cocktails by the open double doors. Rusted base plates held two long stem industrial ceiling fans overhead. The one over the businessmen worked. A short portly Asian in a white tuxedo jacket and black bow tie stood guard behind a dark wood counter. The formal attire's sophistication diminished by the suit coat's tattered sleeves. The middle-aged bartender attempted to conceal a balding head with a greasy comb-over. His thinning black hair sparkled in the bright light.

Roche flicked two fingers at the attentive server. "Some ice please," he ordered in French.

The bartender tilted his head to the side and squinted at the Hawaiian shirted American's request.

Roche snickered. As a Louisiana native, he delighted in the reaction his Cajun dialect evoked in Indochina. The bartender returned with a single ice cube in a bar glass. Roche poured his remaining bourbon on top of the prized ice, as the bartender took an order from a new customer.

Examining the casually dressed patron, Roche concluded a fellow American. Hearing the customer's brazen beer order confirmed his observation.

Looking down the bar at Roche the new arrival asked, "So what brings you to Saigon?"

"Adventure," Roche responded miming a toast.

The curious beer drinker slid down the bar with his amber bottle. Extending a friendly hand he said, "Steve Broda, freelance journalist, just here to cover the transition, yourself?"

Roche gave the ritual greeting gesture a firm shake. "Tom Roche, I'm with the US Military Assistance Advisory Group."

"So you're Roche. The hotel keeps trying to give me your messages. I guess they think we Americans all look alike," Broda chuckled.

Roche examined his clean-shaven drinking companion. The thirty and change Broda appears to be my age, Roche thought. Broda's flat top hair is speckled with more gray, he hoped. Probably five-foot ten and a buck-sixty in weight, he concluded. We do look alike.

"I'm here to supervise how the French are utilizing the US military financial support," Roche offered.

"Not very well, from what I've been told," Broda responded while wiping the lip of the long-necked bottle with a napkin.

Every bar patron in Saigon has an opinion about the Dien Bien Phu disaster, Roche realized. It might be amusing to see how a media reprehensive views the Vietnam crisis. "It must make for good copy back in the States."

"Not really, page three stuff; the sham Army-McCarthy Hearings dominates the front pages," Broda replied.

"What do you mean by sham hearings?" Roche questioned.

"Just that," Broda stated. "Senator McCarthy's interrogation techniques will be his downfall. Not everybody is a Communist. I don't feel any safer now that Charlie Chaplin has been banned from the United States."

"But there are Communists, and we should take every step possible to contain them. The Vietminh are part of the worldwide Communist expansion. The Chinese Communist and Soviet Union intervention in Korea and here in Indochina confirms that. If Communism is not contained in Vietnam, the dominos will tumble. Neighboring countries of Laos, Cambodia, Thailand and Burma will fall under Communist domination. All of Southeast Asia will then be at risk." Roche lectured.

"So, is that the only reason the Americans are backing the appointment of Diem as Prime Minister, because he is anti-communist?" Broda said.

"Diem does have his shortcomings," Roche nodded. "He is a Catholic overseeing a Buddhist nation. He is not very charismatic, but he understands communism must be contained."

The bartender approached the two Americans and their empty containers.

Roche ordered in French, "I'll have another bourbon with lots of ice, and my friend would like a cold beer." The bartender reacted with a smile this time to the Cajun accent.

"You speak French?" Broda asked.

"Since I was a child, I'm Cajun from just outside New Orleans," Roche responded.

"I'm from Jersey," Broda said. "If you don't mind, can we have our second round outside? I can tolerate the smell of the city better than the stagnant air of the Imperil bar."

"Sure," said Roche.

The two men moved to a small rattan table just outside the Hotel entrance. A soft breeze softened the discomfort of the humid air. Car horns barked. An idling lorry spat out diesel fumes. The pungent aroma of Asian cuisine and wet garbage floated in and out. Roche enjoyed a cigarette with his second whiskey. This time two small ice cubes garnished the bourbon.

Pulling out a small pad of paper and a pencil, Broda asked, "Do you mind if I take some notes as we talk?"

"No," Roche said, "As long as it is totally off the record."

"I understand," Broda replied with a nod.

The bartender arrived and looking at both of the men said, "I have a telephone call for Tom Roche?"

"Excuse me," Roche said rising from the table.

"I told you they can't tell us apart," Broda chuckled.

Entering the bright bar, Roche blinked. On the dark wood counter, a black dial phone waited. The receiver off the hook hummed. Picking up the hard plastic handset, Roche said, "Hello?"

"Tom, its Matthews," Roche's colleague replied.

"What is it Matthews?" Roche asked.

"Our banker is dead, apparently a Corsican message. We found his body this evening. He took a small caliber bullet to the back of the head," Matthews answered.

Taking a deep breath, Roche commented, "Looks like the French have just raised the ante for playing poker in Saigon."

"Be careful Tom," Matthews warned.

Hanging up the phone, Roche reached into his front pants pocket. He confirmed the presence of his Baby Browning pistol. A large pop outside the doorway caused him to flinch. Instinctively, he pulled out his gun. A woman screamed. Cautiously he approached the entryway. His pistol concealed against his pants leg. A small crowd gathered around Broda's table. Hunched forward the journalist hugged the small tabletop. Blood drained out of a small hole in the back of his head. Calmly Roche put his gun back into his pocket and returned to solitude of the lobby bar.

"Bourbon," Roche said to the wide-eyed bartender. He slammed down the warm whisky in one gulp. The clamor of a growing crowd flowed into the empty bar. In the distance emergency vehicles wailed. Poor bastard, he thought. Broda came to Vietnam seeking a story and became one. "Another," he ordered.

I just had a drink with that unfortunate civilian casualty, he realized. I guess the least I can do is write a notification of death letter to his family. That is if Broda has one, he thought. I have plenty of experience, he regretted. The sympathetic letters I had written for the marines that perished under my command slowly became standardized. It became a form letter. He was brave; died for a worthwhile cause; your sacrifice was not in vain. Sipping on his whisky he thought he could tailor fit a death letter for Broda's next of kin without much effort.

CHAPTER THIRTY NINE

It was midday. In front of the Continental Hotel's curbside cafe, Saigon's traffic flowed. A chaotic mix of vehicles, bicycles and motor bikes drifted down Dong Khoi Street. Through aviator sunglasses, Petru observed the sputtering stream. The large army-green lenses concealed two black eyes. The spectacles' bridge rested on a crooked broken nose. He sipped on an early scotch. Spotting Casta's head bobbing above the migrating locals, he adjusted the uncomfortable sunglasses.

Breaking from the pedestrian herd, Casta joined Petru. Dressed in a blue blazer and white slacks, he pointed at the crystal glass of whisky and said. "Looks like you're starting early today."

Petru answered with a crooked smile. No mention of my disfigurement, he thought. Just as well. The last thing I want to discuss is how the Nazi broke my nose.

Summoning a waiter, Casta looked at Petru's scotch. He shook his head. With an enlightened expression he said, "I'll have a vanilla milkshake."

Petru bruised face puckered at the frothy drink order. Jesus, he thought. I don't need to be reminded about the trend started by Max's savage sidekick.

"The deal with the German is complete, no issues?" Casta asked.

"No issues," Petru mumbled.

"With regard to the German's mysterious opium commando, unfortunately he is on his own. The policy has changed. Our government will be in strict compliance with the Geneva agreement. There will be no re-supply for the tribal mercenary forces, no more munitions for opium. Can you pass that information on to Max," Casta asked.

Enough about Max already Petru thought. His heart raced. He growled quietly through clenched teeth. "If I see the Nazi and his little brown friend again, I'll kill them!"

Holding up the palms of his hands, Casta said, "Take it easy Petru. Let's move on."

Petru snorted. He adjusted the dark lenses. After taking a deep breath, he raised the chilled scotch to his lips and emptied the glass.

"It appears the Americans have stopped their financial investigation into our opium operation." Casta tossed out.

A composed Petru nodded. "The Chinese Banker had many powerful clients that wanted to remain anonymous. I think his termination sent a clear message to the meddling Americans."

"Petru, do you know anything about the escalating violence targeting Americans, grenades tossed into their residences at night, and the bombing of their cars?"

"Casta you know the answer. You're Corsican. The Americans crossed the line. A blood feud has been launched against the entire American community. Those sons-of-bitches should tuck their tails between their legs and run. We are not going to walk away from eight years of hard work establishing profitable businesses and rackets, just because the Americans don't like Communism. Hell, I don't like Communism. I assisted the Gestapo against the Communist French resistance. Then after the war, I worked with the CIA in busting communist skulls on the docks of Marseilles. Just don't fuck with my livelihood or I will send you a bloody message," Petru ranted.

"Was the murder of the American journalist in front of the Imperial Hotel part of this Vendetta?" Casta asked.

Nonchalantly Petru flicked his hand. "That was mistaken identity. It was supposed to be that Roche. Do you know whom I'm talking about? He's been up to the Plain of Jars, snooping around the opium trade. I wanted to send another clear message."

"Clear message? You gunned down an innocent civilian in front of a Hotel in downtown Saigon!" Casta scolded.

"It doesn't matter that I killed the wrong person. The message was sent." Petru said with a puzzled squint. "Casta, when I killed that Binh Xuyen informant over the arms hijacking, do you really think I thought he was the informant?"

"What are you implying?" Casta questioned.

"It was a set up. Someone had to die. It does not always matter who dies," Petru explained.

"Very well then, let's see how the Americans respond to your various messages," Casta said. Leaning forward, he sucked on the milkshake through a straw. Pulling back, he pointed at the fluted glass. With childish enthusiasm, he announced, "This is really good. I should order it more often."

Petru rolled his eyes.

CHAPTER FOURTY

Night engulfed the Chinese district of Saigon. On the foul streets of Cholon, the establishments that trafficked in vice came to life. Colorful lanterns strung across seedy storefronts beckoned customers. In the shadows and dark alleys, the homeless and fallen sought refuge. Roche seemed out of place. In a white suit, the American walked in the midst of locals and potential sinners. If I'm going to do this, he thought. I need to summon my dark persona. To find the fearless Tom Roche, the Tom Roche who not only kills but also enjoys it. To compensate for his pounding heart, he quickened his pace. A pack of scruffy street children encircled the American. A young decoy hindered Roche's advance. The malnourished six-year old distraction looked up with innocent brown eyes and an open palm. Roche ignored the bait. He spun around and grabbed hold of a boney arm reaching into his pants pocket. Elevating the adolescent pickpocket, he tossed the culprit into the swarm of young thieves. The children scattered.

Roche paused and patted down his pockets. Watch, wallet, money clip, keys and gun intact, he confirmed.

"You want girl?" A teenage prostitute solicited.

"No!" Roche said resuming his journey.

"I'm very good girl, very cheap," she persisted trolling behind the American's fast pace.

Stopping Roche turned. He slapped the young girl with the back of his hand. "I said no!" he growled. She ran off. His demon persona grinned.

Boldly Roche entered the large warehouse. A muffled conversation resonated from the glowing light in the rear of the building. Weaving his way through a maze of stacked shipping crates, he headed in the direction of the voices. Rodent scat littered the floor. The muggy facility reeked like a summer outhouse. The voices grew. The light brightened. He peered out of the labyrinth.

Overhead industrial lighting spot lit a conference in progress. Around a large table, several Binh Xuyen thugs and two Europeans held court. Standing henchmen observed the discussion. From a file photo, Roche recognized Casta, the French Intelligence officer with the pencil thin mustache. The other obvious Corsican wore sunglasses. Most likely, a small time gangster, Roche concluded. A low rumbling growl distracted the American. Glancing to his right, Roche spotted a large guard dog reclining between wooden crates. The wide-eyed mangy mutt's tattered ears pointed into the rafters. A salivating bark ignited the charging canine. Roche emerged from the shadows pulling out his small automatic pistol. He shot the dog. The mutt collapsed at the end of a chain tether. Blood pulsed out of the bullet hole on the top of the dog's head. The tableside spectators remained motionless. The hovering henchmen targeted the intruder with an assortment of small arms. Calmly Roche approached with his hands in the air. A pistol dangled from a trigger finger. Slowly he laid his Baby Browning on the table.

"Who the fuck are you?" Casta asked.

"I'm the United States of America, that's who the fuck I am," Roche said pulling out a cigarette from a pack of Lucky Strikes. He lit the smoke with a Zippo lighter. Taking a drag on his cigarette, he focused on the six guns pointed in his direction. He took another puff and continued, "You want to kill an innocent journalist. You'll have to answer to me. You want to kill a Chinese banker. You'll have to answer to me. It ends now!"

"Yes it does," responded dark sunglasses. The gangster reached into his suit coat. Casta restrained his arm.

"Keep your Corsican dog on a tight leash," Roche taunted. Motioning with his smoldering cigarette towards the dead canine, he added, "You see what we Americans do to wild untrained animals."

Taking his half-smoked cigarette, Roche used the table as an ashtray. He ground the smoldering end into the wood surface. Looking around the room, he said with a shrug, "You can blow up all the empty cars you like, I don't really care about that."

Cautiously Roche picked up and re-holstered his gun. Exiting he stopped at the dead dog and turned back to address the group. "Dinner is on me tonight," he shouted pointing at the canine carcass. "Get used to it, for if we don't contain the Communists, you southerners will be eating a lot of dog. Frankly, I find the meat too fatty for my taste."

As the American left, Casta braced himself for Petru's predictable rage.

"Why did you stop me? We could have killed him right here," shouted Petru leaping out of his chair.

"Do you think he came alone?" Casta responded. "He would not have brazenly strutted in, unless his CIA accomplices knew where he was."

"So what if they did?" Petru persisted.

"An agent comes here to send a message. If he doesn't return, we all become dead men," Casta stated, raising his voice. "If you can't understand that, you are of no use to me." The American was right, Casta realized. He needed to keep a tight leash on his wild dog.

CHAPTER FOURTY ONE

Roche continued down the crowded street at a brisk pace. Breathing heavily and sweating profusely, his white sport coat camouflaged a saturated dress shirt. Adrenaline pumping through his system, he glanced over his shoulder. Amongst the Asian pedestrians illuminated by neon lighted solicitations, he spotted Matthews. The thirty-something Matthews had the boyish good looks of a younger man. The little dab of Brylcreem in his thick black hair sparkled under the colorful lights. I need to keep moving Roche thought. Ignoring his approaching associate, he resumed his fast walk. A winded Matthews jogged up beside him. The two agents continued down the streets of Cholon at Roche's speed.

"Good job," Matthews said patting Roche on the back.

Gulping air Roche muttered, "Thanks."

Grabbing Roche's arm, Matthews slowed him down. They stopped in front of an open-air Cholon bar. Glancing up at pulsing electrified glass tube signage of the Red Lion, Matthews asked, "Do you want to get a drink?"

"Sure," Roche said, "But don't you think we should get to safer turf?"

Matthews waved a hand over his head. On both sides of the street, a dozen Asian men armed with concealed automatic weapons converged on the two Americans. Escorting Roche into the bar, Matthews directed members of the team to stand guard. "This may be the safest place in Saigon to have a drink," he snickered.

The two Americans entered the bar with armed escorts. Jumpy customers stampeding to the exit provided a variety of seating options.

"Bourbon?" Matthews inquired.

Roche nodded coming down from his adrenaline high.

"Two bourbons, in dirty glasses," Matthews called out.

Roche grinned.

An elderly Asian woman with shaky hands quickly brought two whiskeys. Setting the glasses on the table, the nervous server retreated with a slight bow.

Matthews picked up a glass. "Job well done, message delivered."

Roche mimed the toast with a noticeable twitch. "Thanks for the back up," he mumbled. Warm bourbon rolled down the back of his throat. The cleansing whisky washed away anxiety. His heart rate slowed toward normalcy.

"When I walked into the warehouse there were no sentries. I'm assuming you and your boys took care of them?" Roche asked holding an empty glass.

"Yes, there were two thugs at the door. We took care of them, no casualties. I think the Binh Xuyen are getting soft. They saw us approaching and fled. The only casualty tonight was the dog." Matthews informed. He ordered another round, remembering to add ice to the request.

"That was one mean ugly dog." Roche chuckled. "The mutt would have torn me to shreds if he were loose. I didn't see the chain restraint."

The encore bourbons arrive with a small piece of quickly melting ice in each glass.

"This was a good field exercise for the boys," Matthews said motioning to the paramilitary escorts standing watch. "Their training is complete and we will begin to have them infiltrate into the North over the next thirty days. I'm glad we did not have to spray the room. It would have been messy."

"You're glad?" said a smirking Roche, "When I saw that Corsican going for his gun, I thought the show was about to start. I think French Intelligence got the message. The Corsicans will still be trouble."

"The Corsicans will always be trouble." Matthews declared. "Once they find a profitable niche in the new regime they should calm down."

CHAPTER FOURTY TWO

On the outskirts of Saigon, Max disembarked Rene's small plane. The tiny aircraft vibrated behind the single revolving propeller. The prop wash blasted the German with warm air. Sunlight sparked of the concrete runway. The illusion of rolling sheets of water rippled across the hot pavement. Max sucked in the hot humid southern air as Loc exited the idling aircraft.

"There's Casta," Rene shouted from the cramped Cessna cockpit. Extending his arm, he pointed to the Corsican Captain standing in front of the Cap Saint-Jacques Airport terminal. "You wanted to meet in the open, and I could not think of any safer place."

"Thanks Rene," Max said giving a playful salute. Lowering his head, he and his partner left the comforting shade of the aircraft's wing.

"Max!" Rene called out.

Max and Loc turned.

"Be careful," the concerned pilot warned.

Max nodded with a knowing smile. I faced far greater challenges and adversaries than a Corsican pimp's death threat, he thought. Nevertheless, Petru's vendetta is serious. Never underestimate your enemy.

Walking across the windy tarmac, Max approached the modest terminal. Green turf surrounded the pitched weathered red tile roof facility. A pair of swaying palm trees accented the landscaping. Under the shade of twin trees' frond crowns stood Casta. The French Intelligence officer stepped forward extending his hand. Max gave it a firm shake.

"How are you Max and...and..." Casta stuttered. Apologetically he squinted at the tribesman.

"It's Loc," Max informed breaking the awkward pause.

"Of course," Casta declared. "How are the two of you?"

"Just fine Captain. I hear the war is over." Max responded.

"The war may be over, but I don't think the Americans know that yet," Casta chuckled.

"Thanks for meeting with us," Max said. "I'm here on behalf of my friend of the Composite Airborne Command Group. My mystery commando opium contact needs help to continue his resistance efforts. No opium, no exchange, just a French NCO requesting resupply, a basic munitions drop. Can you accommodate him?"

"Max, I'm going north to assist Tai federation troops that fought their way into Laos. If your friend and his forces make it to Laos, I might be able to help them. If they make it to Laos with a couple of hundred kilos of opium, we can help each other," Casta said.

"These men are not going to leave their families behind," Max said. "Can you assist with the arrangement of a resupply drop?"

"No Max," Casta answered shaking his head. "Our tribal allies are not covered by the cease fire. They have no official status. The Geneva agreement prohibits flights in that region. The North is a no fly zone. There will be no munitions drop. I'm sorry. The only option for the commando is to come home. Now if he comes out with opium, I'm very interested." Casta leaned into Max and asked quietly, "Do you know how many kilos of opium he may control?"

Jerking back, Max frowned, "So that is it. You are only interested in the opium?"

"Yes, the war is over. What else is there but the opium?" Casta shrugged. "The financing for the Tai troops' relocation is coming out the profits from last year's harvest. It's an unfortunate reality. Opium funded the growth of this country. It funded the war. And now it is funding our mistakes."

"Do you have any issues if I talk to the Americans about resupplying a French commando" Max politely asked.

"No, good luck in dealing with that strange lot. You can find them at the Imperial Hotel. They stay two to three in a room to save cost, and then throw money around this country as if it was nothing. Just let me warn you, they are a little jumpy these days. There is bad blood between the Americans and French regarding the fate of Vietnam. If you want to make your case in French, talk to an agent named Roche, you'll get a kick out of his Cajun dialect."

Max grinned. "Thanks Captain," he said shaking the Corsican Captain's hand. You warned me the Americans are a little jumpy, Max thought. However, declined to comment about the bounty Petru has placed on my head. Must be a Corsican thing, he concluded.

A slight breeze began blowing dust as Casta departed. Loc dropped and extinguished the second cigarette he smoked during the meeting.

"What do we do now?" Loc questioned.

"We go to the Imperial Hotel and talk to the Americans. According to Casta they don't know that the war is over." Max replied.

CHAPTER FOURTY THREE

The bar crowd at the Imperial Hotel was larger than usual for a Friday evening. Roche approached two Vietnamese businessmen seated under the room's only working ceiling fan. Speaking in French, he asked if they would vacate the table if he bought the next round. The Asians accepted. As they rose, five Americans commandeered additional chairs and swooped in to claim the desirable spot. Securing the location, Roche headed to the crowded counter for beers. He wove his way back to his colleagues with four large amber bottles of 33 *Biere* and drinking glasses. Setting the cold Saigon lager on the table, he overheard Matthews concluding an embellishment of the dog-shooting incident. The Americans selfishly poured their own beers, as Roche took his seat.

"To the Saigon Military Mission," Matthews toasted. The American agents of this covert operation touched glasses. The cold brew went down quickly.

Receiving an admiring look across the table from Allen, Roche wanted to side step any further discussion about Matthews's dog shooting rendition. Shifting the conversation, he asked Matthews, "How are things at the Palace?"

Matthews took a large swallow of cold brew and placed the empty glass on the tabletop. Rolling his eyes, he responded, "Could that Prime Minister be any more incompetent? That man is a dead fish. I tell you guys, I worked with warlords in Burma that had more of a personality than Prime Minister Diem. Did you read in the State Department briefing about Diem's speaking English attribute?"

Flicking an ash into an empty beer bottle, Roche nodded. The table concurred.

Matthews continued. "You sure can't tell what language he understands. Whether the dialogue is in French or English, the dead fish just sits there with that distant look of entitlement. No wonder Diem has so many enemies. It is just a matter of time before one of those fanatic religious sects or crime syndicates eliminates him." He paused to replenish his empty glass. Studying the foam capped golden carbonation, he chuckled, "If those groups don't get to him, I may have to remove him myself."

"Is it really that bad?" Roche asked.

"This is definitely not the Philippines. We all have our work cut out for us here." Matthews answered.

"So all you have to deal with is the potential coup of an arrogant prime minister?" Jensen chimed in as prelude to his own complaints. "We have a small window of opportunity caused by the refugee chaos. Trained anti-communist squads infiltrated the North. Keeping it simple, their first assignment was to contaminate the North's fuel supply. The objective was disrupting bus transportation."

"You were going to put sugar in their gas tanks?" Roche interrupted.

"That's what we should have done," Jensen said. "It would have been easier. Three covert team members inhaled toxic fumes. It was more difficult getting them out then getting them in."

Holding up an empty bottle by the neck, Matthews swung it back and forth.

Roche frowned. "Just because I speak French does not mean I'm the one who always has to get the drinks."

Matthews set down the empty container and squinted in the direction of the double doors. Roche turned to investigate. A stocky blond European and a tribesman stood in the doorway scanning the bar patrons. The quiet American table studied the odd pair.

Approaching the Americans, the European politely asked, "I'm looking for Roche, can you gentlemen tell me where I might find him."

"I'm Roche." He courteously responded. "What can I do for you?"

"My name is Max. My associate's name is Loc. We would like discuss a situation in the North. Do you have a moment?" Max asked.

"I recognize you." Roche said. "I've seen you at the King Cobra Lodge." The German may be a good source of information, he thought or better yet a useful tool. "Sure, I have the time, let's get a table." Turning to his companions, he said grinning, "excuse me gentlemen."

Max grabbed a corner table. Roche went to the bar and retrieved three beers. The American received thankful nods from his guests.

"Do you mind if we sit with our backs against the wall?" Max asked.

"Sure I understand, you have a Corsican bounty on your head," Roche announced.

"How do you know?" Max inquired.

"I'm in the information business. I know many things. I am surprised to see you in Saigon. You are taking a risk." Roche said keeping a friendly tone.

"At Dien Bien Phu, forty-thousand Vietminh tried to collect the bounty on my head. I'm still here. I don't consider a Corsican pimp's vendetta a big threat. It is a matter of perspective," Max said confidently.

"Okay, so what can I do for you?" Roche said, leaning forward.

"I have a friend, a French commando, he is in the highlands. He is going to continue the fight to the end. He is not alone. The partisans are looking for a patron to finance their anti-communist struggle. I have spoken to his countrymen. The French said no. We," Max pointed at Loc, "owe the commando our lives. I told him I would plead his case to anyone who would listen."

"Max, I'm impressed that you came to Saigon with a price on your head on behalf of an idealistic French commando. I will not waste your time. The answer is no. The United States has no interest in establishing a resistance movement based on the French model. It is political. I'm truly sorry." Roche said. Washing down the bitter tasting response, he assessed Max. The German appears disciplined, loyal, and based on his accomplishments fearless, he thought. The perfect candidate, he concluded, to assist with the CIA's dirty work.

"Thank you for your time." Max said nodding. "And thank you for the beer."

Roche held up a hand. "Wait, we have some mutual interests that may be rewarding for both of us. First, I can tell you where to find the Corsican who wants you dead. Does Petru Rossi's whereabouts interest you?"

Max flinched. "Yes it does, but why would you disclose that to me? What is in it for you?"

"Let's just say the enemy of my enemy is my friend. There is bad blood between us and the Corsicans." Roche said.

"I'm assuming the second area of interest we have in common is opium?" Max asked.

Roche nodded. "You're right Max. We recognize the importance of opium to the economy of the highland region. We can compensate you for your assistance in helping us understand those economics."

"If you can help me expedite the business I have here in Saigon with the Corsican, I will be glad to assist you with the economics of opium around the Plain of Jars," Max responded.

"If you like, you can stay here at the Imperial Hotel and we will inform you as to the location Mister Rossi. Is that agreeable?" Roche said, concluding the negotiation.

"I won't be going anywhere until I know where the Corsican is," Max said. He pulled out a cigar. Leaning back in his chair, he added, "Allow me to buy the next round."

CHAPTER FOURTY FOUR

Overhead a string of red paper lanterns glowed. Max looked up scanning the face of the two-story House of Butterflies. Grunts and groans flowed out of open second story windows. Escaping drapes fluttered in the night breeze. Somewhere in the interior of the labyrinth, my unsuspecting prey is fornicating, he thought. This isn't my first trip to the low budget brothel, he reflected. The pleasure palace created for the benefit of the French Forces accommodated my humble Legionnaire's salary. The gratification I seek tonight is not sexual, he realized. Killing Petru will be just as rewarding, he concluded.

"Are you ready to do this, partner?" asked a stone-faced Max.

Loc patted his concealed weapon.

"Let's go in and see how good the American's information is," Max said. Taking a deep breath, he cautiously opened the large wooden door. Standing in the dimly lit foyer, he paused. His eyes adjusted. A dozen young girls playfully pounced. Inhaling the sweet stench of cheap perfume, he looked over the cackling prostitutes' heads. Scantily clad women filled the room. On a worn out red sofa, four young village girls huddled together. The scared children held tightly onto each other. Submissively they stared at the stained floral pattern carpeting the floor. Max thought about his childhood. The Nazis evacuated millions of German children to rural camps. If you showed fear or weakness in the harsh National Socialist institutions, you did not stand a chance, he reflected. There was no compassion in the Hitler Youth camps nor is there any sympathy for the new arrivals at the House of Butterflies. The new girls would have to adapt if they wanted to survive, he thought. He had.

Through a beaded doorway, a heavy pimp mama in a yellow oriental silk gown made her entrance. The tight dress's flower motif bulged around her flabby midriff. Theatrical cosmetics filled the creases of her middle-aged features. Heavy rouge reminiscent of an aging clown smeared the madam's sagging cheeks. A cigarette holder extended between her tightly clenched smoke stained teeth. Posing, she tilted her head back exhaling a scented plume.

The trained girls silenced.

"Welcome gentlemen, what is your pleasure?" Mama inquired in a husky voice.

Frowning at the sales pitch, Max pulled out a five-hundred-piastre note. Handing it to the proprietor he growled, "I'm here for the Corsican."

Instinctively she pocketed the bribe. Over her shoulder she declared, "We don't want any trouble."

Two wide bouncers in sleeveless undershirts splashed through the beaded curtain. Their baggy black trousers fastened somewhere on the underside of large bellies. Grease from an interrupted meal glistened on the scowling men's jowls.

"Why don't you gentlemen choose one of these nice girls instead?" The madam said snapping her fingers. The sharp crack signaled the trained girls to show their wares. Pulled up skirts exhibited young thighs. Flipping black hair exposed bare taut shoulders.

Pulling out another piastre note, Max barked, "Where is the Corsican?"

The mama snatched the crisp bill. Glancing in the direction of brothel security, she nodded. A thug's greasy paw grabbed Max's arm. A confident Loc pulled out his gun. At the end of the tribesman's rigid extended arm, the pistol barrel targeted the goon's oily noggin. The thug released his grip and retreated. Sheepishly he stood alongside his obese companion. Flowing down the staircase a girl's whimpering plea interrupted the failed negotiations.

Glancing at Loc, Max received a confident nod. The German unsheathed his Soviet sidearm. Cautiously he ascended the creaking wood staircase in search of the woman-beating Corsican. At the top of the stairs, he peered down a long corridor. On either side of the hallway, doors separated the tiny rooms in which the girls plied their trade. Active bedsprings squeaked. Light laughter flowed under closed doors. A muffled crash resonated from unit two-sixteen. Max approached. From within, male grunts conversed with a whimpering female. The doorknob resisted. The cheap lock snapped with little effort. Through the door crease, Max saw Petru. Kneeling on a small bed the boney naked Corsican glistened. In front of the pumping Petru, a nude girl on all fours wept. Her sweaty hair concealed the source of the dripping blood staining white sheets. Targeting the back of Petru's head, Max entered the small room. In a demented state of bliss, the Corsican sodomized his victim. To announce his presence, Max tapped his pistol on the back of Petru's head. The Corsican gasped. The battered girl rolled onto the floor and crawled weeping into the corner.

I squeeze the trigger and it's all over, Max thought focused on the Corsican's greasy black hair. I've never killed anyone for my own satisfaction, he realized. The Canadian sergeant during the battle of Caen, was the first life I terminated, he reflected. I killed or wounded many more of the enemy that day. I was seventeen, a soldier. That was war. Who knows how many lives I've ended? He visualized the Communist wave attacks in the Red River Delta. I was a professional soldier. The charging Vietminh became targets to challenge my marksmanship. I should just terminate the Corsican and his bounty now, he thought. You never hesitate. However, this is different. This is personal. "I told you, if I saw you again, I would kill you. So turn around to die," Max announced. I want to see the life drain from the Corsican's dark eyes, he concluded.

A large silhouette appeared in the doorway. Taken off guard by the new arrival, Max turned quickly to investigate. A large shirtless and barefooted Asian stood at the door. "Get out of here!" Max yelled. The Asian did not react. Max shot him. As the weapon discharged, Petru's sharp elbow nailed Max in the forehead. Stumbling back, Max watched Petru's naked white ass jump out of the window. Off balanced, Max staggered to the windowsill. In the alley below, Petru's wiry nude frame stumbled in and out of the shadows. Squeezing off a single shot, Max saw his prey collapse.

Feeling the growing knot on his forehead Max snorted in disgust. Why did I hesitate? I should have followed my military instincts, he thought. You never hesitate. Walking over to the half-naked body in the doorway, he wondered, is this one of Petru's henchmen or just a nosy customer? Could be a civilian casualty, he realized.

The whining girl curled up in the corner gulped for air. Glancing at the young whore, Max spotted Petru's coat draped over the room's only chair. Searching the pockets, he found the Corsican's wallet. After pulling a wad of bills from the billfold, he threw the empty folder to the floor. Randomly dividing the cash, he offered half the currency to the naked girl. She accepted, clutching the generous fee next to her battered face.

Max peered into the hallway. The flanking doors were ajar. Curious eyes investigated the commotion. Max fired a shot into the ceiling. The hallways doors slammed shut. A cloud of white plaster sprinkled down. Stepping over the corpse, Max exited the room. Descending the stairs, he found Loc standing guard over two profusely sweating bouncers. The painted madam stood defiantly with folded arms.

"Loc, you good?" Max asked.

Loc nodded.

Handing the balance of Petru's currency to the lacquered faced woman, Max said, "For your troubles."

In front of the whorehouse, Max holstered his pistol. Walking at a brisk pace, he and Loc blended into the pedestrian traffic.

"Did you kill him?" asked a winded Loc.

Pulling Loc into the doorway of a closed shop, Max said with a slight shrug, "I shot him but I need to confirm that he's dead."

"Let's go back then," Loc said with a nod.

Looking up from the shadows at the crime scene, Max studied the second floor windows. Visually he traced the Corsican's leaping escape to the dark side of the alley. There was no body.

Squatting down, Loc touched the wet ground. Rubbing his thumb against his forefingers, he said. "You did hit him, this is fresh blood."

The House of Butterflies lit up. Light shot out of every porthole. Patrons and employees flowed by open windows. Police sirens wailed.

"Let's get out of here," Max whispered. You never hesitate, he reflected, unless you are a fucking amateur.

CHAPTER FOURTY FIVE

The C-119 transport hummed. Grinning Roche glanced around the empty cargo hold. The higher elevations and cooler temperatures of the Plain of Jars will be a welcome change, he thought. It's been a hot muggy Saigon summer. Turbulence shook the Civil Air Transport or CAT flight. Roche leaned back in his harnessed seat. He marveled at the unlimited resources his employer provided for his clandestine operations. The expansion of the Asian Airlines CAT into Laos will fulfill my covert transportation needs, he realized. The Agency owns the controlling interest in Civil Air Transport, he assumed. The only thing I really need to know about the Asian Airlines complex corporate structure, he concluded is it allows the CIA to play the deniability card.

Exiting the aircraft at dusk, Roche dropped his satchel on the red clay tarmac. He closed his eyes and slowly tilting his head back took a long deep breath of the crisp mountain air. God, that was refreshing, he thought. Throwing the small bag over his shoulder, he began the short walk through the frontier town of Phong Savin. The storefronts he passed reminding him of a western movie set, only with pitched palm roofs. The orange sun slipped below the jagged horizon. Roche's short-sleeve Hawaiian shirt flapped in a cool breeze. Chilled he accelerated. Before him under a red sky, the silhouette of the King Cobra Lodge grew.

Ascending the bowed wooden stairs of the Lodge, Roche paused. Under the raised structure, something big black and dark stirred. Instinctively he dropped his bag and pulled out his sidearm. A small Asian man crawled out from the shadows. Dressed in soiled rags, the malnourished skeleton twitched. "Jesus," Roche mumbled inhaling the stench of urine. Snorting he placed his gun hand over his sour expression. The poor kneeling wretch placed a wooden bowl at the American's feet. Holstering his gun, Roche picked up his bag. Reaching into his pants pocket, he searched for coin. Fumbling a handful of loose change, he studied the bobbing shaved headed beggar. Wait a minute, he thought, this addict is Japanese. This is a former Imperial soldier who stayed in Vietnam after the end of the Second World War, he realized. "You don't look so invincible now, do you?" Roche mumbled. He recalled his mud Marine days during the Battle of Pelelui. The haunting image of Japanese snipers intentionally targeting stretcher-bearers surfaced. A wicked grin emerged, he kicked the beggar's bowl and grumbled, "Fucking nip."

Proceeding up the rickety stairs, Roche searched for cleaner air. On the wood-planked landing, he took deep cleansing breaths. Tossing the satchel over his shoulder, he entered the small lobby. The barroom clamor from the adjacent saloon permeated. Behind the front desk, a tiny Laotian man in an oversized long sleeved white shirt and skinny black tie grinned.

"I need a room for a couple of nights," Roche shouted over the noise.

"No problem sir, we have plenty of rooms," the desk clerk responded.

Paying the bill in advance, Roche inquired, "Do you know of a German called Max?"

"Yes sir," the clerk responded. "Everyone around the Plain of Jars knows Max. Did you know that he and his partner Loc walked out of Isabelle?"

Roche chuckled at Max's notoriety. "I'm aware of his exploits," he said. "Is he here tonight?"

"No sir, I have not seen him in over a week. He has taken up residency in a house near the refugee camp." The clerk answered handing a room key attached to small lacquered bamboo stalk.

Roche handed the clerk several bills, "'Thanks for the information," he said. "And please have my bag taken up to the room."

Roche stood in the doorway of the highland saloon. A smoky haze lingered over the heads of the bar room patrons. The American caught a whiff of spilt beer and unhygienic clientele. The loathing gazes from the Corsican customers greeted him. Most of this boisterous crowd has a Mediterranean origin, he thought. The mobsters and French war veterans all have the same goal, as me he surmised. We all want to fill the void in the opium trade created by the *Deuxième Bureau's* withdrawal.

Puffing out his chest, Roche strutted up to the bar and ordered a whisky. Turning to face the hostile room, he calmly sipped the bourbon with a crooked grin. Amongst his audience, he spotted Casta. The French Intelligence officer with the annoyingly thin mustache, sat at a nearby table with seedy companions. One appeared to be African; one was Eurasian, the other French or probably another Corsican. The large Negro seems out of place, Roche thought studying Casta's colleague. The well over six-foot tall black man's open shirt exposed a barrel chest, accented with a patch of silver growth. Closely cropped spiraled gray hair encircled his large round head. Must be from French North Africa, Roche concluded. Casta made eye contact and leaning forward conversed with his tablemates. French Intelligence is probably announcing my presence, Roche concluded. No doubt, retelling his version of the dog-shooting incident, he thought. Casta's table erupted in sinister laughter.

"Kill any dogs lately?" Casta yelled at the American.

Roche grinned. He took a sip of whisky and responded. "No, but speaking of dogs, whatever happen to that two legged Corsican dog, I told you to keep on a tight leash?"

A red-faced Casta blurted out; "Fuck you!"

The African got up flinging his chair against the back wall. Bumping the back of Casta's seat, he charged the American. Leaning back, a snickering Casta did not attempt to restrain his companion.

"Sit down Hakeem!" Max called out from the doorway.

Clenching his fist, the snorting Hakeem stood his ground. His massive chest expanded and contracted with each breath. Shaking his head, the rage slowly subsided. Grinning wide, Hakeem politely nodded at Max and retreated to his table.

Accompanied by Loc and three Tai tribesmen, Max entered the bar. Max and Loc dressed as Saigon businessmen in light colored suits. Their tribesmen entourage wore black pants and tunics, with blue turbans. Smiles and nods from the other customers welcomed the cadre. The bartender immediately grabbed five ice-cold beers from a galvanized tub.

"Thanks Jimmy," Max said to the plump happy Buddha bartender. As he took the bottles of chilled brew, he added, "Please send a *pastis* over to the Gray Gorilla and put it on my tab."

Standing next to Max, Roche questioned, "The Gray Gorilla?"

"It's Hakeem's nickname. He actually is a pretty good fellow. His size is intimidating. Laotians believe that a large man is a cruel man. That is not the case with the Gray Gorilla," Max explained.

"Good to see you Max," Roche said glancing at the Negro.

"I heard you flew in today. We left Saigon in a hurry and did not have time to thank you for the information about the Corsican. It proved invaluable to me, not so well for the Corsican." Pointing at Roche's empty glass, Max added, "Do you have time for another drink? I owe you some information."

"Sure can use one, let's grab a table. This time I'd like to sit with my back against the wall, if you don't mind?" Roche said.

Looking in Casta's direction, Max mumbled, "I understand."

Max, Loc and Roche made their way towards an empty table against the back wall. Passing Casta's group, the Gray Gorilla lifted his glass of milky soft yellow liqueur. Max winked.

Max and Roche sat with their backs against the wall. Loc sat next to his partner. The three Tais seated themselves at an adjoining table and immediately started smoking. A young bar girl timidly approached the German.

"Not tonight Chimmy," Max said to the barmaid.

Chimmy wilted. With down cast puppy dog eyes, she retreated.

Pulling out a cigar, Max lit it with his Legionnaire Zippo lighter. After taking several large puffs, he asked Roche through the dissipating smoke, "Can you confirm that Petru is dead?"

Roche flinched. "You don't know?" He questioned. "I assumed you killed him and disposed of the body."

"I shot him." Max answered, "But could not verify the kill."

"I'll look into it when I return," Roche said tapping out a Lucky Strike. Glancing at Casta's table, he added, "It appears the *Deuxième Bureau* thinks he is dead."

"I'd appreciate anything you can find out," Max said sucking on his large cigar. "So you want to talk about opium?" He asked leaning back.

"I know a little about the trade," Roche responded. "What can you tell me about the business around the Plain of Jars?"

"It is simple. If you want to get into the narcotics trade in this region, you only need two things. The first is a Laotian connection. The second is air transportation. Since you flew in on a C-119, I'm assuming you have already taken care of one of the requirements." Max said puffing on the stogie. Tilting his head back, he politely exhaled into the rafters.

"What's the competition like?" Roche questioned.

Sweeping his hand in the direction of the bar's clientele, Max said, "Most of it is drinking in front of us. With French Intelligence abandoning their opium monopoly, it appears there are ample profits for all. There are several small charter airlines, mostly Corsican affiliated or owned. You probably saw the dozen or so single engine Beavers and Pipers when you landed. Most modified with auxiliary gas tanks. These small planes are trying to fill the opium transportation void created when the French Air Force pulled out."

"Any serious competition?" Roche persisted.

"Not that I know of. All the players dealing with the supply appear satisfied." Max answered. Flicking a large white ash on the floor, he glanced at Loc. His partner looked bored. Max shot him a wink. The tribesman grinned.

"Max, do you know a Captain Yang Mo?" Roche inquired.

"I know of him," Max nodded. "Yang is a tribal leader from this region. He served as a French officer with the Expeditionary Forces. I've heard he was a good military man but it has been rumored that he shorted the wages of some of the Meos under his command." Rubbing the stubble on his chin, Max pondered the Americans interest in Yang. I assumed the CIA was getting into the lucrative trade, he thought. It appears the United States is going to put Captain Yang Mo into business. "What is your interest in the Captain?" He probed.

"Max, you said there are two prerequisites to get into the opium business. You're correct Civil Air Transport fulfills the transportation requirement; Captain Yang may become our Laotian contact. I am aware of the graft the Captain was involved with at the expense of his troops. That makes him a good candidate for the proposed venture. I'm meeting with him in the morning, or I should say, interviewing him in the morning. I would like you to attend. I would compensate you for your time." Roche asked looking at both Max and Loc.

"Why do you need us?" Max politely questioned.

"First because your connection with the Black Tais." Roche acknowledged glancing at the three Tais seated at the adjacent table, "The Tais are closely related to the Captain's people. Second, if it goes well tomorrow, I'd offer you a job acting as a conduit between the Captain and me. My employer has unlimited resources but limited personnel. We work better contracting out services. You would be on the Civil Air Transport payroll with a good salary and a healthy stipend. Does this proposition interest you?"

"We have an interest." Max said glancing at Loc. "But let's see how the interview with the Captain goes before we come to an agreement. As I said before, he does have a reputation."

CHAPTER FOURTY SIX

Sporting a colorful Hawaiian shirt and aviator sunglasses, Roche stood in front of a small hanger at the Phong Savin airport. He was early for the morning meeting. In the ascending sunlight, he felt the warming rays of the new day. A light breeze pushed pockets of cold air out of the shadows. Absorbing the cool blast, he watched a cloud of blowing red dust dissipating over the windy plateau. The rural community unfolded. Strategically placed paddy fields sparkled in the angled sunlight. Random clusters of two-thousand year old stone jars cast long shadows on the rolling lush landscape.

Pivoting he admired the megalithic jars scattered across the plain. The hollowed out boulders varied in height and diameter from three to ten feet. Why would an ancient civilization hewn lipped urns out of solid rock, he wondered. Burial site, he pondered, no that's too easy. I can rule out the local legend about a race of giants creating the jars for rice wine to celebrate a victorious battle, he realized. The most plausible speculation, he concluded, was that the jars collected monsoon rainwater to assist caravan traders during the dry season. Commerce is a motivating force, he thought as an opium smuggling Beechcraft taxied for takeoff.

Frowning at the high-pitched revving twin-engine aircraft, Roche wondered what the smugglers ultimate destination would be. One thing is for certain, he realized that the cargo's value would increase exponentially the further it traveled. Just the short flight to the Laotian capital of Vientiane, would triple the opium's worth. It would increase one hundred fold once it reached Marseille. What an amazing product, he thought. I wonder what the ancient caravan's profit margins were.

Out of the dusty wake of the Beechcraft's takeoff, Max, Loc and three Tais appeared strutting across the red clay tarmac. The westernized Loc wore his light colored suit, with no tie, in contrast to his Tai brother's black pajamas. In a long-sleeved shirt with the cuffs rolled up to the elbows, Max prominently displayed his Soviet pistol in a shoulder holster. Seeing Max's exhibited sidearm, Roche patted the small Baby Browning pistol concealed in the front pocket of his baggy chinos.

"Morning Roche," Max said.

"Morning gentlemen, glad to see we all made it," Roche said to his guest straightening out his windblown hair.

The Tais acknowledged the greeting with a nod and a nervous smile.

"Looks like your prospect is on time for his job interview," Max said motioning to several approaching Laotian military vehicles.

In the front seat of the lead vehicle sat Captain Yang Mo. There's my pigeon, Roche thought. He recognized the Captain from his file photo. His briefing on the Captain had been extensive. His military record over-shadowed his questionable ethical reputation. The Captain's first combat experience came in his teens fighting the Japanese. For the last eight years, Yang waged war for the French Expeditionary Forces against the Vietminh. Looks like I'll be dealing with a true warrior, Roche concluded.

The small framed Captain exited the vehicle in a tailor made Laotian officer's uniform. He strutted with overwhelming self-confidence. Observing his candidate through the dark green tinted lens, Roche caught the flash of the Captain's gold Swiss watch. Bingo, Roche the poker player thought focused on the expensive timepiece. That's the *tell*, I was look-ing for. Life, like poker is a game of skill, not chance. That is if you can read your opponents. Wrapped around the Captain's left wrist sparkled his desire for wealth, a grinning Roche realized. The true warrior would be exploitable.

The tiny warrior approached. Roche extended his hand and shaking the officer's callus palm said, "Captain Yang, thank you for meeting with us. I am Major Tom Roche with the US Military Advisory Group."

The stoic faced Captain acknowledged the introduction with a slight nod. Turning his back to Roche, he walked over to Max with hand extended.

"Captain Yang Mo," he said introducing himself to Max. "You must be the German who walked out of the Valley. It is a pleasure to finally meet you."

"Yes, I'm Max Kohl, and this is Loc, who also walked out of Isabelle," Max said with a firm grip.

The Captain then added, "It is a pleasure as well. Please let's go inside to discuss the American's potential venture."

You arrogant bit player, Roche thought. I'm about to offer you an opportunity to achieve unlimited wealth and power, and you turn your back to me. With a smirk, he concluded at least the Captain likes Max.

One of the Laotian soldiers unlocked the hanger door and the large group entered the corrugated tin structure. The Tai and Laotian escorts lingered at the entrance. Max, Loc and the Captain headed for an office in the rear of the building with Roche trailing. In the office, ten dining room chairs encircled a large hardwood table. The four men seated themselves. Their respective companions stood attentively along the plywood wall.

"Max, is that a Tokarev pistol you are carrying?" The Captain asked pointing to the German's sidearm.

Politely un-holstering his weapon, Max handed it to the Captain for closer examination. "Yes it is, it is a fine handgun. I not only carry it as a useful tool but as a trophy. It is a souvenir, I picked up on the journey out of the valley," Max said.

"Gentlemen can we get down to business?" Roche announced.

The Captain with a sour face handed the pistol back to Max. Leaning back in his chair, he addressed Roche for the first time, "What is your proposal?"

"Thank you for your attention Captain. The proposal is simple. We will assist you in becoming a wealthy and powerful man. In exchange, all we ask is your support in maintaining an anti-communist agenda in this region. We will initially provide weapons and some seed capital to help you get started in the opium trade. Air transportation will be available and the trafficking in narcotics will be tolerated." Roche paused to let the proposition sink in. "We are aware of your influence with your fellow tribesmen. We would require a certain re-investment of your profits in the recruitment of additional troops to the cause. If necessary, training for the troops will also be provided." Roche then asked, "Do you have any questions?"

The Captain sat up in his chair giving the American his full attention. He started to speak, but then closed his mouth pondering the proposal.

Roche grinned. There it is he thought studying the speechless Captain. I've seen the same reaction before. You are not the first egomaniac to realize that your quest for power has a financial backer. Now comes the fun part, he realized. The manipulated tools must never forget who was in charge. In a harsh tone, he said. "It is a basic proposal that I think even you can comprehend. However, there is one point that I want to make sure you understand. Whether you accept or reject this offer, never turn your back to me again."

Swallowing hard, the Captain responded, "My apologies Major, no offense was intended. We both have the same objective in eradicating Communism, and should not let my lack of etiquette hinder those efforts. I would fight Communism with or without the resources you are so generously providing, however I have a great deal of interest in your proposal."

"Apology accepted" Roche said. "Are we in agreement then?"

"Yes, I am very interested, Major."

"Good, all arrangements will be made through Max." Roche said, making the bold assumption that Max wanted the job. A glance at a subtly nodding Max confirmed his supposition. "You and I will have very little contact going forward, Captain. All communication will be through Max and Loc."

Loc beamed at his inclusion. Rubbing his nose, he shielded a blushing smile.

"Gentlemen, it has been a pleasure," Roche said rising from the table.

The Captain took great effort in shaking Roche's hand. He accented his appreciation with a modest bow.

Roche watched the Captain strut out of the warehouse. On the other side of the cold war chess game, he wondered if his Soviet and Communist Chinese counterparts had similar issues. The Agency entices ethnic warlords and criminals into the anti-communist cause by exploiting their greed and quest for power. It worked well for them in Burma. The same formula should work in Northern Laos. My Communist adversaries must have a tougher sell to convince their puppets, he thought, with that bullshit redistribution of wealth ideology.

CHAPTER FOURTY SEVEN

In the French outpost of Muong Sai, Laos, a young radio operator with elevated feet pawed at the cover of the April issue of *Cinemonde.* The prized magazine featured the buxom American beauty, Marilyn Monroe. There she is, he thought, looking at me with sleepy eyes and those puckered glossy red lips. Pausing from the fantasy, he adjusted the earphones that buzzed with monotonous static. It is going to be another long boring day, he realized. The hissing transmission searched the airways in the hopes of picking up a distress signal. At least I have you to keep me company; he thought examining the image of the doe eyed Miss Monroe. A gentle finger traced the actress's plunging neckline. The constant crackling went silent. He dropped his feet and the dog-eared magazine to the floor. "This is Muong Sai please identify yourself," he said sitting erect.

A distorted and broken voice faded in, "This is Sergeant Jean Guillian of the Composite Airborne Command Group."

"Thank god, Sergeant," replied the enthusiastic operator. "Do you know your position? We may be able to arrange a helicopter evacuation."

"Muong Sai, I'm not contacting you for transport, I'm requesting a munitions drop," Guillian said.

"Sergeant, the war is over. I repeat the war is over." The young radioman said frantically waving his hands over his head.

"No, it is not!" insisted Guillian.

Rushing in the officer in charge grabbed the operator's headset. "Sergeant this is Lieutenant Claude La Monde of the 21st Artillery Air Observation Group, how many are with you?"

"We number about three hundred troops and two thousand civilians and are very low on ammunition and food. I'm requesting a munitions drop," Guillian replied.

"That will not be possible, the best chance for your troops will be to fall back to Laos or to the 17th parallel. We may also arrange a helicopter evacuation for you and any other French personnel. Time is running out, the bamboo curtain is coming down. Do you understand?"

"Lieutenant I will not leave these people exposed to Communist reprisals. They have been loyal French allies. As a Parisian Jew, I survived the attempted extermination of my people. I will not abandon my Meo community to a similar fate. Please help us. I'm begging you. If we are going to evacuate, we will need a provisions drop, a munitions drop and logistical support. If you are going to forsake your *Montagnard* allies, let us die fighting with a munitions drop," Guillian pleaded.

"I'm sorry Sergeant; there is nothing I can do. The war is over. I repeat the war is over."

"Fuck you Lieutenant. I repeat f-u-c-k y-o-u."

"Good luck Sergeant, Adieu." La Monde said not knowing if his last words were received. Taking several deep breaths, he reached for the clipboard containing the list of unaccounted for commandos. To the hum of empty static, he scanned the long list of names. So many abandoned men sacrificed for a forsaken cause, he thought. In the status column next to the name, Sergeant Jean Guillian, La Monde with a shaky hand wrote, "*Disparu Au Combat.*" Placing the pen behind his ear, he examined his poor penmanship. The Missing in Action label is premature, he realized. However, the defiant Jew chose his fate.

CHAPTER FOURTY EIGHT

It had been awhile since Roche had driven outside of Saigon. A light rain began to fall. He rolled up his window. Invading precipitation dampened the backseat's upholstery. Looking over his shoulder, he remembered the missing back passenger window. I still need to get that fixed; he realized chuckling at the Corsican's attempted intimation. The haughty gangsters have regressed to shooting at parked cars, he thought. It's more of a nuisance than a threat.

The late morning sky darkened. The rain intensified. The overwhelmed windshield wipers battled the deluge. The rubber blades methodically sloshed back and forth. Slowing down, Roche got a blurred vision of the displaced. On both sides of the narrow asphalt road, the refugees huddled. Families squatted under frail tarp lean-tos. A few wax paper umbrellas provided shelter. Most of the rabble just endured the showering rain. Pedestrian traffic wandered across the paved street. Roche proceeded at a snail's pace. The drenched crowd slowly parted as he approached. A tiny man laden down with sacks of rice balanced on a wooden yoke across his shoulders hindered the vehicles progress. Idling behind the laborer, Roche placed his hand on the car's horn. Pausing to blast his presence, he admired the coolie's stamina. The old man soaked to the bone in black pajamas with a pointed hat trudged forward in sandaled feet. The load is twice his size, Roche realized. Poor bastard, Roche thought, he doesn't need me forcing his pace. The overburdened coolie slowly migrated to the side of the road.

Passing the flowing throng, Roche smiled to himself. The Agency's propaganda campaign was a success, he concluded. Nothing like nudging the relocation provision in the Geneva Accords with an anti-communist promotion, he thought. North Vietnam's large Catholic population was an easy target. The thousands of leaflets proclaiming, "Christ has departed the north," and "the Virgin Mary is going south," worked, he concluded. We are not only draining the Communist population base, he thought. But with a little assistance to the displaced, we will insure loyalty in the anti-communist cause.

In the center of this refugee city of approximately one-hundred-thousand, Roche pulled into a gravel-paved lot. Several smoldering oil drums billowed out smoke. In the torrential rain, collies fed camp refuse into fading flames. In front of the Bien Hoa administration tent, Roche parked. A cloud of blowing rubbish smoke engulfed the vehicle. Jesus Christ, Roche thought pinching his nose, It's bad enough the whole place smells like a shit-house. Do we really have to add the smell of burnt garbage to the equation?

Hopping over puddles, Roche raced for the shelter of the pitched white canvas structure. Entering the administration tent, he ran a moist hand through his wet hair. The sound of rain danced on the heavy fabric. A square wooden table not quite in the middle of the canvas room waited. The off center arrangement avoided a dripping leak. A strategically placed bucket caught the trickling water. On the table rested a floral printed enamel pot of tea with matching cups. Staring down at a steaming cup of tea with an angelic face, sat a striking young girl in a black smock top and baggy trousers. Her long black hair drawn back in a loose ponytail covered her ears. Next to her sat a clean cut and educated looking young Asian man wearing a short sleeve button down shirt and slacks, no shoes but a decent pair of sandals. His slick black hair shined. He is obviously, an aid worker, Roche concluded. I'd say he is in his early twenties, the American calculated. However, who could guess the ages of these Vietnamese?

Brushing the remnants of the storm off his shoulders, Roche approached. The young man sporting a wide grin stood to greet him. The young girl remained seated, her gaze focused on the misting tea.

"Hello I am Harry Han with Catholic Relief Services, I will be assisting you as a translator this afternoon," the young man informed with only the slightest hint of an accent.

Roche knew his real name was not Harry, and appreciated that he had given himself an English name for ease of conversation. "Pleased to meet you, Harry. I'm Major Tom Roche with the US Military Advisory Group." Shaking the young man's hand, he added, "Please call me Tom."

"This is the young girl we told you about, her name is Mei," Harry said. Mei did not look up but blinked hard at the sound of her name.

Taking a seat Roche lowered his head to make eye contact with the stunning girl. In decent Vietnamese, he said softly, "Hello Mei, pleased to meet you."

Timidly Mei smiled.

Optimistically Roche studied the shy girl who apparently escaped a labor camp in the Thai Nguyen province. She could be a valuable source of information for American Intelligence, he thought. The Communists have controlled that region for several years. This little beauty might give us insight as to how the Vietminh plan to govern the partitioned North. Besides that, he chuckled; she is pleasant on the eyes. Looking at the translator, he asked, "Harry, we were told that she was released from a Vietminh re-education camp. Before we question her about that experience, I would like to know how she made it out of the North,"

As Harry translated, Roche topped off Mei's teacup. He then poured some for himself. Pulling out a cigarette, he noticed, a quick side-glance from the girl suggesting a desire to smoke. Obliging her expression, he offered a Lucky Strike. She accepted and leaned forward for a light. Leaning back in her chair, she took several enjoyable puffs. Eloquently she blew the smoke over her head. After taking a sip of tea, she casually flicked an ash into the water pail.

She is no common peasant, Roche thought observing her smoking etiquette.

Through the translator, Mei spoke at length how several of the prisoners released with her and her friend, were Catholic dissidents. They joined rural Catholics in their attempt to escape the North. The Communist blocked the small group's attempts to make it to any major city, and French evacuation. The only hope was to make it to the coast. In a small wooden boat, they were spotted by a French Naval vessel and rescued.

Pulling out a damp pad of paper from his shirt pocket, Roche took some quick notes. I'm not surprised that the Communist are obstructing the evacuation from the rural parts of the North, he thought. I'll follow up with the US embassy, he concluded and have the State Department make a formal complaint to the International Control Commission. Glancing up from the moist reminder, he said, "Harry, ask her why she was released from the re-education camp."

After several exchanges in Vietnamese between Harry and Mei, Harry concluded, "She doesn't know."

"Ask her how long she was in the camp and what was her offense," Roche asked.

Once again, the two locals conversed back and forth. Roche tried to comprehend the dialogue with his limited Vietnamese. They are talking too fast for me, he realized and leaned back to await the translation.

"She says about six months, but doesn't know why she was detained," Harry replied.

Roche shifted in his chair, just when he thought things were going well. With a slight frown, he said, "Ask her to tell us what life was like in the camp."

Harry took notes while Mei responded to his question. Roche still could not follow the Vietnamese conversation but could tell that Mei concluded with a question.

Taking a deep breath, Harry referring to his notes said, "The initial focus of the camp was education based on Marxist-Leninist teachings. The goal was to prepare the camp's inhabitants to become productive members of a new workers society. In order to do this hard work, discipline and lack of food were required. She said she could recite some communist lessons, but she doesn't know what they mean."

Her rhetoric confirming Roche's information about the Vietminh re-education process, she no doubt was there.

"Do you want me to have her recite some of her communist lessons?" Harry asked.

"No," Roche said. "The last thing I want to hear is that bullshit." The comment startled Harry and caused Mei to stare down into her teacup.

"Sorry," Roche said. "Tell Mei, no thank you, we are not interested in her communist lessons, but would like her to continue." Roche then took a sip of tea as Harry translated his request.

Looking up she spoke again to Harry. Roche observed Harry's expression change to one of concern. When she finished, Harry touched her arm before translating. "The land owners in the North needed to be punished. There were deaths, many deaths. To eat you had to work; many died working. If you could not work, you starved; many died of starvation. An illness or injury always resulted in death. An old female landowner hung herself to escape this world. When it was determined that the camp commissar was a landowner, he was tortured to death in front of the inmates. There are apparently many land owners in the North." Swallowing hard Harry looked at Roche and added, "She said death was very busy harvesting the incarcerated at Camp Number Seventeen."

This information pleased Roche. What a flawed ideology, he thought. The possibility that the Vietminh would implement a Land Reform based on the wave of terror that Communist China implemented a few years earlier was good news indeed. Grinning he stroked his chin. The partitioned North would create an unprecedented economic crisis with their ignorant reforms, he concluded. Looking at the stoic expressions of Harry and Mei, Roche realized his joyous expression. He quickly frowned to compensate for his lack of compassion.

The rain increased. The drumming downpour pounded the canvas shelter. A steady stream flowed through the leak in the tent. The bucket catch basin overflowed. The interview had reached its conclusion, however Roche did not want to leave in this downpour. From his time in this country, he had learned that the skies could clear in five-minutes or it could continue to rain for hours. Hoping for the five-minute scenario, Roche decided, to wait it out. "Harry, thank you for your assistance," he said. "And thank the young lady for her time. This was very informative."

As Harry translated, Roche lit another cigarette and handed Mei the nearly full pack of Lucky Strikes, and a book of matches. Retrieving the gift, she showed her gratitude by looking directly at Roche. A crooked grin slowly emerged from her soft lips. Once again, she stirred Roche's curiosity. What is this seductive creature's background? He wondered. She definitely is not a rural peasant. Thinking her natural beauty would make for a good photo opportunity, he said, "Harry, we are having some refugees tell their stories to the international press this Friday. Tell Mei I would like her to join us. We are particularly interested in her information about the Communist Land Reform Program, and her re-education camp experience." As the translator relayed the request, Roche wondered why he had not thought of using her sooner. With the media spot lighting the mass northern exodus, this eye-catching girl would be perfect to demonize the Vietminh transition.

CHAPTER FOURTY NINE

Max flapped the bottom of his sports coat in the heavy humid air of Saigon. The discomfort magnified by the bright late afternoon sun. He walked back and forth, in front of the Marine guards at the US Embassy gate. I wish I could remove my jacket, he thought. The price of concealing a shoulder-holstered pistol in the tropics is expensive, he concluded.

Squatted down on his haunches in the shade of the sentry's box, Loc enjoyed his nicotine addiction. The tribesman puffed away eyeing his German partner's pacing.

Stopping in front of the crouching tribesman, Max asked, "How about a cigarette?"

Pulling out a pack of smokes from the inside coat pocket of his oversized suit, Loc handed them up to Max. "Leeches?" Loc questioned grinning.

Snorting out a laugh, Max responded, "No, something to kill the time, while we wait for our boss."

Max lit the cigarette and inhaled the warm smoke. He spotted Roche walking briskly across the courtyard.

As Roche approached the main gate, he called out, "I'm sorry I'm late, busy day."

Max grinned. He liked the American. "Take your time. We are not in a hurry."

A sweat-moistened Hawaiian shirt dominated by large white flowers clung to the American. Joining the contract employees at the sentry box, Roche took a deep breath. Perspiration rolled down his face.

"Cigarette?" Max offered.

"Thanks," Roche accepted leaning forward to light the cigarette from Max's lighter. Exhaling Roche said, "Welcome back to Saigon boys. Are you planning to shoot up any more brothels?"

Max smiled, "It depends, can you confirm the death of Petru Rossi?"

"I wish I could, Max. If he still is alive, he is lying low. My staff examined all the hospital records at the time of the incident and found nothing. Our relationship with French Intelligence is civil but we still have issues with the Corsicans and the Binh Xuyen. Saigon is still a covert battleground. You need to be careful. I would avoid the Continental Hotel and the Cholon district. I'd give you the same advice, if I could verify Petru's demise."

"Thanks for the update," Max said.

"One other thing, the confirmed death that night was not just a customer at the House of Butterflies. He was a Binh Xuyen soldier, a local gangster," Roche said inhaling a relaxing plume of smoke.

"I'm glad to hear there were no civilian casualties," Max mumbled.

"So tell me how is the arrogant Captain?" Roche asked.

"He's a shrewd son of a bitch," Max responded. "He's starting to make a good profit in the opium trade."

Upon hearing the word opium, Roche flinched with a sour expression.

"Sorry," Max caught himself. "He is starting to turn a profit; however he short changes his soldiers. He's using his growing influence for extortion purposes. His power within the Laotian Army and in the Plain of Jars region is growing. I think you picked the right man." Max dropped his half-smoked cigarette. His shiny leather shoe ground the smoldering canister into the asphalt. The cigarette left a bitter taste. He preferred cigars.

"Is he still controllable?" Roche asked.

"He is as addicted to power as addicts are to opium. That makes him very controllable," Max answered. Observing Roche roll his eyes, he realized he used the forbidden word again.

As Roche and Loc finished their cigarettes, a group of locals escorted by embassy staff exited the building. The assemblage headed towards the gate. A staff member acknowledged Roche with a wave. Roche waved back.

The usually quiet Loc squinting hard at the gathering asked, "Who are those people?"

"They are very fortunate individuals, refugees from the North who have made it to freedom." Roche explained. "There is a Catholic priest who witnessed the burning of his church and the execution of most of his congregation; a husband and wife who lost a child during their escape; and a young girl who endured the hardships of forced labor in a re-education camp."

"I know that girl from somewhere!" Loc said pointing to an attractive dark haired Asian. Staring at her, trying to recall, he asked, "Max, do you recognize her?"

"No, but I wish I did," Max replied looking the petite beauty up and down. Grinning mischievously, he added, "I would gladly pay a healthy sum for a few minutes of her time."

"Claudine," Loc murmured. "Claudine," he said again in his normal tone. Turning to face the refugees, he looked right at the young girl and shouted, "Claudine!"

The crowd all turned around and stared at the three men. The embassy staff gave puzzling looks and shrugs at Roche.

Roche placed a sympathetic hand on Loc's shoulder and informed, "You are mistaken. Her name is Mei."

"No," Loc emphatically replied. "She was stationed at Claudine. She was with us at Dien Bien Phu."

A stunned Max opened his mouth. Squinting hard at Mei, he tried but failed to recognize her. Turning to Roche, he asked, "Did you know this?"

"No," Roche replied. "The girl was a mystery to me, I knew she was not a rural peasant but I had no idea she was a Field Brothel prostitute."

Two Peugeot sedans pulled into the compound. The embassy staff assisted in loading the refugee passengers.

Loc walking towards the vehicles shouted, "Wait!"

The embassy staff looked past the tribesman. They sought Roche for direction.

Displaying an open palm, Roche called out, "Hold up a minute."

Mei jumped the informal queue pushing her way into a vehicle. Sitting stone-faced in the back seat of the opened door sedan, she ignored the commotion.

"Hang on Loc, let me handle this," Roche shouted. He broke into a jog to catch up to zealous tribesman.

Roche looked at one of the embassy staff. "Excuse me...."

"It's Johnson, sir." The man responded, quickly.

"Yes of course, Johnson. Do you speak Vietnamese?" Roche asked.

"Yes sir."

"Good, can you tell Mei that everything is fine. My friend would like to talk to her," Roche said.

Speaking in Vietnamese, Johnson coaxed the young girl out of the vehicle. Reluctantly, Mei complied looking at the ground. Loc approached her.

"Johnson," Roche whispered. "Translate their conversation for me."

Johnson positioned himself within listening range.

Loc Beamed. "Mei, I recognize you from the Valley. I would never forget your face. I'm Loc. I was with the Tai Auxiliary troops. That is my partner Max," he said glancing over his shoulder at the German. "He was with the Foreign Legion. We walked out of Isabelle on the last day," he explained, exaggerating the accomplishment.

Mei spoke quietly, "You will get me in trouble. They treat my little sister and me very well at the refugee camp. We receive rice and warm milk every day. I don't want to go back to the front."

Loc smiled, "The war is over. There is no more front. We are but a few who survived. It is good to see you. Celebrate our good fortune with us tonight."

"Will they let me go?" Mei asked.

"It does not matter what they want. If you want to go with us tonight my partner can fix it," Loc said.

"I'm no longer a whore," Mei stated with a stern expression.

"And I'm no longer a Tai soldier," Loc replied. "The war is over."

"I need to buy a gift for my little sister. Can you help me?" Mei asked. "It is very important."

"Come with us and that is the first thing we will do," Loc said.

"Let's go then," Mei said. "These Americans are too polite. They make me nervous."

Loc went over to talk to Max. After receiving the translation of Mei's conversation from Johnson, Roche joined them.

"Roche," Max said. "Do you have any objection if we take the young girl with us tonight?"

"What are your intentions?" Roche asked raising his brows.

"Dinner, drinks, what you Americans call a night on the town," Max replied.

"And to buy her friend a gift," Loc chimed in.

"Guys, I'm responsible for her," Roche informed.

"Then join us," Max offered.

Roche paused to contemplate the invitation. "I appreciate the offer," he responded. "But regrettably I have to decline. Just promise me you get her back to the refugee camp tomorrow."

"You have my word on it," Max said. Giving Roche a firm handshake, he added, "Thanks."

Roche headed back towards the embassy. Loc waved for Mei to join him and Max. As she approached, Max tried to comprehend how someone so petite and beautiful could have survived the valley. The sexual aura of her swaying hips and seductive stride faded into the background. Max looked beyond the symmetric beauty of her youthful face into the depths of her dark gemstone eyes. There it is he thought, examining her gaze, the spark for life. She was more than a survivor of a labor camp or Claudine, her quest to exist far exceeded anything this world would throw at her. If death took her too soon, death would be making a mistake. Reaching out for her hands, Max gently held her callused fingers. Respectfully he nodded to his kindred spirit. Fuck the world, he thought, we are here to stay. Tears welled up in Mei's dark eyes. Embracing the German, she wept. Pulling out his handkerchief, Max carefully wiped away her tears. She hugged Max even harder a second time. Turning she squeezed Loc, with the same intensity.

Still holding onto Mei, Loc asked, "So what is this gift we need to buy for your friend?"

A sniffling Mei replied, "I need to buy my Little Sister an ivory comb."

CHAPTER FIFTY

In the back seat of a blue and white Renault taxi, a wide-eyed Mei peered out of the cabs porthole. The upscale boutiques of Saigon's shopping district sparkled. Standing on the crowded sidewalk, Max paid the cab fare. An exuberant Mei shot out of the tiny taxi. In her black smock top, baggy black pants and farmers sandals, she scrutinized the window displays. Loc shadowed her quest. I need to stay close, a lingering Max thought. My European presence should dissuade elitist shopkeepers from embarrassing the girl in her peasant attire. Observing Mei's determined gaze light up, a whelming joy rose in the back of Max's throat. Grinning he watched her rush into a specialty shop.

"Give me some money, Max," Loc said, impatiently holding out his hand.

"I understand," Max replied placing a wad of bills in his partner's open palm.

Stuffing the cash into his pants pocket, Loc ran into the boutique.

Not a bad way to spend the afternoon Max thought. I came to Saigon to enjoy some of my newfound opium wealth and this is a pleasant distraction. Standing in the shade of an overhead awning, he watched Loc and Mei emerge from the store. Mei glowed. She shuffled forward transfixed on the ivory comb in her upturned palm. Glancing up from the treasure, she smiled at Max. Speaking in Vietnamese, she extended her arm displaying the prize.

"She said thank you, this is identical to the comb that was lost in the North." Loc translated.

Max smiled back at her and then said to Loc, "Now that we got that out of the way, tell her we would like to buy her some new clothes that she can wear to dinner tonight."

Loc translated for Mei who graciously accepted the offer with a smiling nod.

In a nearby clothier, Loc purchased a white *Áo Dài* dress. The traditional Vietnamese female attire consisted of a tight long sleeve blouse, with long panels in the front and back, worn over loose fitting trousers. Rather than wait for alterations of the long slacks, Loc bought a pair of high-heeled sandals. Modeling the dress for her new friends, Mei spun around. Max and Loc stood transfixed with open mouths. The outfit accentuated every seductive curve on Mei's shapely figure. Pleased with the results, Mei playfully patted Loc's chest.

French colonial architecture blanketed the skyline. Outdoor cafes dominated the fashionable neighborhood. Loc and Mei strolled down the congested sidewalk. Max loitered behind the couples slow pace. Mei blended in with the female pedestrians in her traditional attire. Strutting Saigon businessmen dressed as westerners. Buddhist monks in saffron robes and the mustard-colored uniformed soldiers of the Saigon police added color to the flowing herd.

Max tried to eavesdrop on the Mei's and Loc's Vietnamese conversation. My quiet partner has found his voice, he thought. No doubt Loc is smitten, he chuckled. I can't blame him, she is special, he realized. Did he just say milkshake? Max wondered. Grabbing Loc by the arm in mid-sentence, Max leaned forward and asked, "Why don't we stop for some ice-cream?"

Sitting on wobbly bamboo furniture in the shade, of an outdoor cafe, Max summoned a waiter. I'll get Loc and his date milkshakes, he thought. I'm ready for a beer, he concluded. A young server in a long-sleeved white shirt and black bow tie approached. What the hell, Max snickered. "Thee vanilla milkshakes, please." He ordered.

As the rush hour traffic of Saigon flowed by, the three survivors of the deadly Valley sucked on the thick refreshing taste of frosted vanilla. Lost in thought, Mei siphoned the cold creamy sweetness through a straw.

Gently she caressed the ivory comb in the palm of her hand. Looking up from the fluted glass, Max saw Loc reach over and softly squeeze Mei's free hand. She reciprocated the bold gesture by interlocking her fingers with his. Feeling like an intruder, Max pivoted away from the budding romance. Enjoying the frothy treat, he watched the setting sun illuminate the Pearl of the Orient. There is apparently more to the pleasures of life then liquor and whores he thought sucking on the straw.

From the outdoor cafe, they walked just a few blocks to the Hotel Majestic for dinner. Mei stumbled in the elevated footwear. She leaned on Loc for support. The infatuated tribesman blushed. Across the congested Dong Khoi Street, the Majestic glowed in fading sunlight. Locking arms, the three veterans plunged into the meandering stream of bicycles, motorcycles, and cars. Crossing a Saigon street required patience and skill. After a calculated advance, the trio sprinted onto the sidewalk.

In the hotel's posh restaurant, an astonished Mei followed the tuxedo-clad maître d'. Her pivoting head tried to absorb the magic atmosphere. At a prominent table, a Vietnamese headwaiter pulled out her chair. Confused she look at Max for guidance. The German winked. His open palm invited her to sit. Grinning she sat down. A server placed a napkin on her lap. She flinched.

Taking his seat, Max said to the waiter, "Tell her not to worry. This is her night and she can do whatever she wants."

"Yes sir," he responded. After translating for Mei, he added a respectful bow.

Giggling, Mei shielded her nervous delight with a cupped hand. Mischievously she grinned at her escorts.

"I'll have a steak with fried eggs," Max ordered. He looked across the tabled at his wide-eyed Asian dinner guest. I know Loc is not fond of heavy western cuisine, he thought. "My friends will have *pho*," he instructed the waiter. Mei and Loc will enjoy the Vietnamese beef and rice noodle soup, he concluded.

Max dug into a sizzling slab of beef adorned with eggs. He observed Loc and Mei meticulously garnish the steaming bowls of *pho* with basil, lime, bean sprouts and onions.

"We used to grow basil and onions in my vegetable garden when I was a child," Mei said to Loc. "Tomatoes were my favorite. There is something so rewarding about watching vegetables ripen on the vine."

Chomping on the juicy steak, Max listened. His limited Vietnamese comprehended a conversation about the joys of gardening. Barracks eating habits quickly devoured the steak. Using a piece of sourdough bread, he mopped up the last of the egg yolk and meat sauce from the empty plate. Popping the flavored bread into his mouth, he saw Mei and Loc had hardly touched the soup.

"This is too much food," Loc said.

Shrugging Max responded, "Don't worry partner, we all deserve one night of excess. Are you ready to get drunk?"

Max led the way into the adjoining lobby bar. Westerners and some of Saigon's elite occupied the glossy rosewood tables and hand carved chairs. Every man in the room paused to get a glimpse of the sultry Mei. Max stood guard over an empty table. Rushing forward, Loc pulled out a chair for his apparent date.

"Three beers, a pack of cigarettes, and a cigar," Max shouted out to the bartender.

As the drinks and smokes arrived, Max pulled out his lighter. He lit Mei's cigarette, and his cigar. Loc fended for himself with the communal Zippo.

Raising a glass to his companions, Max said, "Constantly enjoy life, you're longer dead than alive."

Loc translated for Mei, the German toast that he had heard many times. Mei nodded her approval.

Picking up Max's lighter, Mei rubbed her thumb along the recognizable inscription and spoke to Loc in Vietnamese.

"She said the three-thirteenth were very brave men," Loc translated.

"Yes they were," Max said, smiling at the young girl.

Loc translated another Mei comment, "She said before the surrender, she heard the three-thirteenth from Isabelle attacked without ammunition."

There are many stories of heroism that surfaced in the aftermath of Dien Bien Phu, Max reflected. But none of them come close to bayonet charge of my Legionnaire brothers in the three-thirteenth.

"She says she is not sure of the ritual," Loc relayed. "But we should drink to the spirits of the brave men of three-thirteenth."

Max's throat tightened. My god is she special, he thought. Only someone who was in the Valley would know what we endured; what brave men died for. The former Nazi Mueller confessed to me on his last night, Max recalled. If he was going to die, it had to be as a German. Crazy bastard, Max thought visualizing his bald wide shouldered *kamerad* leading the suicide charge.

Looking into Mei's soft eyes, Max grinned and nodded. Standing up, he lifted his glass towards the ceiling in the noisy room. Glancing around, he quickly silenced the barroom chatter. In a load emotion laced voice, he toasted, "To the brave men of the third battalion, thirteenth brigade Foreign Legion."

The screech of chairs scooting across the wood floor preceded a room full of patrons respectfully standing with raised glasses. "Thank you," Max whispered to the clink of glass. "And thank you Mei," he said taking his seat. I needed that reminder of the honor associated with my military service. Touching his glass to hers, he said, "Mei, to the heroines of Claudine."

Graciously smiling at the compliment, Mei nodded before taking a sip of beer.

Loc slapped the table hard and said, "To the Tai Federation!" Tilting his head back, he drained his beer glass.

"I'll drink to that," Max declared. After two large gulps, he slammed an empty glass onto the table.

Both Max and Loc turned to Mei. Studying the full glass in front of her, she took a deep breath. Wrapping her hands around the chilled container, she lifted it to her lips. Closing her eyes, she slowly poured the gold carbonation down her throat. Completing the task, she grinned with moist lips and slammed the drained schooner on the table.

"Well done, Mei!" Max exclaimed, "Barkeep another round for the survivors."

Empty beer bottles, drinking glasses and an overflowing ashtray cluttered the polished wood tabletop. Max paid the bar tab in the empty lounge. It had been a good day, he thought. He rose with the euphoric sense of inebriation. I'll get two rooms for the night, he decided watching his partner assisting Mei to her feet. The love-struck Loc can spend the night with the young girl, he concluded. I can always get my own girl sent up to my room.

After procuring two rooms in the luxury hotel, Max handed the key to a suite located on the first floor to Loc. Before ascending the stairs to his accommodations, he hugged Mei goodnight. She seemed confused. Sensing her bewilderment, Max spoke to Loc, "Tell Mei I want to thank her for a wonderful day. That we will all have breakfast before we take her back to the refugee camp in the morning."

After Loc translated, Mei firmly hugged the stocky German a second time. Max climbed the stairs. Mei really is a sweetheart, he thought. I never really thought that much about the BMC girls, he realized. Recalling his last experience with the mobile brothel, he could not visualize the courtesan's face. I remember standing in line, entering a small room, and lustfully anticipating the encounter. The exhausted naked young girl covered in sweat, I recall. I can't picture her face, he realized. Maybe I never looked into her eyes, he wondered. Or maybe I couldn't see beyond satisfying my own urges, he concluded. Sliding the room key into the door lock, he decided against having a girl sent up.

Loc walked the young girl down the hall.

"Oh my," Mei whispered entering the opulent suite. On a lacquered table in the entry, a crystal vase displayed fresh cut orchids. Tiny painted rosebuds flowed across the interior walls. A softly rotating ceiling fan's breeze rippled on the bleached white bedspread of a large wood framed bed. A wall mirror over the dresser magnified the magnificent room.

"How many people will sleep here tonight?" Mei asked.

"Just you," Loc replied.

"You are not staying?" Mei asked.

"No, I'll show you how the bath water works and then I'm going to sleep upstairs with Max," He explained.

"You can stay with me if you want," Mei said.

"Mei you are no longer a whore; you are my friend," Loc said.

That simple revelation welled up in Mei's dark eyes.

"Now let me show you how the hot water works." Loc continued, "It is truly amazing."

Mei embraced the tribesman. In heels, she had a few inches over him. The height differential did not hinder the affectionate pause. Softly she wept. Tenderly he stoked her long silky locks. Exiting the compassionate cuddle, she kissed him on the cheek. He reacted with a shy nervous smile.

Loc held her hand as they entered the tile-floored bathroom. Mei wiped away tears with her free hand as Loc demonstrated how the bathtubs hot and cold water worked.

"And when you're done washing, you can use as many towels as you like." He said, pulling a fluffy white towel from the rack.

"What do I do with the towel when I'm done?" She asked.

"Max said to leave it on the floor," Loc said. Looking at Mei's puzzled expression, he added, "I don't understand a lot of these western customs either. They seem so wasteful."

"Thank you for explaining Loc, and thank you for such a wonderful day," Mei said.

In a trance, Loc strolled down the thick carpet of the first floor corridor. Gently he stroked his kissed cheek. What a beautiful girl, he thought. I'm glad I passed on the invitation to stay, he concluded. After all Mei has been through, he realized she needs compassion to heal, not the lust of another soldier.

Loc wandered into a deserted lobby. He froze. Something is wrong, he detected. Quietly he approached the front desk. Squatting below the counter, two staff employees trembled. The sound of heavy footsteps faded up the stairway. "Phone!" Loc commanded. A shaking hand emerged from the curled up employees and pointed in the direction of a dial telephone. Leaping over the front desk, Loc picked up the receiver. "Number!" he grunted.

"Two-fourteen," a trembling clerk whimpered.

Dialing the number, Loc said at the click of reception, "They're coming."

From the second floor, gunshots rang out.

Pulling out his pistol, Loc concentrated on the descending footsteps echoing down the stairwell. An armed Asian goon in a gray suit stumbled off balance into the lobby. Loc shot the fumbling target three times in the chest. The victim collapsed on the polished marble floor. Hopping over the front desk, Loc approached the blood-splattered body. He kicked the victim's sidearm across slick stone surface. A loud rolling thump tumbled down the staircase. Another well-dressed Asian corpse flowed into lobby.

From the top of the stairs, Max called out, "Loc, you good?"

"Yes partner," Loc replied.

Coming into view, in just his briefs, the broad shouldered Max brandished his Soviet pistol. Bending down, he examined his kill and confiscated the dead man's wallet. He repeated the monetary extraction on the bloody victim staining the marble floor.

"Who are they?" Loc asked.

"Hired assassins," Max snorted. "Let's get out of Saigon. Roche was right. This is a battlefield."

"What about Mei?" Loc asked.

Appearing composed, Max said, "Looks like we'll miss breakfast. We're checking out early." Pulling the currency out of the dead men's wallets, he tossed the wad of cash on the front desk counter, adding, "Don't worry Loc, we'll get your girl back to the refugee camp as promised. Then head to the airport. We apparently have too many enemies to get a good night's sleep in this town. Hell, I slept better at Isabelle."

CHAPTER FIFTY ONE

Winded, Rene walked at a brisk pace down a dusty road on the outskirts of Phong Savin. A late afternoon sun hung above wispy clouds. I haven't seen the German in over a month, he thought sucking down rural air. Grinning he reflected on Max slamming Petru's greasy head into the table. I could hear the Corsican's nose crack from across the room, he recalled. The arrogant Corsican was an ass and deserved what he got. At a fork in the country road, he stopped to study a hand-drawn directional map. Flowering weeds swayed in a warm breeze. A cluster of shanty wood hovels beside the trail creaked with life. What possessed the German to take up residency out here with the locals, he questioned. Glancing up from the crude drawing, Rene spotted an approaching young mother holding a baby. Another dirty toddler clung to her soiled black skirt. Extending a dirt incrusted open palm, she motioned to her mouth and the mouth of the child. Out of rough dwellings, a desperate refugee audience emerged. Rene looked at the pitiable mother. I'm sorry *amoureux*, he thought. If I donate to you, I'll draw a crowd. Waving her off with the back of his hand, he accelerated down the road.

A gang of junkyard dogs rummaged through a pile of roadside garbage. Rene slowed down. The alpha of the pack investigated the French pilot's intrusion with a rippled muzzle. Brandishing saliva-dripping fangs, the mangy mutt emitted a shallow growl. Rene pulled out his pistol. I don't want to shoot any dogs, he thought, but if they charge, I won't have a choice. Standing his ground, the intimating canine defiantly pivoted his snarling scowl at the passing Frenchman. After several distance gauging glances over his shoulder, Rene holstered his side arm. Several farm residences littered the hillside. Rene referenced the map.

"Over here Rene!" Max called out from the porch of a raised thatch roofed long house.

Looking up, Rene spotted the cigar smoking German. "Max, good to see you," He called tossing the map aside. "I have a message for you." He informed walking up the dwelling's narrow pathway.

"Do you have time for a beer?" Max asked as Rene ascended the creaking stairs.

"Sure Max, I need to wash down some of this red dust," Rene responded glancing around at the German's home. Several non-matching chairs and a single long bench furnished the large planked wood porch. An open doorway exposed the longhouse's interior. Three Tai men sat on a wooden floor cleaning an assortment of disassembled small arms. Female voices laced with laughter resonated from the back of the large room. The aroma of smoked meat flowed out of the house. Must be dinner, Rene concluded. It smells good.

"Beer!" Max hollered over his shoulder. A barefooted young Tai girl in baggy black pajamas, wearing a very big smile, appeared with a large amber bottle of brew.

Returning the girl's smile, Rene took the surprisingly cold beer. After touching bottles with Max, he poured the rejuvenating freshness down his parched gullet.

"Max?" Rene asked swiping his lips. "Just how many people live here?"

Max grinned. "Beside Loc and myself," he paused to calculate. "About ten, sometimes twelve; it depends on the women." He said with a wink. "There are three Tai Auxiliary veterans who marched out of Isabelle with Loc and me. The other men are also Black Tais related somehow to the three. Don't ask me how they are related. One of the girls is someone's sister; she and a friend of hers do the cooking. The other girls come and go adding to the atmosphere." Max informed puffing on a stogy. After a satisfying exhale, he asked, "So what is the message that the best bush pilot in Northern Laos came all the way out here to deliver?"

Sitting down in one of the chairs, Rene smiled at the compliment. "I'm afraid it is not good news." He answered. "It's about Guillian, your commando friend. I was in Luang Prabang yesterday picking up a shipment. The radio operator at the airport asked me if I knew a German in Phong Savin. I said 'yes and why do you ask?' He told me he received a message from a desperate Sergeant Jean Guillian of the Airborne Command Group." Rene took a large swig of beer. Setting the bottle down on the wood deck, he reached into his shirt pocket and pulled out a crinkled note. Unfolding the paper, he leaned forward resting his elbows on his knees. "Tell the German at Phong Savin I need a favor." He read. "I need a jungle escort out of the North. The village has been evacuated; population hiding in inaccessible mountains near the wall of heads." Looking up from the page, he shrugged, "That's all it said. Does that make any sense to you?"

"Yes," Max answered in a solemn tone. "He could fight his way out with his three hundred warriors, but he's trying to bring out the whole village. That's..." Max paused, "I don't know, two thousand Meos?"

"That's crazy," Rene responded, "Just plain crazy."

"I guess it's a lot easier to fight to the death, if you are not with your wife and child." Max reflected.

"What are you going to do?" Rene asked.

"I'm going to return the favor." Max said taking a swig from the cold bottle.

"It's a suicide mission. You can't evacuate two thousand villagers from the North. The Meos are not covered by the cease-fire. Even if you avoid one or two communist patrols, it would just be a matter of time before the Vietminh annihilate the slow moving herd of women and children." Rene reasoned.

"Thanks for the reassurance." Max smiled. "Do you need another beer?" Before Rene could answer, Max shouted through the door, "Two more beers Mee."

"You are not invincible, Max." Rene informed accepting the fresh bottle.

"Tell that to the forty-thousand Vietminh who surrounded me at Dien Bien Phu, or the Corsican who put a price on my head. I'm still here enjoying sunsets and cold brew." Max responded displaying the perspiring amber bottle.

"Death will eventually catch up to all of us; it is just a matter of time." The pilot declared. "But why..." He asked squinting. "Why are you going to do this?"

"The same reason you are going to assist me," Max grinned, "The brotherhood."

"The brotherhood?" Rene questioned. He flinched. "Who said I was going to do anything?"

"Rene, you knew what the message said. You took time away from your lucrative opium smuggling business to run down here to tell me. You volunteered to fly me in before you even knew my answer," Max replied, raising his eyebrows.

"Look, I'll fly you in, but that's it," Rene stated.

"That is all I ask," Max triumphantly replied.

"So what is this brotherhood?" Rene asked.

"The brotherhood of combat veterans," Max answered. "When I fought for Germany, I fought for some bullshit National Socialist agenda based on racial superiority. I was too young and naive to comprehend. When I fought for the French, it was for twenty piastres a day to protect colonial business interests that did not benefit me. The Vietminh are no different, fighting for the redistribution of wealth. The only thing now that I will always fight for is my fellow soldier. Guillian saved my life when I came out of the jungle." Wincing Max continued with a delicate tone. "Did you know he was a Jew? He lost most of his family in a German concentration camp." Pausing Max diluted the difficult dialogue with a swig of beer. "For those of us who have been duped to fight the wars of others and have come to that realization, the only thing that is worth fighting for is your *copains*." Discovering that his cigar had gone out, he relit the remaining stub with his lighter. Rubbing the lighters engraving of his former Legionnaire battalion, he showed the etched image to Rene and said, "You're an Air Force veteran. You know exactly what I'm talking about."

"I do understand Max," Rene said. "Do you think you could pull this off?"

"Hopefully I won't be escorting Guillian and his Meos out alone. I'll put the word out. The brotherhood is a large fraternity. Hell, I got you to volunteer with not much effort," Max chuckled.

Rene respectfully bowed. He took several gulps of beer. The back of his hands wiped lingering foam from his lips. Squinting at the German, he questioned. "How did you know Guillian was a Jewish survivor? Does he have numbers tattooed on his forearm?"

"No, he was not permanently marked. His family went to a labor camp, not Auschwitz. He told me briefly about the experience to explain his initial resentment to my heritage. We don't dwell on it. Frankly, I really do have more of a difficult time with the fact that he is French." Max answered.

Rene laughed and toasted, "To the brotherhood."

"To the brotherhood," Max echoed.

The veterans leaned back in the rickety chairs. Slowly sipping on the chilled beverage, they watched the setting sun ignite the horizon a blazing orange.

CHAPTER FIFTY TWO

The wind howled across the plain. It was a cold overcast highland morning. Walking towards the Phong Savin airport, Max angled his face away from the blasting headwind. It's been two days since Rene delivered Guillian's appeal, he realized. That makes his radio transmission plea five days old. My Jewish brother has little time left, Max thought. Once I know the cargo capacity of Rene's twin-engine plane, he calculated, I'll have a better idea as to how many men and munitions I can fly in. Maybe Rene could ferry in a second group of mercenaries. He wondered. The more men we can transport in, the better the odds of getting out.

A recently constructed hangar facility shielded Max from the pounding wind. Lifting his head, he squinted in the dusty haze. Waves of crimson powder rolled across the red clay tarmac. A swirling spire of trash passed in front of the corrugated tin Civil Air Transport facility. A windblown Roche stood in the open bay doorway of the Asian Airline's hangar. What is the American agent doing here? Max questioned. Casually dressed in a colorful floral printed shirt and khaki slacks, Roche spotted the German. Smiling wide, the American summoned Max with a friendly wave. Max nodded and dove back into the flowing wind.

"Good morning, Roche," Max said offering his hand. "What brings you to the Plain of Jars?" he asked shaking hands.

"I heard a crazy kraut was going to defy the Geneva agreement and fly North of the seventeenth parallel to evacuate a village. I just had to have a look for myself," Roche answered.

"How do you always know what is going on?" Max asked shaking his head.

"'I told you, I'm in the information business. It's my job to know. Besides everyone in this frontier town was talking about the German financing a rescue mission with his opium profits," Roche said.

"Well, I can't be that valuable to you." Max grinned. "You didn't come up here to talk me out of it. So what brings you to Northern Laos?"

"I came to offer some assistance in your crazy undertaking. I'll provide you with a 'sterile' C-119 aircraft and crew. All the identification removed. It can carry fifty volunteers. I'll provide the munitions. You won't have to spend your life's savings after all. The aircraft will be loaded and ready in the morning," Roche said. "Also, Captain Yang Mo with twenty five of his best jungle troops will be joining you. I broke protocol and spoke directly to him last night."

"What...why...," Max stuttered. "Why would you do this?" He questioned. "I pleaded the case of the French commando to you before and received a quick no."

"Max, when you asked me to sponsor this commando's continuation of the war with a weapons drop, the answer was a political no. When I heard you were going to return a favor for a fellow soldier, I wanted to contribute. This is personnel." Roche paused. His jovial manner took on a serious tone. "Don't let my Major rank fool you. I was a mud Marine in the Pacific. Like you and your commando friend, I spent my time in hell. When you have been baptized by fire, you don't always know what the right thing to do is. Nevertheless, you always take care of your buddies. I wish I could do more."

"You do understand." Max said. "But how did you convince Captain Yang?"

"It was easy, but I suspect his motivations are complex. You can argue it was a calculated move in his quest for power. If successful, he would become legendary with the mountain tribes. It could also fuel the recruitment efforts for his growing army. His rhetoric when I spoke to him last night was that of a true warrior. He viewed this opportunity as a challenge." Roche answered.

"Thanks my friend, you really increased the odds for success," Max acknowledged.

"I won't be here in the morning, but I'll be back when you come out to celebrate. I missed your reunion with that darling Mei. I don't want to miss out again," Roche said. "And one other thing. Since I'm supplying the munitions and transportation, you have to buy the drinks when you come out."

"You're on, *ami*," Max responded.

CHAPTER FIFTY THREE

The sky was black. In the predawn darkness, a corrugated metal hanger at the Phong Savin airport glowed. Through open hangar doors, escaping industrial lighting illuminated a sterile transport plane. A buzz of activity loaded the aircraft with crated munitions. Passengers and crew milled around inside the large cold tin shed. To combat the chill, Civil Air Transport provided hot drinks. Grasping a warm ceramic mug Max sipped slowly on strong black brew. This would be my last civilized pleasure for some time, he realized. Beside the German, Loc enjoyed a cup of tea. Twenty squatting Tai tribesmen dressed in black with blue turbans smoked whilst drinking courtesy beverages. For the Tai volunteers, this is a redemption mission, Max concluded. The tribesmen had left their families and way of life behind in the Communist North. On a back wall, a topo map depicted the mountainous highland terrain. In front of the large diagram, Captain Yang discussed logistics with the American flight crew and the opium smuggling pilot Rene. No one knows the highlands better than Rene, Max thought. Although his flying skills are not required, Rene's expertise is invaluable. The CAT flight crew is a strange lot, he surmised. The boisterous Americans are cocky and overflowing with self-confidence. No doubt still relishing their past victories in Europe and the Pacific, he concluded. Clustered together within listening range of the planning session, the Captain's twenty-five seasoned jungle fighters attentively stood. We just might pull this off; Max realized observing the Captain's combat proven troops.

Out of the darkness, Hakeem dressed in jungle fatigues lumbered into the brightly lit facility. With a puzzled look, Max asked, "Hakeem, what are you doing here?"

"Going to rescue a village and a Jewish commando, how about you?" Hakeem answered.

"Hakeem, I appreciate the gesture, but this is going to be rough." Max informed.

"Max, I may have gotten a little soft living the good life in Laos," Hakeem said patting an overhanging belly. "But I was once a soldier like you."

"This is not going to be a typical military exercise. The jungle is more of a threat than the Vietminh," Max responded.

"Max, I was in a Moroccan Rifle Regiment during operation *Camarque*. I know what rough is. I owe a lot of favors to dead men, that I will never have the chance to repay. If I can help you pay your debt to this commando, it will help me feel better about some of my outstanding obligations. I need to do this," Hakeem said.

Max placed his hand on Hakeem's shoulder. "Welcome aboard Gray Gorilla."

Standing in front of the wall-mounted map, the Captain called out, "Gentlemen, your attention please."

His twenty-five men gave him their full attention. The rest of the mercenaries lingered toward the diagram. Max stood in the background. I'm glad the Captain has taken the reins of leadership, he thought, and the responsibility that comes with it.

"Thank you, I'll be brief." The Captain said in a confident tone. His voice resonated throughout the metal hangar. "We'll depart shortly. The plan is to travel light. We will parachute drop one set of provisions in Northern Laos this morning on our flight out. This is for resupply on the return trip. This will be provisions only, no munitions." He paused pointing to the planned drop zone on the map. "Two things will happen. One, we find the provisions on our way back, which will help us on the trek to Muong Sai. Two, the provisions are discovered and confiscated by a local tribe. If that is the case, we will seek them out for assistance on the journey. If they refuse to offer us hospitality, we will insist that they do. Another set of provisions with munitions, we will hide at the drop off landing strip. If we are pursued on the return, it will be a good place to make a stand."

Once again, the Captain referred to the map. "On the march in, we will try to avoid all Communist patrols traveling light and using the dense jungle as cover. Once we make contact with the civilians, I need to evaluate the situation to determine our exit strategy." He paused and then added, "Good luck gentlemen."

The aircraft taxied to the edge of the dark runway. In the cargo compartment of the flying Boxcar, Max jerked. The plane accelerated. The German's stomach dropped. They were airborne. This is it, he thought stroking the barrel of a bolt-action rifle. There is no turning back. Looking around the tight quarters, he saw the solemn expressions of men deep in thought. How many would be returning, if any, he wondered. Sitting upright, the Captain focused straight ahead. I've encountered many officers like Yang, Max reflected. The Captain will not ask his men to do anything that he wouldn't do. However, everyone is expendable.

An hour into the noisy flight, the cockpit door opened. Two Civil Air Transport crewmembers walked into the aft section. Dressed like well-groomed bookends, the two Americans wore short-sleeved white shirts, black epaulettes sewn on their shoulders. Each had a plastic pocket protector displaying an array of pencils and pens. Their military flat top haircuts and aviator sunglasses made it difficult to tell them apart.

"Move to the front!" one hollered in broken French with a twang.

That must be the one they call Buck, Max concluded. The cowboy was the only CAT employee who attempted to speak French. Glancing down at a pair of pointed-toe black boots peeking out of the American's pant legs confirmed it.

"We are about to parachute drop your return provisions," Buck informed with his strange accent.

Moving forward, Max nodded. Buck and his associate opened the cargo door. A sobering cold blast flooded the cabin. The chilled air slapped Max's face. The brisk sensation felt good. When I'm trekking through the sweltering jungle, it would be comforting to reflect back on this moment, he reasoned. The crewmembers pushed two large crates out of the aircraft. Walking back, Max got a quick glimpse of the parachuted supplies floating down towards the carpeting green below. Holding up his hand, he politely signaled to Buck not to close the door. My survival depends on reconnecting with these supplies, he thought. Braced he looked down at the provision drop zone. I need to find a recognizable landmark, he thought. That saw-toothed ridge west of the supplies will work, he concluded. "*Merci* Buck," he said emphasizing a southern drawl. The cowboy chuckled.

Several hours later, Buck stuck his head out of the cockpit door. "Brace yourselves for landing," he shouted over the drone of the aircraft in his unique French. Loc translated the warning for the benefit of the Tai mercenaries. Max grabbed onto the cargo netting draped along the interior of the fuselage. The plane descended quickly into a bumpy landing. Buck and his twin exited the cockpit. The Americans ran past the harnessed passengers. The rear cargo door popped open. Sunlight and heavy tropical air engulfed the cabin. The flight crew hastily began pushing cargo out the door. Sensing the urgency, the mercenaries quickly disembarked.

Besieged by the deafening whine of the twin prop engines, Max and the Tais formed a bucket brigade. The wooden boxes passed down the line to a growing pile of crates. The focused Captain gestured to his Laotian troops with hand signals. Simultaneously the Laotian's divided into two groups. The units disappeared into the tree line along the landing strip. While the Laotians secured the airfield, the last piece of cargo made its way down the human conveyor belt. Buck shouted an inaudible farewell from the security of the empty plane. The aircraft's engines revved. Buck offered a big thumbs up and a smile before slamming the cargo door shut.

As the plane taxied down the jungle runway, the Captain shouted to Max, "Where is the storage bunker?"

Max pointed up the runway, "About ten yards in from that dead palm tree," he replied. "But I don't think it will be big enough. I appreciate the Americans' generosity, but this is an excessive amount of munitions."

The Captain smiled. "Don't worry; we'll hide what we can." Turning and looking up at the departing aircraft, he said, "They were in a hurry and so are we. We'll secure the supplies, have a quick meal and depart."

CHAPTER FIFTY FOUR

Surging uphill clawing growth grabbed at Max. I can't be that far off the blistering pace set by Captain Yang, he hoped. Balancing on the slick incline, he glanced skyward into the darkening jungle canopy. It's going to be dark soon, he realized and locating the campsite in the thick brush would be impossible. Over his shoulder, he saw his black friend drenched in sweat. In the diminishing light, Hakeem stumbled forward aimlessly. "We need to pick it up, Hakeem," Max said, "Night's approaching."

Panting heavy, the Gray Gorilla lethargically waved a massive paw forward.

Dusk turned to night. In a small jungle clearing the tips of cigarettes glowed. Thank god, Max thought stumbling into the dark campsite. Squatting down in a loose circle, Loc smoked with his fellow Tais. The Laotians slept. Everyone stirred as Hakeem crashed through the dense brush. Taking off his pack, the African collapsed on the wet ground. Removing his load, Max took out two tins of canned meat and a cigar. Opening one of the cans, he handed it to the reclining African and said, "Bon appetite." On the moist ground, Max leaned back against his pack and lit the cigar. After several puffs, he whispered in the direction of the Tais, "Loc, do you have any purified water?"

Loc rose, picked up a canteen and handed it to Max. "We boiled this at dusk," he informed.

"Thanks," Max responded taking a swig of warm water before handing the canteen to Hakeem.

Hakeem quenched his thirst. Between gulps, he asked, "How much further Max?"

"We should be at the wall of heads by tomorrow," Max replied.

"I don't know if I can keep up this pace," Hakeem exhaled.

"You won't have to. Once we hook up with the villagers, you can trek with the women and children," Max chuckled.

"That's something to look forward to," Hakeem muttered. Pulling a poncho out of his bag, he wrapped it around his large torso. Resting his head on the pack, he added, "Don't let me sleep in. I wouldn't want to miss breakfast."

Max opened up his canned meal. Tilting back his head, he tapped the slimy protein into his mouth. The large African began to snore. Leaning forward with a stiff back, Max removed his jungle boots and socks. The chilled air comforted his barking dogs. Re-lighting his cigar, he sat back enjoying the smoke. I'm feeding Blacks and rescuing Jews, he realized toke-ing on the stogie. Blowing smoke rings into the starry night sky, he thought racism was an absurd philosophy. The membership in the brotherhood confirmed it. With a satisfied grin, he wiggled his toes in the cool night air.

Max hiked at his own pace. Over his shoulder, he kept an eye on the drifting African. The Laotians and Tais, cut a decent trail to follow. This is familiar turf, he realized. I'm getting close, he thought sniffing for the decaying stench of the spiked heads. Catching a morbid whiff, he came upon the decapitated display. Scattered upwind of the exhibit, the Laotian and Tai forces hydrated and smoked. The Captain closely examined the decomposing remains. Suddenly three Meo warriors appeared. The mercenaries flinched.

The intruders in black blood stained rags scrutinized the troops. One held a combat knife. Another brandished a spiked bamboo stock spear. The knife wielding Meo cast a stoic gaze upon the German. The Meo's gaunt features brightened. From the depths of despair, a toothless smile emerged. Chue walked over and hugged the German. Max reciprocated with a genuine embrace of friendship.

"It's alright Captain, this is who we were looking for," Max informed holding the frail warrior.

"Hello brothers," Loc said tossing Chue a half-full pack of Lucky Strikes.

232

The Meo quickly tapped out three cigarettes. Leaning forward the three tribesmen lit the cigarettes off a single match. Squatting on their haunches, they sucked on the nicotine treat. The Captain also lit up. The Laotian troops followed the Captains lead. Hakeem staggered into the jungle smoking den. A row of severed heads acted as a backdrop. "Luck Strike means fine tobacco," the African mumbled.

Tossing his cigarette aside, the Captain questioned Chue in a tribal dialect.

Leaning into Max, Loc translated, "Chue says the villagers are a short day's march away. They are hiding in a very inaccessible location."

Interrupting the Captain, Max said to Loc, "Ask Chue where his weapon is."

"They have very little ammunition. This has become his weapon." Loc relayed.

Chue held up a long knife.

Hakeem handed the Meo his submachine gun saying, "He can have mine for now. I'll use my sidearm."

Max winked at Hakeem for the generosity that lightened the African's load by ten pounds. Loc and one of the Tais gave pistols to the other two Meos.

Looking at Chue, Max said out of the side of his mouth, "Ask him when they last ate."

Chue and the other two Meos looked at each other, before mumbling in unison.

"It's been two days," Loc informed.

Max pulled out canned tuna from his pack and handed it to the Meos.

Addressing Max in French, the Captain said, "We have to get moving. It'll take us a day in, and I still don't know how many civilians we are escorting out. If these three haven't eaten in two days, I don't know what kind of shape the villagers will be in."

Max looked at the dining Chue and said to Loc. "Ask him if we can make it there tonight."

Loc translated.

Chue licked out the bottom of the can. Finishing his meal, he looked at Max. Tuna oil glistened across the tribesman's soiled face. Flashing his unique smile, he nodded.

Shouldering his pack, Max walked over to the reclining Hakeem, "Break time is over, my friend," he said pulling up the exhausted African. "We will be trekking in the dark, so stay close."

CHAPTER FIFTY FIVE

High stepping in darkness, Max focused on the tight formation in front of him. Behind him, the African announced his presence with a panting breath. The slow jungle march evolved into a climb. The mercenary force clawed up a steep rock faced ridge. One by one, the party eventually came to rest on an elevated plateau. Under the starlit sky, Max peered into the rustling dark surroundings. From the shadows, Guillian's Meo warriors slowly emerged. Thin and battle weary from surviving on the run, the ragged sentries still projected the resolve of warriors who spike the heads of their enemy. A tall bearded French commando stood amongst the tribesmen armed with automatic weapons, lances and crossbows. In tattered oversized army-green fatigues displaying the rank of sergeant, the lanky Guillian broke ranks. In the still mountain air, he quietly approached the German. The two friends embraced.

Patting Guillian on the back, Max whispered, "Don't worry my brother, it is my turn to lead you to safety."

The men parted.

A solemn Guillian said in a dry a raspy voice, "I'm glad you got my message."

"I wish we could have come sooner." Max replied. "My attempts to procure your village a weapons sponsor fell on deaf ears. The French are pulling out, and the Americans had no interest in financing an insurgency based on the French model."

"I appreciate your efforts. I thought we could continue fighting. It wasn't so much the lack of munitions, but the village was dying. The Vietminh reprisals began immediately forcing us to flee. My men would have fought on to the end, but not at the expense of their families." Guillian said.

"How is your wife and son?" Max gently probed.

"They are fine," Guillian answered motioning towards the darkness. H'Liana emerged. Strapped on her back, a wide-eyed baby peered out of a blue cloth pouch.

The baby boy appears healthy, Max observed. A soft smile shielded Max's concern for the withered middle-aged looking mother. She has lost the glow of youth, he realized. Poor thing, he thought. She obviously nursed the baby at the expense of her own wellbeing. He tenderly touched H'Liana's fragile forearm. The timid girl looked down and mumbled her gratitude. No translation is necessary, Max realized. Over her shoulder, Max spotted the Captain patiently waiting for an introduction. Turning away from the village girl, he said, "Sergeant Guillian, this is Captain Yang Mo, the leader of the expedition."

"Pleased to meet you sir," Guillian said, shaking the Captain's hand.

"As well Sergeant," the Captain replied. "Time is as much an adversary as the Vietminh. I need to assess your circumstances to formulize a strategy."

"I understand sir," Guillian replied.

"How many villagers will be attempting to flee the North?" the Captain asked.

"My rough estimate is about thirteen hundred. The journey to this remote haven has taken its toll. About a third of the villagers have chosen to stay." Guillian informed.

"Good, very good," the nodding Captain responded. "And what is the current status of food supplies?"

"We have about two weeks' provisions left for the community. We have been forced to ration our limited supplies," Guillian answered.

The Captain nodded motioning to one of his commandos. The subordinate handed him a map. The Captain unfolded the diagram and laid it across a fairly flat boulder. The mercenaries and Meo warriors huddled around the rock. A Meo brought over a small kerosene lamp. A sooty glow illuminated the strategy session.

Twenty yards in the dark distance an elderly couple, the tribesman Pao and his wife, Ying watched the glimmering boulder conference. Pao weighed just over a hundred pounds, his petite wife less. He had a slight gray mustache, whiffs of silky gray hair across his balding head and the weather-beaten complexion of a hard life. Ying looked like a wrinkled boy. Her stringy silver hair tucked up under a blue scarf. Nudging him with boney fingers, she said, "You should go over there with the other warriors and find out what the plan is."

Pao glanced at his wife. In the depths of her dark eyes, he saw the village girl he married so many years ago. She was beautiful. You still see me as the warrior I use to be, he realized. Looking back at the strategy session, Pao spotted a large intimidating black man. The stiffness of his years rippled through his frame. Ying nudged again with a reassuring smile. He took a deep breath. Timidly he walked over to the group carrying his crossbow. The massive black man looked down at him. Pao's heart raced. He flashed his crossbow. I'm a warrior just like you, he thought. The black man stepped aside granting access.

Looking up from the dimly lit map, the Captain addressed the troops. "It is good that our numbers have diminished by those who have chosen to stay. Those choosing to go can only carry the essentials of water and food. I suggest they have a good meal out of your stored supplies before our departure. If we travel light, we can make it to the hidden provisions at the landing strip in a few days. If we are not pursued, we may be able to radio for an airlift of..." he paused, "maybe seventy five of the weakest civilians, most likely women and children." As he spoke, he pointed on the map the landing strip location. "The villagers can keep to the trail. Guillian, you and your Meo warriors, and the mercenaries and I, will shadow them from the jungle, if we can. I understand the terrain will not always allow us to do that. In assessing the situation, we only have one choice if we encounter the Vietminh. That is to hug the enemy. With so many civilians, we would not stand a chance if we were to make a stand. The results would even be worse if we attempted to flee. The Communist superior firepower and mortars would just annihilate us at a distance. If we lure them in, we may stand a chance in a hand to hand engagement." The Captain paused. Looking directly at Pao, he said in native dialect. "A Communist is no match for a Meo warrior at close range." Pao responded by lifting up his crossbow with the resolute expression of an experienced veteran. His gesture earned him approving nods from the group. The black man towering over him placed a hand on Pao's shoulder.

The Captain continued, "Any questions?" There was silence. "Good, let's all get some sleep. We have a long week in front of us."

The group dispersed. The warrior Pao strutted towards Ying. Walking tall, he no longer felt the stiffness of years.

CHAPTER FIFTY SIX

It was late afternoon. The migrating refugees slowly moved south. Yesterday they trekked well into the night. No one spoke. Brush rustled under the tedious advance. Beneath the harsh tropical sun, Pao and Ying drifted towards the back of the procession. Ying took quick shallow breaths. Her pace decelerated. The stragglers wandered into a stagnant crowd of their neighbors.

"What is going on sister?" Pao asked a young mother.

"I don't know," She replied. "Everyone just stopped."

The tiny Pao tried to peer through the assembly. "Stay here and rest," he said to his wife squeezing her hand, "I'll go investigate."

Weaving his way forward, Pao's stomach dropped. On the surrounding hillsides, a large contingent of heavily armed Vietminh herded the villagers into a compact assemblage. Wedged in with the exhausted collection of men, women and children, Pao looked back in search of Ying.

The Communist handlers walked amongst the Meo, brazenly taking whatever they wanted. Venturing into the terrified flock, a Vietminh thief showed his delight by holding a pillaged silver necklace over his head. Communists abandoned their post to partake in the spoils. Bullying his way through the crowd, a soldier knocked over women and children. Determined to hold his ground, Pao flexed his small frame. The soldier chuckled at the defiant old Meo. Without hesitation, Pao raised his crossbow and shot the young man in the throat. Clutching the wooden arrow lodged in his windpipe, the gurgling soldier's bulging eyes stared in disbelief. Dropping the crossbow, Pao pulled a six-inch blade from his waistband. Grabbing a handful of oily black Communist hair, the old man took pleasure in dragging the razor sharp knife across the man's throat.

The blade cut deep into bone. I once had three sons, Pao thought. They died defending our people from the likes of you. Squatting down over the carcass, he cleaned his bloodstained knife on the dead soldier's uniform. Picking up the crossbow, Pao stood up. Around him, the victim's oblivious colleagues robbed and looted. Meandering deeper into the crowd, Pao stepped over Communist dead concealed at the feet of the Meo villagers. A looter discovering a fallen comrade dropped his plunder and fired into the crowd.

At the crack of gunfire, Max squeezed off his first shot. His sniper's rifle barked. A Vietminh officer's head exploded. Lying in waist high elephant grass, Max took out a second target, then a third. A dust cloud arose above the stampeding civilians. The surrounding jungle spat out round after round at the ambushed Vietminh. Small arms fire popped. Motionless causalities lay on the ground. The Meo's fled into the jungle. In the clearing dust, a tiny old man shot a crossbow at a fleeing soldier. The speared communist crawled for cover. The yellow feather tail of a projectile stuck out of his back. Slow prey, Max thought squeezing off another head shot. Timing is crucial, he realized. The villagers did their part embracing the enemy, he concluded. It's time for the professionals to take the stage.

Leaving the sanctuary of tall grass, Max ran towards the battlefield. Behind a lone palm tree, he tossed his rifle. Pulling out his side arm, he methodically began shooting Communist at close range. Calculating each shot, he ignored the bullets that buzzed by. Rapid precision fire was his talent. Like an artist, he pivoted around the small tree trunk, hitting target after target. Six, seven, eight, he counted before feeding a fresh magazine into the pistol.

The Gray Gorilla charged right by Max. "To die far away, we are the Africans," Hakeem sang out swinging a machete in the midst of the communist swarm. Powered by a massive black arm, the wide blade sliced through flesh and bone. Dismembered Communists wailed.

Max followed Hakeem into the bloody arena. He shot two Vietminh at point blank range. Backhanding another with his pistol, he heard the crack of a shattered jaw. As the soldier grabbed his dislocated chin, Loc plugged him with a pistol round. Two Laotian commandos fell. Swirling dust engulfed the close quarter's engagement. The Vietminh's carbines became useless. A communist officer drawing a holstered pistol took three in the chest. Dropping to his knees, he joined the growing mass of casualties.

Three Vietminh broke and ran out of desperation. Straddling a corpse, Max ignored the grunts, groans, shrieks of agony and crack of handguns. For him the theater went silent. Time stopped. Methodically he feed a fresh clip into his Tokarev. Extending his arm, he fired three quick rounds. Three targets collapsed at the edge of the tree line. Spitting out of the side of his mouth, he thanked his Nazi mentors for honing his marksman talent.

The cries and moans of the wounded and dying quickly returned. "No prisoners!" the Captain yelled. Sporadic gunfire followed the ordered executions.

Scanning his surroundings, Max made eye contact with Loc. The tribesman's sweat soaked head sparkled. Max winked. Loc smiled. My partner made it, he thought. He searched for Hakeem. Covered in speckled blood, the Gray Gorilla sat on the burgundy saturated stage. In a deep voice, the African continued singing the Moroccan soldier's chant. Max spotted Captain Yang Mo wiping off a bloody combat knife on a pants leg. Yang's embracing strategy worked, Max concluded. The loss of civilian bait was minimal, he calculated examining the fallen villagers. Squatting amongst the wounded, Guillian comforted his damaged neighbors.

"Max, Sergeant Guillian!" The Captain called out sheathing his blade, "I need to speak to you."

As Max and Guillian approached, the Captain said to Guillian, "Sergeant, round up the healthy civilians. Give them five minutes to retrieve anything of value from the battlefield. Then get them moving south with your Meo warriors." Turning to Max, he said, "Assess our casualties. Confiscate any useful munitions. Let's try to clean this up quickly, so we can catch up to the Sergeant."

Both Max and Guillian nodded before departing.

Max, Loc, and the other mercenaries robbed the dead of water, food and munitions. Canteens, food tins and weapons littered the quiet battlefield. Two man teams totted off the dead Vietminh. A tandem-swinging toss sent the corpses into the depths of a deep overgrown ravine. The death collectors passed over the civilian victims. Grieving relatives huddled around the Meo fallen. Guillian convinced the clustering mourners to abandon the dead and dying. Out of the dense forest staggered groups of villagers. The surviving civilian bait picked up confiscated water and food and continued the slow march south.

Loc pocketed the cigarettes of a Vietminh officer. Max looked down at the corpse. The yellow-feathered tail of a wooden arrow protruded from the cadaver's chest. As Max and Loc prepared to lift the body for disposal, the old crossbow-shooting warrior approached. The tiny man placed a sandaled foot on the victim and retrieved the arrow. Grasping the blood tipped projectile, the silver haired warrior nodded at Max and Loc. I saw you in action *kameraden*, Max thought. I admired you fearless contribution the victory, he acknowledged heartily patting the aging warrior's back.

Seeing Hakeem sitting beside a bloody pile of mutilated dead, Max hollered, "Hakeem, we have to get moving."

Hakeem responded by displaying the shining pumping crimson red of a belly wound.

Max shook his head. My friend is about to die, he realized. Walking over to the large African, he asked. "Are you going to try to make it out?"

"No," Hakeem said softly. "You and I both know the outcome of being gut shot."

"Let me move you into the shade. What can I get you?" Max asked.

"I'm fine right here. The sun feels good." Hakeem answered catching a painful breath. "I sure feel like a *pastis*. You wouldn't happen to have any French liqueur with you?"

"I'll see what the bartender has behind the counter," Max said wryly.

"I may need a grenade in case I get impatient waiting. I don't know if I'll have the strength to shoot myself," Hakeem said. Lifting his concealing paw, he glanced at the steady stream of blood.

Max handed his stoic friend the explosive. I've seen strong men grimace in agony from belly wounds, he reflected. Hakeem is camouflaging extreme pain, he realized. Swallowing down the lump in his throat, Max placed his hand on Hakeem's shoulder. "Consider all your past obligations paid in full, my black brother." He mumbled.

Hakeem winced. He touched Max's comforting grasp with a blood-covered hand. "When you get these people back to safety, have a *pastis* for the Gray Gorilla at the King Cobra."

"Consider it done, my friend," Max said.

Leaving the dying man, Max joined the mercenaries in retrieving useful communist munitions. A resolute Guillian firmly herded the remaining stragglers towards the exit. Hakeem leaning up against the dismembered bodies of his kill enjoyed his last cigarette. The African's life slowly drained away. A piercing cry caused the groundskeepers to jump. Sitting in the middle of the path, the old crossbow warrior wept hysterically. The tiny tribesman rocked back and forth with the dead body of an old woman.

Before Guillian could get to the old man, Max intercepted.

"Guillian," Max called out. "I'll make sure he joins the parade. Let's give him a little time. He has earned it."

"Understood," Guillian said leaving the arena.

The mercenaries concealed the dead villagers in the jungle. They disregarded Hakeem in the distance and the grieving old man in the middle of their activities. An hour after Guillian's departure they regrouped to reload and hydrate.

Walking over, Max discovered Hakeem peacefully reclining in a puddle of blood. The hot tropical sun shone brightly on his lifeless African eyes. Max pried the hand grenade out of his friend's massive paw. You did not need this after all, he thought. You bled to death quickly. "To die far away, we are the Africans," Max mumbled closing his friend's eyes. Five mercenaries would not be returning.

Max and Loc approached the grieving old man. "Tell him it is time to go." Max instructed Loc. "And that he is one of us now." Loc translated. Max handed a communist Makarov pistol to the old warrior.

"He asked if we could help him place his wife's body facing west." Loc relayed.

Loc and Max gently lifted up the old woman's body. Pao placed the Soviet pistol into his waistband.

Loc explained the ritual, "A violent death is a bad thing, and requires a hasty funeral. These deaths create negative spirits."

"Why do we have her facing west?" Max asked repositioning the body.

"West is the direction of death. If she would be facing east, she would be blinded by the morning sun," Loc answered.

"Well let's reposition Hakeem before we go then." Max said.

CHAPTER FIFTY SEVEN

The dark woods seemed to lighten. The dense foliage thinned. Instinctively Max glanced over his shoulder to check on his black friend's progress. With a heavy sigh, he realized Hakeem no longer existed. In the penetrating sunlight of a small clearing, he plopped a boot on a fallen log. To the buzzing of gnats, he lit a cigar stub. Puffing away, he lifted up a pants leg. With malice, he ground the glowing red tobacco tip into the slimy leech feasting below his knee. The fat worm sizzled. Guillian approached and revealed a large bloodsucker attached to his calf. Max handed him the cigar.

"Max," Guillian said removing the parasite, "We need to talk."

"What is it?" Max questioned.

"These people cannot maintain this pace. Many will not survive," Guillian pleaded.

"But many will, Guillian. That is the point. If we stop now we all die. You need to motivate your neighbors. We are two days away from a possible airlift rescue of your weakest civilians. There are also ample provisions stored to feed all. The American was very generous with his contribution. We will all eat well," Max said.

"I'm concerned about my wife and child," Guillian confessed.

The Captain interrupted the conference. "Any issues, Gentlemen?" He probed.

Max thought for a minute. "Captain in order to maintain this pace, I think it would be wise if we let the Meo warriors assist their families on the march. The mercenaries can continue with the shadowing strategy."

Stroking his chin and gazing into the sunlight the Captain nodded and mumbled, "I agree."

Guillian responded with a quick nod. Turning he quickly disappeared into the dense brush to inform the Meo troops.

Two days later, a colorful patchwork of family units ate and rested along the shady side of the dirt runway. A gentle morning breeze swayed the tall trees that surrounded the small-unclaimed red clay sliver. Wood from provision crates fueled small cooking fires. The pleasant aroma of hot food hung in the air. From the hidden supplies, village elders dispersed tinned rations, canned milk and Chesterfield cigarettes.

Strutting down the narrow strip, the Captain scanned the picnicking survivors. He easily spotted the tall bearded Guillian. The French commando and his wife sat cross-legged on a red and blue stripped blanket. Guillian bounced a giggling baby. His wife stirred a blackened tin of beans in a smoldering fire.

"Sergeant," the Captain said, "I need to speak to you."

Guillian handed the baby to its mother. Rising quickly, he said, "Yes Captain."

"I estimate we can airlift out one hundred civilians. I'll leave the selection to you. Once the passengers have been determined, I want you and your Meos to rearm yourselves and relieve the mercenaries guarding our perimeter." Leaning forward the Captain quietly added, "Now would be a good time to say your farewell."

"Yes sir," Guillian replied.

It was mid afternoon. Max, Loc and the mercenaries approached the jungle airstrip. The adopted Pao walked amongst them as an equal. In the shade around the weapons bunker, the men dropped their gear and collapsed. Sitting on the wet ground, Max leaned up against an empty supply crate. Curling up beside him, the old warrior fell asleep. After drinking his remaining water, Max lit a cigar. All I want right know is a brief moment in the shade, he thought. Around the German, the other fighting men smoked, ate and slept. We should be in Northern Laos by late tomorrow, Max realized. Taking a big puff on his cigar, he closed his eyes and exhaled.

Nudged out of tranquility, Max opened a sleepy eye. Loc handed him an open can of rations. "Thanks partner," Max mumbled. A slimy gelatin coated compressed meat in the unmarked tin. Dipping two fingers into the pale pink mixture, he feed his face. God this is good, he thought. Avoiding the sharp edges of the container, he quickly devoured the meat. Sucking on his moist fingers, he looked over at the feasting Loc.

"What kind of meat is this?" Loc asked.

"It's called Spam," Max informed twisting a tiny key around another rectangular can.

A puzzled Loc chewed on the meat. Using the back of a hand, he wiped his greasy lips. "Is Spam an American animal?" He questioned.

Max laughed, "No, but it definitely is an American creation." Sampling the second tin, Max chomped down on a glob of the manufactured meat. Between bites he added, "It's some kind of pork that you don't have to refrigerate."

Tilting his head to the side, Loc studied the mysterious meat. After a quick shrug, he continued his consumption.

After eating and a short nap, Max stood up under the protective shade of the jungle canopy. Around him snored the bulk of the mercenary volunteers. Empty ration tins littered the ground. Between the discarded cans, an intricate circuit of ant trails crisscrossed the moist soil. In the distance, the Captain and two Laotian commandos rearmed themselves from the large weapons cache.

After rubbing his face, Max wobbled towards the Captain on stiff legs. Peering into the open crate stocked with ammunition tins, he commented, "For the forty of us and estimated three hundred Meos this is a lot of fire power."

"Do you think this all was for us?" The Captain questioned.

"Who else would it be for?" Max shot back.

"It is for the next war," The Captain replied.

"Next war? The war is over. The country is divided as North and South posture for the upcoming election," Max commented.

"There is always a next war." The Captain said. "I was fighting the Japanese when I was a teenager. I've been fighting the Vietminh ever since." Placing a hand on Max's shoulder, he informed, "Peace is the pause that exists briefly between conflicts. Sustainable peace is only a myth."

I prepared for war as a boy, Max reflected. At sixteen, I went to war. If I stayed in the Legion, I'd be fighting in Algeria. The Captain is right there always is another war. That still does not explain the American's generosity, he realized. "I don't understand." Max questioned. "Why would the American have us bring in such a large stockpile of weapons?"

"Deniability Max, deniability," the Captain answered in his blood stained combat fatigues. "Your rescue of Guillian gave them an opportunity to have someone else bring in the weapons. If our mission failed, it was just a bunch of fanatic mercenaries violating the Geneva accords. If our mission succeeds, one plane in, one plane out, some provisions, we take some of the munitions; that is a small commission to pay for the insurance of deniability."

"You knew this all along?" Max asked.

"Yes," the Captain answered. "The Americans commission to deliver weapons, paid for us to rescue an entire hill tribe from extermination. I'd say it is worth it."

"I was motivated because I owed these people." Max stated. Raising a brow, he asked, "Why are you doing this?"

"It is a worthwhile cause." The captain responded. "These Meos are closely related to my people. Actually, I came from a village much like this one. But if you really want to know why I did this?" The Captain hesitated. Puffing out his chest, he declared, "It is because I can."

"You got us this far with limited casualties," Max said. "I have confidence that you'll get us safely South."

Both men looked up to the drone of an aircraft. Max pointed to a speck just above the saw-toothed ridge on the horizon. Nodding, the Captain acknowledged the sighting.

"Let's get the passengers ready, the crew will not want to stay on the ground long," the Captain instructed.

Barely clearing the treetops, the flying boxcar set down hard kicking up chunks of crimson mud. The twin-engine plane pivoted. A back draft swept clean the campsite. Blankets and empty tin cans went flying into the surrounding forest. Engulfed by the blast, a tight cluster of women, children and elderly stood patiently at the edge of the runway. The aircraft's idling engines drowning out the cries of terrified children.

The rear cargo door popped opened. Buck and another crewmember jumped out. Carrying several heavy tarps and some tools, they approached Max. "Where are the munitions?" Buck hollered over the noise.

Pointing towards the weapons cache across the runway, Max replied, "Just in from that dead palm tree." Buck's companion nodded and ran towards the storage bunker.

"Thanks," Buck said. Glancing towards the idling aircraft, he added, "Board your passengers as quickly as possible. It shouldn't take us long to reseal the weapons against the elements."

Walking towards the cargo door, Max saw his assistance wasn't necessary. The orderly Meos hastily boarded the plane. A well-rested Pao stood beside Max watching the proceedings. Spotting Guillian's thin wife in the crowd of passengers climbing aboard, Max smiled affectionately. The fragile village girl proudly held her healthy son. She is going make it, Max thought. As the last passenger climbed into the aircraft, an American peered out. The crewmember waved at Pao to board. The old warrior snorted in disgust. Brandishing the soviet pistol, Pao declared his mercenary status. Max chuckled. The mistaken crewmember apologized with exposed palms.

The returning Buck pulled a cigar out of his breast pocket protector. He handed it to Max and said, "A gift from Major Roche, he says not to smoke it until you are in Laos."

"Thanks," Max said rolling the Cuban Montecristo between thumb and forefinger.

Patting Max on the back, the departing Buck said, "Good luck *hombre.*"

The plane airlifted towards safety. Clearing the treetops, the freedom flight faded into the red sky of the setting sun. The Captain placed his hand on Max's shoulder. "Try to get some sleep," he said. "We depart for Laos at first light."

Walking down a well-defined trail into Northern Laos, Max saw a colorful procession of refugees snaking down the hillside before him. Terraced farms appeared. The Vietminh and the jungle were no longer a threat.

Max spotted Guillian and accelerated. He came up behind the commando. "I don't know about you, but I'm looking forward to clean sheets and cold beer when we get to Muong Sai," Max announced puffing on an expensive cigar.

"Max, where did you come from?" asked a startled Guillian.

"Change of strategy, the Captain wants to exhibit a heavily armed escort as a deterrent to any mountain bandits. Looks like we will walk to freedom together," Max said.

"Do you know how much longer we'll be trekking?" Guillian asked.

"You should be reunited with your wife and son tonight," Max declared.

"You did it Max," Guillian exclaimed patting the German's back. "You actually did it."

"We all did it, my friend," Max mumbled.

"Thanks Max."

"You did the same for me," Max responded.

"Max, you risked your life coming back into the North, not only to save me but the entire village. I just helped you on your escape from the jungle. I didn't even like you, you're German for Christ's sake," Guillian said.

"But you did help me, that's what's important," Max commented. "The fact that you are a Jew makes that even more significant. You ignored the sins of my Nazi affiliation to rescue a fellow soldier. I was just returning the favor."

CHAPTER FIFTY EIGHT

High ceiling fans circulated the humid air at Saigon's Continental Hotel bar. Below the revolving blades, Thong Doan Tu sipped on single malt scotch. His flabby face puckered. Western sophistication has a bitter acidic taste, he thought. The obese, middle-aged Thong leaned back in an overburdened rattan chair. The wicker support creaked. I'm proud of my size, he concluded releasing the strained button of a tailor made white silk suit coat. My weight is a symbol of wealth, he reasoned. Leering across the table at his new mistress, he grinned at the young Vietnamese beauty in a form fitting long sleeved *Áo Dài* dress. A successful man should flaunt his possessions, he proudly surmised.

Sipping on the sharp golden whisky, he reflected on his recent appointment to Deputy Director Refugee Resettlement. It sounded good. My modest skimming of the Northern refugee's aid is making me rich he snickered. My only qualification for the lofty post was being a member of the Roman Catholic Church. I'm not even a good Catholic, he realized. I only embraced the Western religion to appease my wife. Inhaling his extra-marital lover's seductive sweet perfume, he looked up into the raised ceiling. Embracing Catholicism is a small price to pay for my wife tolerating my indiscretions.

The young mistress looked down at a glass of red wine. Her long black hair tied in a bow at the base of her slender neck. Thong traced the side seam of her tight blouse from her hourglass waist up to her shapely breast. His lustful urges stirred. Although she never refused my advances, he thought. I wished she were more sensual during our sessions. Why shouldn't she be? He wondered. I am good to this northern refugee. I often joked that I assisted at least one refugee's integration to the social issues of Saigon, my new mistress, Mei.

After checking his watch, Thong lit a cigarette. The parade is about to start, he realized. Sitting proud and erect, he puffed away. Foreign businessmen and journalists entered the lounge. The new arrivals gazed in awe at Thong's trophy. Leaning forward, he gently lifted Mei's chin. This should give the audience a better view of her flawless features, he thought.

Mei looked straight ahead. She labored not to show expression. This is the start of a very long night, she sighed. I will be on exhibit here for most of the evening. My workday will conclude coupling with this disgusting man, she realized. At least the sexual encounter will be brief. It always is. Tomorrow will begin with the boredom of confinement, she thought. I'm not allowed to leave the flat unless Thong summons me. I've escaped the North only to become a prisoner in Saigon, she concluded. The apartment is just a labor camp with drapes.

Mei stared blindly across the crowded room. The gawking bar room patrons nothing more than a colorful blur. Thong slowly turned her chin. I'm being viewed as a concubine, she painfully realized. Why wouldn't I be, she concluded. I am a whore. Thong pivoted her flawless features in the direction of the doorway. Two men entering the bar broke her trance. Focused on the new arrivals, she smiled. The fat man's hand dictated her view. Sadly, she looked down into the glass of red wine. Thong firmly grabbed her chin. Lifting her head, he glared into her face. Through watery eyes, Mei stared back. Tears rolled down her cheeks.

"What is the meaning of this?" Thong demanded.

Before she could respond, Loc approached the table. Sobbing Mei impulsively leapt into the tribesman's arms.

Max looked down at Mei's escort. Rage distorted the wealthy man's face. A large vein across a flabby forehead pulsed. The obese Asian attempted to stand. Firmly grabbing a soft shoulder, Max forced the man back down. Confused, Thong's head jerked back and forth. Looking up he snorted at the German.

"Relax, they are old friends." Max said pleasantly. "Allow me to join you for a drink while my partner catches up with Mei."

"Why would I ever want to drink with you?" The fat man barked.

Opening his suit coat, Max exposed his holstered Soviet sidearm. "Because if you don't want to drink with me. I'll fucking kill you," Max answered.

Turning to the embracing couple, Max said, "Loc, why don't you take Mei outside while I drink with lard ass."

Max pulled out a chair, as the couple exited. Sitting down, he scanned the Continental hotel bar. Open mouthed, squinting, frowning and whispering patrons responded to the unfolding drama. This is the lion's den, Max thought. I wonder if a desk clerk or other hotel employee is informing the phantom Petru that I'm in Saigon. Just as well, he realized, all rescue missions have a degree of risk. He reached into his inside coat pocket. The fat man twitched. Pulling out a cigar, Max chuckled. Pointing a large stogie across the table, he asked, "Cigar?"

The man shook his head.

After lighting his cigar, Max leaned back and called out a beer order.

In front of the hotel, heavy pedestrian traffic flowed. Sheltered from the stream by a large potted plant, Mei firmly clung to Loc. Squeezing him tight, she realized he was the only man who ever showed her true compassion.

"It is so good to see you again Mei, I missed you," Loc said breaking the embrace.

Mei looked down at the ground. Tears choked her voice. "Loc, I am so ashamed for you to see me like this."

"Like this? You look beautiful," he said.

"I didn't want to be a whore, but there was nothing else I could do. My little sister is contaminated and needed medicine. That man in there helped me get the penicillin she required. This is how I have to pay him back," Mei informed through subsiding tears.

"How is your little sister doing?" Loc asked.

"She is getting much better. I have to do this for her. There is no other way," Mei responded.

"Come with me to Laos, Mei? We can bring your little sister," Loc asked.

"Loc, why would you do this for me?" Mei asked, "I'm..." She started to weep, "...a whore."

Loc hugged her. Gently he pulled her head into his shoulder. Stroking her silky hair, he whispered in her ear, "You are not a prostitute, you are my friend. We all had to do whatever it took to survive." Looking into her moist eyes, he said smiling, "Come north with us. We need someone to tend our garden."

"You have a garden?" Mei asked.

"We will now," he said grinning.

"The fat man will not let me go," she said.

"Do you want to come with me?" Loc asked.

"Of course I do. But I don't want to make trouble for you and Max." Mei said. "Thong is rich and influential. His power scares me."

"Mei, that man is nothing," Loc said scowling. "I'll talk to Max. I told you before my partner can fix anything."

"Loc, I don't want to see that fat man again."

"And I don't want you to see him," Loc said.

Ushering Mei back into the hotel, Loc said, "Wait here in the lobby. I've got a plan."

Max saw Loc approaching. He turned to his large table companion and whispered. "If you want to live to go home to your wife and children tonight, be very careful what you say to the tribesman. He may just kill you out of spite."

Thong's heavy breaths accelerated. A high-pitched wheeze accented each exhale.

Ignoring Mei's panting escort, Loc addressed Max, "She wants to go back with us and bring her little sister."

Max rose from his chair. "That is great news," he declared seeing his delighted partner trying to hold back a nervous smile. Placing a reassuring hand on Loc's shoulder, he added, "Let's get out of here."

Exiting, Loc did not even look in the direction of Mei's sponsor.

Max stood over the seated Thong. He put out his cigar, grabbed his half-full beer glass, and downed it with several large gulps. "Thanks for the beer," he said. For enjoyment, he slammed the empty beer glass on the table. Thong broke wind. Max laughed. Departing the crowed bar the German strutted past the curious patrons flexing his broad shoulders.

On the polished marble floor of the hotel's lobby, Mei and Loc held hands. Behind them bursting with color, towered a large floral arrangement. To the sweet scent of fresh cut flowers, Max approached his friends. With puffy eyes and a soft smile, Mei embraced the German. In her tight grasp, Max stroked her long silky hair. Loc is one lucky fellow, he realized; she really is a beauty.

Assuming Mei would not understand, Max spoke to Loc in French. "Let's get as far away from the Continental Hotel as we can before getting a taxi. Just be alert. I'm concerned someone in the hotel may try to contact Petru." Looking over at the puppy eyed Mei, he added. "No need to alarm your girl."

"I understand," Loc said.

The trio walked down the crowded streets of Saigon. It was dusk. The setting sun reflected off the glass storefronts. Glancing over his shoulder, Max squinted in the blinding light. Is someone following us? He wondered. "This way," he said to his companions, leading them down a side street. Holding hands, Mei and Loc followed close behind. Signaling Loc to wait, Max backtracked. He scanned the flowing masses. Standing on the crowded sidewalk, he watched the indifferent pedestrian traffic. No stalkers, he concluded. A satisfying grin spread across his face. Mei's extraction from Saigon was much easier than anticipated, he concluded.

Returning to his waiting companions, Max found Loc and Mei whispering in Vietnamese. Feeling slightly envious of his partner, he asked, "Do you have any idea what her little sister looks like?"

"No I don't know what she looks like," Loc answered. Lowering his voice, he added, "But I do know she is contaminated."

Max shrugged. I have no interest in a girl infected with the sickness of Venus, he realized. Probably just as well, he thought. The last thing I need right now is a woman contaminating my life.

CHAPTER FIFTY NINE

Thong Doan Tu finished his scotch with a single gulp. He ordered another. The whisky provided comfort in a barroom full of the gawking whispering voyeurs. Squeezing the empty bar glass, he vowed, he was
not going to let that savage and the obnoxious European intimidate him.
They had no right to claim my property, he thought. That little whore is
mine. I'm a wealthy and powerful man, he concluded. I'll save face no
matter what the cost. His scotch order arrived. He exchanged glasses with
the waiter, and swore he would be drinking with his prize tomorrow at
the same table. Of course, Mei would be punished he thought. I was too
lenient with the girl. I never flogged her like my other domestic servants.
Sipping on the bitter scotch, he envisioned whipping a naked Mei. A sadistic grin emerged. Rising with an alcohol-induced sense of confidence, he
threw a wad of bills on the table. His head held high, he walked to the front
desk of the hotel and requested the use of a phone. Calmly, he placed a call
to the administration office at the Bien Hoa refugee camp.

"This is Thong Doan Tu," he said into the receiver.

"Yes sir," a surprised voice responded.

"I need to speak to the camp police immediately," he said waiting patiently for the connection.

"This is Sergeant Le Chi Cao. How may I assist you sir?"

"This is Thong Doan Tu, do you know who I am, Sergeant?"

"Yes sir, Deputy Director," the sergeant responded.

"Sergeant we have a very delicate matter that needs to be handled with
the utmost confidentiality. Can I count on your discretion?" Thong asked.

"Sir, you can count on me. How may I assist you?" the sergeant
inquired.

"There is a young girl in the infirmary, her name is Lan. I have very reliable information that she may be a Communist infiltrator from the North. I need you to remove her from the medical unit and hold her in detention until I arrive. In addition, there may be some undesirable characters trying to make contact with this girl, another girl who came from the North, a Meo and a European. I ask that you and your men be cautious, but detaining these individuals is necessary. Force may be required, and I understand if you and your men have to exercise it. I will take full reasonability for this delicate matter and will compensate you and your men for your assistance," Thong said.

"Sir, consider it done. The communist girl will be in custody upon your arrival. If her cohorts appear, they will be incarcerated as well," the sergeant said.

CHAPTER SIXTY

Floating in darkness, Max heard a low moan. It's raining he thought. His head throbbed. A pulsating pain hammered his jaw. The distant growl of pain increased. It's me, he realized. I'm the one groaning. Attempting to examine his injuries, he realized he couldn't move. Falling rain drowned out distant voices. Slowly he drifted towards the comforting darkness. Thunder crashed. He lifted his aching head. The room was bright. It smelled of fresh wood. Blinking he saw Loc slouched forward in a metal chair, his hands cuffed behind his back. Loc's chest pulsed. He's still alive, Max concluded. Attempting to move, he felt shackled restraints. In torn bloodstained uniforms, half a dozen battered policemen leaned against plywood walls. Mei! Max recalled. We were getting Mei's friend from the refugee camp. To the pounding of the torrential storm, he heard women weeping. Painfully he turned to investigate. Sitting on the wood floor in a holding cell, Mei and Lan wept. The caged girls held onto each other. Their faces shielded by intertwined black hair. A torn blouse exposed Mei's bare shoulder. We must be in the refugee camp police station, he concluded.

The door in front of Max opened. A middle aged, hefty police sergeant walked into the room. Max recalled the sergeant encouraging his men from the distance during the one sided struggle. The pieces of a fractured time line fell into place. Only one question needs to be answered, Max thought. Glancing up with a heavy head, the fat man from the Continental Hotel entered. So it was you, Max thought. The phantom Petru Rossi is still a mystery.

The sinister smirking fat man waddled to the holding cell. Mei slowly stood to face her former master, the left side of her flawless features red and swollen.

"You will have to be punished my little flower," the man said in a playful tone. His large sweaty noggin glistened. "You are my property and will remain my property until I decide differently."

Trembling Mei sucked back tears.

Thong continued, "Your punishment will begin now as you watch my questioning of these Communist infiltrators." Turning to the sergeant, he said, "If you don't mind attaching the magneto to the German's...ears."

Max's stomach churned. His breath accelerated. The image of defiant Vietminh prisoners breaking under the preferred torture device of the Colonial French surfaced. A shabby officer produced what appeared to be a black field telephone. The policeman wrapped two electric leads around Max's ears. Another officer attached the wires to the magneto and calmly placed his hand on the crank awaiting further direction. The sergeant looked over at the fat man. Chubby nodded with a crooked smile. The officer cranked the device setting Max's ears ablaze. His body stiffened. Electricity ripped through his insides. Jerking violently, he attempted to distance himself from the intense pain.

"Stop!" screamed the caged Mei. "Please stop!" she pleaded.

Max gritted his teeth. The violent experience receded. The bright room spun. Hyperventilating, he drifted towards comforting darkness. A sweaty hand raised his head. "You are not so arrogant now, are you?" the fat man said holding up Max's chin. "I think we need to increase the voltage to soften you up a little more before I begin my questioning."

I can't handle another jolt, Max realized. The painful echo of the last shock lingered throughout his body. Shifting in his restraints, he knew the fat man would break him. Should I give him that satisfaction? Max's pride debated with the realization of pain.

The door burst open and slammed hard against the wall. An intruder in a white dinner jacket, bowtie and black slacks rushed into the room. His hair and clothes soaking wet.

"What is the meaning of this?" Roche shouted. "Release my friends immediately!"

The bewildered policemen sought guidance. The gapping Sergeant scanned the room for his alibi. The obese man quietly tried to exit the stage. Following the Sergeant's gaze, Roche spotted the escaping instigator.

"You, fat man, come here," Roche commanded. "What is your name?"

"I am Thong Doan Tu, Deputy Director." Thong mumbled bowing sheepishly.

"That is *former* deputy director, you're fired," Roche said. Scowling at the confused sergeant, he barked. "I said to release my friends. If I have to ask again, you will be terminated."

Feeling his handcuffs removed, Max gently rubbed his chafed wrist. Beside him, Loc's unshackled arms dangle lifelessly. Woozy, Max remained seated. A freed hand investigated his swollen jaw. Delicately he touched a tender ear. Slowly rising, he used the metal chair for support. Peering around at his assailants, he instinctively reached for his gun. Unarmed he used an extended finger and thumb to mime a comforting shooting sequence. A released Mei ran to comfort Loc back to consciousness.

"Max, do we need to get you a doctor?" Roche asked.

Stretching his aching body, Max attempted to shake off the memory of electric pain. Taking a deep cleansing breath, he reached over and tore a tattered shirt off an officer. The policeman retreated with a shout. Using the end of the shirt, Max removed blood from the inside of his mouth. Slowly he began wrapping the shirt around his right hand. Taking a half step back, he paused. Grinning wide with blood stained teeth, he lunged forward punching the deputy director on the side of the head. The large man teetered backwards with disconnected eyes. His knees buckled and his lifeless body hit the hard wood floor with a thud.

That was satisfying, Max thought slowly unwrapping his hand. Flexing his fist several times, he politely tossed the rag back to the shirtless officer. "What's with the dinner jacket, Roche?" he asked massaging his ears.

"Dinner at the Palace tonight," Roche answered. "I received an urgent message from this kid at Catholic relief services, Harry Han. He said you were requesting the release of a patient from the infirmary. It was a good excuse to pass on dessert tonight and see if I couldn't help expedite the paperwork."

Max turned to look at Mei comforting his partner. "Loc, you good?" he asked.

Peering out of Mei's embrace, a bruised and bloody Loc smiled. "I'm good partner." He mumbled.

"Sergeant," Roche called out.

"Yes sir." The sergeant responded stepping out of the shadows.

"Your mistake tonight was that you bet on the wrong horse," Roche said.

"Yes sir," the sergeant responded.

"Sergeant, I'm asking you to place the deputy director here under arrest. We've suspected his embezzlement of aid funds for some time. We need to set an example that this will not be tolerated," Roche said. "Can I count on you Sergeant?"

"Yes sir, my pleasure!" the sergeant responded.

"One other thing Sergeant," Roche said glancing around at the battered occupants. "Thong has caused us all a great deal of discomfort this evening. If the former deputy director was to slip and fall on the way to his holding cell, I think we would all understand."

"Yes sir." The Sergeant nodded.

CHAPTER SIXTY ONE

A black rotary telephone surrounded by empty beer bottles chimed. The longneck amber glass vibrated. Floating in an opium-induced slumber, Petru Rossi stirred. Focused on the swirling blades of a creaking ceiling fan, he blindly searched for the annoying phone. Toppled bottles rolled off the nightstand. Glass exploded on the hard wood floor. Triumphantly, he lifted the receiver silencing the annoying ringtone.

"Hello," The Corsican mumbled.

"Petru Rossi?"

"Yes," Petru answered.

"This is Francoise at the Continental Hotel. Sir, we have been trying to reach you all night."

"What is it?" mumbled Petru.

"The German and the tribesman were in the Lobby bar this evening," Francoise responded.

"Were they looking for me?" Petru asked.

"I don't believe so, sir," Francoise replied. "They left with a high priced whore, the tribesman called her Mei."

"Thank you for the information," Petru said dropping the receiver near the phone's cradle.

Grinning Petru lay back and contemplated his vengeance in the muggy opium smoke filled room. The dream session numbed the bullet floating in his back. I'm going to bleed the German, he fantasized and that milkshake drinking savage. Corsican patience always prevails. My honor will be restored.

CHAPTER SIXTY TWO

R olling green hills rippled under a cloudless blue Laotian sky. A summer breeze danced in treetops. A network of dusty red trails flowed across the pastoral vista. On a quiet crimson path, Roche and another American agent strolled through the rural experience. The tranquility of the Plain of Jars is a welcome reprieve from the issues of Saigon, Roche thought. Life is far more easygoing on the outskirts of this opium hub, he concluded, It will good to see Max again, he realized. The German is more than a useful CIA tool. He is a friend.

"How much further?" asked Roche's impatient colleague.

Roche glanced over at the tall and lanky Walker. The young agent's dishwater blond hair cropped G.I. style. Examining the acne faced adolescent, Roche questioned the twenty-five year age stated in Walker's dossier. "We're here," Roche declared pointing down the dirt path to a raised long house.

From the elevated porch, three menacing dogs charged. Threatening growls encircled the two Americans. Frozen in a cloud of red dust, Roche looked up from the snarling entrapment. A tiny old tribesman appeared on the porch. Grumbling the old man slowly descended the stairs. A Soviet pistol holstered in the waistband of his trousers. The dogs greeted the old Meo with wagging tails. Petting the mangy mitts, the wrinkled leathery-skinned tribesman scowled at the intruders.

"We are here to see Max," Roche said politely.

Raising his hand, the old man signaled the Americans to wait. Mumbling under his breath, the tribesman and the pack of tail wagging canines disappeared into the long house.

A shirtless Max peered out of the doorway. His inquiring squint retreated behind a big smile. "Come on up Roche," he said waving a welcoming hand. "Let me grab a shirt."

Roche and Walker climbed up the bowed wooden stair treads. Standing in the cool shade of the raised wooden deck, Roche turned to admire the view.

"Always good to see you, Roche," Max said walking through the open doorway. "It's been awhile," he added tucking a starched shirt into baggy chinos.

"As well, Max. This is Jack Walker, I wanted you both to meet," Roche said.

Max gave Walker a firm handshake.

"I've heard a lot about you," Walker said.

"Most of it is true." Max said grinning. "You gentlemen care to join me for a beer?"

"I thought you'd never ask." Roche added.

"Have a seat," Max offered motioning to an array of blistered dining room chairs. Plopping in the only windsor chair, he looked over his shoulder and called out, "Three cold beers, please." Pulling several cigars out of a leather pouch, he offered them to his guests. Roche accepted. Walker declined.

"Who's the old man?" Roche asked, puffing on a large stogy. "I thought he was going to shoot us."

"That's Pao. Don't let his age fool you. He is one of the best men in my crew. He proved himself in battle on our march to freedom." Max said respectfully.

A barefoot young Asian girl in black cotton pajamas pranced out of the house carrying three glistening bottles of beer. Her long radiant hair tied back with a bow. The loose fitting maternity smock top announced her pregnancy. The glow of motherhood enhanced her natural beauty. A gawking Walker stood to accept his beer.

"Mei!" Roche exclaimed.

Mei nodded with an innocent smile.

"It is good to see you," Roche said slowly in Vietnamese. He rose hugging the young mother-to-be.

Blushing Mei graciously slipped back into the house.

"I'm glad that young girl has finally found a home. She has had a very rough start in her short life. I assume she is still with your partner?" Roche asked.

"Loc has been smitten with her since he recognized her that day at the embassy. It was only a matter of time before those two would hook up. As you could see, Loc made their relationship official," Max said.

"Where is Loc?" Roche asked.

"He's around back with some of the other Tais tending to a vegetable garden for Mei. She does not have many requests, but her garden is very important," Max replied.

"Are you ready to discuss business?" Roche asked. "Or do you want to finish our beers first?"

"We can drink and talk at the same time," Max said. "Besides I need to feel I'm doing something for the monthly Civil Air Transport stipend."

Roche smiled, "I need for you to keep an eye on young Walker for me," he said leaning forward patting Walker's back. "Armed with a degree in agriculture from Kansas State College, he will be providing farming assistance to the hill tribes. I need for you to escort him into the highlands."

"You *do* want me to earn my wages." Max said taking a large swig from the chilled bottle. "You realize this is the start of monsoon season?" Turning to Walker, he asked, "Do you have any experience with the Meos?"

"Very much so," Walker said sitting erect. "I spent my childhood on my father's Baptist mission in Burma. I learned several tribal dialects and an appreciation for the customs of the indigenous people."

"So this will be a humanitarian undertaking?" Max questioned.

"Most definitely," Walker responded. "We should be able to significantly increase the morphine content of the Meo's opium harvest."

CHAPTER SIXTY THREE

It was late afternoon on a cool cloudy day. Dark clouds threatened rain. In the back office of a charter airline hangar at the Phong Savin airport, the gray sky shrouded an open window. The room's only occupant reclined comfortably on an army cot. A sweet stench lingered. To combat the tension from a bumpy morning flight, he had smoked a bowl of opium. Opiate is a much better alternative than scotch to elevate my fear of flying, he thought. Footsteps echoed in the adjoining warehouse. That must be the courier, he realized sitting up on the collapsible bed. Out of habit, he straightened the lapels of the wrinkled white suit draped over his skeletal frame. The small room floated. The phantom pain from the bullet lodged next to his spine only a memory.

The door to the office slowly opened. Two Binh Xuyen thugs and another Corsican entered the room. "Petru?" the Corsican messenger questioned.

"Yes," Petru mumbled with sleepy eyes.

"I hardly recognized you," the messenger mumbled. "You've lost some weight."

Petru squinted at his countryman. The healing process has aged me considerably, he realized. My face has lost elasticity and my prized slick black hair has thinned into a comb-over of oily strands. "What information do you have for me?" he slowly asked.

"I'm afraid it is not good news. The German is not in Phong Savin. Max and the tribesman, with most of their crew headed into the highlands a couple of days ago. I don't know how long they will be gone," the messenger informed. Glancing over at the two thugs, he added, "I guess you will not need their services?"

"Not necessarily," Petru said with a crooked grin. "I didn't come up here to kill Max. I came up here to bleed him."

CHAPTER SIXTY FOUR

Through holes in the thick foliage, Max looked up at the switchbacks that scarred the mountainside. He got a glimpse of Loc and the Tai escorts ascending. I'm not that far off their pace, he concluded. Inhaling the soft sultry aroma of the impending storm, he looked skyward. Distant lightening sparked behind stagnant black clouds. Gusting wind flowed down the jungle trail. "Shit," he grumbled. It's going to rain, he realized accelerating. The torrential seasonal rain could extend our ten-day journey, he realized. Behind him, Walker sped up as well.

Bringing up the rear, a winded Walker proclaimed. "This is beautiful country."

"You must be looking at something that I can't see," Max responded turning up another sharp bend in the highland trail.

"For opium production, the elevation is perfect. Opium poppies, like the Meo, thrive at three thousand feet or more above sea level," Walker informed. "We tried to establish poppy fields with the refugee population around the Plain of Jars. The plants withered and died. The displaced tribesmen didn't fare any better. The Meos lack the immune system to deal with the lower altitude's tropical diseases."

"You sure seem passionate about opium," Max said.

"Yes, I am. It is truly an amazing product." The zealous Walker proclaimed matching the German's stride. "A poppy field is ready for harvest in the initial year of planting, and can remain productive for ten years. Tending the fields does not require much labor. But the real attributes are in the finished product." He paused to catch his breath. "Compact and easily transportable opium is a non-perishable. Its value increases with age. I don't know of any other crop with all those qualities."

Slowing his pace, Max asked, "Have you ever been to an opium den and smelled the sweet smoldering scent of slow death?"

"I don't like to think about that side of the equation," Walker responded. "All vices come with a price. I've seen the bottle suck the life out of alcoholics and the infecting aftermath of brothel services. Hell, in the US right now doctors are debating that cigarettes cause cancer. I'll leave it to my missionary father to preach about the wages of sin."

"I don't disagree with you," Max said. "But opium extracts a heavy toll. In the Legion I saw soldiers dance with the pipe. The pleasure is short lived. They wrestle with the beast for a while. The beast always wins. I've never saw an exception."

"For someone who monitors the product for the Agency, your convictions surprise me Max," Walker said.

Max stopped and turned around on the jungle path. Looking directly at Walker, he said, "I'm a soldier of fortune. Death is a byproduct of my profession. It doesn't mean I enjoy it. It is something I've been trained to tolerate. As for your precious opium, you forgot to mention the best attribute. With the Meo women tending to the poppy fields, it allows the Meo men the opportunity to fight and die." Turning his back on the wide-eyed young American, he resumed trekking.

Catching up to the German, Walker blurted out, "For a just cause!"

"What?" Max asked, not breaking stride.

"It allows the Meos to fight and die for a just cause," Walker explained.

Moving forward Max said, "The graveyards are full of young men who died for causes defined just by men who avoided the battlefield. As a survivor, I can tell you the causes I was duped into fighting seem insignificant now."

A strong wind rustled through the treetops. The sky darkened. It started to rain.

CHAPTER SIXTY FIVE

Small plumes of smoke rose out of the rainforest. The wet terrain sparkled in the late morning sunlight. The thin mountain air was moist from last night rains. On the churned muddy trail, Max trudged forward with heavy feet. His boots covered in muck. Catching a whiff of distant cooking fires, he took a deep breath. We are getting close, he realized. Ignoring the fatigue from a rain soaked sleepless night he accelerated. Huffing and puffing behind Loc and the Tais, he entered the Meo settlement. Dipping a shoulder, he released his pack in the middle of the village thoroughfare. The jungle clearing buzzed with construction activity. Ax wielding teams hacked at tall timber. Women sat in circles weaving palm fronds. On a stilted platform, men framed a longhouse. The entire population labored to establish adequate shelter for the rainy season.

Max, Loc and the Tais arrival prompted a work stoppage. The villagers slowly congregated around the visitors. The shy crowd mumbled. An elderly couple bowed in front of Max and Loc. Hands reached out of the throng to touch their benefactors. Max glanced at Loc. The tribesman smiled nervously.

Slowly turning Max smiled at the happy faces of the rescued community. Observing ruddy cheeks and plumper bodies, he took a proud breath. I should have brought Pao, he thought, the old warrior would have enjoyed seeing his former neighbors.

The toothless Chue flashed his unique smile.

"It good to see you brother," Max mumbled patting Chue's shoulder. "You've put on weight," he added examining the warrior.

A confused Chue, sought Loc for a translation.

Max patted Chue's belly as Loc translated. Chue and the audience chuckled.

A grinning Guillian waded through the crowd. The tall lanky commando towered above his shorter neighbors. He shot a curious squint at the adolescent looking Walker before nodding respectfully at Loc and the Tais. With outstretched arms, he approached Max. The German and Jew embraced.

"It's always good to see you Max," Guillian said softly.

"The feeling is mutual," Max mumbled.

Gazing in Walker's direction, Guillian asked, "What brings you to my world?"

Glancing over his shoulder at Walker, Max said quietly, "Another gift from the Americans. His name is Jack Walker. He is here to help you establish your poppy fields."

Guillian chuckled. "*Don't mistake me*, I appreciate your American employer's generosity. We could not have reestablished the community without Roche's help. However, the Meo's know how to grow poppies."

Max shrugged. "I'll leave it up to you." He commented. "But the enthusiastic kid seems knowledgeable."

Guillian nodded.

Max waved for Walker to join them. "Jack Walker, I'd like you to meet Sergeant Jean Guillian." Max said as the men shook hands.

"Pleased to meet you, Walker," Guillian said. "However the Meo know how to grow opium. Their ancestors were cultivating poppy fields in China before they migrated to theses highlands three hundred years ago."

"*Then mine should be an easy task*," Walker said in a familiar tribal dialect.

Guillian nodded respectfully.

Walker continued. "I would like to survey the area. Do you know of any outcroppings of limestone? Opium grows best in rich alkaline soil."

"I'll have Chue show you around," Guillian said, turning to instruct the tribesman. As Chue and Walker departed, Guillian playfully asked Max, "Are you ready to get drunk and have your feet washed?"

"I'd like to see H'Liana and Etienne first," Max said.

"That is kind of you Max, it will make my wife happy."

Walker led the way. A lethargic Chue followed. Over his shoulder, Walker informed, "I want the poppy fields to be within walking distance from the village, preferably with a southern exposure for optimal sunlight."

Chue stopped. "You speak our tongue?" He questioned.

A grinning Walker slowly nodded. I never grow tired of the shock my linguistics skills provoke, he thought.

"This way," an invigorated Chue offered.

Following the tribesman, Walker scanned the sloping terrain. To steep, he concluded. The delicate seeds would wash away. Squatting down he sifted a handful of moist soil through his fingers. The objective is producing high-grade opium, he reflected. Increasing the harvest's morphine content increases the cash crops value. If you are going to grow it, he snickered. You might as well grow the best. Chue waved him forward. Approaching Walker came upon a sunny plot with a slight grade. Standing beside Chue, he scanned the slopping terrace. An August planting assures a December harvest, he thought. Patting his tribal escort on the back, he declared, "This site is perfect.

Woven palm leaf matting blanketed the moist ground. Angle bamboo poles provided shade in a hastily constructed lean-to. Under the slanted roofed shelter, the Meo's entertained their guest. Loc and his Tai's kinsmen puffed on Chesterfield cigarettes with their Meo relatives. Local liquor flowed. Max sat cross legged in his stocking feet. Sucking on a thick maduro cigar, he watched a pack of village boys chiseling the mud off his boots. A soft flowing breeze swept the shelter clean of tobacco smoke. Guillian sipped white whisky out of a wicker-encased bottle.

Taking a swig of Meo moonshine, Max sighed. "Is it safe to smoke?" He questioned.

"An acquired taste," Guillian snickered examining the reed bottle.

"It's really good to see the community taking root in Laos," Max commented.

Shaking his head Guillian grumbled, "Northern Laos comes with the threat of the Pathet Lao. Once the settlement is restored several scouts will join Captain Yang Mo's growing army," he said frowning.

"You sound as though you have some regrets?" Max asked.

"These people have an opportunity to become prosperous once again. Surrounded by uninhabited mountains with fertile land, the Americans induce us to grow opium to fuel the conflicts that will never end. The Captain is a warrior, much as I used to be. He guided us to safety with very few casualties." Guillian paused to reflect. "That's very few causalities *so far*. Who knows what the future Meo death toll will be under his banner."

"Guillian, you built a fence out of the heads of your enemies. You vowed to fight the Communists to the death. Your son was going to carry on after your demise. Why the change of heart?" Max asked.

"The spiked heads around our border was a no trespassing sign." Guillian stated. "The *montagnards* are a proud race. My adopted family will fight to the death anyone who threatens our existence. We always will. As far as Etienne's legacy, I hope my son will become the man who stands up for his family, for his people." Guillian took a large swig from the basket bottle. "We will pay our obligation to the Captain with interest. His request to gather information on the communist Pathet Lao is reasonable. The village would have been exterminated without his assistance."

"I understand, Guillian," Max said. "Now you know why I became independent on my quest to exist."

"You need to find a wife and have children. It changes your perspective. I no longer want to fight to survive. I want to live. I joined the French Military after the big war out of anger. I was enraged at what the Germans did to my country and my people. I swore never again would I be loaded on a train like livestock and sentenced to forced labor. I wanted to possess the warrior skills necessary to repel any future invaders. Those skills served me well in these remote highlands. But there comes a time when you realize if you continue to fight, you will eventually die young," Guillian said. "Sorry Max, sometimes I get carried away."

"You don't have to apologize to me, my friend. There are few moments in my life when I have been content with my existence. In fact there are very few times, I made my own decisions. I didn't have to. A soldier's creed is to follow orders." Max took a sip of whisky to lubricate a crackling voice. Focused on the former commando, he concluded. "One of my choices that I am proud of was walking a Jew and his adopted family out of North Vietnam."

"Why don't you stay with us Max? There is more to life than monitoring the opium trade for the Americans. You could start your own family here." Guillian offered.

"I appreciate the invitation, but I already have a family in Phong Savin. The foul winds of war have blown a collection of misfits to the western edge of the Plain of Jars. We call it home. Like your expanding family, we will have a new addition soon. Loc and Mei's first child is three months off. We even have a grandfather. The old warrior Pao is quite the character," Max said.

Across the lean-to four boisterous old men erupted in laughter. The extremely animated group embellished war stories. Through long bamboo straws, they sucked *Rượu cần* from a communal clay pot. The rice wine fueled the bloviating dialogue.

"That may be us one day, recalling the days of youthful glory," Guillian commented.

"I sure hope these are not our best days," Max chuckled.

"They can only get better, my German friend," Guillian said. Picking up the wicker bottle of white whisky, he raised it in the air and said, "To the future."

Max took the bottle, repeated the motion and said, "*L'Chayim,*" the Jewish toast to life.

CHAPTER SIXTY SIX

Mei stood under the lee of the raised wooden deck's overhang. The big house seemed empty. It was late in the day. A heavy sun beat down. Last night's visiting rain had washed the sky a deep blue. Scanning the surrounding mountains, the petite Vietnamese beauty tied back her long black locks with a simple bow. Breathing in the clean moist air, she thought of Loc. My husband and the German should be returning soon. For the first time, she felt a child fluttering within her womb. My man will be pleased, she thought.

Sprawled on the planked wood porch, the old Meo warrior Pao snored with an open mouth. A black skullcap corralled wisps of silver hair. A crossbow rested on his lap, a bottle of white whisky by his side. Grandpa started drinking earlier than usual today, Mei concluded. I hope he remembered to tether the dogs, she thought. Lan's gardening assistance is contingent on the animals being restrained.

The pudgy Lan in black pajamas stomped onto the deck. Looking skyward she asked, "Do you think the rains will delay Max and Loc's return?"

Extending a flexed finger over her lips, Mei whispered, "Quiet." Her dark eyes shot a glance at the napping Pao. Softly she answered, "I'm hoping they'll be back tomorrow."

Blistered wood treads creaked as the girls gently descended into the tropical sunlight. Lan's face puckered in the warm rays. My little sister does not share my gardening joy, Mei realized. Walking past three reclining junkyard dogs tied up on the side of the house, Lan paused. Taking a deep breath, she gave the docile animals a wide berth. Mei smiled. The only thing Lan fears is large dogs, Mei reflected.

In the back of the pitched palm frond roofed longhouse, furrowed rows of rich soil nurtured Mei's garden. Rooted in the dark moist earth, sprouting cucumbers, rich green bok choy and ripening tomatoes bathed in sunlight.

"Let's work next to each other pulling out weeds," Mei said. Kneeling down in damp dirt, she used a small table knife to extract the unwanted growth.

The dogs started barking. Admiring a plump cucumber, Mei ignored the howling mutts. Three long shadows spilled across the small garden. Mei blinked into the glaring sunlight. Towering silhouettes of two large males flanked the outline of a skinny frail man leaning on a cane. Mei looked at Lan. Her little sister scowled into the blinding rays.

"I told you the German and the tribesman wouldn't be here." A wide Asian thug mumbled.

"I didn't come to kill Max and Loc. I came to bleed them." The frail Frenchman responded in accented Vietnamese. Shifting his weight on the glossy bamboo cane, he moaned. "The kraut's tormenting bullet is reminding me how much I'm going to enjoy this." Grinning wide he said, "Go wake up the old man on the porch, I want him to watch."

Mei tried to stand. The malnourished Frenchman with dark sunken eyes and oily black hair struck her hard with his cane. The blow sent her to the moist earth. Placing the tip of the cane in her back, he pinned her and her unborn child in the dirt. Breathing heavy, Mei sucked in the garden's soil. Sweat rolled down her face. Her baby stirred.

A thug shouted, "The old man is gone."

Screaming Lan lunged at the other wide Asian brute. Snickering he repelled her charge with a massive backhand. Groaning she collapsed at his feet. Reaching down, he pulled her up by the hair. Rhythmically he slapped the suspended girl. Lan's painful cries faded with each smack.

Mei bit her lip. Her pounding heart competed with the pulsating thrashing. The Frenchman shifted his full weight onto the cane. The tip pinned Mei to the ground.

"Harder," The Frenchman mumbled. "Slap her harder." He grunted. "Do her," he panted. "Do her now."

The thug dropped the tenderized Lan. Reaching down he tore off her black smock top. Tossing the bloody rag aside, he squeezed his crotch for stimulation.

The Frenchman twisted the bamboo staff. The jabbing tip digging deep into Mei's back. Lan wept. Fabric ripped. The dogs howled. The rapist rhythmically grunted. The Frenchman panted and snorted like an animal in heat. Mei took a deep breath. An overpowering recognizable sweet fragrance filled her nostrils. Petru Rossi, she thought. I will never forget the revolting stench of the important gangster from the House of Butterflies.

The rapist cried out in pain.

The pinning cane shifted. Mei leapt to her feet. Off balance, Petru fell backwards. I'm no longer the village girl who accepted my brothel fate, Mei realized. She pounced on her assailant. I survived Dien Bien Phu, a Communist labor camp, and sex with a countless number of uncaring men, she reflected. No one, and I mean no one is going to kill me, my child or little sister in my garden. Kneeling on the chest of the important gangster, she pressed the dull gardening knife into the soft skin under the Petru's chin. She stared into his dark sunken eyes. He twitched with fear. The full force of her resolve drove the small blade into his mouth. Clutching his throat, he jerked violently. Mei tumbled back into the garden. Resting on her elbows, she scanned the battlefield. Naked displaying deep purple bruises, Lan slowly crawled under the raised long house. Lying face up in the garden the rapist gasped for life. A wooden arrow protruded from his bloated belly. Pulsing blood leaked out around the projectile. Flaying on the wet ground, Petru gurgled blood. Frantically he tried to dislodge the small knife jammed into his mouth.

Slowly Mei crawled past the men. Under the house, she hugged the trembling Lan. Three dogs came tearing around the house kicking up chucks of earth. Petru Rossi let out a high-pitched scream as two of the snarling dogs ripped into his torso. Glistening blood splotches accented his shredded white suit. The third dog continued to growl while gnawing on the slowly dying Asian thug.

Pao came into view. Walking erect, he confidently brandished a crossbow. Approaching the bloody carnage, he casually tossed the bow aside.

Placing two fingers in his mouth, he produced a shrill whistle. The carnivorous dogs ceased. From the waistband of his trousers, he drew a Soviet pistol. Strutting over, he silenced the moaning intruders with several headshots.

CHAPTER SIXTY SEVEN

It was a lazy Sunday afternoon on the outskirts of Phong Savin. Black monsoon clouds crept along the horizon. Sunlight slowly retreated across the rural vista. The prelude to the tempest produced a comfortable breeze and the pleasant odor of approaching rain. On the raised deck of a Laotian long house, Max and Roche leaned back in wooden chairs. Their elevated feet rested on the porch's railing. They drank cold beers and puffed on expensive cigars.

"Have you ever seen one of these storms blow through?" Max asked.

"Yes, it is an impressive show of nature," Roche responded transfixed on the dark horizon.

Max turned to flick cigar ash on the wooden deck. Three of the Tais and Lan sat comfortably on the planked flooring playing the Vietnamese card game, *Tien Len*. The modest betting kept the competition interesting. Empty beer bottles encircled the players. Smirking Lan revealed a winning hand to surprised laughter. Wagging a victorious finger at the men, she retrieved her winnings. I'm happy to see my little sister is enjoying life after the assault, Max thought.

At the end of the porch, the old warrior Pao sat on the deck with three dogs. The intimidating canines looked passive. The black white stocking Pasha reclined across his legs. Grandpa scratched the happy mutt behind the ears. He paused to take a sip of potent rice liquor from an old bottle. His peaceful gaze focused on the procession of assembling black clouds.

Loc sat on a wooden bench. Mei rested her head on his lap. They conversed in whispers, as he stroked her long black hair.

Over background laughter, Roche said, "Max, I must say, you've done pretty well for yourself up here. I envy your situation."

"We have all paid the price to enjoy at least one quiet Sunday." Max said, "But as you know, the fortunes of these people changes as quickly as the weather."

The salivating aroma of roasting pork drifted across the veranda. The bubbling Meo dialogue of the cooks resonated within the longhouse.

"Smells good," Roche commented. "Do you always eat this well?"

"The two Tai girls are excellent cooks. So yes, we eat well. The pork tonight, however, is special, on account of you staying the night. You need to come north more often," Max answered.

"I'd like to. Things in Saigon are progressing, but we still have a long way to go. The French have conceded. They are moving onto another war in Algeria. The only internal threats left are the Binh Xuyen criminal organization and the Corsicans," Roche said. Taking a puff on his cigar, he glanced over at Pao. "Thanks to your crew, we have one less Corsican to deal with."

"My issue with Petru was personal. The Corsicans operating in Laos seem content. Smuggling narcotics is mother's milk to the Corsican clans. They are making a fortune." Max said.

"Max, they may seem satisfied now, but always be careful when dealing with the Corsicans. They never forget," Roche warned.

Loc shouted, "I felt my son kick!"

The porch occupants all tuned to investigate. Even the dogs elevated their ears. The beaming tribesman tenderly rubbed Mei's pregnant belly.

Touching the back of her husband's stoking hand, Mei corrected, "You mean our son." The porch filled with laughter.

A childish grin spread across Loc's downcast face. "I felt our son kick," he declared giving the mother-to-be an apologetic kiss.

Crashing thunder exploded. Everyone flinched. The dogs scurried into the long house. In the open doorway the two petite cooks appeared. Drying their hands on stained aprons, they looked into the stormy skies. Lightning flashed. A thick mist blanketed the surrounding mountains. A gusty wind sent playing cards flying. Large raindrops spotted the perimeter of the planked deck. God's spigot released a torrential downpour. Driving rain invaded the covered porch.

Max and Roche withdrew from the railing. Standing in a protected location, they puffed on their gourmet cigars. Remaining seated, Pao lit up a cigarette. Everyone else retreated for the shelter of the main structure.

"It's a good thing you decided to stay the night, nobody is getting out in this weather," Max said flicking a large white ash on the wet floor.

"This is a hell of a storm." Roche commented. The dirt road in front of the long house turned from a muddy stream into a murky river. "You never know what will hit this country next."

"One thing is certain." Max said motioning in the direction the complacent Pao. "The inhabitants know how to endure."

"There is more to life than just enduring, Max," Roche said. "You should find a woman and settle down."

Max puffed on his cigar, contemplating the appropriate response. Grinning through the dissipating smoke he declared, "The last mistress I had was Isabelle, and I walked out on the bitch."

####

Book Two
Fool's Errand

"Anti-Communism will remain a useless tool unless the problem of nationalism is resolved."
Marshal Philippe Leclerc de Hautecloque
Commander-in Chief in Indochina, 1945-47

CHAPTER ONE

Returning to her seat in the deluxe service cabin of the Air France flight, Elaine adjusted her skirt. The leggy blonde flashed her perfect gams at the elite cabins only other passenger. The oily complexioned middle-aged French businessman took the bait with a lustful gaze. Bingo Elaine thought, I've found a guide to navigate through customs and baggage claim.

"Can I get you anything before we land, Miss Favreau?" The very attentive steward asked.

"A glass of red wine," Elaine responded, to the thin attendant in a double-breasted navy blue jacket, white shirt and narrow blue tie. A pair of wings pinned over his breast pocket gave the ensemble an official military quality.

"So you waited until the conclusion of our journey to partake in the fine French wines Air France has to offer," he said.

"My adventure is about to begin," she responded. "I thought a toast to the Pearl of the Far East would be appropriate."

"If it is adventure you seek, Saigon won't disappoint you. However with our defeat in the North, the Pearl has lost some of its charm," he said.

As the attendant walked away, she smiled. Our defeat? It was a French loss. It would have been inappropriate to inform him that I'm American, she thought. An American translator with apparently no hint of an accent, she proudly concluded.

After thanking the attendant for the wine, she raised her glass in a quiet toast in the direction of the gawking businessman. He beamed like a love struck schoolboy. Sipping on the exquisite merlot, she closed her eyes. The smooth sophistication flowed past her glossy red lips. I'm about to fulfill my addiction for excitement, she realized. I need this. Just like last summer in Paris, when I convinced father to extend my college graduation gift for another year in that wonderful city.

The planes intercom crackled. Elaine chuckled at the latest innovation in air travel. The static broadcast seemed to indicate preparations for landing. It would have been just as easy for the attendant to tell the few passengers aboard this empty flight, she thought.

Upon landing, she struggled with her oversized leather satchel. As predicted, the French businessman offered assistance. Strutting down the aisle, her free hands straightened out her silk gown. Behind her, waddled the surrogate baggage handler.

"I hope you find what you are looking for Miss Favreau," the flight attendant said cracking open the cabin door.

Graciously, she smiled thank you. Stepping through the doorway, she ran into a wall of sweltering moisture. Oh my god, she thought standing at the top of the gangway gulping thick humid air. Her knees turned to jelly. Panting she felt her hair and make-up wilt. Her Parisian dress slowly died.

"Is there a problem Miss?" the Frenchman behind her asked.

After a sobering pause, Elaine mumbled, "No." Racking a moist hand through her damp hair, she proceeded down the stairway. High heels clicked on the hot sparkling metal treads. Each step the tropical sunlight intensified. A hundred yards away, waves of heat lapped at the blurry terminal. I can make it she thought. Sweat flowed down her taunt skin. Under the shielding lee of the open-air facilities overhang, she sighed. Inhaling she got a whiff of the overcrowded terminal's occupants. Do these people ever bathe? She wondered with a sour face. The musty stench intensified. Dangling from the raised ceiling, fans swirled at full capacity over the noisy clamor of the Asian rabble. A few birds seeking escape darted back and forth through the rafters.

"This way Miss," her loaded down French escort said motioning with his head. "I've done this drill before. It's a little intimidating the first time."

"Thank you for your assistance, I'd be lost without you." She said touching his arm.

Through the short statured crowd, she followed close behind his bullying advance. Ignoring the locals waiting on line, he dropped his load in front of the immigration desk. "Give me your passport. I'll get us out of here *tout de suite*." He said sucking in his gut. His head jerk back at the sight Elaine's documentation. "You're an American?" He barked.

"Yes," Elaine said, awkwardly holding out her passport.

"My mistake mademoiselle," he said. No longer acknowledging her presence, he quietly cleared immigration and exited.

Watching the middle-aged pompous ass disappearing into the crowd, Elaine shook her head in disgust. Just as well, she thought. It will alleviate the awkward moment, when I'd have to abandon him.

After clearing customs, Elaine stared into the dark haired pale-skinned cackling throng.

"Pretty lady you need car?" one enterprising entrepreneur shouted out in English. Other offers for transportation services buzzed about in French and German.

Gazing over the sign-waving mob, she did her best not to make eye contact. A wiry Caucasian towered over the rolling waves of locals. Over his head, he held a make shift sign that read, ELAINE FAVREAU across the top, and just below it the name KELLY TAYLOR. Thank god, Elaine thought. Dropping her oversized satchel, she used both arms to get the frail man's attention. He appeared to be in his late twenties, wearing a white long sleeve shirt with the sleeves rolled up just past his boney elbows. His highwater light colored slacks exposed white socks and a scuffed up pair of black leather shoes. Who is this lackey, she wondered, definitely not the sophisticated Foreign Service representative I'd envisioned.

"Elaine?" He questioned with a friendly smile.

"*Oui*," Elaine responded.

"Please to meet you, I'm Mark Johnson," he said in English. Extending his hand, he added, "Welcome to Saigon."

She placed the handle of her heavy satchel into his inviting palm.

Wrinkling his brows, he turned to relay her travel bag to a porter. "Did you meet Miss Taylor on the flight?" Johnson questioned wiping an unshook hand on his trousers.

"Miss Taylor?" Elaine questioned.

"Yes, Kelly Taylor, she is also a clerical contract employee. I assumed the two of you would have met during the long journey." Johnson answered displaying the greeting sign in the direction of arriving passengers.

"I was fortunate to travel Deluxe Class, so regrettably did not have the opportunity to meet Miss Taylor," Elaine said. Johnson face puckered in response to the expensive travel accommodations. I had better explain, Elaine thought. "Since this was my first trip to the orient, my father wanted to make the long journey as pleasant as possible, by paying for the additional fare."

A slightly overweight woman in her early thirties approached the two Americans in the noisy terminal. "I'm Kelly Taylor," she exclaimed sporting a wide grin. Dropping her travel bag, she grabbed Johnson's hand and vigorously shook it. She startled Elaine with an oily palm repeating the introduction ritual.

Is Saigon a very big mistake, Elaine wondered examining Kelly Taylor and Mark Johnson? Just look at this girl, she thought. Kelly's dishwater blonde hair was pulled straight back into a taut ponytail. A large shiny blemished forehead dominated a round face. Various food stains accented the scruffy gal's baggy fitting white dress.

"Ladies, if you could give me your luggage claims I'll retrieve your baggage and we should be on our way," Johnson said. After receiving the tickets, he relayed them to a porter with instructions in Vietnamese.

Standing in uncomfortable silence, Johnson scratched his crew cut head. Glancing around he mumbled, "Please wait here, I just want to make sure there are no issues with your bags."

Breaking the silence, Kelly asked, "First time in the tropics?"

"Yes, why do you ask?" Elaine responded.

"You are not dressed appropriately," Kelly answered. "Before transferring to Saigon, I was stationed in Jakarta. You'll learn quickly to wear light, loose fitting attire."

You're wearing a stained two dollar cotton dress with flats and giving fashion advice, Elaine thought. She mustered up a slight smile at the frump dog's suggestion. How much longer must we wait, she wondered. Fidgeting through her purse, she sought solitude from the opinionated Kelly Taylor. Retrieving a cigarette, she took her time with the lighting ceremony. Puffing away in silence, she awaited the geeky Johnson's return.

Johnson and the Vietnamese driver tried to figure out the optimal configuration of luggage placement in the Embassy's Peugeot sedan. Casually smoking, Elaine ignored the frustrated glances. Even the bubbly Kelly Taylor, who only had two small suitcases, volunteered her expertise. The trio moved Elaine's various bags around attempting to find the magical combination. Rope securing an open trunk resolved the dilemma. Kelly and Elaine rode in the back seat separated by several bags. One of Kelly's small suitcases rested on her lap. Johnson sat up front with the driver. Elaine's hatboxes hindered the driver's ability to shift gears.

Gazing out the passenger's window of the hot cramped vehicle, Elaine pouted. The tarnished Pearl of the Far East flowed by. A warm breeze on her face provided some relief. Did I make a mistake? She questioned. I came for adventure and am greeted by a rude Frenchman, shabby companions and this sweltering heat. It was that interviewer at the Foreign Service department, she concluded, painting a picture of blowing palm trees, exotic pagodas and a colorful people. A sulking Elaine began to focus. French colonial architecture dominated the thoroughfares. In front of crowded Parisian outdoor cafes, a vibrant people conducted commerce. Buddhist monks in saffron robes accented the steady flow of costumed pedestrians. A wide smile replaced Elaine's puckered lips. Saigon is alive, she realized. I'm going to experience it.

The overloaded sedan drove through the gates of the US embassy. Elaine noticed three men having a conversation in the courtyard. The bleached blond tan Aryan wearing a light colored suit caught her attention. The jacket accentuated broad shoulders and a muscular frame. His thick fair hair fluttered in the breeze. Oh my, she thought. He appears to be about thirty years old, she estimated. I sure wish he had picked me up at the airport she fantasized.

In front of the chiseled blond, a clean-cut American in a Hawaiian shirt and baggy khaki trousers listened intensely. The casual clothing seemed out of step with the man's closely cut flat top salt and pepper hair. The third man was a small unique looking local with dark brown hair and a pale yellow almost white complexion. In a short-sleeved white shirt with black slacks, he looked bored puffing away on a cigarette. Hawaiian shirt acknowledged the passing sedan with a casually wave.

"Who is that?" Elaine questioned.

"That is Tom Roche. He is with the Military Advisory Group." Johnson said. Glancing over his shoulder, he winked at Kelly.

"I don't understand?" Elaine questioned. "Is this some inside joke? Why did you wink?"

"It means that is his cover," Kelly said. "You will figure this out soon enough."

Even more intrigued now by the stocky blond, Elaine asked, "Do you know who he was talking to?"

"I think the tribesman name is Loc. The German is Max Kohl, he is well known as the man who walked out of Isabelle." Johnson said.

"Isabelle?" Kelly questioned.

"He's referring to Dien Bien Phu, Isabelle was the southernmost garrison." Elaine informed recalling the catastrophic defeat covered in all the Paris newspapers. Sarcastically she added, "You will figure this out soon enough, Kelly."

CHAPTER TWO

Max placed the almost empty beer bottle on the wobbly table. He picked up the smoldering cigar balancing over the tabletop's edge. Placing the moist end of the stogy in the vice grip of back teeth, he puffed away. The smoldering stub contributed to the cloud floating over the heads of the crowded King Cobra Lodge. Leaning back, he rested his chair against the back wall. Beside him, the Laotian barmaid readjusted her chair. Cuddling up to his firm torso, she draped a young arm across his chest. His shoulder holstered Soviet Tokarev pistol, impeded the embrace. Across from the whore, sat the eighty something year old Pao. The tiny old Meo warrior in the black tunic and pants of his people weighed in at just over a hundred pounds. His thinning gray hair concealed under a blue turban. In his waistband, he proudly displayed a Makarov pistol.

It was harvest time in the Laotian highlands. This year's bountiful crop was exceptional. Thanks to the American's agricultural assistance, the morphine content of the opium had increased significantly.

The colorful crowd clamoring before Max consisted of other French war veterans, Corsican businessmen and local gangsters. Even a few Meo tribesmen sporting red and blue turbans celebrated with overpriced brand name liquor. Then of course, there were the Americans. A boisterous table of four Civil Air Transport pilots, pounded down beers, laughing uncontrollably. Max recognized Buck, the tall lanky cowboy. The Texan spoke a twangy version of French that rolled out of his large Adam's apple as a growl. At least he makes an attempt to communicate, Max thought. The other pilots could care less. Like most Americans, they are just plain cocky, he concluded. It's been over ten years since they took credit for defeating

Germany and yet they still celebrate as if it was yesterday. I guess I can't blame them he thought, losers need to forget, victors don't have too.

Catching Max gawking, Buck rose from his chair with a grin and a bottle of beer. He sauntered over with a stiff back as if he just ridden into town on a horse.

"Hello Maximilian," Buck said hovering over the table. Nodding at Pao, he added, "*Grand-pere.*"

"Evening Buck," Max responded motioning towards an empty seat, "Care to join us?"

Pulling out the chair, Buck sat down. Leaning back, he yelled, "Barkeep another round!"

Oh how the Americans like to flaunt their wealth, Max thought, over tipping and driving up the prices in Laos on liquor, cigarettes and whores.

Leaning forward Buck said, "Roche would like to meet with you in Saigon." Pulling out a folded paper from his breast pocket, he slid it across the stained tabletop adding, "This is the updated CAT flight schedule, no urgency, whatever works for you in the next couple of days."

"Thanks," Max said picking up the timetable.

A tray of glistening amber bottles arrived. Buck handed the petite server a large denomination *paistre*. "Keep the change," he announced grinning at her wide-eyed response to the gratuity.

Touching bottles with his host, Max asked, "Tell me Buck, where did you learn to speak French."

"Mrs. Clifford," Buck said delightfully flexing his eyebrows. "Old Colonel Clifford returned from the war with a bride half his age. To the victors go the spoils and Mrs. Clifford was quite a prize. The French beauty was so top heavy; it seemed she had a restless poodle strapped across her chest. I took her high school French classes. For four years, I stared at the strained buttons of her taut blouses with an erection. In spite of my infatuation, I learned a second language." He took a satisfying reflective swig of beer. "And now I find myself with a useful language skill in a country without a descent pair of breasts." Looking over at Max's bargirl, he added, "No offense intended mademoiselle."

Max chuckled, the Americans are a strange lot with their obsession of the female bosom.

A distant thunderous roar shook the saloon. Max leapt to his feet, toppling the young barmaid to the floor. Pulling out his pistol, he squinted at the bewildered Texan. The standing bar crowds' heads jerked back and forth in search of an answer. In the midst of the nervous silence, Max observed three men at a nearby table smugly drinking. A bottle of Johnny Walker prominently placed between them. He recognized two of them as local Corsican smugglers. What is your story, he questioned focused on the Corsican's well-groomed Vietnamese companion. In a grey silk suit accented by a thin red tie and matching red pocket-handkerchief, the snickering Asian sipped on the golden liquor. His perfectly parted slick black hair shined in the barroom light. He appears to be in his twenties, Max estimated, but guessing the ages of the locals is always difficult.

"It's the airport!" informed a Chinese merchant seated by the window. The crowd surged across the room to confirm. The barroom noise slowly reappeared as whispers.

"Adios Max," Buck said chugging his beer. The Texan joined his fellow Americans in the investigating race to the airport.

Re-holstering his weapon, Max gave a slight shrug to the seated Pao. He assisted the fallen working girl to her feet. Reseating himself, he glanced at the floor in search of his cigar stub. Scanning the stained wood planks, he could smell the faint aroma of burnt caramel. Over the odor of stale beer and cigarette smoke, the fragrance of burning opium permeated the bar. Abandoning his quest, Max pulled out a new cigar. A smuggler detonated a competitor's opium shipment, he concluded. The cost of trafficking in Laotian jam has just gone up.

Pao tugged on Max's sleeve and pointed in the direction of the water closet. Max nodded. The tiny warrior waddled through the crowd towards relief. As Pao exited, Rene Bergot stormed into the saloon. Soot covered his face and clothing. Framed by the open door, the tall thin pilot scowled at the patrons. His chest pulsed with rage. Max grimaced. Rene was the target of the blast, he realized. I'm sorry my friend, he thought.

Rene focused on the two Corsicans and the Asian sipping scotch. The snorting pilot charged. Slamming his soiled hands on their table, he howled, "You sons of bitches, I know it was you!"

"Careful, fly boy," a Corsicans calmly warned.

"I know a plastique explosion, you blew up my fully loaded Cessna," Rene barked.

"If you are looking for employment, we can always use another bush pilot," the Corsican offered. His table companions snickered.

"Go to hell!" Rene shouted. The veins in his neck pulsed.

The two Corsicans rose from the table. Reaching into their suit coats, they drew pistols. The barroom crowd retreated to safer vantage points. A shrill whistle pierced the tense standoff. The investigating audience discovered the tiny Pao blowing hard through the two fingers in his mouth. Max placed his hand on the old man's shoulder silencing the attention getter.

"Rene," Max called out, "always good to see you my friend. Would you care to join us for a drink?"

Rene glanced down at the targeting side arms. He took a deep composing breath. Slowly he walked over towards Max and Pao.

Good my friend, Max thought. Remember your military discipline. Lose your temper, lose your life.

Hugging the Frenchman, Max whispered, "It will be alright."

"Max," one of the Corsican yelled. "Control your *copain.*"

"Kiss my ass," Max said softly to a chuckling audience. He handed several *paistres* to the bargirl. "Chimmy please get us a beer and a scotch." He asked. A shaken Rene took her vacated chair. Chimmy pranced back with the drinks. "Thanks," Max whispered waiving off his change and the girl.

Sipping a scotch with a shaking hand, Rene mumbled, "Goddamn, Guerini syndicate."

"Rene," Max said. "You knew it would be only a matter of time before a big fish would start to gobble up the guppies in this opium pond."

"That's easy for you to say Max. You're backed by the Americans." Rene commented.

"Don't forget my reputation," Max said touching his beer bottle with Rene's glass of scotch.

"To the man that walked out of Isabelle," Rene toasted. "Thanks for coming to my rescue."

Pao politely tapped Max on the shoulder and pointing towards the toilette sign. Max nodded. The old man slowly rose using the wobbly table for balance. He just pissed, Max realized. How many times does he have to go?

Strutting by the Corsicans' table, Pao glared at the three men. His weathered hand patted the pistol tucked into his waistband. Passing their puzzled expressions, he accelerated towards the facilities. Observing the old warrior's defiance, Max chuckled. I wonder if the three gangsters have any inkling as to how many men's lives Pao has ended, he thought.

Max turned to Rene and asked, "What are you going to do now?"

"Well I'm not going to work for the Guerini brothers and their mystery political sponsor," Rene answered.

"Who do you think is backing them?" Max asked.

"You tell me, you're employed by the Americans," Rene questioned.

"It's not the Americans. That is not their style." Max responded. "When French Intelligence abandoned their opium monopoly, the Americans could have easily stepped into their shoes but didn't. I also, think we can rule out the new Prime Minister Diem. The American's puppet is closing the opium dens and has enacted sweeping reforms."

"Max, all I know is that the independent operators are slowly being eliminated with plastique explosives, arrests and seizures." Rene said.

"Arrest and seizure is a business risk. The export of the drug is illegal. Careless smugglers pay the price," Max commented.

"I agree Max, but the Guerini cartel continues to grow. The Corsican syndicate operates with absolute impunity, no arrest and no seizures. The only way you can do that is with a strong political alliance." Rene said and then glancing over at the well dressed Asian drinking the Corsican's scotch added, "I bet you that slick monkey knows."

CHAPTER THREE

Wispy clouds accented the deep blue Laotian sky. The stagnant afternoon air held moisture from a brief morning shower. Shielded from the sun in a conical leaf hat, Mei in short baggy black pants picked red tomatoes from the vine. A crude willow basket collected the fresh fruit. Damp soil soothed her bare-feet. Harvesting several plump beefy tomatoes, she paused scanning the dark rich earth. This is where the assassin shot by Pao's arrow bleed to death, she reflected. "The fruit that springs from the blood of your enemies taste the sweetest," she mumbled. Stretching she turned tilting back her pointed head cover and looked down the sloping hillside. Somewhere under the waist deep elephant grass and flowering weeds lay the bodies of Petru Rossi and his henchmen, she realized.

The tall grasses swayed from the touch of a summer's breeze. Mei dug her toes into the moist dirt. Closing her eyes, she felt the soft wind caress her angelic features. It's been over seven years, she reflected. I was fifteen standing in the family garden and sold into a brothel fate. She grimaced at the image of her broken peasant father telling her it would be good for her and the family. Bastard, she thought. There is nothing good about servicing a never-ending line of large white men. Yes, I was once a whore, she thought holding her head high in the summer wind. I sucked and coupled with the indifferent French troops in the valley of death, only to show them compassion during the communist assault. I became a person during those dark bunker days, she realized. I became a nurse.

"Mei," Lan called out from an open window of the raised residence. "May wants to be fed."

Glancing up Mei saw her former mobile brothel companion bouncing the baby. Seeing her finicky daughter, she smiled and answered, "I'll be right in."

Walking into cool shade, Mei passed two sleeping dogs. Adjusting the basket of fresh tomatoes resting on her hip, she scurried up the wooden stairs. Her creaking assent woke the napping Pao. Leaning back in a hard wood chair, the old Meo warrior licked his lips eyeing the bright red produce. Beside Pao, his constant companion Pasha reclined in the open doorway. The mangy black dog with white stocking feet and a graying mask extended an ear skyward. Reaching into the basket, Mei chose a beefy tomato for her adopted tribal grandfather.

"Thank you," he mumbled biting into the juicy sphere.

With a long stride, Mei stepped over the reclining mutt. The cheery Pasha's happy tail pounded the wood deck. Entering the longhouse over the thumping dog, she heard the whining of her hungry child. A shirt-less Max and singlet wearing Loc sat at the dining room table cleaning hand guns. Lan playfully tossed May. Placing the harvest basket on the table, Mei smiled at her cigarette-smoking husband. Why must you go to Saigon? She wondered. I already miss you; she realized feeling a twinge of sadness.

Untying the cloth strap under her chin, Mei placed the palm coolie hat over the produce. Sitting beside her husband, she unbuttoned her smock. Lan handed the fluid baby into Mei's dancing fingers. Mother's milk silenced the suckling child. Stroking the black wispy hair on the tiny head, Mei beamed. All was right in her world.

The pudgy round faced Lan meandered behind Max. Placing her hands on his broad shoulders, she initiated a seductive massage. The German's taut muscles scarred with the tracks of a professional soldier flexed. Uncomfortable he fidgeted under Lan's flirtatious kneading.

Mei shot a snickering glance at her husband. Loc grinned back. Coddling the breast-feeding child, Mei tried not to laugh. My little sister is smitten, she realized. I found the love of a good man, she thought and so should Lan.

CHAPTER FOUR

The slow random metal pecks of a manual typewriter echoed in the small cluttered office. On the paper-strewn desktop, a large black stapler resting on its side held down a towering stack of files. An array of pencils and pens stood at attention in a leaping tiger handled white ceramic mug. The gold metallic letters 'LSU' embossed the mug's curved surface. The tiny room's only picture, a black and white photo of six smiling helmeted US marines in sweat soaked fatigues. In the photo with a tropical backdrop, a much younger and thinner Tom Roche proudly displayed a tattered Japanese rising sun flag.

Hunched over the Remington typewriter, Roche's flexed index fingers poked at the keyboard. Glancing down at crude notes scribbled on a legal pad, he cracked his knuckles. Taking a deep breath, he returned to the tedious hunt and peck task. *It's bad enough, I have to deal with the Corsicans, the Binh Xuyen criminal organization, and the incompetent Prime Minister Diem, but having to type is really too much to ask,* he thought. Craning his neck, he discovered he had typed off the page. "Goddamn it," he mumbled. Grabbing the carbon paper interfaced text with extreme prejudice; he ripped it out of the machine. Wadding up the mistake with a blackening hand, he threw the smeared ink mess into the wastebasket. Leaning back in a squeaking swivel chair, he plopped a scruffy pair of penny loafers on the crowded desktop. A black smudged palm pulled a pack of Lucky Strikes from the breast pocket of a floral printed shirt. *Time for a break,* he concluded lighting up.

"Mister Roche," a shy female Asian embassy staff member whispered from the doorway.

"What is it?" he barked spinning to confront the intrusion.

The wide-eyed petite girl dressed in western business attire swallowed hard. Softly she answered. "The German and the tribesman are here to see you, sir. The guards detained them at the gate as you requested."

"Thanks," Roche responded. Spinning back around, he put out the cigarette in an overflowing ashtray. Standing up he pulled out a side drawer, and retrieved his Baby Browning pistol. Placing the small gun in the front pocket of his baggy slacks, he realized being armed was proper etiquette for a covert meeting. This meeting is just the reprieve I need from all this clerical bullshit, he realized scowling at the silent typewriter. Besides it will be good to see Max and Loc again, he concluded. Picking up a large brown package from the cramp accommodations only other chair, he headed down to the appointment.

It was a muggy afternoon. Roche walked across the forecourt with the package tucked under his left arm. At the gate Max puffed on a large dark cigar. Squatting on the concrete sidewalk, the much smaller Loc enjoyed a cigarette. Studying the crouching tribesman, Roche shook his head. I'll never understand how the locals find that bent knee repose relaxing, he pondered. As Roche approached, Loc easily elevated out of the stoop.

"*Ami*, always good to see you," Max said.

"As well kraut," Roche said shaking the German's hand. "Congratulations Loc," He announced repeating the handshake ritual. "I hear you are a father."

Loc's head jerked back. Smiling he responded, "Thank you, sir."

"How do you always know what's going on?" asked a squinting Max.

"I told you before; I'm in the information business." Roche chuckled. Handing the brown paper package to Loc, he said, "Just a little gift from the Central Intelligence Agency for your daughter. I hope Mei and baby are doing well."

"My family is fine, thank you again." Loc said trying to suppress the nervous grin common among the mountain tribes.

Lighting up a cigarette, Roche asked, "So tell me about the economy in Northern Laos?"

"It was a good year for the regions only cash crop." Max informed. "Rivalry amongst the transporters of the product is heating up. One player in particular is methodically eliminating the competition. The net result of the turf war is the price for the product in Phong Savin has increased to seventeen-hundred *piastres* a kilo or let's see in US dollars..." Max paused and looking up to calculate the exchange rate added, "just a little over twenty one dollars a kilo."

"Is our franchisee at risk?" Roche asked.

"No not at this time," Max answered shaking his head. "The Corsican cartel is focused on easier prey; smaller players. They are backed by the Guerini Brothers out of Marseille, are you familiar with them?" Max asked.

"Yes very much so," Answered a nodding Roche. "The Guerini syndicate is the reason the demand for the product continues to rise. As the dens in Saigon are being shut down, the Corsicans are opening up new laboratories in Marseille to enhance the products value." Taking a puff of nicotine, he added quietly on the exhale, "Heroin."

"The question I can't answer is who their Vietnamese political backer is. I'm told it has to be someone fairly high in the Diem regime. Since you are in the information business, you probably already know." Max said smiling.

"We have some suspects but that is about it at this time. If you find out please let me know." Roche said.

"You really want me to earn my salary don't you?" Max said.

A Peugeot Sedan loaded down with luggage pulled through the Embassy's gate. Rope tethers secured an open truck bursting with baggage. Roche waved at a wiry man hanging out the front seat passenger-window of the cramped car. The skinny passenger waved back.

"Who was that?" Max asked.

"That gentlemen," Roche responded, "Is the answer to my prayers. Those are the new contract employees that will alleviate my typing woes."

The Peugeot Sedan stopped. The vehicle's metal doors swung open. A female passenger in the rear of the vehicle pivoted around to exit. A long pair of shapely legs came into view. A tall attractive blonde emerged into the embassy forecourt. Placing her hands on her lower back, she stretched.

"That is just not right," Roche mumbled.

Max placed his hand on Roche's shoulder and said. "It looks like your prayers have been answered. Do you think she can type?"

"Who cares," Roche chuckled.

"I don't understand," Loc questioned. "She a very big woman."

Max and Roche laughed. Roche clarified, "She's big in all the right places, Loc."

The leggy beauty caught them glaring. Max and Roche turned away. Loc continued to observe.

"She come this way," Loc informed.

Max and Roche glanced over their shoulders. High heels clicked on the rough concrete. Strutting towards the embassy gate, she smiled. Her wrinkled silk dress flapped in the warm breeze.

"Sorry to trouble you gentlemen, but I need a light." She said flashing an unlit cigarette with a nimble wrist.

Reaching into his pants pocket, Max retrieved his Zippo lighter to oblige. Leaning forward she accepted the flame from his extended hand. After several puffs, she grabbed his wrist and casually turned it to read the lighter's inscription: *3e Bataillon/13e Demi-Brigade de la Legion Etrangere.* "You were with the three-thirteenth," She asked exhaling.

"Yes I was, I'm Max Kohl," he said. Motioning towards the tribesman and American he added, "This is my partner Loc and I believe you will be typing for this gentleman. This is Tom Roche."

"Pleased to meet all of you, I'm Elaine Favreau" She said.

"Elaine!!" Johnson called from the pile of baggage surrounding the sedan. "We need some assistance with your luggage, please."

Rolling her eyes, she ignored the interruption and inhaled deeply on the fresh cigarette. Tossing it on the ground, she daintily extinguished it with the pointed toe of a high-heeled shoe. Looking up she said. "Mr. Roche, I am looking forward to working with you." She took a few steps towards the vehicle. Pausing she turned back and added, "I hope to see you again Mr. Kohl."

"I bet she can't type," Roche mumbled focused on her swaying hips. "And I guarantee you by tomorrow afternoon ever male staffer at the embassy will know her name."

"I still think she too big," Loc said.

CHAPTER FIVE

Like a room full of chirping crickets, the secretarial staff at the US embassy banged away on manual typewriters. Three large second story windows framed cascading Saigon rain. The splatter of falling water accompanied the clamoring machines. A large clock hung on the back wall. The long hand clicked off another minute. Below the timepiece, a framed color photo of Dwight David Eisenhower. The commander-in-chief's image gazed across two parallel rows of a dozen female occupied desks. Strategically placed elevated fans churned humid air. The manufactured breeze sent a loose sheet of paper across the linoleum flooring.

The rogue page floated under Elaine Favreau's desk. The sultry blonde sat behind an idle typewriter. On the edge of her desk perched, John Matthews. He sure is confident, she thought looking up at the suit and tie wearing thirty-something Matthews. There is apparently no shortage of Brylcreem in Indochina, she concluded observing his thick black hair fashioned into a watered down pompadour.

"I know Saigon is a little frightening at first, but once you become acclimated it truly is an amazing place." Matthews said.

"I know what you mean," Elaine responded. "I had the same reservations when I first arrived in Paris, but quickly fell in love with the city."

"You'll find that Saigon is like a distant cousin to Paris, with a unique oriental flair." He commented.

"You make it sound so intriguing. I can hardly wait to explore its wonders," she said.

In the adjacent workstation, Kelly Taylor harshly banged away on a typewriter key board. No doubt, the carbon papered text would be legible on all pages.

Glancing over at the industrious Miss Taylor, Matthews abandoned his perch. Clearing his throat, he said. "Well I better get going. It was a pleasure meeting you Elaine. Let me know when you are free. I'd love to show you the city."

"Thank you, John." Elaine said to the third Saigon orientation offer she received that day. "Unfortunately, I'm still a little fatigued and disoriented from my long flight, you understand?"

"Of course," He nodded. "Just let me know when you're available."

Eyeing the exiting Matthews, Kelly stopped her fanatical pounding. "Elaine," She said puckering her face, "Have you filed those reports for Mr. Roche?"

"No Kelly," Elaine responded. "I would have had to leave the room to do so, and since I've been seated next to you since you last asked. It has not been done."

Kelly snorted. Her fanatical fingers returned to punishing the key board.

Elaine rose. Straitening her polka dot dress, she glanced around the room. Squints and stares greeted her. Collecting a stack of manila folders, she headed to the file room. In her exiting wake, whispers replaced the chirping typewriters.

Entering the windowless space lined with grey metal drawer cabinets, she took a deep breath. I hope the male welcoming committee will not be able to find me here, she thought. I might even get some work done today. Sitting down in a metal folding chair, she slipped off her red high heels. God, that feels good, she thought massaging swollen stocking feet. The price of fashion in the tropics is painfully expensive, she realized. In nylon stocking feet, she stood and went about the mundane chore of orderly storage. Half way through the boring exercise, she came across a folder labeled; MAX *KOHL CONFIDENTIAL*. After glancing over her shoulder at the empty doorway, she pulled out the file to peruse its contents.

Stapled to the inside leaf were two black and white photos. One a head shot of a defiant looking teenage Max in a French Foreign Legion kepi. The other more current of the German in jungle fatigues with a rain forest background. Aided by an extended finger, Elaine scanned down the summary page; *Max Kohl Ground personnel Civil Air Transport - Phong Savin, Laos.* She continued, born *1926, Nuremberg, Germany.* That makes him twenty-nine years old, she calculated. He is only a five years older than I am. Perfect, she thought recalling the age difference of the middle-aged professor she targeted in her college days at Penn State. What a disaster that turned out to be, the poor man left his wife and lost his job. Besides that, he was a terrible lover. Turning the page, she skimmed through Max's Military background, let's see *Hitler Youth marksmanship awards,* okay. *Captured at the Battle of Caen France at seventeen,* Elaine had to look at that again. He was only seventeen, I wasn't even driving then, she realized. *Recruited from Allied prisoner of war camp into the French Foreign Legion after the war;* Elaine rubbing her chin thought of Gary Cooper in the film Beau Geste. How romantic she reflected. *Distinguished himself by being one of the few Europeans to break out of the siege at Dien Bien Phu and escape to Laos.* "The man who walked out of Isabelle," she whispered. Looking up from the text, she checked her surroundings before continuing. *Successfully lead a covert team into the Communist controlled North and extracted the Meo village that aided him on his escape.* Courageous and honorable, she concluded. *Eliminated a Corsican Assassination attempt on his life with extreme prejudice;* Elaine's hand began to shake; *eliminated a Binh Xuyen assassination attempt on his life with extreme prejudice.* Elaine closed the folder and took a deep breath. My god, she thought, Max Kohl is no college professor or struggling French artist.

CHAPTER SIX

It was a bright sunny Sunday morning. A Citron taxi pulled in front of Saigon's famed Notre Dame Cathedral. Exiting the cab, Elaine joined the Catholic stream of worshipers entering the ornate facility for mass. A dark wide brimmed hat shaded her symmetric features. A wide glossy black belt cinched a form fitting white cotton dress tightly around her waist. Over her shoulder dangled a gold chain-strap attached to a quilted leather Chanel handbag.

Entering the church, she participated in the admission requirement by dipping a finger into the marble bowl of holy water and making the sign of the cross. The thing she liked most about the Sunday Catholic ritual was the service would be completed in less than an hour. A small weekly insurance premium for eternal life, she rationalized. The other inducement the religion offered was that it catered to her sense of fashion, in particular the veiling requirement for women. There was no better forum to exhibit one's hats.

Parading down the center aisle in search of an open pew, she thrived at the attention she received from Saigon's religious elite. Anticipating her approach an acne-scarred Frenchman scooted his family over relinquishing the desirable aisle seat. She genuflected and sat down. In the obnoxiously wide hat, she graciously nodded to her benefactor for his Christian kindness. He smiled at her with crooked teeth. His chubby wife glared in distain.

Whispers and rotating heads from the congregation announced the arrival of the Ngo family. Impeccably dressed in a grey suit, the bachelor Prime Minister Diem strolled down the aisle. His younger brother Nhu, Nhu's young wife and three children followed. Madame Nhu, the unofficial first lady of South Vietnam regally strutted in a tight long sleeved silk dress.

The formfitting gown accented a petite figure with nary a trace of the three children it bore. A simple long black lace mantillas draped over a classic bouffant hairstyle fulfilled her female head-covering requirement.

Once the rulers of Vietnam situated, the multi-language congregation rose to start the one-hour Latin service. Spotting Tom Roche in the crowd, Elaine grinned, it makes sense she thought. With his Cajun accent, he is no doubt a good Catholic boy from Louisiana.

The fifty-minute ordeal concluded with a departing hymn. Elaine shuffled out of the stuffy church with the flock and a sense of accomplishment. The warm sun felt good. An orderly taxi queue had already formed in front of the cathedral. "Shit," she mumbled at the long cab line. Glancing around at the parishioners mingling in front of the church, she spotted a cigarette smoking Roche.

"Good morning Mr. Roche," she said. "I'm glad to see that I'm not the only Catholic that works at the Embassy."

"Good Morning Elaine, and please call me Tom," he replied.

"Well Tom, do you have a cigarette for a former parochial school girl?" She asked.

Roche smiled flicking a pack of Lucky Strikes in her direction. A single canister popped out of the soft box. Accepting the gift, she leaned forward as he lit it.

Exhaling a relaxing plume, she asked, "So does your friend Mr. Kohl come to the embassy often?" Roche flinched. Too quick, she realized. I should have slowly steered the conversation. Identifying a potential suitor was a mistake. Male predators do not like hearing about the competition, she concluded.

"Max?" Roche responded. "You're referring to Max Kohl?"

"Yes," Elaine said. "I met him with you on my arrival. He seemed quite pleasant."

"Max, I guess you could say is a contract employee like yourself. We do meet periodically here in Saigon but he resides in Laos. I do consider him a friend, but Elaine...how do I say this," Roche took a long toke on his cigarette. Exhaling he continued. "Max is a very unique individual. He is pleasant enough, but like most of us, he has a dark side."

So the former legionnaire regularly visits Saigon, she thought. That's all I need to know. Reaching over, she touched Roche's arm and said, "Thank you Tom for your insights, there are so many interesting characters here in Indochina, like you."

He grinned at the compliment.

"Tell me Tom do you know Prime Minister Diem?" she asked.

"We've met on several occasions; however I doubt he would remember me. Every time I've been introduced to him, he always replies that he is pleased to meet me." Motioning with his smoldering cigarette to a crowd gathered behind Elaine, he said. "It appears the Ngo family is still holding court."

Elaine turned. On the green manicured lawn, Catholic well-wishers paid homage to their benefactors. An apparent team of well-dressed security personnel surrounded the ruling family. Elaine focused on the petite Madame Nhu. The Asian woman has an incredible sense for fashion, she thought. Making eye contact, Elaine smiled. Madame Nhu said something to an aid, who took charge of the children. Leaving the informal receiving line, she approached the Americans. Two members of the security team followed.

"I'm so sorry to interrupt," Madame Nhu said. "I am *Trần Lệ Xuân*, I could not help but admire your purse, is that a Chanel bag?"

"Please to meet you Madame Nhu, I'm Elaine Favreau, and this is Tom Roche. And yes this is the handbag that has taken Paris by storm. It came out last February." Elaine said handing the quilted bag for the first lady to admire.

"My dear," Madame Nhu said stroking the stitched leather. "For as much as I detest the French, I still admire their style." Draping the gold chain strap over her shoulder, she twisted from side to side mimicking a walking motion. Handing the purse back, she said. "Thank you Elaine it was so nice meeting you," then turning to Roche added, "It is nice to see you again Major Roche."

"Madame Nhu," Roche nodded.

"Elaine, unfortunately I have some family obligations this afternoon," Madame Nhu confessed, playfully rolling her eyes. "But we need to get together; I'd love to hear what other trends are emerging out of Paris."

"It would be my pleasure," Elaine responded.

As Madame Nhu walked away with her escorts she turned and said, "Elaine I'll have someone contact you this week through the US Embassy to make the arrangements."

"I'm looking forward to it," Elaine replied.

Elaine calmly took another puff on her cigarette, and whispered to Roche, "It seems that Madame Nhu remembered you."

"Elaine this is big," Roche declared bobbing his head. "We have been trying for some time to get someone into the inner circle of Ngo family. It may be just girls talking about purses, but you need to be briefed and prepared for your upcoming rendezvous." Taking one last drag off his cigarette, he flicked the butt into the street adding, "You may have typed your last memo."

CHAPTER SEVEN

The C-119 flying Boxcar hummed along peacefully in the clear blue skies above landlocked Laos. Beneath the soaring advance, sharp mountains and deep ravines blanketed the chaotic topography. The pilots spotted a river traversing in the depths of a canyon and a carved out patch of green from a tribal village's farm. Random smoke strings fluttering skyward, identified the existence of numerous hill tribes. The aircraft decelerated. The topical forest receded. A plateau of rolling hills, speckled with random clusters of carved out boulders appeared. The transport made a rough landing skipping along the isolated but heavily trafficked dirt runway at the Phong Savin airport. Jostling around with Red Cross humanitarian freight, Max held onto to a cargo netting for balance. The only other passenger his tribal partner, Loc. Max observed his Tai companion's child like enthusiasm. Loc is anxious to see his family, he thought. How much longer can I count on him as backup? Max wondered. It will be difficult without him. Since we walked out of Dien Bien Phu, we have relied on each other to navigate through the minefields of Indochina.

"Do you think Mei will like the gift?" Max asked preparing to exit.

"Very much," Loc replied hugging Roche's maternity present. "It's good to be home."

Max smiled. I would have wanted to spend a few days in Saigon to enjoy that city's pleasures, he thought. Loc is no longer interested, he realized. The only thing that concerns the tribesman is Mei and his daughter May.

Hopping out of the rear cargo door, Max waived adieu to the cowboy pilot. The twin-engine aircraft continued to produce a deafening drone.

Teasing his partner, Max yelled, "Do you want to stop at the King Cobra for a beer, before we head over to the longhouse to deliver your package?"

Frowning at the invitation, Loc hollered, "No!"

The aircraft suddenly silenced. Max and Loc began their trek to the frontier town of Phong Savin. Passing the last hanger facility of the airport, two familiar Corsicans in wrinkled business suits stepped out of the late afternoon shadows.

Sucking on a cigarette, Tino leaned into Max. Beside Tino, the greasy Carlo scowled. In a low gruff tone, Tino stated, "I need to speak to you."

Max quickly surveyed the surroundings for a possible ambush. Not wanting to converse in the open, he pushed Tino aside and headed back into the shadows. "What do you want?" he said in a solemn tone.

"We want you to deliver a message to your American sponsors." Tino answered. "In order to continue a transport operation out of Phong Savin without governmental intervention, we will require a twenty percent tariff on all jam exported."

"I'll deliver the message," Max conceded. "It may be an easier sell, if I could tell them who in the government is requiring this graft."

"Don't ever question us you *Boche* errand boy," Carlo barked. "If it was up to me, I would have relayed our terms through one of the whores at your longhouse."

Max frowned at the unprofessional outburst. He placed a restraining hand on Loc's shoulder. The touch revealed the insult had no affect on the tribesman.

"Max, I apologize for Carlo's sudden display of emotion, he was a close associate of Petru Rossi." Tino explained. Glancing at Carlo, he added, "We all must put the past behind us in order to maintain stability in this lucrative trade."

"I understand," Max said slightly pulling open his suit coat. Grinning he added, "Carlo, if you would like to pay your respects to the deceased pimp Petru Rossi. I can point you in the direction of his shallow grave. It is easy to find. Just follow your Corsican snout to the stench of urine. Occasionally I find satisfaction in pissing on his interned remains."

Carlo lunged. Max's extraordinary hand speed pulled out his Soviet side arm. The German slammed the pistol's butt into the charging Corsican's face. The blow toppled a wailing Carlo to the ground. Dropping the maternity package, Loc revealed his targeting sidearm. So much for Corsican patience, Max thought. Nothing trumps the disciplined reflex of a German infantryman.

Carlo came to rest at Max's feet on all fours. Blood flowing from his mouth produced a glossy burgundy puddle. Broken teeth accented the small crimson pond.

Re-holstering his weapon, Max calmly addressed Tino, "I'll deliver your message, but I ask again, who in the government are you working with?"

"Max I don't know," Tino responded looking down at his crippled companion. "I can tell you they are well connected within the Diem regime. They have enough pull to have our smuggling pilots released if arrested and have our competitors incarcerated. We will extend the same privileges for your operation for a twenty percent fee."

"Thank you," Max said. "I'll relay your request." Glancing down at Carlo, he warned, "If you ever insult my family again, I'll kill you, no hesitation."

Max picked up the brown paper package. He and Loc slowly exited the conference. On the red clay thoroughfare of the frontier town, Loc concealed his weapon.

Taking the package, Loc asked, "What did you mean your family?"

Proudly grinning, Max explained, "I meant our family, you know Mei, your daughter May, our grandfather Pao and little sister Lan...the family."

Loc chuckled, "I like that."

The highland night pushed the fading sunlight aside. Yawning at the end of the long day, Max felt chilled on the red clay pathway. Loc accelerated down the last hundred yards toward their raised thatch roofed residence. Illuminating kerosene lamps dangled along the porch. The old warrior Pao sat guard on the top step. A loaded crossbow cradled across his lap. Pasha reclined at his side.

Ascending the creaking stairway, Max patted the seated Pao on the shoulder. "Good job," he said. The mangy Pasha hopped up and down on the splintered wood-planked deck. A wagging happy tail hindered access.

"Mei," Loc called out over the whimpering hyperactive mutt. His bare-footed woman in black pajamas ran out the open doorway. She wrapped her arms around her returning husband.

Observing the happy couple, Max grinned. My partner is a lucky man, he thought. She really is a beauty. Motherhood only enhanced her voluptuous figure, he realized.

The short pudgy Lan carrying Mei and Loc's daughter joined the festivities. The baby's wide brown eyes gawked at all the commotion. Taking the infant, Loc lifted May over his small frame. In the sooty glow of kerosene light, he examined his daughter. Relieved of the child, Lan wrapped herself around Max's arm.

Max grimaced as the snuggling former child of the Saigon streets patted his chest. I know you have a big crush on me, he thought. Why did I sleep with her, he regretted. That one coupling was a big mistake, he realized. Being drunk is not an excuse. Timidly he returned the embrace. Smiling into her round face, he concluded last thing I want to do is break your heart.

"I sure can use a beer," Max said subtly dismissing Lan with the errand. Sitting down on the porch next to Pao, he hugged the overactive Pasha into submission. The black dog plopped down beside him on the deck. Max pulled out and lit a cigar. Seeking attention, Pasha emitted a disapproving whimper. Blowing smoke into the night sky, Max chuckled. Scratching behind the dog's ear, he appeased the fussy mutt. A curious Pao tugged on Max's coat. The old man pointed at dried blood on the sleeve. Splatter no doubt from Carlo's split lip, Max concluded. Pao patted the German's leg. His weathered face gave a reassuring nod.

"Thanks little sister," Max said as Lan handed him and Pao cold bottles of brew.

Ripping paper caught Lan's attention. She joined Loc and Mei's unwrapping of the American's maternity gift. After the third sigh of delight, Max turned around. The girls in awe admired miniatures clothing.

Those Americans are a strange lot, Max thought picturing Roche purchasing baby clothes.

"Max," Loc called out holding up a stuffed animal. "What is this?"

"It's called a Teddy bear," Max informed.

"What is it for?" Loc questioned.

"It's for entertaining the baby," Max responded. "She...plays with it I think...I really don't know."

Turning back around, Max took a big swig of beer. The stuffed bear evoked an uncomfortable reflection of a lost childhood. Staring into the starry sky, he reflected. My participation in the Hitler Youth stared at age six, he recalled. At ten years of age, I officially joined the *Jungvolk*. There was no stuffed animals, no place for toys. Physical strength, military preparedness and racial purity were all that mattered. I lectured my parents about the folly of Christmas, he bitterly recalled. After all the Christ Child was a Jew. He pictured his weeping mother and terrified father listening how the archaic religious celebration was out of step with the Third Reich. They had too, he realized. I would have reported them to the Nazi authorities. That holiday season, my Catholic parents quietly observed the winter solstice out of fear.

Lan joined Max at the end of the porch. Looking down at her, he realized she had begged on the streets of Saigon as a child until she was old enough to sell herself. My lack of childhood memories seems trivial in comparison, he concluded. Putting his arm around her, he hugged the young girl out of genuine affection. Don't worry *Little Sister* he thought, life can only get better.

CHAPTER EIGHT

Roche exited the silent smoke filled conference room. The hairs on the back of his neck prickled. Standing in the darkened embassy hallway, he carefully closed the heavy wood door behind him. A cloud of cigarette smoke escaped over his head. The metallic click of the doorknob echoed down the late night corridor. From the enclosed chamber muffled dialogue resumed. Roche stood at attention, the polished wood door inches from his face. Unable to decipher the ongoing discussion, he slowly turned scratching his head. The three hour debriefing had drained him.

"How did it go?" Matthews asked.

"Jesus!" Roche exclaimed jumping back. "What are you doing here?" He asked catching his breath.

Seated in the shadows of the deserted hallway, Matthews rose asking, "What did you think of the Assistant Secretary of State?"

"Just another bureaucrat," Roche shrugged. "I don't think he appreciated my candor."

"Such as?" Matthews probed.

"I told the room flat out, that the Prime Minister was an ass," Roche declared.

Matthews's face puckered.

"Of course I backed up my conclusion with fact." Roche clarified. "We propped up this political appointee, with US taxpayer greenbacks. And the ass Diem just sits back with this smug sense of entitlement stirring up the hornets' nest."

"I know it's late. But I have a bottle in my desk, are you up for a drink?" Matthews asked.

"Bourbon?"

"Is there anything else?" Matthews responded.

The two agents walked through the lonely dark late night halls of the US Embassy. Matthews confiscated two coffee cups on the way to his small office. Inverting the mugs, he released a tablespoon of stagnant java on the waxed flooring.

"I must apologize for a lack of ice," Matthews said flipped the light switch in the cramped office. Extracting a fifth of Jim Beam from the bottom desk drawer, he poured generous servings into each mug. Toasting his fatigued colleague, he mumbled, "To Democracy."

Touching a lipstick-stained mug with Matthews's handled cup, Roche nodded. Avoiding the wax red stain, he took a gulp of the warm comforting liquid.

Matthews sat down in a swiveling desk chair. Leaning back, he placed a pair of black laced wingtips on the desk. Roche took a seat in an uncomfortable folding metal chair.

"You summarized a year of covert activity and millions of tax payers' dollars by calling the State Departments chosen leader of Vietnam an ass?" Mathews questioned.

"At least I didn't lie," Roche smirked. "Diem is an ass. The Assistant Secretary responded on behalf of Diem, with all the same excuses; eight years of civil war, the country being split at Geneva and the never failing justification for incompetence; predatory communism. I told the Assistant Secretary in no uncertain terms, we needed to pick another horse. The French are backing the Emperor Bao Dai, and Uncle Sam is going all in on an ass that has little authority beyond the gates of his own palace."

"How was your candor received?" Matthews asked.

"The Assistant Secretary is a politician," Roche shrugged. "He changed topic. He inquired about the pacification of the armed religious sects that control the Mekong Delta. Unfortunately I diluted the good news by editorializing on how expensive it is to bribe fanatic Buddhists because the US chose a Catholic to rule."

"Is it good news?" Matthews questioned. "Are the *Hòa Hảo* and *Cao Đài* conceding?"

"Let's just say, they've accepted the graft. Once again, it would have been cheaper if Diem had allowed them a voice in the new government. But that ass of a Prime Minister continues to appoint family members and Catholics."

"But that is good news?" Matthews probed.

"The jury is still out," Roche commented. "There are a few zealous holdouts that will never compromise, and that is dangerous. There is one General the locals call *Ba Cụt*. That means, *short third*, and refers to the self-amputation of his third finger. He hacked it off as a teenager in protest of the French occupation. The General is a ruthless psychopath and no amount of money will lull him and his follower into submission. If the populous does not embrace Diem quickly, dissidents like Short Third gain traction." Roche took a sip of whisky. Looking over the glossy stained lipped mug, he asked, "So that is how my debriefing went. What did you tell them about the Vietnamese National Army?"

"I was a little more diplomatic than you," Matthews answered grinning. "I said the Armies loyalty to Diem was questionable. The big showdown will come when the Prime Minister tries to implement his promised reforms. There is no amount of bribe money that will persuade the Binh Xuyen criminal syndicate to abandon their Saigon financial empire."

Roche tilted his empty coffee mug in Matthews's direction. Matthews obliged with a healthy refill.

"How did Elaine perform in the meeting?" Matthews asked topping off his cup.

"How do you think she did?" Roche responded. "That girl is a pro. She was her usual charming seductive self. Eloquently describing the inner circle of the palace as she playfully flirted with the Assistant Secretary."

Matthews took his feet off the desk and leaned forward. In a quiet tone, he asked, "Tom, do you have any intentions when it comes to Elaine?"

Roche flinched. Where did that come from? He wondered. Matthews must be joking, he concluded. Snickering he responded, "Every white male in Saigon has intentions when it comes to Elaine. I'm just one of the pack."

Matthews frowned.

He wasn't joking, Roche realized. Taking a sip of whisky to wet his palate, he clarified, "I must say I enjoy her playful flirtations. However, I never mix business and pleasure. I'd like to say we are good friends, nothing more."

Matthews nodded slowly, "Thanks Tom, I consider you a good friend as well. I wouldn't want to step on your toes."

Squinting at his colleague, Roche asked, "You're not thinking of pursuing her? Are you?"

Matthews responded with a mischievous grin.

"Matthews you're a married man, nothing good will come out of this."

"Easy Roche," Matthews said still smiling, "Nothing will probably come out of this at all. I just wanted make sure, that I wouldn't be treading on your turf." Leaning back in his chair, he added, "As far as my stateside wife is concerned, she is well aware that I partake in the local cuisine whilst on assignment."

"I would not put Elaine in the same category as the oriental dishes you've sampled after negotiating a fixed price," Roche commented.

"I definitely agree with you there my friend. I don't think Elaine is out of my price range but I'd like to find out," leaning forward resting his elbows on his knees, he said quietly, "Don't worry Tom, the cost of losing my wife and children would be way to expensive."

CHAPTER NINE

E laine stared at the large clock over the picture of President Eisenhower. The minute hand clicked. It was five minutes after three. This is it, she thought. Clutching a stack of papers, she headed towards Tom Roche's office. Outside his door, she placed the folders on a metal grey file cabinet. Her free hands brushed her white cotton dress and aligned the wide glossy black belt buckle. Looking down she unbuttoned the top bottom. Too much? Too little? She thought examining her amble cleavage. Perfect, she concluded. Picking up the documents, she took a deep breath and barged into Roche's office. Dumfounded she stood open mouthed in the small empty room. Where is he meeting the German? She wondered. Proceeding down the corridor, she peered into the vacant conference room. Dashing through the embassy hallways, she scrambled in search of the illusive Tom Roche. From a second floor window, she spotted Roche and the intriguing Max Kohl in the courtyard. Change of plan, she thought. Back at her desk, she dropped off the stack of documents. Grabbing her purse, she bumped into the persistent John Matthews.

The polished Matthews stood uncomfortably close after the impact. In a starch white long-sleeved shirt and red and blue stripped rep tie, he leaned forward and whispered softly at the base of her neck, "Is someone planning to play hooky this afternoon?"

Inhaling his coffee breath and sharp cologne, Elaine sighed. Not now, she thought. I don't want to offend an influential member of my adoring audience but don't have the luxury of time, she realized.

Matthews grabbed her firmly by the shoulders. Out of the side of his mouth he said with a confident growl, "I say let's call it a day and blow this Popsicle stand."

Politely smiling, she twisted out of his clutches. Pulling the trump card out of the excuses deck, she whispered, "Female trouble."

Matthews's self-assured expression melted. Taking a step back, he coughed into a fisted hand. "I understand," he grumbled making a hasty retreat.

Tucking the small handbag under her arm, she observed the fleeing Mathews. "Works every time," she mumbled victoriously. Casually she strolled downstairs toward the courtyard for the planned coincidental encounter.

"Gentlemen," she said approaching Max and Roche's patio meeting. "I hope I'm not interrupting but once again I'm in need of light." She flashed a single cigarette delicately placed between her fingers.

Max and Roche smiled. Max once again pulled out his lighter fulfilling the request.

"Thank you," she said, taking a puff. "If you could appease my curiosity, why do the two of you always meet in the courtyard?"

Max looked at Roche for guidance. After receiving an acknowledging shrug, he opened his sport coat revealing a shoulder holstered weapon.

"You see Elaine," Roche explained. "We prefer not to have armed contract employees within the embassy. It would set a bad precedent."

Oh my, he's armed, Elaine thought. A rabble of fluttering butterflies invaded her abdomen. She swallowed back surfacing enthusiasm. Calmly she responded, "Of course I understand." A long cigarette toke dispersed the fluttering swarm sensation. With a doe-eyed innocence, she looked at her boss and asked, "Tom, actually I'm glad I ran into you. If you don't mind after the last few late nights I was hoping to leave a little early today?"

"Of course, Elaine I understand," Roche responded.

"Well once you gentlemen conclude your business; perhaps you could join me for a cup of coffee?" She asked. It is a single invitation, she realized.

"Unfortunately, I have other commitments. It's up to you Max," Roche said with raised brows.

"Well I like coffee," Max said. "I like it strong; however I only drink it in the morning. But I would be more than happy to accompany you."

The terrace lounge of the Continental Hotel hummed with late afternoon cocktail chatter. Large arched windows supported a raised ceiling. Crystal chandeliers hung down illuminating Saigon's privileged minority. The maître d' sat the attractive couple at a very prominent table. Other than the Asian servers and the inescapable humidity, this is just like Paris, Elaine thought.

"Mademoiselle?" asked the tuxedo-clad waiter holding a small pad of paper and an anxious pen.

"I was going to order coffee, but on second thought," Elaine turned to Max and asked. "What are you going to have?"

Max looked at the waiter and said, "I'll have a beer."

"Well then I'll have a *pastis*," Elaine blurted out. The server flinched. Turning to Max, she explained, "Although it's a little early for me, I fell in love with the French liqueur when I lived in Paris."

Max gazed into the vaulted ceiling. A grin slowly appeared on his distant expression. Refocused on Elaine, he said quietly, "I had a very good friend and *pastis* used to be his favorite libation."

"Oh, he doesn't drink it anymore?" Elaine questioned.

"No he is dead," Max said.

Responding to the sobering revelation, Elaine slid her hand across the white linen tablecloth touching Max's coat sleeve. "How did he die, Max?" She asked.

After a calculating pause, he answered, "He was gut shot doing me a favor and bled to death quickly in the warm sun. Before he died he asked me to get him a *pastis*."

Reaffirming her touch with a slight squeeze, Elaine said "I'm so sorry Max."

Looking down at her hand, he smiled.

The waiter approached. He served a glass of dark transparent yellow liqueur and jug of diluting water to Elaine. In front of the German, he placed a large glass mug of sparkling brew.

Griping the cold glass handle, Max said, "The Gray Gorilla would be happy to know I'm drinking with a pretty lady who loves *pastis*."

"The Gray Gorilla?" Elaine asked with a playful frown.

"Yes, Hakeem was North African from Morocco, he loved his nickname." Max clarified. With a reflective smile he added, "That big black bastard would charge into battle swinging his blade while singing the Moroccan Soldiers chant."

"Big black bastard?" Elaine questioned sipping on the liqueur.

Max laughed, "My apologies for the barracks dialogue."

"No apology necessary," Elaine chuckled, "I've said worse"

"Enough talk about the deceased," He said. "What brings you to Saigon?"

I can't give him the standard response, she realized. He would find my clever discourse about action, adventure and romance trite. "I really don't know," she answered.

"I appreciate your honesty," Max said. "As for me, I wake up each morning and know how I got here but I still question why." Touching her petite liqueur glass with the foamy beer mug, he winked and toasted, "to the uncertainly of life."

Blushing at the wink, she reciprocated the toast. He is different from any man I have ever known, she realized. I need to proceed with caution, she thought. Recalling her infatuation with the college professor, she felt a pang of remorse. The academian turned out to be a pompous ass, and an old pompous ass at that. Then there was Emile, she reflected. The Parisian artist I fell in love with. The oil painter was only interested in my monthly allowance. His art sucked, she concluded. However, never right out of the gate have I encountered anyone like Max Kohl.

A buzz of activity engulfed the couple. The waiter presented Max with a bottle of champagne. Busboys set up a bucket of ice beside the table.

"Compliments of the gentleman at the bar," the waiter said to a puzzled Max.

Examining the label, Max shrugged. He handed the bottle back to the server and squinted in the direction of the bar. A thin well dressed European with a receding hairline and straight thin moustache graciously nodded.

"Who is that?" Elaine questioned bathing in the attention the table received from the late afternoon corkage ritual.

"That is Captain Ghjuvan Casta of French Intelligence, the *Deuxième Bureau*." Max responded.

"This is an expensive bottle of Dom Perigon," Elaine said quantifying the gesture. Raising the broad-bowled stemmed glass, she added, "It's my turn to propose a toast." Champagne danced around the shallow bowl. "To life itself," she toasted. Delicately the crystal champagne saucers clinked over white linen. Religiously she took a soft sip of the luxurious beverage. Glancing up, she caught Max tossing back the sparkling wine with a single gulp. His face puckered. Apparently, to cleanse his palate, he took a swig of beer.

"I take it you don't like champagne?" Elaine questioned.

"I prefer beer," Max informed.

Max is a man who knows what he likes, Elaine concluded. Apparently, he likes beer.

Casta in a lightweight doubled-breasted gray suit strolled from the bar. His thinning dark hair slicked back. "Max, sorry to interrupt. But I just wanted to introduce myself to the ravishing Miss Favreau." Boldly he reached down and elevated her hand. He gave it a soft kiss. "Mademoiselle," he whispered looking up from the caress. "I am Ghjuvan Casta."

Delightfully shocked, Elaine forgot her social graces. Jerking her hand back, she blurted, "How do you know my name?"

"Miss Favreau, when such a beauty as you arrives in our little corner of the world, everybody knows." Casta replied with a charming smile.

Elaine blushed with the discovery of celebrity. "That is very kind, Mister Casta, and thank you for the champagne,"

"My pleasure," Casta said. Turning to Max, he added, "Good to see you back in Saigon. I trust you delivered our message."

"Captain Casta," Max said nodding.

"Max, Mademoiselle," Casta said bowing, "My apologies for the intrusion."

"What a pleasant man," Elaine commented as Casta strutted back to the bar. "He is the first polite Frenchman, I've met in Saigon."

"Casta is not French," Max clarified. "He is Corsican."

"Is there a difference?" Elaine asked.

"There is a difference if you're Corsican." Max responded.

"I still can't get over the fact that he knew my name." Elaine said. The attentive waiter refilled her champagne coupe.

"I suspect he knows a lot more about you than just your name," Max said leaning back in his chair.

"What do you mean?" She asked.

"He probably has a file on you. You work for the US embassy. You spend time at the palace. For French Intelligence that makes you a person of interest." Max explained.

"This is all so exciting Max," Elaine said sipping champagne. What a wonderful afternoon, she thought glancing around the room. Is it the alcohol, my unexpected notoriety, or Max, she wondered. Regardless, I feel invincible. Reaching over she grabbed Max's firm forearm. Looking deep into his blue eyes, she said. "Take me to dinner Max. Show me the city. I want to see your Saigon."

Flowing with the masses through the clock tower entrance of the Ben Thanh night market, Elaine hung on firmly to Max's arm. A maze of hawker stalls peddled everything from dry goods to produce. A confusing network of light bulbs and frayed electrical cords dangled overhead. Passing a row of severed pigs' heads, Elaine buried her face in Max's shoulder. Brushing a hog head, she grimaced. The crowded pock marked surface, taunted her high heels. Stumbling she clutched Max even tighter. "Sorry, it's these damn shoes." she confessed.

He grinned examining her footwear. The surging crowd drifted by. He scanned the tightly packed kiosk over the heads of the shorter locals. "This way," he said guiding her to a peasant sandals vendor. The boney proprietor in a stained white singlet stood at attention. A sweeping hand identified his low-budget merchandise. Max offered a handful of loose change and pointed at the nicest pair displayed. The skinny hawker weighed the offer in a cupped hand. After a short deliberation, he flashed a single gold tooth in a wide smile.

"Try these on," Max said, dropping the sandals on the ground.

Pulling off her expensive heels, Elaine slid her feet into the comfortable flat wear. "God this feels so much better," she said. "Thank you."

Reaching down, Max picked up her high heels and said. "Good, now let's get dinner."

Walking through the labyrinth, the consumer goods kiosk abruptly ended. Food stalls flanked the narrow walkway. Sweat soaked cooks toiled over fired stoked woks and charcoal grills. Steam erupted. Grease sizzled. Runaway smoke carried the pungent aroma of cheap cuisine. Elaine swallowed down surfacing bile. I can't eat here, she thought.

Max led her out of the confusion to the dining room situated under the starry sky. Three men in t-shirts smoked and drank around a table cluttered with beer bottles. A family of five dinned around another small hard wood table. The husband shoveled a noodle dish into his mouth at close range. His wife tried to persuade their three small children not to gawk at the white arrivals. Approaching the only unoccupied seating option, Max pulled out a small wooden stool for Elaine. He took a seat beside her. A slight breeze swept the air clean of foul food odors. A grinning boy wearing only shorts and sandals suddenly appeared. Holding up two fingers, Max said, "Beer." The nine year old scurried off into the glow of the distant night market. He immediately returned with two bottles of 33 Beer.

After wiping the bottle opening with her handkerchief, Elaine took a large gulp of the refreshing brew. "I can see why you like beer so much," She said placing the cold bottle next to her cheek.

"It's funny," Max said pausing to chug down half the bottle. "How your body sets the priorities when it is pushed to the limits. At Dien Bien Phu, I was hungry until the water ran out. When I was thirsty, I forgot about my hunger. Then days without sleep, I forgot about my thirst." Taking another large gulp of beer, he continued with a smile. "Now the reverse is true. After I caught up on my sleep, I was thirsty. After quenching my thirst, I was hungry. And after I appeased my appetite..." Max finished the bottle and holding it over his head added, "I needed a beer."

Chuckling Elaine questioned, "So you put beer up there with food, water and sleep?"

Receiving a fresh bottle from the nine-year-old server, Max examined the glistening bottle, "No doubt about it, beer is in the top five essentials for life."

"What's number five?" Elaine questioned sipping on the bottle seductively.

"That's easy," Max chuckled, "*Schweineshaxe!*"

"What???" Elaine blurted out.

"*Schweineshaxe*, roasted pork knuckle," he said licking his lips.

Shaking her head, she conceded, "Must be a German thing."

"No," he clarified, "Bavarian."

Out of the flow of gawking on-lookers, a young mother approached Max. Holding a naked baby, she stood submissively. The begging teenager held out a shaking soiled palm. Subtly, Max pulled a *paister* out of his coat pocket. Waiving her off, he slipped her the currency.

"I saw that," Elaine said smiling. "Why didn't you just give her the money?"

"Elaine you have a lot to learn about mingling with the locals. I may not know about the Champagne tasting ceremony. But donating to the less fortunate requires skill. The trick is not to draw other solicitors." He explained.

"You may have dissuaded other beggars. However we do have an audience." Elaine said pointing her bottle towards the thoroughfare. A curious group of about twenty locals respectfully observed the white beer drinkers.

"Show them your peasant sandaled feet," Max challenged.

Taking up the dare, Elaine lifted a leg displaying a sandaled foot to the crowd. Snickering applause followed. Chuckling Elaine stood up and took a slight bow.

A sampling of food from various stalls cluttered the small table. Max slammed down the oriental grub like a lumberjack. Elaine prodded the recognizable rice and noodle dishes with cautious chopsticks. She avoided eye contact with the large fish head and prawns.

"Max?" she asked sampling the oily chicken and rice entree, "Could we go to the Cholon district after dinner? I want to see the dark side of Saigon."

Using a paper napkin, he wiped his greasy lips. "Cholon offers many excesses and forbidden pleasures, what is it you want to see?" he asked pulling out a cigar.

"Madame Nhu talks constantly about reforming the city and restoring Vietnamese traditional values. I want to see the plight of the depraved. I would like to see an opium den. Is that possible?"

"You'll find everything is possible in Cholon, for a price. Your request is a simple one. However I must warn you, a smoking den is not a pleasant place," he replied puffing on his post dinner cigar.

If I'm going to converse intelligently with Madame Nhu about her reforms. I must see the moral corruption for myself, she rationalized. Sitting upright on the wobbly stool, she said, "Let's do this. I want to get a glimpse of the opium beast."

Stepping out of the Citron taxi in front of the dimly lit nondescript doorway, Elaine beamed. I'm about to enter into the exotic excesses of the orient, she realized. Visualizing elaborate silk tapestries, raised lacquered beds and reclining patrons puffing away on hand carved ivory pipes, her heart raced.

"Stay close to me," Max said opening up the creaking door.

Following Max into the dark interior, a sweet burning smell engulfed Elaine's senses. It was too sweet, to sharp. Her eyes watered. The back of her throat burned. I can't see, she realized squinting into the dim hazy atmosphere. She jumped. A wiry Asian man appeared out of the shadows. His greasy hair glowed in the unnatural light. In a wrinkled black suit, he smiled greedily at the potential upscale customers. Elaine' eyes adjusted. A middle-aged woman peered out of a barred window into the foyer. Frayed and torn Chinese paper scroll adorned the walls.

Max handed the seedy greeter a 500 *piastre* note and said, "Just tourist my friend, wanting to take a look around."

The oily man smiled pocketing the entrance fee. In Vietnamese, he informed the opium-dispensing cashier. She retreated into her cage. The doorman's welcoming arm gestured down a long hallway.

Elaine clung to Max. The planked floorboards creaked. The corridor led to a maze of hallways and dark rooms. Passing open doorways, the nauseating sweet smell intensified. A faint gurgling sound resonated.

Respecting the silence of the opium worshipers, Elaine spoke with a church whisper. "This is not what I pictured."

"You wanted to look at the beast, well there it is," Max said in front of the doorway of a lighted room. A dozen half-naked men reclined in the crowded enclosure. Taut skin stretched tightly over their sharp bones. One of the breathing corpses rolled onto his side. The movement rippled across the skeletal inhabitants. Distorted limbs and torsos readjusted to a stagnant repose.

A sleepy head slowly rotated to examine the intruders. Dark tombstone eyes housed in sunken sockets stared right through Elaine. "Oh my," she gasped covering her mouth. Her stomach dropped. Clinging on to Max for balance, she mumbled, "Let's get out of here."

The couple set a brisk retreat towards the exit. Passing the slimy doorman, Elaine said, "Thank you."

Max chuckled at Elaine's departing etiquette. The Americans are a strange lot indeed.

Outside Elaine took a deep breath. The smell of diesel fumes and wet garbage cleansed her senses of the sweet burning stench of slow death.

"Thank you Max," Elaine said. "I just needed to see for myself." Taking another deep breath, she smelled her long blonde locks. "Damn, that stink is in my hair," She said brushing the fabric of her dress with an open palm. "Why do they do it, Max?" Elaine asked shaking her gown.

"I suspect escape," he answered. "The patrons of this establishment are likely common laborers. The work is hard and demeaning. For a few *piastres* they can escape the harsh realities of their own existence with a dream session. I've seen the same thing in the Legion. Legionnaires enjoy the dream stick for a while. Then they wrestle with the pipe. The pipe always wins."

"How about you Max, have you ever tried the pipe." Elaine asked.

"No, as I told you before I prefer beer." He said grinning. "The Legion was my escape from reality. I was uneducated, with no family, and no Third Reich. I feared being one of the many unemployed in Germany. The effects of enlistment could have proved just as deadly as the pipe. Fortunately when I walked out of Isabelle, I kicked the habit."

I'm no different, Elaine thought. I've escaped the reality of becoming a common housewife in Harrisburg, Pennsylvania. My father funded my addiction for an exotic lifestyle, she realized. Dad paid for a year in Paris and a deluxe class ticket to Saigon. "Max I want to thank you again. This will help me converse more intelligently with Madame Nhu and her proposed reforms." She said, "However, I have to ask you why this den? You could have taken me to a more...upscale establishment."

"Elaine," Max responded, "You wanted to see the beast, why distort the view."

The couple strolled down the dark side street towards the main thoroughfare. Max handed Elaine her high-heeled shoes. "Hold these for just minute," he whispered.

"What is it?' She questioned.

Ignoring the inquiry, he squinted into the depths of a narrow side alley. The sparkle of hand held steel blades emerged. In wide stances, three teenage street punks flexed. The alpha extended and upturned arm. Flicking his fingers, he growled, "Your money."

Calmly, Max stepped in front of Elaine. In a fluid motion, he pulled out his side arm. Tauntingly he brandished it in front of the would-be-assailants. The terrified children cut and ran.

Max smiled holstering his weapon. "Are you alright Elaine?" He asked.

Overcome Elaine stood open-mouthed. Instinctively she embraced Max squeezing him hard.

Patting her softly, Max said, "I think the tour of the Cholon district has come to an end."

In the security of the crowded thoroughfare, Max waived down a *cyclo* taxi. The shirtless driver's face shielded by a pointed coolie hat. Max sat down first on the tiny padded bench of the man-powered tricycle. Elaine sat across his lap. Behind them, the tiny driver stood upright on the pedals. Every ounce of his wiry frame set the cycle rickshaw in motion.

Sitting across Max's lap with her head resting on his chest, Elaine watched the colorful nightlife of Saigon drift by. I'm in my own dream session, she thought. "Max?" she questioned. "How did you know those street thugs would appear?"

"When I said I wasn't educated, I meant as defined by civilized society. I am well versed in the ways of war. The walkway and alley was an obvious ambush venue. I didn't know with certainty but am always prepared." He explained.

"I'm sure glad you were," She said, snuggling up. "When do you have to go back to Laos?"

"Why do you ask?"

"Because I need an escort to the palace this Saturday night. There is a reception for the Assistant Secretary of State, I don't know of anyone else I would rather go with then you." She explained playfully patting his chest. He sat quietly. Is he thinking about his Laotian responsibilities, she wondered. Does he have another woman? She questioned. I am not going to let him get away, she decided. Sitting up she stared hard into to his blue eyes. "Well Max, are you going to help out a fellow contract employee?"

"Before I concede," Max responded. "I have to warn you, I have no social skills."

"And I know nothing about armed conflict," she said. "We will make the perfect couple," and with that she kissed him.

CHAPTER TEN

ugging on the starched shirt collar, Max shifted his broad shoulders in the white dinner jacket. How the tiny Asian tailor could measure me and produce a tuxedo in less than three hours is truly amazing, he thought. It really should come as no surprise, he concluded. The industrious Vietnamese hauled heavy artillery into the remote jungle and defeated French colonialism.

"You look wonderful," Elaine whispered.

Glancing at the plunging neckline of her long dark blue silk evening gown Max decided to forgive his stunning date for tardiness. "My apologies for my earlier frustration," he said.

Hugging his arm, she replied, "I'm the one who should apologize. I should have informed you about being fashionably late."

Must be an American tradition he thought still baffled by Elaine's explanation. It still makes no sense at all, he concluded. If everyone came late to make an entrance, then everyone would arrive at the same time.

Diplomatically Elaine nudged Max into presenting their invitation. Reaching into his inside coat pocket, he flinched. Where is my pistol, he wondered. That's right, he realized tonight I'm unarmed. Feeling vulnerable, he handed the invitation to the receptionist.

Entering the large banquet hall, Max holding Elaine's soft hand paused at the top of a small staircase. So this is it, he thought. I'm about to peek behind the curtain at the people that sleep on clean sheets, eat the finest foods, and make the decisions that decide the fate of the masses.

A polished marble floor glistened under the feet of Saigon's ruling class. Large geometrically placed floral arrangements decorated the room's periphery. Roman columns supported the raised ceiling. Dozens of ceiling fans circulated the guest's perfumed aroma. Rolling laughter accented the buzz of polite conversation. A string quartet played classical music. The mingling crowd consisted of informal cliques centered on race and language. Just like a French Foreign Legion bivouac, Max chuckled. In the corner, Prime Minister Diem, his older brother the Archbishop, and his younger brother Nhu and his wife Madame Nhu chattered amongst themselves. Isolated from the festivities, the heir apparent rulers of Vietnam seemed bored.

Taking a deep breath, Max locked arms with Elaine and plunged into the party.

"Champagne?" a smartly dressed waiter asked. Balanced over his shoulder by an upturned hand, a silver tray of saucer shaped crystal glasses sparkled.

Retrieving a glass Elaine asked, "By any chance can we get a beer?"

The waiter nodded and quickly exited into the crowd. Taking a sip of sparkling wine Elaine winked at Max. The waiter reappeared with a single glass of pale lager amongst the bubbling champagne. Taking the beer, Max nodded to the server and lipped a silent thank you to Elaine.

Madame Nhu broke away from the Ngo family inner circle. The party volume lowered. Polite turning heads observed the first lady of Vietnam greeting the attractive blonde couple.

"Elaine you look exquisite," Madame Nhu said. The two women gingerly hugged. Breaking the embrace, Madame Nhu extended her hand, "And you must be Mister Kohl. Elaine has told me so much about you."

"Madame Nhu," Max said delicately shaking the petite hand.

"My husband would love to meet you," she said. "He is a fond admirer of the Third Reich." She hollered across the room, "Honey, come here, there is someone I'd like you to meet." The boisterous solicitation silenced the festivities. All watched the attentive husband adhere to his young wife's request.

The Prime Minister's short brother in a white dinner jacket, black slacks and a bow tie slowly migrated across the ballroom. He looks like the maitre'd at the Continental Hotel, Max thought tugging on a his tight shirt collar. Spotting Roche in an American cluster, Max shrugged. Roche snickered.

Max shook Nhu's sweaty hand. The flash of a photographer's bulb startled the German. Temporality blinded, he blinked. Beside Max, Madame Nhu and Elaine posed. Immediately the women began speaking amongst themselves. The conversation centered on Elaine's gown and Madame Nhu's jewelry.

Turning to the two silent men, Madame Nhu locked arms with Elaine and said, "Please excuse us while we go powder our noses."

Elaine looked at Max and whispered, "Sorry," emphasizing the abandonment apology with a submissive shrug.

"Are you a German veteran of the big war, Mr. Kohl," Nhu asked in a slow methodical tone.

"Yes," Max responded.

"I've always been impressed with the Third Reich, in particular the Gestapo. The German Secret Police were extremely efficient in enforcing the will of your Fuhrer." Nhu mumbled with sleepy eyelids. "Were you in the *Waffenn* SS by any chance Mister Kohl?"

"I was with the 12th SS Panzer Division *Hitlerjugend*," Max responded.

A smile awoke on Nhu's drowsy face, "The Murder Division," he exclaimed delightfully bobbing his head, "The boy-soldiers that did not take prisoners." Yawning he concluded, "Very impressive Mister Kohl."

The Murder Division! Max's insides shuddered at the sound of the Allies' derogatory labeling of his unit. That fucking Canadian characterization, he thought. Breathing heavy, he shifted his shoulders in the snug dinner jacket. Moisture flowed under his arms. Looking down at the lethargic Nhu, rebuttals to the insult raced through his psyche. Should I inform this slant-eyed maggot, that prisoners were killed on both sides of the conflict? And regardless which side initiated the atrocity; it is not an *impressive* consequence of war. It's a good thing I'm not armed, he realized visualizing securing Nhu's greasy noggin in a headlock and blowing out his brains I wonder if he would find that impressive?

"The motto of the *Waffen SS* holds true today; 'My honor is loyalty'." Nhu said focusing his disconnected guise across the crowded ballroom. "Were you in the *Waffenn* SS by any chance?"

Baffled by the repeated inquiry, Max squinted hard at Nhu. The slick Asian's pale face slowly rotated back into Max's purview. The familiar tracks of the opium beast appeared in the creases around the hollow eyes of the Prime Ministers chief advisor. *So the pious reformer dances with the pipe,* Max thought smirking at the irony.

After a dry cough, Nhu re-started his rambling dialogue about the efficiency of German National Socialism. Max ignored the rant. Nhu acted as both orator and audience in his Nazi homily. *So much for worrying about my lack of social skills,* Max thought. He raised the nearly full glass of beer and emptied it with several gulps. The sleeve of his tuxedo, wiped away the foaming residue on his lips. *Nhu's Nazi infatuation is amusing,* he realized. *What this poppy smoker doesn't understand, is the racial ideology of the National Socialist classifies him as an untermenschen, something less than human, a little yellow monkey. A well dressed monkey, but an inferior being none the less.*

A well-groomed Asian tapping on Nhu's shoulder terminated the fascist sermon. Leaning in, he whispered into Nhu's ear. Glancing up the intruder with perfectly parted jet-black hair smirked at the German.

I recognize you, Max realized. *You are the slick monkey who blew-up Rene's Cessna,* he reflected. Max frowned at the messenger with a declaration of war. Nhu and his subordinate just walked away.

"What was that all about?" Roche asked.

"Apparently the Prime minister's chief advisor loves Nazis," Max said grinning. "Oh and one other thing, if you want to know who the Corsicans have allied themselves with in the new government, it's the Prime Ministers brother. That slick young man who interrupted Nhu's incoherent admiration for National Socialism, I recognized from the Plain of Jars."

"Yesterday I would have found that information valuable. However the Prime Minister's actions this afternoon overshadow its significance. That arrogant aloof bastard ordered the removal of the Chief of Police of Saigon. He has drawn a line in the sand. The Binh Xuyen are not going to walk away without a fight." Roche explained.

Seeing the stress in his friends tired features, Max asked, "Saigon is the only safe haven in this chaotic country. Do you really think something is going to happen here?"

"The French gave the Binh Xuyen the brothels, opium dens and casinos. Hell, they even gave them the police department to enforce their criminal empire. In exchange the Binh Xuyen eliminated all Communist activity in Saigon." Roche looked around the crowded ballroom. In a hush tone, he added. "Be careful Max, the fuse was lit this afternoon. The city is a powder keg that is about to be blow."

"Thanks for the warning *ami*," Max said. "Do you think I have time for another beer before the explosion?"

Roche smiled, "As long as the queue at the bar is not too long." Pointing at open casement doors leading to a courtyard, he added, "There is a bar in the garden that no one is using because of the rain. Let me shake a few more hands and I'll join you out there for a drink."

"If you spot Elaine while you are making your rounds, please inform her about our plan," Max asked.

"No problem," Roche said immersing into the mingling mass.

Max set his empty glass on a lacquered table next to a large floral arrangement. Peering around, he searched for Elaine. With a shrug, he headed towards the courtyard. Standing in the doorway to the garden, he felt the cooling night air softened by a recent rain. The wet cobble stone path reflected the glow from an overhead strand of colorful lanterns. Large droplets fell off the surrounding foliage. A protective tarp shielded a small bamboo bar. The only patron waving a threatening finger berated the young bartender. Growling insults flowed out of the obese guest. The grievance centered on an inappropriate scotch. Max approached. The young server kept bowing to no avail. Standing behind the irate guest, Max rubbed his chin. This whining ass sounds familiar, he reflected. This couldn't be Mei's former keeper, he thought. Recalling the eclectic shock torture at the hands of the fat bureaucrat, he gritted his teeth.

Becoming impatient, Max cleared his throat. The fat man blindly flashed the back of an indignant hand. "Excuse me," Max growled tapping the man on the shoulder, "I'd like to get a beer."

The annoyed man abruptly turned around. His snarling expression melted into fear. Max head butted his former adversary. Thong Doan Tu dropped to the wet ground. Stepping over his reclining victim, Max winked at the wide-eyed bartender and said, "I'd like a beer, please."

The young server reached into a bucket of iced beer and pulled out a cold bottle. Several smiles appeared and quickly vanished as he opened and poured the beer into a glass. Pointing to Max's forehead, the happy bartender handed Max a bar towel. After blotting his head with the white cloth, Max examined a small crimson stain. This not my blood, he realized. Taking the beer, Max nodded thanks to the barkeep. Thong moaned. Looking down at the fat piece-of-shit floundering on the wet stone surface, Max thought about Mei's forced couplings with this pig. Snorting in disgust, he set his beer on the counter and instinctively reached for his gun. I'm unarmed he realized with a chuckle. Just as well, he rationalized. "It's your lucky day chubby," he mumbled. Grabbing the counter top for balance, he silenced the groaning victim with a swift kick to the rib cage. Picking up his beer, he took big satisfying gulp. Looking into the puzzled bartender's face, he said, "It's a family matter."

Standing in the open doorway with the courtyard at his back, Max heard Thong stumbling to his feet. Sipping on his fresh beer, he grinned. Assaulting the other guest probably wasn't proper etiquette, he realized. I better find Elaine and make an early exit to avoid the Americans any embarrassment, he thought. Across the room mingling with the minions, he spotted Elaine firmly attached to Madame Nhu's side. Elaine gave Max a quick wave. Showing an open palm, she signaled for him to wait. Over the clamor of the cocktail chatter, Max heard a very familiar faint shrill whistle. Dropping and shattering his beer glass on the marble floor, he ran towards Elaine. Her confused expression turned to shock. Grabbing her shoulders, he wrestled her to the ground. A deafening explosion rattled the ballroom. A large crystal chandelier in the center of the banquet hall came crashing down. The room went pitch black. Another blast pounded the party. Shards of glass rained down. Howls of pain and cries of terror resonated in the darkness. On the cold stone floor, Max grimaced shielding his date from the stampeding masses.

"Don't panic," Max whispered into her soft ear. Large chunks of ceiling plaster fell. "It should be over soon."

"How did you know?" She questioned.

"The familiar sound of an incoming round," he answered. "You were right, with your social skills and my knowledge of armed conflict, we make the perfect couple."

Dust thickened the air. Shadows moved about. The crunching sound of glass under foot competed with the moans of casualties. Slowly rising Max took off his jacket and wrapped it around Elaine. Shuffling his feet, he guided her towards an exit.

"Should we stay and help?" She asked.

"Let's get you to safety first, and then assess the situation." He answered.

They joined the slow steady drip of party survivors milling around on the wet palace lawn. Sirens wailed in the distance. The bruised and bleeding continued exiting. The obese Thong stumbled onto the grass holding his side. That fat man's face covered in blood. Max grinned. Just another causality of these chaotic times, he thought. I wonder if a broke a rib.

"You two alright," Roche said dusting off his shoulders.

"Sure Roche," Max said. "I counted five mortar rounds."

"There were six," Roche said, pointing to a small crater on the palace grounds. "I don't think there is much more we can do here tonight. I'd say the party is over. I have an embassy car waiting, be more than happy to give you two a lift."

"Thanks *ami*," Max said.

The trio walked through the soiled crowd. Draped in Max's white dinner jacket, Elaine clung to the German's arm for support.

"Where are you staying at Max?" Roche asked, approached the vehicle.

"The Hotel Majestic," Max answered.

"Good, that is close by; we'll drop you off first." Roche said opening the rear door.

"How about you Elaine?" Roche asked.

"Hotel Majestic," She responded.

CHAPTER ELEVEN

The pre-dawn horizon glowed in anticipation of the tropical sun. Standing on the fourth floor balcony of his Majestic Hotel room, Max awaited the new day. Clad only in boxer briefs, he enjoyed the warming humid air on his naked flesh. Puffing on the first cigar of the day, he reflected on his late night activities with the seductive Elaine Favreau. After a steady diet of professional local flesh, the coupling with the busty Elaine provided some much needed variety. What are you suppose to do? He wondered. The required etiquette of the local prostitutes is easy, he concluded. You paid them and they left.

Taking a puff on the cigar, he looked back into the hotel room. In a sea of churning linen, the alluring Elaine slept. Long golden blonde locks spilled across the pillows. Perfumed scented perspiration glistened on the bare torso. A flat stomach pulsed. What a beautiful creature, he thought.

A distant blast greeted dawn's first light. Sporadic gunfire crackled. Max looked out over the balcony. A plume of black smoke rose above the silhouetted skyline.

"What is it?" Elaine asked turning on her side.

Grinning at the naked American, he answered, "The battle of Saigon."

Rolling on her back, she gazed into the rotating blades of a ceiling fan. "Do you think we'll have time for breakfast?"

"I don't see why not," he replied.

It was late morning. In a corner of the deserted Majestic Hotel cafe, the restaurant staff whispered about the day's tragic events. Holding Max's callus hand, Elaine in a dark blue cocktail dressed strolled into the restaurant. A nervous waiter broke away from the gossiping cluster. The server waved an inviting arm at the sea of vacant tables. Max in khaki slacks and a long sleeved white shirt, surveyed the seating options. Choosing a table just inside the doorway, he pulled out a rattan chair for the overdressed Elaine. A morning breeze flowed through the open doors. Placing a small satchel containing his pistol next to the table, he once again felt the security of being armed.

"Breakfast *a la Francaise*," Max said to young waiter. The boy nodded.

Leaning forward in her chair, a wide-eyed Elaine asked, "Max how safe do you think the city is?"

"It appears from our balcony that the battle ground is the Cholon district. We should be safe if we keep our distance." Max said attempting to defuse her enthusiasm.

Enjoying the breads, jams and strong coffee, the blonde couple turned to watch a single blue and white Renault taxi making its way down the empty streets. The small vehicle screeched to an abrupt termination in front of the hotel. A disheveled white man in blue jeans, white t-shirt and beige photo vest jumped out of the cab. A large zoom lens camera dangled from a neck strap. Jogging into the cafe the photographer glanced over at the waiter's conference and shouted, "A pot of black coffee, please." Sitting at a table across from Max and Elaine, he loaded film into the expensive camera. Looking up from the task, he smiled at Max and Elaine. "Bonjour," he said in accented French.

"Good morning," Max responded. "Can you tell us what's going on?"

"If you're feeling adventurous you can see for yourself. I'm heading back to the European quarter off the Boulevard Gallieni where you can get a front row view." The American replied.

Elaine reached over touching Max's arm said, "Let's go, this sounds exciting."

Frowning at Elaine's naive enthusiasm, Max looked back at the scruffy unshaven young journalist and asked, "A front row view of what?"

"The Vietnamese Nationalist slugging it out with the Binh Xuyen. I have a friend who has a flat in the European quarter. From the security of his balcony, you can see all the action." He responded.

"Count us in," Elaine exclaimed.

A tiny taxi sputtered down the empty street. Extending an arm into the back seat, the photographer said, "I'm foreign correspondent John Merle by the way."

Max acknowledged the introduction with a firm handshake, "Max Kohl and Elaine Favreau."

Approaching the one-mile divide between the European quarter and the Chinese suburb of Cholon, the vehicle flowed through fleeing pedestrians. The nervous cabbie glanced at Merle for guidance. Over his shoulder, Merle informed, "My friend's apartment is just another two blocks. We'll make better progress on foot." Cautiously, he opened the car door into the escaping horde.

Holding on firmly to Elaine, Max followed Merle through the crowd. Nationalist troops ran in one direction. The homeless staggered in the other. The salvaged possessions of the displaced cluttered the street and sidewalk. Traumatized families huddled around what remained of their possessions. Children wailed. Mothers wept. Fathers twitched nervously with despair.

Entering the ornate security gate of an upscale colonial French apartment building, the grating sound of confusion faded. A tense doorman guarded the quiet solitude of a marled floor lobby. Merle nodded at the attendant before leading his guest up a sweeping circular stairway. The click of Elaine's spiked heels echoed through the stairwell. Muffled party laughter resonated. Flexing a knuckle, Merle rapped on apartment 3G. The third floor flat hummed. A portly middle-aged graying man in a starched white dress shirt answered. Bottled laughter escaped. Sporting a big smile and holding a celery stock garnished cocktail, potbelly welcomed the new arrivals. Gawking at Elaine's plunging neckline, he spoke pleasantly in English.

Unable to comprehend their host's greeting, Max nudged Elaine for clarification.

She translated, "He said they are having Bloody Marys, but we could have something else if we like."

Max shook his head to decline. The Americans cackled amongst themselves in their native tongue. Left out of the conversation, Max surveyed the plush apartment. Oriental rugs blanketed the polished wood floor. Tapestries hung on the walls. Bamboo and rattan furniture cluttered the large room. A high-fidelity phonograph provided a jazz soundtrack. Sunlight and celebratory conversation flowed in from two open casement doors. Wandering over to investigate, Max walked upon a semi-circle of six American men sitting on a small terrace. Their feet propped on the wrought iron railing. The skyline in front of them burned. The men politely turned to acknowledge Max's presence with a nod or a smile. As Elaine approached, the balcony audience jumped up. Like schoolboys they scurried around to make room for her. She took the center chair. Potbelly handed her a tomato juice cocktail. Merle elbowed his way to sit beside her. Standing behind his seated date, Max tried but could not comprehend the lighthearted English dialogue. It was too fast and laced with slang.

While Elaine entertained her American audience, Max looked across the face of the upscale building. Behind decorative balustrades, European spectators sat comfortably with a glass of wine or a cocktail enjoying the battle. Two balconies over a white gloved Vietnamese server poured champagne. On the street below, a military transport burned. Oily soot reached into the sky. A lifeless body lay on the ground. Sirens wailed. Gunfire popped. A Nationalist vehicle raced down the road. At the end of the thoroughfare, it drew fire and crashed. The Binh Xuyen rooting French observers cheered. The journalist Merle hollered out to the French terrace, "Wait until the second half!" Both balconies broke out in laughter. The witty remark earned Merle a pat on the leg from a snickering Elaine.

Is this what aristocrats do, Max wondered, find amusement in the masses risking their lives? Is it all just a game, a sporting ritual? Do they not comprehend the magnitude of what is in front of them, he thought. This is real. Men kill. People die. Looking down at the combatants scurrying about on the stage below, he realized, he had played that role. I was a soldier in the trenches, fighting the battles for others.

The balcony audience shouted out encouragement to the players. Max lit a cigar. The American voyeurs salivating exuberance, is sickening, he thought. Puffing away, his stomach churned. What is wrong with these people, he wondered. Biting down hard on the stogie, he snorted cigar smoke through flared nostrils.

"I hope they make it," Elaine exclaimed, pointing at a barefooted couple running for safety with three small children.

In her revealing silk dress, she looked grotesque. I've seen enough, Max concluded. It's time to exit this macabre theater. Stepping quietly back into the plush apartment, he ran into potbelly holding a pitcher of Bloody Marys.

"You sure I can't get you anything?" potbelly asked slowly in French.

Max dropped his smoldering cigar in the pitcher of tomato juice accented with vodka and left.

CHAPTER TWELVE

It was late morning. Max's head throbbed. Sipped on strong black coffee, he hoped the java would provide relief. Through heavy eyelids, he tried to focus on the rural vista in front of his Laotian long house. A single farmer toiled in ankle deep paddy water behind a water buffalo. I need to stick to beer, he realized. That local white whisky comes with a hefty delayed penalty. Stepping out of the raised porch's shade, he glanced into the bright sunlight. That was a mistake; he concluded retreating into the cool shadows with his morning brew. Slouching in a chair, he took a deep breath. In the distance, a red dust trail emerging on the dirt road. What is a vehicle doing out here he wondered? Whoever it is, they are sure in a hurry.

Lighting a cigar, he sucked on the relaxing smoke. The dusty automobile wake closed in. The red billowing cloud came to a screeching halt at his gate. Puffing on his cigar, he stared into the dissipating crimson haze. Behind the wheel of a military jeep sat Tom Roche. The American's spiked flat-top hair a reddish hue. Removing sunglasses, Roche exposed the spectacles' clean imprint. Stepping out of the open-air vehicle, he shook his soiled head. A hand stroked the bristles of cropped hair. In a settling plume of red dust, he walked toward the house. Patting down his soiled fatigues, he spat.

"Too early for a beer, Roche?" Max asked from the comfort of his slouched position.

Smiling through dirt encrusted lips, Roche answered, "No but I could use some water."

Fearing nausea, Max remained seated. Over his shoulder, he yelled, "Lan, some water for our guest."

The round faced Lan ran out barefooted in her baggy black pajamas. With a sour expression, she handed Roche a fruit jar filled with cool well water.

"Thanks," Roche mumbled. The inconvenienced Lan stomped back into the residence. Pouring half the water into a cupped palm, Roche bent over the railing and splashed his face. Standing erect, he downed the refreshing liquid with two large gulps.

"What happened to you?" Roche asked looking down at the sluggish German.

"Slow morning, I was up late last night drinking with the old man Pao. I hate to admit it but the tiny Meo drank me under the table." Max's scratchy voice responded.

"Well Max what I came to ask you was not going to be easy. The fact that you're hung-over does not help the situation." Roche said raising a brow.

"What is it *ami*?" Max asked slowly sitting up.

"After weeks of fighting, the battle for Saigon is about to be decided. Much to my surprise, the Vietnamese Nationalist rallied around the incompetent Prime Minister and are about to crush the Binh Xuyen. The gangster army has made their stand in the Cholon district. The final assault by the Nationalist is just days away." Roche said.

"So what is your difficult request?" Max questioned.

"Three Americans are in the Binh Xuyen citadel. They wouldn't survive the assault. The Nationalist having corralled their adversary, are going to level the district with artillery." Roche informed.

Rubbing his forehead, Max asked, "Three Americans?"

"Yes," Roche said, "A journalist: John Merle, a photographer: Alec Russing and," Roche swallowed, "Elaine."

"Elaine!" Max exclaimed.

Nodding Roche said, "Like a moth to a flame, she is drawn to the unknown, but naive about her peril."

"Roche the sex was good, but it wasn't that good," Max said leaning back in his chair.

Roche snickered. In a serious tone, he said, "Max, I have a forty-eight hour window to send in a team and abstract the three adventurers. The Nationalist offered their assistance, but they are amateurs at best. Over five hundred civilians have already been killed in the crossfire. A Nationalist team would have little chance of success."

Max called into the house, "Lan some whisky, please."

The barefooted Lan skipped out of the house grinning at Max's discomfort. She handed him an old bottle of the local moonshine.

"Thank you," Max said pouring the murky liquor into his coffee cup. After tossing it back, his face puckered. "I hope that makes me feel better." Sitting upright, he asked, "What is your plan?"

Roche nodded in gratitude. "We go in through the back door, taking a raft across the Saigon-Cholon canal. Entering the stronghold, we locate my naive countrymen and exit unmolested before the sky falls in."

"We? You said we?" Max questioned.

"You, me and three members of your crew," Roche explained, "I think it's a five man job."

"You're going in?" Max asked.

"I'm not asking you to do anything I wouldn't do. Elaine is just your former lover. She still is my secretary," Roche replied.

Rising from his chair and stretching Max said, "Let's get this over with." Grinning he added, "I like the arrangement with the local girls. You pay for sex upfront. You don't always get what you pay for but you know the cost."

CHAPTER THIRTEEN

The sky was black. Small arms fire popped. An inflatable raft slipped into the brown liquid of the Saigon-Cholon canal. Across the waterway fires burned. Flames reflected off the murky water. Max paddled quietly. His blond locks concealed under a black bandana. In camouflaged Tai soldier fatigues, Loc rowed beside the German. The rubber boat drifted past the twisted metal and concrete remnants of a bridge. The old Meo warrior Pao clutching a crossbow, snorted at the smoky stench floating above the surface. Dressed in black with a blue turban, a stone faced Vue squinted at the smoldering inner city ruble. This was Vue's first trip to civilization. The seasoned jungle fighter was not impressed. In marine fatigues, Roche operated a simple rudder to navigate the short distance. The American's face painted various shades of dark green.

Pushing a bloated floating corpse aside, Max studied the approaching shoreline. A ten-foot log at the water's edge emerged from the shallows. What the hell, Max thought. A large crocodile slithered onto the shore. The armored skin streamlined reptile methodically pranced on webbed feet. Waving its massive tail the croc disappeared into the debris that lined the embankment.

Jumping out in the shallow water, Max pulled the raft and crew onto the muddy shore. "What's with the crocodile, Roche?" He inquired.

"One of the Binh Xuyen kingpins had a private collection of tigers, snakes and crocodiles he kept on display at the New World Casino." Roche answered.

"Casino?" Max questioned.

Roche pointed to the shell of a structure at the top of the ten-foot embankment.

Max nodded and cautiously led the team past the crocodile's layer. An asphalt boulevard capped the short debris cluttered incline. On the pockmarked street, twenty dead Binh Xuyen soldiers in the private army's mustard-colored uniforms and green berets laid face up. Max snorted at the battlefield odor of death. The smell triggering the image of the French hillsides littered with the bloated corpses of German soldiers and livestock. You never forget the stench, he thought. Flies buzzed about the sidewalk morgue. A half-a-dozen street children rummaged through the pockets of the deceased. Two of the squatting youths glanced up to examine the heavily armed five-man team. The others could not be bothered.

Turning to Loc, Max said, "Ask them if they've seen any white people."

Approaching the children, Loc translated. A boney shirtless boy wearing a confiscated green beret strutted towards the men. A sack slung over his bare back bulged with plunder. Inhaling deeply on the cigarette between his soiled lips, he exhaled. In broken French, he declared, "I know where the whites are hiding." Grinning with tobacco stained teeth, he extended an open palm and asked, "How much?"

Max rolled his eyes. "I'm in no mood to negotiate," he growled.

Roche stepped in. The American placed a large wad of *paistres* in the street punk's extended hand.

Wide-eyed the youth looked down at the fortune in currency. "The high school," he exclaimed. "Whites are trapped in the high school."

Roche turned to Max and said, "The Petrusky high school has become a Binh Xuyen garrison. It is less than a mile from here, if we cut through the casino."

Leaving the young vultures, Roche led the strung out team single file down the smoke filed boulevard. Abruptly he stopped and raised a fisted hand over his shoulder. Ten Binh Xuyen soldiers rounded the corner. The uniformed thugs froze. The two groups sized up the opposition.

Obvious deserters, Max realized brandishing a submachine. These fleeing men have no fight left in them. No discipline, he thought. You can dress a hoodlum in a uniform with a jaunty beret but that does not make him a soldier. The Binh Xuyen mobsters blinked first. Lowering their weapons, they advanced. Increasing their pace, they broke and ran out of sight.

In front of the three-story carcass of New World Casino, Roche shouldered his weapon. Peering through a window frame, he scanned the dark interior with a flashlight. The probing beam sparkled off shattered glass. Green felt gaming tables littered the red-carpeted floor. Bricks flowed down a staircase. Beneath a gaping hole in the plaster ceiling rested a pile of second story debris. Glancing over his shoulder, he nodded and climbed through the window. The three tribesmen followed. Max brought up the rear. In a tight line, the team advanced behind Roche's investigating flashlight. Crunching glass echoed in the empty hall. Roche stopped. The floor came to life. The illuminating ray captured a slithering ten-foot Burmese python. In the muggy dark atmosphere, Max chuckled. Just like a night patrol in the tropical forest of Tonkin, he thought, complete with menacing inhabitants. Giving the reptile a wide berth, the team pressed on. What is behind me? Max wondered glancing into darkness. He placed a hand on Pao's shoulder. The old warrior relayed the signal forward. In the dark silence, a distant moan closed in. A low threatening growl purred. Roche's small beam spotlighted an Indochinese Tiger dragging a one armed man. The cinnamon brown and black stripped regal beast paused with its prey. Defiant yellow eyes stared into the light. The large headed feline snorted. Blood dripped from bristled whiskers. The shoulder of the big cat's quarry secured by the vice grip of massive jaws. The terrified open-eyed victim dangled helplessly. The stump of his severed arm pulsed. The tiger's meal opened and closed his mouth without a sound. The carnivorous animal pranced back into the darkness with its prey. A slick trail of red marked the journey. Eight years of jungle fighting, Max thought and I have my first wild tiger sighting in Saigon.

Using his submachine gun, Roche cleared the remaining broken glass from a back window. Leading the team out of the Casino, he pointed down the smoldering boulevard, "The high school is just down the street." Turning to Max, he whispered, "Should we have killed the tiger?"

Max shook his head. No reason to announce their presence, he thought. The man would die anyway. The tiger would expedite the inevitable quietly.

Clinging to the shadows on the dark side of the thoroughfare, the team cautiously advanced. Passing the dark shelled frame of a clothing shop, a voice called out, "Max!"

Max stopped and looked at Loc and Vue. The tribesmen shrugged. The German squinted into the blown out window frame of the storefront.

"In here," the pleasant voice informed.

Stepping over bricks and splintered wood, Max carefully peered into what remained of the shop. The trunk of a dust covered man reclined on the floor, half buried in debris.

"What is it?" Roche whispered from the sidewalk.

"I don't know," Max mumbled. Crouching down beside the man, he flicked his lighter. "Do I know you?" Max asked studying the soiled face of a Binh Xuyen officer in the flickering light.

"No," the man replied. "But I know you. Hell, every Binh Xuyen soldier in Saigon was looking for you at one time. We all were hoping to claim the bounty that the Corsican Rossi had placed on your head. I see death has not found you yet."

Flipping his lighter shut, Max stood up. To the sound of crunching glass, Roche stepped through the window frame shinning his flashlight on the casualty.

Blinking into the beam of light, the officer asked, "How about a cigarette? Those street children picked me clean at dusk. Little roaches took my smokes."

Roche pulled out a cigarette and lit it. After taking a puff, he held the smoldering canister of nicotine just out of the man's reach and asked, "We are here to retrieve some Americans. Do you know where we might find them?"

Even in the dark environment the grin on the trapped man was visible. Nodding he said, "You are here for the leggy white woman. She was at the high school yesterday, that's all I know. I don't blame you for tracking her down, she is quite the looker." Extending his arm toward the cigarette, he twisted his hand to show an open palm seeking payment.

Paying the fee, Roche handed him the cigarette. Turning to Max, Roche whispered, "At least she was alive as of yesterday. Let's get out of here."

Staring at Roche, Max gestured in the direction of the confined informant.

"Leave him," Roche mumbled.

Inhaling the stagnant dust laced with the aroma of charred wood triggered Max's deeply warehoused memory of his own claustrophobic ordeal. On a French battlefield, he had spent some time in a shallow grave of bricks and mortar. Looking down at the glowing tip of the cigarette in the darkness, he asked, "How bad is it?"

"My foot is crushed, but I'll live," replied the incapacitated smoker.

"Death is closer than you think," Max said ignoring the impatiently scowling Roche. "Loc, Vue, I need some help."

Loc and Vue climbed through the window. Roche shined his flashlight on the victim. Looking around through the debris, Max found a ten foot piece of pipe. He and Loc slightly leveraged up the entrapping pile as Vue pulled the soldier free.

"Can we go now?" asked an annoyed Roche.

"Sure," Max said stepping back onto the sidewalk.

From within the shop the freed man said, "Thanks Max, I owe you."

"Good luck," Max whispered into the darkness.

Concealed by bushes, Max parted the brush. A few windows of the dark single story Petrusky high school glowed from faint internal lighting. A soldier mingled around sandbagged bunkers at the entrance. Other than that the shelter looked deserted. Crouching back down, Max whispered to Loc, "Tell Pao we need him to infiltrate the school and find out where the white people are being kept."

Loc translated. The old man rubbed dirt on his face. Handing Max his crossbow and pistol, he approached the entrance as a shell-shocked civilian.

Roche whispered, "Are you sure he is up to the task?'

Max smiled, "never underestimate a Meo warrior."

Pao quickly returned from the reconnaissance mission. In the dirt, he sketched out a map of the school and the classroom objective.

"Ask him if they are held as captives or just seeking shelter from the storm," Max said to Loc.

Pao shrugged his shoulders in response.

"What do you think Max?" Roche asked, "Should we try and negotiate a release?"

Checking his watch, Max said, "We don't have the luxury of time to find out and I'm not willing to risk the element of surprise." Checking his weapon, he added, "We should assume they're hostages."

"Let's do it," Roche said.

The team scampered along the shadows of the campus. Beneath the windowsill of a glowing classroom, Roche pulled a small mirror from a pant leg pocket. Holding it up to the window, he grinned. Crouching down, he handed the mirror to Max.

Max scanned the room through the reflective glass. A small kerosene lantern identified ten scruffy civilians sleeping on the floor. Curled up beside Merle, Elaine slept. Fast mover, Max thought. Next time Merle, you can rescue the long legged damsel when she gets too close to the flame. Turning the mirror slightly, he confirmed the presence of four Binh Xuyen soldiers, two with Tommy-guns, the others with holstered side arms. Squatting down, Max held up four fingers. His other hand tapped out a one, four, two, three shooting sequence. He pointed at Loc. His partner nodded. He pointed at Vue. The jungle fighter blinked his acknowledgement. Looking at Roche, he signaled for the American to break the window.

Grabbing the barrel of his submachine gun, Roche paused. Max unholstered and checked his pistol. Both men looked at each other taking several deep breaths. Roche rose and with his full force swung the weapon shattering the glass barrier. Leaping up Max shot the first expressionless thug in the forehead. Pivoting he got off another head shot on the other Tommy-gun carrying guard. The back of the targets head splattered across the classroom's black board. A round to the chest sent the third hostile tumbling into the screaming civilians. The forth target attempted to unholster a pistol. A bullet slammed into his shoulder. Spinning out of the way, Max realized the fourth guard still posed a threat. Loc and Vue leapt through the window. A quick burst of automatic weapons fire lit up the room.

Roche surveyed the battlefield. Loc had finished the job of eliminating the fourth hostile and stood watch at the door. Using the barrel of his gun, Roche cleared the remaining glass from the window frame. Vue ushered a bewildered Elaine to the window. Her head jerked back and forth.

Startled by a green faced Roche, she mumbled, "Tom? What the..."

"Let's go honey, times a wasting," he said.

Jumping out of the window, Elaine landed in Max's arms, "Max?" she questioned. Focused on the mission, he ignored her and placed her on the ground next to a very serious old man carrying a crossbow.

"Merle, Russing let's move," Roche called out to the American journalist.

A red-faced Frenchman stuck his head out the window shouting, "Murders, murders, you just gunned downed four men in cold blood!"

Pointing his submachine gun at the irate frog, Roche said, "Do you want to make it five budrow?" Glaring up he added, "This place is about to be leveled. You can ride out the firestorm with your gangster allies or flee. The choice is yours."

Pushing the Frenchman out of the way, Merle hopped out the window followed by his camera toting associate.

"Roche," Max called out. "Scurry towards that stinking canal with your countrymen. I'll bring up the rear with the Tais."

Roche nodded. "Let's go ladies," he barked leading the sprint to the waterway with Pao.

Loc and Vue joined Max on the ground below the windowsill. "Any soldiers coming?" Max questioned.

Loc shook his head.

Maybe we didn't have to kill these men after all, Max thought. No need to ponder that now, he concluded. "Let's get out of here," he declared. Befuddled French faces poked out window. "*Bonne chance,*" shouted a departing Max.

Max and the Tais easily caught up with the American delegation. A winded and stumbling Elaine hindered progress on the deserted war torn streets. Handing Loc his weapon, Max tossed the big-busted beauty across his shoulders. His former lover grunted and groaned from the jarring escape. Carrying comrades off the battlefield is never pleasant, Max thought. Hearing Elaine whining discomfort, he grinned. Serves you right sweetheart, he mused.

"Forget the Casino and the raft," Roche said between breaths. "We'll get to the canal and swim for it."

At the water's edge, Max put Elaine down on the muddy shoreline. She collapsed. Placing his hands on his knees, he inhaled the foul stagnant canal stench. Elaine screamed. The winded party flinched. Roche shined his flashlight at the reclining woman. At her feet, a large wharf rat elevated on back haunches threatened. Whooshing wind preceded a projectile impaling the rodent. Pao swaggered over with an empty crossbow. The old Meo picked up the speared rat. A dying tail twisted and turned around the wooden arrow. Stepping on the vermin, Pao retrieved the projectile. The tiny man grinned at the open-mouthed Elaine.

"Let's get wet," Roche said removing his boots. Holding his automatic weapon and footwear over his head, he waded into the liquid filth. Russing followed holding his camera high in the air. A splashing Merle swam free-style. Elaine shot the brown water-spraying journalist a look of disgust. Stretching her neck above the foul surface, she gingerly dog paddled.

Scanning the shoreline, Max picked up the remnants of a wooden crate. He tossed it into the water. The tribesmen placed boots and weapons into the floatation device.

Treading water behind the group, Max kept a close watch on Pao. The old Meo clung to the box. The other two tribesmen pushed it across the short waterway.

Max emerged and plopped down on the water's edge next to Roche. The tribesmen stood in ankle deep water retrieving boots and weapons from the wood box. The photographer blew on his camera between breaths. In the limited light, Max gazed at his former lover. Exhausted Elaine gasped for air. Her wet blouse clung to her heaving chest. All form and no substance, Max thought. Focused on her shapely breast, he grinned. No substance he concluded, but a hell of form. Reaching into his breast pocket, he pulled out a saturated handful of tobacco. With a sour face, he tossed the waterlogged cigars back into the canal.

Breaking the silence, Roche asked, "Did you get off all four shots? It did not sound like it."

"Yes I did," Max responded. "That happens sometimes with my rapid fire. The sound is deceiving."

"That was an amazing display of marksmanship my kraut brother," Roche said with a bow.

"The National Socialist taught me well," Max responded.

"If the Nazis taught you to shoot, where did you learn your battlefield compassion? I was surprised when you freed that Binh Xuyen officer." Roche questioned with a curious squint.

"As a boy-soldier, I spent two days pinned under the ruble of a French cafe during the Battle of Caen." Max said quietly to soften the harsh recollection. "A French speaking Canadian soldier released me from the tomb." Taking a deep breath he confessed, "It was my first lesson in empathy."

"Excuse me!" Merle interrupted in English. "Was that rescue really necessary?"

Roche translated for Max. The German chuckled. Loc relayed Merle's inquiry to Vue and Pao. The rescue team exchanged snickering glances. A faint high-pitched whine escalated into a shrill whistle. The silhouetted skyline across the canal erupted with deafening man made thunder. The artillery barrage pounding the Cholon district accelerated. Flames and debris shot into the night sky. Splintered wood and chunks of concrete rained down. The surface of the canal splashed and churned.

The group rose and slowly backed away from the turbulent water's edge. The bombardment intensified. Merle placed a consoling arm across Elaine's trebling shoulders. She repelled the advance by dipping and relocating next to Max. Tenderly she grasped his hand. Looking down into the soft eyes of the soaking wet temptress nuzzling up beside him, Max winked.

CHAPTER FOURTEEN

Roche focused on the sweeping second hand of a small desk clock. Quarter to ten, only fifteen more minutes until the briefing, he calculated. Time for my shot, he realized. Out of the large bottom desk drawer, he pulled out a half full bottle of bourbon. He took a healthy snort. The warm whisky burned the back of his throat. That should calm my inner demon, he hoped. I can't afford to lose my temper.

"Excuse me, Tom," Elaine said standing in the doorway.

"Yes Elaine," he said catching his breath. Hastily he re-filed the bottle of Jim Beam and spun around in the squeaking swivel chair,

Stepping forward she entered the tight enclosure. The office seemed to shrink with her occupancy. "I don't know how to say this diplomatically," She said holding a hanger with a starch white shirt a black tie. Innocently shrugging she continued, "I overheard the Assistant Secretary of State make a negative comment about your casual dress. I thought business attire may be more appropriate for this morning's session." An outstretched arm extended the shirt in his direction. She looked down at the floor.

"Thanks Elaine," Roche said accepting the professional costume, "That's very thoughtful."

"It's the least I can do for you saving my life last week," Elaine said looking into his eyes.

"Oh, I can give you a few other repayment suggestions," Roche chuckled.

"Tom," Elaine snickered as she exited.

Watching the long legged Elaine strut away, Roche focused on her perfect bottom. Her cotton dress swayed back and forth to the beat of a seductive stride. Max gets to sleep with her for the rescue mission, Roche thought, and I get laundry service and fashion tips. Examining the shirt and tie he realized it was a friendly gesture, She was looking out for him.

Taking off his Hawaiian shirt, he quickly dressed. Sliding his arms into the starched long sleeved shirt felt awkward. Fastening each button increased the confining sensation. Flipping up the stiff collar, he draped the tie around his neck. Pausing he tried to remember the knotting sequence.

"Let's go Tom," Matthews said standing in the office doorway, "We don't want to be late for our dressing-down." Out of the side of his mouth, he mumbled, "Nice tie."

Tugging on the tight collar, Roche joined Matthews on the walk to the embassy conference room. Opened double doors framed Robinson, the Assistant Secretary of State perched at the head of the long table. The focused bureaucrat read from a stack of papers. The agents quietly entered and took distancing seats. Robinson's large forehead glistened with sweat. A pair of glasses clung to the tip of his noise. Beside the documentation, a coffee mug disrespected the cork coasters strewn about. The polished wood table top stained with cup rings.

"Gentlemen," Robinson said peeking over the tops of his balanced spectacles. "I'll be brief. I'm aware there are splits, or should I say differences of opinion within the U.S. mission here in Vietnam with regard to the Prime Minister." Leaning back, he interlocked fingers over his chest and lectured. "The two of you have been very outspoken about the incompetence of Diem. The current administration appreciates your candor in bringing his shortcomings to light."

"Sir...," Matthews coughed.

The palm of Robinson's raised hand terminated the exchange. "I'm not going to debate the issue. I'm here to dictate the United States policy." He declared. Slowly he removed his reading glasses. After enjoying his silencing power, he informed, "Diem has proved himself as a worthy leader. He displayed courage eradicating the Binh Xuyen criminal organization from Saigon. Simply put, he is our man. The United States will use all of the resources available, to support Prime Minister Diem's efforts to stabilize, secure and strengthen a Free Vietnam. That includes," Robinson paused tilting his large head in the agent's direction, "the services of the Central Intelligence Agency without dissent."

Staring at the large sparkling forehead pointed at him, Roche realized how naive the Washington bureaucracy was to the situation in Vietnam. At least my memorandums predicting the dire consequences of backing Diem are being read, he thought, otherwise I would not been called in on the carpet.

Leaning back in his chair Robinson continued, "The next order of business in a laundry list of tasks is to establish Diem as the leader of a non-communist Vietnam. We will be by showing the world that he is the peoples' choice through the democratic process. The people of Vietnam will decide in the upcoming election between the competent and moral Diem and the corrupt French puppet Bao Dia."

French puppet? Roche thought. At least the French controlled Bao Dia. The American's marionette pulls his own stings, while dictating terms to the puppeteer.

Robinson rose and said, "Gentlemen, as promised, I said I would be brief. Thank you for your time." The agents stood up. Leaning over the glossy tabletop, he shook Matthew's hand. Reaching in Roche's direction, he repeated the ritual. "Tom, I wanted to compliment you on placing Elaine Favreau within the palace inner circle. She has been an invaluable asset in communicating our suggestion for stabilizing this country."

Shaking Robinson's hand, Roche bit his lower lip. You pompous diplomat, he thought. Don't you realize that the U.S. is pumping hundreds-of-millions of dollars of aid into the Diem government. And with all that leverage, you are relying on a secretarial contract employ to relay your desires.

CHAPTER FIFTEEN

The rising sun cast long shadows across the terraced rice paddies and rolling hills of the Plain of Jars. The sunlight illuminated the thousands of megalithic jars scattered across the landscape. The historical significance and mystery of the large hollowed out lipped boulders lost on the current region's opium smuggling inhabitants. Standing off the red clay runway at the Phong Savin airport, Max inhaled crisp highland air. He caught a whiff of cigarette smoke. Beside him, Loc puffed away. The drone of a taxiing twin-engine plane contaminated the tranquil atmosphere. The prop wash of revving engines kicked up red dust. Glaring into the cockpit, Max received an apologetic shrug from the silhouette behind the controls. The obnoxious Twin-Beech idled at the edge of the runway.

Tugging on Max's long sleeved shirt, Loc pointed to a reflective spark hovering over the horizon. Max squinted at the incoming flight. The approaching spec materialized over the treetops. An unmarked C-47 Skytrain set down hard on the red clay tarmac. The large transport skipped down the runway kicking up crimson plumes. The morning rays flickered off the metallic beast. Snorting white smoke the aircraft taxied towards the Civil Air Transport corrugated tin hangar facility. The flight terminated with a sputtering cough. Max glanced down at Loc. The tribesman took one last satisfying toke before flicking his cigarette. In the cool morning breeze, they strutted to greet the passengers.

The door behind the wing on the long fuselage popped open. A shaved head popped out. The curious noggin surveyed the Laotian highlands. Apparently satisfied, the bald American in a short-sleeve white shirt hopped out of the aircraft. Other lean and muscular civilians disembarked. The arriving passengers milled about the red clay surface. This is supposedly an archeological survey team, Max chuckled. Who decided on that cover for the Special Operation Unit, he wondered. In a defiant stance, the covert team members scrutinized the approaching German and tribesman. To assist in the analysis, Max showed the palms of his hands. Loc did the same.

Stepping out of the pack, a snowcapped haired agent in khaki trousers and a tight muscle revealing t-shirt said, "You must be Max."

"Yes, I'm Max Kohl, and this is Loc," Max informed. "We're here to assist you with your archeological endeavors."

Snow top chuckled. Extending his hand, he said, "Jim Dugan, I'm in charge of the mission."

Shaking the hand with a firm grip, Max said, "Pleased to meet you Jim, I must say your French is excellent."

"Thank you Max," Dugan replied nodding in the direction of his mingling colleagues. "We have undergone extensive training for this assignment. The preparations included daily language lessons in French and Laotian. We also studied the successes and failures of the French Indochina military campaign." Addressing Loc, he added, "Our brief education taught us to respect the fighting capabilities of the tribal people. We look forward to establishing a solid alliance to defeat the communist Pathet Lao."

I've heard this dramatic cant before, Max realized. Whether it was the Americans demonizing the Pathet Lao. The French anti-Vietminh rhetoric or the German National Socialist propaganda about the threat of Communist Russia, it was the same dialogue. The only change in this never ending performance was the actors.

"Max, if you don't mind," Dugan said, "I would like to meet with Colonel Yang this morning and observe his growing Meo army. My boys have enough to keep them busy establishing our base of operations at the airport. That flying boxcar is loaded to the gills with communication equipment and combat supplies."

"That should not be a problem," Max responded. "The Colonel's Laotian infantry battalion and Meo self-defense forces are bivouacked on the outskirts of Phong Savin."

"My review of the Colonel and his exploits has been extensive," Dugan commented. Pointing a serious finger at Max asked, "What is your impression of the man?"

Smiling at the notion that his opinion had relevance, Max replied. "Don't be fooled by his boyish looks and small stature. He is a warrior and a leader of men. He would not ask his troops to do anything that he wouldn't do, however everyone is expendable." Rubbing his chin Max recalled his combat experience with Captain Yang. "Your intelligence probably covered my involvement with Yang rescuing a Meo village from Vietminh reprisals."

Dugan nodded.

Max continued. "First hand I observed a brilliant strategist focused on the mission. The loss of life to accomplish the task was secondary to achieving the goal."

Squinting Dugan asked, "Do you know anything about the Colonel's rumored corruption?"

Max snorted. "I've been to Saigon and got a peek behind the curtain at the ruling class. When they enhance their wealth off the regional hostilities, it is called good business. When the men who fight and die in the trenches attempt to prosper off the conflict, they are labeled corrupt. From my perspective Colonel Yang is a good businessman."

CHAPTER SIXTEEN

In the warm dust of the Laotian military compound, an army jeep skidded to an abrupt termination. Max jerked forward. Stepping out of the vehicle, he swatted at the billowing cloud of red. Thousands of men in the green fatigues of the Laotian troops and sandaled tribal soldiers in black smock tops and short black pants stood in formation. Three tribesmen lay prostrated on the ground in front of the assemblage. Sharply dressed in an officer's uniform, a strutting Colonel Yang Mo ranted. A black beret drooped over his small head. His rolled up shirt sleeves displayed a gold Swiss watch. The expensive timepiece sparkled in the late morning sunlight. Yang acknowledged Max's presence with a friendly raised brow. Refocusing he continuing to berate the men at his feet.

Jumping out of the vehicle, Dugan placed a palm under his chin and grabbed the side of his head. A startling yank cracked his neck into alignment. "Looks like they were expecting us," he exclaimed stepping forward.

"Wait a minute Jim," Max said politely blocking the advance. "I don't think the muster is for our benefit."

Whispering to Max, Loc clarified, "The three tribesmen are deserters, apparently forsaking their military obligation to return to their village."

Deserters? Max questioned recalling a warm day in the summer of 1944. On a table of a bombed out cafe in Northern France, his legs dangled above broken glass, splinted wood and loose bricks. In a water filled tin cup, he stirred chunks of hard bread. Sniveling he sucked back the urge to weep. A dirty spoon attempted to soften the pathetic meal. The back of a dusty sleeve wiped his sniveling nose. He inhaled the rotting stench of death. Investing the crunch of broken glass, his watery eyes gazed upon Sergeant Franz. Covered in soot, the battle hardened thirty-year-old sergeant stepped into the fire-gutted structure. The wrinkles of his black-ened face showed fatigue. The fire in his brown eyes burned with the deter-mination of a professional soldier.

"Are you alright Maximilian?" Franz asked. Dipping a shoulder, he removed his pack.

Max swallowed hard on knotted emotions. On the edge of tears, his voice crackled, "Did we have to kill them?"

"I'm afraid so my sharpshooting *kamerad*," The consoling sergeant replied. He plopped his steel helmet on the table. Running a blackened hand through the sweat soaked bristles of cropped hair, he added, "Cowardice is not tolerated in the *Wehrmacht*, regardless of the age of the deserters." Placing a hand on Max's shoulder, he asked, "Were the boys friends of yours?"

"We went through basic training together, I knew them but not well," Max answered. Attempting to gain Franz's respect, he clarified, "They weren't boys. They were soldier."

"That's right," Franz grinned. "And soldiers know the penalty for battlefield desertion." Rubbing a soiled chin, he reflected. "The sentenced passed upon our colleagues today was justified. The execution of the Canadian prisoners last week was a crime." The seasoned veteran looked at the teenage soldier. "Max we are German soldiers. We follow orders uncon-ditionally, however stay disciplined and true to the profession." Pausing his sooty face softened. "When I was with the *Afrika Korps*, Field Marshall Rommel forbid any reprisals against civilians or prisoners of war. Although in combat, the temptation for retribution always exists, just remember we are soldiers in the finest fighting force to march across the face of this planet not fanatics. When we meet our maker, we do it with pride."

A handgun popped. Max refocused. Yang shot the first man in the back of the leg. Methodically Yang crippled the second tribesman in a simi-lar fashion before firing a small caliber round in the third deserter's thigh.

Holstering his side arm, Yang dismissed the troops. Several Meo sol-diers ran over to assist their wounded colleagues.

Swaggering over Yang reached up and patted Max's shoulder. "Always good to see my German brother," he said cheerfully. Slapping Loc's back, he added grinning, "even though I may be more closely related to Loc." Extending a hand to Dugan, he said, "You must be the military advisor my American allies promised."

"Jim Dugan," Dugan responded firmly shaking the little man's hand.

"Mister Jim please let's discuss my growing supply needs," Yang said motioning toward a cluster of grass roofed huts.

The visitors followed behind the strutting Yang. The foot traffic of an army had ground the courtyard into a fine powder. Yang changed course to avoid the deserters' bloodstains. Outside an open-air hut, they stomped their dust-clad boots before entering. A table made out of waste wood sat at a slight angle in the center of the shack. Under the table were several stools.

Pulling a stool out from under the table, Yang sat down. He motioned with a wave of his arm for his guest to join him. "What are my American allies proposing to do about the twenty percent tariff proposed by the Corsicans on my opium?" He asked.

Max uncomfortably shifted his weight on a tiny wobbly stool. Dugan's face puckered at the mention of opium. Americans sure do not like the sound of that word, Max thought recalling Roche's bitter reaction.

A deep cleansing breath washed away Dugan's sour face. Diplomatically he responded, "Colonel, I'm not here to discuss your various business ventures. I'm here to assist you in organizing the tribal population of Laos against the threat of Communism. Famine is on the horizon in several Northern provinces due to the recent rice failure. I see this unfortunate event as a recruitment opportunity of the eligible young men in the surrounding hills. We can induce them to act as intelligent gathering commandos by feeding and clothing their families. The United States will provide the humanitarian aid. You will provide the inspiration to your countrymen to join in the anti-communist cause against the Pathet Loa."

"What of training and munitions?" Yang asked.

"The United States will provide the relief aid," Dugan repeated. Leaning back, he boastfully informed, "I will provide you with the military training and munitions you require."

Beaming Yang said, "Excellent Mister Jim, I'm looking forward to a mutually beneficial relationship." Then looking at the smug Dugan, he asked, "Now what are we going to do about the opium tariff?"

Dugan rolled his eyes fidgeting on the three-legged stool.

Touching Dugan's arm, Max clarified, "Colonel Yang any issues with regard to your non-military endeavors you can discuss with me."

"Well then Max," Yang insisted. "What are you going to do about the Corsican extortion?"

Turning to Dugan, Max asked, "Jim could you excuse us for a moment?"

"Sure Max," Dugan responded, "I'll be right outside."

Dugan exited. Max, Loc and Yang sat quietly. After verifying Dugan's absence, Max informed, "Colonel the Americans are in denial when it comes to their involvement in the opium trade. Don't ask me why." He paused and accented the commentary with a shrug. "The only reason Loc and I are in their employ is insulation and deniability from illicit drug trafficking. Also you must understand, that if you go to blows with the Corsicans over their proposed fee, you risk losing the Americans as your sponsor. Just the mention of the word opium makes them cringe. God only knows how they would react to an opium war."

"I appreciate your explanation Max, but it still does not solve the Corsican issue," Yang stated.

"Here is how I see it." Max offered. "The twenty percent is the cost of insuring that one hundred percent of your product makes it to market. I would propose paying the Corsican and there Vietnamese backers in product. That way the twenty percent would be calculated based on quantity not quality. You exclude the product with the higher morphine content from the equation, reducing the cost of your insurance."

Yang nodded. "You will make this proposal to the Corsicans?" He asked.

Grinning Max answered, "That is what the Americans pay me for."

CHAPTER SEVENTEEN

It was an unseasonably clear sunny morning in the central city of Hue. Rain had visited this former capital of Vietnam the night before. The city hummed under a crisp clean dawn. Phan a thin wiry twenty-four year old transit worker finished buttoning his clean white long sleeve shirt. Hastily he tucked the shirt's tail into black slacks. Slipping into sandals, he walked over to the small table next to the door. Picking up his tattered billfold, he confirmed the presence of his identity card. Satisfied he placed the wallet in the front pocket of his trousers. Taking a deep breath, he pushed his rusty bicycle out the front door of his small apartment. This is a great day for the people of Vietnam, he thought peddling in the flowing stream of morning rush hour. We the people have a chance to speak as to the future of our nation, he thought. Lorries coughed white smoke. Car horns barked. A distance red-light halted the procession of taxis, delivery trucks and automobiles. Phan joined the other bicycles and scooters weaving through the idling maze. Straddling his bike, he planted his sandaled feet on the asphalt. Cross traffic raced by. He snorted at the polluted air. A large political banner strung across the intersection caught his attention. A picture of a youthful smiling Prime Minster Diem rippled in the wind. The words democracy, republic, and human rights jumped out of the text. After a quick glance at the red traffic light, he scanned the campaign posters dominating the busy thoroughfare on this Election Day. In vain he searched for at least one image of the Emperor Bao Dai. A truck's horn howled. Phan flinched. Joining the surging traffic, he blindly waved an apology to the impatient horn blower.

Chaining the bicycle to a light pole, Phan grinned at the short line outside his designated polling station. This should not take long, he concluded. Joining the queue, he shuffled forward. Amongst the photographic images of the beaming Prime Minster Diem plastered around the open doorway, he spotted a poster depicting a cartoon caricature of the Emperor Bao Dai. It mocked the monarch as obese with his hand around a sleazy blonde, while a Frenchman stuffed money into the Emperor's blotted pockets. The caption read, *'Bao Dai, puppet king selling his country.'* What does that mean? Phan wondered. He shook his head. It does not matter, he realized. Bao Dai was Vietnam's ruler, mandated from heaven. God chose the Emperor, he thought. Casting my vote will make it official.

Inside the door, an administrator sat hunched over a small table. A few wisps of greasy hair graced the top of a balding head. Phan stood beaming.

The clerk mumbled, "Identity card."

Retrieving his wallet, Phan produced the documentation with a smile. The bureaucrat used a ballpoint pen to scan a long list of voters. He checked off Phan's name. Blindly he handed back the identity card. Reaching down the emotionless official retrieved a ballot and envelope. In a monotone voice he instructed, "Tear off the half representing your candidate. Place it in the envelope and present it to the Commission Chief for review before inserting it into the ballot box."

"Thank you," Phan said to the top of the administrator's head.

Examining the ballot, Phan frowned. This can't be right, he questioned. Bao Dai's half of the ballet, framed a somber picture of the Emperor in green, the color of misfortune. Below the photo it read: *"I do not depose Bao Dai and do not regard Ngo Dinh Diem as the Head of State charged with the commission of setting up a democratic regime."* Diem's half bordered in lucky red around a smiling Prime Minister surrounded by happy people, declared: *"A vote for Diem is a vote for democracy."*

Dragging his sandaled feet on the floor littered with green paper, Phan tore his ballot in half. He placed his green choice for Bao Dai in the envelope. The discarded red ballot slowly drifted to the sea of green paper at his feet.

"I believe you've made a mistake," informed the scowling inspecting commissioner.

Phan nodded and reexamined his placement of the ballot in the envelope. It looks appropriate; he concluded handing the envelope to the Commissioner.

The Commissioner snorted and tore Phan's attempt at the democratic process into pieces. Two men in black suit coats stretched uncomfortably across broad shoulders approached.

"Is there a problem here," a thug growled.

The Commissioner nodded. Phan's knees turned to jelly. He began to pant. The henchmen each grabbed an arm. Hoisted into the air, Phan could not speak. A sandal slid off one of his dangling feet. The line of voters parted as the thugs ushered the suspended youth out the polling station. There is no hope of rescue, Phan realized gazing upon his fellow citizens. Slammed onto the sidewalk, Phan stared at the creased pants legs of his hovering assailants.

"For freedom?" One of the ruffians chuckled.

"No let's do this one for democracy," responded his snickering colleague.

"Very well then for democracy," the thug concurred.

A massive paw grabbed a handful of Phan's hair and jerked back his head. He yelped. Through teary eyes, he got a glimpse of a bottle of red liquid. Chili sauce flowed down his titled nostrils, igniting the back of his throat. A firm grip held his face under the red liquid fire. Surfacing vomit attempted to expel the molten flavoring. Released Phan collapsed on the concrete pavement.

The pedestrian traffic gave a wide berth to the laughing brutes. The empty bottle clinked off sidewalk. "Let's do the next one for freedom," an assailant chuckled.

Phan crawled into the gutter. Cupping a hand, he inhaled stagnant puddle water. Weeping he looked up. The smiling image of Prime Minister Diem returned the teary gaze. The caption on the campaign poster declared: *Ngo Dinh Diem, Hero of the People.*

CHAPTER EIGHTEEN

In the cluttered confines of his embassy office, Tom Roche stared at a fifth of bourbon. Lightly shaking the half-full bottle, he watched the swirling golden liquid. If I'm going to wash down the sins of others, he thought. I might as well do it in the hallowed darkness of a confessional. Tilting back in the swiveling desk chair, he flipped off the light. Regaining balance, he unscrewed the plastic cap on the square bottle. What more could I have done? He thought. The current administration had determined that Diem was their man. The United States assisted in creating the Republic of Vietnam for Diem to govern. Reflecting on the corrupt regime, he took a large swig of whisky. What a poor choice we have made, he concluded. The warm liquid flowed down the back of his throat. The entitled Diem is a prick he snickered. God only knows how the prick will rule with the democratic title of president. Leaning back, Roche placed his feet on the paper-covered desk. He tossed back another healthy jolt of Jim Beam. It's the little things that determine the character of the man, he always believed. Small actions become a man's tell. It determines how you play the cards you are dealt. Hell, Diem was dealing from a stacked deck in this election with the red and green ballots. Even with that inside lane, he had to cheat, getting more votes than voters. I made my issues with the dangerous man and his family well known through the proper channels, Roche surmised. People listened to me before the Battle of Saigon, and now I'm being labeled as a malcontent.

"Tom, there you are," Elaine said standing in the doorway.

Jerking forward, Roche dropped his feet to the floor. A large stack of papers cascaded off the desk. "Elaine!" he said, "You startled me."

"Well that's what you get for drinking by yourself in the dark," she said placing her hands on her famous hips. Extending an upturned hand in his direction, she wiggled her fingers. "Come with me, I'm in need of an escort to the conference room. The embassy is providing champagne to celebrate Diem's victory in the referendum."

Rolling his eyes, he mumbled in a raspy voice, "No thank you Elaine, I prefer drinking alone."

Stepping into the office stall, she put her hands on his shoulders. Her pulsing grip initiated a seductive massage.

Closing his eyes, he floated in darkness to the fragrant aroma of her distinctive perfume.

Kneading at his tense muscles, she leaned forward and purred, "I won't take no for an answer."

Reaching back, he patted a manipulating hand. I'm no match for her persuasive powers, he realized. "Sure, why not," he conceded.

As he stood, she hugged his arm and said, "This will be fun."

The couple strolled down the empty embassy hallway. Under the amorous affect of bourbon, he flexed his arm in her grasp. This will never amount to more than playful flirtation, he realized but the fantasy dance is rewarding. Entering the open doublewide doorway of the conference room, Roche stood proudly with the sultry Elaine dangling on his arm. The room resonated with laughter and cocktail chatter. A large wooden conference table dominated the room. At one end its polished lacquered surface reflecting a dozen tall dark green champagne bottles standing in formation. Broad-bowled stemmed glasses sparkled. Across the surface empty bottles and random glasses reclined as dead soldiers. Around the glossy varnished wood battlefield, thirty members of the embassy staff selfishly indulged in free alcohol.

Observing the festivities, Roche snickered. This is not a celebration, he realized. It is an excuse for the expats to get drunk.

Roche poured some champagne for Elaine and himself. Across the table, the bigheaded assistant secretary of state peered at Roche suspiciously. Picking up his glass of sparkling wine, Roche mimed a toast in

Robinson's direction. Nodding at the gesture, Robinson stepped forward pulling out a silver pen from his breast pocket.

"Your attention please," Robinson said tapping the pen against an empty green bottle. The room slowly hushed. "Now that we are all here," he declared tilting his large forehead in Roche's direction. "I would like to propose a toast." He raised his bowled glass over the table. The embassy staff mimicked his motion. "To the people of Vietnam, whose voices were overwhelming heard in this free election supporting the leadership of President Diem. Ladies and Gentlemen to democracy," Robinson raised his glass slightly higher before taking a sip.

The other attendees murmured, "democracy."

Leaning over to Elaine, Roche whispered, "Sorry Elaine, I can't do this. I need to return the solitude of warm whisky."

Grabbing his arm, Elaine tilted her head and flashed deep brown eyes. In search of comfort, he returned her gaze. Her charm is not working, he thought. Even the seductive Elaine Favreau cannot numb my gut retching sense of hypocrisy, he realized. Politely shaking off her grasp, he headed for the double doors.

Terminating Roche's escape at the doorway, Robinson questioned, "Tom, leaving so soon?"

I've dealt with warlords and criminals for the anti-communist cause, Roche reflected snarling at the political appointee. A grin emerged as Roche asked, "Where did you go to college Mr. Robinson?"

A multitude of wrinkles appeared up and down Robinson's big forehead. "Duke...I went to Duke University." He muttered.

"Did you ever cheat in college? Have someone else write a term paper or maybe have the answers to a quiz or examine?" Roche prodded.

"Tom I'm not following your logic here," Robinson questioned.

"The logic is simple," Roche replied chuckling. "If you know the answers to an examine you try for a B or if you are bold go for a B-plus. If you stuff the ballot box in a free election, you should aim for sixty percent of the vote. If you get over a hundred percent of the vote like that son-of-a-bitch Diem, you're not allowed to use the word democracy when toasting the election."

A vein appeared across the vast surface below Robinson hairline. The purplish blood vessel began to pulse. A constipated Robinson growled, "Tom, I will not tolerate disparaging language when referring to President Diem."

Grinning at the beet red politician, Roche asked, "Do you consider the term jack-ass disparaging?"

"Why yes! Yes I do," Robinson shouted.

"Just checking," Roche said sidestepping around the fuming bureaucrat. Quickening his pace, he preceded down the lonely dark corridor.

"Tom!" Elaine shouted out from behind.

Turning around, he barked, "What is it Elaine?"

"Easy," Elaine responded holding up her hands, "Just thought you could use a drinking companion while considering your career options."

"Very funny," he chuckled. "As for our current job security, Washington has set this country on a course through treacherous waters and placed a dangerous man at the helm. It's only a matter of time before the ship goes down and we all will be seeking other employment."

"Tom, really," Elaine said playfully frowning. "The house of Ngo does have its short comings but I've become very close with Madame Nhu. I can assure you the family intends to use the power they've been given to reform Vietnam."

Standing in the shadows of the quiet corridor, Roche examined the naive Elaine. A soft blue form fitting cotton dress clung to a tempting frame. A wide black belt cinched tightly around a slender waist matched patent leather high heels. A string of pearls resting on the nape of a taut neck complimented pearl earrings. The girl knows how to package herself, he thought. However, when it comes to intuition about the tyrannical hunger of a despot family, she is no more than a contract employee blinded by the elevation of her station. "I hope you are right, Elaine," Roche said resuming his escape.

"What about that drink? Tom," she called out.

"Some other time," he mumbled.

CHAPTER NINETEEN

The morning sunlight crawled into the open window. It slowly crept across the lacquered hardwood floor of the upscale Saigon flat. Jostled by the illuminating dawn, the naked houseboy leapt out of his master's bed. He wrapped a sarong around his slender waist. Quietly on the balls of his bare feet, he strolled across the polished surface. Entering the small kitchen, he lit the gas burner under a teakettle. My finicky master likes to awaken to the aroma of coffee, he thought. Carefully he filled the bottom of a coffee cup with sweet milk. After shoveling rounded teaspoons of ground coffee into the small tin brewing chamber, he placed the perforated metal filter on the cup. Slowly he poured hot water onto the hat shaped disk. The steaming liquid seeped into the rich chocolate grounds.

"Where is my coffee?" growled the master.

Flinching, the manservant hastily placed the misting cup on a saucer. His bare feet pounded the hardwood flooring in the race to the bedroom. Propped up on an elbow, the young lord accepted the morning brew. A white sheet covered his thin naked frame from the waist down. His signature perfectly parted jet-black hair tousled about from the late night coupling.

"I will be traveling today," he said taking a sip of the hot sweet concoction. "Pack my bag and lay out the sharkskin suit and," he paused with a squint before adding, "black tie and white handkerchief."

The half-naked boy nodded and carefully retrieved the attire from a large armoire. Smiling he relished the thought of three and possible four days of unmolested sleep.

Sliding into the fine fabric of the sharkskin suit coat, Tommy adjusted the thin black tie and secured the white pocket-handkerchief. With perfectly parted jet-black hair, he stood in front of the full-length mirror admiring his boyish good looks. Not bad for a gook, he thought stroking the tailor made garment. Oh the games we've been forced to play to access the American's power, he realized. Glancing up, he smirked at the reflection of the crucifix hanging over his bed. Looking at the nailed image of Christ on the cross, he chuckled. If Catholicism is the admission fee for wealth in the new Vietnam so be it, he concluded. The ramblings of Hail Marys and Our Fathers are really no more than Buddhist mantras to recite whilst meditating; the rosary, prayer beads. Lifting a leg, he allowed the houseboy kneeling before him to slip on a patent leather shoe. Glancing down he used the boy's naked shoulder for balance. Squeezing the soft flesh, he realized that being Catholic was a good cover for his sexual preferences.

"Where will you be traveling today?" asked the kneeling boy.

"Phong Savin?" Tommy mumbled using the palm of his hand to primp the back of his head.

"You're not going to Laos this time?" the boy asked.

Inhaling deeply Tommy sighed in disgust, "Phong Savin is in Laos," he grumbled. No wonder the whites treat us with contempt, he thought. The country is populated by morons. But unlike the majority of my countrymen, I am educated, speak three languages and figured out how to play the American's game. I've earned the privilege to loot and pillage whenever I can. However it does pay to be white he realized, thinking about the stocky blond German. Hell, that blue-eyed Nazi veteran is no more than a brigand. Tommy snorted looking at his reflection. Then tilting his head to the side mumbled sarcastically, "But because of his light-skinned European origin the kraut gets an invitation to the Palace reception."

CHAPTER TWENTY

Sheets of rain cascaded down from the night sky. Plodding along the deserted runway of the Phong Savin airport, Max avoided the growing puddles on the slick gummy red soil. Wiggling his toes, he grinned. At least my feet are dry, he thought. To the pounding of water careening off his poncho, he squinted in the wet darkness. Blurred lights illuminated the Corsican airline hangar.

Through wide-open bay doors, Max entered the brightly lit corrugated sheet metal structure. Rainfall reverberated off rippled tin. Flipping back the poncho hood, he shook the moisture from his bleached blond locks. The clean aroma of fresh cut wood lingered in the recently completed facility. Elbow deep in the engine of a Cessna, an Asian mechanic labored. A smoldering cigarette attached to his lower lip. At the grease monkey's feet, an assortment of tools and engine parts blanketed the concrete floor. Behind the Cessna, a line of collies passed bundles of opium towards the cargo door of a twin-engine plane. Several armed local thugs monitored the progress. In the corner, five Europeans played poker. A cloud of smoke hung over the round gaming table. Probably grounded pilots, Max concluded. Nobody is flying in this weather. Recognizing the pistol-whipped gangster Carlo, Max grinned.

Max approached the card game. Standing patiently, he observed the betting. Water dripped off his raingear. Displaying a pair of queens, a coffee drinking pilot confiscated the currency and coin pot. The smug players mumbled amongst themselves and dealt out another hand. Don't mistake my politeness as weakness, Max thought taking off his poncho. Shaking the wet tarp, he sprayed the table occupants.

"What the hell!" Carlo shouted pushing away from the table.

"I'm here to discuss business, who do you boys take your orders from?" Max asked folding the moist poncho over his arm.

Scowling at Max, the gangly Carlo snorted. A roving tongue under his cheek confirmed missing teeth. Slowly he extended a finger and pointed to a plywood office in the back of the hanger.

"Thank you," Max said with a slight nod. Carlo mumbled an inaudible comment to his companions. Snickers followed. Rolling his eyes Max thought, what are these gangsters or a bunch of schoolchildren? No military discipline, he concluded.

Max rapped on the thin rough wood office door with a knuckled fist. He paused and entered the small room. The well-groomed Asian associate of the Vietnamese government sat behind a metal desk. The young man's glistening black hair side parted perfectly. In a sharkskin suit, a white pocket-handkerchief and thin black tie, he scanned down an open ledger. His left hand identified numbers. His right hand input the digits into a manual adding machine. Pulling back the calculators handle, he advanced paper tape. The small paper roll flowed off the front of the desk and spilled into a curling pile. The young man momentarily glanced up at the intrusion.

Tearing the paper tape from the calculator, the accountant examined the tally. Looking up, he said, "Thank you for your patience," and motioned to a folding metal chair. "Please be seated Mister Kohl, you can call me Tommy."

"Tommy?" Max questioned sitting down.

"It will make our discussion go smoother. I won't have to grimace every time you mispronounce my Vietnamese name," Tommy said pulling out a cigarette from a pack of *Gauloises*.

"Very well Tommy and you can call me Max." Max responded.

Tommy took his time with the cigarette ritual emphasizing the use of a gold lighter. "Max I recognize you from the formal event held for the Americans at the palace. I must say you are very well connected for a common soldier." Tommy commented puffing on dark tobacco.

Smiling at the subtle insult, Max replied in a commanding tone, "I'm here to discuss payment of an insurance premium. Our terms are simple.

We will pay a twenty percent tariff in jam for immunity from Vietnamese prosecution. Any violation of this agreement by you or your Corsican partners will result in either me or one of my well connected associates killing you." Rising from the flimsy metal chair, he extended his hand adding, "Do we have a deal Tommy?"

Open mouthed, Tommy attempted to speak. After several attempts he said, "This is not how it is suppose to play out. We are not offering a service. We are demanding a twenty percent tax on all opium exported from Phong Savin."

Placing both his hands on the paper-covered desk, Max barked, "The tone of your request implies extortion, if that is the case..." Standing up, he pulled out his Tokarev pistol and said with a shrug, "I'll just kill you now."

Beads of perspiration appeared across Tommy's shiny forehead. Staring down the barrel of the Soviet sidearm, he stuttered. "You...you... realize there are twenty...twenty heavily armed men just outside this office?"

Chuckling Max said, "Do you think I came here alone? The hangar is surrounded by common soldiers, like me." Squinting into Tommy's twitching dark eyes, he added, "Now are you offering insurance from Governmental intervention or trying to strong-arm the Laotian Army into paying extortion?"

Swallowing hard and motioning towards the empty chair with a shaky hand, Tommy responded, "Please be seated, let's discuss your terms."

Lowering his weapon Max stated, "There is nothing to discuss, my terms are non-negotiable."

"Max your proposal to pay the tariff in product is acceptable, and the Republic of Vietnam will turn a blind eye towards your operation's smuggling activities. However I cannot guarantee total impunity. Politically, we like your American sponsors need to maintain an untainted image," Tommy said adding with a shrug, "You understand."

"If one of your Corsican shipments and pilots are sacrificed to maintain your governments reforming persona, I'll understand. However, if the Republic of Vietnam interferes with the Laotian Army's smuggling operation, I'd consider it a violation of our agreement. I need to feel we are getting something for turning over twenty percent of our harvest." Grinning Max added, "You understand."

Rising from his chair Tommy said, "I understand Mister Kohl."

"Good," Max responded waving his pistol towards the exit. "Now you can walk me to the door."

Draping his poncho over the gun, Max poked the pistol barrel into his escorts back. The two men exited the small office and entered the warehouse. The tinny sound of the downpour echoed inside the metal facility. The poker players turned to investigate Max's departure. Carlo rose from the table. Tommy waved his hand to defuse interaction.

Stopping in front of the large open hangar bay doors, Max peered out into the dark. Sheets of rain poured down. Tossing his poncho over his shoulder, he holstered the pistol. "It's going to be a wet night," he said putting on the raingear. Extending a hand, he asked, "Do we have an agreement Tommy?"

Tommy examined Max's open palm. Glancing into the hanger, he searched for assurance from the puzzled faces of his heavily armed associates. Turning he peered into the downpour attempting to locate Max's back-up. Gingerly he shook the German's hand.

"I'm glad that is settled," Max said. "Would you like to join us for a drink to celebrate our successful negotiation?"

"Us?" Tommy questioned.

Max motioned with his head towards the darkness. The silhouettes of poncho covered soldiers moved into view.

Rotating from left to right Tommy scrutinized the contingent of men before saying, "No thank you, unfortunately I have to return to my numbers."

"And Tommy just remember," Max said placing the poncho's hood over his head and stepping into the rain, "any violation in the agreement makes you a dead man."

CHAPTER TWENTY ONE

The tracks of Max's mud clad boots joined clumps of muck strewn across the wood-planked floor. Resembling a happy Buddha, the plumb King Cobra bartender instinctively pulled an iced bottle of beer from a galvanized tub.

"Thanks Jimmy," Max said over the rolling barroom clamor. Bellying up to the counter he retrieved the cold brew. "Also a shot of Schnapps, I need something to combat the damp chill."

The portly server took his time in pouring the clear alcohol into a stainless steel hourglass shaped jigger. Dumping the measured portion into a bar glass, he added a calculated bonus. Max slammed down the warming spirit with a gulp. Feeling the soothing affects, he turned resting his elbows on the counter. Seeking shelter from the pouring rain Corsican mobsters, Vietnamese strongmen, Laotian hookers and grounded pilots cavorted. Amongst the European opium smugglers, the Air American aviator Buck sat in a dimly lit corner. The Texan's pointed-toe black boots propped on a chair. In the comfortable repose, Buck nibbled on the ear of a young flat-nosed whore. Small chest, Max concluded eyeing the working girl. The American was right. There is not a descent pair of breast in the highlands. Visualizing the voluptuous Elaine Favreau, he grinned. There is an exceptional bosom in Saigon, he realized.

Scanning the crowd, Max spotted the fair-skinned Rene Bergot. The pilot sat against the wall at a paper-cluttered table. Even in the soft light Rene's perpetually sunburned faced glowed. A smoke string danced from a fresh cigarette balanced on the rim of a full ashtray. Using a yellow pencil on a scratch pad, the French smuggler performed basic math. After a quick sip of scotch, Rene input the results into a hard cover ledger.

"Have you made enough to retire?" Max said casting a shadow over the pilots bookkeeping exercise.

Squinting up through the smoke, Rene beamed. Placing the pencil in the crease of the open ledger, he rose extending a hand. "Max! I was hoping I would bump into you." Shaking hands, he answered, "Haven't made enough to retire yet, but according to my calculations, I can afford to get us both drunk tonight."

"Any time you're buying Rene," Max said pulling out a chair, "I'm drinking."

Clearing the table of papers, Rene placed the unorganized stack in a satchel. "So what are you doing out on a wet night like this?" He asked.

The tip of a fresh cigar hovered over the flame of a Zippo lighter. Max took several igniting puffs. "Conceding to the terms of the opium tariff to keep the peace," he responded.

"It is a tough business. I hate the risk," Rene commented. Take a sip if scotch, he grinned. "But I love the profit margin."

"What and for whom are you flying these days?" Max asked.

"Well I'm still independent," Rene answered rapping on the wood tabletop. "With the insurance proceeds from the Cessna explosion I was able to upgrade to a twin engine Beechcraft." Smirking he added, "In case you are wondering, the insurance company would not reimburse the loss of opium."

Max chuckled, "So tell me how is business?"

"It's phenomenal. It did not take long for everyone in Southeast Asia to figure out what the French knew all along. Opium pays the bills. There was a lull when the dens in Saigon were being closed, but the new government in need of cash reopened them. Turkey the other big grower of the valuable poppies is being pressured out of business by the West. That leaves this remote corner of the world, the Golden Triangle, the leading producer of opium."

"The Golden Triangle?" Max questioned.

"It extends across the mountains to Burma. But Max, I'm just an independent dealing in the scraps that fall off the table in Laos and that is making me a wealthy man."

"Well I'm glad you're buying the drinks then." Max said nodding thanks. "But Rene you've already lost one plane and a full load. As an independent you're exposed." Glancing over, he subtly motioned to a table of hard men in light colored suits, no ties.

Rene looked over at three greasy Corsicans drinking in a cloud of cigarette smoke. One had a young girl sitting across his lap, the other two conversing in a guttural growl. Behind them, a wide Vietnamese strongman stood guard. The Asian thug's large scanning head slowly rotated back and forth.

"Those are the boys who had your Cessna destroyed," Max informed quietly.

Leaning back in his chair, Rene sipped scotch. "A cost of doing business," he conceded. "The Corsicans sent me a message and it was received. The pie was smaller then but thanks to American intervention the equation has changed."

"How so?" Max squinted.

"In their attempt to win the hearts and minds of the Meo with refugee supplies, the Americans have eliminated the incentive for the tribal people to grow anything but opium. In the wake of the generous humanitarian efforts, a network of crude landing strips has expedited the transportation of the regions only cash crop." Pausing Rene waived his empty bar glass over his head getting Jimmy's' attention. After placing the silent drink order, he looked at Max and added, "Times have changed since we did our weapons for opium exchange with Guillian back in fifty-four."

Puffing on his cigar, Max felt a warming comfort at the reference to the lanky French commando Jean Guillian. "Have you run across my Jewish brother on any of your highland junkets?"

Snickering Rene answered, "A couple of months ago I negotiated a deal with his Meos on a rough mountain airstrip just below their village. It should come as no surprise, that the tribe that adopted a Jew grows the most potent opium in the Golden Triangle and commands top dollar for the jam."

The crash of splintered wood and shattered glass silenced the barroom. Max flinched hard. Knocking over his chair, he jumped to his feet.

Standing defiantly, he clutched an amber beer bottle with a cocked arm. The cowboy lay sprawled across the floor. Hovering over the Texan, the Corsicans' Vietnamese henchman snorted with clenched fist.

"Stay out of this Max!" said a side glancing Corsican with an extended hand. "It's between Bao and the cocky American."

"Get up!" Bao grumbled in broken French.

Shuffling through the retreating patrons, Max moved closer to investigate. It did not matter what sparked the confrontation, he realized. About once a week, the alpha dogs drinking at the King Cobra watering hole needed to flex. More than likely, the Corsican handlers had turned their Vietnamese dog loose for sport, he concluded. The roly-poly bartender casually placed a black billy-club on the counter.

Slowly the face down Buck rose to his knees using a chair for balance.

"Get up!" Bao barked.

"The Americans drunk," Max said holding the empty bottle. "He is no match for your trained gorilla."

Boa snarled at the German. The Corsican pulled back the flap of his suit coat to reveal a sidearm. "I said stay out of this Max," out of the side of a crooked grin, he added, "It will be over quickly."

Max chuckled at the sight of the pimp pistol and mumbled, "Don't bite off more than you can chew."

Climbing up the chair Buck stood on wobbly legs. His head hung low. Glancing at Max, he winked. Breathing heavy, Buck swayed back and forth using the chair for support. After inhaling deeply the wiry Texan locked his knees. In a flash, he slammed the chair on the top of the thick-necked Asians' head. Tumbling backwards Bao hit the mud crusted floor with a thud. Like a cat, Buck pounced on his prey. Straddling the disoriented thug's chest, the cowboy twisted back raising a tight fist high over his head. An arced swing delivered a sledge-hammer blow right between the Asian's dazed eyes. A spasm rippled through Bao's body before going limp.

Standing over the lifeless form Buck shook his hand. He scrutinized the Corsicans through a swollen sucker-punched eye and growled, "You fucking frogs got a problem?"

A Corsican reached inside his coat for a sidearm. Max threw the brown bottle. The empty glass container careened of the Corsican's greasy head and shattered against the wall. Dropping to a knee the Corsican tenderly investigated a growing knot.

"Enough!" The bartender shouted pounding the counter with a night-stick. "You want to drink; drink. You want to fornicate. I'll get you a girl. We have only two rules at the King Cobra. No opium smoking in the lobby and no fighting!" Pointing the truncheon at a cluster of working girls, Jimmy waved the baton signaling them to clean up the mess.

The young girls began to pick up the upturned table and chairs. The presence of young female flesh on the battlefield defused the confrontation. In defeat, the Corsicans attempted to revive the disoriented Bao. Without success, they each grabbed a lifeless leg and dragged the massive dead weight towards the door.

"Thanks partner," Buck said placing his hand on the German's shoulder. "The frog was right. It was over with quickly."

Max nodded, but he had doubts. You never know how the fanatical Corsicans will react. Breaking Petru Rossi's nose, triggered the haughty gangster's inbreed desire to restore his misguided conception of honor. Reflecting back on Rossi's attempted vendetta, Max smiled. The cost of failing to kill me over a bloody nose was an unmarked grave, he thought. Even a feared *Unione Corse* hit-man like Rossi was no match for the aging Meo warrior Pao or my feisty little sister Mei. Rubbing his chin, Max smirked. If the Corsican thumped by the empty bottle wants to restore his honor, there is a plot reserved next to the pimp Petru Rossi.

CHAPTER TWENTY TWO

Topical sunlight punished the stationary compilation of metal. Wedged deep within the overheated Saigon traffic jam, a Citroen taxi sputtered. In the sweltering back seat, Elaine checked the time. "Damn it," she mumbled. The imprisoned cab had not moved in fifteen minutes. I'll make better progress if I walk, she concluded. The sweaty Vietnamese driver flinched as she handed him the fare. Exiting in the middle of the vehicular maze, the reflecting sunlight bleached her vision. Blinking, she inhaled the stench of diesel. The snarled vehicles purred and coughed. Frustrated horns blared. Timidly she squeezed between the stagnant trucks and cars. A scooter carrying a family of five buzzed by. That was close, she gasped. Her heart raced. I should have stayed in the cab, she realized. There is no need to get killed going to a photo shoot. Peering around a large lorry, she saw the security of the sidewalk. Holding her breath, she scrambled through the billowing white smoke of a high-pitched whining motorcycle.

Standing safely on the concrete pedestrian path, Elaine shook the hem of her cotton dress. Looking up at the clock tower entrance to Ben Thanh Market, she grinned. I don't have that far to go. I'll be fashionably late, she concluded. In a loose fitting dress and flats, she strolled comfortably into a slight breeze. I would never admit it, she conceded, but that frumpy Kelly Taylor's fashion advice works in the tropics.

On the bank of the Saigon River, the towering sixty-foot tall Trung Sisters Memorial cast a long shadow. The reflective pond at the base sparkled. At the top of the new monument, the sculptured images of the first century sibling heroines of Vietnam stood defiantly in opposite directions. Around the stoned column, photographers buzzed around snapping pictures of the photogenic Madame Nhu. The first lady posed in a form fitting *ao-dai* dress. Approaching the blatant self-promotion, Elaine gazed skyward at the shrine. Madame Nhu compares herself to the Trung sisters? Elaine questioned. The sibling heroines donned suits of golden armor and rode elephants into battle to repel Chinese invaders, she recalled. From the back seat of a chauffeur driven Mercedes, the fashionable Madame Nhu's objective is eliminating abortion, divorce, contraceptives, and beauty pageants from the Vietnamese culture. Drawing similarities is a reach she chuckled.

Elaine smiled at a wide shouldered sweating bodyguard in Madame Nhu's security detail. The stone-faced Asian in sunglasses and uncomfortably warm black suit stepped aside. Elaine meandered to join Madame Nhu's handpicked admirers in the hot sun. Glancing around at the wilting crowd, she concluded that being late was probably good. This should be over soon, she hoped. More than likely, I'll be offered a ride back to the embassy in an air-conditioned Mercedes Benz.

The photographers reloaded for a second round. Madam Nhu walked over to her admirers. The audience universally bestowed compliments. The repetitive praise evoked a slight nod and an insincere smile from the overheated First Lady. Madame Nhu sat down in a canvas director's chair. An umbrella attendant provided shade. Another servant fanned the tiny woman.

"Madame Nhu," Elaine said ducking under the umbrella. "I apologize for being a little late this afternoon; however what I've seen so far looks..."

"You're dressed inappropriately," barked Madame Nhu.

"Madame Nhu?" Elaine questioned. Who is this? She wondered. Squinting she examined the distinguishable features of the petite First Lady of Vietnam; the round face, bouffant hairstyle and high cheekbones.

"I invite you as a guest to this event, you come late and are dressed like an American housewife." said the sharp-tongued Nhu. The umbrella attendant's hand quivered. The fanning servant's breathing accelerated. The worshiping entourage retreated.

"My apologies Madame Nhu," Elaine said in a firm tone. "I just thought on this warm day..."

"You thought wrong!" Madame Nhu snapped. Over her shoulder she growled, "Duc, escort Miss Favreau off the premises."

You bitch, Elaine thought. You pompous little bitch. How dare you talk to me like that. I'm an American citizen. Duc grabbed her upper arm. "I got the message," Elaine said to her reflection in the thick man's sunglasses. He tightened his grip and escorted her to the adjacent street. Standing on the curb, she shook herself free. Staring defiantly at the rough escort, she blindly stuck out her arm to hail a cab. Please, somebody stop, she thought. Car brakes squealed. Squinting hard at the brut, she jumped into the backseat of an old dented taxi.

"US Embassy," she said to the driver. Slumping down into the torn vinyl upholstery, she burst into tears.

The rusty cab coughed in front of the Embassy gate. Sniffling, Elaine hastily paid the fare. The old driver lit up. I over paid him, she realized. Who cares, she concluded. Holding a wadded up handkerchief under a runny nose, she presented her identification card to the Marine guard.

"Everything alright ma'am?" the acne faced young Marine asked. Bending down he attempted to make eye contact.

Tears surfaced with her voice. She settled to answer with a couple of quick unflattering nods. Seeing traces of mascara on the hankie, she grimaced. I must look atrocious, she concluded.

Walking across the courtyard, she took several deep breaths hoping to suppress emotions. I cannot afford to be seen like this, she realized. Entering the embassy, she quickened the pace. Glancing down an interior corridor, she got a blurry glimpse of the dowdy Kelly Taylor. Not now, Elaine thought. You are the last person I want to see.

Standing her ground, Kelly shouted "Elaine!"

Sidestepping around the wide framed Kelly, Elaine waived a dismissive hand.

"Elaine, what's the matter?" the persistent Kelly softly inquired.

Why does she always have to sound so cheery? Elaine thought. Rounding the corner, she saw Tom Roche in a Hawaiian shirt and baggy khaki pants standing in the doorway of his tiny office.

"I take it the photo shoot promoting Madame Nhu as the next great heroine of Southeast Asia did not go well?" Roche asked with raised brows.

"Tom..." Elaine said. Wrapping her arms around him, she melted into a comforting embrace.

Gently patting the back of her head, he whispered, "Don't feel bad Elaine. We all have days like this."

"I must look awful," she said separating.

Prying the crumpled hankie from her hand, he said, "Let's have a look." Tenderly he wiped off smudged mascara. "As ravishing as ever," he said with a wink.

"Do you still have that bottle of Jim Beam you keep hidden in your office?" she asked. "I sure could use a drink with a friend."

"Sure Elaine," he said picking up a stack of files from the chair next to his desk. Successfully he balanced it atop another large pile. Retrieving the fifth of bourbon from the bottom drawer, he motioned with an open hand towards the empty chair. As she sat down, he poured the whisky into two coffee mugs.

"How do you do it Tom?" she asked accepting the libation. "I mean how do you tolerate dealing with these self centered, ego centric despots? As far as I'm concerned, I'm through with that Nhu bitch"

Leaning back in his squeaking swivel chair, he took a sip of bourbon and snickered, "They don't call us diplomats for nothing. If I lost my temper every time an assignment caused me grief or crossed the line, there would be dead bodies all along the Iron Curtain. One of them most likely would be mine." Lifting his cup, he asked, "So tell me what happened?"

Taking a pausing breath, Elaine sat in reflective silence. Quietly she mumbled, "Madame Nhu insulted me."

"What did she say?" Roche probed.

Sheepishly she confessed, "She said I was dressed like a common housewife."

"I can see why you got so upset." He chuckled. "How did you respond?"

"I didn't have time to respond," she answered. "Before I could, the bitch had one of her goons escort me out."

"That's a good thing," Roche informed. "Elaine you were sent into a hornets' nest this afternoon. The State Department has been increasing the pressure on the Diem regime to clean up their act. Your run-in this afternoon is a result our government's policy changes towards the House of Ngo."

"Thanks Tom," Elaine said. Tipping an empty mug in his direction, she sought a refill. Leaning forward, he poured a healthy serving. "Still Tom how do you it? How do you maintain self-control?"

Settling back into a comfortable repose he answered, "It's just something I was trained to do. I take on the persona the assignment or situation requires." Rubbing the back of his neck, he counseled. "Elaine you came to Vietnam as a contract clerical translator. Nobody expected you to perform as well as you've done. Just focus on the task at hand, which is Madame Nhu. If anything, today's events have given you the appropriate perspective."

"Thanks again Tom. I'm a little bit embarrassed the way I reacted. I really need to work on controlling my emotions," she confessed.

"If you really want some pointers on discipline, military discipline, just study our friend Max. He is always focused," Roche commented.

"Speaking of Mister Kohl, do you know when Max will be back in Saigon?" She asked gulping on whisky. "I never had a chance to properly thank him for saving my life."

Roche recoiled. "What..." he mumbled. "I assumed...I mean I thought the two of you...hooked up the night of the rescue."

Grinning Elaine said, "Let's just say I got my first lesson in German military discipline that night, as our friend refused my gratitude."

CHAPTER TWENTY THREE

Strapped into the transport, Max leaned back into the cargo net. He closed his eyes. The drone of the twin engines lulled him towards sleep. One more stop and then we head for home, he thought. The relaxing fog of slumber rolled in.

"Buck! One of your monkeys just hit me with a handful of shit!" Dugan cried.

Max stirred. An open eye investigated. A Laotian soldier suppressed a childish grin. Dugan sat red-faced, primate feces splattered across his jungle fatigues.

"Goddamn vermin!" Dugan hollered throwing a jungle boot at the cage housing the mischievous cargo. The boot ricocheted off the soiled chain link enclosure. Three monkeys scrambled in a high-pitched frenzy. Colonel Yang troops laughed.

Returning to his eyes closed repose, Max chuckled at the enterprising passengers and crew. The tall lanky cowboy trafficked in exotic birds and monkeys. The balding stocky co-pilot acquired the primitive weapons of the Meo. The lances and cross-bows resold in Bangkok produced a hefty profit. The smile on Max's face subsided. He thought about Dugan's collection. The American trafficked in severed Pathet Lao ears. Dugan paid tribesmen one-thousand kip, (two dollars), for each cartilage flap accompanied with a bulbous Communist cap. Opening his eyes, Max glanced over at the blood stained burlap sack besides Dugan's stocking feet. Business was good.

Feeling the plane decelerate, Max firmly grabbed the cargo netting. The touchdowns on the crude short runways were brief but violent. The airplane skidded to an abrupt termination on the mountainside tarmac.

Quickly, Max unharnessed to disembark. Hoping out of the noisy aircraft onto moist fertile soil, he took a deep breath. An exotic fragrance accented the crisp clean highland air. Along the steep grade, Meo women in bright red turbans and blue long sleeved blouses, waded knee deep in dark green opium fields. White flowers blanked the crops. Above the poppy meadow, pitched raised wooden structures clung to the foliage-draped hillsides.

"Colonel," Max said to a stretching Yang. "Go easy on your recruitment efforts this afternoon. If any issues arise let me intervene."

Reaching up Yang patted the broad shouldered German. "Don't worry Max. This village is special to me as well."

Dugan interrupted, "Is there a problem here gentlemen?"

"No problem Mister Jim," Yang replied. "These are the people Max and I rescued from Vietminh reprisals."

"This is the village with the French Jew?" Dugan blurted.

"His name is Guillian," Max barked, "Chief Sergeant Jean Guillian."

Taking a step back, Dugan flashed his palms. "Okay Max, Chief Sergeant Jean Guillian." Out of the side of his mouth he mumbled, "Jesus you Germans are so touchy when it comes to Jews."

Turning his back to Dugan, Max proceeded up a stepped inclined pathway. Leaving the warming sunshine, he plodded uphill. Dense growth flanked the narrow trail snaking up the mountainside. He paused to the rumbling of sandaled feet. A herd of Meo women stampeded downhill with empty wicker baskets strapped on their backs. Happy faces gleamed with anticipation. Winning hearts and minds, Max thought.

In the enthusiastic women's trailing cloud of dust, a dozen Meo warriors in soiled black tunics and short baggy pants swaggered. The sandaled soldiers proudly brandished French bolt-action carbines and pillaged Chinese burp-guns. A balding senior with wisps of gray hair and criss-crossing cartridge belts paused to indentify Max. The cackling of his trailing comrades faded into silence. A Meo warrior holding a blood stained gunnysack, stepped out of the pack. Flies buzzed around the moist bag. A French submachine gun slung over his shoulder. Revealing a toothless smile, Chue dropped the rancid bag and embraced the German.

It's good to see you brother, Max thought ignoring the stench of decay. He heartily patted the small soldier on the back.

Chue stepped back. Placing a hand on Max's shoulder he said, *"Nam lu."*

Nodding Max accepted the tribal greeting to get drunk. I fought beside you against overwhelming odds my friend, he thought. I'll drink with you anytime.

Squatting down Chue retrieved snarled ears that spilled of the coarse cloth sack. Tossing the amputated trophies over his shoulder, he pointed towards the airstrip.

"Yes Chue," Max said. "After you collect your bounty, we will all get drunk."

The Meos shuffled downhill to collect their prize money. Familiar faces nodded. Max bowed respectfully at the passing troops. There is no greater bond between men than the one forged in combat, he realized. Snorting at the lingering odor of decay, he continued the steep climb. Barking dogs announced his arrival. The sharp fragrance of the flowering poppies triggered a sneeze. Pausing in the deserted steeply angled town square, he looked around. A middle-aged Meo woman struggled. A load of firewood strapped to her arched back. Focused on the ground, she glanced sideways with a curious squint. A crooked toothed smile appeared on her round wrinkled face. Approaching Max, she spoke in a musical rambling of her native dialect. Grabbing his hand, she placed it on her sweaty forehead.

"The feeling is mutual mother," Max said softly.

"Max!" Guillian called out from the raised porch of a hut. "I was hoping you'd be on the flight."

Looking down at the grateful woman, Max gave her a quick wink. Walking towards Guillian, he shouted, "Good to see you as well my friend. How are your wife and son?"

"That's kind of you to ask. H'Liana is fine and Etienne is no longer a baby. You won't believe how big he's gotten. He is so much larger than the other *Montagnard* children his age."

"It must be that kosher blood pumping through his veins," Max chuckled. Ascended a rickety stairway, he hugged the commando.

Breaking the embrace Guillian said, "Unfortunately Max our reunion is going to take on a serious tone. I need to ask for a favor."

Pulling a cigar out of his breast pocket, Max bit off the tip and spit it over the porch railing. After lighting the stogie, he exhaled a cloud of smoke. He chuckled, "The last time you asked me for a favor, it was to escort you and your adopted community out of communist Vietnam. I responded to that request without hesitation. Do you really think I'm going to say no?"

Guillian snickered, "Alright my *Boche* friend, since you put it into perspective, we might as well drink while I humbly exploit your goodwill."

In the local dialect, Guillian called over his shoulder into the modest residence. A puffy eyed sniffling H'Liana came onto the porch carrying an old bottle of white whisky and two bamboo stock flask. That petite high-cheeked boned Meo beauty avoided eye contact. She set down the liquor and bamboo beakers. A colorful sleeve wiped her flat runny nose as she rushed back into the hut.

"Are you having family issues?" Max questioned.

Squatting down on his haunches, Guillian generously poured the murky moonshine into bamboo mugs. "Have a seat, that's what I need to talk to you about."

Plopping down on the deck next to the crouching host, Max shook his head. "How you find squatting like that comfortable still baffles me."

Smiling Guillian handed the German a whisky. "After escaping the French fueled war of North Vietnam, we find ourselves involved in this American financed struggle in Laos. I'm not stupid. I realize that this conflict is in its infancy and will only escalate." After taking a big swig of whisky, he proposed, "Max I want you to take H'Laina and Etienne with you this afternoon."

Flicking a cigar ash onto the ground, Max grinned. "Guillian we're not dead yet. You and your family are always welcome to join me and the collection of misfits that reside on the Plain of Jars."

"I accept your hospitable offer, with one caveat." Guillian responded. "Take my wife and son with you today and I'll join you once the Meo recruits from this village are established under Colonel Yang's command."

"So you know about the recruitment quota required from each village?" Max asked.

Smirking Guillian responded, "I don't know the specifics, but speculate that right now on the runway Colonel Yang is bartering with American guns, rice and money to uproot the fighting men of the community."

"Is it going to be a difficult sell?" Max questioned.

Shaking his head Guillian said, "No, the tribe owes Yang a debt of gratitude which they will repay. Hell, I owe him as well and that is why I'm going. Once I fulfill my obligation under his banner, I'll reconnect with my family."

"I understand," Max nodded, "H'Liana and Etienne will be fine in Phong Savin. Loc's daughter is about the same age as Etienne and Pao and Loc speak the same dialect as your wife."

Smiling pleasantly, Guillian rose pulling a wrinkled envelope from his pants pocket. Squatting back down, he handed the sealed letter to Max. "I'd like you to hold this for me until I see you again in Phong Savin. If for whatever reason I don't make it, please read."

Max stuffed the letter into his breast pocket and said, "I'll just hold it. I'm not much on reading."

"Very well Max" Guillian said taking a satisfying breath. "You probably saw the poppy fields are in the flowering stage?" Receiving a confirming nod, he continued, "So we have not harvested this year's crop. I still have thirty kilos of opium from the last harvest. I'd like you to take the jam to help with my family's room and board."

"That's not necessary," Max responded, "Besides Mister Jim does not allow opium on any flights he's on."

Guillian flinched. "You're kidding! The Americans established our poppy fields." Wrinkling a brow he asked, "What was that gangly CIA agent's name?"

"Walker," Max informed chuckling.

"That's right, young Mister Walker. He grew up on his father's Baptist mission in Burma. His tribal linguistic skills were overshadowed by his passion for growing opium."

Nodding Max said, "The Americans are a strange lot. They traffic in exotic animals and antique weapons and Mister Jim pays a bounty on the severed appendage of Communist. But they distance themselves from the drug trade." Taking a swig of whisky he added, "That is they distance themselves for appearances."

"Those are all side ventures," An enlightened Guillian informed. "The Americans are in the business of cultivating the indigenous people to fight their wars. Just like we grow opium, the Americans nurture the Meos to feed the flames of their anti-communist addiction. The fire of war constantly fueled with men and munitions will never burn out. All soldiers in a never ending conflict eventually die."

Max concurred. "I've learned from drifting on the waves of war, that death is a fickle bastard. When I was introduced to him on the battlefield as a boy, death scared me. During my Legionnaire days in Indochina, I respected him. It was on my march out of Isabelle that he pissed me off." Inhaling deeply on the cigar Max puffed out his chest. After a long satisfying exhale, he continued with a gruff tone, "Before I stumbled into your hillside community on my escape from Dien Bien Phu, death taunted me. With no food or water and a fungal rash that made each step a painful accomplishment, the Grimm Reaper whispered in my ear to call it quits. To lay down and become part of the jungle landscape." Looking at Guillian, he chuckled, "It wasn't that I didn't want to give him the satisfaction. I didn't want to leave this world with a rotten crotch. Nevertheless, death is death. He chooses the time and place. I heard that Jean Paul is no longer with us. Death punched his ticket in Algeria."

"JP is dead?" asked a startled Guillian.

"Unfortunately yes," Max answered. "He was pushing forty and the oldest of the five Isabelle survivors who walked into your village that day in '54'. The tank crewmember had this stubbornness for life that the younger Frenchmen lacked. I was just as surprised when I heard the news."

"He die in combat?" Guillian questioned.

Snickering Max answered, "Heart attack." Taking a sip of moonshine, he added grinning, "It should come as no surprise, the pale-horseman has a morbid sense of humor."

"To the hell with death," Guillian said.

"I'll drink to that," Max responded raising the bamboo carafe.

"Better yet, let's drink to life," Guillian said. "It has the same affect."

Touching flasks Max said, "*L'Chayim.*"

Tilting his head back, Guillian laughed. "I appreciate the sentiment but your Hebrew pronunciation needs some work."

CHAPTER TWENTY FOUR

It was mid-day in Saigon. The dark sky churned. Lighting flashed. Thunder cracked. A blue and white Renault taxi idled at the US embassy gate. The thunderstorm unleashed a torrential rain. Behind the wheel of the four-door compact car, a small Asian cabby puffed away on a cigarette. Feverously, he cranked up the driver's window. Out the water stained back seat window, Max spotted a lone figure. A blurred silhouette battled the driving rain under a red oilpaper umbrella. Misplaced steps detonated puddles.

Swinging the car door open, Max scooted over on the frayed vinyl upholstery. Roche in a saturated business suit flew into the cramped vehicle.

"Jesus, it is really coming down today," Roche said. Quickly, he closed the umbrella and the passenger door. Leaning forward, Roche said to the driver, "Presidential Palace."

The cabby flinched. Sitting erect, he smiled with a confident nod and popped the clutch. The rear powered Renault sputtered forward.

Patting Max's leg with a moist hand, Roche sat back and asked, "So how is my kraut brother?"

Chuckling Max responded, "Just fine *ami*, thank you for setting this up."

"Max, I got you the audience you requested, but the show is yours. I'm attending for appearances only," Roche informed. Puckering his face, he waived his hand at the growing cloud of cigarette smoke. "I want to warn you in advance, that I cannot be dragged into the negotiations. If any concessions are asked of me in my capacity as a representative of the United States, I'll be forced to leave the room."

"I understand *ami*. I hope it doesn't get to uncomfortable for you," Max said. Grinning he added. "I'd hate for you to feel the discomfort I felt during the Battle of Saigon. Remember when I risked my life to extract Elaine and the American journalists."

Nodding Roche replied, "Fair enough Max, your right. Let's get your friend out of jail."

"This way gentlemen," said the young Vietnamese beauty.

Roche and Max followed her down a marbled floor hallway. Focused on their guide's well-rounded bottom, they ignored the large oil paintings decorating the high walls. The tight floral printed silk dress swung back and forth. The seam line of nylon stockings accented perfectly shaped calves. The click of high heels on stone kept a seductive beat.

Stopping abruptly at an open doorway, she turned. Catching a glimpse of the gentlemen's lustful stares, she shielded a flattered giggle with a cupped hand. Clearing her throat, she swung a welcoming arm into the plush room.

Playfully, Roche backhanded Max on the shoulder, as they entered. The dark wood paneled office resembled a big game hunter's trophy room. Mounted animal heads and tiger skins adorned the walls. Beside an elaborate carved wooden desk resided an elephant's foot umbrella stand. In front of the desk, the German and American starred at the tall back of a red leather chair. A wisp of cigarette smoke floated up from behind the shielding backrest. A faint squeak accompanied the chair as it slowly rotated. Max grimaced. Slumped down in the oversized glossy red leather seat, Tommy impeccably dressed in a light gray suit, enjoyed a smoke.

"Hello Max," Tommy smugly said leaning forward extinguishing a cigarette.

"Hello Tommy," Max responded.

Roche flinched. "You two know each other?" He questioned.

"Yes Major Roche," Tommy replied extending a friendly hand in the direction of the empty chairs in front of the oversized desk. "Max and I have already had the pleasure of completing a successful negotiation in Northern Laos." Grinning at the German, he added, "If I recall, you accelerated the discussion by stating your terms and then adding the caveat that they were non-negotiable." He paused to ignite a fresh cigarette. Exhaling in Max's purview he said, "Here are my non-negotiable terms for expediting the prison release of the convicted dope smuggler Rene Bergot. I require ten thousand American dollars and the confiscation of his twin-engine Beechcraft. In addition, the bush-pilot will come to work for the Guerini syndicate for the three year term of his prison sentence."

"Let me get this straight," Roche interrupted, "Rene was arrested for smuggling opium and beside the graft, you want him to come to work for you smuggling opium?"

Holding a silencing hand, Tommy continued, "Rene will be compensated for his services at the same rate as our other pilots. To insure that Rene fulfills his three year obligation, I require a guarantee." Leaning back into the oversized chair, he interlocked his fingers across his shallow chest. "If Rene decides to flee from the employment obligation, I'll have you killed, Max."

"You arrogant little shit," Roche growled, "How dare..."

Max grabbed Roche's arm. "Tommy," Max announced, "Your terms are acceptable." Standing up, he extended a hand over the desk. Arrogantly the slick Asian slowly presented a petite paw. After a firm shake, Max tightened his grip, "Tommy in case Rene does flee and you are forced to collect on the guarantee. Are you going to be the one to kill me?"

The haughty peacock swallowed hard. He grimaced, the vice grip intensified.

"Well?" Max said flexing his forearm. The delicate fingers in his grasp cracked.

Wincing Tommy tried to ply Max's hand loose. Surrendering he mumbled, "No."

"I didn't think so," Max said releasing his hold.

Slumping down in the plush leather chair, Tommy massaged his damaged paw.

"So where do we make the cash for pilot exchanged?" Max inquired.

Still rubbing tender fingers, Tommy took a deep breath. Sheepishly he responded, "He is still being detained, where he was arrested. Your friend is at the town of Xuan Loc about fifty miles north of Saigon." Pausing to wipe his shiny brow with a pocket-handkerchief, he asked, "How long will it take you to procure the ten-thousand in cash?"

Max squinted. I need to contact Rene's bank, he thought. Then I'll need to convert the funds to US dollars, he realized. "That may take some time," He responded.

"We can have your bribe by tomorrow," Roche blurted.

"Very well then gentlemen," Tommy said. "Tomorrow it is. We can meet at the police station in Xuan Loc and make the exchange. And Rene Bergot can start work for his new employer on Monday."

Exiting the trophy room, Max whispered to Roche, "I thought you were not going to get involved in the negotiations."

Placing his hand on Max's shoulder, Roche responded, "I didn't want you to have to deal with that arrogant little prick any longer than you had to. I can front you the money. I know that you and Rene are good for it."

"Thanks *ami*," Max said.

"But Max are you sure Rene is willing to go to work for the Guerini syndicate? They are more than likely the ones who set him up." Roche asked proceeding down the palace's marble hallway.

"Without a plane, he has few options. With harvest season approaching, he can make back some of what he lost here today. Besides I actually hope he flees the country. Then I can deal with Tommy and his life threatening guarantee." Max said.

"Be careful Max," Roche responded. "I've dealt with hundreds of young pups like Tommy. He may not have the stomach to carry out his threat. But he has powerful friends that will."

Exiting the palace under a dark cloudy sky, Max stopped and turning to Roche said, "Tommy is not the only one with influential friends. Thanks for attending the negotiations today." Grinning he added, "even though it was just for appearances."

A blue and white taxi wove its way through the afternoon traffic of Saigon. A fickle sun appeared in the swirling black sky. Random sunlight reflected off the wet surface streets. Max and Roche sat shoulder to shoulder in the back seat of the compact cab. The temperature had dropped at the expense of increased humidity.

"At least this cab is better than that ashtray smelling rust bucket we rode to the Palace in." Roche commented. Taking a deep breath he added, "Since you're going to be staying the night in Saigon, you should try to see Elaine," Subtly he glanced sideways to gaze a reaction. "She's always asking about you."

"To tell you the truth," Max confessed. "I was hoping to avoid her."

"You're kidding!" Roche exclaimed. "You are the envy of every male staffer at the Embassy... including me. We all would like to take a sip of that tall drink of water."

"Roche as you know things in Laos are not going well. We get our information from the same tribal sources. The Pathet Lao guerrilla forces are amassing troops along the Plain of Jars northeastern rim. For the first time in my life, I have a family in Phong Savin that depends on me. I can't afford to dull my military edge with the issues of the complex Elaine Faverau." Max said.

"If the Communist launch a coordinated offensive on the Plain of Jars, I will personally see to it that you and your adopted family will be evacuated out safely," Roche offered.

"Thanks Tom," Max said patting the American's knee.

"Hell, I spent many fond nights enjoying the hospitality of your collection of refugees. I'm not going to turn my back on friends." Grinning he reflected. "Don't forget, I was the one who introduced Mei to Loc."

"And now you're trying to connect Elaine and me," Max snickered. "Roche you missed your calling. Instead of trying to eradicate Communism, you should have been a matchmaker."

A slight drizzle began to fall. The tiny taxi pulled in front of the embassy's security gate. Looking out a portal, Roche said, "It looks like you won't be avoiding Elaine on this trip."

Roche paid the fare. Max climbed out of the tiny metal box. Standing on the sidewalk, Elaine held a black umbrella. In a white cotton shirtdress, she tilted her head with a schoolgirl grin. Max smiled. What a beauty, he thought admiring how stunning she looked in the simple gown.

In the light rain, Elaine dropped the umbrella and ran to the German. Wrapping her arms around his neck, she planted a big moist kiss on his dry mouth.

Enjoying the seductive caress, Max opened an eye. Peering up at the curved embassy building, he saw every window framing a curious onlooker.

"Welcome back to Saigon," Roche said patting Max on the back.

"Hello Tom," Elaine said breaking the kiss and snuggling up against Max.

Reaching down, Roche picked up Elaine's umbrella. He handed it to the disorientated German with a wink. Whistling a simple tune, Roche headed towards the embassy security gate.

"Don't let me go Max," Elaine whispered. Rain began to fall on the shielding umbrella. "I only feel safe when I'm with you."

Max caught a pleasant whiff of perfume. Maybe it's worth another try, he thought. Her soft frame pressed against him. What have I got to loose, he pondered. I've enjoyed the excesses of clean sheets and hot meals since walking out of Isabelle. Why not the tender affection of a woman.

"Max," she cooed clinging to his chest. Heavy raindrops pounded the umbrella's canopy. "Stay with me tonight," she whispered. "I have a small flat just around the corner and I've planned a steak and potato dinner. I've stocked up on lots of beer." Glancing up, she looked deep into his blue eyes.

"What kind of beer?" Max asked rubbing his tongue against the inside of his cheek.

Playfully, she slapped his chest. "Cold beer," she announced. "Is there any other kind?"

CHAPTER TWENTY FIVE

The sun was bright. The sky blue. A haze from distant fires hung in the air. A slight breeze carried the charred aroma of the approaching Communist onslaught. Standing at the edge of the Phong Savin Airport, Max dropped his duffle bag. Extending his arms, he halted the progress of his adopted family. A desperate Cessna buzzed by taking flight. Holding her daughter, Mei bowed and pivoted to shield the child from the escaping aircraft's prop wash. A large bag tethered to his back, Loc placed a reassuring hand on his wife's shoulder. Beside the tribesman, H'Liana defiantly stared across the red clay runway. Her taut flat-nosed face challenged the soiled blast of air. A bright bandana, dominated by red, covered her hair. Large silver looped earrings decorated exposed ears. Strapped to her back, a blue cloth pouch trimmed with orange fabric. Her wide-eyed son Etienne peered out of the Meo papoose. Pao took this brief pause to drop his satchel. Looking back, the old man whistled loudly across the smoldering countryside. Lan joined her grandfather and shouted, "Pasha! Pasha!"

"Let's go!" Max called out slinging the green canvas sack over his shoulder.

The small contingent of refugees surged across the dirt tarmac. A lone cargo plane sparkled in the afternoon sun. Dismantled hangar facilities cast skeletal shadows. This opium boom town has gone bust, Max thought. The Meos will still grow it. The Corsicans will still buy and sell it and governments will turn a blind eye. But Vientiane, the Laotian capital will now be the regions opium hub.

Blinking at the sunlight reflecting off the lone C-47 transport, Max held up a shielding hand. Buck stood next to the open cargo door. The tall lanky Air America pilot wore a short-sleeved white shirt with black epaulettes, a pair of blue jeans, shiny black cowboy boots and a white Stetson hat. The anxious Texan feverously tapped a pointed-toe boot on the red clay surface. Sporadic gunfire echoed in the surrounding hills. Looking up from a clipboard at the colorful passengers, Buck smiled. A red-tipped wooden match poked out the side of his mouth.

Calmly removing the match from clenching back teeth, Buck said, "Let's see." Using the moist end of the sulfur tipped toothpick, he scanned the passenger list. "Max, Loc, *Grand-pere*, Mei and child, Lan, the Meo girl and child..." Looking around he asked, "Where is the dog?"

Shaking his head Max, sighed, "When the shelling started last night all the dogs got spooked and ran off."

"That's too bad," Buck mumbled. Looking at his watch, he informed. "We are cutting this a lot closer than I'd like. However, we still have two more passengers we're waiting for." Tucking the clipboard under his arm, he gazed across the vacated airport and added, "Let's get your family aboard. Hopefully we will not have to wait too long."

As his family climbed into the plane, Max squinted at the cowboy. "What's with the Tom Mix outfit?"

The Texan grinned. "How do you know about Tom Mix?"

"His westerns were very popular in Germany before the war," Max responded. "So what's with the get up?"

Proudly sticking out his chest, Buck informed with a twang, "Well I'm from Texas. And if I'm going to die today. I'm going to do it with my boots on." Lifting a denim pant leg, he exposed a cut-back-heal and pointed-toe boot. Reaching down, he slapped the red dust blanketing the glossy black leather.

"Alright cowboy," Max chuckled joining his boarding family.

Under a metal ribbed arched ceiling, a center aisle lead to an open cockpit door. Benches ran along the sides of the cabins interior. A dozen privileged locals sat in silence. Recognizing a Laotian Air America mechanic, Max nodded. The employee smiled nervously. Graciously, he huddled his family closer together. Several evacuees gasped at the distance roar of manmade thunder.

"Max I want you to wait with me upfront," Buck informed patting the German's back. "When we are ready to take off, I'll need for you to close the cargo door. I'm going to leave it open until the last minute to expedite our departure."

Max trailed behind the cowboy to the front of the plane. He peered into the doorway of the small cockpit. A stoic co-pilot sat stone faced, beads of sweat sparkled on his oily forehead. On the other side of the windshield, crimson dust blew across the dirt runway.

Buck strapped himself into the pilot's seat. Patting the co-pilot on the knee, he mumbled, "Don't worry Jay, we shouldn't be on the ground very much longer."

Hovering behind the pilots, Max squatted down for a better view. At the end of the runway, a green-patchwork of strategically placed paddy fields glistened. The twin prop engines sputtered to life. On the horizon, mortar fire erupted. Both pilots checked their watches.

"I don't think our last two passengers are going to make it," Jay muttered.

No one responded. The three men in the stuffy cockpit watched advancing fireworks. All of them jerked violently. A hangar facility adjacent to the runway exploded. Sheets of rippled tin and fractured wood shot across the red clay tarmac.

"We weren't hit Jay," Buck said taking a breath, "it will be a bumpy take-off but I'm still planning to fly out of here in..." he paused checking his watch, "...ten minutes."

A black junkyard dog wandered out of the dust floating across runway. Max mumbled, "Pasha."

"Is that your dog?" Buck asked over his shoulder.

"Sure is," Max responded.

Checking the time, Buck said, "My two American passengers still have...nine minutes to catch this flight. If you want to risk it you can get the dog."

Max squeezed the Texas pilot's shoulder. Into the cabin he hollered, "Loc! Pao! Pasha is on the runway!"

From the cockpit, Max saw Pao attempting to whistle over the humming aircraft. The mangy mutt froze. Extending an ear skyward, Pasha wagged a white tipped tail. After a few joyous leaps, the dog broke into a sprint towards his master. Pao carried the happy dog into the cargo hold. Nervous laughter greeted the hyperactive canine.

Looking back at the commotion, Buck chuckled. "That dog better not shit during the flight."

The sound of rolling thunder interrupted the cockpit defecation warning. A wave of random explosions marched across the scenic landscape. Dust and smoke engulfed the aircraft. The filthy haze poured into the passenger cabin. The women gasped. The children cried. In soiled darkness the deafening bombardment rippled by.

"We still flying out of here?" Max asked over the coughs and whimpers of the passengers.

"I'll tell you in a minute," Buck said revving the engines and squinting forward.

Settling dust revealed small fires burning across the runway. Out of the swirling smoke staggered Jim Dugan. Across his shoulders lay another American.

"Loc!" Max called out into the murky fuselage. "Man down!"

Through the soiled cockpit glass, Max and the flight crew observed. Loc sprinted out. The agile tribesman hurdled over smoldering debris. Dugan collapsed at the sight of assistance. Loc relieved him of his wounded burden. How does someone so small possess so much strength? Max questioned. The tiny Loc heaved the heavy casualty across his back. A stumbling Dugan followed the tribesman to the aircraft.

"We going to do this?" Jay asked.

"We sure going to try," Buck said making the final preparations for take-off.

Dugan secured the cargo door. The passenger cabin went dark. Max harnessed himself into the jump seat.

"Hold onto your hats boys and girls, we're in for one hell of take-off!" Buck called out over the shrieking twin prop engines.

Another artillery barrage danced across the landscape. The cargo plane at full throttle bounced down the pitted, cluttered tarmac. Amongst the blast of incoming fire, Buck pulled back on the plane's yoke. Through gritted teeth he mumbled, "Come on you metallic bitch get me home."

A rapidly expanding column of fire blocked the runway. The red clay beneath dropped. Buck hollered, "Yeeee Haaaaa," and flew directly into the inferno. Banking hard to the left, the metal thoroughbred passed through intense heat. The fire baptism was brief. Climbing into the cool blue skies above the Plain of Jars, the flying boxcar left a victorious smoke corkscrew in its wake.

A big grin spread across Buck's face. Petting the control panel, he whispered, "Good girl." Taking a triumphant breath, he asked, "Do you have a cigar Max?"

Max balked at the strange request. Pulling a cigar out of his breast pocket, he questioned, "You're going to smoke?"

Grabbing the stogy, Buck answered, "I like to smoke after sex."

"Sex?" Max mumbled.

"I just fucked death and feel like lighting up," the Texan responded.

Laughing Max said, "Enjoy the smoke cowboy, you've earned it." Unfastening his harness, he rose and squeezing the pilots shoulder informed, "I'm going to check on the passengers."

Max exited the cockpit. Bucks back teeth bit down hard on the unlit stogy. After humming a familiar tune, the cowboy broke into song.

"The stars at night are big and bright..." echoed behind Max as he entered the cargo hold. The American casualty lay on the floor of the cabin. His head rested on Lan's lap. Firmly, she held his hand while gently stroking his sweaty hair. Utilizing the plane's first aid kit, Mei cleaned his wounds. Sitting in the aisle observing the nurses, a sweat soaked Dugan drank from a canteen. Looking up at Max, he blinked several times. Pouring water into a trembling cupped hand, Dugan splashed his soiled face.

"Who are the girls?" Dugan questioned.

Squatting down beside Dugan, Max responded proudly, "That's Mei and Lan, they are my *Little Sisters*."

"They apparently know what they are doing, I can't recall a field medic dressing wounds any better." Dugan stated.

"The girls have extensive field experience from the valley of death." Max informed.

"Dien Bien Phu?" Dugan questioned.

Sitting beside the American, Max nodded. "How bad was it?" He asked.

The fatigued Dugan took a deep breath. "It was not good," he muttered observing Mei stitching up his wounded colleague. "The Laotian regulars literally dropped their weapons and ran from the Pathet Lao guerrillas. The only troops that stood their ground were the Meos. Your friend, Colonel Yang and his *Montagnard* army came to fight. Those *Yards* performed admirably in the face of overwhelming odds."

"And the Colonel?" Max questioned.

Stoically looking into Max's eyes, Dugan said, "Colonel Yang successfully retreated to Padoung with most of his Meo soldiers. However Max," Dugan paused placing his hand on Max's shoulder, "your Jewish friend did not make it."

Slumping back from the weight of grim news, Max looked over at H'Liana. Guillian's wife in her colorful tribal clothing bounced her giggling child. Guillian's son innocently sprang up and down trying to pet the tail wagging Pasha.

"Is that his wife and child?" Dugan whispered.

Nodding Max recalled Guillian's prophecy. All soldiers in a never ending conflict eventually die.

"I know he was a good friend of yours Max, I'm sorry. The Jew was one of the best commandos I ever saw in combat. If it was not for him and his contingent of Meos, I would not be here." Taking a calming sip of water, he added, "I'm not a wealthy man but I will make sure that his wife and son are established before I head stateside. For what I owe the Jew that is the least I can do."

CHAPTER TWENTY SIX

The air was cool. The hum of the aircraft soothing. Max fumbled through his overstuffed duffle bag. Beneath his rolled up clothes, he felt two kilos of opium. Reaching past the drugs, he grabbed an accordion file folder. Pulling the document pouch to the surface, he glanced around the cabin. All the children slept. The high-strung Pasha reclined at Pao's feet. The wounded American rested with a sedated gaze. Dugan's head bobbed towards slumber. The other passengers sat quietly with disconnected eyes.

Opening the cardboard folder pouch, Max looked at neatly bundled stacks of Vietnamese piastres, Laotian kip and American greenbacks. Elaine's letters filled a compartment. In a side slot was Guillian's correspondence. Extracting the wrinkled envelope, Max closed the file folder. An attached elastic band sealed his life savings and lover's letters. Taking a deep breath, he broke the seal on the envelope. Reverently, he read Jean Guillian's last communication.

Max, if you are reading this as instructed, I'm dead. I'd like to say it was a great life, but it wasn't. It started out with so much promise for me as the heir apparent to the family department store business in Paris. Under German occupation my father was forced to sell the family business that his grandfather had started. The proceeds from the sale were held by the bank based on the new anti-Semitic laws trickling into my world. The biggest mistake my father made was becoming an outspoken critic of the new collaborating government. The fascist responded to his outrage by allowing the family to be deported to a labor camp. As I've told you before my mother and me were the only survivors. Now that you are reading this, the only Guillians are my mother and my son Etienne.

I became a commando to escape the past. I took refuge amongst the ridge running Meo, where I found a wife who bore me a son. It's important to me for my mother to know that she has an heir, when so many European Jewish lineages have been terminated.

I've told you before that my mother was never the same after the war. I have no predictions how she will receive this news. I'm hoping my mother will take H'Liania and Etienne in as part of the family, just like the Meos adopted me.

Max, I hate to ask you for one last favor seeing as given my current circumstances I can never repay you. However one positive aspect for you is that I will never be able to ask you for anything ever again.

Pausing Max grinned at his Guillian's levity. Even from the grave, Max thought. The Jew had unique way of looking at life. Turning to the next page, he continued.

I need for you to contact my mother Celine Guillian through the family attorney. He has been handling her affairs since he successfully recovered much of the family wealth. His name is Olivier Masson or at least it was during the war. Before that he went by Hassan. He may have changed it back. Like a lot of French Jews, he hide behind an alias during occupation. I'm assuming your American employer at the US embassy can help you expedite this request.

If my mother is too far out of touch with reality to accept H'Liana and Etienne into the family, see to it that they are returned to their highlands. And if your travels take you in their direction look in on them for me. When Etienne comes of age, let him know who his father was.

Stopping to catch his breath, Max took several quick snorts. He gazed upon Guillian's family. The young mother, H'Liana proudly sat in the colorful costume of her people. A drawn back red bandana framed the taut skin of her youthful face and dark eyes. Etienne slept peacefully across her lap. Glancing at Max, she flashed a nervous smile. He grinned. How am I going to tell her, he pondered? It doesn't matter what I say, he realized, the young girl will be crushed. I'll worry about that when we land, he concluded. Returning to his dead friend's correspondence, he continued to read.

I know I can count on you Max, I always could. We never had the discussion about the anti-Semitic agenda of the German National Socialist and I'm glad we never will. When I saw you for the first time staggering out of the jungle on your escape from

Isabelle; I saw a German through contempt filled eyes. When we walked out of the Communist north with my Meo family, we did it as brothers.

Adieu my friend,

Sergent-chef Jean Guillian.

Carefully folding the letter, Max put it back into the envelope. He tucked the document in his button down breast pocket. Patting the secured correspondence on his chest, he mumbled, "Adieu my brother."

CHAPTER TWENTY SEVEN

In front of the plane's cargo door, Pasha wagged a white tipped tail. At the other end of the cabin, Buck sporting a white Stetson, peered out the cockpit. He gave a big thumbs-up to Dugan. The American unlatched the barrier. Sunlight and the late afternoon humidity of South Vietnam flooded the plane's interior. The anxious dog leapt onto the tarmac of the Cap St. Jacques airport. Lifting a hind leg, the mutt took a healthy piss. After relieving himself, Pasha stood over the urine pond with a pointed ear. Detecting the high-pitched wail of an approaching siren, the dog pointed his snout to the sky and howled. The bewildered passengers remained seated. On a canvas stretcher, Max and Loc carried the wounded American towards the noisy sunlit opening.

"You got him?" Max asked lowering his end of the stretcher to the disembarked Dugan.

Nodding Dugan cautiously pulled the stretcher out of the aircraft. White uniformed paramedics rushed out of an ambulance to assist.

From his elevated vantage point, Max saw ground personnel pushing a short gangway towards the plane. Under the tropical sun, an ambulance's flashing red light pulsed. Pasha barked at the paramedics loading the casualty. Dugan petted the dog before jumping into the back of the ambulance. Looking up at Max, the American saluted. Max returned the respectful gesture. The obnoxious wailing siren faded with the departing ambulance.

Under the protective shade of the aircraft's wing, Max assembled the twenty refugees. A warm breeze blew across the noisy open airfield. The windblown audience stared into the open cargo door. Strutting down the short gangway, the cowboy pilot chomped on the slimly end of a cigar. Still displaying the wide grin from his satisfied sexual encounter with death,

Buck hollered, "Let's move 'em out!" For emphasis, he swept both his arms in the direction of the terminal.

At the end of a taut rope leash, the enthusiastic Pasha led the procession. The scruffy dog pulled the pudgy Lan out of the pack towards the terminal.

Walking alongside Max, Buck asked, "Do you and your family have a place to stay?"

"We'll figure something out," Max answered. Adjusting the duffle bag strung across his back, he motioned over his shoulder at the other Laotian refugees.

"They are all taken care of," Buck reassured. "The Air America employees and their relatives are headed to Vientiane."

Glancing over at Guillian's widow, Max felt his stomach churn. I've got to tell her, he thought. Entering the pitched tiled roofed open air terminal, Lan distracted Max's heavy heart. In a tug-of-war with Pasha's leash and a uniformed customs official, she sought backup. Max surged forward. Buck politely intercepted the German's advance.

"Let me handle this," Buck said walking into the confrontation. "What seems to be the problem here, chief?" He asked chewing on a cigar.

The short Vietnamese official looked up at the towering Texan's protruding cigar. In broken English, he informed, "We quarantine dog!"

"How much?" Buck inquired.

"No bribe!" the official defiantly responded, "We quarantine dog!"

Biting off the end of the cigar, the cowboy chewed hard. Out of the side of his mouth, he spat a saliva moist wad of tobacco. The maduro spitball splattered across the customs official's patent leather shoe. "You ain't quarantining shit," he declared. Slowly he removed his white Stetson. Handing the hat to Lan, he pleasantly said, "Please hold this for me darlin."

Standing behind the clenched fist Texan, Max inquired, "How are the negotiations going?"

Staring at the small bureaucrat, Buck responded. "I'll tell you in a minute after I beat the crap out of the only non-corruptible official in Southeast Asia."

"Before you break his jaw, let our boss have a crack at him," Max said pointing to Roche jogging towards the debate.

"Gentlemen," a winded Roche said flashing his diplomatic passport at the terrified customs agent. "I apologize for any misunderstanding. This is my dog and therefore immune from local regulations." Placing his passport back in his Hawaiian shirt pocket, he slowly took control of the leash. Pulling out a money clip, he added, "I'd like to compensate you for the inconvenience."

"I already tried that!" Buck blurted.

Roche shot a frown at the lanky cowboy. Looking back politely at the official, he shuffled currency awaiting a monetary response.

"Go! Go!" the customs agent said waiving his hands in disgust. Walking away, he grumbled Vietnamese obscenities.

"Thanks for the diplomacy lesson," Buck said twisting the saturated stogy in the corner of his mouth. Extending a finger, he lifted the brim of his hat. "I'm buying. Would you gentlemen care to join me?"

Grinning, Max placed a hand on the Texan's shoulder. Looking over at the timid H'Liana coddling her son, he said, "Another time cowboy. I have an unpleasant task I need to perform."

"What is it Max?" Roche asked.

"*Sergent-chef* Jean Guillian is no longer with us," Max responded solemnly.

"I understand," Roche nodded. "I've arranged transportation for your family. Let me handle them, and you..." he paused to swallow, "do what you have to do."

Deep green grass landscaped the front of the airport terminal. Twin palm trees stood in a colorful white and yellow flowerbed. The cloudless sky was royal blue. Holding H'Liana by the hand, Max and Loc led her over to a shaded patch of turf. Etienne waddled beside his mother. The rest of Max's adopted family loaded their worldly possessions into the staff cars provided by Roche.

Taking a deep breath, Max stopped. Looking down, he smiled into the face of the young widow.

Puzzled, H'Liana squinted into Max's blue eyes. In tribal dialect, she spoke softly to Loc. He responded by shaking his head.

"She asked if we are planning to leave her here in this noisy place," Loc translated.

"No," Max said looking into her confused expression, "And tell her, she is now and will always be a member of our tribe." Swallowing he added, "For Guillian is dead."

Before Loc translated, tears welled up in her dark eyes. In crackling French, she said, "I understand, my husband teach me."

Placing a hand on her petite shoulder, Max said, "Guillian was a good ..." before he could finish his condolence, H'Liana melted. Slumping down onto the moist turf, she wept.

The bewildered Etienne observing his mother began to cry. She hugged him into her detached lament. Rocking back and forth, she wailed.

CHAPTER TWENTY EIGHT

A warm afternoon breeze flowed through the residential canyon of mid-rise apartment buildings. Suspended by bamboo poles, colorful Saigon laundry flapped. On the urine stained concrete terrace of a fourth floor flat, a reclining Pasha panted. Beside the moist foul smelling dog, Pao fought to stay awake. It was another uncomfortable muggy urban day.

Carrying a plastic pail full of water, Mei stepped onto the sunlit balcony. Looking around at the flower boxes that lined the lanai railing, she smiled. In rich brown earth tiny green sprouts bathed in sunlight. Utilizing a tin can ladle, she watered her garden.

"Can I get you some water grandfather?" Lan asked from the doorway.

Looking up at her with a detached expression, Pao blinked several times. Ignoring her query, he refocused his sleepy-eyed gaze at the fluttering clothes.

Lan shot a puzzled frown at Mei.

"What is it little sister?" Mei asked.

Lan walked onto the deck. Straddling the family dog, she leaned into Mei and whispered, "I'm concerned about Pao."

Glancing down at the comatose old warrior, Mei quietly responded, "He has his good days and bad days. He'll be fine, besides Max is coming over tonight. Pao always perks up when Max is here."

"Max is coming!" Lan exclaimed, "Why didn't you tell me?"

"I just did," Mei giggled, "I guess Pao is not the only one that perks up in Max's presence."

"I just hope he doesn't bring that American cow with him," Lan said puckering her face.

"Elaine?" Mei questioned. Putting down the watering can, she touched a piece of fluttering laundry.

"Yes Elaine," Lan said frowning, "With her big chest and sweet stench. I don't know why Max has to stay with her. I bet she can't give him a baby."

Placing a hand on Lan's shoulder, Mei counseled, "One thing I've learned little sister is you will never figure out the white people. They are a very confusing race." Evoking a smile out of Lan, Mei added, "I know Elaine is helping Max find little Etienne's grandmother in France. Maybe that is why he stays with her."

Beaming Lan said, "That is probably why Max stays with her. Because I just know she's unable to give him a baby."

"Now that you've figured that out, you can help me take in the laundry," Mei asked.

Pao slowly rose. Placing his hands in the small of his back, he stretched his old bones.

"Did we wake you grandfather?" Lan asked.

"When did we get chickens?" Pao asked looking at the confused girls.

"Chickens?" Mei inquired.

"I'm going to take a walk," he informed. Slowly he shuffled through the doorway. Looking over his shoulder, he added with a sly grin, "I just can't get comfortable out here with all the clucking hen chatter."

Laughing Mei said to a snickering Lan, "I told you, he has good days and bad days."

The smell of roasted duck permeated throughout the small fourth floor apartment. Behind a sheeted partition, Lan put on a new *Ao Dai* dress. On the other side of the cloth divider, H'Liana in colorful tribal garb hummed a simple tune to her son and Mei's daughter. The catchy melody enticed Lan to whistle along. Pulling back the draped screen, Lan received an approving smile from the shy widow.

"Loc!" Mei called out from the tiny kitchen. "Can you go check on Pao. He's not back yet from his walk."

From the balcony, Loc stuck his head into the flat. A smoldering cigarette attached to his lower lip. Firmly grasping a wet sudsy dog, he answered. "Give me a minute, I'm not done bathing Pasha."

"I'll go," Lan replied receiving a thankful nod from Loc. Entering the stagnant stale air of the stairwell, Lan avoided the rusty hand rail. I need to look my best for Max, she thought. I just hope he missed me as much as I missed him. It's been weeks since he paid us a visit, she calculated. Recalling Max showing up with that large white woman, she frowned. Why did he bring her? She wondered visualized Elaine prancing into the apartment and handing out gifts to the family acting all nice and friendly and then leaving with Max.

Exiting the dimly lit apartment building, Lan looked left and right. Dusk approached. Street hawkers along the sidewalk set up shop for the nightly trade. A small crowd gathered at the end of the block. Lan quickened her pace to investigate. Approaching the chuckling onlookers, Lan followed their cruel gaze. Three teenagers taunted her grandfather. A snickering boy wiped his ass with Pao's tribal cap. His companions pushed the old man back and forth.

Lan's heart raced. Out of breath, she opened her mouth gasping for air. A quick side-glance spotted empty Coke bottles beside a vendor's cart. Grabbing a thick glass bottle, she charged. Snorting like a wild animal, she knocked over a spectator. Breaking the female shaped container against a light pole, she swung jagged glass at the face of the ass-wiping clown. Felling resistance, she knew she had cut the boy. His accomplices grabbed her from behind.

Wading through the crowd, Max peered over the pointed hats and black haired heads of the undersized locals. Pao lay on the asphalt. Two street punks restrained an enraged Lan. A third teenager investigated a gash across his cheek. Instinctively, Max reached for his shoulder holstered pistol. Feeling the comforting power of the weapon, he calculated a shooting sequence. Three easy head shots. Visualizing the terminations, he fired an attention getter into the air. The crowd let out a simultaneous cry. The mob dropped to the ground or ran for cover. Brandishing a pistol, Max strutted onto the impromptu stage. Grabbing the cut ringleader by the throat, he lifted the wiry young thug. The two punks holding Lan ran. Pao slowly rose. Gasping for air the teenager's eyes bulged. His feet dangled above the black asphalt. Max elevated the instigator higher before slamming the terrified boy into the blacktop. Placing a black leather shoe on the boy's chest, Max re-holstered his pistol and smiled at Pao. A confident grin appeared on the old warriors face. Pao could have easily killed the boys, Max realized.

Waving the heavily breathing Lan to join him, Max wrapped an arm around the little fire cracker. He kissed the top of her head. It's time to teach the neighborhood a lesson, he thought. The pedestrian audience slowly reappeared to catch the final act. Extending a forefinger and thumb, Max symbolized a handgun. Pointing the index finger barrel at the boy, he winked at Pao. Lifting up his smock, Pao revealed a pistol. The old warrior aimed the weapon at the boy's head. The street punk pissed his pants.

An irate fruit stand vendor yelled, "Let the boy go or we call the police."

"Now you want to call the police?" Max questioned. "Why didn't you call the police when my family was being harassed?"

"The boys were just having fun. The old *Moi* does not belong here. He belongs in the jungle," declared the brazen spokesman.

The crowd murmured in agreement.

Looking down at the wide-eyed boy, Max recalled when he was that age. In his jaunty *Jugendbund* uniform, he taunted old Jews. The young wolves of the Hitler Youth beat Jewish shopkeepers. Glancing around at the bigoted Asian audience, he could see the faces of his anti-Semitic German neighbors. The haunting regret of past sins, churned in his belly. He released the boy under his foot. The youth jumped up and sprinted away. Bending down, he picked up Pao's skullcap.

Approaching the outspoken fruit vendor, Max said, "One day events that you have no control over may uproot you from your home. You will find yourself adrift as an outcast in another land. When that happens, just hope the local inhabitants show more compassion than you did today. Believe me, it is a tough lesson to learn. It takes time."

Swinging open the creaking door, Max walked into the small apartment. Lan and Pao followed. Inhaling the smoked flavored aroma of roasted duck, Max shouted, "Smells good!"

"Max!" Mei exclaimed hastily drying her hands on an apron. Rushing out of the kitchen, she leapt into the German's arms.

Closing his eyes, he affectionately embraced the kindred Dien Bien Phu survivor. We both walked away from the valley of death, he thought. Mei's journey through a communist forced labor camp was far more treacherous. The petite beauty is special, he thought. Her quest to exist far exceeds anything this world can throw at her.

"We were beginning to worry about the three of you," Loc said extending his hand.

Releasing Mei, Max slapped Loc's hand out of the way and embraced the tribesman. Patting Loc on the back, he quietly said, "Always good to see you partner."

Timidly standing against the wall in the crowded room, H'Liana smiled nervously. Approaching the shy widow, Max placed his hand on her soft cheek and said, "Bonjour H'Liana."

Touching his hand against her face, she responded in a soft voice, "Bonjour monsieur." Covering her mouth with a cupped hand, she giggled.

Pasha leapt up and down. A happy tail hammered everything within range. Reaching down, Max petted the hyperactive mutt on the head and muttered, "Good boy."

Lan handed Max a bottle of beer. He placed his free arm across her shoulders. She beamed. Raising the cold brew towards his family, he declared, "It is good to be home."

Snuggling up under his arm, Lan patted his chest and asked, "Then you stay with us?"

"I will tonight Little Sister," Max answered basking in the appreciative glow of his displaced companions. I'm sure glad I came alone, he thought; Elaine will never understand my bond with these people. Hell, she really doesn't understand me.

CHAPTER TWENTY NINE

Galvanized hinges and a padlock secured a large plywood barrier across the storefront. A young Vietnamese realtor fumbled with a set of keys. A cigarette glowed between his lips. His prospective tenants stood patiently. On his third attempt, the broker unlatched the plywood door. He pulled back the wooden barrier. Stagnant air escaped. Late afternoon sunlight poured in. A musty dust blanketed the vacant Saigon shop. Completing his task, the realtor squatted down on the sidewalk. Shutting out the world, he enjoyed a smoke.

Ignoring the disconnected realtor, Max looked at Loc and asked, "What do you think?"

The tribesman shrugged.

Mei walked past the men to investigate the family opportunity. Standing in the center of the empty space, she slowly turned. We can easily paint over the stained walls, she assumed. Looking down, she examined the black and white checkered linoleum flooring. A good wash and wax will bring this back to life, she concluded. She peered into the doorframe of the back room. Stained white tiles covered the floor and walls of the small enclosure. The fixtures consisted of a squat toilette in the corner and a tarnished porcelain sink. "Perfect," she whispered.

Returning to her husband and Max, Mei quietly asked, "How long is the rent agreement?"

"I don't know," Max responded.

"How long is the agreement with the American dairy?" She questioned.

With a slight shrug, Max said. "I don't know that either, but Roche said it is a very good deal. We can buy the ice-cream directly from the new factory and sell it to the public at a good profit."

Nodding confidently, Mei said, "We should make both agreements for the same length of time."

"That makes sense," Max said. "What do you think of the shop?"

"I don't know," Mei squinted. "When do people buy ice-cream?"

"Late afternoon?" Max guessed.

Mei stepped outside. Framed by the doorway, she looked left and right studying the flow of pedestrian traffic. Seeing a small crowd at a bus stop two shops down, she smiled.

Coming up behind her, Max asked, "What are you looking for?"

"Fish," she chuckled. "Never go fishing in a pond where there is no fish."

"So Mei," Max asked, "Are you going to let your husband and me roll our opium profits into the ice-cream business?"

"Do you think we can buy sweet milk from the American dairy?" She asked.

"I don't see why not, I'll ask Roche. What are you thinking?" Max questioned.

"The more lines you have in the water. The more fish you catch." She said. "We can sell coffee with sweet milk in the morning and ice-cream with fruit in the afternoon."

"I like that," Max said looking over his shoulder at Loc.

The tribesman proudly nodded.

"Roche has asked me to run an errand for him tomorrow," Max informed. "When I return, I'll have him assist with the agreements. The only thing we need to come up with now is a name for our ice-cream shop."

"Isabelle's!" Loc blurted out.

CHAPTER THIRTY

On the outskirts of Saigon, Max flexed his foot on the accelerator. The two door red Peugeot convertible purred. Green rice stalks flanking the dusty road became a blur. Clean agricultural air swirled behind the windshield. Max patted the satchel of money on the passenger seat. Looking through the insect-pitted glass at the long road in front of him, he grinned. It would be awhile before the complexities of working the clutch and shifting gears came into play. Leaning back with one hand on top of the steering wheel, he coasted before flexing his foot again. Thank god, the traffic of Saigon is behind me, he thought. This should be a simple errand. He glanced at his watch. I'll deliver the funds and be back in the city before night fall, he thought. Well before the nocturnal Viet Cong take control of the night.

Local pedestrian traffic appeared. Downshifting, he winced at the grating sound of grinding gears. A single file line of a dozen peasant farmers plodded along. Slouched over, the coolies staggered forward in bodies broken by hard labor and lack of food. Pointed hats shielded the sun. Soiled black cotton pajamas clothed malnourished frames. Poor bastards Max thought. Do you think they really care about the political struggle for this country? "Winning the hearts and minds," he mumbled. The sports car's dusty wake engulfed farmers procession. If you really want to give them what they need, Max concluded. Just leave them alone. An uninterrupted daily struggle to survive is all they want.

Fronting the thoroughfare, a sprawling bamboo-fenced community baked under the tropical sun. Orderly rowed thatched roof huts stood at attention. This must be the *agroville* Max thought, steering onto a gravel paved entrance road. Why the Saigon government feels the need to uproot and isolate selected inhabitants from the Communist is beyond me. Two armed soldiers waved Max through the gate. One pointed in the direction of an administration building. Across the hot dusty compound, thousands labored in the sweltering heat. Uniformed troops provided security from the shade of completed structures. Barbwire around the perimeter of the compound sparkled. Is the razor wire keeping the communist out or the secluded population in, Max pondered. He swung the vehicle in a wide turn in front of the administration building. At least I won't have to deal with reverse when I exit, he thought. I'll drop off the Americans' under-the-table contribution, take a quick piss and be back in Saigon well before dusk. Exiting the car, he stretched in the sea of industrious construction.

"That's a beautiful vehicle you have there," commented an army major in clean pressed military fatigues.

Glancing at the swaggering Asian officer, Max responded, "Thanks, but it is not mine. It belongs to my employer."

The major nodded. "You must be here to see Mister Tuyen. He is in the administration building."

Reaching into the convertible, Max retrieved the satchel. He got a glimpse of the major salivating at the bag of money. "Tell me," Max asked, "Just how many people live in this community."

"Right now, about three thousand. Once completed that number should double." The major informed in a rehearsed response.

"All these workers are residents?" Max questioned.

The major chuckled, "No, in order to meet our completion dead line, we imported ten-thousand laborers." Rubbing his chin he added, "The additional workers are fulfilling their civic responsibility by contributing their time." Looking at his watch, he offered, "If it is not too late after you meet with Mister Tuyen, I would be happy to show you around."

"Thanks," Max said, "but once I deliver the package I'm heading back to Saigon."

"I understand, but feel free to tell your American employer what you have seen here. We are winning the support of the peasant population."

Arbeit macht frei, Max thought. Calling slave labor civic duty had the gruesome irony of the Nazi slogan *work will set you free*.

Entering the starched white concrete administration building, a seated slouching guard greeted Max. Unfolding his arms, the sentry flicked a thumb in the direction of a back office. Peering into the open office doorway, Max grinned. Behind a metal desk sat the arrogant little shit Tommy. Mr. Tuyen chose Tommy because it was easier to pronounce, Max chuckled.

Looking up from his paper work, a mischievous smirk spread across the well-groomed henchman. In a clean starched short-sleeved white shirt, he leaned back in his chair and said, "Hello Max."

"Tommy," Max mumbled tossing the satchel on the paper covered desktop.

Leaning forward Tommy unzipped the bag. "You don't mind if I count it? Do you?"

Max shrugged. "Do whatever you like. I'm going to take a piss and head back to Saigon. For all your efforts in the countryside, it becomes a dangerous place once the lights go out."

"The facilities are in the back," Tommy informed.

After relieving himself, Max glanced at his watch. I'll easily be home before nightfall, he thought. Gravel crunched underfoot, as he approached his vehicle. Tommy with that cocky smile held the car door open. Two workers hastily washed the insect graveyard from the windshield.

"Have a pleasant return trip," Tommy said as Max climbed in behind the steering wheel. "We may have had our differences in the past, but I'm glad the Americans were able to find you employment as a trusted bag man." He added slamming the door shut.

Turning over the ignition, Max looked up at the confident Asian and said, "Better get back to your numbers boy." Flooring the gas pedal, he left the self-important Tommy in a cloud of dust.

After navigating through the rural pedestrian traffic, Max opened up the vehicle. Leaning back, he cruised down the long deserted roadway. Behind him, the sun slowly set. Warm wind tousled his blond hair. The vehicle decelerated. He pumped the accelerator. The car sputtered. This is the last thing I need right now, he thought. The speedometer and the convertible Peugeot slowly died.

Coasting to the side of the road, Max tried several times to restart the vehicle. "Damn," he mumbled hitting the steering wheel. Exiting the car, he slammed the door shut. Flipping his sports coat over his shoulder, he scanned barren fields of rice. The palm of his hand measured the setting sun and horizon. Another hour of daylight, he estimated. One hour, he realized before the Viet Cong rule the night.

Opening the car's trunk, he scowled at the spare tire in empty compartment. Just great, he thought closing the hatch. Looking up he noticed a discoloration around the vehicles gas cap. Squinting, he examined a white powder residue. Rubbing it with an extended finger, he took a sample. The tip of his tongue detected a sweet taste. That arrogant son-of-a-bitch Tommy spiked the gas tank with sugar, he realized.

It is what it is, he thought. I have about an hour to put some distance between myself and the vehicle, he concluded. An abandoned car will attract the Viet Cong like flies.

At a brisk pace, he hiked down the roadway. At dusk, he headed into the paddy fields. Beside a shallow irrigation trench, he stopped. To evict any occupants, he stomped around a patch of waist high elephant grass. Tossing his sports coat on the matted turf, he sat down and pulled out a cigar. Rolling the stogy in his mouth, he realized he could not light up. What the hell, he thought reclining back and looking at the evening sky. I spent weeks in the jungle hunted by Vietminh; ten hours in a paddy field *es machts nichts*, (It's nothing).

CHAPTER THIRTY ONE

Morning sunlight raced across the flat low-lying terrain. An intricate patchwork of rice paddies, tributaries and canals sparkled under the advance. The illuminating warmth flooded a matted down patch of waist high elephant grass. The warm rays nudged Max into the new day. Blinking into the bright light, he shielded the sunlight with his pistol. Inhaling the heavy moist air, he cautiously peered over the tall green blades. In the surrounding flooded fields, peasant farmers in the midst of the sheeted water tended to rice stalks. Standing up in the deep grass, he stretched his sore frame. Just like the roaches in my apartment, he thought. The Viet Cong scatter once you turn on the lights. After holstering the sidearm, he picked up his grass stained sport coat. Throwing it over his shoulder, he plodded towards the main road. Rubbing the fresh mosquito bites on the side of his face, he realized he got a few hours of sleep.

In the distance, a bus billowed down the rural road. To intercept it, Max ran waving his arms and shouting. Flagging down the vehicle, he smiled. My agricultural ordeal is about to end, he thought. I can hitch a ride to the nearest town and hire a car to take me home. Hell, I could be in Saigon by late afternoon.

The bus came to a screeching halt. Max looked up into the insect splattered windshield. A curious wide-eyed driver peered down. Giving the man a thankful nod, he put on his soiled sports jacket. Straightening out the lapels, he climbed aboard. Handing the driver a one-hundred-piastre note, he looked down the aisle of the crowded transport. In the front row, two local police officers stretched out. One slept. The other examined Max over the sunglasses resting on the tip of his nose. Walking past the officers, Max grabbed an overhead handrail. The vehicle jerked forward. Next to Max, a young mother breast-fed her baby. A caged chicken at her feet clucked. Pivoting to give the mother and child privacy, he looked down at a seated local. A Coca Cola bottle crate rested on his lap. Across the tarnished red wooden, box the companies white scripted logo prominently displayed. The tops of female shaped coke bottles clanged.

Involuntarily Max's dry mouth swallowed. "How much?" He asked the cola peddler.

The nervous man shook his head.

Fumbling around in his pants pocket, Max retrieved a crumpled one-hundred-piastre note. Handing it to the hawker invoked a smile. After pocketing the money, the vendor pulled out a bottle of cola. A skilled palm opened it on the side of the box.

A captive audience watched Max grab the warm bottle. Tilting his head back, he poured the sweet carbonated liquid down his parched throat. The day is starting out better than expected, he thought licking the rich taste across his lips. Handing the empty bottle back, he nodded his appreciation. The vendor quickly opened a second bottle. No doubt I won't be getting any change back, Max realized. I guess I'm about to find out how much cola one-hundred piastres buys in the Mekong Delta. Taking the second bottle, Max handed it to the passenger beside him. A startled grin conveyed gratitude. To the pleasant murmurs of the rural bus passengers, Max handed out bottles of Coke.

The vehicle skidded to a jolting stop. A pistol-brandishing gunman burst through the door. The sleeping policemen surrendered. In black pajamas with a red headband, the communist hijacker fired a round into the rusty ceiling. Orange flakes floated down. A woman screamed. Babies cried. The hijacker barked at the trembling sheep. The terrified herd scurried to disembark.

Shuffling forward, Max lowered his head. He counted ten heavily armed men outside of the bus. Un-holstered his pistol, he placed it in his coat pocket. Stepping off the bus, he saw the police officers bound and kneeling by the roadside. Alongside the transport, passengers stood shoulder to shoulder. Max fell into the forced lineup. The pistol-waiving communist demanded identity cards. The assembly nervously obliged. Spotting

Max, the hijacker smirked. Grabbing the German's lapels, he yanked Max out of the lineup.

Glancing left to right, Max calculated a shooting sequence. You're the first, Max thought ignoring the youth jerking on his sport coat. Prioritizing the killing order, he studied the facial expressions of potential targets. These are not amateurs; he concluded examining the determined resolve of hardened men. Sighing, he realized the equation was unsolvable. Looking down at the vintage French revolver in his face, he grinned. Death has found me, he realized. The pistol waving youth scowled at the smiling German. "So you are death?" Max questioned. Chuckling he added, "I thought you'd be taller."

From the front of the bus, a limping Viet Cong approached. He waived off the pistol-toting subordinate. "Hello Max," he said.

Frowning, Max studied the hobbling Communist officer. Could this be the Binh Xuyen soldier I assisted during the battle of Saigon? He wondered.

"You don't remember me do you?" The cripple asked.

"Your crushed foot gives you away," Max responded. "But what is a Saigon Binh Xuyen soldier doing under the Communist banner?"

"Where do you think we would go?" The hijacker chuckled. "The Binh Xuyen started out as river pirates from this region. We regrouped along with every other adversary the Americans' Catholic marionette drove out of Saigon. We will take our country back. It's only a matter of time." He paused as a Viet Cong soldier handed him the passengers' identity cards. "Excuse me a minute Max," He said examining the cards one at a time. Half way through the deck, he mumbled, "I know you are armed, don't do anything stupid." After finishing the review, he handed the cards to his subordinate and instructed, "Give these back to the passengers, they'll need them." Reaching into the pocket of his baggy black trousers, he pulled out two sheets of paper. In a monotone voice, he added, "Pin the verdicts onto the policemen before passing sentence." Leaning into Max, he clarified, "Policemen in this region have been warned many times to abandon their jobs and seek other employment. If not they must suffer the consequences."

The sandaled soldier walked away with his orders. Passing in front of the line of passengers, he handed the driver the stack of identity cards.

The nervous driver bowed. Grasping the paper verdicts, he approached the bound and kneeling police officers. On the backs of the condemned, he pinned the sentence. A teenage executioner un-sheathed a machete. The wide blade lifted skyward. A female passenger gasped. The heavy knife caught a spark of sunlight on its downward path. The honed edge cut clean. A severed head plopped in the dust. A woman screamed hysterical. Two civilian witnessed collapsed. The bus driver took a knee and vomited. The second policeman melted. Slumping forwarded he wept. A wide bloody blade silenced his whimpers.

The Viet Cong officer said, "I'm going to need your pistol Max."

Slowly, Max retrieved the handgun from his coat pocket. Holding the handle with thumb and forefinger, he surrendered the weapon. The officer nodded graciously. Pulling out the clip he handed the unloaded gun back.

"Thanks," Max said.

"Last time our paths crossed you warned me that death was close. I'm returning the advice. If you stay in Vietnam death will find you, Max." Grinning the officer added, "But best of luck."

The limping officer led his Viet Cong cadre past the traumatized passengers and decapitated corpses. Wading into waist high grass, the patrol vanished into the rich green countryside.

CHAPTER THIRTY TWO

An overflowing 'In Basket' rested on the edge of a clean desk. All around typewriters chirped. A large clock hung over the picture of President Kennedy. Checking the time Elaine sighed. Three long hours before lunch, she calculated. Taking a sip of strong black coffee, she closed her eyes. Only two hours until an early lunch, she pondered.

"Elaine," Roche said.

Startled, she returned to reality.

In apparently his favorite white and blue Hawaiian shirt, Roche hovered over her desk. He tossed a manila envelope in front of her and said, "This just came in from our Paris branch. It's the information you requested about Guillian's mother. It makes for some interesting reading, however," he paused examining her idle workstation, "if you have the time, we can discuss it now over a cup of coffee."

Leaping to her feet she grabbed her purse. Touching his arm she exclaimed, "Bless you Tom Roche; let's go."

The breakfast crowd had long since evacuated the small cafe. Sitting outside on a wicker chair, Roche slowly stirred a quickly dissolving cube of sugar into rich dark coffee. In the shade of an overhanging canvas canopy, he watched a focused Elaine. Mesmerized, she scanned the five-page memo. Her jaw dropped. "I take you got to the part that estimates her wealth." He commented.

"This is unbelievable," Elaine responded. Placing a completed page face down on the table, she continued to read.

"I know Max just wanted assistance with contact information about the family attorney. But since we have the resources I wanted to find out what he was walking into." Roche said placing his spoon aside and tasting the coffee.

Setting the last page on the pile, Elaine leaned back. Taking a deep breath, she commented, "So they did an extensive search three years ago to find Guillian, or I should say Jean, and was told he was missing in action."

"The way I'm interpreting the information..." Roche said lighting the cigarette dangling from the corner of his mouth, "...this Jewish attorney Olivier Masson..."

"It's Hassan; Olivier Hassan, he changed his name back sometime after the war," Elaine corrected.

"That's right, Olivier Hassan," Roche echoed correcting himself. "He controls a sizable trust with no heirs. Guillian's mother is in poor health and apparently mentally incapacitated. He has been using estate assets to find an heir any heir, a distance cousin any blood relative."

"You think that would not be that difficult," Elaine pondered. Reaching forward she stole one of Roche's Lucky Strikes.

"Elaine, we are talking about European Jews. Unfortunately the Holocaust has reduced the Guillian blood line to a Meo-Jewish offspring in Southeast Asia," Roche clarified igniting Elaine's cigarette.

"I'll talk to Max," Elaine said enjoying the smoke. "You know Max, he could care less about the potential inheritance. He is only focused on fulfilling Guillian's final request of notifying Etienne's grandmother."

"Our German friend does have a fanatical sense of loyalty and obligation." Roche chuckled.

"Tell me about it," Elaine grumbled. "That adopted family of his is like the in-laws that will never accept you."

"So I may still have a chance to win your affections?" Roche asked with a raised brow.

Grinning widely, Elaine responded, "You had your shot Tom. You just didn't take it."

CHAPTER THIRTY THREE

The Saigon bus terminal awoke. Triggered by morning sunlight, rusted and aging transports snorted exhaust. Mei's long black hair flowed down her back. Her forehead rested on Loc's shoulder. He stroked the back of her head. She closed her eyes. Please understand that I have to do this, she thought. I should only be gone for a week, she rationalized.

Kissing Loc one last time, Mei smiled into his concerned eyes. Tossing a rough cloth travel bag over her shoulder, she joined the orderly passenger shuffle. Boarding the bus, she took the first available seat. Sliding over on the torn vinyl bench, she stuck her head out the open window. Spotting her husband, she waved. The bucket of bolts jerked forward. She blew Loc a kiss.

The bouncing rural bus slowly stopped beside a towering cluster of bamboo. The transport idled impatiently. A handful of peasant farmers exited. The vehicle coughed to life. In a cloud of dust, it rambled down the rural highway. Standing in short black pants and a baggy white top, Mei glanced up from under a pointed palm frond hat. The other travelers dispersed into the flat green countryside. Standing alone in the shade of bamboo trees, she stretched after the long journey. The familiar country air smelled clean, fresh and pure. A warm breeze caressed her face. Overhead, wind rustled through dense foliage. I'm home, she realized recalling images of her mother and younger brothers. No need to dwell on the father that sold me, she concluded.

Mei checked the straight razor in her waistband. Clutching the rough gunnysack, she started on the ten-mile journey to the village of her birth. Her sandaled feet plodded down the narrow path. Swarming birds performed in the blue sky. The trail intersected with a drainage ditch. Stagnate canal water reeked of decay. A bowed wood plank connected the banks of the narrow channel. She tested the board's stability. Traversing the plank, she chuckled. Taun had fallen into the muck at this very crossing, she recalled. My little brother was such a handful. I wonder if he is married by now, she thought. Skipping up the last embankment towards the village gate, she stopped. The simple stone archway over a grass encroached walkway seemed much smaller than she remembered. Framed by the ancient entryway, she placed a hand over her mouth. What has happened? She wondered. Tall weeds blanketed the town square. Deserted mud and palm frond roofed structures displayed the wounds of neglect. She followed a trail of trampled growth to the village well. Grasping the familiar hand pump, she filled the concrete washbasin. The operational well is still being used, she realized. "Hello!" she called out. Wind brushing across flowering weeds answered. A damp handkerchief wiped her face with cool undrinkable water. Pulling a plastic bottle out of the gunnysack, she drank fresh water. A few strokes of the pump, refilled the plastic container. I hope that I will be able to boil this, she thought.

Blazing her own path through the knee-deep growth, Mei strolled through the lifeless community. Passing empty hollow huts, she visualized the former residents. On the outskirts of the ghost town, a small hovel clung to the sloping terrain. An angled planked wood door hung by a single hinge. Her heart raced. Taking a deep breath, she gingerly pushed the barrier. It collapsed. A cloud of dust rose up in the roofless structure. Waving a hand in the soil plume, she peered into her childhood home. It was picked clean.

In the back of her former residence, she scanned the sloping hillside. Weeds covered the family's small vegetable plot. Wading into the waist deep foliage, she stood in the location of her garden. This is where my father sold me, she realized. My mother wept. I never said goodbye to my brothers, she recalled with a heavy heart. Wiping a sniffling nose, she pulled back the unwanted growth in search of her grandfather's grave. Invading weeds shrouded the unmarked concrete headstone. Two addition gravestones resided beside her grandfather's marker.

The setting sun extended Mei's shadow across the family cemetery. It was joined by the darkened shapes of approaching men. Glancing over her shoulder, she saw a heavily armed Viet Cong cadre. A limping soldier in a baggy black peasant uniform, a chest rigging holding ammunition and a floppy jungle hat led the patrol. His followers were similarly dressed. Some wore conical hats. Others knotted red headbands. Resting an AK-47 across a relaxed arm, the leader stood beside Mei. His thirty armed followers encircled the three graves.

"Ancestors of yours?" he asked nodding at the gravesites.

Looking around at the chiseled faces, Mei swallowed with a dry mouth. She thought of her daughter May and her loving husband Loc. Gazing into the spokesman's eyes, she saw a raised brow soliciting a response. "My grandfather," she said softly.

"Mei?" One of the communist rebels asked.

Squinting in the direction of the questioning soldier, a smile spread across her face. "Taun!" she exclaimed to her younger brother.

CHAPTER THIRTY FOUR

The fading light of a kerosene lantern cast a soft glow in the deserted *đình làng* (communal house). The rebel patrol dispersed along the dried grass mud covered walls. Squatting, they enjoyed a hot bowl of sticky rice. With two small bowls of the steaming protein, Tuan pointed his sister in the direction of his designated corner. Sitting on the earthen floor, the siblings used fingers to shovel the warm meal into their mouths.

"I never thought I would ever see you again," Tuan said with a mouth full of rice. "Every year at Tet, I would gaze out at the village gate hoping to see you return. During the holiday, mother set a plate for you in anticipation."

"What happened to our mother?" Mei asked.

"Mother and father rarely spoke after your departure. Father tried to find you once. He was gone for a week and returned empty handed. Shortly after that mother died with a broken heart."

Looking down into the empty wooden bowl, Mei wept. They didn't know, she thought. Tuan placed a comforting hand on her shoulder. All these years, I've blamed them for my brothel fate. It was not their fault. They were simple farmers who were duped into selling their daughter. Sniveling, she smiled at her younger brother and said, "I've had a good life. I'm married to a good man. We have a beautiful daughter May."

"That makes me happy Mei," Tuan said squeezing her shoulder. "Unfortunately my world collapsed two years ago. Shortly after our father's death government troops arrived. The promise of good pay enticed us to abandon our crops. In the adjoining province, we constructed a stockade. The pay never came. We were told to relocate within the barbed wire fortress. To abandon our homes, our fields and our ancestral graves. Those who resisted were arrested as communist sympathizer. They took our brother."

"Are you a communist little brother?" Mei asked recalling her re-education camp ordeal.

Snickering Truan responded, "I don't know what that means." Glancing around at the Viet Cong cadre, he added, "None of us do. The choice was being an exploited caged animal in a government stockade or fighting to return to a traditional way of life. The old men, women and children were rounded up and herded into the government pen. The able-bodied men rallied to fight for land, village and family."

A low grating moan emerged from a darkened doorway. The dining occupants stirred. The groan faded.

"What was that?" Mei whispered.

"A casualty from a raid last week," Truan responded. "Poor fellow is in bad shape."

"Let me see," Mei said rising to her feet. "I may be able to help."

Accompanied by the limping leader, Mei peered into the dark room. In the limited light, she snorted at the familiar rotting odor of infection. It triggered an image of the hospital bunker at Dien Binh Phu. Her escort lifted a smoldering lantern. Reclining on a grass mat, a sweat covered boy twitched and moaned. His body fought to stay alive. Squatting beside him, Mei pulled back a wool blanket. A fresh wave of stench escaped. Swallowing back an exiting bile of sticky rice, she pinching her nose. Her free hand carefully unraveled warm and blood soaked bandages around a mangled arm. Motioning for the officer to lower the lantern, she completed the examination. The victim's disconnected eyes rolled around in the flickering light. Standing, she nodded in the direction of the doorway and exited with the officer.

"If he is to have any chance of survival," she said quietly. "The limb has to be removed."

"Do you know how to do it?" the officer questioned.

"I've seen it done before," she responded. "Do you have a carpenter's saw?"

"How do you know about this?" He probed.

Thinking about the French doctor she assisted in the valley of death, she paused. "Does it really matter?"

Looking into her confident eyes, he slowly shook his head. "What else do you need?"

Under the starry sky, Mei washed amputation splatter from her face and hands.

"Thank you," said the approaching limping leader.

"He is young," she said, "and at least now has a chance. In the morning before I leave, I'll show you how to change his bandages."

"Leave?" The Viet Cong officer questioned. "Mei, I can't let you go. You are of value to our struggle."

Squinting into the silhouetted face of the commander, she could not see his resolve. But it was there. I've been a prisoner much longer than you've been a guard, she thought. It's a role I detest but one I know how to play. Slowly nodding her head, she accepted the arrangement. An early escape is my only chance of seeing my family again, she realized.

CHAPTER THIRTY FIVE

Elaine neatly stacked the back issues of LIFE magazine on the coffee table. Placing both hands on her famous hips, she glanced around her small apartment. Never looked better, she thought. H'Liana with her head covered in a red and blue plaid bandana, sat on the edge of a cushioned chair. The tribal widow quietly mumbled familiar French phrases. Etienne scurried around the small room with the vigor of youth. Max came out of the bedroom combing back wet blond hair.

"You should put on a sport coat," Elaine diplomatically instructed.

With a slight shrug, Max retreated. Returning in business attire, he patted the young Etienne on the head. Plopping down on the sofa, he smiled at the rambling H'Liana.

Terminating the French lesson, the soft-spoken H'Liana addressed Max and the standing Elaine, "When attorney comes, please do not inform him I understand a little French. It will help me determine his intentions."

Max grinned. A rap on the door caused a puzzled Elaine to flinch. Composed, she glanced at her reflection in the entry mirror. Taking a deep breath, she answered the door.

The frumpy Olivier Hassan, in wrinkled white suit with a short wide red tie, staggered into the small flat. Around a protruding potbelly, shirt buttons strained. Atop the bulging spare tire rested the pointed tip of the crimson necktie. Standing in the entryway, the obese Frenchman sighed. Continuous sweat permeating from his furrowed baldhead. A saturated handkerchief attempted to ebb the flow. A large bright red acne scared pineapple nose dominated his sunburned face.

"Monsieur?" questioned a concerned Elaine. She gestured for her overheated guest to take a seat.

Waddling past her, he collapsed in a cushioned chair. The furniture painfully creaked under the weight. In a parched raspy voice, he asked, "Some water please, if you don't mind?"

Elaine handed him a hastily retrieved glass of cold water. Hassan placed it next to his pulsating head. He closed his eyes. Slowly he began to sip the water. His hydration accelerated. Several large gulps emptied the glass.

Taking a deep breath, he said, "My apologies for the rude entry. I am not use to this topical heat."

"I'm Max Kohl," Max said standing. Catching a foul whiff of the sweaty Frenchman and heavy cologne, he snorted. Holding his breath, he extended a hand across the coffee table.

"Yes of course," Hassan responded offering a flabby dead fish hand-shake. "You are the German mentioned in Jean's correspondence."

You arrogant pompous ass, Max thought. Mentioned? The letter was addressed to me. Sitting back onto the sofa, Max dried his moist palm on the front of his slacks. Gesturing to Elaine, he said, "This is Elaine Favreau whom you corresponded with."

"Mademoiselle," Hassan said nudging his massive weight slightly forward.

"And this," Max said waving an open palm towards the colorfully dressed Meo, "Is Sergeant Jean Guillian's widow; H'Liana."

"Such a lovely young creature," Hassan responded. Leaning back in his chair, he handed the empty water glass to Elaine. "The tribal people all seem so innocent and naive. It really adds to their beauty and charm." Taking a replenished glass of water from Elaine, he nodded his gratitude. Smiling at the gawking boy standing in front of him, he continued, "And this must be Etienne. There is no mistake, he has the Guillian jaw." Turning he addressed Elaine, "Mademoiselle, I can't tell you how happy you have made Jean's mother by finding her grandson. The poor woman has suffered so much since the..." he paused and glancing at Max mumbled, "German invasion."

"In your correspondence you mentioned some concerns about Etienne's legitimacy," Elaine questioned. "Are there any issues?"

Wiping off his moist shiny head, Hassan responded, "That is why I came to Indochina. There is no doubt that Jean Guillian wrote the letter, you so graciously provided. We had a handwriting expert compare it to the few letters Jean had sent his mother. Now that I see young Etienne with the Guillian jaw line, it confirms that the boy is Celine Guillian's grandson." Shifting his fluid mass in the over-burden chair, he cleared his throat. Lowering his voice, he continued, "The only real issue is Jean's widow. I'm assuming she would be willing to relinquish her parental rights for the good of the boy. In Paris he would be given an education and opportunities that would be difficult for most of us to comprehend. Of course we would compensate her for this incredible sacrifice."

Discipline, Max thought, don't lose your temper. Inhaling deeply, he pondered a civilized response to the Jewish attorney's insulting assumptions. Before Max could speak, the timid H'Liana found her voice.

"Excuse me Monsieur," H'Laina said in soft confident tone. "If you are asking me to sell my son, the answer is no."

Max grinned. The stunned Frenchman stared at the tribal widow with an open mouth.

"My apologies H'Liana," Hassan responded in a high-pitched nervous crackle. Coughing hard he continued, "I just thought in these troubling times that a court appointed guardian might be more suited to looking out for Etienne's needs in the secure environment of France."

Leaning towards Max, H'Liana whispered, "What is court appointed guardian?"

"It's like a new mother or father," Max responded.

"And what does secure environment mean?" she asked.

"He meant France is a safer place," Max clarified.

Sitting back up, H'Liana focused on the Frenchman and said, "I Etienne's mother. No one will raise him better than me. I carry him and run when Communists shoot at us. I fed him when I have nothing to eat. I carried him over great distance to be here. I don't believe court appointed would do that."

"H'Liana" said a pleading Hassan, "What I meant to say..."

"I'm not done talking," H'Liana interrupted with focused dark lethal eyes. "You say France is safe place. Jean tell me how Max's people conquer France in six weeks. My village fought Communists for eight years until France abandon us. My husband tell me how Frenchmen betrayed his people the Jews to survive. So I don't want to hear any talk about how court appointed or secure environment is good for my son." Grabbing the wandering Etienne, H'Liana held her son in front of her and added, "You tell Jean's mother that her grandson is very safe with me. No one love him like I do. And you tell her no one love her son more than me. You go and tell her that." Standing up she picked up her son. She held him close. Kissing the top of the boy's head, she squinted hard at the Frenchman. "There is nothing more to say, nice meeting is over." She ran into the bedroom.

With a heavy sigh, Hassan looked at Elaine and said, "I wished you would have warned me that Mrs. Jean Guillian spoke French."

Standing up Max said to the seated attorney, "What difference would it have made? You came here to take her son." Walking over, Max opened the door and added, "A little friendly advice counselor, never underestimate a Meo. And never try to take a cub away from its mother. Meeting adjourned."

CHAPTER THIRTY SIX

Squatting down Mei touched the warm cheek of her one-armed patient. His fever is breaking, she thought. Slowly rising to the rolling groan of the amputee, she gingerly walked through the communal house. It was late afternoon. The Viet Cong cadre blanketed the floor. In preparation for a nocturnal sortie, they slept. Cautiously Mei stepped over and around the boy soldiers. Sunlight poured into the mud and grass structure. The open doorway framed rolling grass hills and a blue sky speckled with rain clouds. Pausing at the exit, she turned to the clean smell of an approaching storm. Surveying the rustling bodies strewn on the dirt floor, she searched for her brother. In his designated corner, Tuan lay curled up in a ball. With an open mouth he snored. Sweat covered his face. He was always a sound sleeper, Mei recalled. It was always difficult to wake him to do chores. Her father always joked that a thunderstorm couldn't wake Taun. Farewell my brother, she thought.

Standing in front of the crude structure, she inhaled the cooling air. Black clouds challenged the afternoon sunlight. Visualizing her daughter her heart sank. It had been a long two weeks since I held May, she realized. It's now or never, she thought. Studying the skeletal remains of the village, she formulated an escape route.

"Thinking of home Mei?" the commander whispered from behind.

Startled she turned. The Viet Cong officer shadowing her gaze of freedom grinned. Her stomach churned. With a polite smile, she nodded.

"Not a day goes by that I don't think about returning to my former life," he quietly confessed. Reaching into a breast pocket, he pulled out a wrinkled pack of Chesterfields. Delicately he retrieved two cigarettes and politely offered her one.

Accepting the prized luxury, she leaned forward. He lit it with a match.

Standing beside her he exhaled. Looking into the darkening sky he commented, "Looks like rain."

After several puffs, she nodded in agreement.

"Mei, I know I've asked you to make an incredible sacrifice," he said. "But if we are to return the land to the people, we all have to pay a price."

Please, Mei thought. I know the communist rhetoric better than you. Six months in a re-education camp taught me a worker's society is a lie. I've seen the land reforms in the North, she recalled. The inmate ranks at Learning and Transformation Camp Number 17 swelled with beaten and tortured farmers.

"Your silence betrays you," he said grinning. "You are too smart to be enticed by a simple Communist promise." Taking a puff, he continued. "It may surprise you, but I don't believe it either. In this struggle a variety of political and religious groups have all picked up arms. The objective is replacing the American's Catholic dictator. We are fighting for a government that represents all the classes. In order to achieve that goal, we've embraced the peasant population." Flicking his cigarette aside, he looked into her eyes, "Mei I've seen the way you cared for my men. It is your sense of compassion that I'm appealing to." Placing a hand on her shoulder, he said, "Thank you."

"I appreciate your honesty," She said. Continuing the charade, she added. "But we are up against a formidable foe."

"The question is not if we will be successful. But when," he responded. Confidently he mumbled, "Death by a thousand cuts. We will slowly bleed our powerful enemy."

Mei dropped her cigarette. A sandaled foot ground it into the moist soil. "I came out here to fetch water," she informed. Looking up at the stormy sky, she added, "I better get going."

"I don't want you going alone." The commander gruffly responded.

Mei followed Tuan through the deserted village of their youth. Across their shoulders, bamboo yokes balanced wooden buckets. They waded through the field of weeds towards the community well. A gusting wind swayed the growth. Mei felt a drop of rain. Focused on the back of her brother's head, she realized he would never understand. He is young, full of zeal, fighting for a way of life that no longer exists.

"Some things never change," Tuan said plodding forward. "Remember when we use to do this as children."

"The buckets don't seem to get any lighter," Mei chuckled. She dropped the empty wooden pails in the tall grass besides the well. Scanning the foliage, she picked up a large stone.

Tuan feverishly cranked the cast iron handle. Well water gushed into a positioned pail. Filling the second bucket, he gazed into the dark sky. Forgive me brother, Mei thought slamming the stone into the back of his head.

Dropping to his knees, he turned. Blood flowed down his back. He smiled. "Kiss my niece for me, *Chi gái* (big sister)." He muttered before collapsing face down in the tall grass.

Running towards freedom, tears rolled down her cheeks. Lighting flashed overhead. The black clouds barked. And the sky released a torrential rain.

CHAPTER THIRTY SEVEN

In front of the Continental hotel, a tiny taxi skidded to a stop. Through the water stained back window, Elaine watched the pedestrian traffic flow by. Paying the fare, she glanced at her watch. My embassy job presumably started fifteen-minutes ago, she thought. I'll be late once again, she realized. Stepping onto the sidewalk, she got a glimpse of the grotesque French attorney. Sitting at a sidewalk table in front of the hotel, Hassan enjoyed a late breakfast. An assortment of breads and pastries lay upon a linen tablecloth. A napkin stuffed into the shirt collar of his short-sleeved white shirt. A trickle of jam hung from the corner of his mouth. Spotting Elaine, he waved her over.

"Mademoiselle," he said slightly elevating his massive frame. Slumping back to his seated repose, he motioned towards an empty chair. "I'm so glad you accepted my invitation for breakfast."

"Monsieur, I must say I was surprised with the request and a little curious." Elaine said turning over a coffee cup. Immediately, an attentive Vietnamese waiter filled it with steaming java. Politely, she pointed to the corner of her mouth and cleared her throat.

Like a trained toad, Hassan flicked his tongue at the gob of misplaced jelly. Smacking his lips, he picked up a piece of bread. Methodically, he began to apply layers of butter across the porous surface. Glancing up from his handy work, he said, "Elaine I could tell by your dress and the way you carry yourself, you have a certain sense of style. Needless to say I feel it is something your German lover does not fully appreciate."

"Monsieur!" Elaine exclaimed.

Applying a coat of apricot jam to the butter based bread, Hassan continued, "Elaine, when we met in your apartment, I said the opportunities available to the young Etienne could not be fully comprehended. However, I think you understand what is at stake here," pausing he took a large bite out of the apricot glazed creation. "Mmmm, this is so good," he mumbled. Closing his eyes, he chewed slowly. After several enjoyable swallows, he continued. "When your lover's countrymen took away my freedom, I was forced to do without for four long years. I know it may be hard for you to believe but I was reduced to skin and bones. Since that time I'm committed to indulge in all the excesses this world has to offer." Picking up his coffee cup, he blew across the steaming black surface. A side-glance admired the young Vietnamese females dining at the adjacent table.

"What does this have to do with me?" She questioned.

Sipping coffee, he responded. "I was wrong to assume that the tribal widow would give up her son. My objective was and has always been to give some joy to Celine Guillian in her final days. The poor Holocaust survivor has suffered so much. I won't see her denied the reunion with her grandson." Placing the coffee cup on a saucer, he reached over touching Elaine's hand. "Elaine, I'd like to solicit your assistance in this endeavor. Help me convince H'Liana that it was her late husband's final wish to reunite the family. I'm proposing that you accompany H'Liana and her son with me to Paris. Of course I'd compensate you handsomely for your time. However, the true reward for your service would be seeing the house of Guillian reunited."

Leaning back in her chair Elaine felt drained. What about Max? She thought. What about her career with the state department? The image of her blond blue-eyed German lover faded. Fond memories of the Champs Elysees, the Eiffel Tower, and the Seine surfaced.

"Cigarette, my dear," Hassan asked pointing a pack of *Gauloise* in her direction. A quick twitch exposed a single tobacco canister.

Reaching forward, she accepted the offer. A well practiced flick of his lighter, ignited the dark tobacco. Elaine inhaled deep. The nicotine rush had a soothing affect. Leaning back she pondered the life-changing proposal. I can just quit my job, she realized, that's easy enough. But what of Max, where is the relationship going? Could he leave Saigon or is he destined to become just another lover in a list of memorable affairs?

Taking another long drag on the cigarette, Elaine exhaled and said, "I'm going to need some time to think about it. I need to talk to Max and try to council H'Liana as well."

"I understand," Hassan responded. "I can give you until the end of the week to decide. I would need to start making Air France travel arrangements by then."

Grinning she asked, "Would that be deluxe service accommodations?"

"Most definitely," Hassan responded with nod.

After the enticing breakfast proposal, Elaine walked down the crowded sidewalk. She kept pace behind the bobbing shaved heads of two Buddhist monks in saffron robes. No time like the present, she thought. I'll meet with H'Liana to gauge her reaction to Hassan's change of heart. Late morning sun reflected off the glass storefronts. She blinked. I might as well take the day off, she concluded. I may not be working for the State Department too much longer. One thing I won't regret is ending that flirtatious charade with the married John Matthews. I will no longer have to parry his inappropriate advances, she thought. Standing on a street corner, she waited for the light to change. After I give my notice. I'll tell Matthews flat out. I'm not interested and never was. With a wide satisfying grin, she surged forward with the crowd. Under the tropical sun, the herd migrated across the intersection.

I wonder if we would be staying in an estate on the outskirts of Paris, she pondered. I bet the wealthy Celine Guillian has several residences. A luxurious flat in the heart of the city or perhaps a villa in the south of France. Overcome by the possibilities, she stopped under the shade of a shop's tattered canvas awning. In the middle of the pedestrian thoroughfare, she closed her eyes. Feeling the masses flow by, she imagined a walled gated mansion behind a large circular driveway. Servants, she surmised, lots of servants tending to our needs. Assisting the adorable H'Liana's assimilation to Paris would be rewarding, she concluded. My workday would be short. There would be lots of free time to become reacquainted with the City of Light. I could explore my creative side; take up painting, writing...

all the things I always wanted to do. Opening her eyes, she mumbled, "I can make this happen."

The pedestrian traffic thinned. Saigon's commercial district faded. Mid-rise residential buildings dominated the skyline. Laundry flapped from balconies overhead. On the stoop of an apartment building, a cadre of loitering local teens gawked at the passing blonde. Elaine accelerated. She cringed at the boy's catcalls. I wish Max was with me, she thought. Max! She realized. What do I do about Max? The pursuit and capture of the German's affections has not lost its allure. Could I convince him to go with me, she wondered. Snickering, she concluded Max is an independent. No one could every convince him to do anything he didn't want to do. Hell that what makes him so damn attractive, she thought.

In front of Loc and Mei's apartment building, Elaine stood on the buckled and uneven sidewalk. Her cotton dress clung to a clammy frame. I'll worry about dealing with Max latter, she concluded. Taking a deep breath, she entered the stagnant stairwell. In anticipation of facing the in-laws, her stomach churned. Ascending the creaking stairs, she thought Mei and Loc are pleasant enough just distant. The old Pao is like Grandpapa Favreau, she concluded, docile but annoying. Snorting, she visualized the spiteful Lan. What did I ever do to that pudgy china doll? She wondered. I know she intentionally spilled her drink on me during our last dinner, she recalled. That was no accident. Lan didn't fool me with that smirking apology, she reflected. I still don't know why Max coddles these refugees. At least the shy H'Liana is sweet, she acknowledged while lightly tapping on the apartment door. After a long pause, she thought no one was home. Rapping on the door a second time, she heard movement within the flat. The door opened to an investigating crease. A moist dog snout poked out. A sleepy eyed Pao peered through the crack.

"Bonjour Pao," Elaine said softly, "Is H'Liana in?"

Slowly the old man opened the door. The tail wagging Pasha greeted Elaine with intrusive sniffs. Clinging to the wall, she tried to avoid flinging stings of saliva. Chuckling Pao restrained the happy dog by the collar.

"H'Liana?" Elaine inquired.

Jerked about by the dog, the tiny old man nodded. A boney finger pointed towards a beaded doorway.

"Merci," she said quietly.

Through the beaded curtain, Elaine saw the young widow dressed in her traditional colorful clothes. Sitting on the floor, leaning up against a bed, H'Liana caressed her cheek the sergeant stripes sewn on a tattered green military shirt. Gently rocking back and forth, she hummed a simple tune. The widow occasionally paused to softly converse with her dead husband's garment.

Oh my, Elaine thought. Her eyes welling up with tears. It's not about me, she realized. This poor, poor displaced woman lost the love of her life. Fighting the rising knot in her throat, Elaine gave into the harsh reality and wept.

Looking up a startled H'Liana, exclaimed, "Mademoiselle!" Standing up, she hastily folded her husband's shirt. Placing the prized possession on the bed, she gave it a tender pat.

Walking through the dangling strung beads, the tall blonde embraced the petite Meo. Both women offering and seeking compassion.

CHAPTER THIRTY EIGHT

Bow-tied waiters balancing steaming dishes on serving trays scurried about the smoke filled restaurant. On a small stage, an Asian women's trio in tight fitting long silk dressed of blue, red and yellow plucked and strummed traditional instruments. The melodic sound wove into the commotion of clanging dishes, boisterous diners and rolling laughter. In Vietnamese, Roche questioned the maître'd'. Politely standing behind the American, Max tried to comprehend the dialogue. Looking over his shoulder, Roche gave a confirming nod to the German.

Following the tuxedo clad greeter, Max and Roche received curious and suspicious stares from the Asian diners. The tuxedo guide pulled back a red sliding door decorated with the serpentine image of a black dragon. Bowing, he extended a welcoming hand into the private dining room. Roche dismissed the maître'd' with a handful of crumpled currency.

Three couples sat around a linen covered round table. A vapor mist hung over a centered wooden Lazy Susan. On the rotating tray, white bowls decorated with a blue bamboo accent, offered rice, noodle and seafood dishes. Looking up from empty dinner plates, two of the young Vietnamese men in dark suites squinted curiously. The three attractive painted female escorts smiled seductively at potential westerner customers. But Mister Tuyen or Tommy as he liked to be called twitched with concern.

Stepping into the room Max said softly, "Hello Tommy."

Ignoring the greeting, Tommy looked past Max. With a high-pitched cackle, he said, "Major Roche this is highly inappropriate. If you would like to schedule a meeting, please have your embassy set it up with my office."

With blinding speed, Max slapped the arrogant Asian peacock. Tommy groaned. The other dinner guest pushed back from the table.

"Do I have your attention now?" Max asked shaking his wrist. Tommy used a napkin to blot leaking blood. Max placed a finger in the sugar bowl. Touching it to his tongue, he said. "You know why I'm here."

Roche slid the private dining room's door open. "I think it would be better if you would leave us alone with Mister Tuyen." He informed. "We have some urgent business to discuss."

The party shuffled to the doorway. Max took off his sports coat revealing a shoulder holster and pistol. Flexing his broad shoulders, he said to the departing guest, "This should not take too long."

Wide-eyed and panting, Tommy looked up at the two intruders. In a squeaky voice, he said, "Gentlemen, I'm warning you as a representative of the Vietnamese government you are about to make a serious mistake, with dire consequences."

Roche chuckled, "Tommy you don't think I came here without clearing it through the proper channels. Exposing your sexual preference for boys made you expendable. Max may have his own issues but I'm here for two reasons. The first is the cost of a US embassy Peugeot convertible. Although the sugar in the fuel system could be repaired. By the time we retrieved the car it was stripped and a total loss."

Beads of sweat sparkled on Tommy's forehead. He slowly nodded accepting the cost of replacing the vehicle. Taking a big dry gulp he asked, "What is the second reason?"

"Per my agreement with your government, I'm here to make sure Max doesn't kill you." Roche responded.

Max nodded. Carefully, he draped his sports coat over the back of a chair. Picking up a napkin, he tightly wrapped it around his hand. Focused on the binding, he said, "I'm not happy with the terms. I wanted to kill you. But we all have to compromise in these chaotic times. Per the settlement with your government, I'm going to beat you within an inch of your life."

"Max..." Tommy pleaded, "Please no...I..." Speechless he buried his face in the palms of his hands and sobbed.

"Max," Roche said with a wink. "Perhaps Tommy can compensate you for the inconvenience of stranding you in the Mekong Delta."

Looking up, Tommy inhaled through a sniffling nose. "Yes, yes, I can pay you. How much?"

Max looked over at Roche and shrugged. "Let's see," he said. "What did you charge me for helping out my friend Rene...oh yes, ten thousand US dollars. That seems like an appropriate penance for trying to kill me."

"Are we all in agreement then gentlemen?" Roche asked.

Tommy bobbed his head. Max shrugged.

"Good," Roche said. Reaching down, he pulled a large prawn from a rice dish. Smacking on the spicy shellfish he said between bites, "We will expect payment by Friday."

CHAPTER THIRTY NINE

Late night food hawkers lined the sidewalk. The aroma of pungent spices and smoked meat hung in the humid air. Walking through curbside diners, Max's stomach growled. He stopped. At his feet bamboo skewered strips of chicken sizzled over glowing charcoal. A squatting boney man used a palm fan to stoke the coals. The grill a converted five-gallon military gasoline can. Flicking his finger, Max ordered a dozen sticks of spicy marinated poultry.

Clutching a meat bouquet, Max continued down the sidewalk. He chewed on a greasy chicken strip with an open mouth. God this is good, he thought. At these prices he chuckled, Tommy's ten-thousand-dollar penance will last me forever.

Approaching Elaine's apartment building, Max picked at his teeth with a bamboo skewer. Under the glow of a streetlight, Loc sat on the stoop of the building. The tribesman drank a bottle of coke through a straw.

Max tossed the large toothpick into the gutter. With an inquisitive squint, he asked, "What are you doing here partner?"

Setting the coke bottle down on the moss stained concrete step, Loc rose and answered, "I'm sorry Max. It's bad news. Pao expired today."

"What happened?" Max asked softly.

In a solemn tone, Loc answered, "Pao had really slowed down since Mei's return. After a long day of painting the shop, we all wanted to go out for dinner. He insisted on staying home tonight. He liked sitting on the balcony with Pasha and his white whisky. We brought back his favorite noodle dish and found Pasha wailing over his dead master."

Placing his hand on Loc's shoulder Max said, "Let's go in. Elaine is home, we can talk upstairs."

"Max," Loc said with an apologetic shrug, "If it's all the same to you I'd prefer talking here."

"I understand," Max said realizing it was a family matter. "So how are the girls taking Pao's death?"

"Not well," Loc answered. "He was very special to Mei and Lan after he killed the assassins in the garden. Mei feels he hung on just long enough for her to return."

"How about H'Liana?" Max asked.

"I'm very concerned about her," Loc said taking a breath, "Pao was the only link she had to tribal life. She lost her village, her husband and now Pao. She realizes there is no going back, but she does not like Saigon. In fact, she thinks that is what killed Pao."

"What do you think?" Max asked.

"I think she may be right. He aged very quickly once we left Laos. I'm Tai, so I know how hard it is to assimilate, but she refuses to try. She insists on wearing traditional clothing." Loc responded.

"I respect that. She comes from a proud honorable people. Look how they took us in when we stumbled out of the jungle." Max said. Frowning he questioned. "Has anyone in your neighborhood given her a hard time about being Meo?"

"Not since Pao made that street punk piss his pants," Loc chuckled.

Laughing Max sat down on the stoop and commented, "You realize he could have easily killed those three teenagers."

"How about the time he killed those Binh Xuyen hit men," Loc recalled fondly. "Hell he was drunk at the time."

"He was the best warrior I ever knew," Max said with a lump in his throat.

"What do you want to do with the body?" Loc asked.

"I'm going to bury him in the highlands," Max responded.

"How are we going to do that?" Loc asked, "There is Laotian civil war going on."

"The war hasn't slowed down the flow of opium. The hub of the drug trade may have shifted from Phong Savin to Vientiane, but today there are more landing strips across the highlands than when we were in the business." Pausing, Max rubbed his forehead with greasy fingers. "Rene owes me a favor," he mumbled. "I'll get him to fly me close to where the wall of heads once stood and lay our friend to rest." Patting Loc on the knee, he added, "I'll do it. You stay here with the family. After Mei's Mekong Delta adventure, I don't want them worrying about both of us being gone."

"Do you remember the Meo burial position?" Loc asked.

"I'll make sure our friend is entombed facing west," Max responded with a confirming nod. "We don't want him to be blinded by the rising sun." Clearing his throat, he rose. Slapping Loc on the back, he said, "Now for a western tradition, let's go drink to the memory of our *kamerad*."

CHAPTER FOURTY

Staggering up the dimly lit stairwell, Max grimaced at the light emanating from under the door. She's still up, he thought. Inebriated, he fumbled with the key. Opening the locked door, he entered the small one bedroom flat. Elaine sat at the dining room table with a cup of coffee in hand. A short yellow silk robe loosely draped over her naked frame.

"I worry about you," she said. "I never know if you will be returning."

Tarnished by the sense of loss, Max thought not now. I'm in no mood for another of your relationship discussions. With a slight shrug, he realized it is what it is. Maybe it is time to part ways. "Pao died today in his sleep," he informed. "I plan to bury his body in the highlands. I leave tomorrow and if all goes well, should be back by Friday."

"I'm so sorry Max," she said slowly shaking her head, "I know you two were very close."

Turning, Max walked through the beaded curtain into the tiny kitchen. He grabbed a bottle of beer from the icebox.

"How is the rest of the family reacting?" Elaine asked.

Searching the lime-green tiled counter top, Max quickly spotted a bottle opener. Popping open the beer, he staggered into the dining room. Sitting down across from Elaine, he took a large swig of the cold brew and said, "Everyone is saddened from the loss, but H'Liana is distraught."

"That sweet young widow has endured so much," she said reaching across the table. Touching his hand she asked, "Is there anything I can do?"

"No," Max said softly, "That is very kind of you to ask. But you have to realize that when it comes to the death of a loved one, my family has lots of experience. We mourn the loss, hold dear the memories, and move on, because gone is gone."

"That is so sad," Elaine said. She started to weep.

"That is the reality of our existence," Max said squeezing her hand.

Sniffling she asked, "What memories will you cherish of Pao?"

Leaning back in the hardwood dining chair, Max gazed into the pulsing white metal blades of the ceiling fan. Reflecting back on a sun baked jungle clearing, he visualized the Meo villagers corralled by a communist patrol. Hug the enemy, he thought, recalling the strategy to draw the Vietminh into a hand-to-hand engagement. While calculating a shooting sequence from the security of dense foliage, he got his first glimpse of Pao. In the midst of the civilian bait, the tiny man stood defiantly. His terrified neighbors trembled and wept. Dropping his eyes, Max focused on the naive Elaine and said, "I met Pao on the battlefield." Taking a sip of beer, he continued, "I watched with admiration as the old Meo used a steady hand and a crossbow to kill his enemy."

"Oh my," Elaine responded staring into the mug of coffee. Swallowing hard, she looked up and confessed, "I met with H'Liana this morning. Pao answered the door." With a surfacing crackle, she echoed, "He answered the door on his last day."

Pulling back his hand, Max asked with a frown, "What were you doing there?"

Startled by his response, she leaned back and said defiantly, "Because I had breakfast with Hassan today and wanted to gauge H'Liana's reaction to his new proposal"

Max looked into her watery brown eyes. With a cynical nod, he asked, "What did he offer you?"

"He said he was wrong for thinking about taking Etienne away from H'Liana. He wants to unite both of them with the grandmother, per Guillian's dying request." Elaine responded.

"Of course he was wrong, and yes re-uniting the family was Guillian's last wish," Max said taking a swig of beer. In a harsh tone, he repeated. "But what did he offer you?"

"Three years salary," she blurted out. "He offered me three years salary to escort H'Liana and her son back to Paris."

"Did you counter his offer?" Max asked fondling the beer bottle.

"Counter his offer?" Elaine questioned. "I wanted to talk to you first. To do what's best for all concerned."

"Do you think this would be good for H'Liana and child?" He asked.

"Yes, Yes I do," She said bobbing her head. "The displaced H'Liana is confused by Saigon. She appreciates your family's empathy but feels like her and Etienne are intruders."

"Do you think Paris would be any different?" Max snorted.

"The grandmother's wealth will soften the transition and Etienne would be raised in a life of privilege with all it entails. So yes" Elaine declared, "Paris is a better option."

"I agree with you, H'Liana should take advantage of this opportunity but for other reasons. Etienne is not only the last of the Guillian line, but more than likely the last of H'Liana side of the family as well. The widow has a strong sense of family and having her son connect with the grand-mother may be just what she needs. The reason she is learning French is not to assimilate but to one day educate her son about his father's heritage." Max said finishing the beer.

"I think she will understand," Elaine concurred.

"She will do what is best for her son."

"But what about Hassan?" Elaine asked. "I don't trust him."

"No doubt, the attorney has his own agenda. So you need to be pre-pared. Get a legal recommendation from your Paris branch. They should help navigate through the French courts if it has to come to that." He said and added with a smirk, "but by all means counter his offer. He is a Jew and expects it."

"Max," Elaine said with raised brows, "What about us?"

"It looks like you have made up your mind. I'm not going to compli-cate the situation by trying to talk you out of it," he grinned.

"You could have at least tried," she said choking back tears.

"I'll mourn the loss, hold dear the memories, and move on." Max mumbled as Elaine started to weep. Standing up, he walked to her side of the table and ran his fingers through the back of her hair. She rose trembling and wrapped her arms around his neck melting into a consoling embrace.

CHAPTER FOURTY ONE

Under a blue sky, a single engine Cessna skipped across the top of the jungle canopy. A towering limestone pinnacle rose out of the green ocean. The foliaged draped landmark sparkled in the morning sunlight. From the cramped cockpit, Max grinned at the rock signpost. We are getting close, he realized. Looking down, he admired the captivating beauty of the unforgiving terrain. To the buzzing sound of the aircraft, he mumbled, "You are a formidable foe." I bested you once, he thought reflecting on his escape from Isabelle. I wouldn't want to give you a re-match. Glancing over his shoulder, he smiled at the white sheets wrapped tightly around Pao's corpse. You'll soon be home my friend, he thought.

A small landing strip of red earth peeked out of the encroaching rain forest. With little effort, Rene made an abrupt landing on the sliver of real estate. "Close enough?" He hollered over the whining Cessna.

"Good job," Max said unbuckling his seatbelt. "These are Pao's highlands."

Rene cut the engine. Max hopped onto the moist soil. In the distance, monkeys howled. All around tropical insects clamored. Max closed his eyes. He inhaled the damp distinct sent of his former adversary.

"Max!" Rene called out tossing a pickaxe and two shovels onto the ground. "Can we pick up the pace?"

Walking past the digging tools, Max returned to the plane to unload the body. "You fly-boys sure don't like being grounded." He said tossing the small dead bundle over his shoulder. "Follow me while I search for an appropriate plot."

Picking up the tools, Rene commented, "Let's not wander to far from the plane."

"This should be perfect," Max declared under the protective shade of a large banyan tree. Carefully, he laid the body on the ground. He placed his shoulder holster and pistol on the wrapped corpse. After removing his shirt, he grabbed the pickaxe. Broad shoulders swung the pointed head. Stroke after precision stroke churned a rectangular plot in the red clay.

"Jesus, Max," Rene said comfortably leaning forward on the handle of a grounded spade. "How do you stay in such great shape?"

"Calisthenics," Max replied on the upward arc. "I still keep a rigid routine." To the rhythm of the pickaxe, he continued, "It helps me start the day." Shaking off a large clump of spiked earth, he looked at Rene. With a sweaty grin, he said, "Now let's see how well you work a shovel."

Stepping forward, Rene chuckled. He flinched at the crack of a snapping twig. Both he and Max turned. A dozen black skull-caped mountain bandits stood under the banyan tree. The squinting sandaled brigands brandished vintage weapons. Max studied the malnourished chiseled faces forged by perpetual war. The paths life leads us on, he thought. Loc could easily be standing amongst these men. The Meos are an honorable race. Let's just hope this group hasn't lost all compassion with everything else that has been taken from them.

Rene whispered out of the side of his mouth, "I think they're just curious. Otherwise they would have killed us by now."

"Or maybe they were just waiting for us to finish the grave." Max said softly. Turning, he located his holstered pistol on the wrapped body. The intruder's heads pivoted to follow Max's gaze. "Do you know any tribal dialects?" Max asked returning his focus to the one sided standoff.

"Besides, what do you want for the opium," Rene whispered. "The only other phrase I know has to deal with fornicating with the smelly vagina of someone's mother."

Max laughed. The bandits surged forward cocking weapons.

"Do you have any liquor in the Cessna?" Max asked showing the palm of his hands.

"I have a bottle of twelve year old Johnny Walker Black Label." Rene informed. "I was saving it for a special occasion,"

"Well since this may be our last day, let's break it out," Max whispered. Stepping forward he said to their guest, "*Nam lu.*"

The drinking greeting did little to calm the bandits. A senior in the group stepped forward. Under the security of his targeting associates, he walked over to Pao's body. Squatting down, he unraveled the sheet. Startled, he jerked back. The armed contingent mumbled at the sight of the dead Meo warrior. Around Pao's peaceful expression, wisp of silver hair flickered in the warm breeze. The tiny corpse wore a black jacket embroidered with red and blue trim. His pistol tucked neatly in the red sash around his waist. Pao was to be laid to rest in his finest attire. The inquisitive bandit squatting over the body titled his head with a puzzled expression.

"*Yawg,*" Max informed. The term his family used for their adopted grandfather.

Slowly rising the bandit pulled out Pao's pistol. Softly speaking in his native tongue, he walked over and handed the sidearm to Max. Pointing at the gun and then the grave, he shook his head with a soft frown.

"I think he's trying to tell us we shouldn't bury Pao with a weapon." Rene speculated.

With gun in hand, Max realized the situation was defused. Placing his hand on the bandits shoulder, Max nodded his appreciation. Out of the side of his mouth, he said to Rene, "Get your expensive scotch. We are about to give my grandfather a proper wake."

CHAPTER FOURTY TWO

The sky was dark. The airport deserted. A single engine Cessna taxied over towards the empty Cap Saint-Jacque terminal. Max's soiled hand, patted the pilot on the shoulder.

"Any time my friend," Rene responded over the revving sound of the aircraft. "Hopefully next time we meet it won't be for a funeral."

Grinning, Max stepped down onto the tarmac. Against the propeller backwash, he wrestled with his sport coat.

"Don't forget this," Rene said placing Pao's Makarov pistol on the empty passenger seat.

"Thanks," Max said tucking the handgun in the small of his back. A grateful salute bid adieu to the departing Cessna.

What are the odds in catching a cab at three AM, Max wondered? With a shrug, he walked around the closed terminal. Gravel crunched with each step. I'll get a room, he decided, and head into Saigon in the morning. At least then, I can get a shower and wash off the dirt from Pao's grave. Picturing the tiny Meo warrior, his crossbow, white whisky, and dogs, he grinned. Today was a good day, he thought. My friend is once again residing in his beloved highlands with his wife and sons.

Walking to the front of the airport, Max let out a sigh. The parking lot lay barren. A single empty black Mercedes sedan sat under an illuminating light pole. There were no taxis, no porters, nobody around.

Max took a deep breath. Should I head back to find Rene at the hanger facilities, he pondered? What the hell, he concluded sticking to the gravel walkway. It's just a short walk to town.

Passing in front of the dark terminal, he thought about the complex Elaine. Such a lovely creature, he reflected. But so difficult to comprehend at times. I still don't understand why we have to be fashionably late to every event. It makes no sense. And she eats so slowly, he recalled. I'm tired of watching her pick at food from across an empty plate. It must be an American...

The sharp sting of pain proceeded darkness. Disoriented with a throbbing head, Max heard distant moaning. Poor bastard, he thought. As a groan rolled out of his throat, he realized he was the poor bastard. Sharp gravel dug into the back of his head. His face was moist. Warm liquid wet his lips. Where am I? What is going on? Slowly with an uncoordinated hand, he tried to investigate. His wrist was slapped hard. Just as well, he conceded. He drifted back into the comforting darkness. Laughter nudged him towards consciousness. Probing hands went through his pockets. His pistol and wallet removed. I'm being robbed, he concluded. I need to get up. His motor skills did not respond. Jesus, they took by Tokarev pistol, my trophy. He slumped forward to a seated position. The empty parking lot, he recalled, the single black Mercedes. I'm at the airport. We buried Pao today. I was coming home, he concluded. His head hung forward. Blood flowed down his face. On the gravel path laid a four-foot piece of wood. The fresh cut two-by-four splattered with blood. Next to the wooden club, an assailant stood in a pair of black shiny shoes. Max tried, but could not lift his head.

"Get him to his feet," commanded a familiar voice.

Two sets of massive hands grabbed Max's upper arms. Lifted up, he hung like a rag doll. His knees wouldn't lock.

"Did you really think I was going to pay you ten-thousand dollars," said a whiny high-pitched voice.

Tommy? Max thought that arrogant peacock. Slowly raising his head, Max saw the well groomed Asian. Tommy flashed a straight razor. The polished blade sparkled under the parking lot lighting.

"You asked me once before if I would be the one to kill you," Tommy said with a playful tone. "I'm here to inform you yes; yes I'm the one who is going to kill you tonight." Placing the sharp blade under Max's chin, the skinny Tommy lifted up Max's head. Smirking, he added, "Death has finally found you, Max Kohl. And let me tell you, it is not going to be pleasant."

Looking at an accomplice, Tommy instructed, "Bind him tightly, when I start removing pieces of Mister Kohl. I don't want him flailing about."

Hyperventilating, Max tried to regain consciousness. Focus, he thought, dig deep clear your head. We buried Pao today, he thought. His countrymen made sure there were no weapons in the grave.

A goon pulled Max's limp hand behind his back. Max reached for Pao's Makarov pistol. Gripping the handle, he felt rejuvenated. Locking his knees, he wobbled. Flexing his arm, he spun free. Placing the pistol under the thug's chin, he got a blurred glimpse of a terrified henchman. The gun barked. The target's head erupted. Skull fragments and brain tissue shot into the night sky. No time to focus on kill shots, Max rationalized. He got off two quick rounds to his left and blindly fired in Tommy's direction. Dropped to one knee, he scanned the battlefield. Only three assailants, he concluded. Using his coat sleeve, he wiped the blood from his eyes. To his left a belly shot thug pleaded for life. Max terminated his pain with a head shot. Sprawled out on the gravel walkway, Tommy wailed like a ten-year-old girl. Gripping a blood soaked thigh, the peacock kicked up rock fragments.

Max stood up. His head throbbed. "Remove pieces of Mister Kohl?" He asked. Raising the pistol, he squeezed the trigger. The gun popped. Tommy's head jerked. The path of the bullet marked a blood trail along the peacock's cheek and missing ear. Pulls a little to the right, Max thought glancing at Pao's weapon.

"I'll pay! I'll pay!" pleaded the weeping Tommy.

Adjusting for the weapons imperfect calibration, Max shot off the other ear. Much better, he concluded.

"Help! Murder! Murder!" Tommy screamed cupping the sides of his bloody head.

Staggering over, Max reached down and grabbed a handful of Tommy's slick black hair. Pulling the head back, he looked into a sweat glistening face. "Do you know why death cannot find me?" he asked pointing the gun into a tear-filled eye. "It's because I am death," Max informed. Squeezing the trigger, he released a ten-thousand dollar projectile through the young man's brain.

CHAPTER FOURTY THREE

C arrying two large leather suitcases, Max entered the Tan Son Nhat Airport. The Asian rabble parted. In a light colored suit and sporting a white teardrop-shaped crowned fedora, he bullied his way forward. The felt hat's downturned brim concealed the bandaged sixteen stitches across his forehead. His refugee family followed his luggage-totting wedge. Loc kept pace, a cigarette smoldering out of the side of his mouth. In a black suit, the tribesman held his daughter. The young May in a white lace dress, scanned the terminal commotion. A red bow accented her straight black hair. Arching her back, she tried to avoid her father's cigarette smoke. Drifting behind, Lan and Mei in white *Ao Dai* dresses flanked the colorfully dressed H'Liana and Etienne. Under a red and blue bandana, the tribal widow concealed her black hair. Large silver looped earrings dangled from pierced lobs. Her indigo dyed skirt and smock top elaborately embroidered red, yellow and green. In all her *Montagnard* splendor, she walked proudly. Dark focused eyes refused to acknowledge the curious airport audience.

In front of the Air France ticket counter, Roche in a Hawaiian shirt enjoyed a smoke. Beside the American, the fat Jewish attorney sporting a blue blazer blew his pineapple nose into a white handkerchief. Even in the mild morning's temperature, Hassan large moist baldhead sparkled.

Max dropped the luggage at Roche's feet. Where is Elaine? He questioned scanning the crowd. A group of inquisitive French tourists hindered H'Liana's advance. Amateur camera flashes captured the image of a blinking Meo mother and child.

"Watch the bags," Max said to Loc and Roche.

"I'll take care of the luggage," Roche said picking up the suitcases.

Loc flexed to repositioned the child bundled in his arms. With a better grip on his fluid daughter, he counseled, "Patience Max."

Glancing back over his shoulder, Max winked. Pushing his way into the photographer's siege, he confiscated a camera. Aiming the photographic device at the gawking assembly, he flashed a photo of open mouth onlookers. Handing the camera back to the startled French traveler, he had made his point. The gathering scattered. Lan and Mei giggled. The focused H'Liana chuckled. Reaching down, Max picked up the young Etienne and carried him over to the ticket counter.

"Where is Elaine?" Max asked setting the boy down.

"She using the toilette," Hassan informed wiping a sweaty forehead. "Once she returns we can head over to the passenger lounge." Neatly he tucked the statured handkerchief into his navy-blue blazer's breast pocket. As if rehearsed, he pulled out a piece of coconut candy. Bending down, he handed it to Etienne. Throwing back his shoulders, he took a deep satisfying breath.

Little Etienne eyed the rectangular piece of *keo dura* with delight. Slowly, he began to unravel the vegetable oil soaked outer wrapper. Biting into the edible rice paper cover, he broke the candy in half. He offered the freed piece to his adopted sister, May. Patting her son on the head, H'Liana beamed at the unselfish gesture. Loc and Mei nodded their appreciation. The children sat on the airport floor enjoying the treat. The adults shot bewildered glances at Hassan.

I might as well get this over, Max concluded. Leaning into the attorney, he whispered, "Hassan I need to have a word with you. Do you have a minute?"

Squinting with a closed eye, Hassan responded, "Yes, Mister Kohl."

Max wandered out of the groups listening range. Hassan followed. From under the brim of the white fedora, Max asked, "Do you know what I'm about to say?"

"I have a very good premonition," Hassan responded.

"Do I need to say it?" Max questioned.

"No, monsieur," Hassan answered.

Lifting his head, Max looked deep into the attorney's eyes and said, "Convince me."

Taking a quick breath, Hassan avoided Max's penetrating stare. Timidly, he responded, "You are holding me personally responsible, for the well-being of Elaine, H'Liana and Etienne. And if any misfortune was to fall upon them through my actions or events out of my control you will hunt me down and kill me." Completing the difficult dialogue, he gazed at the German.

Nodding, Max patted the attorney on the shoulder. "Could not have said it better," He replied glancing around the crowded terminal. "Now where is Elaine?" He questioned.

Checking his watch, a composed Hassan responded, "We still have plenty of time. If you like I can take everyone over to the passenger lounge. You no doubt would like to say a private farewell to Miss Favreau."

"No," Max responded shaking his head. "Elaine and I have already said goodbye. I'll send Lan to check on her."

Lan skipped through the crowded terminal. The panels of her traditional Vietnamese gown swayed back and forth. I'm finally going to get rid of that American cow, she thought. Humming a pleasant tune, she entered the women's airport lavatory.

Just inside the door, a pudgy Vietnamese washroom attendant in baggy black pants and a wrinkled stained long-sleeved white blouse sat on a metal folding chair. An idle bucket and mop leaned against the tile wall. Slouching like a propped up corpse, the middle-aged women remained motionless. In front of the comatose attendant, western female travelers primped. The tall white women applied makeup in front of water stained mirrors over a row of porcelain washbasins. Along the other wall, partitioned squat toilette stalls. The large women conversed in whispers.

Looking left then right, Lan searched for Elaine. A women vomiting in the corner stall silenced the washroom chatter. A wide smile spread across Lan's face. The American cow is sick, she concluded. Slowly peering into the corner stall, she found Elaine in a dark blue dress with white polka dots. Kneeling on the urine stained tile floor, Max's lover threw up. Seeing the glamorous Elaine like this Lan felt compassion. It is one thing to think bad thoughts about a rival, it is another thing to see them distressed, she realized. Turning, Lan hastily wet her handkerchief.

"Missy?" Lan whispered handling Elaine the damp hanky.

"Merci," Elaine responded blindly accepting the damp cloth. Standing up, she wiped her mouth and face with the moist fabric. Seeing Lan, she flinched. "Thank you Lan, I'm feeling much better now." She said slowly.

"I tell Max you sick but better now." Lan said turning away.

"Wait Lan!" Elaine called out, "I feel much better, no need to alarm Max."

Turning her head to the side Lan studied Elaine's guarded expression. "You baby sick?" she questioned.

Startled, Elaine said, "No! No!" Walking over to an open sink, she began to wash up.

"You have baby," Lan said placing her hand on Elaine's shoulder. "Don't worry Missy, I no tell Max."

CHAPTER FOURTY FOUR

I n the corner of the passenger lounge, a young attentive bartender in
a bowtie stood guard over a bamboo bar. Displayed on glass shelves,
a mirror reflected a limited selection of liquor. In the large room a handful of elite passengers awaited departure. A large plate glass window provided light and a view of an Air France airliner being loaded with luggage.
Isolated on a bench, Hassan sipped on a morning glass of champagne.
Elaine and Roche stood beside the bar in deep conversation. Loc, Mei and
Lan entertained the children.

Looking down at the petite H'Liana, Max tenderly touched her taut
cheek. "I'll miss you."

Reaching up, she patted his large callus hand, "This is not goodbye.
Elaine read my husband's final letter. He asked you to visit us when Etienne
is older. My son and I will wait."

Grinning Max said, "I hope our paths will someday cross."

With a wrinkled brow, H'Liana responded, "No hope, my husband
asked you to visit. So you visit. My husband tell me you are special. He said
you are a man of his word. So Etienne and I will wait."

"Paris is very far," Max informed.

Squinting up at Max, H'Liana responded, "The journey to Paris is long,
but easier than traveling through the mountains of my people." Glancing
over at Elaine saying goodbye to Roche, H'Liana added, "You come see us
and Elaine."

Following her gaze, Max looked over at his former lover and said,
"Elaine and I have parted ways. We are very different people from different
tribes."

Focusing on Max, H'Liana chuckled, "You are both white people. I'm Hmong, a savage who found love with a French Jew. So don't tell me you are from different tribes. Now go over and say goodbye to Elaine. You tell her that you will come to Paris to visit." Pausing a soft smile spread across her taut features. "Max although I find her customs and dress confusing, I can tell she has a good heart."

"Farewell Mademoiselle," Max said. Leaning forward, he kissed the young widow on the cheek. He softly whispered, "Until we meet again."

Approaching the two Americans, Max interrupted the conversation. Over his shoulder, Roche acknowledged Max's presence with a wink and continued his dialogue, "The station chief's name in Paris is Kennedy, same as our President's. He is aware of your arrival. If you need anything just contact him."

"Thank you Tom," Elaine said touching his arm, "Thank you for everything."

Roche hugged his former secretary and said, "Good luck sweetheart." Patting Max on the back, he added, "I'll leave you two alone."

"Well Mister Kohl," Elaine said as Roche departed. "I was wondering if you were going to say goodbye."

"A friend convinced me it was the right thing to do," Max said. "I'll always cherish the time we were together."

"I never felt safer than when I was in your arms," Elaine said smiling. "You have an aura about you Max. I know I'll never have to worry about you." Reaching up, she tenderly touched the bandage under the brim of his hat, "You have a strange relationship with death. Even when he finds you, he just walks away."

Tenderly grabbing her extended hand, he questioned, "Do I need to worry about you?"

Glancing over at Roche, she said, "I have friends in high places that are watching my back." Taking a gulp of air, she added, "I still would feel safer having you by my side." With watery eyes she asked, "Come with me Max."

Hugging her tightly, he quietly repeated, "I'll always cherish the time we were together."

Weeping into his broad chest, she mumbled, "I love you Max Kohl."

CHAPTER FOURTY FIVE

A single string of smoke wove its way into the humid starry Saigon sky. The aroma of the smoldering fumes lost amongst the foul odors of the urban center. On the moss stained concrete balcony of his small apartment, Tom Roche snorted above a small fire. At his feet, flames danced in a metal trash bin. On a hard wood dining room chair, he fidgeted in search of comfort. Jesus, I wished it would rain, he thought. Unbuttoning his Hawaiian shirt, he flapped the moist floral printed fabric. A damp palm wiped beads of sweat from his face. Shaking his hand, he resumed tossing papers into the trashcan furnace. Ten pages seems to be the limit, he concluded. Consuming flames leapt above the rim. He took a sip of warm bourbon. Setting the glass down, he reached under the chair and picked up an overstuffed unmarked manila envelope. A large rubber band corralled the packet's press clippings and photos. A grin of remorse spread across his face. I could have labeled the envelope, *I told you so*, he realized. But one shouldn't gloat when people are about to die.

Releasing the elastic band, he dumped the contents in his lap. On top of the pile, he unfolded the torn off June Life magazine cover. Under the magazine's block lettered LIFE font, a doe eyed Shirley MacLaine in a green lace bra smiled seductively. A flicking wrist tossed the glossy picture of the perky breasted Miss MacLaine into the hungry flames. In the flickering light, he studied a page from the MacLaine issue. The glimmering illumination eerily danced across the black and white image of a mediating Buddhist monk ablaze. It had been five months since the ritualistic suicide had shocked the world. The disturbing photo still haunted Roche. The single self sacrificing act of protest exposed the hypocrisy of the American's anti-communist efforts. Roche took a big gulp of whisky. Seven years of propaganda reduced to bullshit by a single match. *A single death is a tragedy, a million is a statistic*, he reflected on the Stalin quote. The commie bastard was right about that, he conceded.

Leaning back in the heavy chair, he stuffed the horrific image into the front pocket of his khaki slacks. I sure not going to burn it, he reasoned. That wouldn't be right.

Taking a soothing sip of Jim Beam, he continued to feed the fire. Grabbing an eight by ten glossy photo, he paused. The glowing light reflected off the black-and-white image of four partygoers in formal attire. Roche snickered at the uncomfortable expression on the cool and calculating Max Kohl. My sharpshooting associate can stare down death, he thought, but a photographer's flash captured a rare moment of social anxiety. The broad shouldered German dwarfed the sleepy looking Ngo Nhu. The evidence of Nhu's poppy smoking addiction etched in the creases of a pale face. Just another drug lord turned user, Roche concluded. Nhu's infamous bride posed beside him. Roche squinted at Madame Nhu's China Doll features. The photo captured her seductive Oriental charm, but not her dark character, he thought. Just below the diamond studded cross displayed in the plunging neckline of her evening gown, he realized a black heart pumped the blood of a viper. The petite bitch referred to the self-immolation of the monk, as a Buddhist barbeque, he recalled. A sharp burning pain shot through his gut. The house of Ngo rose to power in the protective shadow of the United States, he thought. The penance for America's Vietnamese sin is going to be expensive, he concluded. Locking arms with the venomous Madame Nhu was Elaine Favreau. Ah Elaine, Roche smiled. I miss you already. His abdominal pain subsided. He pawed at the image of the stunning long legged thoroughbred. Recalling Max's assessment of Elaine, he chuckled. "The sex was good, but it wasn't that good," he mumbled. Not pursuing Elaine is on a long list of regrets, he realized.

Carefully, he tore the image of Elaine from the glossy print. It would make for a nice keepsake. Flinging the remaining photo and papers into the smoldering wastebasket, he leaned back. The fire crackled. The pre-dawn glow on the horizon signaled the start of the day. Rubbing the stubble on his chin, he scanned the moss-stained balcony. His personal files reduced to ash. Standing, he stretched his sticky frame and checked his watch. I'll have time to shower and shave before I make the delivery, he concluded. Miming a toast to the sunlight peeking over the horizon, he downed the last of the liquid corn.

CHAPTER FOURTY SIX

It was a damp gloomy Paris afternoon. A black Citroen DS hovered over the pockmarked *Rue des Rosier*. A mist collected on the steeply curved windshield. One hand griped the top of the steering wheel. Leaning back, the portly Oliver Hassan casually steered the futuristic designed vehicle through stop and go traffic. In the roomy back seat, H'Liana in colorfully embroidered traditional Meo clothing shared a padded leather armrest with Elaine. Standing on the front passenger seat in a black suit with a red bowtie, seven-year-old Etienne tugged on a stiff shirt collar. Kosher butchers, restaurants and bakeries drifted by. Jewish men in long black wool coats and wide-brimmed black fedoras dominated the pedestrian population.

Hassan expertly squeezed the vehicle in a tight curbside space. A three-story mansion stood out from the boulevard fronted with apartment buildings and boutique hotels. On the front stoop of the large residence, a plump middle-aged woman stood under an umbrella. A white apron shielded her black smock dress, atop her head an unflattering gray haired bun. She gave an acknowledging wave.

"*Grand-mère*," Etienne exclaimed pointing at the umbrella greeter.

"No," Hassan chuckled. "That's Ada, the housekeeper."

Exiting the vehicle, Hassan pulled a *kippa* out his white suit coat pocket and placed the saucer shaped Jewish cap on his head. Can I trust him? Elaine thought. I should. He paid me the three years' salary as promised. Would he know a discretionary doctor? She wondered. How would he feel about assisting with the illegal termination of my pregnancy? I need to be assured that a back office abortion would be a safe procedure. It would help with the ultimate decision, she realized.

Under a slight drizzle, H'Liana whispered, "I little-bit scared."

Elaine gazed into the young Meo's innocent dark eyes. I'll worry about my problem latter, she concluded. "Don't worry little sister, I'm here to protect you," Elaine said with a reassuring smile. Did I just call her my little sister, Elaine thought? I must have picked that up from Max, she realized. It's no longer about the money, she concluded. This refugee is counting on me. By God, no one is going to take advantage of her on my watch. "Let's do this together," she said inter lacing fingers with the H'Liana's petite callus hand.

Under the protective overhang of the front door, Hassan and Etienne waited with the housekeeper. Elaine and H'Liana casually strolled up hand in hand to meet Jean Guillian's mother.

There was a damp chill in the mansion. In the foyer, a large marble spiral staircase swirled into the raised ceiling and beyond. Along the ascending plaster stairwell wall, contrasting rectangular shading accounted for lost artwork. At the base of the stairs, a grandfather clock stood at attention. The oak centurion marked the passing of time on a roman numeral dial.

"This way," Ada said to Hassan with an inviting hand.

The guests followed the servant into a parquet-floored parlor. A massive fireplace dominated one wall, above the stone mantle the shadow imprint of a missing painting. Provincial furniture on a Persian carpet surrounded an oak coffee table. Filtered light from the overcast day trickled in from high arched windows.

"How is Madame doing today?" Hassan questioned.

"She is napping, but should be able to join you shortly," Ada responded. "This is not one of her better days." She whispered.

Hassan nodded.

"Monsieur, would you prefer coffee or tea?" Ada asked.

"Coffee, please," he responded.

Looking at Elaine, Ada asked, "Mademoiselle?"

"Coffee is fine," Elaine answered.

Ada turned to walk away.

Elaine squinted hard and barked, "Wait a minute." Turning to H'Liana, she asked softly, "Would you like coffee or tea?"

"Tea," H'Liana whispered, "And a glass of milk for Etienne."

Sternly looking at the domestic servant, Elaine informed, "Mrs. Jean Guillian would like some tea and your employer's grandson would like a glass of milk."

Ada exaggerated a curtsey and left the room.

"What was that all about?" Hassan questioned.

Smirking Elaine responded, "Just earning my wages counselor."

A curious Etienne wandered into the fireplace hearth and peered up into the chimney. Elaine and H'Liana sat themselves on the sofa. Hassan sat across from them on a cushioned chair.

Feeling an uncomfortable lump at the base of her back, Elaine reached into the sofa cushion. She pulled out a rock-hard dinner roll. Displaying the stale bread in an extended hand, she asked Hassan, "What is this?"

With a shrug, he answered, "Unfortunately since Madame Guillian's labor camp ordeal she hoards food." Taking the chunk of unbreakable bread, he placed it into a coat pocket. "It's an obsession. I should have warned you. At every meal she hides more food than she eats."

Out of a simple white porcelain cup, Elaine sipped on rich dark coffee. Breads, cheeses and thinly sliced pastrami cluttered the tabletop. The grandfather clock in the foyer chimed the marking of three o'clock. Grumbling whispers and the descending shuffle of leather soles on marble stair treads announced the arrival of Madame Celine Guillian.

Following Hassan's lead, Elaine rose to greet the elderly women. Assisted by Ada, Celine in a light blue flannel housecoat shuffled forward with an arched spine. Tangled long silver hair hung over a downcast gaze.

"Always good to see you Celine," Hassan shouted.

The old woman's pale wrinkled features squinted.

Hassan wiggled his fingers at Etienne. The boy walked over to the attorney. "Celine, I'd like you to meet your grandson." Hassan declared grasping the infants shoulders.

The old woman seemed annoyed. She looked up. Focused on the boy, she smiled. A shaking hand covered an open mouth. "Oh my," she mumbled. Her shoulders fell back. She lifted her head. Color flowed in the pale crevices of a weathered complexion. Blushing with watery eyes, she muttered, "My son Jean has returned."

"No," Hassan said, "This is not Jean, this is..."

"Mousier," H'Liana interrupted the attorney, "Don't correct her. Let her enjoy the moment."

Ada assisted the frail women into a chair. Seated, Celine held her arms out towards the boy.

Young Etienne looked at his mother for guidance. H'Liana said softly, "Go give your grandmother a hug."

The boy cautiously embraced the old woman.

"You really gave me a fright Jean," Celine said patting the boy's head. "But don't worry it will be our secret. I won't tell your father when he comes home." Pulling a flaking croissant out of her housecoat pocket, she said, "Now that you are home we can eat. Our family will never go hungry again." Beaming with joy, the disillusioned old women rambled on in a musical tone about another time.

Choking on tears, Elaine watched. It was a charade, she realized, but that didn't matter. The bond between mother and child is eternal, she realized. She placed a tender hand on her pregnant belly and vowed to her unborn child, "I will raise you on my own if I have too, and my precious; you will never go hungry."

CHAPTER FOURTY SEVEN

The white tiled bathroom sloped towards a floor drain. Moss hid in the crevices of the stained grout. A squat toilet occupied a corner. Under a wall-mounted mirror, toiletries and a handgun cluttered the rim of a porcelain washbasin. Attached to a corroded pipe, a showerhead aimed at the center of the room. Roche braced himself for the chilling spray. The trick was to lather up quickly in the water warmed in dormant pipes. This morning however, the American agent extended the bathing ordeal. In a sobering stream of cold water, he washed away the affects of a sleepless night and fifth of bourbon. A distant thump penetrated the sound of rushing water. He turned off the spigot. Water dripped. He stood motionless. His hand on the valve. A muffled rapping interrupted the overhead dribble. Grabbing a white towel, he wrapped it around his naked waist. Reaching for his Baby Browning pistol, he knocked over a jar of Lucky Tiger butch wax. "Shit," he mumbled exiting the bathroom. Leaving a trail of wet footprints on the polished wood floor, he stared at the front door. The entrance barrier thumped.

"Who is it?" he questioned with gun in hand.

"It's Max."

Roche sighed lowering the weapon. Unlatching the door, he scolded. "You're early."

"Call it German punctuality," Max responded entering the flat. "You seemed unusually tense about today's errand. I didn't want to add to your anxiety by being late."

Holding onto the white towel sarong, Roche flashed the pistol and said, "No more apprehensive than usual. I still shower armed." Casually waiving the Browning towards the kitchen, he said, "Why don't you make us some coffee while I get dressed?"

To the aroma of coffee, a barefoot Roche entered the tiny kitchen. An un-tucked white short-sleeved shirt hung over a pair of khaki pants. His short bristled salt-n-pepper hair waxed into a flat square. Sitting at the dining room table, he put on shoes and socks. Accepting a steaming mug of java, he slouched back and inhaled the pleasant sent. "You Germans sure know how to make a great cup of joe," he declared sipping on the strong black brew.

Max nodded. Pointing his misting cup at the smoldering trash bin on the balcony, he asked, "Burning evidence?"

Roche stood and tucking his shirt into belted pants responded, "My own personal files about today's activity. I don't want to leave a trail in case things go awry."

"What is today's agenda?" Max asked.

"It's confidential," Roche calmly responded. "But what I can tell you is I'm delivering graft to a Vietnamese General. After that I need to observe and report." Placing an empty cup on the table, he asked, "What are you packing?"

Casually Max flipped open his sports coat exhibiting his Tokarev. Reaching behind his back, he pulled out Pao's Makarov handgun. "Call it battlefield preparedness," Max said brandishing the side arm, "My personal armament policy has changed after the confrontation with Tommy Tuyen."

"That's understandable," Roche said lifting a foot onto a dinning chair. Pulling up a pant leg, he holstered his small gun in an ankle holster. Standing, he shook the limb to cloak the weapon. Picking up a bulging sealed manila envelope off the table, he added, "Let's get this over with."

CHAPTER FOURTY EIGHT

It was early Sunday morning, All Souls Day on the Catholic calendar. On the grounds of the Presidential Palace, Max walked beside a focused Roche. Helmeted troops buzzed around the compound. Armed soldiers peered out from second story windows. Max glanced at the American. I hope you know what you doing, he thought.

In front of a nondescript doorway, a stone-faced Vietnamese Colonel awaited. He nodded at the American and shot a suspicious side-glance at the German. "This way gentlemen," he informed.

Max and Roche followed the escort down a long linoleum floored hallway. The pounding of the Colonel's army boots echoed off Spartan walls. Stopping in front of a frosted glass door, the Colonel's flexed knuckle rapped on the translucent barrier. The door swung open. The Colonel clicked his heels and retreated down the long corridor.

Glancing at Max, Roche winked and entered the room. Half a dozen officers of various ranks lounged around the small office. A Vietnamese General grinned. His polished laced boots resting on top of the room's only desk. Remaining in his relaxed repose, he pointed at the overstuffed envelope tucked under Roche's arm. Roche tossed the package next to the General's elevated feet. Glossy boots dropped to the floor. The General tore open the package and poured denominated bundles of currency across the desktop. Sitting upright, he counted the quantified bundles of cash.

Ignoring the digit mumbling General, Max scanned the distant harsh expressions of the other Asian officers. These are hard men, he concluded. I've seen the same mask worn by Corsican hit men and members of the *Waffen SS*, he realized. These are not soldiers who do their duty. These are men who kill because it is enjoyable.

"This should cover our expenses," the General announced. "My sources have informed me that our Catholic targets our attending Mass at Saint Francis Xavier. You gentlemen are welcome to accompany the extraction team," he offered. His sweeping arm introduced the occupants as the team.

"Thank you General, however, we would prefer to observe from a distance." Roche responded.

"Very well," the General said checking his watch, "Let's say about nine AM then, outside the church after the Catholic ritual. It will give our guest a chance to receive the Body of Christ one last time."

Two army jeeps and an armored personnel carrier sped through the quiet Sunday morning streets of Saigon. Keeping a respectful distance, Roche in an embassy staff car followed. He sighed. "The hard part is over Max," he informed. "You never know how these things will play out."

"Since I'm on a need to know basis, what else do I need to know?" Max questioned.

Grinning Roche responded, "If all goes well, the General's men pick up the targets. We observe. I report in and the US Government buys us breakfast."

"Do I at least get to know what we are having for breakfast?" Max chuckled.

Roche slapped Max on the knee and said, "Anything you want my kraut brother. Anything you want."

Roche double-parked in front of Saint Francis Xavier. Mass was in session. A muffled congregation's hymn escaped the stone structure. On the quiet church grounds, helmeted troops spread out.

Lighting a cigarette, Roche leaned against the car and enjoyed a smoke. The tall arched doors of the church swung open. Worshippers poured out. Heavily armed greeters startled the exiting flock. Soldiers wadded into the dispersing congregation in search of specific prey. Swallowing hard, Max flinched. On the rich green grass of Saint Francis Xavier, an army officer shackled the President of Vietnam, Ngo Dinh Diem and his brother Nhu. A swift kick in the ass silenced the protesting Ngo brothers. The arresting troops dragged the leaders of Vietnam across the lush landscape. At curb-side, soldiers hoisted the Ngo siblings onto an armored personal carrier before stuffing them down a turret.

Tossing his cigarette into the street, Roche mumbled, "Their being exiled from the country."

Roche is just rehearsing the United States explanation, Max thought. I'm not buying it, he realized. The President and his brother are about to be assassinated.

Opening the passenger door, Roche slid into the front seat. He pulled a hand held radio microphone out of the glove box. Switching on the unit, he said, "The package has been delivered."

The radio crackled. Through the static a single word responded, "Acknowledged."

Roche turned off the unit and closed the glove box.

Leaning into the driver's window, Max asked, "Why me, Tom?"

"Because I could trust you Max." Roche answered. "Very few people knew the plan. Besides it could have gone the other way. And if it did, I wanted to be close to the man that continues to elude death."

CHAPTER FORTY NINE

It was late morning on this event filled All Souls Day. At the Continental Hotel's curbside cafe, Max and Roche enjoyed a heavy breakfast of eggs, ham and an assortment of breads and pastries. A slight breeze pushed humid air across the shaded linen covered table. The formally dressed servers seemed unusually cheerful. Whispers carried the rumored news of the Ngo brothers deaths. A table of well-dressed Catholics abandoned their post Sunday services brunch.

Placing his palms on the table's edge, Roche pushed himself back. He pulled out a crumpled pack of Lucky Strikes. Lighting a cigarette, he leaned back in the rattan chair. Waving a hand over his head, he got the attention of a waiter. The smoldering tobacco canister between his fingers pointed to an empty coffee cup. "So tell me Max," he asked inhaling smoke, "have you heard from our gal?"

Utilizing a folded piece of sourdough toast, Max sponged up the last of the egg yolk from his greasy plate. Squinting he questioned, "Elaine?"

"Yes! Elaine," Roche frowned. "Has she written you?"

Max popped the piece of egg-flavored bread into his mouth. Chewing the last of his breakfast, he swallowed and casually answered. "I received a couple of letters, nothing of importance. She is doing fine. H'Liana's has become proficient in French. Etienne's grandmother is happy." Grinning he added, "And apparently very wealthy."

Sipping his coffee, Roche peered over the steaming cup and asked, "That is all she said?"

"That about it," Max shrugged. "To tell you the truth, I don't know how to respond."

"So you don't know?" Roche asked placing his half full coffee cup in the table.

"Don't know what?" Max mumbled.

The glowing tip of Roche's cigarette intensified. Exhaling, he quietly informed, "Elaine is with child."

"Well I'll be damned," Max said sitting back scratching his cheek. "How do you know?"

"As I told you before, I'm in the information business. That is what I do," Roche answered grinning. "The station chief in Paris checked in on Elaine at my request. He was glad to do it after hearing all the internal office clamor about the seductive Elaine Favreau. After their brief encounter, he informed me that the glow of motherhood replaced her hour glass figure." Taking a deep breath, he concluded, "Given the estimated timing of her due date. It is safe to say your child was conceived in Saigon."

A grin slowly migrated across Max's face. Slowly he pulled two cigars out from an inside coat pocket. He tossed one across the table. Lighting a cigar, he slumped back in his chair. Crossing his legs, he looked up into the Saigon skyline and took several satisfying puffs.

"Well Max what are you going to do?" Roche asked blowing a cigar smoke plume.

Still lost in celebratory smoke, Max's calm expression focused on the blue sky. Flicking accumulated cigar ash into an empty coffee cup, he answered, "Well it looks like I'm going to have to answer her letters."

CHAPTER FIFTY

In the thick upholstery of the commercial airliner's seat, Roche closed his eyes. The aircraft accelerated. The humid air of Saigon quickly cooled. Ten years, he thought in his relaxed repose. Ten years and hundreds of millions of US dollars wasted. Vietnam is less stable than when the French departed. Such a beautiful country, he reflected, so many resources, rich in culture and tradition. The opportunity squandered, he realized because Uncle Sam cast Ngo Dinh Diem as the lead marionette. An unstable government now faces a formidable communist insurgency.

The drone of the jet engines lulled Roche towards sleep. Vietnam was like an innocent prom date, he visualized. The blossoming debutante plied with alcohol in the form of American aid and propaganda. Uncle Sam the indifferent chaperone watched as the House of Ngo raped the country. President Diem's assault distorted by the presumed anti-communist banner under which the potentate ruled. Picturing the bloody international press photo of the shot and stabbed bound Ngo brothers, a sarcastic grin spread across Roche's face. Suicide, he chuckled. They reported the cause of death as suicides. Well that is someone else's public relation nightmare, he concluded. I'm heading home.

The Ngo brothers paid for their exploitations with life, Roche realized. The United States penance for their Indochina sins would be more expensive. The moral cost of adding assassination to the CIA resume could not be quantified, he concluded. However by terminating Diem the US would not be doubling down in Southeast Asia but would be going all-in.

Someone brushed Roche's arm. Cracking open a sleepy eye, he saw the smiling face of a stunning Asian stewardess.

"Your Jack Daniels sir," she said quietly to camouflage the mispronunciations of her second and possibly third language.

"Thank you," Roche said intercepting the glass of golden brown whisky. The deserted passenger cabin was crisp, clean. Leaning back, he admired the slender flight attendant wheeling the drink cart down the aisle. Her thin hips swayed back and forth. She could be fifteen he thought, or even thirty. I've learned the language, studied the culture and history and still cannot estimate the ages of these people. Still analyzing the flight attendant's tightly knit covered bottom, he lifted his glass in her direction. I'll drink to that; he chuckled sipping on the cool comforting whisky. God this is really good, he thought. Twirling the ice filled glass, he realized the days of drinking warm bourbon in Southeast Asia were over.

"I never understood you Americans and your fascination with ice," Max said from the window seat.

"Do you want to go there, kraut?" Roche playfully questioned. "You Germans eat pickled cabbage with every meal."

"Fair enough, *ami*," Max said touching a bottle of Schlitz with Roche's chilled whisky glass.

"How does it feel to be going to Paris?" Roche asked leaning back.

"I'm a little apprehensive," Max said, "It was tough saying farewell to my family."

"Are you concerned how they will fare without their German guarding angel?"

"Not at all," Max responded. "I didn't look out for them any more than they looked out for me. We were all orphaned and came together to heal. And like all families, there comes a time to cherish the memories and move on."

"Do you think the ice-cream venture will be a success?" Roche asked sipping on ice chilled Jack.

Smiling Max patted the American's knee, "Not to diminish your gift of providing the opportunity *ami*, but Mei would become successful at any endeavor. It's amazing considering her lack of education, but the petite beauty has a head for numbers and a sense for business."

"Mei truly is an amazing woman," Roche said with a respectful nod. "But Elaine is also special in her own right."

"Indochina has transformed all of us, Elaine is no exception. My only hope is that we can have the same relationship with child as Loc and Mei." Looking forward Max softly said, "What else would you need?"

"Are you going to get there on time?" Roche asked.

"The baby is due tomorrow, but I won't get there until Wednesday," Max answered. Taking a satisfying swig of beer, he added, "I'll get there in plenty of time. Elaine is always fashionably late."

CHAPTER FIFTY ONE

T he small ice cream parlor smelled of fresh paint and the sweet cool scent of frozen dessert. An orderly queue waited in front of a raised counter. Families digging into serving bowls topped with fresh fruit occupied all three tables. Wearing a soda jerk paper hat, red bow tie and bib apron, Loc scooped out a vanilla cone order. The shy tribesman did not make eye contact with the customers peering over the glass countertop.

"Who's next?" Mei called out assisting her husband with the afternoon rush.

"This is a very good day," Lan said making change out of a cigar box cash register.

A very good day indeed, Loc thought. He glanced over out his stunning wife. In a white server's uniform the bubbly Mei attended to patrons with a glowing smile. I have a lot to be thankful for, he realized. My German Isabelle brother supplied the capital. Roche the agreement with the American dairy. All we have to do is dish out ice cream and collect money.

"We're getting low on chocolate," Mei uttered out of the side of her mouth.

Loc nodded. Walking through the beaded doorway into the storage room, he wiped his hands on the apron stained with the day's success. Sitting on the tile floor playing with a doll, his daughter ignored the intrusion. The lethargic Pasha reclined in front of the cooler. Affectionately, he rubbed the top of May's head. Straddling the sleeping dog, he retrieved a five-gallon carton of chocolate.

Returning through the beaded curtain, Loc froze. His customers stampeded out of the shop. Just inside the doorway, a scruffy looking officer of the law stood tapped a black nightstick into an open palm. Stocky and bordering on obese, the policeman lustfully looking Mei up and down. The billy club kept a steady beat. With a sinister grin, he paused. Using the baton, he pushed up the patent leather visor of his military cap and surveyed the premises. His skin was dark, oily. His plump round cheese grater jowls pitted and scabbed.

"Are you the owner?" the officer growled at Loc.

Holding the cold five-gallon container, Loc slowly nodded.

Chuckling the policeman snorted. Nodding in Mei's direction he asked, "Is this fine specimen your wife, little man?"

Stone faced Loc stood in place. Mei and Lan submissively focused on the checkerboard linoleum floor. Through the beaded curtain, a wide-eyed May investigated alongside the family dog. Brandishing teeth with a rippled snout, Pasha emitted a low rolling growl.

Walking behind the counter, the uniformed thug pulled out the cigar box, "This is how it's going to be jungle man." He informed. Grinning at the take, he stuffed the currency in his pocket. Dipping a finger into the vat of vanilla, he paused to suck on the cold sweet glob. "I'll make my rounds about once a week and extract an appropriate fee for my security services. If I'm not satisfied, I'll report you as a communist sympathizer. And while you are rotting away in prison, I'll see to it that your wife is serviced by a real man." Squinting harshly, he stared into Loc's disconnected expression. "Do we have an understanding?"

Unblinking, holding the large container of chocolate ice cream, Loc remained motionless.

"Simpleton," the officer mumbled exiting the parlor.

Setting down the frozen container, Loc walked to the door. Peering out, he observed the policeman heading north. Returning to the counter, he removed his paper hat, unclipped his bow tie and pulled the apron off over his head. Squatting down, he reached under the counter and retrieved a MAB pistol. Standing up, he checked the chamber and clip. He placed the sidearm into a front pants' pocket. With an extended hand, Mei offered her husband a straight razor. He took the blade with a nod. Through the beaded curtain, he bent down and kissed his curious daughter. A confused

Pasha looked up at his master with a tilted head and pointed ear. "Good boy," Loc mumbled petting the defiant mutt's head.

Turning around, he hugged Mei. "I'll be back," he whispered.

"I know you will," she softly responded.

Stepping onto the sidewalk, Loc turned north to track his prey.

Blending in with the rest of the herd migrating in the urban jungle, the tribesman had no problem stalking his quarry. Stopping in front of the plate glass window of tailor's shop, he watched the reflection of the strutting cock. The officer confiscated an orange from a fruit vendor. Dusk turned to night. The officer after a long day of shaking down locals entered the Blue Sky Bar. Squatting down in the shadows in the alley across the street, Loc waited. Patrons flowed in and out of the seedy watering hole. A cadre of street children stopped to examine the crouching tribesman. A flash of a pistol satisfied their curiosity. It was early morning. The trash strewn about the alley came to life. A sewer rat scurried into the neon light cast by the Blue Sky Bar. Loc's target staggered into the deserted street. The policeman paused to urinate in front of the building. Keeping to the shadows, Loc pulled out Mei's straight razor. The jungle fighter pounced. A firm hand covered the officer's mouth. The honed edge of a razor cut deep into flesh and bone. On the short journey, the slicing blade severed the officer's windpipe. Wrapping his arms around the gurgling victim, Loc tossed the body into the dark alley. Blood pumped out of a deep gash that traversed below a gapping mouth and shocked expression. Squatting down, Loc wiped Mei's blade clean on the policeman's uniform. He retrieved his day's receipts and an extraction bonus. The officer's existence faded. The graveyards are full of men who threatened my little corner of this planet, Loc thought. The only difference between you and them is that they were professionals and you are a fucking amateur. After spitting on the corpse, Loc removed his blood splattered shirt and dropped it on the ground. Concealed by the pre-dawn shadows, he headed home to his wife and daughter.

***

Book Three
Hard Rice

"For those who fight for it,
life has a special flavor the protected will never know."
Unknown defender of Khe Sanh in Vietnam

CHAPTER ONE

I t was 1982, the year of the dog. A common wind blew across the Indochinese Peninsula. A social order rooted in Marxist-Lenin doctrine prevailed. Thirty years of war had scared the hills, mountains, tropical forest and delta wetlands. The rusting debris of retreating armies littered the landscape. The foreign devils were gone. The Japanese departed in 1945. The French evicted in 1955. From the rooftop of their embassy in Saigon, the United States departed in 1975. Saigon was relabeled Ho Chi Minh City. In the seven years since the Americans departure, millions of inhabitants fled. Many escaped into the sea as boat people. From land-locked Laos, refugees flowed into Thailand. Across the communist landscape labor camps blossomed. The American collaborators spared execution, needed reeducation.

It was two AM. In waist high elephant grass along the bank of the Mekong River a sickly Chong Yeeb lay face down. The cold steel of an M-16 comforted his cheek. The air was muggy. Crickets chirped over the sound of flowing water. Can I make the long swim into Thailand undetected, he wondered. Examining the night sky, a shard of pain jolted his empty belly. Above clouds shielded the moonlight. Through breaks in the billowing canopy, stars sparkled. His callused hand pulled back razor sharp growth. Peering through the brush, he got a glimpse of Yai. On matted weeds, the scrawny Yai laid face up; through heavy eyelids, he studied the heavens. Yai's chest pulsed with shallow breaths. The opium water is numbing the effects of the poison Yeeb concluded releasing the foliage. The concealing elephant grass sprang back. Utilizing the automatic weapon as a crutch, he propped onto his knees. A sparkling ribbon of water flowed south. He felt dizzy. A diesel stuttering patrol boat chugged against the current.

The voices of cackling Communist resonated off the river. Searchlights illuminated the Laotian shore. The surrounding bushes seemed to float, to drift, to spin. With a throbbing head, Yeeb lay back down. Taking sobering breaths, he enjoyed the serenity of twinkling stars. I am Cheng Yeeb, he reflected proudly, of the Cheng clan. I returned to Communist Laos for proof and I have it, he realized. A blind hand shook the sealed Mason jar tethered around his neck. Tarnished-yellow powder sloshed in the glass container. It's been ten days since Yai and I scrapped the yellow poison that blanketed the rocks of the dead village. Ten days of trekking, he thought. The vomiting and diarrhea had passed. I will survive the yellow death for a second time. Now I can tell the story of the Communist extermination of my people with evidence. The West should listen to me, they have too. I speak English.

Reflecting on his former life brought the empty realization that his wife and children no longer existed. It has been three years, he calculated. That wound will never heal. Closing his eyes, he could still hear the Soviet helicopters cutting through the morning air. The yellow smoke sounded like rain. Crops wilted. Chickens ran in frenzied circles. Hogs twitched. Light headed, I ran like a drunkard with a precious child under each arm. I raced past the bodies of convulsing relatives and neighbors, he visualized. My wife staggered with the baby. My family made it to the forest and hide in a cave, he recalled. Just outside the cavern, I buried my three children. Under the night sky, tears welled in Yeeb's eyes.

"Yeeb," Yai whispered through the weeds. "The patrol boat has passed."

Yeeb swallowed. Tossing the rough twine tethered jar on his back, he grabbed the M-16 and slithered forward. The sleepy eyed Yai crawled beside him. The growth was thick. Snarled branches clawed at the escaping Hmong patriots. Yeeb could smell the murky brown river. I'm close, he thought. Sliding forward the earth gave way. Tumbling down a crumbling embankment, he fell into a soupy mire of silt. Yai implanted beside him. Weak and exhausted, Yeeb clawed himself free from the muddy grasp of the Lao People's Democratic Republic. On all fours, he crawled over the fifty yards of muck to the water's edge. Upriver a watercraft sent a shimmering strip of rippling light downstream. No time to rest or find a flotation device, Yeeb concluded sucking on chilled air. Untying the hemp rope sling of his rifle, he attached his sandals to the twine. Yai secured an antique French revolver and flip-flops to his belt. In silence, the two men slid into the current of the Mekong River.

The glass container of poison bobbed beside Yeeb's head. The heavy M-16 tugged on his back. Dipping below the dark surface sent a jolt of fear down his spin. Surfacing, he took a quick breath. Wet darkness engulfed him. Up and down, the silent strokes carried him forward. His heart pounded. The gasp of air above the water was not enough. The Kingdom of Thailand was not getting any closer. Gulping for air, he choked on water. Flaying under the stars, the M-16 with seven rounds of ammunition in its clip rolled off his shoulder. Freed from the burden, he treaded water inhaling clean crisp air. Rhythmically, he began to repeat the simple breaststroke towards the Thai shoreline. The jar of poison still tethered around his neck.

CHAPTER TWO

It was a dreary Sunday morning. A hung-over Paris stirred under the glow of gray skies. Strutting down the *Rue de Berri*, Max's brown polished wing-tips pounded the moist concrete. The broad shouldered middle-aged German walked tall. He ignored the few staggering survivors of a Saturday night in the city of lights. The flanking shops were closed. Curled up on entrance stoops, the less fortunate slept under cardboard blankets. The encompassing mist leaned towards rain. Max placed a folded newspaper over his thinning blond hair. His khaki suit began to wilt. Just before the *Champs-Élysées*, he stopped in front of an iron-grated doorway. 'Casino' arced in scripted font over the entrance. Glancing up at the simple signage, he smirked. Just enough bait to snag naive tourists, he thought. I charge them an entrance fee for the privilege of loosing. Pressing the buzzer, the barred door cracked opened with a familiar click. Standing in the scuffed black and white checkerboard tiled foyer, Max waved a moist newspaper at the gatekeeper.

The wide doorman grinned. In a charcoal suit, he swung open the transparent barrier. "Good morning Mister Kohl." He said in a raspy voice.

"Good morning Henri," Max replied. Squinting he asked. "Have you been here all night?"

With a sleepy nod, Henri responded, "Most the staff pulled an all-nighter." Raising his brow, he informed, "The boys from Marseille are still at the twenty-one table. They fell out of favor with lady luck around three AM."

Max patted his employee on the back. "That is a good thing."

"These Corsicans don't like to lose," Henri mumbled.

Stepping on the plush red carpet Max acknowledged the doorman's commentary with a soft nod. Over his shoulder, he chuckled, "Then they shouldn't gamble."

A buxom cashier stood behind a greeting counter. The stunning brunette's voluptuous figure accented by a black lapelled form fitting red satin vest. Taking a deep breath, she straitened her black bowtie and conjuring up a smile said, "Good morning Mister Kohl."

"Thanks for staying the night Angeline," Max answered.

"No problem," she responded. "I let the husband deal with the baby for a change."

What's her baby's name? Max thought. Is it a boy or a girl? Playing it safe, he asked, "How's the little one doing?"

"Growing like a weed," She commented. With an enlightened expression she added, "Casta needs to see you. Our last two customers want to raise the table stakes."

Glancing across the gambling club floor, Max replied with a thumbs up. Black vinyl covered the empty baccarat and poker stations. The only active gaming table was poker twenty-one. Its rich green felt surface jumped out of the sea of dark plastic shrouds. The dealer sat stone faced. Across from him, two thirty something Corsicans with dark features and slicked back black hair scowled at upturned cards. The player's dark gray designer suits only varied slightly in shading. A big haired redhead, baring a shoulder, tried to sleep on her betting escorts shoulder. Curled up on three empty poker chairs, a thin blonde with a beak nose snored with an open mouth. A skimpy red silk dress failed to conceal her charms. Along the back wall, Ghjuvan Casta stood in front of a dark oak bar observing the gaming. Max spotted his Corsican partner and gave a light wave. With two fingers, Casta signaled Max to join him.

Giving the gamblers a wide berth, Max walked along the wall. Studying his partner, Max noticed the long night seemed to have aged Casta. The wiry Corsican looked thinner in a pinstriped suit. His gray bordering on white hair cropped short and his signature pencil thin mustache a crooked silver line. I wonder how old he is, Max thought. Let's see, I met Casta in Saigon in 1954 when he was a captain in the Deuxième Bureau. That's twenty-eight years ago and he was pushing forty back then. Mid to late sixties, Max calculated. The journey through life makes for unusual relationships, he concluded. Our first transaction was a weapons for opium trade to arm the hill tribes. Casta got his opium, the Hmong small arms and I ended up with the *Unione Corse* hit-man Rossi's bounty on my head. "Long night Casta," Max said giving his partner's hand a firm shake. Looking down at his gripping hand, Max chuckled at the irony. Twenty-eight years ago the Corsican syndicate wanted him dead and today they are doing business. Glancing over at the active table, Max said, "I hear your kinsmen want to raise the limit in the hopes of getting back into lucks good graces."

"What do you think?" Casta asked.

Focused on the players, Max studied their dark mysterious eyes. "I've never been able to read a Corsican," He mumbled. "But if these Marseille boys want to risk more of their heroin profits, I'm willing to dance."

Casta signaled the solemn croupier to raise the stakes.

Max turned and placed his hands on the lacquered wood counter. "A cup of coffee Lucky," he said to the attentive Asian bartender. As Lucky poured the steaming brew, Max added, "So Lucky how is Kia and your sons Toua and Lue adapting to Parisian life."

The light-skinned Lucky acknowledged the bosses recognition with the child like innocent smile of the Hmong. Looking down, he answered softly, "Fine Max."

Max turned and took a cautious sip of the strong coffee. He grinned. His three Hmong employees all called him Max. It seemed only fair since he named them Lucky, Bear and Sparky.

"That what I'm talking about!" exclaimed a Corsican gambler.

The proclamation got the attention of the sleepy audience. The hook nosed blonde sat up. Casually, she straitened the flimsy red gown over exposed nipples. Blinking with heavy make-up smudged eyelids, she cracked an unflattering disconnected grin.

"Looks like our customers are on their way back to finding the magic," Casta said with a shrug.

Leaning into his partner, Max whispered, "Addicts never can duplicate the initial sensation of euphoria, no matter how hard they try. The patience of the house odds always prevails." Downing his warm coffee with a single gulp, he placed the empty cup on the polished surface and said, "Just in case my theory is flawed, let me see how much cash we have on hand."

The flowing chips on the active table reversed course. The Marseille boys bathed in the rejuvenating glow of good fortune. Keep playing, Max thought entering his Spartan office. Stacked in the corner were boxes of brand liquor. Two oil paintings depicting sad clowns hung on the wall. A large wooden desk cluttered with papers anchored the small room. The facsimile machine perched on a gray vertical metal filing cabinet hummed as it coughed out a scroll of onion paper. With a curious squint, Max unraveled the fax. Looking at the single sheet, he smiled. The stiffness from his morning calisthenics faded. He flexed his aging frame and read. *'Need a cuckoo to escort hard rice across the fence. If interested meet me in Los Angeles... Ami.'* "Ami" Max mumbled visualizing Tom Roche. Apparently, the CIA operative wants to come out retirement, he concluded. I can do this, Max thought studying the brief text a second time. Hell, I need to do this. What do I tell Eva and Elaine, he questioned thinking about his daughter and wife? If I'm going to do this, I need to go to Nice and say goodbye to Eva, he realized. And Elaine, he pondered. I can entice her with a stateside trip, he calculated. She can go to LA with me and then head off to Pennsylvania to visit her mother.

Grasping the fax invitation, Max walked over to the wall and pulled back the hinged oil painting of a depressed circus performer. Recessed in the wall was a cold gray metal combination lock safe. He spun the numbered dial.

Casta entered the small room and happily declared, "No need to check our funds partner. Lady Luck is teaching our patrons an expensive lesson."

Ignoring the update, Max reversed the dial's rotation and blindly handed Casta the fax.

"What is a cuckoo?" Casta questioned.

"It's a medium sized slender bird," Max mumbled opening the steel box.

Snorting Casta blurted, "In regards to the facsimile?"

"Its military slang for a German sharpshooter," Max informed reaching past the neatly stacked bundles of francs and US greenbacks. From the back of the vault, he retrieved a leather shoulder holster wrapped around a pistol. "The English word is sniper," he continued. "Cuckoo refers to German shooters who popped out of trees to delay the advancing allies."

"Are you are going to do this?" Casta asked waiving the onion paper scroll.

Pulling out a Soviet made Tokarev handgun from the leather sheath, Max enjoyed the comforting grasp of the familiar tool and mumbled, "I really don't have a choice,"

"Max!" Casta exclaimed. "We are not the men we were in our youth. You cross the fence you may never come back."

"Speak for yourself old-man," Max chuckled aiming the Tokarev at an imaginary target.

"Don't worry Max," Casta said. "I'll keep milking this cash cow until you return."

"Thanks," Max responded taking of his suit coat and strapping on the friendly shoulder holster.

After a hard swallow, Casta said solemnly, "In case you don't return. There is something I need to know. We never spoke of this although we knew it was always there."

"Petri Rossi?" Max mumbled.

Casta nodded, "It really doesn't matter one way or the other. Petru had a lot of enemies before he vanished in fifty-five. I just need to know," Pausing he asked softly, "Did you kill him?"

Holstering his pistol, Max answered, "No." Putting on his jacket, he added, "But in a shallow grave on the Plain of Jars, I buried his Corsican carcass."

CHAPTER THREE

U nder a low gray sky, the morning drizzle took a turn towards rain. Max emerged from the bowels of the Paris Metro with an added spring in his step. The weight of a holstered shooting iron felt good. A reminder of my youth, he thought. Large droplets fell off the art nouveau Metro sign marking the Saint-Paul station. Spinning to get his bearings, Max opened an umbrella. The precipitation, the humidity, and the comfort of being armed rekindled images of Saigon. Pausing under the protective canopy, he inhaled the wet city aroma. Walking in the summer rain, he grinned. Those were the days, he thought. Living on the edge added a special flavor to life. Is it only a taste a young man can savor, he wondered. I guess I'll find out when I cross the fence.

Meandering through idling wet cars, he crossed the street. Stepping onto the sidewalk of the *Rue des Rosier*, he took a deep breath. The Star of David marked the doorways of restaurants and bakeries. Wide-brimmed black fedoras dominated the pedestrian traffic. Rubbing the back of his neck, he passed a kosher butcher's shop. The scowling proprietor stood in the doorway. The old butcher wearing the saucer shaped cap of his tribe and a blood stained apron scowled at the German's Arian features. Max ignored the scrutiny. I might have been young and foolish when I bought that anti-Semitic Nazi propaganda, Max thought. But I bought it. With a hateful brush I slapped that six-pointed star across Jewish storefronts, he reflected. The haunting image he dreaded surfaced. A sharp pain churned in his gut. Boney kneed in the short black pants of my Deutsche *Jungvolk* uniform, I taunted the Jewish baker, he recalled. Pummeled by the young wolves of the Hitler Youth the old man laid on the sidewalk in front of his bakery. To gain favor with the older boys, I pissed on the Jew. Why he always wondered? What honor is there in humiliating a man who makes bread and cakes? Being part of a mob does not dilute the sin, he realized. The memory is my penance. It has accounted for many a sleepless night, he reflected and considerable angst on a rainy day in Paris.

Most of my Jewish taunting companions paid the ultimate price for fanaticism, Max realized. The Reich fed the boy soldiers of the 12th Panzer *Hitlerjugend* into the fire of war. Left behind to slow the inevitable rising tide of the allied forces in France, few survived. The murder division, he snorted at the Canadian label of his unit. There were atrocities on both sides, he always concluded. But the victors always have the advantage of writing history.

In front of a three-foot wrought iron gate, he stopped. Glancing from under the umbrella canopy, he admired a three-story mansion. A rarity in this densely populated Jewish quarter. "The Guillian estate," he mumbled under the pounding of rain. *Sergent-chef* Jean Guillian, Max reflected with a comforting grin. "If your travels take you in the direction of my family look in on them for me," he mumbled the quote from Guillian's final letter. I owe you far more than that my Jewish brother, he thought rubbing a sniffling nose.

The mansion's blister white panel door slowly opened. A petite middle-aged Hmong woman cautiously stood on the stoop. A simple black smock dress graced her slender figure. Her hair fashionably cut into a short bouffant. Squinting into the falling rain, she questioned the man at her gate. "Max?"

"Hello H'Liana," Max responded with a short wave.

"What a pleasant surprise," she said waving him in. "Let's get you out of the rain."

Accepting the invitation, he unlatched the ornamental garden gate. The clang of the decorative barrier resonated as he approached the stoop. Under the protective overhang of the entryway, he dropped the umbrella. Bending down, he greeted her with a soft peck on the cheek. Reaching up, she latched onto his broad shoulders and buried her face into his hard chest.

"Oh how I look forward to your visits," H'Liana whispered accenting the sentiment with a flex. Breaking the embrace, she playfully patted his chest and questioned, "So what were you doing standing in the rain at my gate?"

"A warm rain always takes me back to our Indochina days," he confessed. "I was thinking of Jean."

H'Liana gasped and patted her heart. Gazing into the falling rain, she smiled. Taking a deep breath, she swung open the front door and asked, "Do you have time for coffee?"

"I'd prefer a beer?" He responded.

"Of course you would," she chuckled.

Standing in the open doorframe, Max collapsed and flexed the umbrella several time over the stoop. In the large foyer, he set down the taut moist canopy on the marble floor. There was an empty chill in the mansion. The adjoining room was dark. Starched white fabric shrouded the furnishings. A large marble spiral staircase wove its way into the raised ceiling. Along the ascending plaster stairwell rectangular footprints accounted for pilfered artwork. Most of the Guillian estate confiscated by my occupying countrymen was returned, Max thought, but not the paintings.

Max followed his host into a parquet floored parlor. A massive fireplace dominated one wall. Above the stone mantle the shadow imprint marked another Nazi theft. Provincial furniture on a Persian carpet surrounded a dark wood coffee table. Cascading water trickled down high arched windows.

"Let me get us a couple of beers," H'Liana said grinning. "I like this. Drinking with a guest is the Hmong way."

The widow quickly returned with two pointed bottles of Kronenbourg 1664. She handed one of the emerald glass bottles of brew to Max.

A gentle clink resonated as Max tapped her bottle. "L'Chayim," He said before taking a swig.

"To life," she mumbled. Taking a cushioned seat, she took a sip and asked, "So tell me Max are you still uncomfortable walking through the Jewish quarter."

535

Slowly nodding he answered, "It always churns up the ugly sins of my youth. It was something that your husband and I never spoke about." After taking another healthy swig he added, "I'm glad we never did."

"In the Hmong culture when a woman marries into another clan, they become her family. After all these years, I still don't feel my neighbors have accepted me into the tribe." She confessed.

"Then why don't you move?" Max questioned. "You and I both know you have the resources to live wherever you want."

H'Liana looked puzzled. "Move?" she mumbled. "I could never move. This is the ancestral home of the Guillians. This is my husband's village. Jean lived her as a boy and so did his father and his father before him. After the Holocaust the only one left in the blood line is my son," she said. "The flame may flicker but it still burns."

"How is Etienne?" Max asked about the sole heir to the Guillian fortune.

"He's definitely embraced the French way of life," she answered. With a sad shrug, she added, "He vaguely remembers his Hmong childhood."

"Don't fault him for a lack of memories," Max said. "He was just a child." Leaning back in the soft cushioned chair, he gazed up into the rafters with a wide smile. "I remember when he was born. Jean was so proud."

"Those days seem like a dream now," she responded. "It is funny how I reexamine them with a different prospective. I was so young and naive back then. A village girl who didn't know a world existed beyond the mountains of Laos." Squinting she asked, "What was your American friend's name? The one you called *Ami?*"

"Roche," Max answered. "Major Tom Roche."

"I used to think those flowery shirts he always wore were the dress of his clan. What a happy people they must be to dress in colorful floral prints." she said giggling.

"Roche and his Hawaiian shirts," Max commented with a playful snort. "Don't feel bad H'Liana, I found his casual wear unique and slightly odd."

"And that tall lanky pilot that flew us out of Plain of Jars?" she questioned waving a nervous finger.

"Buck!" Max answered, "The Texan."

Nodding in agreement, she recalled, "He wore those big black sharp pointed boots and that wide brim hat. I had never seen a cowboy before. I assumed that is how his tribe dressed."

Laughing Max informed, "Your assumption was right on that one. I think all Texans dress like that."

To the pleasant murmur of levity the front door clicked. Squeaky leather soles on hard stone rolled in from the foyer.

Beaming H'Liana smiled. "That is Etienne," she informed. Looking in the direction of the arrival, she said softly, "Etienne?"

"What!" her son barked from the entryway.

Embarrassed, she looked down.

Scowling at Etienne's response, Max said in a firm tone, "Etienne!"

"Uncle Max," Etienne responded. Appearing in the arched entrance to the parlor, he said pleasantly, "I didn't know you were here?"

Etienne in his late twenties was tall like his father at a little over six feet. There was little trace of his Asian ancestry in his dark features. His eyebrows were thick, his eyes and long hair a dark brown. A firm chin anchored a perpetual five-o-clock shadow. Exposed by and unbuttoned wide collared blue silk shirt, several gold chains sparkled. Black leather pants completed the fashionable ensemble.

Max stood to greet his adopted nephew, and asked, "Do you have time for a beer with your uncle Max?"

"Of course I do!" responded Etienne.

"Can you get us a few more beers?" Max politely asked H'Laina. She smiled, nodded and collected Max's empty bottle. Standing beside Etienne, Max watched her exit. Once she departed from view, he smacked the back of the boy's head hard.

"Oww!" Etienne cried out rubbing his noggin. "What was that for?"

"Where do you get off talking to your mother like that," Max scolded. "You were too young to remember, so let me inform you since I was there. I saw your mother drained from breast feeding you when she was starving. She carried your plump little kosher ass out of Tonkin with communist bullets buzzing overhead. I suspect she didn't do it so that one day you could walk in here dressed like a pimp and disrespect her." Looking up

Max got a glimpse of H'Liana with three beers slowly retreating from the parlor. He winked at her. She smiled.

"I'm sorry Uncle Max," Etienne replied still rubbing his head.

"Don't apologize to me," Max growled, "Apologize to your mother." Playfully he grabbed the boy's puffy silk shirt. Flicking the fabric, he asked, "Is this a blouse? And if you are going to wear jewelry at least make it silver. You're half Hmong for Christ sake."

Slouching Etienne focused on the parquet flooring. Max placed an arm around the boy's shoulder. Etienne accepted the olive branch and hugged his uncle. Breaking the embrace, he looked at Max with a curious squint.

To answer Etienne's expression, Max pulled back his suit coat exhibiting the sidearm.

"What does this mean?" H'Liana asked setting fresh beers on the coffee table.

"It means," Max answered grabbing a cold bottle, "That I have an errand that requires the tool of my former profession." Taking a long hard gulp from the bottle, he wiped his moist lips and announced, "I'm going back to the land of your births."

Etienne accepted the news with an open mouth. H'Liana walked over to the fireplace. Stretching up on the tips of her toes, she pulled down a small urn. Setting it down next to a green beer bottle, she pulled off the bell shaped lid. Taking a deep breath, she reached in. Between thumb and forefinger she retrieved a small piece of yellow cloth. Delicately she handed it to Max.

Looking down he smiled. In the palm of his cupped hand was the three chevrons of *Sergent-chef* Jean Guillian.

"You and Jean survived many a battlefield," H'Liana said with teary eyes. "When you cross the fence Jean will be with you once again."

CHAPTER FOUR

It was late Saturday night in southern California. There was a chill in the cool summer air. In front of a modest three-bedroom tract home, plastic five-gallon buckets cluttered a concrete driveway. A middle-aged Hmong in black slacks and a wrinkled white cotton shirt filled the pails from a green garden hose. Like most tribesmen, he was light skinned, thin and short in stature. Graying temples on dark brown hair showed his age. Laughter woven into Vietnamese dialogue flowed out of the brightly lit carport. In the open-air shelter, the tribesman's petite Vietnamese wife supervised teenage girls sorting carnations into dozen and half dozen bouquets. Short black hair framed his wife's China doll features. She wore a pink sweater to combat the cool summer night. The couple's young Asian helpers wrapped the sorted flower stems in plastic. The finished product placed into the watered pails. The cackling girls turned shy as a burly neighbor wandered into the light. Pot bellied with a crew cut, the large man rubbing his head said, "Evening Loc...Mei, what are you doing?"

"Good evening Norbit," Loc answered turning off the water spigot. "Tomorrow is mother's day. We will be selling flowers on street corners."

"Shit," Norbit mumbled. "I didn't get Gracie anything." Enlightened he asked, "How much?"

"Five dollars for half dozen, ten dollars for dozen," Loc answered.

Pulling a crisp ten-dollar bill from a fat weathered wallet, Norbit said, "Thanks Loc you really are a lifesaver."

"My pleasure," Loc replied handing a plump bouquet of white and red carnations.

"Good evening Norbit," Mei said. "I hope Gracie likes the flowers."

"Thanks Mei," Norbit responded. Shaking his head, he commented. "Where do you Chinese get the energy for all your ventures? You always have your fingers in a money making scheme."

Looking at Mei, Loc grinned. She smiled back. No matter how many times I've told Norbit that I'm Hmong and Mei is Vietnamese, he thinks all Asians are Chinese. Responding to the innocent mistake, Loc answered, "Not much effort in this task. Our nail salons are closed tomorrow, so employees who want to make a little extra can. We sold out last year by noon."

Shrugging Norbit confessed, "I wish I had your drive." Displaying the dozen fresh carnations, he added, "Thanks again for keeping me out of the dog house with Gracie." Turning to leave he said, "Good night Mei." Bowing in the direction of the young Asian girls, he added, "Ladies."

Loc's neighbor faded into the darkness. What a strange people Loc thought, surrounded by opportunity but too lazy to take advantage. Gazing across the driveway full of five-gallon buckets, he grinned. Every year when they wax the school's floors, I pull these perfectly good containers out of the elementary school dumpster, he recalled. Maybe next year I'll sell the buckets on the street corners for a dollar, he pondered. Pure profit.

The front door swung open. Peering out with a sense of urgency his daughter May called out, "Long distance phone call dad. It's Uncle Max!"

Loc looked at Mei. Her face expressed concern. He ran into the house. Mei followed. The screen door slammed behind the couple. Loc picked up the idle receiver.

"Hello?" Loc questioned into the crackling static.

"Bonjour partner," Answered the familiar voice.

"Bonjour partner," Loc echoed. Shadowed by his apprehensive wife, Loc asked, "Is it bad news?"

Max chuckled. "The only death to report is my youth."

Loc laughed. Mei sighed in relief.

"Ami contacted me," Max informed. "He's putting a team together for a munitions drop in Laos."

"Just like the good old days," Loc responded.

"They weren't that good," retorted a snickering Max. "Opium is not part of the transaction this time. Payment will be the satisfaction of arming our Meo brethren."

"Hmong brothers," Loc corrected. "Meo is a dated term."

"My apologies to your noble race," Max said. "Well I'm meeting Roche next week in Los Angeles..."

"I'm in," Loc interrupted.

"Just like that?" Max questioned. "I haven't even asked you yet."

"How long did it take you to ponder the request?"

"Fair enough," Max acknowledged. "It's just that we are not as young as we used to be."

"And we are not getting any younger," Loc said.

Mei listened. The usually shy Loc conversed with confidence. Loc and the German are committed to each other, she thought. Bonded in battle, they were inseparable at one time. The years and distance had not diminished the relationship. Before I crossed paths with Max and Loc's partnership, I lived a nightmare existence, she realized. I hated all whites, she reflected. The large intimidating French soldiers only focused on satisfying their perverted pleasure. It was a hot muggy Saigon afternoon in the spring of 1955, my fortunes changed. In the courtyard of the US embassy, I spotted the floral shirted American interrogator. The one they called Roche. He was conversing with a wide shouldered yellow haired white and my tribesman. My tribesman who proclaimed, he would never forget my face. Mei grinned. The recollection invoked tears of joy.

Hanging up the wall phone, Loc said, "Max asked me for a favor."

"I heard," Mei responded wiping moist eyes. "Don't worry; I'll be able to run the family business."

Loc wrapped her in his arms and confessed, "I have to do this."

"I know," she responded with an affectionate squeeze.

CHAPTER FIVE

The bright summer moon illuminated a towering cast iron gate encrusted with an olive leaf motif. In front of the barrier, Max turned off the ignition of the rental car. To the crunch of gravel, he guided the compact red Renault to a silent termination. Behind the bared obstacle a cobble stone driveway twisted up the plushy landscaped hillside. Exiting the vehicle, he confirmed the address from the hotel concierge's hand written directions. No need to announce my presence, he thought examining the obstruction. Using the metal foliage accents as footholds, he scaled the gate.

Hoping down onto the uneven cobble stones, he realigned his white suit. Not bad for a fifty-six year old man, he thought running his fingers through thinning blond locks. The salty aroma of the French Rivera caused him to pause. Looking up into the starry sky, he took a deep cleansing breathe of the seaside air and proceeded up the private road. In the dark distance, the faint thumping beat of modern music. Rounding the final bend of the pathway the party noise intensified. Behind a circular driveway clogged with overpriced vehicles, a brightly lit two-story villa pulsed with life. Walking through the maze of BMW's, Mercedes Benz's and an occasional red Ferrari, Max spotted the gatekeeper. In a sharkskin suit and tie, a bald black man with a barrel chest scowled at Max's weaving approach.

Leaving his perch in front the entry door, the black man flexed his intimidating frame. Beads of sweat glistened on his large slick head. He growled, "Where the fuck do you think you are going?"

Chuckling, Max showed the palms of his hands and said, "I'm Eva's father here to see my daughter."

"And just who the fuck is Eva?" The thug barked.

Squinting at the comment, Max calculated his options.

With a well-rehearsed motion, the guard pulled back his suit coat revealing a side arm. Smirking he mumbled, "I suggest you turn around and go home, pops. This is a private affair."

Max sighed in defeat. He turned away but quickly spun back around with his Tokarev pistol drawn. Touching the barrel on the black man's sweaty noggin, Max watched the thug wilt. God this feels good, he thought. Looking down his extended arm, he felt the familiar comforting power of the weapon. His heart raced. After taking a deep breath to dilute his enthusiasm, he asked softly. "Did you ever kill anyone with your sidearm?"

The black man gave a negative twitch.

"Well I have," Max informed. "This pistol has been with me for many years and served me well. It is a Soviet made Tokarev. I took off a Communist I killed in 1954. As a Legionnaire, I earned roughly about five dollars a day to kill men. I did it without hesitation. Even after the war the Tokarev was a useful tool, sending men who opposed my agenda to their maker." Looking into the black man's subdued gaze, he asked with a nod, "What's your name?"

Swallowing hard the guardian responded, "Rocco...they call me Rocco."

"Well Rocco can I count on your assistance in retrieving my daughter?"

Slowly Rocco nodded, "Yes sir."

"Good," Max said waving his pistol in the direction of Rocco's concealed weapon. Rocco carefully extracted his gun with thumb and forefinger. Max confiscated the pistol and warned, "One more thing Rocco...don't ever call me pops again."

Max followed Rocco up the three steps to the large arched oak entry door with a grated speak easy portal. Over the muffled beat of loud music and high-pitched laughter, Max asked, "Tell me Rocco is there any other security issues I need to worry about."

Glancing over his shoulder at the seasoned handgun, Rocco shook his head and politely said, "No sir." Then turning his back to the entry, the black man added, "Sir, I must warn you as a father to another father, the festivities after a successful photo shoot can get rather decadent."

Nodding Max holstered his pistol. His stomach churned. Remember your military discipline, he thought. Eva's twenty and legally an adult, he concluded visualizing the image of his little girl.

"What is your daughter's name again?" Rocco asked leaning in to compensate for the party noise.

"Eva," Max responded. "Eva Kohl."

Flinching back, Rocco blurted out, "Your Max! Max Kohl, the German who walked out of Isabelle!"

Max chuckled with an uncomfortable nod. After all these years, he thought my youthful defiance of death is still remembered.

"Let's go find your daughter Mister Kohl," Rocco said turning and opening the large vibrating oak planked door. A wave of popular music escaped.

Standing in the polished marble foyer, Max's stomach thumped to the load beat. He squinted behind the broad shoulders of his escort. His vision distorted by the limited lighting and a haze of cigarette smoke. The vestibule was crowded. A mostly male audience of a dozen spectators, focused on taut young female flesh intertwined on the polished surface. To the voyeurs' delight two naked girls panted and moaned in a sexual performance. The performers encouraged by grunts and groans.

Bullying his way through the satisfied assembly, Rocco led Max past the reception floorshow down a short hallway. In the corridor a large oil painting depicting the Mediterranean seascape hung over a hallway table cluttered with beer bottles and used cocktail glasses. The passage led to the heart of the festivities. In a crowed dark-wood paneled room, scantily clad women clung to well dressed men. Wailing guitar riffs poured out of speakers housed in the rafters of the raised ceiling. Along the far wall, three sets of open casement doors invited in comforting cool summer's night air.

Scanning the occupants in search of his daughter, Max snorted at a familiar sweet stench. The dragon's breathe, he realized. Tilting his head, he spotted a young man slouched down on a bright red leather sofa puffing away on an ivory dream stick. The ne'er-do-well with bare feet propped up on a coffee table, a blue blazer over a naked torso and sleepy eyes, inhaled the opium beast. "There will always be demand for the product," Max mumbled recalling an enthusiastic CIA agent's prediction from his past.

"I don't see her sir," Rocco informed. Leaning into the German, he offered. "If you would like to wait here, I can check the bedrooms."

"Thanks Rocco," Max responded.

As his black escort exited, Max wandered over toward an open casement doorway. A lighted swimming pool active with nude bathers glowed on a terrace that overlooked the distant sea. Frolicking topless amongst the late night swimmers, he spotted Eva. Mesmerized, he watched his long-legged blonde daughter splashing about with a childish innocence. Such a beauty, he thought, just like her mother. Walking to the glimmering water's edge, he squatted down and called out, "Eva!"

Turning to investigate, Eva's face lit up as she exclaimed, "Papa!" Plunging in the glistening water, the high-cheeked boned model churned a splashing path to her father.

Emerging at his feet, she gulped for air. Looking up, she asked joyfully, "Papa what are you doing here?"

"Hello *liebchen*," Max said. "I didn't want to embarrass you princess, but your papa is going out of the country on business. I wanted to say goodbye."

"Oh papa," she said touching his brown leather shoe. "You will never embarrass me."

"Would you like to go back to the hotel and have a beer with your papa?" Max asked.

"Always," she said patting his shoe. "Just let me get my things," she added turning to swim across the pool.

Standing up Max pulled a cigar from his inside coat pocket. He lit it as Rocco approached.

"I see you've found your little girl," Rocco said.

Looking into the shadows across the glowing water, Max grinned at Eva dressing and mumbled, "She not little anymore." Returning the black man's pistol, he said, "Thanks for your assistance Rocco." Squinting he asked, "I'm curious, how did you know about my Isabelle exploits?"

Rocco holstered his weapon and replied, "My father was in a Moroccan Rifle Regiment in Indochina."

"We are the Africans, we come far away to die," Max mumbled with respect.

After a reflective pause, the bouncer's harsh features faded. A soft grin emerged. Nodding he commented, "You know the Moroccan soldiers chant."

Taking a comforting puff on the cigar Max thought of his black-brother Hakeem. The Gray Gorilla growling out the chant as he charged into battle. "I know it very well," Max mumbled.

"Well I need to return to my post," Rocco said extending his hand.

Max gave the large black paw a firm shake and said, "Thanks again."

"It was my pleasure." Rocco said. Tilting his head, he asked, "Would you have shot me?"

"Without hesitation," Max chuckled.

Snickering Rocco returned to guard duty.

Eva's high heels clicked on the stone terrace. The tall wet haired blonde hugged her stocky German father. Patting his chest she said, "I'm sorry you had to find me in this environment."

Grasping her hand, he squeezed it and said, "You don't have to apologize to me *liebchen*." Glancing through the casement doorway at the depraved celebration, he added firmly, "Just promise me you won't dance with the pipe."

"Opium papa?" she questioned.

He nodded.

Flashing the famous smile that had graced the cover of many a European periodical, she said proudly. "You don't have to worry about that. I'm a Kohl and us Kohl's prefer beer."

"Thank you princess," he said kissing her damp forehead.

CHAPTER SIX

I t was late afternoon at the Los Angeles International Airport. Standing across the corridor from the women's restroom, Max watched the travelers flow by. Denim and white tennis shoes, he thought examining the casually dressed American passengers. Hovering over his Louis Vuitton luggage in a blue blazer and white slacks, the bleached blond German invoked a few inquisitive glances.

Waiting for his American wife, Max thought about her relaxed sense of punctuality. In our twenty years of marriage, he realized we have never been on time. Glancing at his watch, he concluded, Elaine's fashionable tardiness would always trump his inbreed German military desire for promptness. She did give me Eva, he thought, and for the gift of my daughter I'll always be in her debt. "And always late," he mumbled snickering.

Fondly, he reflected back to that muggy Saigon afternoon when he first encountered the alluring Elaine Favreau. In the courtyard of the US Embassy, a pair of shapely legs pivoted to exit a Peugeot Sedan overloaded with luggage. A tall blonde emerged. Placed her hands on her lower back and stretched. A wilted silk dress clung to a shapely moist frame. She grabbed my attention, he recalled and never let go.

In the crowed LA terminal, a cadre of gawking flight attendants in bright red uniforms with matching pillbox hats stopped in front of the grinning German. One of the giggling twenty-something-year-old girls asked with a squint, "Excuse us, but we were wondering who you are?"

Max looked at the wide-eyed stewardesses. Beaming smiles solicited an answer.

"You look very familiar," she added. "Are you famous?"

Max chuckled. I was once in Indochina, he realized. Before any of you were born, I gained notoriety in a war that no one remembers; nor even cares about. Ninety-thousand French troops and half-a-million Vietnamese Communist perished for naught. "Sorry to disappoint you ladies," he replied with a German accent. "I'm just an attentive husband waiting for my wife."

Glancing over red pill-boxed garnished heads, he saw Elaine emerge from the women's facility. The tall sultry blonde paused to get her bearings. Even after the long journey from Paris, she looked exquisite. At fifty-years-of-age, she weaved through the underdressed crowd in a quilted silk jacket synched tight around a slender waist. Fashionable shoulder pads enhanced timeless hourglass curves. Her light chestnut hair pulled back into a tight bun. With stiletto heels clicking on the airport's terrazzo floor, she approached her husband. The uniformed female audience dispersed.

"What was that all about?" She asked.

Picking up their designer luggage, he slung a strap over his shoulder. "Inquisitive Americans," he mumbled.

"Let me help you with the bags," she offered reaching for his Pullman suitcase.

"I got it," he informed jerking the bag out of her reach.

Standing her ground in the congested terminal, she asked, "Max, did you pack your Tokarev?"

He nodded. A spark of excitement danced across his wife's face. Like a moth to the flame, he realized. The Elaine Favreau, I encountered twenty-five-years ago is still drawn to the dark side of my existence.

Surrounding arriving and departing passengers buzzed. The airport's crackling intercom announced the arrival of a Chicago flight. Amidst the commotion, Elaine wrapped her arms around her husband's neck and planted a big kiss on his surprised lips.

Returning her passionate caress, he realized she shared the same exuberance for the unknown challenges that lurk in shadows.

Holding him tight, she whispered, "So your business in LA requires a side-arm?"

Looking down into her wide brown eyes, he replied, "I don't know with certainty but am always prepared."

"Welcome to Los Angeles, Mister and Misses Kohl!" a greeter called out.

Still embraced, the Kohl's tuned. In a bright yellow golf shirt, baggy khakis and white tennis shoes, Tom Roche stood beaming. The retired CIA operative had aged considerably since his Saigon days. A close-cropped ring of white hair encircled a balding head. The wrinkles from failed anti-communist efforts etched deep around his dark eyes.

"Tom!" Elaine exclaimed releasing her man to hug her former boss.

"*Ami,*" Max said giving a firm handshake to his ex-employer.

"Jesus," Roche said, "Don't you two ever age. You both look the same as our Indochina days."

"That's kind of you to say Tom," Elaine responded.

"Here let me help you with the luggage," Roche offered reaching for a bag.

"I wouldn't take Max's Pullman," Elaine chuckled, "My husband is packing heat."

Roche laughed. "Still toting around that Soviet pistol, Max?"

Nodding Max questioned, "You still arm yourself with the Baby Browning?"

"Absolutely," Roche responded. "A craftsman doesn't throw away his tools when he retires."

Oblivious to the parting masses, the three covert alumni strutted through the crowed terminal.

"I'm looking forward to meeting Sandy," Elaine said to the luggage toting Roche. "I'm sorry that you and Cathy did not work out."

"Sandy had planned to greet you," Roche said, "But decided to take her son to Disneyland today."

"Her son?" Max questioned.

"Yes," Roche chuckled. "The second wife came with nine-year old baggage. He's not a bad kid," he added shifting the designer strap over his shoulder, "Just fucking annoying."

"Tom!" Elaine exclaimed as Max laughed.

"So tell me Elaine?" Roche asked. "What are your plans for the next couple of weeks?"

"Well, while the two of you try to recapture the excitement of your youth. I plan to check out the haute couture fashions along Rodeo Drive. Then next week plan to visit my mother in Harrisburg."

CHAPTER SEVEN

The dimly lit lounge at the airport Holiday Inn had a cool and inviting atmosphere. The late afternoon patrons consisted of a boisterous flight crew around a corner table and two businessmen at the bar. A bored young waitress made idle chatter about the end of her shift with an adolescent bartender in a black vest and bowtie. Behind the young servers, shelves of liquor bottles displayed in front of a large mirror glowed in the soft light.

The bartender flexed to attention as Max and Roche entered. The German and retired agent slid into a polished dark brown leather booth. The cocktail waitress approached. Leaning forward displaying ample cleavage, she lit a candle in a red frosted holder.

"Gentleman, what is your pleasure?" she asked.

"Jim Beam and water," Roche said and then looking at Max with a squint added, "A draft beer."

Pulling out several cigars, Max asked, "An ashtray as well, please."

At the end of a fat cigar a flame danced out of a tarnished Zippo lighter. Max took several satisfying tokes to ignite the beast. Placing the lighter encrypted with his former Legionnaire battalion on the table, he asked between puffs, "You're not smoking?"

Slumping into the squeaking leather cushion, Roche sheepishly responded, "Sandy made me quit."

Max shrugged. Leaning back, he blew a satisfying plume of smoke into the air.

"Fuck it," Roche mumbled. In the direction of the bar counter, he shouted, "Add a pack of Marlboros to the order."

"Ah that's the Major Roche I remember," Max commented, "Taking charge and toppling governments and anything else that opposes his agenda."

Roche paused as the drinks and red and white packet of nicotine were served. The waitress's firm bottom swayed back to her post. The two veterans touched glasses. Ceremonially they mumbled in unison, "To our friends we left behind."

After taking a sip of the chilled bourbon, Roche commented, "To tell you the truth, I don't know if I'm the same man who confidently strutted through the underbelly of Indochina. That's who I used to be. That is who I wished I still was. My dark side has been dormant since I retired from the Company."

"Is that why you wanted to do this?" Max asked as Roche tapped out a cigarette, "To once again feel the comforting power of a demon persona."

With closed eyes and a smoldering Marlboro between his lips, Roche inhaled the addicting vapors. After a gratifying exhale, he answered, "I'm doing this for past sins, not only my own but my governments." Taking a few long overdue quick puffs, he flicked the ash and continued. "Max what we are doing is highly illegal. If we are successful, we will be risking our lives. If we are caught substantial prison time."

"*Ami*, we have always risked our lives. That is nothing new. The solution for a lengthy incarceration is simple," Max said taking a swig of cold brew. "Just don't get caught."

"I've always appreciated your confidence Max. Maybe that is the reason you've eluded death all the years." Roche said miming a toast.

After nodding at the compliment, Max asked, "Can you give me an outline of the plan?"

Slamming down the last of his whisky, Roche waived the empty glass over his head. Once the bartender acknowledged the silent order, he answered, "A year of planning is about to be executed over the next four weeks. The less you know will be helpful for your legal defense if we are apprehend. What I can tell you is pretty simple. We secure the operational funding this Thursday over breakfast. You and I fly to Baltimore to secure the product." Roche paused as his bourbon and water arrived.

After taking a sip, he continued, "We make contact with the rest of the US team; assemble the players in Bangkok to collect the package and then..." With raised eyebrows he concluded, "The over the hill gang rides into the Laotian highlands for one last mission."

CHAPTER EIGHT

The air conditioner rattled. Morning sunlight advanced around the edges of thick drapes. A ray of invading light ran across the generic hotel room. Sitting on the unmade bed, Max flicked a black sock. He dressed quietly. Behind him under a painting of a California mission, Elaine slept. Always a late riser, he concluded glancing over his shoulder at his naked wife. Several pillows shielded her face. A starched white sheet did little to conceal her seasoned but still seductive frame. Max grinned, reflecting on their late night session. Their coupling was not routine. Or should I say couplings, he proudly pondered rubbing his chin. Standing in stocking feet, he picked up the holstered pistol off the nightstand. Strapping on the shoulder harness, he knew what had sparked his wife's passion. If I knew a covert mission would inflame her desires, he chuckled. I'd fly into Laos on a regular basis.

Pouring half a cup of water into the courtesy coffee pot, he anticipated strong brew out of the premeasured packet. I know it's selfish, he thought. But if Elaine wants coffee, she can order that thinly flavored java water from room service. What the Americans call coffee.

To the sound of random drips, Elaine stirred. "Is that coffee I smell?" she asked with a sleepy smile.

Damn, Max thought. It looks like I'm going to share after all. "Good morning sunshine," he said.

Hugging the pillows behind her head, Elaine propped herself up and questioned, "It was kind of sad seeing how much Roche has aged?"

Max took a sip of the precious coffee. Indifferently, he shrugged and handed his wife the warm cup. "He's got ten years on you," he informed.

Puckering her lips, she softly blew on the black misting surface. After taking a cautious sip, she asked, "I don't look that old?" she questioned. "Do I?"

There it is, Max thought. Elaine's vanity always floats just below the surface of all conversations. With a wink, he answered, "You are still turning heads sweetheart."

Ignoring the compliment, she patted the underside of her chin and asked, "It's my neck isn't it." Pinching soft skin, she frowned.

"I don't think your neck has anything to do with the lustful stares you invoke," He chuckled. "I suspect your admirers focus on other attributes."

Setting the ceramic cup on the nightstand, she sat up on the bed. Hugging her knees, she said, "Roche greeted us with an un-tucked golf shirt and tennis shoes. What is it with Americans and their casual dress? It as if my countrymen have traded appearance for comfort."

"You shouldn't criticize Roche's dress," Max responded. "He hasn't changed. Remember his signature aloha wear in Saigon?"

"That was different," Elaine responded. "In Southeast Asia, I used to admire his Hawaiian shirts and chinos. It was a defiant statement that he was an American. And in that tropical heat it was practical."

"The only difference between then and know is that he was young," Max informed.

Slowly nodding her head, she conceded, "We all were." In a serious tone, she added, "I know I'm not going to change your resolve. Believe me I tried over the years." Focused on her man, she continued, "After seeing a balding paunch bellied Roche, I'm concerned about your mission." Her voice crackled. With welling tears, she forged ahead, "I told you once I would never have to worry about you. I saw you in action. I witnessed your relationship with death. Even when he finds you he walks away. But Max... that was twenty years ago."

Max picked up the coffee cup and downed the last swallow. Bending down, he softly kissed her forehead. Lifting up her chin, he grinned into her teary brown eyes. "No need to worry, Misses Kohl. This is what I was trained to do. As far as performing like a young man, I'm surprised you would question my capabilities after our late night sessions."

Elaine cracked a smile and tenderly placed his hand next to her blushing cheek.

CHAPTER NINE

It was a cool sunny Southern California Thursday morning. Standing in front of the entrance to the Holiday Inn, Max puffed on the first cigar of the day. The automatic glass door behind him slide open and shut. To the swish of the electronic glass barrier, guest wandered in and out of the hotel. Two cab drivers leaned against idle yellow taxi's awaiting fares. Under the shaded hotel entrance canopy, a husband and wife in matching Hawaiian printed attire argued while loading their children into a weathered white sedan. A black Lincoln Towne car turned into the facility. Making is way up the curved entryway; the polished luxury vehicle's chrome hood ornament sparkled. It rolled to a curbside termination. Max's investigating stare into the vehicle, revealed his reflection in tinted glass. The front passenger door swung open. A young Asian in a black suit with dark sunglasses hopped out and opened the back door. A short pudgy old Asian man slowly pulled himself out of the back seat. With close-cropped silver hair, he blinked at the inquisitive glaring cab drivers. The Hawaiian dressed family stopped quarreling to gawk.

The chubby old man squinted in Max's direction. A big smile lit up across his weathered features. "Hello Maximilian," he blurted out with a raspy tone.

"Good Morning General," Max replied tossing a smoldering stogy into the gutter. Stepping down off the curb, Max embraced his old friend. There is no greater bound between men than the ones forged in combat, he thought. Warmly he squeezed his *copain*. He visualized a young Captain Yang cleaning a bloody blade after a brutal skirmish in Tonkin. That was almost thirty-years ago he realized breaking the embrace.

"So how is my German brother been after all these years?" Yang asked playfully patting Max on the shoulder.

"Life has been good Yang," Max said. After a brief reflection, he added, "I have a daughter."

"Then life has been good to both of us," Yang said. "I have nineteen children." Shrugging he informed. "Unfortunately due to the Americans relocation agreement, I could only keep one of my wives." Leaning into Max, he whispered, "I kept the young one."

"You always were a brilliant strategist," Max responded.

Chuckling Yang said, "And you were the finest marksman I ever saw." After a respectful bow, he asked, "Tell me Max, do you still arm yourself with the Tokarev?"

In front of a flight crew boarding an airport shuttle, Max un-holstered his concealed weapon and handed it to Yang. Yang griped the familiar weapon and commented, "For as much as I detest the Soviets, I must admit, they make the finest small arms on the planet." Extending his arm, he aimed the pistol at the star that crowned the scripted Holiday Inn signage. "I can still see you pivoting around that lone palm tree methodically picking off targets."

Humbly nodding, Max retrieved and holstered the weapon. The portals of a passing shuttle bus, framed the shocked expressions of the departing aircrew. I need to be more careful, he realized. Los Angeles is not the place to be brandishing a hand gun.

Yang's assistant retrieved a black leather gym bag from the back seat and stood at attention. Yang gestured with a sweeping hand towards the sliding glass door and said, "Let's go have breakfast with Major Roche and discuss our venture."

CHAPTER TEN

T he brightly lit hotel coffee shop was half full. Across the back wall, a stack of inviting white plates started a buffet line of stainless steel roll top chafing dishes. The aroma of crisp bacon and fresh coffee accented the cool air-conditioned atmosphere. A teenage hostess clutched large laminated menus. In a white golf shirt and Levis, Roche pointed her in the direction of a quiet corner table. Roche, Max and Yang sat down and simultaneously turned over ceramic coffee mugs. Yang's assistant stoically stood in the corner. The well-groomed Asian scanned the diner through dark sunglasses. The black gym bag firmly in his grasp.

"Any issues Major Roche?" Yang asked.

Roche delayed a response. A pudgy middle-aged waitress in a light blue white collared dress poured steaming black coffee from a glass pot. A plastic badge on the food stained gown introduced her as Bonnie. After nudging her customers to order the buffet, Bonnie conceded and took their individual breakfast request.

After a gentle sip of the hot java, Roche peered over the mugs misting surface and responded, "The package is ready for delivery and the seller is expecting payment."

Nodding in the direction of the black satchel Yang said, "The funds have been procured and..." he reached into his inside coat pocket and retrieved a fat white envelope. Sliding it across the table, he continued, "This should cover your teams travel expenses."

Roche nodded and tucked the envelope under the edge of a plastic place mat.

"Who ordered the oatmeal?" Bonnie questioned balancing a serving tray over an upturned palm. Yang nodded. "Yogurt and granola?" she asked. Roche flicked an acknowledging finger in her direction. "Then the three eggs, ham and hash-browns must be yours," she said placing the overflowing platter in front of Max. "Anything else gentlemen?"

The three men mumbled no thank you.

Turning she looked into the stone face of Yang's standing bodyguard. "Are you sure I can't get you anything?" She cheerily asked.

He did not answer. His chiseled features adorned with aviator sunglasses pivoted into Bonnie smiling purview.

Her expression melted into concern. "Well..." Bonnie squeaked, "Enjoy your breakfast Gentlemen."

With the barracks etiquette honed in his youth, Max used a fork and knife to dig into his greasy breakfast. Chomping on the ham, egg and fried potato mixture, he commented, "Oat meal and yogurt? Really?"

"Enjoy it while you can Fritz," Roche responded. "You are not that far behind us in age."

Yang's body guard flinched. Dropping the satchel, he reached into his jacket. Max mimicked the motion. Roche pushed back from the table. Yang turned to investigate.

A tall burly man in a workman's uniform walked towards the isolated table. An embroidered Pepsi logo patch over one breast pocket, Jimmy scripted in red stitching over the other. Disheveled gray hair covered his head. Coke bottle thick eyeglasses magnified and distorted his facial features. Showing the palms of his hands, he approached.

"It's alright," Yang said rising to hug the intruder. "Mister Jim always a pleasure."

Max looked at Roche and whispered, "Jim Dugan?"

Roche nodded.

This is Jim Dugan? Max thought; the former head of covert operations in the Laotian highlands. The man who organized a tribal army of over thirty thousand troops to fight communism. Why is Dugan dressed like a laborer? He wondered shifting uncomfortably in his chair.

After speaking to Yang in Laotian, Dugan reached across the table and said, "Hello Max."

Giving the hand a firm shake, Max grinned, "Good to see you again Dugan."

"Major Roche," Dugan said repeating the hand greeting gesture.

"Jim," Roche acknowledged.

"Mister Jim, please join us for breakfast." Yang said motioning towards an empty chair.

The men reseated themselves. Yang's bodyguard returned to his vigilant watch. Turning over a coffee mug, Dugan informed, "I just have time for a quick cup of joe. I need to get back to work."

"Bonnie!" Roche called out, "Some coffee please."

The shaken waitress raced to the table holding a misting glass pot.

"Thank you," Dugan said to the apprehensive retreating Bonnie. After scanning the coffee shop, Dugan said quietly. "I need to book my flight."

Roche retrieved the fat white envelope. Pulling out a healthy stack of hundred dollar bills, he relayed the currency to Dugan under the table. "That should get you to Bangkok."

"Thanks Tom," Dugan said hastily tucking the crisp bills in a pant pocket. After a gulp of coffee, he added, "I wished I had more time to catch up but I need to go." Standing, he flashed a wide smile. "We'll catch up in Bangkok. I know a great bar in Patpong to rehash the exaggerated tales from our youth."

Yang rose and quietly conversed with Dugan in a tribal dialect. Occasional laughter permeated from the dialogue.

Leaning into Roche, Max asked quietly, "What does Dugan do these days?"

Roche shrugged, "He delivers Pepsi."

"What happened?" Max asked frowning.

"He was in charge of a clandestine war that we lost," Roche snorted. "Now if we would have been victorious in Vietnam and on the smaller stage of Laos, Dugan would be living the good life in Southeast Asia. His self-imposed penalty for defeat, is delivering sugar water." Glancing over at Dugan and Yang's reunion, he continued. "The consequences for the failed US efforts in the Laotian Civil War were far more onerous on our hill-tribe allies." Swallowing hard, he mumbled. "Since the war ended in 1975 over one-hundred thousand Hmong have been exterminated by the Pathet Loa. When the Communist took power the vowed to hunt down the American Collaborators and their families." Shaking his head, he repeated, "American Collaborators."

"Can we count on Dugan?" Max questioned.

Nodding his head slowly, Roche pondered the question. "I don't see why not. He speaks French, Laotian and several tribal dialects. And he knows the remote terrain of Northern Laos better than any westerner."

Dugan clicked the heels of his work boots together. Standing erect, he bid adieu to his companions with a playful salute.

CHAPTER ELEVEN

Early morning sunlight got its first glimpse of the Maryland countryside. Rolling hills of green ebbed and flowed. Clusters of swaying trees accented white fenced grazing pastures. A burgundy rental car purred down a black asphalt country road. Leaning back in the passenger seat, a sleepy Max blinked at the light reflecting off a passing bright red barn. Inhaling the fresh plastic and leather scent of the new vehicle, he commented, "Now I know why you identified our Baltimore flight as a redeye."

Roche chuckled, "It's an efficient use of time. If there are no glitches this morning, we can catch the three o'clock flight back to LA."

"What do we need to be concerned about?" Max questioned.

Roche glanced into the back seat at the black leather gym bag. Focusing forward down the empty road flanked by tall trees, he responded, "Traveling with half-a-million in cash."

"Fair enough *Ami*," Max said.

"I trust Matthews," Roche commented. "However I've bought betrayal from good men with a lot less." Glancing at Max, he asked, "Do you remember Matthews from our Saigon days?"

"I remember him," Max answered. "He was a pretty boy. His thick black hair held in place with the greasy assistance of Brylcreem. He was quite the swordsman with the local ladies, I recall. Elaine told me he attempted to sway her on several occasions with his charm."

Roche snickered. "Don't hold his attempts on Elaine against him. Back in fifty-five, every male staffer at the US embassy was infatuated with the long-legged Elaine Favreau."

The vehicle decelerated. Roche turned off the asphalt serpent onto a gravel path. To the crunching of small stones, the car traveled adjacent to a split rail fence. Half a dozen horses in the distance foraged on deep green grass. The dusty country road terminated atop a hill. A massive two-story farmhouse surrounded by trees anchored an equestrian complex. A barn, outdoor arena, equipment shed and workers quarters basked in the rising sun.

"Is this spread Matthews?" Max asked.

"Sure is, been in his family for several generations." Roche answered parking the vehicle under the canopy of a towering white oak.

Exiting the automobile, Max inhaled crisp clean rural air. "This is beautiful country," he commented.

Roche nodded slinging the bag of money over his shoulder.

Ascending three creaking stairs, Max and Roche stood on a covered planked wooden porch that surrounded the white farmhouse. Roche's flexed knuckle rapped on the glass pane of a windowed door. No response invoked a harsher second rapping; rustling from within signaled success.

A petite hand pulled back the thin veiling curtain on the windowed door. A sleepy looking young Vietnamese girl blinked with a squint at Roche.

"We are here to see Matthews!" Roche shouted through the glass.

The young Asian greeter cracked open the door. Peering out of the crevice beneath a latched chain, she informed with a heavy accent, "Daddy asleep."

"*Well wake him up sweetheart,*" Roche barked in Vietnamese, "*and inform him Major Roche is here.*"

The door closed. The latch released. The barrier swung open. A barefoot young Asian woman stood on a polished wood floor. Her fisted hand clutched the front of a short yellow silk robe. The floral printed loose gown barely concealed the seductive taut skin of a twenty-year-old.

"I'll go wake daddy," She said. With the vigor of youth, she sprinted upstairs.

Roche commented out of the side of his mouth, "Looks like the Saigon swordsman is still active."

Max chuckled.

Assisted by a dark oak banister, John Matthews slowly descended the stairway. A protruding potbelly flowed out of a loosely cinched light blue terrycloth bathrobe. Matthews paused on his decent to rub his sleepy face. The wiping hand concluded by corralling wisps of gray hair dancing across the slick surface of his balding head. Looking down at his visitors, he snorted out a smile and said, "Morning boys, would you like a cup of coffee?"

"Sure John," Roche said.

Turning to look up the stairwell lined with paintings of posing horses, Matthews called out, "Cherry! A pot of coffee please."

Shuffling down the last few stair-treads in a pair of tattered slippers, Matthews yawned. On the polished wooden foyer flooring, he extended a hand, "Good to see you again Tom."

Roche gave his former colleague a hearty handshake, "As well John." Motioning in Max's direction, he asked, "Do you remember Max Kohl?"

An enlightened expression spread across Matthews's sleepy face. Giving Max a firm handshake, he said, "You're Elaine Favreau's German. It is a pleasure to meet the man who landed that stunning thoroughbred. You realize Max; you terminated my aspirations with that blonde beauty."

"So I've been told," Max mumbled.

To the pounding of bare-feet on wood treads, the three men looked up. Cherry in tight jeans and a tube top ran down the stairs. At the base of the stairwell, Matthews slapped her perfect bottom. She giggled prancing towards the kitchen. "During my tenure in Southeast Asia I became addicted to the local cuisine," a gloating Matthews informed.

In the rustic country kitchen, pots and pans dangled on chain tethers from a raised ceiling. Cherry slung back her long black hair and poured coffee into ceramic mugs adorned with sunflowers. Waiting for the hot brew, Max, Roche and Matthews sat in Windsor chairs around a circular oak table. The dinette set tucked in the alcove of a bay window. Through the paned glass, rolling grasslands extended to the tree line across the horizon. A nine-by-twelve inch manila envelope occupied the center of the glossy tabletop. The black leather gym bag containing half-a-million in US currency situated on a vacant chair.

The young Asian served the steaming mugs of java. Matthews wrapped his arm around her thin waist. Leaning back in the spindled back chair, he closed his eyes and puckered his lips. She obliged the solicitation with a quick peck. "Thanks for the coffee, Cherry," He said. In Vietnamese, he added, "*Why don't you go down to the stables for awhile? Your papa has some business to discuss and doesn't want to be disturbed.*"

"Ok daddy," she said scurrying out of the kitchen.

Matthews inhaled the aromatic steam from a misting mug and let out a pleasurable sigh. Sipping the coffee, he slid the beige envelope in Roche's direction and pointed at the money satchel. Receiving a nod from Roche, Max reached over and grabbing the wrinkled leather bag tossed it into the host's lap.

After a quick peek into the satchel, Matthews held the bag with extended arms. Bouncing the contents, he commented, "Seems about right." Dropping the bag to the floor, he added, "You realize Tom. I'm giving you an employee discount."

Insincerely Roche shrugged pulling out a pair of reading glasses. With the spectacles perched on the end of his nose, he opened the envelope and began to read the Bill of Lading. Scanning the boxes on the form, he read; *Port of Loading-Karachi/Pakistan; Place of Delivery-Bangkok/Thailand; Exporter-Security Shipping (PVT) LTD; Consignee- Hilltribe Relief Agency. Description of Packages and Goods-Partial Container: Two (2) Crates Agricultural Implements and Spare Parts; Shipped on Board- 06/12/1982.* Checking the shipping date again, Roche peered over the top of the reading glasses and questioned, "The package has already been shipped?"

A smirking Matthews responded, "I knew you'd come through with the funds." Taking a sip of coffee, he added, "Besides if you didn't, I could easily mark up the price for the Stinger Missiles in Asia. Like I said, at two-hundred-thousand dollars apiece you are getting a discount."

"Tell me about the *Kalashnikov's*?" Max asked.

The pot bellied Matthews responded, "Your five-hundred large bought you two portable surface-to-air missiles, two-thousand AK-47s and six-hundred-thousand rounds of ammunition. The Stingers were difficult to skim off the *mujahedeen* supply line flowing into the Afghan civil war. The assault rifles, a piece of cake." Slowly rising Matthews walked over and refilled his sunflower mug. Standing in the middle of the kitchen with the terrycloth robe draped over his soft plump torso, he continued, "There are so many weapons being funneled to those Muslim freedom fighters from the US, the Brits, Saudis, Egyptians and even the Chinese, that the global cost for an AK-47 has dropped substantially." Pausing he squinted at Max and said, "Just so were clear, the automatic weapons you procured are the Chinese copy of the Russian AK-47."

"I assumed so," Max said, "The Chinese Type 56 is just as reliable as its Soviet counterpart."

"So tell me boys, what are you up to?" Matthews asked. "Tom you were always more noble than me. I can assume you're not enhancing your retirement."

Leaning back in the wooden chair, Roche studied his aging colleague and responded, "Your strongest suit during our time together in Saigon was your intuition. So you tell me."

"Thanks for the softball," Matthews responded. "You're planning to take the munitions *across the fence* to arm another army of *carbine soldiers*.

Roche nodded and mumbled, "Laos is the destination and the small in stature boy partisans of the Hmong are the beneficiaries." Chuckling he added, "Your right; it was a softball." Glancing at the bill of lading, he asked, "There was one other piece of hardware I requested?"

Grinning Matthews responded, "Ah yes the long rifle. I think you will be pleased." Raising his coffee mug, he said, "Be careful my friends, we are not as young as we used to be."

CHAPTER TWELVE

Interstate 405 was packed. Under the Southern Californian sun, the compilation of colorful vehicles flowed north and south at just under sixty-five-miles-per-hour. Nuzzled within the metallic southern stream, Roche hit the brakes on the midnight green rental car. "Son-of-a-bitch," he hollered flipping an extended finger at a light utility vehicle.

Max chuckled, "I knew your dark side would eventually come to the surface."

"Do me a favor Max," Roche said. "When I pull up alongside that non-signaling bastard, pull out your pistol and blow his head off."

"I like to oblige you Major, but we are coming up to the Garden Grove exit," Max said.

"Just as well," Roche mumbled. Glancing over his shoulder, he began the tedious task of merging towards the off ramp.

The vehicle decelerated. Roche asked, "So when is the last time you saw your adopted family?"

Leaning back in the wine-red upholstery, Max smiled. He thought about Loc and Mei. "I guess it was about six maybe seven years ago." Looking at Roche, he asked, "When was the fall of Saigon?"

"April 30, 1975," Roche snorted.

"So it was the winter of seventy-five. Elaine and I came to the States to see how the new immigrants were acclimating to life in Michigan," Max clarified. "I want to thank you once again for getting them airlifted out of Vietnam."

Roche nodded.

"Why Michigan?" Max questioned.

Roche chuckled, "The original relocation policy was to scatter the Indochina refugees across the country. But it didn't take long for them to resettle together in ethnic enclaves mostly in Texas and California."

"Judging from the winter weather in Michigan, I can see why they chose to relocate," Max commented. Looking at the passing retail businesses lining the street, Max thought about Lan, the short pudgy firecracker. "But I haven't seen Lan since our Saigon days," he mumbled. "That's over twenty years ago."

"Lan is in California?" Roche questioned.

"Yes," Max answered. "She immigrated a couple of years ago as one of the *boat people.*"

The recognizable retailers flanking the thoroughfare thinned. Passing a boarded up automotive service facility, Roche turned into a small strip center. K J's Lounge anchored the center as an end unit. A door propped open by a bar stool invited customers into the dark windowless slump block watering hole. Adjacent to KJ's was the Park Avenue Laundromat. Visible through a large pane glass window, frontend loading washers and dryers lined the walls of this narrow deep coin-operated space. A few active machines churned clothing behind round portholes. A bright red for lease sign and a phone number adorned the adjacent storefront. In front of the vacancy, Roche turned and parked between faded lines.

Examining the last retailer, Max beamed. A scripted neon sign read, 'Isabelle's Nails'. Exiting the vehicle, Max stretched in warm California sun. Looking at Roche over the car roof, he asked, "Can you give me a minute before you enter?"

"Sure Max," Roche responded with a knowing nod.

Max took a deep breath and shook his arms. Slightly composed, he opened the glass door to the nail salon. The jingle of a dangling bell announced his arrival. A pungent, irritating chemical odor caused him to snort. Along the wall to his right were six manicure stations, four of them active. Seated and facing him from behind Formica tabletops, four Vietnamese girls in white lab coats plied their trade. Goose neck lights illumined the hands of a gum popping American teenager and three rather large female customers. The patrons sat in swivel rolling chairs.

The Vietnamese girls painted, polished and filed nails. The shy Asian girls giggled and whispered amongst themselves while stealing glances of Max. Along the other wall was a small coach, two cushioned chairs and a coffee table. Dog eared magazines cluttered the small table top. Over the waiting area, four small pictures hung on a large white wall. Max smiled at the three framed French magazine covers featuring his daughter Eva. The other picture seemed out of place. It was a black and white headshot photo of an American actress, identified by a label on the frame as Tippi Hedren.

"I'll be with you shortly," a heavy accented familiar female voice called out from behind a beaded curtain.

The beads parted. Mei rushed out. She froze in her tracks and stared at Max with an open mouth. Her signature long black silk locks were gone. A bouffant hair style now surrounded her angelic features. Time had been kind to the petite beauty. A white lab coat graced her slender frame. Tears welled up in her dark gemstone eyes.

"Hello little sister," Max said softly.

Mei burst into tears and rushed to embrace the German. The Vietnamese nail techs began cackling amongst themselves. The customers seemed annoyed but curious as they swiveled around to investigate.

After all these years, she still has it Max thought. He felt the spark of life that was Mei.

Breaking the embrace, Mei looked down at the floor and brushed the tears away. Glancing up at the gawking employees, she said in Vietnamese, *"This is my big German brother Max."* Pointing at the framed magazine covers on the wall, she informed, *"He is the father of my famous niece Eva."* Respectfully the Asian employees bobbed their heads and smiled before quietly gossiping amongst themselves.

"Are you somebody famous?" questioned the beak-nosed frizzy haired teenager. Smacking on a wad of gum, she waited for a response.

"No, we are just old friends," Max responded politely.

Mei looked up at Max with her distinctive mischief smile. Patting his chest, she whispered, "You didn't want to tell her about your famous walk out of Isabelle."

"Ah, Mei," Max exclaimed kissing the top of her head, "You sure haven't changed."

To the jingling of the door's hanging bell, Roche entered the salon. Mei squinted into the American face she hadn't seen in over twenty years. "Major Roche?" she questioned softly.

"Jesus, Mei," Roche said extending his arms. "I haven't changed that much."

Mei hugged her American benefactor, "Thank you for everything *Ami*," she said. Slapping him playfully with the back of her hand, she chuckled, "Next time make it easier for these old eyes and wear one of your bright flower shirts." Looking at both men, she added, "We did not expect you so soon. Loc is at our other salon with Lan. Let me call them?"

"Other salon?" Max questioned.

Leaning into the German, she commented, "We learn from our ice-cream parlors in Saigon, the more lines you have in the water; the more fish you catch."

As Mei, rushed into the back room, Roche mumbled, "What an amazing woman."

"*Ami* ?" Max asked pointing to the studio photo of Tippi Hedren. "Do you know who this is?"

Standing next to Max, Roche pulled out his reading glasses and examined the black and white image. Stepping back, he took off his spectacles, "That is the patron saint of Vietnamese nail salons. About seven years ago the American actress went into a refugee tent city with her personal manicurist and trained about twenty Vietnamese immigrants in the fine art of hand and nail cosmetics. The unselfish gesture to aid unskilled refugees who could not speak English has become a Vietnamese cottage industry." Grinning he added, "Mei and Loc already have two locations."

"Loc and Lan are on their way," Mei announced. "I know how my German brother likes beer, so I told them we would be waiting at KJ's."

CHAPTER THIRTEEN

W alking past the Laundromat, Mei squatted down and picked up a discarded fast food wrapper. Wadding up the trash, she led Max and Roche through the propped open door of KJ's Lounge. A skinny old man perched on a barstool stared down at a sparkling glass of light caramel liquor. In the corner, three off duty painters in white speckled bib-overalls slammed down beers from long-necked bottles. Behind the counter, the thirty something bartender looked up from a folded newspaper with concern.

"I already spoke to Loc," the bartender said quietly to Mei, "he gave me until next Tuesday."

"I know," Mei responded sternly handing him the crinkled wrapper. "This is not about rent Kevin. My friends and I are customers."

Kevin smiled tossing the litter under the counter. Rubbing his hands on an apron, he asked, "What is your pleasure?"

"A pitcher of beer," Max replied.

After filling a plastic jug, Kevin pulled a cellophane bag of shelled peanuts from a metal clipped display. As Roche reached for his wallet, Kevin shock his head. Placing a stack of plastic cups, the foaming jug and bar nuts on the counter, he winked at Mei and said quietly, "No charge."

Mei insincerely nodded.

"You own this center?" Roche questioned pulling back a heavy nicked and scratched wooden chair.

Placing the beer and cups on a wobbly table, Mei responded, "Bank owns the property now. Rent from bar and coin laundry pays our mortgage." Pouring the cold brew, Mei added with delight, "Nail salon very profitable with no rent."

Max took a seat and lit a cigar. After a few quick puffs, he placed his tarnished lighter on the table.

Mei closed her eyes and bathed in the familiar smoldering odor. "Every time I smell a good cigar I think of you Max." Picking up the old Zippo, she ran her thumb across the engraving: *3e Bataillon / 13e Demi-Brigade de la Legion Etrangere* (the 3rd Battalion / 13th Foreign Legion Half-Brigade.) "The brave men of the three-thirteenth from Isabelle attacked the Vietminh with no ammunition," she mumbled. Looking at her companions, she asked, "Do you think anyone still remembers that?"

"Hell," Roche commented, "Most Americans have never heard of Dien Bien Phu."

"We still remember," Max said. "And that's what is important."

Mei squinted at Max and asked, "Are you going to do it? If not I will."

Roche looked puzzled as Max stood. The German lifted his plastic glass of beer towards the ceiling. The boisterous painting crew went silent. Kevin put down his newspaper. The old alcoholic pivoted around on the barstool to investigate. In a commanding emotionally laced tone Max said, "To the brave men of the third battalion, thirteenth brigade Foreign Legion."

"I'll drink to that," slurred the drunk at the bar.

The painters displayed more refined barroom etiquette by politely raising amber bottles of Budweiser.

"Kevin," Max called out, motioning towards the bar's patrons, "A round of drinks for my friends."'

Kevin acknowledged the order with a two finger salute.

"Still picking up bar tabs partner," said the small statured silhouette standing in the open doorway.

"Still drinking milkshakes?" Max responded.

Loc stepped into the dark enclave and hugged his former comrade in arms. Silver temples garnished his dark-brown hair. The tribesman's pale yellow boarding on white complexion showed the creases of age.

"Hello Loc," Roche said embracing the Black Tai. "Looks like you are living the American dream." Patting the short tribesman on the shoulder, he added, "You immigrated six years ago and already own two salons and a strip center."

Tipping his head sideways, Loc grinned, "You know Roche in Indochina I always had a hard time comprehending your Cajun French. And now that I speak English, I realize after twenty-five years you just talk with a funny accent."

Roche chuckled, "It's a quirk of the Louisiana tribe."

Loc leaned down and gave a quick peck on the lips to Mei.

"Where is Lan?" She asked.

Smirking Loc mumbled, "She is at the salon putting on fresh make-up for her reunion with Max." Turning to the German, he informed, "Max, I must warn you Lan is very excited about your visit. She has been driving us and her husband crazy since we got your call."

Max took a deep breath. *After all these years, I was hoping her infatuation would have faded away. I still regret my one and only coupling with the little spark-plug twenty-five years ago*, he realized. "It's probably a good thing I didn't bring Elaine," Max said reflecting on Lan's disdain for his American lover.

"It's a good thing for Elaine," Loc said playfully as Mei chuckled.

The fearless Lan peeked into the open doorway of KJ's. Her head retreated and after a long pause, she strutted into the bar. She was heavy. A silk floral printed dress stretched tightly around a fluid torso. Her black hair with wisp of gray teased into a high riding cotton-candy bouffant. Thick theatrical make-up filled the crevices of age. Bright red glossy lipstick distorted the size of her tiny mouth.

Max looked through the middle-aged women. He saw the young Lan who swung a broken coke bottle at the street thugs taunting their grandfather. *This is the girl who fed shell shocked Frenchmen during the Communist bombardment of Dien Bien Phu*, he reflected. *This was Lan. This is my little sister.* Stepping forward, he met her in the middle of the lounge and squeezed her tight. *He always cared for her*, he realized, just not romantically.

"Bonjour Lan," Max said trying to ignore the strong floral scent of cheap perfume.

"I speak English," Lan said defiantly placing fisted hands on wide hips. "I American now." Tilting her head, she probed, "You miss me Max."

"Of course I do," Max replied.

"You still with that large white woman?" She questioned.

"I'm still married to Elaine," Max responded.

"I forgot her name," Lan informed. "She give you many children?"

"We have one daughter, Eva," Max answered.

"Only one," Lan pondered rubbing her chin. "Very pretty daughter," she said with a nod. "I see magazine covers, she very attractive. Look like you, not like her mother."

Max chuckled, Lan hadn't changed. "So tell me about your husband?" Max asked.

"We have four boys," Lan said sticking out her chin. "My husband good man," Leaning into Max, she whispered, "But he a little slow."

Mei hugged Lan's arm. "Little sister," she said in Vietnamese. "We'll catch up with Max and Mister Roche latter. They have important business to discuss."

"I understand," Lan replied. She quickly planted a big wax red kiss on Max's cheek and whispered, "Thank you for everything big brother."

CHAPTER FOURTEEN

"Well, it's good to see Lan hasn't changed." Max said re-ignited his stogy.

Roche tapped out a cigarette from a red and white pack and pointed the exposed nicotine stick at Loc.

"No thanks," Loc responded shaking his head, "I quit."

The corner of Roche's mouth unsheathed the exposed cigarette. "So did I," he mumbled. Using Max's lighter, he detonated his renewed addiction. After a satisfying drag, he called out, "Kevin a Beam and water, please."

"I'll be right with you," the bartender replied.

The sunlight pouring into the lounge retreated. Dusk approached. KJ's cliental shifted as the happy-hour crowd punched in. Lining the counter the drinking crowd consisted of locals stopping by for a quick snort. After a flurry of activity, Kevin brought over the complimentary bourbon and another foaming pitcher of draft beer.

As Max refilled his plastic cup, he said, "You don't have to do this Loc."

"Neither do you," Loc responded taking a sip of cold brew.

"Can you still move undetected like a cat?" Max asked grinning.

"Old cats are just as silent," Loc answered, "Just a little slower." Leaning back, he asked, "Tell me Max, can you still get off three shots and make it sound like one blast?"

"I've seen a lot in my long years Max," Roche interjected, "But nothing like your lightning-quick marksmanship skill during the Battle of Saigon."

"Thanks *Ami*, but those reflexes faded with my youth." Max responded. Clenching a smoldering stogy in a tight grin, he added, "I still can hit every target."

"I know you can partner," Loc said nursing a beer. "I've never seen you miss."

"Once again Loc, you will be donating the next month to the cause," Roche cautioned. "That's thirty days give or take if we are successful." Exposing his palms, he added, "If unsuccessful your commitment could be extended with a lenient sentence to ten to twenty years."

A focused Loc glanced back and forth between his companions. "With all due respect brothers," He said gruffly, "don't question my dedication to this undertaking again. I'm a Black Tai whose village was annihilated in the 50's because my people sided with the French against communism." Looking at the German, he said, "Max you could always have gone back to Nuremberg." Glancing at the American, he commented, "And Roche you could always return to your beloved New Orleans. I no longer have a homeland. In Saigon I was wealthy. Mei and I had six ice-cream parlors. Our children went to private schools. But I was still a Meo, a savage. Do you have any idea how offensive that term is? It sounds like the noise a cat makes." Solemnly Roche and Max shook their heads. "It's never been easy being Hmong. When the French and Americans returned home after their failed Southeast Asian excursions they abandoned their hill tribe allies to communist reprisals." Tossing back a gulp of beer, he squeezed the plastic cup. "What I don't understand is the West's lack of compassion or even acknowledgement of the chemical extermination being inflicted on the Hmong?"

"It's called politics," Roche responded leaning back in the hard wood chair. "Where your culture values honesty, our politicians focus on getting re-elected. Politicians bend the narrative to fit their agenda. If that doesn't work, they...what's the word...lie. And if you get caught in lie, you play the trump card; call for an investigation." Leaning forward, he translated, "Investigation means you delay the truth to a point in time when nobody cares."

"I still don't understand?" Loc questioned with a puzzled face. "Why would the US want to ignore the plight of their loyal Hmong allies?"

"The communist regimes of Laos and Vietnam do not have the capabilities of producing chemical weapons." Roche informed. "That points the accusing finger at the Soviets. The previous administration wanted to enhance the integrity of the USSR. A strategic arms limitation treaty signed by Russians who test biological weapons on the Hmong has no credibility. The music plays on, the politicians dance. The investigation into the Yellow Rain that killed tens-of-thousands of Hmong get's extended as inconclusive. Bee pollen is suggested as a possible natural explanation. Common pesticides were proposed. The motivation and reliability of the opium trafficking Hmong gets questioned. All the while the bureaucratic gears grind slowly towards a conclusion that nobody but the Hmong want to hear." Roche sighed and slammed down his whisky to dilute the bitter taste of reality.

"Call it bee excrement if you like," Loc said. "But nobody pisses on my brethren without paying a price."

"Once again honor and commitment is only found in the trenches of common soldiers," Max said miming a toast.

"Let's do this," Loc said.

CHAPTER FIFTEEN

The air was dry, the sun a simmering dot. Dust devils danced on the adjacent unplowed fields. A warm breeze carried the drone of a single engine biplane across the flat southwestern terrain. At the end of each monotonous pesticide strafing, the crop dusting pilot flirted with the power line obstacle at the edge of the cotton field. Like a row of headless robots, the transmission towers stood defiantly with outstretched arms teasing him to come closer. Not today, Buck thought releasing the last load of aerial application. Heading for home, he bid adieu to the power line guardians with a perfectly executed aileron roll. Coming out of the three-hundred-and-sixty-degree revolution, he shifted his weight in the tight open-air cockpit. Sciatic pain ran down his leg. I'm getting too old for this, he realized.

On the outskirts of Casa Grande, Arizona, Buck landed the agricultural biplane. It was late afternoon, the hottest time of day during the hottest time of year. The sheet metal facility looked deserted. Tumbleweeds converged around the rusting skeletal remains of antiquated farm implements. The only sign of life, the rattling of an overworked window air conditioner. The lanky Texan hopped out of the tiny plane. Standing on the powdered dust of the dirt runway, he stretched. Reaching into the leg pocket of army fatigues, he pulled out a pint bottle of Jim Beam. Examining the golden bourbon in the harsh sunlight, he grinned. Closing his eyes, he took a healthy swig of the warm liquid. Sloshing it in a closed mouth, he cleansed his senses of the insecticide taint. After a satisfying swallow, he headed with a slight limp towards the sparkling corrugated sheet metal oasis. The shade of the hangar offered some relief. Entering the facility, he froze. Three men stepped out of the back office. "Fuck me," he mumbled grinning.

"Hello cowboy," a stocky blond said with a German accent.

"Max!" Buck exclaimed. "I thought you were dead."

Next to Max, a balding man with a slight paunch in a Hawaiian shirt and chinos laughed, "Aw come on Buck, didn't you learn in Indochina that our kraut brother is invincible."

"Major Roche," Buck blurted out. Squinting at the small Asian, he added, "Loc!" Swallowing back surfacing emotion, he said with a crackle, "Its good seeing you guys again."

"We are in search of a bush pilot and thought you might have an interest," Max said wiping a moist brow. "Do you know of a cool dark venue that serves beer, where we can discuss our proposal?"

Beside the interstate highway, a solitary windowless adobe structure cast a shadow across a pockmarked parking lot. A bleached red font sign identified the establishment as The Tavern. In front of the watering hole, a dozen motorcycles stood at a slight angle. The dust-covered bikes had bedrolls strapped to handle bars and wrapped around passenger backrests. Leaving the cool comfort of the air-conditioned rental car, Max examined the row of muscular chrome beast. A German Iron Cross adorned a towering backrest.

"Bring back memories of your Third Reich days?" Roche asked.

"It's funny," Max said, "how the German military symbol of honor and valor has been denigrated to represent rebellion and non-conformity."

"If it's any consolation, this part of the motorcycle is called a sissy bar." Roche informed.

Turning Max said, "Let's go drink *Ami.*"

Max opened the blistered wood door. A blast of cold air engulfed the four Indochina alumni. Sunlight and the late afternoon heat flowed past the men into the dark enclave. A startled biker gang looked up from lighted pool tables to investigate. A jukebox along the back wall produced a static laced rendition of a popular tune. Behind a long bar counter lined with empty barstools, a tense middle-aged female server smiled at the new arrivals.

"Shut that fucking door," growled one of the bikers.

Ignoring the harsh welcome, Buck pointed to an empty table and said, "The beers are on me."

"I'll take a coke," Loc said.

Buck nodded and approached the barkeep. "A pitcher of Bud, a coke, a shot of Jack and a pack of Marlboros," he ordered.

After paying the tab with his last twenty dollars, Buck joined his friends with the drinks. Examining the rough clientele, he asked, "Does this remind you of the King Cobra bar in Laos?"

"No," Max responded filling his glass. "The patrons at the King Cobra were professional killers, this gang of punks, amateurs."

To the laughter of his friends, Max downed the small glass of beer. "I don't understand you Americans, your coffee tastes like thin tea and your beer like soda water."

Dropping the shot of Jack Daniels into his beer glass, Buck responded, "I know what you mean Max. That is why I drink beer with a whisky garnish."

"So what has the best Air America bush pilot been up to the last twenty years," Roche asked.

"It's been rough," Buck responded sipping on the boilermaker. "With two ex-wives, four estranged children and the IRS up my ass, I've been forced to seek employment that pays in cash or under the table."

Leaning back, Max pulled out a cigar. Lighting it he took several puffs. "Our proposal meets your compensation requirements, however..." pausing, he leaned across the table and added, "It's illegal and besides your life you may be risking jail time."

Snickering Buck responded, "Just like the old days." Tapping on a red and white pack of Marlboros, he inquired, "What does it pay?"

Looking at Roche and then Loc, Max responded "We'll we're not charging for our involvement. However the services for a seasoned pilot that's familiar with the various landing strips scattered across the Laotian highlands pays ten-thousand dollars."

Buck lit a cigarette, after a puff he said, "The ten thousand would help with my IRS situation. But it won't solve my child support problems."

Squinting he questioned. "If you're not getting paid for this venture, why are you doing it?"

Max shrugged, "We all have our reasons," he said. "As for me, a friend asked me once to look on his family from time to time. His adopted family was the Hmong"

Smiling Buck said, "I wish I didn't have to charge you, but given my circumstance I have to." Downing his drink, he added, "I'll do it for the ten large."

"How much do you need cowboy?" Max asked.

"Fifteen will get me close." Buck responded.

"Then let's make it twenty," Max said.

"Thanks Max," Buck nodded. "I appreciate the generosity. However I must warn you I'm not the man I use to be." After a hard swallow, he confessed, "I have a problem with the bottle."

Reaching over Roche placed a hand on Buck's shoulder and said, "Who doesn't have a drinking problem after what we did in Indochina."

"Well now that that's settled," Max said standing up. "Let me get another pitcher of this watered down American beer."

Max turned away from the bar counter with a fresh pitcher of beer. A greasy biker dipped a shoulder colliding into the German.

The thug barked, "You better watch where you're going pops."

Max brushed off the encounter.

"Didn't you hear me old man?" the outlaw growled. Accenting distain, he shoved the middle-aged blond in the back.

A drenched hand clutched a half-full pitcher of beer. Max squinted at the instigator. The obese biker was wide. A sleeveless denim vest exposed a grim-reaper motif tattooed across a chest and bloated belly. Just below the beer gut, a holstered revolver hung at an angle. Long black curly hair flowed from a balding head. The particles of past meals laced into the fabric of a scruffy beard. The thug stood defiantly puffing out his decorated chest.

Max placed the glass jug on the bar. Shaking his wet hand, he reached over the counter for a bar towel. Slowly he began wrapping his right hand with the moist rag. Come on and bite he thought. Take the bait. The thug glanced at the towel wrapped decoy. Max unleashed three lighting quick left jabs.

Nothing stings more than unexpected blows, Max thought. Stepping into the staggering tree trunk, he released a cocked rag cushioned right-hand pile-driver.

The biker flew backwards. His face exploded. The back of his head slammed hard into a hanging billiard table light. Down lighting swayed back and forth. The thug collapsed face up on the stained and tattered green felt pool table. Disconnected eyes danced in the pulsing light. Blood flowed out of a shattered nose. Shaking off the towel wrapping, Max grabbed the moaning broken nose victim's revolver. Wearing the mask of death, he scanned the outlaw biker gang calculating a shooting sequence. Trying to prioritize retaliatory threats amongst the targets all he saw was the wide-eyed fear of exposed charlatans.

To the twang of jukebox music, Satan's Disciples slowly began to migrate towards the exit. The last two disciples assisted their bloody fallen leader into the blistering sunlight.

"Shut that fucking door," Loc barked.

Tossing the small revolver onto the concrete floor, Max shook his bruised knuckles. Turning towards his standing companions, he started to laugh.

"What's so funny?" Roche asked holstering his Baby Browning.

"Satan's Disciples?" Max snorted.

The covert team appreciated the irony.

The weathered but relieved female bartended placed two foaming pitchers of cold brew on the table. "These are on the house boys," she informed. Quietly she probed, "Who are you guys?"

Grabbing a pitcher, Max drank from the jug. After several gulps, he smiled with a frothy mustache and replied, "Common soldiers, ma'am."

CHAPTER SIXTEEN

Black clouds challenged the rising sunlight. In the cool morning air of the Laotian highlands, a Hmong woman in a grungy green bandana crawled out of a jagged rock hole. Balancing a baby in her arms, she looked at the dark sky. "The summer rains?" she questioned softly to the squatting sentry.

On his haunches using a weathered M-16 for balance, Va-Meng looked up at the sooty faced woman and nodded. She smelled of smoke. We all carry the smoldering stench of the cave fires, he realized. The woman scurried back into the ground. Scanning the mountainous tropical vista, he caught the scent of the approaching rain. The tail end of the monsoon season, we will attempt to escape, he rationalized. The sanctuary of the cave is a blessing but it lulled me into complacency. There is no future for my family hiding in a hole, he concluded. Chai is thirteen years old and becoming a woman. The two White Hmong families we share the cave with have no boys. The only thing my Black Tai family has in common with the other occupants is fear of the communist predator. Gen will be eight and old enough to carry his own weight. And Nu; he paused with pride visualizing his eleven year old son. Even if the family does not survive the journey to Thailand, he realized, the feisty Nu would make it. My family, he thought picturing his wife. Shaking his head, he closed his eyes. His empty stomach churned. I haven't touched May La in years, he realized. The haunting image of her forced coupling with the Vietnamese occupiers surfaced. He spat in disgust. Our bond now is one of survival, he concluded but she will always be the mother of my children.

From out of the ground emerged two of Va-Meng's White Hmong neighbors. They placed pots and jars around the caves entrance in anticipation of rain. In black cylindrical hats, May La and Chai climbed out of the cavern. The mother and daughter bowed in respect to the head of their household. Va-Meng's women unfolded a large tarp as drops of precipitation began to fall. Frayed hemp cords secured the canvas sheet between trees to catch the precious water. The summer rain accelerated.

Water and fire, Va-Meng thought tilting his head back with an open mouth. His parched tongue caught large refreshing drops. The cleansing downpour washed his soiled face. Our food is meager but hot. The Hmong women undressed and placed their raggedy clothing under the protection of the stretched tarp. Under the flow of the morning shower they washed. Out of the thick surrounding growth, Nu plodded up the soggy steep grade. His black frayed smock and trousers were soaked. In the drawstring of his waistband, the boy proudly displayed a French revolver. Seeing his father, the boy lifted up four small dead songbirds. My son and his sling shot will feed us for another day, Va-Meng realized. Another day of substance to ponder our escape, another day to wait for the Americans to return, he thought.

As the young hunter approached, Va-Meng stood. With an extended arm, the boy presented the dead birds. To show his appreciation, Va-Meng rubbed his son's moist hair. To get his wife's attention, he whistled and displayed the game that required cleaning. May La acknowledged her responsibility with a submissive bow.

Leaving the birds on a wet rock, father and son got out of the rain. Through the small opening, limited light flowed into the cavern. The high jagged limestone ceiling stained with the soot from cooking fires. Palm fronds carpeted the rough floor. A fire pit deep with white ash glowed in a dark corner. The other inhabitants stirred in the shadows. The endless whine of babies echoed off the enclosed coarse rock. A hand on his son's shoulder Va-Meng paused as his eyes adjusted. The shadows faded. The forms of the displaced slowly appeared. No one spoke. The hunted quickly learn the virtue of silence. An old man sat slowly scratching the scabs of his balding head. A middle-age man poked the smoldering coals of the fire pit. Ash rose around the end of the probe. A woman tenderly bounced a sweat glistening child. The trembling baby arched its back trying to free itself from the comforting grasp. Va-Meng realized the convulsing infant cried for the numbing pleasure of opium. Addiction was the cost of quieting toddlers during the journey to this den.

Va-Meng nudged his son towards their family's corner residence. They shuffled forward. During the summer months, a morning beam of light terminated over their grass mats. The overcast skies limited today's glow. The filtered light still illuminated the smoky haze floating over the youngest family member. With the butt of his weapon, Va-Meng poked his reclining eight-year old son. Gen leapt to his feet with a bow. He took his father's automatic weapon. Sitting cross-legged, the boy used a rag to wipe the moisture from the tarnished weapon. Nu sat beside his brother and cleaned his antique revolver.

Va-Meng ran his fingers through wet hair. Seven rounds, he thought studying the rag stroking his weapon. Two bullets left in the handgun, he reflected glancing at Nu drying off the pistol. Is that enough for the journey south, he pondered. Does it even make a difference? He wondered. Va-Meng reached for a glass mason jar perched on a rocky ledge over the family's quarters. A rusty lid sealed a curled document wrapped in wax paper. He twisted the container in the ray of sunshine. The jar sparkled. If the Americans return, all I have to do is show them this, he thought.

CHAPTER SEVENTEEN

Spewing white smoke, a tuk-tuk wove through the night traffic maze of Bangkok. Colorful overhead neon lighted signage cast reflecting shades of red, blue and green. The glowing compilation of coughing metal slowly surged forward. The sputtering motorized three-wheeled rickshaw slid past and overcrowded diesel bus in search of a clear path.

Max grasped onto the flimsy tricycle's canopy for balance. A white handkerchief shielded his nose and mouth. Beside him, Loc leaned back on the padded vinyl bench and snorted at engulfing toxic fumes.

Goosing the throttle, the driver hopped over the curb and onto the sidewalk. The unorthodox exit startled six tiny men with expensive cameras dangling from neck straps. The Japanese tourist began snapping photos of the baby taxi. The flash of a Nikon blinded the exiting German. Regaining sight, Max saw the Japanese photographers bowing apologetically. *"Es machts nichts,"* he muttered to the retreating camera totting pack.

Max examined the congested street. So this is the famous Patpong, he thought. A bustling night market occupied the narrow thoroughfare. The real draw flanked the brightly lit tourist stalls hawking silk ties, knock-off watches, T-shirts and wood carved elephants. Above the kiosk canopies, the red light district's bars solicited customers with catchy names. Hot Stuff, The Kings Table and the inviting Lucky Pussy sparkled in scripted neon. At the end of the street, Max spotted The Knock Out Bar.

"What do you think partner?" Max asked placing his hand on Loc's shoulder.

"Sex is like opium," Loc answered. "There is always a demand for the product."

"You want to see show?" asked a teenage boy in white short sleeved shirt and dirty slacks, "Very good show; very cheap." He produced a large cardboard sign and mispronounced a laundry list of show features, "Ping-pong valls, Vazor Vlades, Darts, Vannans..."

"No thanks," Max said a waving dismissing hand.

"Show is free for you," the youth insisted pointing a finger at the German's barrel chest. "You like you pay. Don't like it free."

Max and Loc walked away. "What was he peddling?" Loc asked.

Max chuckled, "A performance where a young girl pulls things out of her vagina."

"Sounds entertaining," the tribesman replied sarcastically.

Max led the way in the tourist stream flowing down the crowded sidewalk. The catch phrase Go Go Girls in varying font adorned the walls of windowless venues. Two Thai girls in black bikinis and high heels sat on bar stools beside the open door to the Lucky Pussy. As Max passed one asked, "Blondie you want to buy me drink?"

"*Nien danke*," Max mumbled glancing into the establishment. A dozen local girls danced on a stage in front of deep purple velvet drapes. To the sparkling rotation of a mirrored ball, the prancing ponies swayed to the beat of a popular song. In swimwear and high heels each girl could be easily identified by potential customers by numbered plastic disk attached to their scanty outfits.

Max smiled. He thought of the Laotian bar girl Chimmy. Is it the humidity, he wondered, the smell of cheap perfume or abundance of young Asian flesh. It doesn't matter what triggered the dormant memory, he realized. The recollection felt good. Chimmy wasn't just a whore, she was my whore. Paying for her insatiable talent was a bargain. What became of her? He wondered. Mei survived the harsh profession and Indochina, he thought, I hope Chimmy did too.

"Is this the place?" Loc asked,

Looking up Max squinted at a pair of neon boxing gloves and The Knock Out spelled in bold red illuminated glass tubes. A young female hostess in a black bra and satin yellow boxing trunks waived them in.

Across the front of her satin shorts, red Thai lettering spelled out Muay Thai, the combat sport of Thailand.

An elevated boxing ring dominated the large boisterous barroom. A bar counter surrounded the roped arena. Male patrons sat on encircling stools. Female bartenders in bras and satin Muay Thai shorts poured overpriced liquor. In the center of the ring, a lady-boy in heavy makeup and a tight silk gown lipped-synced the American county song, *Stand by Your Man.* The she-male's emotional laced pantomime of the country classic, lost on a few members of the heckling audience.

"Over here Max!" Roche called out from a dark corner.

Max spotted the three Americans standing over a round table waving. Roche dressed in his signature Hawaiian shirt and kakis. Buck in a tartan snap button cowboy shirt and blue jeans. The Texan's attire included a large ace of spades logoed pewter belt buckle. The thick spectacled Dugan wore butter colored polyester pants and a tight white golf shirt. Dugan's snug collared t-shirt accenting muscular shoulders and upper arms as well as a slight paunch.

Max and Loc joined their colleagues shadowed by the hostess. As the men took their seats, Roche said, "Another round and Max? Loc?"

"I'll have a Singha," Max said.

"Singha," Loc echoed.

"You buy me a drink too?" The hostess asked seductively dipping a naked shoulder.

"Sure," Max conceded pulling out a cigar.

The young girl nodded in appreciation before skipping towards the counter.

"Max," Roche scolded. "Buying her a drink is a ruse. The equivalent of a twenty-dollar champagne cocktail has just been added to our tab."

Max shrugged lighting his cigar. After taking a puff, he responded. "I know but did you see how she looked at me?"

Everyone laughed. A tray of drinks arrived. Max grabbed a cold amber bottle and said, "To our friends we left behind."

The clink of glass sealed the sentiment.

"So are you both checked into the hotel?" Roche asked looking at Max and Loc.

"The Shangri-La?" Max questioned. "*Ami* you booked us at a luxury hotel."

"I figured if we end up doing jail time, it would nice to reflect back on our lavish stay in Bangkok." Roche responded. "Besides I got a package deal that includes a half day city tour."

"We are not going to get caught," snorted Dugan taking a sip of chilled vodka. "And I'm not going on any fucking city tour."

Looking a Dugan, Roche responded, "I appreciate your confidence Mister Jim but smuggling arms into a neutral country to insight a coup is very risky."

"This is not our first rodeo, Gentlemen." Dugan commented. "When we return to the highlands, we will be doing it with the most powerful tool in any arsenal," After pausing, he informed with a satisfied grin, "Experience." Leaning back in his chair, he continued, "I don't know about you boys, but I've sure wasted my true talent delivering Pepsi the last ten years."

"At least spraying insecticide kept me in a cockpit," Buck declared.

"You are one hell of a pilot cowboy," Dugan said raising his glass. "I remember when you flew us out of Phong Savin in that flying boxcar when the Plain of Jars fell." Looking around the table, he commented, "Max you were there and...Loc..." Dugan stopped and flitching at another revelation, slapped Loc on the knee. "Ah my Tai brother, you ran out in the mortar barrage and rescued me and..." With a frown, he scratched his balding head. "You know I can't remember that other American's name. It sounds like Kelly...no. Anyway...Buck you and your disciplined confidence flew us out in the face of death." Snickering he concluded, "I remember Buck referring to our escape as a sexual experience, the day he fucked death."

"I had relations with a lot of women during by Indochina tenure," Buck said. "But let me tell y'all, Death was the tightest bitch I ever laid."

Max chuckled. "It's been awhile since I encountered that callus whore. After each coupling, I never felt more alive. However the euphoria came at a very expensive price."

"Death certainly is not a cheap whore," Roche commented.

"Speaking of inexpensive sexual entertainment," Buck said. "Y'all interested in joining me for the late night show of a girl shooting darts and smoking a cigarette out of her woo woo."

"I'm in," chimed Dugan.

"Sorry boys," Roche said. "I'm working tonight."

Max squinted at Roche from across the table and asked quietly, "*Ami* do you need back-up?"

Roche leaned forward. His companions huddled around him. Quietly he said, "The package arrived in Bangkok yesterday. I'm meeting with a patsy tonight to arrange pick-up. There are critical hurdles in our operation when we are exposed to the authorities. Clearing Thai customs is one of them. If something goes awry on the docks, we are insulated and can just walk away while somebody else takes the fall." Leaning back he concluded, "If that is the case, then we would have time to enjoy a half-day city tour of Bangkok."

"*Ami?*" Max questioned a second time, "Do you need back-up?"

Roche shook his head, "I appreciate it Max, but no. Tonight is a cakewalk."

"What does cakewalk mean?" Loc asked.

Roche laughed, "Sorry Loc," he said. "It's a Southern expression for very easy or effortless."

Loc nodded and asked Buck, "Who is y'all?"

Everyone laughed as Buck responded, "It's another Southern expression meaning you and all, basically everyone in the conversation."

"Now that I speak English as an American," Loc said, "I have to say you Southern Americans are hard to understand."

"Well said my fellow Californian," Dugan chimed in. "Well Max, Loc are either one of you up for a late night woo woo show?"

Before Max could decline, the high-pitched wail of a clarinet distracted him. Investigating the haunting sound, he discovered four musicians ringside setting a soundtrack for a Muay Thai bout. Cymbals and drums kept the beat for the addictive high whining sound. Two kick boxers in the ring exchanged blows.

"I'm going to pass on seeing a smoking vagina," Max commented focused on the two conditioned combatants punishing each other. No defense, he realized. The barefooted chiseled youths pummeled one another with kicks and punches. This is the pure combative art of victory through attrition, he thought. Who has the stamina to prevail? A mismatch, he surmised as the kick-boxer in red satin trunks took charge.

Focused on the one sided bout, Max reflected back to a summer day in 1940. The clean air of the German countryside smelled of fresh cut grass. The sky over the soccer pitch was blue. Encouraged by their Nazi mentors, Klaus Ditzen sat astride Max and pummeled him with flabby fist. Fearing reprisal from the camp bully, the other boys of the Hitler Youth cheered. Through watery eyes, Max could see a trickle of blood draining out of Klaus's pudgy nose. At least I got one good shot in, he realized as blow after blow rained down.

"Had enough sweetheart?" Klaus questioned waiving a cocked bloody fist over his head.

The vocal audience went silent. Klaus glanced over at the Hitler Youth commandant for guidance. The harsh leader nodded his approval. A wide grin spread across the bully's flabby face.

What have I got to loose, Max pondered spitting a wad of bloody saliva at the smirking expression. Grimacing, he braced as Klaus unleashed the windmill blow.

Max's tongue investigated the gap left by the molar lost in the summer of 1940. The betting crowd of at the Knock-Out Bar in Bangkok replaced the cheering Nazi youth. The action in the ring reached a fever pitch. A razor sharp elbow sliced a gash over an eye. Blinded by flowing blood, the bleeding combatant clinched his adversary. At close range, the sightless boxer twisted his torso and exploded the spear point of his knee into his foe's rib cage. Dancing on the balls of his feet to the seductive beat of the ringside quartet, the boxer alternated the curving knee strikes. "Don't give up now," Max mumbled. The vision-impaired kick-boxer's only chance of victory a knock out. Red trunk's knees buckled from the rhythmic body shots. "It's just about over," Max yelled. Covered in blood, blue trunks drove his tenderized opponent's head down into the upward thrust of his knee. The crack of a nose punctuated the accompanying music. The match ended with the victorious boy rejoicing. The unconscious loser carried out of the ring.

Examining the battered and bloody victor, Max grinned at the accomplishment. The Thai boxer took a beating but he stood his ground. That's more than could be said about Klaus Dizten, he reflected. On the French battlefield Klaus wailed like a baby. Under fire the large boy cut and ran. He didn't get too far, Max recalled. The blood splatter staining the white canvas boxing ring faded. Max visualized the portly Klaus collapsing. A German officer's bullet executed the fleeing boy for desertion.

CHAPTER EIGHTEEN

In the deserted coffee shop of the Rambutti Palace Hotel, Roche finished a second late night cup of java. He lit up his third cigarette. Caffeine and nicotine, he thought eyeing the smoldering canister between his fingers, one of the better combinations of life. I sure have missed you; he realized sucking the addictive smoke from the filter-tipped Marlboro. Leaning back in the cushioned rattan chair, he raised the empty mug over his head soliciting a refill. In the brightly lit cafe, a young petite Thai waitress rushed to his side. He stared at her focused angelic features as she refilled his cup. Such a timid creature, he thought in his unsuccessful attempt to make eye contact. As the tiny girl retreated, he checked his watch. It was closing in on eleven PM. My patsy is late; he realized blowing on the black surface of the hot brew. Looking up after a cautious sip, he spotted his mark. A twenty-something American female entered the restaurant. The scruffy gal in a faded denim shirt with a dark blue cotton batik sarong wrapped around wide hips looked apprehensive. Standing at the empty hostess station, she dipped a shoulder releasing an army surplus duffel bag. A red bandana pulled back her hair. An oily sheen covered her pudgy face and pock marked forehead.

"Nicky," Roche called out.

Smiling she dragged the green canvas bag across the carpeted floor.

"I'm so sorry I'm late Mister Johnson," she said, "But the travel bus had a flat tire this morning."

"No need to apologize," Roche responded, "And its Bill Johnstone not Johnson. But please call me Bill." Nothing like having to correct the pronunciation of an alias, Roche thought as he took his seat. Getting a whiff of her moist odor, he slowly leaned back. Searching for cleaner air, he asked, "Would you like a cup of coffee?"

"Please," Nicky responded and then humbly asked, "Would it be too much of an imposition if I got something to eat?"

"Not at all," Roche said waving over the only server. "What would you like?"

Closing her eyes, she titled her head back and said softly, "Pancakes, buttermilk pancakes, orange juice, a glass of cold orange juice, a glass of milk and bacon lots of bacon."

"Anything else?" Roche asked as the Thai waitress scribbled down the order.

Opening one eye, Nicky squinted at Roche and asked, "A tall cold draft beer?"

Over his shoulder Roche said to the waitress, "Make that two beers."

"Thank you Bill," she said. "I have been exiting on eggs, rice and fruit for the last three months."

"How much longer is your two year tour of duty?" Roche asked.

"A year and a half," she grumbled. Frowning she confessed, "I'm not going to make it. I signed up with my teaching degree and specifically learned Thai to educate improvised children. And the organization sends me to some isolated village with no supervision or resources and expects me to do the impossible. School is rarely in session. The father of the family I'm been assigned to live with is a pervert. He's all hands, always touching, groping. I don't dare bath for fear of him walking in."

"Have you reported this to your country supervisor?" Roche asked.

"What do you think?" Nicky barked. "They day I arrived; I expressed concerns and was told to be strong. A month later I requested a transfer and was told to stop complaining and to just deal with it." Pausing she glanced around in the pleasant air-conditioned atmosphere and looking at Roche added in a softer tone, "The system is corrupt and I suspect that is why you've asked for my assistance. I only hope the agriculture equipment you are donating to the hill tribe refugees will be put to good use."

"So do I," Roche said appreciating the irony.

The midnight breakfast and assorted beverages arrived. The waitress placed a large misting stack of flapjacks in front of the salivating aid worker. Beside it, a heaping side dish of crisp bacon. A glass of milk, a glass of OJ, and two glistening beer mugs encircled the meal. The aroma of smoked meat hung over the crowded table. Licking her lips Nicky hesitated.

Grabbing a foaming white crowned glass beer stein, Roche smiled and said, "Dig in sweetheart, don't mind me."

Nicky didn't need any more encouragement. Lifting the side dish of bacon, she slid the crisp meat onto the flat cakes. After dousing the large mound with a healthy dose of maple syrup, she used fork and knife to cut and stuff big chunks of the sweet concoction into a ravenous mouth. Occasionally she would take a gulp of milk or orange juice to assist with the rapid consumption. She tasted the beer once but after a sour expression it was removed from the rotation.

Roche leaned back with his beer enjoying the spectacle. A loud belch paused but did not slow down her intake. She probably responded to a television ad about making a difference, Roche thought. The idealistic youth are so naive and unprepared for the corrupt realities of this planet. The underbelly of society is controlled by cruel masters and a far cry from the smiling grateful foreign faces of a sixty-second commercial. Even if she cuts short on her commitment, she's earned the future romanticized bragging rights about the sacrifice she made for mankind. That is if she is not apprehended doing my bidding on the docks tomorrow. Hell, he thought, if someone was tipped-off about the weapons, all they have is a shit-load of munitions and an innocent aid worker. She would walk after a week, he concluded or maybe a month.

Pushing back from the table, Nicky used a linen napkin to wipe off sticky jowls. The sponge tracks of maple syrup on an empty platter were all that remained of the late night meal. Slumping down in her wicker chair and breathing heavy, she reached for the draft beer. Placing the cold glass stein next to her cheek, she sighed, as the waitress cleared the table.

"Are you ready to talk business," Roche asked.

She responded with a sluggish nod.

"Have you cleared relief supplies through Thai customs before?" He asked.

Enjoying the beer, she nodded. After a big swallow, she sat up and said, "It's no big deal. The fact that I speak some Thai is a plus. There usually is an expediting fee involved or what we would call a bribe in the states."

"Are you comfortable doing this?" Roche asked innocently.

"Bill," she snickered, "I've been fighting off the inappropriate advances of the father of my host family for three months. I sleep in a shit-hole village and wake at dawn each day to teach English and American values to a handful of disinterested impoverished children. Assisting a generous donation of farm implements may be the only humanitarian deed I accomplish during my short service."

"How much do you think the expediting fee will be?" He questioned.

"The last time I cleared a container through customs it was tents, blankets, basically disaster supplies. The bribe or fee was five-hundred dollars." She answered.

"American dollars or baht," he asked.

"I don't think that matters," she shrugged.

Roche put a manila envelope on the syrup stained linen tablecloth. Placing an extended finger on the sealed document he said, "This is the bill of lading for the cargo and one-thousand US dollars. Negotiate however you want." Pulling a room key out of his pants pocket, he slid it across the table. "I've paid for your room through the weekend. So before you go back to that shit-hole village enjoy a few hot showers, air-conditioning and clean sheets."

CHAPTER NINETEEN

I t was a smoggy Southern California afternoon. An orange sun drifted in and out of the polluted sky. In front of the Garden Grove location of Isabelle's Nails, a white 1970's four door Chevy Impala sedan skidded to an abrupt termination. Four cocky Asian youths jumped out of the weathered vehicle. Three casually dressed in white t-shirts and blue jeans. The tight knit cotton shirts accented muscular frames. Elaborate colorful tattoos peered out of taut short sleeves. In contrast to his companions, a suave twenty-something wore a light-wool gray suit, starched white dress-shirt and wide red tie. His slick black hair combed straight back. A long scar split his left eyebrow and traveled past a dead eye socket before terminating on his cheek.

A bell chimed. The glass door to Isabelle's' swung open. Two girls in plaid Catholic high school uniforms exited the nail salon. The teenage girls froze at the sight of the Chinese gang members. One of the street punks flayed his arms and growled at the white girls. Dropping their books, the terrified students ran to the mischief laughter of the Asian thugs.

The well-dressed gangster kicked a civics textbook aside with a polished black leather shoe. His troops followed him into the small shop. The swinging door chimed.

Glancing through the beaded curtain of the back office doorway, Mei spotted the new arrivals. It was only a matter of time before the leeches rise to the surface, she concluded. Opening the top desk drawer, she picked up a straight razor. Feeling the familiar grip of the well-honed cutthroat tool, she realized its use was optional. Placing the blade in the front pocket of her white lab coat, she took a deep breath. Now is not the time to negotiate, she concluded. Standing behind the beaded doorframe, she studied the one eyed thug. I've encountered more dangerous adversaries, she concluded. Cautious of the fanatic sense of youthful invincibility, she parted the beads and entered the salon.

The only customer, the portly Misses Odenbach hastily paid for her incomplete manicure and exited the shop. The three seated Vietnamese nail techs looked down sheepishly.

"Are you the owner," One-eye barked.

"Missy not here," Mei informed. "You gentlemen want manicure?" she asked.

Chuckling One-eye said, "We are not here to buy services. We are here to sell you ours."

"I'll tell Missy when she returns," Mei responded. Squinting she asked, "What is your business other then scaring away customers?"

The thug flexed. Mei slowly reached into her pocket and gripped the comforting power of her weapon.

"We represent Wah Ching," He responded. "This is our territory. In order to protect this establishment, we will require a monthly fee."

Wah Ching, Cantonese for Chinese Youth Mei thought. The names and the players change but the shakedown is always the same. "I'll inform the owner," she said reflecting back to Loc and her terminating similar threats in Saigon.

"Friday!" the thug said. "You tell Missy we'll be back Friday for the first installment."

"What time?" Mei asked cordially.

Scowling at the inquiry, he stammered, "I don't know...sometime Friday!" Turning with a straight arm, he pushed open the swinging door. His escorts followed his hasty exit.

Standing on the concrete sidewalk in front of the salon, Mei watched the Impala sedan burning rubber. It merged into flowing traffic. Squatting down, she picked up the scattered papers and abandoned textbooks. To the chiming bell, she entered the shop.

Looking over at her intimated employees, she said calmly, "Don't worry, after tomorrow we will not be seeing those boys again."

Entering the back office, she placed the schoolbooks on top of the cluttered desk. Picking up a small black address book, she flipped through pages. With a telephone handset wedged between her shoulder and head, she dialed the number for General Yang Mo.

CHAPTER TWENTY

Max's cordovan loafers sunk into the plush elevator carpeting of the Bangkok hotel. Beneath his feet the word Saturday was woven into the rich fabric. They must change it out at midnight, he thought of the lift flooring's daily notification. Beside him, Loc studied the blinking numbered overhead lights marking descent. The tight crisp clean quarters accented with the scent of polished wood.

Roche standing at attention stared at the crease between paneled sliding doors. "The package cleared customs." He informed quietly.

"Any issues?" Max asked.

Focused forward Roche responded, "I haven't made contact with our transport security. Once I do, we can get the package out of Bangkok."

The chime of a bell announced a stop. The lift paused on the fourth floor. The doors parted. Roche stepped back. A slick looking Thai in a sharp black suit and entered. Over a breast pocketed white handkerchief, a gold metal nameplate read Shangri La Hotel and a tongue twister name.

"Good morning gentlemen," the employee said. "I trust you're enjoying your stay."

"Yes, thank you," Roche responded.

Max nodded. Loc remained silent. The doors closed.

The employee studied Loc. The chime announced the lobby destination. The doors slid open. The hotel employee pulled Loc aside and asked, "Can I see your room key, please?"

"We are all together," Max informed. "Do you need to see our keys?"

"No," said the embarrassed employee, "If he is with you that's fine."

Watching the employee walking away, Max reflected back to the posh lobby of the Continental Hotel in Saigon. Loc's tribal presence was questioned there over twenty-five years ago. No matter what Loc accomplishes in life, Max thought, he still is viewed as an inferior, a tribesman.

The lobby was active that morning. Sunlight poured down from the elevated ceiling's skylights. A Japanese tour group huddled around the front desk. Piles of luggage littered the white, green and cheery parquet marble floor. A centered planter housed and interior tree that stretched thirty feet towards the windowed ceiling. A uniformed European flight crew occupied one of the many strategically placed soft seating options.

Max elbowed Roche with a playful nudge. He motioned toward an obese American couple. The portly pair argued over the wife's spending habits. In shorts and a t-shirt labeled with a sport's team logo, the husband scolded. Hubby barked and waved a carved wooden elephant in his spouse's sun burnt face.

"What's with you Americans and short pants?" Max asked.

"They're cool and comfortable," Roche responded. "Don't you own a pair?"

"I did when I was a boy in the Hitler Youth," Max retorted.

"Don't worry kraut; I won't be wearing them on this mission."

"Ankle holster?" Max questioned glancing down at Roche's bunched up chino pants leg.

Roche nodded raising his eyebrows seeking a response.

Maxed patted the front pocket of his pleated kakis. "This climate does not allow for a sport coat and shoulder holster."

Max and Roche looked at Loc who also patted a front pocket.

A rhythmic clanging quieted the buzzing chatter in the lobby. A meandering white gloved bellboy in a spiked pith helmet rang a hand-bell. He held an elevated chalkboard. Written in porous white sentiment across the dark green slate was the name Thomas Roche.

"This is not good," Roche whispered. "Shadow me," he said approaching the bellhop.

Max and Loc moved in opposite directions towards the edges of the lobby.

"What is it?" Roche asked the messenger scanning the crowd.

"Doorman needs to see you sir," the bellboy answered.

Never looking at the uniformed boy, Roche handed him a ten baht note and headed towards the hotel entrance. Exiting the lobby's air-conditioned comfort, a blast of humid air laced with exhaust fumes slapped his face. A line of yellow and green taxis waiting for fares queued to his left. In front of him, an idling tour bus coughed out puffs of white smoke. Crowded around the bus's accordion door, a tour group of impatient gray haired seniors pushed and shoved in a race to board the transport.

In a brass buttoned military shirt and a pointed pith helmet, the doorman approached and asked, "Taxi sir?"

"I'm Tom Roche," Roche responded, "Do you have a message for me?"

"Sir a group of..." The doorman paused. Squeamishly he mumbled, "Vagabonds?" Pleased with his word selection, he announced, "Sir a group of vagabonds wanted to see you." The uniformed attendant pointed a white gloved hand down the hotels long entry driveway.

Following the extended arm, Roche spotted a group of raggedy locals milling on the sidewalk. "Thanks," Roche responded. Waving two fingers over his head, he summoned his back up.

"What is it?" Max asked standing behind the American.

"You tell me," Roche responded. "What do you think these local bums want?"

"Not locals," Loc said. "These are my people. They are Hmong."

Placing a hand on Roche's shoulder, Max said, "It looks like we've made contact with our security escort."

The three mercenaries left the shielding shade of the luxury hotels overhanging entrance. The tropical sun magnified the sweltering moist air. Cautiously they approached the scruffy cadre. One of the men laid face up on the sidewalk. His unbuttoned shirt exposed a concave stomach and a well-defined rib cage. Two tribesmen stood with disheveled dark brown hair and soiled faces apprehensively watching the passing pedestrian traffic. An empty plastic liter bottle secured by raggedy twine hung from one of the men's shoulders. The six other Hmong squatted in a row just above the walkways gutter. The crouching men had discounted gazes. All the men were small in stature and extremely thin. Torn and frayed clothing hung off their malnourished frames.

Loc leaned into Roche and asked, "Do you have cigarettes?"

Roche nodded and retrieved a fairly full pack of Marlboros from his shirt breast pocket.

"Thanks," Loc mumbled taking the pack. "*Hello brothers*," Loc said pleasantly in the language of his birth. Walking into the cluster of Hmong, he handed out smokes. Nervous smiles and nods accepted the nicotine gift.

Looking at Max and Roche, the plastic canteen toting Hmong questioned, "Major Roche?"

"I'm Tom Roche," Roche said extending his hand and shaking the man's clammy palm.

"Pleased to meet you, I'm Yeeb," he said with a crooked grin, "And yes I speak English. I was once a Captain in the Royal Laotian Army."

"Max," Max said shaking Yeeb's hand, "Always good to meet a fellow veteran."

Behind Yeeb, Loc squatted and puffed away with his countrymen in a tight circle. Strings of smoke and light laughter mixed with tribal dialogue rose from the crouching huddle.

Leaning into Max and Roche, Yeeb said quietly, "We are here to assist you with transport and delivery."

Roche glanced down at the circle of broken men and asked, "Captain are your men up to the task?"

Yeeb paused to allow a gawking hand holding white couple to pass. He snorted. "The nine of us are armed with a single vintage French revolver and four bullets. But what we lack in munitions, we make up for in skill and determination. All of us have extensive military training and combat experience, dating back to our childhood. Yes Major, we were *carbine soldiers*. All of us have lost wives, children and our way of life. When you have lost everything, you have nothing to lose. Our only objective now is a glorious death. So to answer your question Major Roche, my men are up to task."

Roche nodded respectfully. "Do you and your men want to get something to eat?" He asked.

Yeeb grinned, exposing crooked yellow teeth. "We missed a few meals eluding the cat to get here."

"The cat?" Max questioned.

"The Siamese cat," Yeeb informed. "The Thai authorities are a clever cat and the Hmong its mice. The cruel cat plays with us, taunts us, but never lets us forget its supreme power. Last month a Hmong father wondered out of the refugee camp in search of food for his family and was shot."

"Was the incident reported to the United Nation authorities?" Roche questioned.

"The mice have learned to avoid being mauled, never question the actions of the cat," Yeeb answered.

Max looked down the congested boulevard. Amongst the upscale souvenir shops catering to the area's luxury hotel tourist, he spotted a life-sized mannequin of a Kentucky Colonel. Grinning he said, "Let's go eat."

The air was cool, clean and scented with the aroma of fried chicken. Along one side of the fast food restaurant, tourist stole glances of the gluttonous beggars. Roche and Max sat with Yeeb and three of his men on fixed pivoting seats around a Formica table top. Loc dined at the adjacent table with five of his Hmong brothers. Smacking lips, grunts and belches resonated from the focused men. Cupped hands feed rice and battered encrusted chicken into hungry mouths.

Sucking iced cola through a plastic straw Yeeb sighed with delight. The red and white wax cup vibrated from a noticeable twitch.

"What is it?" Max asked glancing down at the quivering soda cup.

"Yellow rain," Yeeb answered. "I've was exposed to the poison two weeks ago."

"You were in Laos?" Roche questioned.

Grinning Yeeb responded, "I crossed the Mekong to retrieve a sample for the indifferent United Nations investigators."

"You risked your life for those bureaucrats?" Roche questioned.

Shrugging Yeeb responded, "Who knows, somewhere in the West the sample of brown-yellow powder and our cries for justice may fall into the hands of good men."

"I hope your right Captain," Roche said quietly.

"Captain," Yeeb snorted. Sucking comfortably on the cola straw, he studied Max and Roche and continued, "When the war ended in 1975, I had my men disarm themselves and awaited the orders from the victorious Pathet Lao. The Communist quickly informed us we were war criminals and sentenced us to hard labor. They worked us like animals. Groups of starving prisoners were force to pull ploughs for days on end. Overworked death was common. You were forbidden to speak. One day the wives of some of the CIA collaborators were brought to the camp. We watched in silence the soldiers taking turns fondling and raping the Hmong women." He paused and set down the wax cup. "The soldiers violated the women for several days. It was during the prolonged assault that I escaped."

"You fled to Thailand?" Max asked.

Shaking his head, Yeeb answered, "No I went in search of my family. Living on leaves and roots, I made it back to my village. It was occupied by Vietnamese troops. I got a message to my wife. With our three children, we slipped into the jungle. We survived with other displaced families. We were naive to think the remoteness and the concealing forest would dissuade our enemy. The communist could not tolerate Hmong residing in the mountains of Laos. One morning we awoke to Soviet helicopters showering us in yellow rain." Pausing he added with a crackling voice, "My three children got sick and died. After we buried our family, my wife and I fled to Thailand. Crossing the Mekong River and within a hundred yards of the Thai shoreline..." Yeeb closed his eyes and whispered, "She drowned."

"I'm sorry," Roche said feeling the gut retching guilt of his government's abandonment of these loyal allies.

Sucking on the soda, Yeeb wet his dry mouth and said, "Thank you Major, now tell me about this weapon that can swat the helicopters that killed my children out of the sky."

CHAPTER TWENTY ONE

On the outskirts of Bangkok, the traffic thinned. A rickety wood paneled lorry sputtered in its attempt to accelerate. Behind the wheel, Yeeb with a cigarette attached to his lower lip leaned back. A warm breeze flowed through the door-less truck cab. The Hmong driver flexed his sandaled foot on the clutch. Max in the center seat politely pivoted his knees. Yeeb shifted gears. Beside Max, Roche's chino pants flapped in the exposed vehicle. Behind the windblown cabin, Loc and the Hmong security detail reclined on the wood planked and splintered truck bed. The tribal soldiers now armed in addition to the antique French revolver with full bellies and cutlery.

"Slow down," Roche said studying a fluttering crinkled paper with crude directions, "We are getting close."

The late afternoon sun defiantly hung over the horizon. In the bright sunlight, the tired and weathered vehicle passed through the gated opening of a chain-link fence. The diamond-mesh netting capped with swirling razor wire encircled a storage complex. Large corrugated blue, orange and white steel shipping containers were neatly stacked on the cracked and decaying black asphalt paved lot. Sprouting out of crevices in the hard surface, knee high clusters of flowering weeds attempted to survive.

Roche leaned forward and squinted through the insect cemetery on the windshield. Pointing towards the opened mouthed loading dock of a concrete block warehouse, he said, "Back this up to the open bay."

Yeeb nodded and skillfully spun around the high riding bucket of bolts.

Hopping down out the vehicle, Roche scanned the facility. The complex seemed deserted. There was a forklift and utility vehicle parked in front of the warehouse but no signs of life. Glancing back up into the vehicle, he saw Max checking his pistol.

"German vigilance?" Roche questioned.

Climbing out of the cab, Max responded quietly, "The last time Loc and I picked up a package like this, we assisted death in punching the tickets of three hijackers."

Roche nodded. Walking up to the large open bay, he shouted, "Hello!"

A stocky Thai with a half buttoned shirt and sleeves rolled up over his shoulders emerged from the shadows. Flexing exposed muscles, he barked. "What do you need?"

"Take it easy chief," Roche responded waving a carbon imprinted pink document. "We are here to pick up a shipment."

The broad Thai squatted down above the used tire bumpers of the loading bay. Snatching the thin page, he studied the document. Looking at Roche, he said a well rehearsed line, "I'm shorthanded today locating your crates will take time."

Rather than exchange dialogue, Roche pulled out a US twenty dollar bill and offered the expediting inducement. The Thai reacted to the greenback with a sour expression. Forty dollars invoked hope in the worker's facial expression but not closure. Sixty dollars US sealed the deal.

Stuffing the currency into his pocket, the Thai turned and disappeared into the maze of wooden crates stored in the warehouse.

Roche used two fingers to get Yeeb's attention. As the tribesman approached, he said, "Get one of your boys to follow the warehouse worker."

Yeeb nodded. After a short conversation, Pheej in his sandaled feet hopped up into warehouse to track the worker.

"What is it *Ami?*" Max asked.

"Empty warehouse," Roche responded, "Could be a set up."

"The authorities?" Max mumbled.

"No," Roche responded. "If it was we would have been arrested when I handed over the Bill of Lading. Just be alert for a petty shakedown." Leaning into Max, he whispered, "Nobody can see the cargo."

An annoying persistent beep preceded the humming motor of a fork-lift. A levitating crate flowed out of the bowels of the warehouse. With a sharp turn, a faded yellow lift-truck deposited its load in the back of the lorry. Flashing a smile, the Thai driver reversed the forklift and to the pulsing short high-pitched noise retreated to retrieve the second crate.

Pheej returned and placed a fisted hand to the side of his head. Roche nodded and turning to Max said, "The warehouse employee made a phone call."

Stone faced Max turned and walked over to the lorry. Climbing into the truck bed, he placed his pistol in the small of his back. He alerted Loc. Loc cautioned the Hmong escort. Four of the vagabond soldiers jumped onto the asphalt and disappeared behind the colorful mountain of stacked shipping containers. The obnoxious forklift beep announced the arrival of the second crate. Max and Loc hugged the trucks wood side panel to make room.

A black Mercedes entered the complex. The crunch of decomposing asphalt accompanied the luxury vehicle's casual approach. The black sedan coasted to a stop in front of the poised and loaded lorry. Simultaneously the four doors of the polished vehicle swung open.

Shooting sequence, Max thought studying the exiting occupants. Three men advanced, three men remained behind shielded by the open vehicle doors. The sparkling glitter of a fat gold Rolex watch indentified the leader. In a short sleeve shirt with creased tailor-made black slacks, a slick young Chinese man led the procession. Short in stature but not confidence; Max surmised, most likely unarmed and therefore a secondary target. Flanking the strutting Rolex flashing peacock was a scruffy local policeman. The tall lanky Thai officer had a small military cap with a weathered leather visor balanced on top of a narrow head. His un-tucked uniformed shirt hung down over a mismatching pair of pants. A charlatan Max realized, part of the ruse. Getting a glimpse of the imposter's holstered pistol, Max moved the costumed policeman up the list of potential targets. A Chinese thug shadowed the spokesman. The wide Asian had chiseled features, and with the mask of a killer studied the surroundings through dark lifeless eyes. The goon's right arm concealed behind his boss's back. Probably has a gun in hand, Max concluded by the body guard's calculated trailing advance.

Looking at Roche, the Chinese spokesman said with a slight accent, "I need to speak to a Mister Johnstone."

"What do you want?" Roche growled.

Roche's demon persona is surfacing, Max observed.

"Are you Johnstone?" asked the squinting Asian.

"Are you deaf?" Roche responded. "What the fuck do you want?"

The body guard snorted and flexed, puffing out his chest. The costumed policeman flinched. Raising a confident hand the spokesman calmed his troops. Looking down, he rubbed his forehead and said politely, "I think you have mistaken us for local hooligans." Scowling at Roche, he added, "You sir have no idea who the fuck you are talking to."

Chuckling Roche responded, "14K triad?"

The Asian's face puckered. He spat in disgust. "We piss on those Macau dogs. We are Ah Kong."

"Ah, The Company," Roche responded translating the Hokkien name of the Singapore triad. "So now that I know who I'm talking to, I ask once again, what the fuck do you want?"

"You are either very brave or very stupid, Mister Johnstone." The gangster responded. "We are here to extract a tariff for passing goods through our territory."

"How much?" Roche inquired.

Focused on the flexing hit-man, Max slowly reached for the pistol in the small of his back. His periphery vision detected shadows moving in the tall weeds behind the luxury sedan. The setting sun flashed a spark off a blade in the unwanted foliage.

The gangster smiled, "Before we negotiate a fee, I need a peek at your cargo."

Max drew his Tokarev. Aiming at the bodyguard's head, he squeezed off a shot. The bullet grazed the thug's scalp. A bloody trail parted greasy hair. Disoriented the gangster stumbled back and discharged a round into the hard pockmarked asphalt.

My god I missed, Max realized. Larger targets, he concluded. His second attempt hit the confused goon in the chest.

Gasping for air, the henchman dropped his handgun. With both hands, he ripped opened his buttoned shirt. In disbelief, he staggered into the sunlight focused at the blood pulsing out of his sternum. Violently his wide frame jerked. Another slug tore into his back. His knees buckled. His legs folded and his upper body collapsed on the sun-baked asphalt.

The imposter in a cop's uniform frantically fidgeted with the clasp of a leather holster. Unsheathing his revolver, his torso absorbed two quick rounds. The impact twisted the wiry target. A third projectile toppled the twirling corpse.

As Max's pistol spit out the five rounds, the Company spokesman turned towards his vehicle. His shoulders dropped. Vagrant assassins emerged from the tall weeds. The knife wielding Hmong warriors pounced on the remaining three henchmen. Flickering sunlight reflected off honed steel blades slicing through flesh and bone. Defeated the Asian gangster slowly spun back around. To the moans of his dying escort, he said confidently, "You realize you are all dead men."

Ignoring the warning, Max took a deep breath. Compensating for his earlier miss, he shot the defiant thug in the head. The blast created a crimson dot on the man's forehead and blew out the back of his skull. Chunks of brain, bone fragments and blood decorated the polished black Mercedes.

The warehouse worker showing the palms of his hands stood opened mouth trembling. Possessed by his inner demon, Roche reached down and pulled his Baby Browning from an ankle holster. Casually he walked over and shot the unarmed worker in the side of the head. Watching the growing burgundy puddle around the workers lifeless body, Roche snorted. He realized it was a harsh sentence. Squatting down, he retrieved his sixty dollars. "You made the phone call," he mumbled to the corpse, "You paid the price."

Roche looked out across the lot. The Hmong guerrilla fighters displayed the battlefield etiquette of clearing the arena. They pushed the blood splattered Mercedes Benz behind a tower of shipping containers. From the fallen, they salvaged weapons, currency, shoes and anything of value. The stripped clean dead dragged to a growing pile in front of the loading dock.

Max walked over and looked down at the thug missing the back of his head.

"What is it?" Loc asked.

"The last time I killed was the summer of sixty-two. That was twenty years ago," Max said quietly.

"Casualties of war," said a consoling Loc.

"I know," Max responded. "But I don't remember it leaving such a bile taste in my mouth."

"Don't think about it partner," Loc said. "Focus on the mission, that's all that matters."

Max nodded. Bending down he grabbed the ankles of spokesman and dragged the corpse to the pile.

Yeeb, sporting a gold Rolex climbed into the lorry's cab. The vehicle coughed to life. Roche ripped a bloody shirt out of the mound of dead. Using the crimson rag, he left a bogus calling card. On the block building, he painted 14k in blood.

CHAPTER TWENTY TWO

I t was a cool Southern California night. Cruising in a light blue Datsun hatchback, Mei searched for Vineyard Avenue. The identical shake roofed homes flowed in a maze of twisting and curving residential streets. Downshifting she turned around in yet another terminating cul-de-sac. I have to be close, she concluded. She stopped at a deserted intersection. Rolling down the window, she stuck her head out and examined the street sign. Finally she sighed, now to locate the house. Driving slowly, the street numbers on the homes perched behind green manicured turf decreased. The fading numbers painted on the curb in front of a dirt and weed infested lawn marked her destination. Dated vehicles clogged the driveway. Children's toys littered the desolate landscaping. The wood shingled residence was well lit. Several silhouettes moved back and forth behind closed drapes.

Mei took a deep breath of crisp cool air. She locked the compact car. Slinging a black purse over a shoulder, she traversed across the dusty playground. Behind the peeling red paint of the front door children's voices resonated. The buzz of the doorbell quieted the young inhabitants. The door slowly opened. Holding a baby, a Hmong girl smiled before shyly looking down.

"I'm here to see the General," Mei said softly.

Stepping aside the girl allowed access. Mei entered. The house reeked with the oily smell of fried fish. A smoky haze floated below a low ceiling. Steeping on frayed green shag carpet, Mei heard the bottle laughter from a television sitcom.

Following behind the baby carrying twelve-year old, Mei passed a crowded kitchen. Hmong women and children held court around an oval dinette table. In an adjacent room, teenage boys lounged around the glow of a small color television screen. Stopping in front of a hallway, the guide adjusted her grasp on the infant and pointed down the corridor.

"Thank you," Mei said politely.

In the first room down the narrow passage, General Yang in a white singlet sat behind a large desk. The sleeveless undergarment exposed the flaccid softness of age. Random scars marked the old warrior's loose skin. The room smelled like an ashtray. Yang conversed quietly with two men in black suits. Looking up from the conversation, he smiled at Mei. He stood-up. The other men also rose.

"Mei," Yang exclaimed, "So good to see you again after all these years."

Mei bowed slightly, "General Yang."

"Come have a seat," He said waiving the men towards the wall. The Hmong henchmen were short but wide. The seams of their charcoal suit coats stretched to the limits. With slouching broad shoulders, they stood as instructed. Looking at the stoic men, Yang informed, "In my younger days I spent many enjoyable evening with Mei, her husband Loc and the German at their longhouse on the Plain of Jars."

"We were all younger back then," Mei said sitting down in a red leather cushioned chair.

"Let's get to our business at hand," Yang said taking a seat in a high backed chair. "You have an issue with the Wah Ching triad?" he questioned.

Mei nodded, "It is nothing my husband couldn't handle. However with his departure, I seek your assistance."

Yang lit a cigarette. Leaning back in his swiveling chair, he blew a cloud of smoke towards the low ceiling. "The Hmong community under my protection has had to deal with these Chinese punks from San Francisco." He commented studying the smoke stained popcorn ceiling. "Now the Hmong refugees throughout the US pay me for this protection. That is how we are able to fund the expedition your husband has volunteered for. Seeing our past relationship and your husband's current involvement to our cause, I'll handle your Wah Ching threat for five-thousand dollars."

"You're going to charge me?" Mei questioned.

Showing the calming palms of his hands, the General responded, "Mei, the favor you ask does have cost. Look around you. I'm not a wealthy man. If I could do this favor for gratis, I would."

Mei stared at the General.

Breaking the awkward silence, Yang offered, "In addition, for Loc's services in the liberation of Laos, I will reward him with the rank of General once my new regime is established." Sliding open a desk drawer, he pulled out an according file folder. Plopping it on top of the desk, he flipped through certificates organized by military rank and civil service post. Carefully he handed an official looking document across the desk.

Mei quickly scanned the certificate. There was a blank space for a name above the title of General. The signature block formatted for General Yang. She respectfully returned the document. "Reduce the rank to colonel and lower the cost to three thousand dollars and we have deal," she said.

Looking at one of the henchman, Yang asked, "Can you handle this for three large?"

The chiseled faced tribesman nodded.

Opening her purse Mei asked, "Will you take a check?"

Leaning back in his chair, Yang said, "Make it out to the Lao Liberation Front."

As Mei wrote out the check, Yang sucked deep on his cigarette. His pleasant persona faded. Looking hard at the wide henchmen, Yang said with a soft growl, "I want this Chinese threat eliminated with extreme prejudice. Delegate it to one of our street gangs and make sure that all participants are underage." Looking across the desk, he explained, "There is a quirk in the American judicial system that favors youthful indiscretions."

Mei handed him the check, "Thank you General."

CHAPTER TWENTY THREE

It was late in the day, but it felt like evening. From the black sky, heavy rain pounded down on the dark green canvas of a lean-to structure. Stacked wooden cases of AK-47s walled two sides of the shelter. The front opened to the elements. The cascading runoff from the angled tarp roof blanketed the exposed rear. To the drumming sound, Max gazed out at the red clay runway. Tall trees and dense vegetation surrounded the jungle tarmac. Large puddles formed on the narrow slick surface. Glancing over at the idle Twin Beech aircraft, he inhaled the sweet fragrance of the rain forest and shook his head. We won't be flying out tomorrow, he concluded.

Behind Max, a panel from a wood shipping crate rested on top of stacked ammo boxes. Huddled around the makeshift table, Roche, Loc, Buck, Dugan and Yeeb studied a map. A cloud of cigarette smoke hung over their focused gaze. Turning Max walked over to join the session. His treading combat boots on the tent fabric flooring detected a softening in the shelters base.

Spread out on the rough wood tabletop a dated map. Between the frayed and separating creases of the unfolded diagram was the visual representation of Northern Laos. With a smoldering cigarette between his fingers, Roche tapped on the document, "Right here," he said adding another emphasized pat. "There was a landing strip below a Hmong community."

Leaning forward, Buck in a weathered wide-brimmed hat peered down at the location. "Yep," he mumbled raising his head. "I flew there many times, delivering both rice and hard rice."

Puzzled Loc asked, "What is hard rice?"

"Ammo," Buck responded with a smirk. Glancing into space, he stiffened his spine. An extended index finger pushed up the tattered brim of his Stetson. "I remember there were three boys...three Hmong boys. I always assumed they were brothers. Every time I landed on that small sliver of real-estate they would come tearing down from the village." Pausing he looked around the table at his attentive companions and continued. "Well while the villagers unloaded cargo, the two older boys convince their younger brother to approach me." Chuckling he said, "I guess they never saw a cowboy before. Well I'm having a smoke and I look down and see this big headed little boy gawking up at me with an open mouth in awe." Buck shrugged. "So what am I going to do? I end up giving this kid a Snickers bar. He bites into that caramel, peanut, milk chocolate combination and lights up." With a big smile, Buck concluded, "So on subsequent trips I would hand out candy bars to a growing audience of cowboy admirers."

Roche snickered, "Sorry cowboy but your fans are long gone. The village above the strip is deserted."

"Not deserted," Yeeb said softly, "exterminated."

Dugan placed a hand on the tribesman's shoulder during a sobering silence.

"Well...Buck," Roche coughed out. "Are you ready to make another delivery of hard rice?"

The cowboy pulled out a six inch metal ruler from his breast pocket. Laying it on the map he used a flat carpenters pencil to draw a line from their current position to the proposed destination. Using the edges of the map as a scratch pad he made several calculations. The computations resulted with a Buck marking down the number five. Emphasizing the single digit result, he circled it several time with pencil graphite.

"What does the five mean?" Roche asked.

"The number of trips it will take to get us and the cargo into Laos?" Buck answered.

"Shit," Roche mumbled. "How can that be?"

"The payload," Buck answered. "And the heaviest component of that is the AK-47 ammunition."

"It's the cartridge size and weight," Max informed, "What the heavier bullet loses in accuracy it makes up for in penetration."

Scowling Roche said, "Thanks for the update, Fritz." Shaking his head, he grumbled, "With every flight our odds of success decrease."

"Hell Roche," Buck said. "I've been spraying cotton fields and flirting with power lines for the last ten years. Tree top flying through the mountains of Laos undetected is just another day at the office."

Roche chuckled, "Very well cowboy we'll ferry in cargo." Looking at Yeeb, he said, "Captain you and your men will be on the first flight."

Yeeb acknowledged the order with a nod.

Dugan in a tight t-shirt flexed his middle-aged frame. Clearing his throat, he pushed back his coke bottle thick glasses and declared, "I'm going in with the Hmong."

Looking around at the conceding huddled group, Roche said, "We have no objection."

The rain intensified. The green canvas ceiling began to bow. A clean stream began to meander across the hard fabric floor.

"So what is the plan?" Max hollered over the heavy torrential downpour.

Roche answered loudly, "Dugan and Yeeb set up a base camp in the deserted village. We transport in the cargo." He paused and took a final puff of a cigarette. Dropping the smoldering butt onto the moist floor, he exhaled and said through grinning teeth, "And given the opportunity we sucker punch communism."

CHAPTER TWENTY FOUR

The cloudless sky was a deep blue. Below a churning sea of mountain ranges and deep ravines clawed towards the horizon. Afternoon sunlight reached down into the depths of sharp jagged chasms, nurturing draping growth. In the basin of a narrow gorge, a twin-engine aircraft skimmed across the treetops. The low-winged plane with twin tail fins banked hard to avoid a towering limestone pinnacle guarding a canyon.

In the cockpit Max took a deep breath and glanced over at the cowboy pilot. Buck in blue-jeans and his signature sweat stained Stetson had a wicked smirk as he navigated the Twin Beech through the Laotian obstacle course. With sweaty palms, the German looked over his shoulder. Reclining comfortably between gunnysacks of rice, Loc in jungle fatigues slept. Roche seemed tense from the jostling flight. Sitting on the floor next to the crated Stinger missiles, the American coddled a case of Jim Beam resting on his lap. The chiming cling of the whisky bottles in the logoed cardboard box penetrated the drone of the aircraft.

Blinking at the sunshine pouring through the windshield, Max's stomach dropped. Grabbing the underside of the seat, he leaned back as the plane rapidly descended over a saw-toothed ridge. "Are you having fun cowboy?" He hollered.

"The time of my life," Buck responded.

"You actually miss this?" Max questioned.

Focused forward the seasoned pilot said, "It sure beats worrying about child support." After pausing to reflect, he continued, "You know Max, the best years of my life were flying for Air America. I was young. Thought I was invincible. Combine that with a healthy salary and the excesses of Indochina...it makes for an existence that hard to top." Glancing over at the German, he added, "Don't tell me you don't miss those days? You were Max Kohl, the man who walked out of Isabelle."

"I'm still the same person, just older and a little stiffer in the morning." Max chuckled. "And by the way you are flying today cowboy, I can tell you are the same bush pilot that flew me out of Phong Savin under fire."

"Thanks amigo," Buck mumbled. "I must admit it's been a long time since I had a sense of purpose. Returning stateside was a rough transition. I got lost in the herd. I became that annoying drunk telling tales that nobody wanted to hear."

"It wasn't your stories cowboy." Max said. "It was your audience. Very few people even know where Indochina is. Their ignorance precluded them from appreciating your exploits."

Buck laughed, "I'll have to remember that next time I'm buying and no one is listening."

The Twin Beech began a steep climb up the face of a twin peaked mountain. "Hold on tight to the whisky!" Buck hollered.

An inclined patch of brown appeared in a saddleback ridge between matching summits. The small plane hit the edge of the dirt clearing and rapidly decelerated on the uphill runway. The twin props kicked up dust on the narrow strip before stopping just short of the tree line. Buck in a sweat soaked denim shirt leaned back in his seat and proudly declared, "After five landings that was the smoothest one yet."

Standing on the sloping tarmac, Max inhaled the cool clear air. His head slowly pivoted to capture the magnificent vista. A soft breeze caressed his gaze. A waking Loc rubbed his eyes with a fisted hand. The tribesman's chest swelled as he breathed in the familiar atmosphere.

Hopping down out of the aircraft with a tight grasp around the neck of a square bottle of bourbon, Roche joined his companions. Unscrewing the plastic cap, he took a healthy swig and said, "Next time we make a munitions drop we need to bring ice."

Emerging from a jungle path, Dugan with an AK-47 across a relaxed arm led a squad of seven Hmong partisans. His thin gray sweat soaked hair matted and restrained by a side knotted black headband. Sporting a dark green chest rigging over a taut white singlet, he smiled at his colleagues. Through the thick lenses of sweat spotted spectacles, he said enthusiastically, "Welcome to the party boys."

Roche walked over to Dugan and with an extended arm offered the bourbon. Dugan smiled, slung his automatic weapon over a shoulder and accepted the libation. After a quick nip, he handed the bottle to Yeeb. The tribesman in army surplus fatigues nodded in gratitude and after partaking shared the whisky with his men. Some of the Hmong were dressed like Yeeb, others in black pants and tunic tops, all brandishing virgin AK-47's with distinctive curved banana box magazines.

"What is the situation?" Roche asked.

Dugan flexed. "The abandoned village is a long click up a few switch backs, hauling supplies it seems farther. It has a working well that was tested. Water is not an issue. We made radio contact yesterday with the Hmong resistance and Yeeb sent two scouts out to roust up additional guerilla forces." With a playful shrug, he added, "Other than that all I can tell you is this sure beats the shit out of delivering Pepsi and Pepsi products."

Passing the conversing Americans with a hundred pound burlap sack of rice balanced over his shoulder, Max interrupted, "Just point me in the right direction."

"Uphill Max," Dugan responded pointing towards a tight opening in the dense growth.

Focused on his combat boots, Max slowly ascended the thin trail snaking up the hillside. The stagnant air trapped under the blanketing growth was heavy. Beams of sunlight randomly penetrated the thick canopy. Finding a comfortable rhythm, Max methodically took small steps. Rounding a corner the incline steepened. The rice got heavier. Smaller loads and larger targets, he thought. My age has set new limitations, he realized. The days of squeezing off head shots and trekking with arduous cargo are behind me.

The overhead shade slowly retreated. The air got lighter and carried a charred aroma. The coarse cloth sack chaffed the side of Max's head. He looked up from the trail. Around a sloping town square, stilted palm frond roofed structures clung to hillside. Encroaching patches of brush and weeds swayed in the village pathways. Stacked crates of AK-47s and ammo boxes encircled a stone communal well with a metal hand pump. Breathing heavy, he trudged toward the stockpiled supplies. Bending forward, he released the gunnysack of rice onto a rough wood box. Rubbing his shoulder in the center of the ghost town, he felt emptiness. There were no barking dogs; no tribal women dressed in elaborately embroidered costumes and half naked children running about. He squinted at a large rectangular pile of ash. The cremated remains of the communal house, he concluded. A soft wind kicked up a swirling column of soot. The charred whirlwind danced across the town square.

Grabbing the cast-iron handle of the well's pump, Max siphoned a handful of cool water from the ground and splashed his face. God that felt good, he thought. Cranking harder, he bent down and dowsed his head. Shaking the moisture out of his blond locks, he got a whiff of the fragrant forest. The jungle is one hell of an adversary, he thought. Twenty-eight years ago, I stumbled into a village much like this one, he reflected. I must have looked like Christ of the cross when I collapsed in the shade of a pitched roof stilted hut, he chuckled. His face pinched thinking about the infected insect bites that covered his body and the blood sucking leaches feasting on his legs. Reflecting on the jungle rot that tormented his tender crotch, he tugged on the fly of his pants. Grinning he thought about the young Hmong girls in their tight black skirts washing out his wounds. One of the best non-sexual experiences of my life, he reflected. What a noble race of people, he concluded. They nursed me back into the world of the living. It wasn't my first glimpse into the abyss, he realized. But it was the closest I got to the edge. Recalling the cold voice of death, he shuddered. Like a nagging bitch the pale horseman beckoned with morbid council. Fuck him and his horse, Max chuckled.

Max walked past the pile of dark ash. He paused in front of a raised long house. Cautiously he tested the bowed stair treads of the stilted structure. The rotten wood planks creaked with his ascent. Standing on the sloping deck, he looked into the one room vacated residence. Rodent droppings and a larger animal's scat decorated the planked floor boards. Along the high pitched ceiling crest resided several large fruit bats. Max ignored the stale moldy odor. On wobbly legs I staggered up the stairs of a similar longhouse back in fifty-four, he reflected. The room buzzed with activity. Seated amongst the Meo that day was a tall lanky European with leathery skin and a scruffy beard. Draped over his thin frame was a tattered and frayed uniform. On the shirtsleeves the three stripe markings of a *sergent-chef*. Reaching into his pants pocket, Max retrieved the sergeant stripes of Jean Guillian. With the snarled piece of rough fabric in the palm of his hand, he whispered into the deserted hovel, "I got the weapons you requested."

CHAPTER TWENTY FIVE

The setting sun ignited a red sky behind a towering summit. In the fading light the pinnacle's shadow blanketed the ghost town's village square. Reclining on crates of munitions in cool comfort, the mercenaries rested after unloading the last of the cargo. Roche's legs dangled over a case of automatic weapons. On his back, he focused on the darkening sky with a bottle of whisky. Next to the stone enclave of the communal well, the tribal partisans squatted in a loose circle and quietly enjoyed a smoke. Sitting atop the largest stack of supplies, Buck with his pointed-toe boots resting on an ammo box entertained the troops with the pleasant moan of a blues harmonica. A string of smoke danced above a small cooking fire. A Hmong warrior tending the flames used a combat knife to turn rectangular slabs of Spam in an iron skillet. The sizzling manufactured meat added a salivating aroma to the thin air. Balanced over hot coals, the clattering metal lid of a rice kettle battled escaping steam. Hovering over the cook, Loc and Dugan stood holding impatient tin plates.

Fatigued from the treks up and down from the landing strip, Max propped up by a rough wood box puffed on a short stogy. After exhaling a plume of cigar smoke, the German took a sip from a tin cup. The soothing taste of bourbon diluted with chilled well water rolled down his throat. I'm going to be stiff in the morning, he realized.

Loc sat down next to Max and handing him a metal plate of rice and meat mumbled, "Bon appetite partner."

"Thanks," Max responded. Leaning forward, he blew on the misting serving.

"Meal time?" Roche questioned.

Looking over at the American, Max answered, "Service is like the buffet at the Shangri-La. Get a plate and stand in line." With thumb and forefinger, he picked up a fried slab of Spam. He waved the charred mystery meat to cool it. "If I'm not mistaken," he commented. "I think the luxury hotel had a better selection of entrees."

Snorts, grunts and the smacking of lips accompanied the rapid consumption. Max won the contest. Placing an empty platter to the side, he licked greasy fingers. Retrieving the cigar butt balanced on the end of a crate, he took a quick puff. A feather of smoke flew out of the white ash tip. Several brisk tokes brought the stub of rolled tobacco back to life. Leaning back into the hard wood support, he enjoyed the after dinner cigar.

The camp fire began to glow in the growing darkness. Just beyond the small flames' illumination, the dark jungle stirred. To the rustling sound of dead foliage, Max imagined a nocturnal rat foraging. It could be snake, he thought or one of the thousands of vermin that inhabit the moist ground.

In the midst of the campsite, Dugan set down a greasy plate and flipped on a short wave radio. The black box produced an irritating hiss. The cackling terminated as Dugan flexed a thumb on a handheld microphone. Broadcasting across the airwaves, he spoke in Hmong. Hollow static answered his appeal. After repeating a simple phrase, he waited for the box to speak. Dugan's voice took on a monotonous tone with each repetition.

Max closed his eyes. His belly was full. What is more annoying, he wondered; the electrical interference or the recurring tribal dialogue. Max flinched. A static laced voice answered Dugan's call.

The encampment stirred. All focused on the Hmong dialogue flowing out of the soft-lighted instrument panel. The gaunt partisans huddled around Dugan and his high frequency conversation.

"What is it?" Max whispered to Loc.

Bending an ear, the eavesdropping Loc said, "They made contact with Chao Fa."

"Who is Chao Fa?" Roche slurred loudly.

Over his shoulder, Dugan scowled at Roche's outburst. "Shhhh!" he replied with a finger over his lips.

"Sorry," Roche mumbled. Looking at Loc, he solicited an answer.

"Chao Fa is not a person," Loc informed quietly. "It is a mystical resistant force. They are followers of the Lord of the Sky. The Hmong legends I learned as a boy are incorporated in their beliefs."

"I've never heard of them," Roche said looking at Max for confirmation. Max shrugged.

"After the Americans pulled out in seventy-five, desperate Hmong seeking hope became followers." Loc responded. "Hmong legend foretells of the return of a powerful protector. That in times of great despair true believers would be safe from bad giants. Followers will possess magical powers to destroy any threat."

Placing the handheld microphone beside the fading light of the shortwave, Dugan stood. With his hands on his lower back he stretched. His chest flexed with a sense of accomplishment. Strutting towards the fireside audience, he warmed his palms over the rising heat. Focused on the small blue flames flickering out of the coals, he said shaking his head, "The Choa Fa priest I spoke to predicted our arrival a month ago."

"Come on Dugan?" Roche questioned. "You don't believe in that mystic warrior mumbo jumbo?"

Glancing over at Roche, Dugan's thick spectacles reflecting the fires glow responded, "They started clearing an airstrip three weeks ago awaiting a munitions drop." Looking up at the perched cowboy, he asked, "Well Tex, do we have enough fuel in that Twin-Beech for an early morning milk run?"

Leaning forward, Buck replied, "We did catch a favorable tailwind today. It gave us a petro cushion for the return flight. But before I commit to running errands, I need to know the destination and payload."

"I'll be your only passenger and you can determine the limit of the freight." Dugan informed. "The destination is an old Air America strip in the foothills of Phou Bia."

"Shit," Buck groaned.

"Is it feasible?" Roche asked.

"It's a short flight, so cargo and fuel is not the issue," Buck answered. "And spotting the highest peak in Laos will be easy to find. But that mountain is always shrouded in clouds and fog. During my Indochina tenure, a C-130 slammed into the summit. I hated flying into that remote thick misted jungle strip."

"Let's hope for favorable conditions then," Dugan said. Chuckling he added, "Beside our delivery was forecast by the Hmong god of war."

Stepping into the fires light, Yeeb said quietly, "Don't make light of the Chao Fa. I saw them in action. It was about two years ago. Under the cover of morning fog, I was foraging for food on the outskirts of a Vietnamese occupied village. Out of the heavy mist about thirty mystic warriors appeared. Marching in a straight line, they followed behind a young female flag bearer. The partisans dressed in black and wore red and blue arm-bands. The bright red Chao Fa flag decorated with a crescent moon and a sacred pig. As the crimson flag flapped in the wind, so did the Sons of the Sky shoulder length locks." Pausing to clarify, he injected, "Followers do not cut their hair." Looking down into the smoldering embers, he continued, "Heavily armed with American M-16 carbines and M-72 one-shot rockets, they strutted confidently into the village. Not breaking formation, one of the warriors fired off a shoulder rocket. The Vietnamese barracks erupted. Surviving communist staggered out of the ruble. Standing their ground under the protection of the flag bearer, the Choa Fa exchanged fire. Vietnamese mortars prematurely exploded in mid-air over the heads of the Hmong column. Not one Hmong was killed or wounded as they slaughtered the Vietnamese invaders." Looking around at his attentive audience, he added, "After the one-sided encounter the followers of the Lord of the Sky faded into the morning mist."

No one spoke. The fire popped. The distant jungle stirred.

Pocking the fire with a stick, Roche broke the silence, "I don't doubt your story Yeeb. I've seen a lot on the battlefield that defies logic. I had a hard drinking Marine buddy that changed his ways after a pocket bible caught a bullet. As far as the mortars exploding in mid-air, I also have experienced the divine intervention of faulty weaponry." Tossing the small stick across the coals, he watched it ignite. "I'll never question another man's beliefs nor impose mine on him. Hell, when I was thirteen as a good Catholic boy I became a soldier for Christ. The Bishop came to our parish and slapped me as a reminder that I was a defender of the faith. On many a battlefield, I embraced my beliefs to endure. Like the Choa Fa, I believed a higher power was involved in my survival." Glancing around the fireside, he said confidently, "I don't think it is coincidence that I'm still here breathing the Lord's air."

"My parents were Catholic," Max interjected. "But I was a Nazi. As a boy I was a fanatic follower of the National Socialist agenda. I believed in my racial superiority and the prediction that the Third Reich would last for a thousand years. After that revelation turned out to be a crock of shit, I found my own religion in the trenches. One truth I've learned is that in any conflict the enemy of my enemy is my friend." Looking up at the Texan, he said, "It's up to you Buck. If you are comfortable with the logistics delivering hard rice to these mystic warriors, I'm all for it. If the landing strip is blanketed in spittle, abort."

"Let's do this Dugan," Buck responded. "I don't want to anger the gods of war."

CHAPTER TWENTY SIX

A t dawn's first light, a small plane buzzed across the jungle canopy. A deep fog shrouded the rain forest. Under a gray sky, the serrated summit of Phou Bia punctured the white foam.

In the crowed cockpit, Buck looked over at his only passenger and said, "It's not looking good Mister Jim."

"Have a little faith cowboy," Dugan replied. "Our delivery was foretold by a higher power."

"I'll do a quick flyby of the northwest side. If the hidden valley and runway does not pop out, I'm going to abort." Buck informed.

"It's your call," grumbled Dugan.

Taking a deep breath, Buck descended into the billowing mist. A chill shot through the cabin. In fading light the instrument panel glowed. Flanking the aircraft, towering limestone outcroppings rolled by in the haze.

The fog abruptly terminated. Above the bleak sky turned a shade of blue. In a pocket of surrounding mist lay a long thin red clay tarmac. Buck looked over at the surprised Dugan and shrugged as he prepared to land.

"Kind of makes a believer out of you," Dugan said as the plane landed on the inviting runway.

Taxiing towards the tree line, Buck saw the jungle spring to life. Out of the dense growth the Chao Fa followers eerily appeared. Gaunt men, dressed in black. Long ratted hair draped around chiseled faces. They slowly encircled the aircraft. Fearing they would stroll into the props, Buck hastily cut the engines.

"Let's get this over with quickly," Buck said staring into the leather faces glaring up at the cockpit. "These guys give me the creeps."

Dugan released his harness. Crawling over the cargo, he opened the rear hatch. Cool high altitude air flooded the cabin. "Are you coming?" Dugan questioned.

What have I got to lose? Buck thought.

A thin warrior climbed into the plane. Deep sunken eyes studied the cowboy. A slow nod acknowledged the pilot's presence.

"Mornin'," Buck said as he hoped out of the aircraft. Exhaling he saw his breath. Crossing his arms, he confronted the cold. Rubbing his shoulders, he observed the mute warriors form a human chain to expedite the unloading. Good, we should be back in the air soon, he thought. He wandered over to Dugan conversing with a zealot. "What's going on?" He asked.

"This is Xiong a Chao Fa commander," Dugan responded.

Buck nodded at the sharp cheek boned thin officer.

Dugan continued, "He gets his orders from a ...spiritual advisor...a priest. The priest predicted our arrival and apparently an afternoon departure."

"What!" Buck blurted.

The Hmong commander scowled at the outburst.

"Let's indulge them," Dugan mumbled.

Xiong adjusted the strap of the M-16 slung across his back. Pointing to the procession of men and cargo entering the jungle, he invited his American guests to follow.

Dugan answered Buck's puzzled expression by saying, "The commander is a little odd, but I don't think there is any cause to be alarmed. I suspect their spiritual advisor just wants to show his gratitude."

The forest was thick. There was no trail. Buck plodded behind Dugan. Dugan followed behind half a dozen munitions porters. The short thin Hmong in black pajamas struggled up the steep grade. Treading over decomposing undergrowth released a vile smell.

In the cool air, Buck began to sweat. Winded in the thin air, he became annoyed. We should have just flown out of here he rationalized. Dugan could have politely told the commander thanks for the invitation but we have other shit we gotta do.

The procession stopped. The cargo handlers dropped their loads. From out of the deep foliage curious longhaired inhabitants peered out. Night of the living dead, Buck thought as skeletal partisans draped in rags moved slow; methodically. Standing beside Dugan on trampled growth, the cowboy slowly turned detecting a few camouflaged shelters carved in the earth and brush. To the rustling of leaves, he spun around again. On the second pass hundreds of armed emotionless specters appeared.

"Should I be concerned now?" Buck mumbled.

Dugan chucked and addressed the large audience in their native tongue. In the middle of the monologue, he stuck his chest out and pointed at the munitions crates.

Scanning the hard faces of the audience, Buck ignored Dugan's gibberish. In the midst of the tribal dialogue the words "Mister Jim" popped out. A few smiles appeared on the chiseled faces of the rough crowd. From the hillside, a gray haired warrior descended and placed a respectful hand on Dugan's shoulder. Mister Jim hugged his former associate. Patting the old man's back Dugan whispered into his ear.

Breaking the embrace, Dugan looked at Buck and informed, "This is Chang Neng Sang an old friend."

Buck shook the old man's soiled clammy hand.

Chang bowed.

Out of a rustling pile of leaves, an old man crawled out of the ground. His black tunic and pants streaked with dry mud. Wisp of twisted and tangled thin long silver locks flowed out of his balding head. On all fours, he looked up at the reunion. Chang assisted the old man's frail frame to an upright position. The hillside audience bowed in the presence of the spiritual advisor. The silver haired priest stared through the cowboy with disconcerting eyes. Slowly his head pivoted to focus on Dugan. Creases appeared around the corners of the priest's dry lips. The old man bowed. In a deep distant voice, he spoke to Dugan. Dugan hung on every word. Behind Dugan's thick lenses, wide eyes welled up. The shaman pulled a white stone from his pocket and held it to Dugan's forehead.

As the priest chanted, Buck wondered if this is some kind of baptism. Glancing around at the congregation, he realized the ceremony was sacred.

Now would not be a good time to ask Dugan to translate. Nor would it be appropriate to smoke, he concluded.

The priest left Dugan and crawled back into the ground. The armed crowd cracked open the crated AK-47s. Dugan stood with his head hung down. He flinched as Buck tapped his shoulder.

"You all right?" Buck asked quietly.

"This was my destiny," Dugan mumbled lifting his glasses and poking a finger at moist eyes. "The priest informed me that I had the heart of a Hmong warrior. The blood pumping through my white veins served a single purpose. I was summoned to defeat the evil giant."

Seeing Dugan beam with a sense of purpose, Buck remained silent. Many a carnival fortune teller and evangelical preacher can achieve the same results, he realized. A drifting soul in search of significance hungers for answers. Whatever the Chao Fa priest was serving, Dugan ate it up. Who am I to question Dugan's destiny he concluded. I found religion at the bottom of whisky bottle.

CHAPTER TWENTY SEVEN

I t was dusk in the Laotian highlands. The setting sun cast long shadows across the deserted village square. Yeeb and his fellow Hmong partisans squatted across the tops of the munitions crates. Encircling a small cooking fire Max, Loc and Roche sat on ammo tins. A Hmong warrior tended the fire. Lifting the jittery lid of a rice kettle, the cook dumped a can of tuna into steaming rice. A denim jacket slung over his shoulder, Buck followed Dugan into base camp. Max and Loc turned and with quick nods greeted their companions.

"We expected you sooner," Roche said firmly gripping the neck of a whisky bottle. "Any issue with the Chao Fa milk run?"

"Nah," Buck said approaching the fire. "A Chao Fa psychic predicted a late afternoon departure. To accommodate the mystic, we delayed our return flight."

"He was a priest!" Dugan corrected. "His intuition assured a safe journey."

Rolling his eyes, Buck said, "Sorry Dugan, I didn't mean to insult your new found religion." To the fireside audience, he added, "The shaman took one look at me and quickly determined my Southern Baptist roots were not worth converting."

Roche filled a tin cup with bourbon and handed it to Dugan. Mister Jim accepted it with a snort. Scowling at the cowboy, he crawled atop a munitions crate with his Hmong brothers.

Waving off Roche's cocktail offer, Buck said, "Not tonight." Seeing the surprised expressions of his companions, he chuckled. "This is not the first time I've tried to quit," he informed. Taking a seat on an ammo box, he warmed his hands over the fire. Looking into the hot coals, he said, "This is as good as any time for me to confront the alcohol demon." Placing a cigarette between his lips, he stuck a twig into the fire. The end of the stick sparked into flame. He lit the Marlboro. Exhaling, he examined the smoldering canister between his fingers and mumbled, "One vice at time."

"Were the Chao Fa worthy of our contribution?" Max asked.

Slowly nodding his head, Buck answered, "Most definitely." Glancing up at glowing faces, he added, "Their religious fanaticism was eerie but not their resolve." Focused on Loc he asked, "Just who is this San Sai they kept referring to?"

The Hmong cook stirring chunks of fish meat into sticky rice flinched.

Looking up at the cook, Loc winked. "Sin Sai is an ancient warrior." Loc answered. "My father told me the story of Sin Sai as did his father. The tale dates back to the beginning of time. The first people of earth were threatened by a big bad giant." Pausing Loc looked into the fire and grinned. "My father always would say the giant's eyes burned like the fires of hell." After reflecting on the lost memory, he continued. "Sin Sai was powerful, kind and just. He took grains of rice and after putting them in his mouth spit them out. The grains of rice became soldiers in a powerful army. The bad giant was defeated. Sin Sai told the people to stay on top of the mountains and avoid evil spirits. If bad giants threaten, he would return out of the sky. He then left this world in a flash of fire." Leaning back, Loc took a deep proud breath of highland air.

Atop a munitions crate an eavesdropping Yeeb yelled out, "My father would say the bad giant growled like the thunder."

Raising a tin cup in the air, Roche proposed a toast, "To the return of Sin Sai."

"I'll drink to that," Max said miming the gesture. "There are a lot of bad giants roaming this planet."

The snap of underbrush triggered the clicks of automatic weapons charging bolts. Gun barrels took aim at the dark surrounding tree line. The fire crackled. The rice kettle lid fluttered. Just beyond the flickering light, the trampling crunch of foliage escalated. Out of the black dense growth, a Hmong family waddled into the soft fire's glow. Sighs of relief and surprise preceded the securing of armaments.

The father removed his skullcap. Bowing his head, he fidgeted with the piece of black fabric. A rusty M-16 strapped across his back. Behind him his wife with a black cylindrical hat and large silver looped earrings protectively wrapped her arms around two boys and a teenage daughter. The girl buried her face in her mother's shoulder.

"How are you friend?" Dugan asked in a tribal dialect. He slowly rose with stiff joints.

The nervous father flinched at the American's linguistic skill.

Max looked at the Hmong boys clinging to their mother's indigo dyed skirt. They appeared to be ten and twelve years old. The eldest had a French revolver tucked into the drawstring of his trousers. The soiled faces brothers nervously twitched. Big brown eyes stole glances of the campsite. Carbine soldiers, Max thought, victims of perpetual conflict. After war claims the able body youth, you feed it old men and boys. I was a carbine soldier, he realized. The Third Reich called me into service as they desperately scrapped the bottom of the barrel.

Max nudged Loc and pointed his head in direction of the hill tribe family. Loc leaned into the German and whispered, "They are Black Tai like me. My mother wore the same stovepipe hat." Loc paused as the father spoke to Dugan. Translating the dialogue, Loc informed, "The father heard that Americans had returned. He claims he has a ... treaty...an agreement with the American president." Loc paused with a puzzled expression. Leaning closer to the conversation, he added, "He humbly asked if we are here to honor the commitment."

From the comfortable fireside, Roche sprang to his feet and asked, "What does he want?"

Dugan turned away from the nervous father. Looking at Roche, he shrugged his shoulders and responded, "He claims he has a White House document guaranteeing him and his family the full protection of the United States."

"Oh this I gotta see," Roche exclaimed taking a swig of whisky. With an intoxicated smile, he staggered across the moist earth. Peering over Dugan's shoulder, he nodded soliciting proof.

The tiny tribesman placed his black skullcap back on his head. From the cloth satchel strung across his shoulder, he retrieved a glass mason jar. A shaky hand unscrewed the rusty lid. Carefully he pulled a plastic wrapped document from the vessel. Between thumb and forefinger and with the reverence of a priest offering the body of Christ, he presented the contents.

Dugan accepted the cellophane protected text. With Roche breathing heavy beside him, he unwrapped the covering. A colorful lithograph of the White House appeared on the stiff folded paper of a Christmas card. Flipping over the cover labeled *Presidents House*, Dugan read out loud the greeting below the embossed presidential seal, "With all the best wishes for a Merry Christmas and a Happy New Year... the President and Misses Nixon."

"I'll be damned," Roche mumbled.

The tribesman sheepishly grinned with crooked yellow teeth seeking authenticity.

"He has no idea," Dugan said.

Roche looked over at the perched Texan and asked, "Buck can we squeeze another five passengers in on our return flight?"

Squinting into the limited fire light, Buck rubbed his chin. "Let's see," he said. "Dad is a buck fifty at best. The mom and girl are a little over two hundred pounds and the boys are rounding errors." With a slow nod, he added, "No problem Major."

Roche turned to the father with an extended hand and said, "On behalf of Dick and Pat in DC, we will honor the document."

The tribesman shook Roche's hand with a bow. Looking over his shoulder at his family, he proudly stuck his chin out.

Dugan placed a reassuring hand on the man's shoulder. Waving a welcome hand toward the kettle of rice suspended over glowing embers, he said, *"Please eat from our table."*

The man bowed in gratitude and retrieved the sacred greeting card. Carefully wrapping the document in cellophane, he placed it back into the fruit jar chalice. His shadowing wife patted the back of her trembling daughter's head.

A stiff-backed Roche with a square bottle of bourbon dangling at the end of a limp arm raised his other hand. With extended fingers, he called out. "Loc toss me a tin cup."

The metal mug spun out of the darkness into the fire light. Roche plucked it out of the night sky. Filling it with a healthy shot of whisky, he offered it to the tribesman. The father seemed confused. Sticking his nose into the mug, he inhaled deep. His head elevated with a wide grin.

Roche nodded and tapped the bottle with the tin cup. "To your family," he said taking a swig. Turning towards Loc, he asked, "Can you translate that for me?"

"When a host provides liquor *Ami*, there is no translation necessary," Loc responded.

CHAPTER TWENTY EIGHT

The remote night sky sparkled. A streak of a falling star graced the twinkling canvas. A soft chilled breeze flowed down the deserted village square arousing the embers in the fading camp fire. In the glow of the disturbed ash lay Max, Roche and Loc. Perched above a tranquil audience, Buck with cupped hands blew a peaceful blues tune through a harmonica. Wide eyed, the two Hmong boys sitting on ammo boxes stared up at the cowboy. Their older sister enjoyed the instrumental from a distance.

The wailing melody competed with the crack of boards as Pheeb, Dugan and the Hmong partisans took turns with a pry-bar to unwrap the crated weapons. Fueled by Jim Beam, billowing laughter erupted from the warriors.

Laying face up on a canvas tarp beside the fire, Max marveled at the twinkling night sky. Blowing cigar smoke into the crisp air, his chest expanded and contacted. Soothed by Buck's background music and the crackling fire, he drifted comfortably towards sleep. The clanking of tin plates stirred him out of his bordering slumber. Squinting in the direction of the communal well, he spotted the Hmong mother cranking on the rusty hand pump to wash the mess kits. In a stovepipe hat, the frail woman bent over and licked the tuna grease from the platters before rinsing them off. Life on the run has certainly taken its toll on this Hmong beauty, Max thought. She is probably in her late twenties, he guessed. Her face has few wrinkles but her hutched over frame shows the cost of bearing three children with little to eat. Glancing over, Max saw her offspring enjoying the cowboy's harmonica act and grinned. The soothing power of music, he concluded. In the distant shadows, the Hmong father sat contently sipping on a whisky.

"*Ami,*" Max called out to Roche.

Roche took a deep breath and answered with a groggy voice, "What is it kraut?"

"Why this family?" Max questioned, "Of the hundreds of thousands Hmong seeking rescue, why them?"

Roche propped himself on his elbows to respond. Glancing around at the family, he answered, "Call it fate or perhaps divine intervention. Regardless, at the point in time when I needed to do penance for my government's betrayal of the Hmong, we crossed paths with a family in possession of Nixon's Christmas card. Arming the partisan will make me feel good; rescuing this family will absolve me of past sins."

Taking a performance break, Buck wiped his moist lips on the back a denim shirtsleeve. From a tin cup, he took a sip of well water. Looking down into the glowing faces of his new admirers, he winked.

The youngest boy responded with a wide grin.

"What do you think Corky?" Buck asked the boy.

Confused the boy politely shook his head.

"Loc I need a translator," Buck called down into the darkness.

"What do you need cowboy?" Loc responded from the fireside.

"Tell this little hombre his nickname is Corky," Buck declared. As Loc translated the boy beamed. "Now let's see," Buck said studying the older brother with the French revolver. "You're packing a shooting iron like a true gunslinger...How does Hip-shot sound?" The translation caused the boy to sit up and take a deep proud breath.

Steeping into the fire light, the shy teenage girl looking into glowing coals sought recognition. Her hair tucked tightly under a stovepipe black hat. Silver loop earrings dangled from exposed ears. The taut skin of her young flat nosed face shined in the limited light.

Such a beauty, Buck thought admiring the perfect example of blossoming innocence. Just like my daughter at that age, he realized. We were so close back then, he sadly reflected on the lost relationship. "Angel," he said softly gazing at the Hmong girl. "She reminds me of an Angel."

Loc translated. With a shy smile the girl looked up a Buck before quickly turning away and blushing.

"Now that that's settled," Buck said. "We can all board the midnight train to Memphis." Encasing the blues harp with cupped hands, he began to mimic the wailing sound of a train whistle. The tune quickly evolved into the riff of a thundering locomotive express.

With the reproduced sound of a freight train entertaining the children, Loc approached the Hmong father. Squatting down Loc stuck out his hand and said, "I am Moua Loc."

Giving the hand a firm shake, the tribal father introduced himself, "Fang Va-Meng," With a respectful bow, he added, "My sister married into the Moua clan. It is good to see a brother."

"I am a proud Hmong," Loc said. "But after fighting in the French war as part of the Tai Battalion, I adopted the Western way of life."

Humbly looking down Va-Meng informed, "I was born during the time of the French. I am thirty years of age."

"I'm fifty years old," Loc reciprocated. "I reside with my Vietnamese wife and four children in America. In a village called Garden Grove."

"Is it a large village?" Va-Meng asked making eye contact for the first time.

"Very large for a Hmong," Loc chuckled. "In America all the villages seemed connected. It is difficult to tell were one starts and one ends."

"Is it a good place?" Va-Meng asked. As Loc pondered a response, the Hmong father clarified. "Is it like the harmonious time the elders used to talk about before the French?"

Shaking his head Loc said quietly, "Those days will never return little brother. As for life in America it is very confusing for a Hmong. Our virtues of honesty and politeness are many times misunderstood as weakness."

"The Americans are a strange people," Va-Meng commented rubbing a scruffy chin. "They are so powerful and yet they were intimidated by the Pathet Lao."

"Did you work for the Americans?" Loc asked.

Slowly nodding Va-Meng answered, "They supplied my village with food and weapons. We paid them back by sacrificing Hmong warriors rescuing downed pilots. I was a scout monitoring communist troop movements down the Ho Chi Minh trail. The American withdrawal came quickly. There was much chaos. During the evacuation of the base camp, I bargained with an important American for the safe passage for my family. I traded ten bars of silver for the agreement with the President of the United States. In addition to the document, he gave me a leather suitcase. The travel bag was weathered. We placed all our worldly possessions in that cracked and torn hide box. Hundreds of Hmong families stood on a dirt landing strip. There were three large transport airplanes." Shaking his head, he added. "They weren't large enough. The nervous crowd surged forward. Children cried. Passengers were shoved out of overloaded aircraft. The metal birds came to life. The racing engines were deafening. Slapped hard by the prop wash, we watched the fortunate escape into the sky. Scanning the skies for additional aircraft the crowd waited. The next day with the loss of hope, the American collaborators began to disperse."

"How did you survive brother?" Loc asked.

With a dry raspy voice Va-Meng reflected. "Since I can remember there was war. I conceded to the communist victory and chose to live in peace as a simple farmer. Returning home, I found my village occupied by Vietnamese soldiers. The occupiers ruled supreme. They took what they wanted." He paused and rubbing a sniffling nose glanced over at his woman and confessed, "They slept with our wives without protest." Inhaling back surfacing emotion, he continued. "I knew my name was on the list of American collaborators and had to flee. One day while working in the fields my family slipped through the communist grasp. Pursued in the dense jungle we ate leaves, roots and..." He glanced over at his children and grinning injected, "My eldest son Nu became very skilled at shooting birds with a sling-shot." Re-focusing he continued. "On our journey we encountered many fleeing Hmong. We hid in caves and dug holes in the ground to avoid enemy patrols. To quiet the very young, mothers feed their children opium. Sometimes the drug worked too well. Doped babies left this world without a whimper. We passed through dead villages. The crops, water and inhabitants poisoned by the death that dropped from the communist sky." Pointing at the silhouette of the towering mountain, he said, "We found sanctuary there about two years ago. In a deep cavern on the northern slope, we hide. It is a small community of several Hmong families. We were the only Black Hmong. The other inhabitants were strangers from other tribes. We came together fearing extermination from a common enemy. Yesterday a resistance scout informed us that the Americans were returning for a munitions drop. I have waited all these years for the United States to make good on the agreement that cost me ten bars of silver."

Loc studied his countryman in the flicking light. This could have been me, he thought. Had I not partnered with Max all those years ago, I would either be dead or existing on roots and leaves in the back of a cave. Loc placed his hand on Va-Meng's shoulder and said, "Our mission is the priority. There is great risk in completing our task. However, if Roche said he will honor the American president's agreement with you," Loc paused and identified Roche with a nod and a glance. "Then at the conclusion of our business, we will fly you and your family to safety."

Va-Meng picked up his battle-scarred M-16. Laying the tarnished weapon across his lap, he looked into Loc's eyes. "I will fight beside you brother," he said proudly. "The Communist gave the Hmong few choices. We could flee, hide or fight back. After years of running and living in a cave, it will good to once again kill the men who rape our women and children." Looking over at his sons, he added, "Nu is the same age I was when I picked up arms. He will fight beside me as I did with my father."

Loc saw a spark in the humble man's eyes.

CHAPTER TWENTY NINE

Isabelle's nail salon was dark. An adding machine in the back office chirped. A gooseneck desk lamp provided focused light. Scanning down an open ledger with her left hand, Mei worked a ten-key calculator by touch. A small paper roll flowed out of the electric aid and spilled out onto the floor. On the desk top arranged by denomination were neat stacks of cash. Less formal was a heaping pile of personal checks. A closed journal reflected what was reported to the taxing authorities. The ledger Mei updated more fairly represented the profits of the family business. Cash transactions the significant difference between the two sets of books. Tearing off the paper scroll, Mei studied the tally. Grinning she picked up a number two yellow pencil and inputted the results. A good month, she concluded. If only KJ's Lounge's rent check didn't bounce, it would have been better, she thought. I'll have to speak to Kevin in the morning, she grumbled. Leaning back in the swiveling chair, she sighed and glanced at a desk clock. It was eleven-twenty-five. Flinching at this revelation, she cut short the bookkeeping reprieve. It's later than I thought, she realized. With a sense of urgency, she corralled the heap of disheveled checks and filled out a deposit slip. After securing the checks in a zipped blue vinyl bank bag, she placed the cash in her purse.

Standing over the illuminated cluttered work surface, Mei slung the purse over her shoulder. Attempting to restore an assemblage of order, she stacked the loose papers into random piles. Picking up a folded over section of the Los Angeles Times, she paused. Under the headline: *Escalating Gang Violence in Little Saigon* was a grainy black and white photo of a bullet riddled Chevy Impala sedan. The caption clarified that four members of the Wah Ching youth gang were gunned down in an apparent turf war. A sixteen-year old boy in critical condition was the only survivor. Terminated with extreme prejudice, Mei reflected. She tossed the printed results of her three-thousand dollar donation to the Lao Liberation Front into the trash bin.

Turning off the desk lap, she shuffled towards the back door. Exterior light leaked through the crease of the doorframe. Opening the hollow metal door, she cautiously peered into the back alley. Downcast lighting spotlighted her vehicle. The hum from the back of the Laundromat competed with the distant jukebox music resonating from KJ's lounge. The cool air tainted with the odor from the communal dumpster.

High heels clicked rapidly off the loose gravel. Sliding a key into the car's door, Mei heard movement under the vehicle. Startled, she looked down. A pair of black hands reached out shackling her ankles. The concealed assailant pulled hard. A spiked heel snapped as she fell backwards. Her tush slammed hard into the rough asphalt. The momentum whipped back her torso lashing the back of her skull into the blacktop. Stunned, she gazed up into the bright back lot light. A slow hand investigated the biting pain on the back of her head. Her fingers stroked wet matted hair. A large black canvas tennis sneaker slammed into her chest. Trapped under the heavy foot, she heard a low groan. It's me she realized, I'm the one moaning in pain.

A black teenager in a blue headband and flannel shirt looking down said, "I bet you didn't see that coming momma."

A wiry kid crawled out from the vehicles undercarriage and emptied out the bank deposit bag, "This is just paper," he snorted. "I thought you said these chinks were loaded."

"Check the bitch's purse," the pinning thug ordered twisting his heavy foot.

Beside Mei's head the contents of her handbag rained down.

"Holy shit," declared the mugger. "You were right, these zipper heads got bank."

Squatting down the large footed thug placed the blade of a knife across Mei's face. "You sure are pretty for an old gook." He mumbled.

"Cut her Cuzz," his accomplice encouraged.

The back door to KJ's Lounge swung open. The thump a popular tune escalated. "What's going on over there?" Kevin called out. "Call the police!" he shouted back into the dark watering hole.

The teenage assailants ran. Turning on her side Mei, saw Kevin tossing a metal garbage can full of empty bottles at the sprinters. Bottles rolled and shattered across the alley way. The wiry thug with cash in hand did not break stride hurdling the trash can obstacle. Cuzz's large sneakers did not clear the galvanized drum. Off balance with flaying arms, he landed face down in broken glass littering the asphalt.

Using an arm for support, Mei stood. Blood flowed down her back. Bent over with hands on her knees, she took large gulps of night air. At her feet lay the contents of her purse. Elevating her gaze, she saw Kevin kicking the injured predator's knife out of reach. Picking up the empty trashcan, the delinquent tenant slammed the metal barrel on the groaning youth. Reaching down, Mei picked up the bone handle of her straight razor. Limping with a missing shoe, she flicked her wrist exposing a sparkling blade. Under the parking lot lights, she ignored the curious patrons peering out of the lounge. Kevin spoke to her with concern. She did not hear him. Grabbing a handful of blue flannel, she flipped over the moaning gang member. His cut and scraped face twinkled with green and amber imbedded shards. Dropping a petite knee onto his pounding chest, she looked into his twitching eyes. With death looking over her shoulder, she placed the honed edge of the razor next to the boys head. Twenty-seven years ago I drove a small knife into the throat of a Corsican assassin, she reflected. Recalling the killing of Petru Rossi, she grinned. Anyone who threatens my existence pays a hefty toll, she surmised. "Cut her cuzz?" she questioned her prey. The trembling boy pondered an answer with an open mouth. Hearing the wailing of approaching emergency vehicles and feeling the focus of the bar patron audience, she reduced his sentence. A firm hand split his ear and plowed a deep trench across his cheek.

CHAPTER THIRTY

The morning light bathed the towering summit. The penetrating rays defined crevices in the jagged stone face. The early light spilled into an open longhouse window. Creeping across the hardwood floor it stirred Max out of a deep sleep. Blinking up at the pitched palm ceiling above, he smelled the rich aroma of coffee. A soft breeze carried the commotion of distant voices and laughter. Rolling over his stiff torso, he propped himself up on an elbow. Empty bedding blanketed the floor. Angel in the black cylinder hat of her tribe stood in the doorway with three misting tin cups. Floating on the balls of bare feet, she wove her way across the room and placed a mug beside the cowboy's empty high-shaft boots. Snoring under a wide brim hat, Buck did not stir. Gingerly stepping over a sleeping Roche, she smiled at Max. Quickly she looked away and giggled. The beauty of youth, Max thought admiring her dark eyes, firm skin and flat nose. Squatting down, she placed two steaming cups beside the German. "Thank you," he whispered as she pranced away. Sipping on the rich brew, he watched Roche snort to life.

"What is this?" Roche asked blinking and pointing at the metal mug.

"Room service," Max answered talking a satisfied gulp.

The American poured a shot of bourbon into his coffee and mumbled, "Hair of the dog."

Sliding out of the sleeping bag, Max in white boxer shorts stretched his tight frame. Firmly clutching the warm precious mug, he shuffled his stiff joints onto the deck. Chilled mountain air caressed his naked flesh. Leaning on the bamboo railing of the stilted structure, he enjoyed the strong coffee. The ghost town appeared alive. White smoke strings from bogus cooking fires drifted into the morning sky. In the town square, Dugan stood on a wooden crate and supervised the distribution of automatic weapons. An orderly queue of tribesmen snaked through the courtyard. Mountain bandits, peasant farmers, old men and boys waited patiently for an AK-47 and ammunition. Recipients squatted and stood in small clusters admiring their new possession. Others beneficiaries accepted the gift and retreated into the jungle.

"Priming the pump of rebellion," Roche in white briefs said joining the German on the porch.

"I don't know," Max responded. "For me this was a weapons drop and nothing more." Shifting his weight on the bamboo balustrade, he added, "In the first Indochina war hundreds of French commandos stayed behind with the hill tribes. As the bamboo curtain came down dividing Vietnam, they pleaded over the static of fading radio transmissions for support. Fearing communist reprisal they wanted to go down fighting. France abandoned them in 1955." Glancing at Roche, he added, "The Americans repeated the betrayal twenty years later." Flicking the tin cup, he tossed a swallow of cold coffee onto the dirt below. "I know General Yang has higher aspirations but if France and the United States could not defeat communism in Indochina, these tribesmen don't stand a chance."

"I know," Roche said.

Stepping back from the railing, Max took a deep breath. Inflating his chest, he raised his arms over his head and let out a relaxing moan. "Having fought in the trenches like you *Ami*, we both know that what we were fighting for gets blurred and distorted over time. The only true constant is your *kameraden*, your *copains*, your buddies." Focused on the troops below the bamboo banister, he professed, "The *Montagnards* took me in twenty-five years ago on my escape from Isabelle and for that I will always be in their debt."

"Well my kraut buddy, we might not defeat communism in the next couple of days," Roche said with a wicked grin. "But given the opportunity, we'll slap that bitch."

"I like the sound of that *Ami*," Max responded. "A firm backhand across the face of the Pathet Lao is long overdue."

"Let's get dressed," Roche said. "Today we poke the hornet's nest."

Entering the longhouse, Max muttered, *"Guten Morgen,"* to the dressing cowboy.

"Mornin' hombres," Buck replied strapping on his jeans with a pewter ace of spades buckle. "Is something burning outside?" he asked.

"Dugan's sending up smoke signals to announce our presence," Roche replied putting on his army surplus fatigues. "Hopefully the communist take the bait and send out a patrol."

The cowboy's brow wrinkled.

"Don't fret Tex," Roche said buttoning his shirt. "All you have to worry about is flying us out of Dodge once the shit hits the fan."

Adjusting his cowboy hat, Buck smiled and saluted with a finger off the wide brim.

Sitting on the wooden crate of the prized hand-held missiles, Max laced his combat boots. Standing, he stomped the floor to test the fit as Roche picked up a pry-bar.

Squatting down, Roche wedged the cut-shaped tip of the cat's paw into a crease of the shipping crate. The American pounded the hexagonal bar with the palm of his hand. Working his way around the nailed wooden lid, he opened the timber box. A leather rifle case rested on top of the packaged Stinger missiles. Max and Buck leaned over Roche's shoulders as he unlatched the leather container.

"What is it?" Max questioned.

"It's something I asked Matthews to throw into the weapons deal." Roche responded lifting the lid. "It's a Barrett M82 anti-material rifle."

"Designed for targeting military equipment rather than combatants?" Max asked.

Roche nodded.

"Looks like an updated version of a Kentucky Long Rifle," Buck injected. "Davy Crocket named his Betsy and used the weapons superior range defending the Alamo."

Ignoring the Texas history lesson, Roche grunted picking up the weapon.

"How much does it weigh?" Max questioned.

"About thirty pounds?" Roche answered handing the rifle to Max.

"Its heavy," Max said gauging the weight with a lifting motion. He offered the rifle to Buck.

The cowboy threw up his hands, "Don't look at me. I'm just here to drive the getaway car."

Max chuckled and respectfully placed the weapon back in the case. "What's the effective range?" He asked.

"A little over a mile," Roche answered raising his brows.

"My god," Max mumbled.

"If you are going to poke a hornet's nest," Roche said. "It always better if you can use a long stick." Looking at Buck, Roche informed, "At that distance a skilled marksman can neutralize a communist unit of both men and equipment undetected."

"Cartridge size?" Max asked.

"Fifty-caliber feed from a ten-round detachable magazine." Roche informed.

"What if they send in choppers?" Buck asked.

Patting the crated missiles, Roche said, "I hope they do."

CHAPTER THIRTY ONE

A rogue cloud passed in front of the afternoon sun. Its cooling shadow rolled across the abandoned mountainside community. Sham cooking fires continued to feed beckoning smoke into the sky. On the raised deck of the longhouse, Buck stood beside the Hmong mother and daughter. Dangling his feet over the edge of the elevated porch, Corky sat in front of the cowboy's pointed-toe boots. From these cheap seats, they quietly observed.

Around the communal well, a guerrilla band of twelve prepared for battle. A breeze brushed the courtyard with white smoke. The metal click of small arms resonated in the haze. Sitting on the lip of the stone well, Roche knotted a camouflage rag behind his balding head. Beside him, Dugan used two fingers to paint his face a deep green. Loc cranking on the well's pump filled a cupped hand with water and splashed his face. In a small circle, Yeeb and four of his Hmong warriors squatted on their haunches. Clutching loaded AK-47's the tribesmen sucked apprehensively on cigarettes. Va-Meng slung a Russian automatic rifle over his shoulder and checked his son's French revolver. A wide-eyed Hip-shot looked up at his father with childish enthusiasm. Va-Meng spun the six-gun's loaded cylinder. A leather lariat hung from a small eyelet under the pistol's grip. Ceremonially the father placed the tethered revolver over his son's head. Max sheathed his Soviet pistol in a shoulder holster. Taking a deep breath, the German heaved the heavy snipers rifle across his back. Out of the jungle lavatory, the balance of the patrol emerged pulling up trousers. Roche nodded at his companions and the cadre began a slow march out of the village.

Max plodded behind Loc in the loose line of resistance fighters trek-king downhill. Seeing the father and son team of Va-Meng and Hip-shot on the narrow path, Max pictured his daughter Eva. She is so young and full of life, he thought. Why am I doing this he wondered? I have a good life in Paris, a beautiful wife. Looking up into the jungle canopy the sunlight danced above the thick growth. This is not my first patrol, he realized but probably my last. I was and still am a German soldier. The finest fighting force to ever march across the face of this planet, he thought, reflecting back on the words spoken by Sergeant Franz. We are soldiers not fanatics, the *Afrika Korps* veteran preached during the battle of Caen. I didn't choose this profession, Max realized but I excelled at it. I may be older, have a lot more to lose but when I meet my maker I'll do it with pride.

Passing the airstrip, Max saw the dirt tarmac covered in brush. Perched atop the incline the Beechcraft shrouded in camouflage netting. It is a good thing our back door is concealed, he thought. The filtering light dimin-ished. The dense growth thickened. The jungle path faded in and out. The short high pitched call of an exotic bird competed with insect racket. High stepping through damp knee high ferns, Max continued the gradual descent. In front of him, Loc led the way in sweat soak fatigues. The air was heavy. Heat rose from the moist ground. Passing through a cloud of gnats, Max wiped his face with a moist hand and snorted. Heavy drops of perspiration dripped from his head. He tugged on the anti-material rifle's strap. Scowling he stopped to sling the long heavy uncomfortable load over his other shoulder.

The dark woods lightened. Max followed Loc into the penetrating sun-light of a small clearing. Yeeb, Dugan and the Hmong partisans conversed with a scout. The eleven-year old Hip-shot stood tall amongst the seasoned veterans. Max dipped a shoulder releasing the thirty-pound rifle. Placing the gun butt on the damp soil, he held onto the long barrel for balance.

Bringing up the rear, Roche stumbled into the open space. Placing his hands on his knees, he sucked in humid air. Between breaths, he asked, "What's the situation?"

Loc translated, "A communist military unit has been deployed to investigate the smoke. They typically truck in twenty to thirty troops to the trail head and then trek up to the village."

From his crouched position Roche called out, "Dugan how far to the trial head?"

After asking the scout, the dark faced Dugan answered, "Five clicks."

"What do you think?" Roche inquired.

"Take out the truck?" Dugan answered with a question.

Straightening up, Roche placed his hands on his lower back and asked Max, "What do you think kraut? Can you hit a truck with that long range cannon?"

Max chuckled, "It may take me a few shots to see how this weapon performs. But yes *Ami*, I can hit a fucking truck."

"All we need to do today is poke the hornet's nest. Let them know that we're here." Roche said seeking confirmation.

The mercenaries nodded as Yeeb translated the orders to his troops.

CHAPTER THIRTY TWO

In a prone position, Max lay in waist deep elephant grass. In front of him under a blue sky, the rich emerald vista of a deep sharp valley unfolded. Through a telescopic riflescope, he studied the carved out red clay road zigzagging up the dark green mountain face. Lying beside him, Roche with binoculars followed the progress of an orange dust cloud traversing between the sparking rice paddies in the valley's basin.

"I've never used a scope before," Max mumbled.

"Use the folding backup iron sights, if you need to," Roche whispered before loudly smacking a pest on the side of his head.

"Let's try to remain undetected *Ami*," Max murmured.

The tall grass engulfing the ambush patrol swayed under a light wind. The ground beneath them was alive. The moist soil pulsed. A curious insect population investigated the intrusion. Max twitched from a pin prick on the back of his sweaty neck. Blindly, he reached behind his head. Between thumb and forefinger, he crushed the exoskeleton of a frantic six-legged parasite. After wiping the gelatin remains in the dirt, he pivoted the rifle's scope down. Through the magnified glass, he got his first glimpse of a high riding Soviet Molotova truck. Climbing up the steep grade, the faded green and rusty transport rocked from side to side. A rolled up white canvas canopy draped over the vehicles cab. Out of the open wood paneled truck bed, approximately twenty Mao-style soft caps adorned communist heads. The bulbous caps swayed to the rhythm of the jostling ascent.

Feeling Roche's hand on his shoulder, Max whispered, "What is it?"

"A second vehicle," Roche responded softly.

Through the cross-hairs of the telescopic sight, Max confirmed another truck make the turn into his field of vision. "Acknowledged," he mumbled.

The two transports appeared and disappeared crawling up the narrow switchbacks. The lead vehicle made the final cut up the hill into range. Looking past it, Max waited for the second transport. To the coughing of a Soviet engine, he realized this was not the time to be schooled in telescopic targeting. Detaching the scope, he flipped up the backup sights. The second vehicle rounded the corner. Aiming at a dented rusty truck grill, he whispered, "Shooter ready."

Roche crawled out of the muzzle blast zone.

The crack of the long rifle echoed off the mountain's face. A half-inch projectile passed through an overheated radiator and into the engine block. The hood of the truck flew up in a burst of steam. The wheels locked. The vehicle died.

Expecting a bigger kick, the weapon's recoil surprised Max. The manual sights are dead on he realized searching for the lead vehicle. The truck skidded to a stop. Scanning the target, he saw five-gallon gas cans lined up behind the driver's door. Squeezing the trigger, he unleashed a fifty-caliber round.

A fireball erupted out of the side of the vehicle. The truck cab burst into flames. Bewildered men in khaki uniforms poured out of both transports. Black soot twisted into the blue sky from the smoldering truck. Amidst the confusion an officer stood his ground. Waiving a pistol over his head, the commander hollered at the disoriented troops.

Spinal cords, Max thought reflecting back to the backbones strewn across the bloody basin of Isabelle. We reported dead Legionnaires by counting spinal cords, he recalled. All that remained of my fallen *kameraden* after the communist long range assault was a loose column of vertebrae. You had the tactical advantage then, he thought. "But not today," he whispered.

The sniper rifle barked. Max's shoulder felt the kick and a fifty-caliber bullet sent the communist officer flying with an open chest.

They are only targets Max concluded, but the officers have a higher point value. Taking a soft satisfying breath, he whispered, "That was for Muller."

Twenty to thirty communist charged up the hillside. Wading through waist high foliage, they sprayed their advance with automatic weapons fire. Suppressing fire is useless at this range, Max thought calculating a shooting sequence. The Laotian soldier leading the charge jerked back violently. A fifty-caliber round severed his right shoulder and arm. The flaying victim wailed. They are only targets Max reminded himself. Flexing his finger the German sent another plasma-spewing attacker tumbling downhill. The advancing roaches scurried for cover in the shallow brush and behind the few trees decorating the embankment. "Time to retreat," Max mumbled.

Utilizing the thin forest, the hostiles pulsed uphill. Targeted a tree trunk Max launched a penetrating projectile. From behind the splintered tree wound, a casualty staggered into the open and collapsed. Out of the shallow brush, bulbous soft communist caps bobbed up and down. A brave soul jumped out and ran down the hill. Targeting the fleeing man Max hesitated. Two other dissuaded communist joined their comrade in retreat.

Feeling a hand on his calf, Max looked back.

Roche gave him a thumbs-up and mumbled, "Message sent."

Max flinched at the popping sound of small arms fire. Across the hillside battlefield, a possessed green faced Dugan charged downhill. The thick spectacled American running out of control, squeezed out quick burst from an AK47. Trailing Mister Jim, the Hmong partisans advanced with poise.

"What the hell?" growled Roche.

"*Ami*, I got four shots left. I'll need you to spot targets." Max said returning to a firing position. Immediately he blew a hole in the back of an escaping hostile. It's the recoil that will determine my pace, he realized. I need to absorb the kick, set, aim and fire. Glancing at Dugan's progress, he saw the Hmong warriors had overtaken the off balance American.

Scanning the arena with field glasses Roche called out, "Hostile behind third tree up from trailhead."

"Got it," Max replied splintering the timber with a penetrating round.

"One maybe two hostiles in the rock cluster by the ravine." Roche sighted.

"I see one," Max said getting a glimpse of a khaki cap peeking over the stone barrier. Squeezing out a round, he launched chunks of rock and the Pathet Lao bonnet into the sky.

"Second hostile is crawling in the brush to the left of the stones." Roche informed.

"Terminating threat," Max replied neutralizing the target. Ten rounds, he calculated. Swinging the large barrel in the direction of the smoldering truck, he squeezed the lifeless trigger. Looking back at Roche, he asked, "Can you keep this dog barking?"

With a puzzled squint Roche replied, "Where are you going?"

Max rose. His sweat soaked fatigues caked with moist soil. "Someone's got to fetch Dugan," He said. "And if I'm going down there, I sure would feel better with an active fifty-caliber discouraging hostiles."

Roche nodded and crawled into the matted grass sniper's bed. With a fresh magazine, he reloaded the long-range beast.

Max picked up Roche's Ak-47. He pulled back and released the charging bolt. Loc popped up out of the dense brush. Max nodded at the tribesman who had his back since they walked out of Isabelle. Words were not necessary. It had been over two decades since their last battlefield performance. Loc with the graying temples of age smiled with the familiar nervous twitch of a Black Tai.

At Loc's feet Va-Meng and his son crawled out of the brush. The father with a firm grip on an AK-47, rubbed Hip-shot's scruffy hair with a free hand. The boy soldier stood focused, his defiant expression far exceeding his eleven years. Cocking the hammer of the French revolver, Hip-shot grunted.

Studying the boy, Max looked at Loc and slowly shook his head.

"Loc," Roche called out from the snipers nest. "Tell Hip-shot I need him to stay as a spotter."

Loc translated the order. Max handed the disappointed boy the field glasses.

Looking at Va-Meng and Loc, Max winked and started the downhill jog. Small-arms-fire popped in the distance. Rhythmic blast echoed as Roche and his young spotter unleashed the barking fifty-caliber dog.

Sucking in the thick warm air tainted with the aroma of charred metal, Max's feet were heavy. I'm not the man I used to be, he thought feeling the uncomfortable stiffness of age. His sweaty grasp of the automatic rifle weakened. Seeking relief, he slowed down and pulled the weapon close to his chest. In sandaled feet and black pajamas the agile Va-Meng flew by. The nimble tribesman descended the steep grade disappearing into the dense brush. Max's jog faded into a cautious advance. Stopping behind a tree, he leaned up against the rough bark. His heart pounded. He took short shallow breathes. Perspiration rolled down his body. He glanced over at Loc panting behind a tree barrier. Pulsing overhead Roche's big gun kept a steady thunderous beat. A rustling wind blew through the forest. At the base of the hillside, a smoldering vehicle cracked and popped. Taking a deep breath, Max carefully poked his head around the tree trunk. A severed arm rested on the fronds of a pygmy palm. Thick drops of burgundy dangled from the jagged meat of the detached shoulder. Around the wrist of the lifeless appendage, the sweeping second hand of a Soviet watch monitored the passing of time. Ten yards below the bloody limb the owner laid face up. Opened mouthed the amputee gazed into the jungle canopy with lifeless eyes. Beside the corpse squatted a motionless Va-Meng. The tribesman slowly turned and looking at Max placed an index finger to his lips. Max nodded and relayed the message to Loc.

What does he see? Max wondered staring at the crouching tribesman's back. A breeze brushed up the hillside. A few loose hairs on top Va-Meng's head danced in the soft wind. Slowly the tribesman signaled back with a fisted hand and a single finger. One hostile Max surmised. No doubt the communist froze under the fifty-caliber barrage and Dugan's advance, he concluded. Va-Meng extended a second digit. Max conveyed the message to Loc. The battlefield remained silent. Two hostiles Max assumed. He took his right forefinger and pulled the Kalashnikov's fire selector all the way back into semi-automatic mode. The weapon clicked. Va-Meng's hand signal rapidly expanded the digit count to five. Max re-set his weapon's firing option to full-automatic.

Va-Meng looked over his shoulder and gave a slow-motion nod in Max's direction. Max passed the information to a focused Loc. Va-Meng rose and in a wide stance aimed his Kalashnikov down into a jagged stone ravine. Max and Loc quietly stepped from behind the tree trunk protection. Just below them, five Pathet Lao troops gingerly crawled out of the protective cover of a shale rock overhang. After blinking in the bright sunlight, the young soldiers reached back into the tight fissure. Slowly the communist pulled out a wounded colleague. Va-Meng puckered his lips and whistled softly. Jerking heads reacted to the tribesman's subtitle announcement. Smiling down at the frozen expressions of fear, Va-Meng squeezed his trigger hard. The AK-47 cycled fresh rounds into the chamber and spat out spent cartridges. With flanking fire, Max and Loc joined the tribesman's turkey shoot. A deluge of cooper-plated bullets rained down into the tight gully shredding foliage, sparking off rock and ripping into fresh meat. The khaki uniformed targets twitched violently. Round after penetrating round tenderized the five Lao communist.

On full-automatic, it took twenty-seconds to exhaust the AK-47s' curved thirty-round magazine. Empty Kalashnikovs went silent. A mist of gun-smoke floated quietly over a bloody heap of beige rags. A low guttural moan rose from the bullet ridden carnage. Simultaneously Max, Loc and Va-Meng detached spent banana box magazines and reloaded. To the rippling grunts of his enemy's suffering, Va-Meng inhaled the victorious sulfur mist. Pulling back the charging bolt of his weapon, he fired a short burst into the groaning pile.

CHAPTER THIRTY THREE

Through a telescopic sight, Roche scanned the battlefield. Max and the tribesmen have secured the hillside, he concluded. Pivoting the scope past the smoldering truck, he saw Dugan and the partisans exchanging fire with retreating communist. The blurred image of a hostile laying suppressing fire came into focus. Locking the target between the lens's cross hairs, he squeezed the trigger. The heavy weapon kicked hard into his tenderized shoulder. A soft cloud of dust kicked on the mountain trail. "Damn," Roche growled. "I can't hit shit." Concentrate he counseled. "You can do this," he mumbled taking a deep breath. Studying his prey for a second attempt, he flicked his trigger finger. A loud blast rang out. A bolt of pain slammed into his bruised flesh. The oblivious target continued firing in retreat. How does that kraut do it? He wondered. I'm not the marksman Max is, he realized. His talent got them to withdraw. All I need to do is keep this beast howling, he concluded. Hell, maybe I'll get lucky and actually hit something. A hollow click indicated the empty magazine. Thank god, he thought craning his neck. The tense and strained muscle across his shoulder relished the pause. Detaching the magazine box, Roche looked over at Hip-shot. "Ok son," he said waiving the empty cartridge holder. "I need some ammo." He pointed toward his pack.

Hip-shot nodded before scurrying to retrieve fifty-caliber rounds.

Roche rubbed his sensitive shoulder. Sitting up he twisted seeking comfort. Grabbing his chin with one hand and the back of his head with the other, he yanked his spine into alignment. A blanketing shadow interrupted the satisfying crack of adjusted vertebrae. Investigating the towering silhouette, Roche got a glimpse of a startled Pathet Lao. Starring down the muzzle of an automatic weapon, Roche's stomach dropped. The image

J. C. Bourg

was brief. A blast sent the armed intruder tumbling backwards. Roche turned with a nervous twitch. A whisper of smoke danced out of the barrel of a French revolver. The antique weapon firmly grasped in the stiff extended arms of an eleven-year-old boy.

In peasant sandals, Hip-shot ran past the reclining American. Standing at the edge of the sniper's bed, the carbine soldier squeezed off another shot. The recoil knocked him back a step out off balance. Composed, he stepped forward with a downward gaze.

Roche jumped to his feet and stood beside the young shooter. A corpse lay face up in the brush. Two distinctive bloody splotches stained the chest of the victim's green uniform. Scanning the swaying growth, the only hostile Roche detected lay dead. Reaching down into the matted grass, he detached the riflescope. Assisted by magnified sight, he examined the hillside. A lifeless calm blanketed the scrub brush. An occasional communist corpse passed through his sweeping vision. The distant gunfire went silent. Through the sighting device, he saw Dugan and the partisans clearing the battlefield. We did more today than poke the hornets' nest, he realized. Adjusting the telescope, he watched Max and the two tribesmen walking past the dead. Lowering the scope, he rubbed his eye with a fisted hand. Glancing down, Roche smiled at his young buddy and placed a grateful hand on Hip-shot's shoulder. The wide-eyed boy beamed. The young warrior's glow of accomplishment evolved into a mischievous smirk. Dipping away from the American's affectionate touch, he raced to plunder the kill.

Recalling the cold steel of the communist gun-barrel, Roche's heart raced. Jesus that was close, he realized. Light headed his knees buckled. Carefully, he sat down in the sniper's bed. Sweat dripped off his face. He flinched as Hip-shot ran up the hill.

The boy had an AK-47 strapped across his back and the tied laces of a pair of combat boots slung over his shoulder. Hip-shot dropped the victim's weapon and personal effects in front of the hyperventilating American. On the matted grass lay a cheap watch, tattered wallet and two yellow packs of local smokes.

With a shaky hand, Roche reached for the dead man's cigarettes. Igniting the nicotine cylinder, he sucked on calming smoke. That's all I needed, he realized. His pounding heart pulsed closer to normalcy. Tilting his head back, he placed the tobacco wrapper to his lips and took a deep satisfying drag. Through the dissipating smoke, his young colleague helped himself to the smokes. Flicking his lighter, Roche lit the boy's cigarette. "The Surgeon General has determined that cigarette smoking is dangerous to your health," Roche mumbled clicking his Zippo shut. I'm old enough to be your grandfather; Roche realized watching Hip-shot puff away. But after today, he thought tapping off ash, we will be brothers for life. "Welcome to the brotherhood," he said to the squinting puzzled expression of the Hmong warrior.

CHAPTER THIRTY FOUR

The draping growth thinned. The mud slick assent steepened. Flanked by Loc and Va-Meng, Max took short probing steps. He pulled back a tree branch. Holding on the flimsy growth for balance, he peered down a three-foot embankment. Roaring fire shot out from the smoldering truck skeleton's wheel wells. Ignited mud tires billowed out clouds of filthy smoke staining the summer sky. The charred remains of the driver sat upright behind the steering wheel. Playfully small flames danced in and out of the skull's cavities. A wave of putrid heat brushed Max's face. Shielding the stench with the back of a hand, he looked past the truck. Khaki uniformed bodies of Lao communist littered the rough red clay mountain road. Yeeb waded amongst the dead, confiscated weapons slung over his shoulder. Another Hmong Partisan tugged at a dead man's boot. Dugan was missing.

Max turned to Loc and said, "It looks like the show is over."

Loc nodded and signaled with a quick glance in Va-Meng's direction.

"Sure," Max responded. "You can send the father back to check on his son."

As Loc translated, Max winked at Va-Meng. A very capable scout, Max thought. It wasn't luck that kept Va-Meng and his family alive all these years, he concluded. It was the talent and skill of a seasoned veteran. In black pajamas and cheap sandals the tribesman raced uphill. Max watched Va-Meng's agile exit with envy. I once could move like that, he reflected. Now with the fragile bones of age, I'm relegated to traversing on my butt, he thought. Sitting on the edge of the grassy embankment, he slid down to the hard rock road.

The nimble Loc descended with more poise.

Once Max hit the flat trail, the roasting truck's heat intensified. To avoid the toxic aroma of burnt rubber, he held his breath. He gave a wide birth proceeding past the smoldering heap. In misting smoke and floating embers, he exhaled.

Stepping over a barefoot corpse of a Lao officer, Max approached Yeeb. The hunched over tribesman with half a dozen captured weapons strapped across his back nodded at the German.

"Any Hmong casualties?" Max asked.

Grimacing from the heavy load, Yeeb responded with a solemn nod.

"How many?" Loc probed.

"Yai has left us to begin the journey to the village of his ancestors," Yeeb responded.

"Where is Dugan?" Max asked.

Pointing a thin arm and boney finger, Yeeb answered, "Mister Jim is at other truck."

"Thanks," Max mumbled as he and Loc continued down the hillside morgue. "Which one was Yai?" Max whispered.

Reflecting Loc smiled and responded. "At the Kentucky Fried Chicken in Bangkok, he was the one that was infatuated with the fast-food chain's moist towelettes."

Max chuckled, "I remember him stuffing his pockets with the tiny packets." With a respectful tone, he added. "I hope the damp wipes come in handy on his journey towards the afterlife."

A breeze swept the charred air clean. Orange dust floated above the mountain trail. A dead truck blocked the narrow thoroughfare. The hood was open. A puncture wound in the grill slowly leaked fluid into a growing puddle beneath the engine block. Beside the transport lay ten dead men, face up side by side. Dugan with a combat knife in hand and a knee on the chest of a corpse hacked off the victim's ear.

Max's stomach dropped. We are soldiers not fanatics, he reflected. I killed my first man at seventeen he realized, still picturing the Canadian soldier's face during the battle of Caen. I lost count over the years as to many enemies I terminated, he thought. Hell, I probably killed ten men today. It is an unfortunate consequence of my profession. Victories should be celebrated not death's harvest.

"Do you remember the bounty Dugan paid during the Laotian civil war?" Loc asked.

"Yes," Max responded with disgust. "Mister Jim paid the tribesmen one-thousand kip, (two dollars), for a severed ear accompanied with a Pathet Lao cap."

"Bad habits are hard to break," Loc mumbled.

"I've never understood the trophy collecting addiction," Max commented, "Although I saw it practiced by good soldiers on battlefields in France and in Indochina."

The crouching dark faced Dugan admired the prize in a cupped hand. Slowly his head turned. His thick lenses reflected the distant fire. He greeted Max and Loc with a demon possessed grin.

"Dugan!" Max called out. "Time to go, our message was sent."

Ignoring his colleagues, Dugan moved down the line and sliced off another communist ear.

CHAPTER THIRTY FIVE

The night rain continued to fall. An empty pot caught a steady drip from the pitched palm frond ceiling. The clatter of cascading water resonated from the open windows and doorway. A kerosene lantern resting atop the empty Stinger missile crate, cast a glow across the dry crowded room. Soot and the scent of coal oil hung in the humid air. Under the limited light, Roche assisted by reading glasses studied the hand held missiles owner's manual. At his feet the surface to air weapons laid wrapped in plastic. Blanketing the floor, Yeeb and his partisan troops puffed away on American cigarettes while sipping on expensive whisky. Against a windowless wall, the Hmong mother in her stovepipe hat tucked her children into a hard wood floor bed. Loc squatting with her husband quietly conversed in the language of his birth. From a dark isolated corner, the shrill sound of metal on stone pulsed. Still painted with the camouflaged mask of battle, Dugan religiously stroked the blade of a combat knife. Around his neck, a leather shoestring necklace displayed the severed ears of his enemy.

Reclining on a bedroll, Max feeling the effects of shooting the fifty-caliber cannon rubbed his tender black and blue shoulder. Turning on his side and propped up by an elbow, he asked the studious Roche, "*Ami*, what does it say?"

Roche closed the text. Peering over his spectacles, he answered, "I can sum it up with three simple instructions." Displaying an index finger, he said, "One; point and shoot." Showing a second digit, he added, "Two; don't stand behind the shooter." Smirking he concluded waving three fingers, "Three; Don't forget number two."

Max chuckled. He glanced over at the open doorway to sound of Buck stomping his signature rawhide boots.

The cowboy checked the fly of his faded blue jeans. Into the grating sound emerging from Dugan's corner, he hollered, "Jesus Jim, I think your blade is sharp enough."

"Buck," Roche said softly, "Let him be."

The cowboy removed his dripping Stetson. Shaking off the rain, he responded, "Come on Roche, Dugan is acting like a loon."

The irritating sound of metal scratching stone intensified.

"With a little luck," Roche said in a commanding tone, "We will fly out of here in a few days."

"I'm not leaving," Dugan mumbled from the darkness.

"Dugan," Roche shouted. "Now you're talking like a loon." Standing he took a swig of bourbon. "Guys we poked the hornets' nest today. All they know is that a defiant tribe has reoccupied this village. Maybe tomorrow or in the next couple of days they will send out a gunship to investigate." Strutting in the glow of the limited light, he added, "When they do, we point and shoot. If they send additional troops, we unleash the fire power of a well armed resistance." In the direction of the scrapping blade, he informed, "That is our mission and once accomplished, we fly the fuck out of here."

"I'm not leaving," Dugan growled.

Roche snorted. "Jim I understand your commitment. Hell, that's why we're here. I have no idea how this is going to play out. But with our limited resources, we will educate those commie bastards that any excursions into the remote highlands will be expensive."

Dugan stirred in the dark. From the shadows, the middle-age American rose. Sweat rolling down his face smudged his dark mask with ominous streaks. The eerie glow of the lantern light reflected off his spectacles. The thick lenses magnified and distorted hard dark eyes. Gripping a razor sharp trench knife, he stood defiantly.

With a sour expression, Max examined the decorative string of human cartilage draped around Dugan's neck. I've seen this on too many battlefields, he reflected. The pleasure of the kill seduces many combatants. Glancing up, he focused on Dugan's distant harsh expression. We are soldiers nothing more, he realized. Returning to Laos renewed Mister Jim's addiction to the sins the profession tolerates.

Dugan in a low gruff voice said, "In Southern California, I was Jimmy the Pepsi delivery man. In the Laotian highlands, I am Mister Jim..." he lifted the snarled ears dangling over his chest, "... the benefactor of communist kills." Out of the side of his mouth, he growled, "I would rather be respected in hell, than labor for minimum wage in San Dimas." Glancing around the room with a disconnected gaze, he ranted in a tribal dialect. His eyes burned barking out passionate dialogue.

The Hmong children stirred under the covers of their bedding. The partisans stared up at the intense sermon. Buck rolled his eyes. Roche frowned with a concerned squint.

Calmly Max looked at Loc and asked, "Can you translate?"

Focused on Dugan, Loc summarized, "Apparently Mister Jim felt the protective hand of Sin Sai during the battle today. He's bearing testimony to the supernatural power of the Chao Fa."

As a panting Dugan took a deep breath, Roche interrupted the lecture. "Enough Jimmy, we get the picture."

"Nothing any of you can say or do will change my resolve," blurted Dugan. Scowling at a frowning Roche, he offered, "Hell if you want to go home tomorrow please do. I'll see the mission through to its noble conclusion."

Roche looked at the silhouette of the lanky cowboy in the doorway. Buck shrugged. Roche glanced down at Max. The German slowly shook his head. The mercenaries all focused on the squatting Loc.

The short tribesman rose from his crouch. Addressing Dugan, Loc said, "We appreciate the offer Mister Jim. But speaking for myself, I'd like to stick around to witness a chemical spraying helicopter swatted out of the sky."

CHAPTER THIRTY SIX

Rubbing the gray stubble of a sprouting beard, Max took a deep breath of the crisp morning air. Sitting on a rain soaked wood crate, he could smell the clean aroma of wet timber. The seat of his pants wet with moisture. He fidgeted. Not too wet, he concluded. Getting a whiff of Roche's fetid odor, he wondered about his own smell. A soft breeze added smoke from a cooking fire. The Black Tai mother and Angel feed kindling into smoldering flames. Turning away from the smoke, he blinked at the sunlight sparkling off the mud. His eyes adjusted on the empty weapon containers littering the courtyard. The departing partisans have churned the village square into a soupy swamp, he concluded. The weapon revival was a success, he reflected with a grin.

A distant approaching conversation faded as Buck and Loc emerged from the jungle trail. They paused to determine a course across the blanketing sludge. The cowboy gave a big thumbs-up to Max and Roche.

"Looks like the sloping runway shook off the downpour." Max said sipping strong black coffee out of a tin cup. "Do you think today will be the day?"

"Sure hope so," Roche responded patting the plastic wrapped Stinger missiles. "We are just about out of provisions."

"Bourbon?" Max questions.

"That was what I was referring too," Roche chuckled. "Do you think I'm worried about running out of rice and Spam?"

"The years have made us soft *Ami*," Max mumbled.

"Originally I was thinking of booking a massage when we return to the comforts of Bangkok." Roche said, "But now all I'm looking forward to is ice, clean sheets, a hot shower and a porcelain toilette that flushes." Politely smiling at the Hmong girl fanning the fire, he solicited a java refill.

From the small circle of smoldering coals, Angel pranced over through the muck. A red rag shielded her callus palm from a hot galvanized steel coffee pot. She fulfilled his non-verbal request with a soft smile. Raising his cup, he thanked her.

"I still feel empty about Dugan," Roche said blowing on his misting mug.

Max shrugged. "It was his choice," he commented as the shy girl topped off his coffee. "Mister Jim is a warrior not a delivery driver."

"Did you talk to him...say goodbye?" Roche asked.

Cradling the warm tin-cup with cold hands, Max shook his head above the escaping heat.

"I tried to," Roche confessed. "With that streaked camo face paint and those coke bottle lenses, he fondled that communist cartilage necklace. Never looking up from the severed ears, he mumbled something in Hmong."

"Maybe he was saying goodbye," Max responded.

"I doubt it," Roche replied. "The Jim Dugan we flew in with departed after renewing his taste for battlefield blood. Like a relapsing alcoholic, Dugan's killing addiction was rekindled with the first hostile he terminated." Frowning he added, "I don't buy any of that mystic warrior bullshit. The Hmong are fighting for survival. We are assisting with that endeavor, nothing more. Neither God nor Sin Sai has anything to do with this conflict." Looking into the mud, he slowly shook his head, "Given Dugan's age and this environment, his days are numbered."

Buck sat down with mud-encrusted boots and splattered blue jeans. Playfully surveying the surrounding hills, he commented, "I take it you haven't shot down a helicopter yet."

Roche chuckled, "Once we get the signal cowboy, you'll be the first to know."

Buck looked over at Loc, Yeeb and the Hmong father conversing around the fire. "We have an empty seat with Dugan's cancellation," he said. Motioning with a nod in the direction of the tribesmen, he asked, "Is Yeeb returning with us?"

"No," Max responded. "He stayed behind to witness the execution of a rotorcraft and crew."

From out of the dense growth of the surrounding hillside, a flare sizzled skyward. It arced into a glowing descent.

Flicking his wrist, Roche tossed his coffee onto the saturated soil. A wide grin spread across his face. Everyone around the communal well gazed skyward. The flare faded into a wisp of smoke. Roche slapped Max's knee and said, "It's show time; one flare, one chopper." Looking at Buck, he said, "That's your cue to load your passengers Tex. Once we terminate this Soviet helo, we're heading for greener pastures."

Buck stood. Placing two fingers in his mouth, he produced a shrill whistle. Getting the attention of the Hmong family, he said, "Ghost Rider Airlines is ready for boarding."

The family glared at him with puzzled expression. Corky ran over through the mud and looked up at the wiry Texan with big brown curious eyes.

"We're heading out son," Buck said softly.

For the benefit of the Hmong family, Loc translated and quickly defused Va-Meng and his oldest son's combat assistance offer. The mother hastily collected their meager belongings. Pausing she confirmed the presence of the sacred fruit jar holding their ticket to freedom. Heads held high, the tiny family stood attentively in front of Buck.

Towering over the Hmong passengers, the lanky cowboy said to his companions, "Good luck amigos."

"Just don't leave without us Buck," Max said pulling the plastic wrapping off a Stinger missile.

Strolling through the muck towards the mountainside airport, the pilot and passengers departed.

Loc, Yeeb, Max and Roche stood around the communal well. Max and Roche picked up surface to air missiles, the tribesmen AK-47s. Side-glances acknowledged their commitment.

"Let's do this," Roche announced.

The freedom fighter and three mercenaries walked abreast, the rising sun on their backs. Flanked by stilted structures, they cast long shadows across the town square. The air was thin, the grade steep. Strutting uphill through the frontier town, Max felt a relaxed calm.

Focused on the emerging horizon, Roche said out of the side of his mouth to Max, "I'm glad to see that you and Loc have not lost the swagger of your youth. I still recall the day you strolled into Saigon with a Corsican bounty on your heads."

"Its training and discipline, *Ami*," Max mumbled. "Never show fear to a rabid dog or a Soviet gunship. It only enhances their resolve."

To the sloshing of mud, Max heard the distant hum of an approaching helicopter. Beside him, Yeeb grunted at the twirling buzz. Max glanced at the snarling tribesman snorting with rage.

At the summit of the incline, the four men stood defiantly. A Russian Mi-8 helicopter swept towards them from the sea of green below. The bloated assault transport brandished machine guns on side mounted sub-wings.

Max tossed the firing tube over his shoulder. A low growl rolled out of Yeeb's boney neck.

Handing the weapon to the tribesman, Max said, "You take the shot... for your family."

Without hesitation, Yeeb accepted the responsibility. "My people threw spears and shot arrows at communist aircraft," he said hoisting the Stinger into firing position. Balanced in a wide stance, the frail man aimed his weapon at the hovering beast. "I am Cheng Yeeb," he yelled out over the aircraft noise, "Of the Cheng clan." The gunship opened fire. The side mounted PK machine guns tore through the surrounding vegetation. A rough mowed swath of jungle approached the shooter. "These are the mountains of my ancestors," he barked. "And today we take back our sky!" Yeeb's thin frame jerked. An exhaust flame erupted. A five foot, twenty-two pound missile shot into the sky. The rocket's trajectory curved slightly just before impact. A blast of smoke and flame tore off a chunk of the chopper's fuselage. Three flailing men fell out of the wounded bird. The smoldering transport fluttered before spinning out of control. Clipping the face of the steep terrain, it burst into flames. A tumbling compilation of mangled metal and fire careened down the mountain. Detonated munitions popped. The plunging remains broke apart. Twisted metal, bodies and small fires littered the hillside. Billowing black smoke stained the morning sky.

Yeeb casually tossed the empty firing tube to his side. Strutting forward, he pounded his chest with a fisted hand. From deep inside, he released a blood-curdling cry.

The pent-up of rage of one man's pain echoed through the sharp jagged peaks and valleys, Max, Roche and Loc stood respectfully. Yeeb turned with watery eyes and tears rolling down his leathery cheeks. A crooked smirk emerged across his weathered face.

CHAPTER THIRTY SEVEN

Perched atop the moist sliver of red earth, the Twin Beech prepped for takeoff. Standing on the slopping tarmac beside the metal bird's open rear hatch, Max, Roche and Loc said farewell to Yeeb.

"Leave with us brother," Loc said patting the Hmong warrior on the back. "You've had your taste of vengeance."

Breaking the embrace, Yeeb stepped back. "I appreciated the offer; however I have not yet begun to quench my thirst." Grinning he added, "Besides the second Stinger will allow another long overdue swallow." Looking at Max and Roche, he bowed, "Thank you brothers. Thank you for everything."

"Give 'em hell!" Roche yelled.

Yeeb responded with the nervous grin of a ridge running Hmong.

Max shook the tribesman's hand with a firm grip. "It's been an honor," he said.

Yeeb nodded. Flexing a shoulder, he adjusted the missile launcher strapped across his back. "Until we meet on the other side..." He paused and with a casual two finger salute said softly, "*Adieu.*"

Following Loc through the metal aircraft doorway, Roche paused. Over his shoulder, he watched Yeeb disappear into the jungle. "What are his chances?" He asked.

Following Roche's gaze, Max replied with a grin, "Better than most. A well armed warrior with nothing to lose is powerful. I suspect that communist casualties in the highlands will be on the rise."

Sputtering to life, the twin prop aircraft coughed out white smoke. The prop wash sprayed the tree line. A windblown Max turned away from the revving propellers. Blindly he pushed Roche into the cabin. Under the metal ribbed ceiling, the Hmong family sat on a plywood floor. The cabin's interior vibrated to a high pitched drone. Corky with cupped hands over his ears sat cross-legged. Beside the young boy, his mother and sister in their distinctive black pillbox headgear sat erect. Their wide gemstone eyes sparkled with anticipation. Frayed cords through metal eyelets secured the passenger cargo. Roche and Loc crawled in the thick stagnate air to open spaces across from the family and tied themselves in.

Crouching Max made his way to the copilot's chair. A pair of field glasses occupied the seat. "What are these for?" He asked picking up the binoculars.

"I need a spotter," Buck said loudly checking his gauges.

"You think we'll encounter another helicopter?" Max asked strapping in.

"A gunship is the least of my concerns." Buck hollered. "I can out run a chopper." Glancing to determine the size of his audience, he leaned into Max and informed, "If they send out MiGs to investigate your downing of their helicopter and crew, we are in for one hell of a flight."

At full throttle, Buck launched the aircraft into the cloudless blue sky. Yesterday's rain left its mark on the rugged terrain. Rivers flowed with brown water. The rainforest glistened under the rising sun. Skimming along the jungle canopy, the low wing aircraft navigated through small valleys. Smoke from isolated villages and the occasional terraced fields signaled life.

Scanning the sky through binoculars, Max asked, "Do we stand a chance if we encounter a jet fighter?"

"It depends where and when," Buck replied. "We have the advantage of low speed maneuverability to evade and escape. A MiG-21 is armed with a pair of thirty-millimeter cannon, two rockets and supersonic speed."

"Shit," Max mumbled.

"Have a little faith," Buck chuckled, "When a bull rider draws a bad mount, he makes up for it with skill."

The harsh landscape softened. Over a stream in a low-lying area, Max hollered, "Incoming bogey at three-o-clock."

Glancing over at the approaching speck in the cloudless sky, Buck yelled, "Hang onto your hats boys and girls. I'm about to school supersonic Ivan in the fine art of flying."

The Beechcraft dove to the valley floor. Corky hunched over and threw up. His sister quickly followed suit. To the stench of vomit, Buck arched his back, the MiG interceptor breathing down his neck. Hold, he thought taking a deep breath. On the exhale, he banked into a hard turn. A large unguided rocket flew by. The MiG-21 could not hold the tight turn. Feeling the g's of the sharp bend, Buck got a glimpse of the streaking silver jet. In the basin of the rainforest, the unsuccessful missile exploded. A fireball of charred timber erupted into the sky.

"We'll lose him in the briar patch," Buck said racing the twin props towards the mountainous highlands.

The retreating twin-engine plane clipped the treetops of a narrow gorge. Max's head jerked from side to side, "Where is he?" he yelled over the whimpering women.

"He's climbed to a comfortable perch," Buck responded squinting hard at the approaching ridge line. "To avoid a stall, he'll make sweeping high speed passes." On the horizon a metallic flicker of light sparkled. "He's heading right at us," the cowboy informed.

The small glimmering dot in the blue sky swept over the ravine spitting out tracer rounds. In a flash, Buck saw the predator's jet intake pass overhead. "To low for you comrade." He mumbled. "Come on Ivan. I know you want it. Come down and get me."

Twisting in the co-pilots seat, Max tracked the passing bandit and yelled, "He's coming around for another intercept."

"Thanks for the update," Buck responded flying into a sharp box canyon. Banking the aircraft, he flew perpendicular along the jagged rock face. In the angled cabin the tethered Hmong family dangled above Roche and Loc. Hats, satchels, packs and loose change swirled about. Loc grunted as a runaway French revolver clipped the side of his head. Trailing the Beechcraft thirty-millimeter rounds sparked and tore chunks of stone off the mountain.

Flying directly into the approaching wall of sharp stone draped with foliage, Buck mumbled, "Open up honey."

Max flexed a leg. The German feverishly pumped his foot on an imaginary brake.

"I know you are there," Buck whispered. A sliver of light appeared defining a detached limestone pinnacle. "Wider baby," he mumbled.

The MiG launched a second missile. Its twin-engine target suddenly vanished in the shadows of the stone forest.

Flying into the crevice, Buck held his breath. The Beechraft's vertical stabilizer ripped a creeping vine from the towering column. A thunderous blast erupted behind the prop plane's twin tail fins. Emerging into daylight, the cowboy exhaled. Pursuing the escaping aircraft flames and shattered stone shot through the narrow crack.

The climbing MiG flew into the rocket's blazing aftermath. The jet clipped the edge of the precipice. Dislodged shale tumbled into the canyon. The pilot ejected. The abandoned supersonic jet plowed a deep row through the dense rainforest before terminating in a billowing cloud of fire and black smoke.

In the blue sky, a rapidly descended streamer of white silk whistled. At the low altitude, the parachute struggled to deploy. Harnessed to the fluttering fabric, the fighter pilot plunged into the jungle canopy. Branches and tree limbs battled the plummeting pilot's flesh and bone. The bulk of his torso with one arm and a partial leg slammed hard into the moist earth. A torn and frayed white silk shroud floated down covering the mangled remains.

To the relaxing drone of the twin engines, Buck gulped air. Removing his wide brimmed hat, he dragged a denim shirtsleeve across the sweat beads clinging to his forehead. Adjusting the Stetson on his drenched matted hair, he asked over his shoulder, "How y'all doin?"

Heavy breathing and whimpering women answered.

Buck glanced at Max seeking an answer. The German responded by patting the pilot on the shoulder. Buck slowly swung the Beechcraft around to exit Laos. With a slight alteration in the flight plan, the cowboy flew towards the black smoke polluting the sky. A smoldering heap of earth, timber and twisted metal burned at the end of a furrowed row of charred vegetation. Sticking out of the mound, the jet's vertical stabilizer marked the gravesite. The metal tombstone prominently displayed the flag of the Lao People's Democratic Republic.

Flying by Buck dipped his wings and mumbled, "School's dismissed comrade." To ease the tension across his shoulder's he leaned back and flexed. After a satisfying grin, he hummed a familiar tune. In a low voice, he broke out singing softly, *The stars at night - are big and bright, deep in the heart of Texas..."*

CHAPTER THIRTY EIGHT

The passengers in the cabin of the Beechcraft sat in silence. The twin engines hummed. The air was cool. Curled up on the vibrating plywood floor, Loc slept. Craning his neck, Roche looked out of a side window searching for a recognizable landmark. Angel's head rested on her mother's lap. The Hmong mother affectionately stoked the child's hair. A nervous Va-Meng fidgeted with his black skullcap. Hip-shot loaded and unloaded the French revolver, occasionally spinning the chamber. Sitting cross-legged, Corky picked splintered chips from the rough wood floor. Dried vomit decorated the front of the youngest passenger's black tunic. In the cockpit, Max scanned the horizon through field glasses. A focused Buck glided the aircraft through the endless twist and turns of the mountain range.

Tracking the growing stream separating the peaks, a big grin spread across the cowboys face. The tributary merged with a massive river. Flying over the shimmering sheet of glass flowing south, Buck said, "You can put down the binoculars Max."

"What is it?" Max asked, the field glasses dangling over his chest.

"That Fritz is the Mekong River." Buck answered leaning back. "Along its west bank is the Kingdom of Thailand."

The brown waterway glistened. On the sparkling surface two fishermen stood on the opposite ends of a very long narrow canoe. They paused from laying netting to wave. Further, down the channel, puffs of smoke rose from a thin watercraft overloaded with freight.

"We made it," Max mumbled.

Shaking his head, Buck responded, "We made it to the next crisis is all." Over his shoulder, he called out, "Major Roche its decision time."

Roche freed himself from the rope harness. On all fours, he crawled forward. Assisted by the pilot and copilot's seats, he stood. In a wide legged stance, he leaned into the cockpit and asked, "What is it?"

"Our game of tag with the MiG cost us fuel." Buck informed, "We won't make it to the remote airstrip in Loei."

"How about the airport at Udon?" Roche inquired.

"That's what I was thinking," Buck answered. "We'll be flying on fumes but it's feasible." Taking a deep breath, he continued. "You and I both know that airport all too well. Landing there will be expensive."

"What do you mean expensive?" Max questioned.

Roche turned and just inches from Max's face said, "The airport at Udon Thani was the Asian headquarters for Air America. It is now a Thai Air force base. Landing on familiar turf will likely cost each of us five to ten years for arms trafficking."

Peering around Roche, Max asked Buck, "Can we ditch the plane in the Mekong?"

Glancing down at the wide flowing serpent, Buck said, "It's feasible."

Placing a hand on Max's shoulder, Roche whispered, "Max I'll bet you the next round that Va-Meng and his family can't swim. Besides do want to risk their chance at freedom."

Max patted Roche's hand, "Your right *Ami*. Besides five to ten in a Thai prison *es machts nichts* compared to the six weeks I spent at Isabelle." With a reflective grin, he added, "Surviving the siege in the valley of death made me callus to whatever harsh penalties this life may impose."

"My moment came in the fall of 1944 during the Battle of Peleliu in the South Pacific." Roche said rubbing his chin. "I discovered my dark side. It has served me well. If incarceration is the penance for my covert sins so be it."

Buck broke out laughing. Between breaths, he flashed an apologetic hand. "Sorry hombres," he said. "I don't mean to disrespect the depths of your existence, but I've got you both beat." Smirking he continued. "I can do ten years in a Thai prison standing on my head," Looking back and forth between Max and Roche, he prodded, "Do you want to know why?"

His eager audience shook their heads. "It's because I was married to Betty Lou McFarland for five years."

Max and Roche burst out laughing.

Over his companions' spontaneous release of amusement, Buck fueled their delight by adding, "Unlike your adversaries, Betty Lou took my house, took my cars and took my kids."

Gasping for air Max squeaked out, "Did she leave you anything?"

Snorting playfully Buck said, "Oh yea, I got the mortgage payments, the car payments and child support."

Loc stuck his head into the levity. "All right what is so funny?"

Peering back Max said with fading frivolity, "It really isn't funny partner. Our only option is landing in Udon and facing the authorities."

"That's all," Loc responded. Patting Roche on the back, he added, "Major Roche will figure a way out of this, he always does." On wobbly legs, he returned to the passenger cabin and yelled out. "Don't wake me unless it is something important...like another MiG."

CHAPTER THIRTY NINE

G ray clouds blanketing the sky darkened. In the cockpit's fading light, the fuel gauge rested on empty. Buck switched on the aircraft's antiquated communication system. The radio lit up with a hiss. Turning to the emergency frequency, he picked up the handheld microphone. Glancing over at a curious Max, Buck shrugged and then called out, "Declaring Emergency! Out of fuel! Request emergency landing!"

Crackling static answered his plea. He repeated the message.

Out of the speaker box a distorted and broken voice answered, "Runway twenty-one Udon airfield cleared for emergency landing. Please identify yourself."

Confidently nodding, Buck looked at Max and said, "I know where that is. We should make it."

"Please identify yourself," squawked the speaker box.

Rubbing the handheld-microphone against his temple, Buck pondered a response. Emphasizing a Southern-drawl, he replied, "This is Ghost Rider. The bad-ass that out ran the devil's herd over the Plain of Jars. Unfortunately the experience emptied my fuel tanks."

A calm static laced voice replied, "Ghost Rider, runway twenty-one cleared for emergency landing."

The tricycle undercarriage of the twin beech touched down on the concrete runway of the Udon Thani International Airport. Halfway down the extensive tarmac the twin engines sputtered silent. There was no fuel left to taxi. The distant wail of emergency vehicles emerged.

From the cockpit, Max saw the flashing red lights closing in. Glancing up into the overcast gray sky, he grinned. A gloomy welcome, he thought, seems appropriate. Behind him the cabin hatch creaked open. Cool air rushed in. He glanced over his shoulder. Roche tucked a healthy wad of US greenbacks into the liner of Angel's black stovepipe hat. To the sound of the disembarking passengers, Max drew his holstered Tokarev pistol. Feeling the familiar comforting grip, he moaned. *My prize possession is about to be confiscated, lost forever,* he thought. *It was more than a useful tool. It's bite crippled the greasy Corsican hit man Petru Rossi,* he reflected. *The weapon's precision terminated four Binh Xuyen gangsters during the battle of Saigon.* He visualized pilfering the pistol from the communist corpse. *It is not just a weapon but a reminder,* he concluded. *Confiscating the pistol marked the moment on my escape from Isabelle when the prey became the predator.*

"Time to face the music," Buck said placing a hand on Max's shoulder.

"I'm right behind you," Max said respectfully laying the Soviet handgun on the copilot's seat.

Following behind the crouching cowboy, Max stepped over Roche's discarded Baby Browning pistol, Loc's sidearm and Hip-shot's revolver. Emerging out of the hatch, he saw Loc explaining the situation to a bewildered Va-Meng. The tribal father shook his head and retrieved President Nixon's holiday greeting.

Standing beside the aircraft, Buck, Roche and Loc stood with their hands in the air. Each American displayed the dark-blue passport of the United States. Max beside his companions raised his hands exhibiting a Bordeaux-red French *passeport.* The Hmong family also reached for the sky; Va-Meng clutching the Presidential Christmas card.

Leading the charge, two light utility vehicles with flashing red lights and wailing sirens skidded to a halt. The small trucks paused. A trailing military transport arrived. Helmeted Thai soldiers poured out of the transport with weapons drawn. The Thai troops ignored the Hmong family and surrounded the four mercenaries.

Looking down the barrels of targeting rifles, Max chuckled. Roche started to laugh. Buck and Loc joined in. The frivolity faded as a strutting cock in an officer's uniform entered the tight circle.

"Don't you think this is a little excessive chief?" Buck asked motioning to the encompassing troops.

The back of the Thai officer's hand slapped the cowboy hard. Buck jerked back. His Stetson fell to the concrete runway. His companions flexed. The troops surged a step closer. The officer stepped back.

Buck glared at the tiny officer. He wiped a trickle of blood from the side of his mouth with a denim shirtsleeve. "All right Ling Poo," he said. "If that was an attention getter...you got my attention."

Behind the focused troops, a policeman herded the Hmong family into the back of a utility truck. Breaking away, Va-Meng rushed into the circle of armed men. In front of the officer, Va-Meng bowed with his hands in a prayer position. The officer scowled. The tribal father humbly presented the White House greeting card. The officer accepted the document with a curious squint. After a quick examination, he tossed it aside.

"It's alright brother," Loc said in tribal dialect. *"We can fend for ourselves. Protect your family."*

Gazing respectfully across the mercenary line up, Va-Meng said, *"Thank you friends."* He picked up the discarded greeting card. Carefully he brushed off the glossy document and joined his departing family.

Roche made eye contact with Hip-shot. Fifty years separated the two warriors. Roche winked. A confident grin surfaced on the boy's face. The young warrior placed two fingers on his silent lips. Casually he removed the fingers and blew phantom smoke. Roche nodded at the symbolic smoking pantomime. As the vehicle sped off, Corky clutching the tailgate waved goodbye.

Max stood with hands in the air. He winced at being patted down. A hand probed his pants pocket. Swallowing back the bile taste of defeat, he closed his eyes. Tolerating the humiliation of submitting to inferiors, he recalled his capture in during the Second World War. The sting had not dulled over the years.

It was a foul hot August day in the summer of 1944. The sun hung in the clear sky over the scared French countryside. The roads choked with a continuous train of twisted German metal. The flanking hillsides littered with the maggot ridden remains of men and livestock. Birds defecated as they feasted on decaying flesh. Swarming flies disrespected the dead and taunted the living.

A lanky teenage Max stood on wobbly legs. From lack of sleep his head bobbed. Knotted up with hunger, his stomach groaned. A Canadian soldier wearing a scarf over his nose and mouth frisked the defeated boy. After the quick search, the Canadian spun Max around. A large combat boot kicked him in the ass. The momentum shoved Max into the flow of his countrymen headed towards allied incarceration.

Tossed into a red plastic pail, a tarnished Legionnaire lighter clunked. Opening his eyes, Max gazed up into the cool overcast skies over the Udon airport. I'm a survivor, he realized. Always have been and always will be. Grinning Max looked over his shoulder at his shackled hands. Amateurs, he thought studying the child like faces of the Thai soldiers. These are boys doing a job, nothing more. I've been close to death many times, he realized and this is not one of them. A handler shoved him forward. Standing his ground, Max turned to face the uniformed Siamese youth. The German flashed the mask of death. The boy wilted, took a small step back and looked away. Point made, Max concluded joining his colleagues on the quiet march towards an idling paddy wagon.

Welded to the bed of an Isuzu light truck was an open air cage. In handcuffs, Max kept his balance climbing into the rusting pen. Dried liquid stained the diamond plate floor with the stench of urine. Along the bars of one side, Roche and Buck slouched on a rough metal bench. Across from them Max joined Loc on the other long backless seat. The creak of rusting hinges preceded a reverberating clang. The vehicle jerked forward. Under a rotating red beacon, it sped across the runway.

"What now?" Buck asked.

Roche looked around at his handcuffed *compadres* and answered, "There is an insurance card still in the deck. Its Uncle Sam's to play. If the US wants to establish a diplomatic relationship with the Lao communist regime, our mission never existed. Under that reality, there would not be a trial and our incarceration may be brief."

"That doesn't sound very promising," Buck grumbled.

Roche concurred with a nod. After fidgeting on the metal seat, he conceded to his discomfort and said, "If Uncle Sam's insurance card never surfaces. We are at the mercy of the blowing winds of the Thai justice system.

There is a lot of tension between the Kingdom of Thailand and their communist neighbors. Most likely our Thai host will bilk us for information about the Lao People's Democratic Republic and after that determine our fate. If the political tides favor exposing the communist atrocities, we will get a trial, probably get a couple of years slap on the wrist and go home."

"What if the wind is blowing in the other direction?" Buck asked.

"Then my friends we are fucked," Roche answered with a smirk. "To avoid revealing their own exploitation of the Hmong refugee crisis, our Thai allies would just as soon throw us into some shit-hole and forget about us."

"I'm a US citizen," Buck declared sitting erect. "Doesn't that account for something?"

Roche chuckled. "We won't be the first nor the last Americans serving hard time in the Kingdom of Thailand."

"You know," Buck said. "I always feared going to prison and coming out an old man. But when you are already an old man it doesn't seem that bad."

Max shifted his weight on the hard bench. Grinning he commented, "A couple of hours ago, we could have been splatter on the face of a limestone butte. And now," he looked around at the neon lights starting to glow as dusk blanked the provincial capital. "I'm in a city going to jail. The food is going to be rancid, but there will be something to eat. The water maybe contaminated, but I'll quench my thirst. And after we get a lay of the land, we will determine the appropriate course of action." Glancing at Loc, he added, "Keep in mind Loc and I were surrounded by forty-thousand Vietminh and escaped to freedom."

CHAPTER FOURTY

A metal door slammed shut. Overhead single light bulbs illuminated a long concrete corridor. The grating slide of a bolted lock sealed the four arms traffickers deep within bowels of the Thai prison. A half-dozen uniformed tiny men elevated by their station pushed and shoved. The narrow passage terminated at a grated speakeasy door. An escorting guard bumped, Max aside. The jailer wrapped a nightstick on the barrier. In the grilled window, the perturbed face of a flat noised sentry appeared. Chiming keys preceded a metallic click. The heavy door swung open. A wave of stagnate air laced with a feces stench rolled into the corridor.

Turning away from the foul blast, Max mumbled to Roche, "This must be the shit-hole you were referring to."

The guards slammed the prisoners into the concrete wall. Cold stone kissed Max's cheek. A nightstick pressed hard into his back. Looking at the at the back of Roche's balding head, he felt the unshackling of his wrist.

Herded through the open portal, the mercenaries rubbed chaffed wrist. Barred cells flanked a dim walkway. It was difficult to see in the limited light. Most of the pens appeared empty. Encouraged by pokes from jailer's truncheons the prisoners plodded forward in the darkness. A sour faced sentry unlocked the barred entrance to the last cage. Shoved into the dark end chamber, the arms traffickers stood in silence. The entrance slammed shut behind them.

We are not alone; Max realized squinting at the shadows moving across the floor. Stepping forward, he felt a reclining body. Leaning back against the bars, he waited for his eyes to adjust. "Can anyone see?" he whispered.

"I can't see shit," Buck said with a twang.

Slowly the shadows took form. In the far corner, a squat toilette buzzed with flies. Three sheepish men crouched around the stench. Their faces pinched with fear. Across the hard floor, eight men reclined comfortably on grass mats. With cocky expressions, they analyzed the new arrivals. A white porcelain sink stuck out from the far wall beside a single cot.

A moan from corner caused Max to focus on the large wide Thai standing defiantly. The fat man exposed golden teeth with a sinister smirk. Kneeling before him a frail prisoner's head bobbed. Gold teeth's sleepy eyes reflected the oral pleasure. Maybe three-hundred pounds, Max estimated studying the flabby arms exposed by a stained white singlet. No doubt achieved his power through brutality and humiliation.

"Welcome to my kingdom," the obese thug said clutching the back of his concubine's head. "Did they send me a Meo?" He asked squinting at Loc. "Those jungle savages are better than ten year old boys." Looking down at the man kneeling before him, he said, "You can take tomorrow off while I break in the Meo."

Stone-faced Loc showed no anger or fear. Buck flexed with clenched fist.

The ground came alive. Prisoners jumped to their feet brandishing jailhouse shivs. Golden teeth shoved his sexual servant aside. The male concubine crawled over towards the squatting sheep. In a fetal position, he curled up under the porcelain sink.

Loc blocked the advancing Texan with a protective arm and whispered, "Before we cut off the serpents head, let's determine its length."

"Tomorrow my friends," Golden teeth shouted. "I will officially welcome you to my realm." The thug barked in Thai. His followers returned to their humble bedding. His servant emerged from under the washbasin to finish his task.

"It's been a long day," Loc said quietly to his companions. "If you want to get some sleep, I'll stand watch. Remember I slept during the flight."

Max slide down the bars and sat on the cold floor. To the distant moans of perverted pleasure, he nodded off to sleep.

Morning sunlight crept into a small high barred window. It slowly spread a peaceful glow across the cell. A legion of amber cockroaches retreated down the excrement and urine stained concrete toilet. Their morning exodus impeded. Plugging the exit was the flabby head of a gold toothed man. His lifeless eyes focused on the accumulated waste in the pit below. With a broken neck, his twisted torso reclined on its side. Squatting on his haunches at the victim's feet, Loc cleaned his nails with a homemade knife.

Stirring from a shallow sleep, Max glanced over at the corpse. He looked over at the aging Hmong warrior with a satisfied grin. Quiet as a cat and deadly as a viper, Max thought once again admiring his tribal partner's assassination skills.

"Morning Loc," Max said loudly, "Anything interesting happen on your watch?" Strutting through the reclining prisoners, he headed towards the concrete toilet. Straddling the corps the German released a steady stream of urine on the dead man's head.

"No," Loc replied studying the shock expressions of gold tooth's waking henchmen. One of the thugs subtly reached under his grass mat. Loc shook his head. Reaching behind his back, Loc displayed a seven-inch shank made from prison fence wire. "Oh there was something," Loc said over his shoulder to Max. "I snapped the neck of the faggot that called me a Meo. I find that term offensive."

"I'll never make that mistake," Buck said reaching over his head to stretch.

Roche slowly stood and dropped his trousers. Fastened to his inner thigh a large rubber band secured a red and white pack of Marlboros, matches and a wade of US currency. "Smoke?" he asked pulling up his trousers. Retrieved a cigarette, he lit it with the flick of a match. Puffing out his chest, he tossed the smoldering toothpick on the Thai audience.

"Any cigars *Ami?*" Max asked chuckling.

"Max they missed the cigarettes during the pat down." Roche said comfortably blowing smoke across the cell. Laughing he added, "To smuggle in a cigar, I would have had to use an orifice."

"I'll have a cigarette then," Max said. As Roche lit Max's cigarette, he looked down at the crouching Loc and said, "I take it your the new cell boss?"

Loc rose. In front of him the henchmen seemed unsure. The frail sheep appeared cautiously optimistic. "Does anyone speak English?" Loc growled glancing around the crowed cubicle.

From under the rust stained porcelain sink, a thin shirtless man crawled out. "My name is Sanouk. I speak a little," he said. Then bowing his head asked, "Can I stand here?"

"Why are you asking?" Loc questioned.

Swallowing the frail translator answered, "Because Kanda..." he nodded in the direction of the corpse, "charged us for space on the floor."

"Where did the dead man keep his graft?" Loc asked.

The boney Sanouk glanced over at the frayed army cot.

Loc nodded. Looking down at the confused henchmen, he flexed brandishing the jailhouse shank. The men hastily parted. Strutting over Loc lifted the bed. Dog-eared Asian gentlemen's magazines sat atop a fruit crate. Plopping the wooden box on the folding bed, he tossed the pornography aside. Arranged by brand name were neatly stacked packs of cigarettes. Red soft packs of the local Krong Thip Ninety brand dominated the cigarette cache. Grinning Loc reached past the jailhouse currency and retrieved a flimsy box of chocolate bars. "Sorry Max," he said. "No cigars... but we'll have a sweet breakfast."

The four arms traffickers sat on the cot. Leaning against the concrete wall, they devoured the hoarded candy. Before them, the Thai inmates squatted. The twisted remains of the golden toothed Kanda still firmly lodged in the toilette. While Buck thumbed through an Asian gentlemen's periodical, Loc tossed a pack of cigarettes to the crouching Thais. The tobacco chum hit the floor sending the Thais into a feeding frenzy.

Looking up from the magazine, Buck chuckled, "Reminds me of feeding chickens."

Timidly Sanouk approached the cot. Bowing his head in front of Loc, he mumbled, "Are you done with the body, sir?"

"What?" Loc asked with a squint.

"Kanda, sir, can we have his body?" Sanouk clarified and motioned toward the fat carcass.

Buck chuckled and said, "Sure, knock yourself out."

Sanouk did not react. He stood patiently awaiting Loc's reply.

Loc nodded. Sanouk turned and translated for the Thais. Two of the healthier inmates grabbed a lifeless leg and extracted Kanda's flabby cranium from the waste hole. One walked over and clutching a handful of urine soaked hair, forced open the dead man's mouth. He repositioned the face on the edge of the toilets concrete cubicle. A sandaled foot stomped down hard.

"You know I always had a fear about going to the dentist," Roche said observing the inmates dividing up Kanda's golden teeth.

Max laughed and commented, "And I always had a fear about be raped in prison."

A metal door swung open. Light poured down the corridor between the cells. The clang of a night stick dragging across bars grew louder. Two guards stood in front of the sliding cage entrance. One of them shouted out two inaudible words. He banged the cage with a baton and repeated the phrase louder.

"Anybody catch that?" Buck asked.

"I think he's trying to say something in English," Loc said.

Slowly Roche rose from the cot and looking at his friends said. "Let me try to figure out what he wants." Approaching the scowling guards, he shrugged.

A vein throbbed on the side of the jailers head. The tightly wound guard wacked the cell with a baton and shouted, "Villim Johnsin."

Roche nodded at the attempt to pronounce his alias. "I'm William Johnstone," he said accenting the syllables.

The guard grunted. He pointed with his stick to the food slot. Roche placed his hands through the window. The jailer handcuffed the American.

Roche stepped back. The bars slid open. Over his shoulder, he said to his companions, "I hope they are not taking me for a dental check-up."

CHAPTER FOURTY ONE

Diminishing light trickled through the high grated window. Max sat on the jailhouse cot. Between his fingers, a cigarette slowly burned. Just above the cork-colored filter a column of white ash defied gravity. The smoldering vapors shielded the cage's putrid aroma.

Six o'clock Max estimated, maybe six-thirty. It been a very long day, he realized. Glancing down at the crouching Thais, he knew it would be a very long night. They took Roche this morning, he recalled; Loc and the three-hundred pound carcass around noon. Retrieving the dead is no doubt a common occurrence, he concluded, visualizing the shackled prisoner detail hauling off the toothless corpse. Then came lunch or dinner or whatever the fuck you want to call that red rice floating in thin fish broth. It was mid-afternoon, when they came for Buck. Max grinned recalling the guard banging on the bars and mispronouncing the Texan's name. "Melvin Case," he mumbled. No wonder he goes by Buck. It's funny, he thought, I never knew the cowboy's real name. Falling ash singed the German's fingers. "Damn," he grumbled. Shaking his hand, he flicked the glowing cigarette butt. The discarded ember caused a ripple through the crouching Thais. Most ignored the distraction. A few seemed perturbed. Scrutinized his cell mates' reactions, Max wondered, about the long dark night ahead. Who's it going to be? He speculated. Who's going to slit my throat for a couple of cartons of cigarettes or to avenge golden teeth's death? None of the sheep, he easily concluded looking at the frail men huddled around the squat toilet. Focused on the hard faces before him, men glanced down or looked away. But in the corner, where the bared door intersected with the stone wall, two defiant youths held their heads high. A lap dog, Max surmised examining the thug with a deep knife scar traversing across his face. You are dangerous, but not the threat. Your confidence comes from association. But you, Max thought, glancing over at the wiry youth with a shaved head, have killed before and enjoyed it. It's in your eyes, he concluded, that enjoyable disconnect from reality. I've seen it before. The sinister gaze of the Waffen SS, Saigon gangsters and Corsican hit men. Max squinted at the potential assassin. A devilish smirk emerged on boys face. Too young to conceal your tell, Max realized returning the smile.

Taking a deep breath, Max stood. Let's get this over with, he thought. A faint metallic click of a lock resonated in the distance. The shrill creak of rusting hinges proceeded the light rolling down the corridor.

"Max Kohl!" shouted the long shadow approaching the crowded cage.

Familiar with the drill, Max walked over to the barred entrance. He placed his hands through the food service slot. A guard handcuffed his hands. He stepped back. To the grating sound of the sliding door, the young head shaved assassin approached the German. The boy puckered his lips and blew a kiss. Max grinned. Taking a deep breath, the German leaned back and with the full force of weight advantage, head-butted the teen. The toppling youth's face exploded. Max stepped over the body and growing burgundy puddle. The disinterested guards slammed the cell shut.

The room was bright. The block walls coated with thick white paint stained a murky yellow. The stale air was heavy. Jailers ushered Max in front of a gray metal desk. The guards attached the German's shackled hands to the floor with a chain leash. Once secured to an eyelet in the concrete floor, his handlers exited. Behind the desk on a folding metal chair, a Thai army officer casually perused through a manila folder. The rank of major prominently displayed on the epaulettes of a clean and sharply pressed dark green uniform. The major's jet-black hair sparkled in the bright light. The officer blindly flicked ash from a smoldering cigarette into an empty coffee mug. Displayed on the cold gray desktop was Max's Tokarev pistol and Roche's Baby Browning. The interrogator took his time as he carefully thumbed through the documentation.

Max sighed. Glancing to his left, he looked at his reflection in a mirrored window. A one-way portal no doubt, he concluded.

The officer's chair creaked. He leaned back and plopped a pair of glossy black combat boots on the desktop. "Well let me get to know you Mister Kohl," he said looking up from the open file. "It looks like you have quite an extensive resume." From his comfortable repose, he looked down at the documentation and mumbled, "Born 1926 in Nuremberg, Germany." Flipping up the page, his volume increased as he read, "Hitler youth marksmanship awards. Served in the 12 Panzer Division during World War Two; captured at the battle of Caen in France at the age of seventeen." Pausing he looked at Max and with a nod commented, "So you were a carbine soldier Mister Kohl." Returning to the text, he continued to read. "French Foreign Legion service 1945 to 1954. Distinguished as one of the few Europeans to break out of the siege of Dien Bien Phu and escape to Laos." Tossing the folder on the desk, he interlocked his fingers over his chest and added with a smirk, "The information goes dark after your historic escape. Apparently your contract employment service with the Central Intelligence Agency is still classified." With an indifferent shrug, he dropped his feet to the floor. Sitting up in the chair, he asked politely, "Well Mister Kohl can I count on your cooperation?"

Max squinted into the slick Asian's face.

"You see Mister Kohl, if the information you volunteer is helpful to military intelligence, we would recommend leniency in your arms smuggling arrest." The interrogator said playfully. In a commanding tone, he continued, "If however you are not obliging, we would need to push for a murder conviction." Reverting to a pleasant tenor, he added, "And if you are not familiar with the laws in the Kingdom of Thailand. The penalty for murder is execution by firing squad."

"Murder," Max snorted.

The officer chuckled, "Your American accomplices had the same reaction. And note when I refer to the Meo..." He paused and after glancing down at his notes continue, "When I refer to the tribesman Moua Loc as a US citizen, I use that affiliation loosely." Slowly he pulled an eight-by-ten glossy black and white photo from the folder and pushed the picture across the desk top.

Max looked down at the image of a pile of bodies in front of a loading dock on the outskirts of Bangkok. Behind the mound of dead, painted in blood was Roche's bogus Fourteen K calling card.

"You see Mister Kohl as we speak forensics is running ballistic tests on these handguns to the projectiles recovered from the warehouse crime scene," The officer said motioning with an open palm to the sidearm display. "The choice is yours. Cooperation assures you leniency in an arms smuggling conviction. Defiance will certainly mean your life would end seated behind a targeted screen with a bullet through your heart."

Max studying the confident officer asked, "What information would buy me your favor?"

Grinning the major sat erect. "There is a lot of tension between us and our communist neighbor across the Mekong River. The Hmong insurgence has assisted the kingdom in gathering intelligence on the Lao People's Republic next door. Our strategy is simple. A hungry dog is loyal. The Hmong resistance is kept on a tight leash of limited supplies, in particular munitions." The officer paused and leaning back placed interlocking fingers behind his head. Taking a comfortable breath, he continued. "Then you and your American accomplices come along and feed our highland dog." The integrator reached into the breast pocket of his starched uniform. Casually he retrieved a soft pack of cigarettes. Slow and methodically, he went through the cigarette lighting ritual exposing the use of Max's tarnished engraved Zippo. Blowing a plume of smoke across the desk, he asked, "So tell me Mister Kohl, what did you feed our dog?"

Max chuckled and mumbled, "A shit-load of prime beef."

The officer jumped out of the chair and slammed on open palm on the desk top. The hand guns and coffee mug jumped. "Don't play with me old man," he growled. "The stakes are too high. A wild un-tethered Meo canine in Laos could spark a war along the Thai border. If you are not cooperative you will be eliminated." With shiny furrowed rows across his forehead, the Thai major squinted hard.

To the clinking of chain links, Max shifted his weight. "You read my file. You know who you are dealing with," he replied in a grating tone. "I've been close to death many times, shadowed by him; felt his presence, even had him whisper with a cool breath into my ear." Looking over each shoulder, he informed, "He's not here now, which makes your extermination threat a hollow boast." Changing to a softer tone, he continued, "Now if you would like me to re-create a shipping manifest from last week's munitions drop, I would be willing. However since that is the only card I am holding, I'm not going to play it against a cheap death threat or a shallow promise of leniency."

The officer turned and seeking guidance looked at his reflection in the one way mirror. A muffled tap resonated from behind the reflected glass. The interrogator nodded at his image and turning to the German asked, "What is it you want?"

Taking a victorious breath, Max responded, "A pad of paper and pen to fulfill your obligation. I need to be reunited with my friends. Given the international overtones of the situation as a group, we need to speak with a representative from the US consulate." Grinning he added, "And some scrambled eggs."

CHAPTER FOURTY TWO

The cage was small, the room large and bright. An open window framed the darkness of a still night. Thai police officers processing paper work occupied three strategically placed desks. A chirping manual typewriter competed with the nocturnal sound of insects. Perched on top a vertical filing cabinet, a rotating fan churned the humid air. In the holding pen, Max grasped cold steel bars. On the warped wooden cage floor, Roche, Buck and Loc slept.

Max stared across the room at the frosted glass window of the entrance door. His impatient stomach churned anticipating scrambled eggs. Two silhouettes appeared in the opaque glass. It's about time, he thought licking his lips.

The door swung open. The clerical officers flexed. A Thai general in full regalia entered with a tall thin American. The American's dishwater blond hair cropped short. A pair of mirrored aviator sunglasses balanced at the high water mark of a receding hairline. An un-tucked short-sleeve Filipino dress shirt hung over a pair chinos. The American held onto a bulky flour sack slung over his shoulder. There was no serving of scramble eggs.

The policemen stood at attention. The general ignored the officers' ramrod postures. He chuckled from a mumbled comment from the casually attired American. Composing himself the general barked in Thai. An officer scrambled to open the cage. The other policemen hastily exited.

To the grating sound of the cell door creaking open, Buck grumbled from his fetal position, "What is it now?"

Looking down at the stirring cowboy, Max answered, "The US cavalry has arrived."

Aviator Sunglasses shook the general's hand. The high-ranking officer bowed and joined the other Thais in vacating the room.

Ginning at the four mercenaries, the American envoy said, "Good evening gentlemen, I trust your stay in Udon has been pleasant."

Rubbing waking eyes, Roche grumbled, "Who the fuck are you?"

"Well Mister Johnstone or should I say Major Roche," he answered with a smirk. "I'm Ken Roberts, your guardian angel from the state department." Walking over to an empty desk, he poured out the contents of his cloth sack. Passports, wallets, a Baby Browning, a Soviet Tokarev, Loc's pistol, an Ace of spades belt buckle, a harmonica, watches and a tarnished engraved Zippo lighter clanged as they rolled across the metal surface.

Seeing his lighter and prized sidearm, Max smiled and asked, "What does this mean?"

"It means," Roberts clarified. "That you are very lucky or brilliant strategist."

Sifting through and retrieving his personal effects, Roche commented. "Uncle Sam played the insurance card." Looking at Roberts, he said, "I take it the US senator and his delegation arrived in Laos."

A respectful grin spread across Robert's face. "I'm always impressed when a plan takes into consideration all variables."

"What are y'all talking about?" asked a sour faced Buck.

"Bones!" Roche exclaimed. "We got bones for sale."

Roberts knowing nodded.

Roche clarified. "When the communist regimes of Laos and Vietnam need something from the west, they bargain with the remains of missing in action American servicemen. In this instance, to score humanitarian propaganda points and to assure no US involvement with the Hmong insurgence, the Laotian government enticed a California senator with bones."

"A hell of an insurance policy Major Roche," Roberts said. "If you were apprehended during your hard rice delivery, you knew we would have to wipe clean any US participation whether in fact or perceived."

"It was a calculated assumption," Roche replied with a humble shrug. "I was aware the logistics for the Senator's trip was under negotiations. The fact that it is an election year increased the probability."

"Not that it is any of your concern but our concessions to the Kingdom of Thailand to wash clean your apprehension were expensive." Roberts said. "Denying the loss of a MiG and two Soviet gunships is the Laotians' problem."

"Two gunships?" Roche questioned visualizing Yeep with the second stinger strapped across his back.

Squinting at the grinning mercenaries Roberts asked, "You seemed surprised?"

"Not at all," Roche responded proudly.

"We go home now?" Loc asked placing his small French pistol in a front pants' pocket.

Roberts nodded. "There is a C-130 transport headed to Guam tomorrow at midnight, I'm going to babysit you until then. Once on the lovely island of Guam, you boys are on your own."

"I need a word with you," Roche said beckoning with a crooked finger.

Roberts leaned in, "What is it?"

"I can tell by the gate of your confident stride you're a pilot." Roche probed.

Roberts acknowledged the insight with a slow nod.

"Air Force or Navy?" Roche asked.

Playfully frowning Roberts declared, "Don't insult me Major with an Air Force affiliation. I was a naval aviator...a Phantom jock."

"Any wartime experiences with the Hmong?" Roche asked with raised brows.

Roberts chuckled, "I know where you're going Major. I feel for our hill tribe allies who risked their lives to rescue many of my downed buddies. Nevertheless, their fate is an unfortunate casualty of war. If there was something I could do for them, I would."

"There is something you can do," Roche said with a serious tone. Flicking his head over his shoulder at his companions, he added, "We have an errand to attend to. It should not take too long and we will defiantly make the red-eye flight to Guam. I'm just asking you to look the other way for twenty-four hours when we walk out of here."

"You realize you are asking me to jeopardize my career?" Roberts blurted out.

Roche looked deep into Roberts' eyes and confessed, "I sinned during my tenure in Indochina. I'm here paying penance. As a fellow Vietnam vet, I'm asking for this favor."

"Besides turning a blind eye," Roberts answered. "What do you need?"

"How much cash do you have on you?" Roche asked rubbing his thumb against his fingers.

Reaching into his back pocket, Roberts retrieved an alligator skin wallet and pulled out a wade of Thai currency. After arranging it sequentially, he counted it. Offering it with an extended hand he said, "A little over ten-thousand baht."

"Good that'll work," Roche said grabbing the wad of purple, red and green shaded money. "Now we'll meet you at the entrance to the Udon airbase at twenty-two hundred hours."

Roberts dangled a set of car keys in front of Roche and said, "It's the white Toyota in front of the station." Sarcastically he asked, "Is there anything else?"

Snatching the keys, Roche said, "Just five more seats on the flight to Guam."

CHAPTER FOURTY THREE

Through thin drapes, the rising sun glowed below the horizon. The air was moist but cool. A rusted ceiling fan twirled above the cheap hotel room. Empty beer bottles and an overflowing ashtray cluttered a small glass topped rattan coffee table. Max with wet hair and a small white towel wrapped around his naked body paced back and forth. The bottoms of his bare damp feet soiled from the dirty linoleum tiled floor. From the open bathroom door water ran in an active shower.

"Jesus," Roche shouted out from behind a drenched plastic curtain. "Did you use all the hot water?"

Max chuckled probing the ashtray in search of a cigar stub. Discovering an inch long tube of dark tobacco, he smiled. Carefully he lit the butt, anticipating a few puffs of enjoyment. On the second relaxing exhale, he heard a rapping on the hollow wood door. Gun in hand, he leaned into the flimsy barrier and said, "Who is it?"

"Coffee and laundry sir," Answered a Thai accent.

Carefully Max opened the door. A teenage Asian balanced a pot of coffee and cups on a tray in one hand and a wicker basket of folded clean clothes in the other. Cautiously Max allowed him in. The youth entered and scanned the cluttered surroundings.

"Just set them on the bed," Max said offering a fifty-baht gratuity.

Accepting the tip with a nod, the boy said, "You want morning girlfriend. I send one up right away."

"No thanks," Max mumbled pouring a cup of rich dark brew.

Backing out of the room, the employee said, "My name is Joey. You change your mind about girl or you need anything just ring down for Joey."

Max nodded with a disconnected acknowledgement and closed the door.

Roche walked in rubbing his wet balding head with a towel and asked, "Sleep well kraut?"

"Clean sheets, *Ami*," Max responded. After taking a careful sip from the misting cup, he added, "As a German soldier and even in my Legionnaire days, I always cherished the luxury of a starched clean white rectangular piece of fabric to rest my bones."

"I appreciate your passion." Roche said. "But as a marine and during my covert tenure in Indochina it was ice. Nothing accents bourbon, coke or any liquid better than crystallized cubes of frozen water."

"Well are we going to do this today?" Max asked slipping into a stiff clean pair of khaki pants.

"If all goes well, we should be at the Udon airbase well before the midnight flight." Roche said buckling on a wristwatch. "To tell you the truth with the fickle winds of politics swirling about, the sooner we exit Thailand the better."

"I hate to question your planning skills Roche," Max said. "But that Roberts seemed accommodating. Why did you not solicit his help with our errand?"

"Options," Roche said. "No doubt Roberts could grease the skids for a negotiated extraction." Raising his brow, he continued, "If that failed, Roberts would hinder the alternative for a forced retrieval. I hope violence isn't necessary but for me to alleviate past sins failure is not acceptable."

"Let's see if the rest of the team is up," Max said tucking his pistol into his waist band and concealing it with an un-tucked shirt.

Pounding on the adjoining room's door, Roche heard rustling before it slowly swung open. Loc buttoned a starch shirt. Buck sitting on the bed pulled on a pointed toe boot.

"Morning boys," Roche said as he and Max entered the room.

"Mornin'," Buck mumbled with a raspy growl.

Loc nodded.

"Buck here is cab fare," Roche said offering a couple of one-hundred baht bills. "This should get you to the airport. With a little luck, we should hook up with you shortly."

"What are you talking about?" Buck scowled.

Flinching at the defiant reaction, Roche said apologetically, "There is a degree of risk today and the task does not require your flying skills. I just figured…"

"You figured wrong Roche!" Buck growled leaping to his feet. "You're paying me very well to drive the getaway car. Now give me the fucking car keys and don't question my commitment to the mission."

Fumbling in a front pants pocket, Roche retrieved the Toyota keys. Handing them to Buck he said, "You've definitely earned your salary cowboy."

"Thanks Major," said a composed Buck. Shrugging he confessed, "Just so y'all know…" He paused to swallow, "I've never killed anyone."

Snickering, Max broke the confessional silence. Loc chuckled. Roche joined in the levity. The three experienced assassins busted up.

"What's so funny?" Buck demanded.

Max patted the wiry Texan on the back and informed, "You made it sound like virginity is a bad thing."

CHAPTER FOURTY FOUR

It was a crisp rural morning on the outskirts of Udon. The air was clean, the sun bright and the sky a royal blue. With one hand on the steering wheel, Buck maneuvered a mud spattered white Toyota down a red clay country road. In the vehicle's wake a cross breeze shoved a misting cloud of crimson across the flanking scrub brush and flowering weeds. The compact car jumped out of a puddle of orange mud.

"Jesus, cowboy!" Roche said from the passenger seat.

Smirking Buck accepted the commentary and flexed his foot on the accelerator.

"What's that smell?" Max asked cranking up a rear window.

Roche informed, "The stench means we are getting close."

The vehicle rattled over a railroad-tie bridge. The passengers involuntarily sighed in disgust. A channel of raw sewage slowly drifted beneath the crude spanning structure.

No one spoke. The car ascended a rolling hill. From the summit, the densely populated Hmong shantytown rolled into view. Surrounded by barren hillsides, high fences of sparkling razor wire corralled tens of thousands of refugees into a compilation of misery. Between the barbwire boundaries, punishing sunlight reflected off shallow rooftops of plywood, corrugated tin and palm fronds. Colorful sheets of plastic flapped in the dust and smoke. The shit-canal sluggishly snaked out of the hill tribe ghetto. The Thai camp commander's headquarters sat atop the adjacent hill, in the field in front of the white single story building a shrouded helicopter. Next to the administrative office, a row of red-roofed wooden barracks housed camp security.

"Hold up a minute," Roche said to Buck in the idling car. Leaning forward, he pulled out his wallet. Carefully he rearranged the currency and concealed the bulk of the wad in his sock. Pulling down a pant leg, he informed, "Paying bribes is an art form gentlemen. Just like poker, you don't want to show all your cards unless you have to." He nodded at the driver.

Buck shifted the car into gear. The white Toyota slowly rolled down the hill. The clay road terminated at a break in the barbwire. A large tree shaded the entrance. Under the green foliage canopy, three bored Thai soldiers and an officer lounged around a waste wood table. At the tree's base leaned automatic weapons.

To the squeal of car brakes, a slouching officer peered out from under a patent leather visor. Waving an indifferent hand, he ordered a subordinate to investigate. The young soldier approached the vehicle as Roche got out. Tapping on a pack of Marlboros, Roche released a cigarette. Placing the freed cylinder between his lips, the American flashed the soft red and white pack at the guard. The guard grinned. Roche tossed him the cigarettes.

"I hope you speak English my friend," said a strutting Roche.

Stuffing the cigarettes into the breast pocket of his fatigues, the soldier replied, "I speak little. Please talk slow."

Roche took his time and after lighting his smoke asked, "Are you married?"

The guard seemed surprised but slowly nodded.

"Good," Roche said. "Then you will understand. My wife wants me to buy some Hmong needle work, the *pa'ndau*. I even hired a Hmong to help me translate." He said motioning to Loc sitting in the car. "My wife wants the bright colorful embroidery of the Black Tai."

"Five thousand baht," the soldier said holding out a hand. Smirking he added, "You will find Black Meo in back of camp living over graveyard."

Graveyard? Roche pondered paying the entrance fee.

Pocketing the money the guard's tone changed. "No take pictures and no tapestries depicting war. At dusk we enforce strict curfew."

"Strict?" Roche questioned.

Retrieving the gifted pack of smokes, the sentry lit up. On the initial exhale, he delightfully informed, "We shoot any Meo that wonder out of the cage?"

OK fucker, Roche thought grinning with a complaisant mask. I've seen many inferior men corrupted by power begging for mercy when the table turns. Your time will come sooner than you think he concluded humbly smiling at the guard's cocky expression. Turning towards the white Toyota, he hollered, "Let's go boys, times a wasting."

The four mercenaries strutted into the crowded cage, the red dirt at their feet a fine powder. Loc took the lead. Single file, they wove through the shoddy maze. Black smoke from cooking fires cloaked the ghetto's stench. Hungry children cried. Beside the narrow walkway, malnourished families squatted under corrugated tin and plastic tarp lean-tos. The displaced occupied every nook and cranny. Sunken dark eyes inspected the intruders. Buck bumped into the back of Max as the column hit a dead end. Turning to retreat, Buck glanced down at ten boney squatting Hmong huddled around a boiling black cooking pot. Fueled by smoldering charcoal a clump of matted weeds surfaced in the scolding broth.

"Jesus," Buck exclaimed. "They are eating grass."

Max nodded. Politely he shoved the cowboy forward and mumbled, "Our mission is to find Va-Meng and his family."

In faded blue-jeans and pointed-toe boots, Buck led the procession. High stepping, he walked over children sitting in the dust. The path narrowed. The cowboy ignored the women mimicking the Thai *whai* greeting. The women respectfully bowed with palms pressed together in prayer. After a sharp left, the shantytown boulevard widened. The path flowed around a bamboo fence enclosure. Looking down at the wicker-protected obstruction, Buck stopped dead in his tracks. In the center of the enclosure, a decomposing skull stuck out of the ground. Joined by his companions, the four men examined the open-mouthed skeletal head. Smoke from a cooking fire brushed the soiled bone. Leather patches of skin and wisps of long gray hair fluttered.

Loc turned and asked an old woman tending a fire, *"Grandmother what is this?"*

Assisted by a stick cane, she stood. Hunched over in black rags and a face weathered by the hard winds of time, she gave a slight bow and informed, *"The cat forced the mice to live with the dead."* Shaking the stick with a shriveled hand up the pathway, she added, *"When it rains the dead peek out of the mud."* With the stiffness of her years, she turned and mumbled, *"Evil, very evil."*

"What did she say?" Roche asked.

Solemnly Loc answered, "It looks like in the wisdom of the Thais and the United Nations relief agency, they chose to expand the camp over the Hmong graveyard." Shaking his head, he added. "Disturbing a body laid to rest is a very bad thing in my culture."

"In mine too," Buck snarled. "This is bullshit. This hell hole is surrounded by open fields. Some pompous bureaucrat must enjoy pouring salt into the wounds of the Hmong."

Roche placed a hand on the cowboy's shoulder. I feel it too Buck, he thought looking around at this proud race of people reduced to the sadistic whims of new masters. "This is bullshit," he echoed quietly.

"This must be the graveyard where that prick of a guard mentioned we would find the Black Tai." Max commented.

Roche nodded and said, "Let's find Va-Meng." Standing beside the desecrated grave, he scanned the hollow faces and sunken eyes of a growing audience. Behind each Hmong expression of despair, a story Roche realized; the individual tales of sacrifice and loss connected by the human spirit to survive. Rescuing the Hmong family is no longer a token gesture for past sins, he concluded. When a man saves your life, you owe him your future. I'm indebted to an eleven year old Hmong nicknamed Hip-shot, he realized.

A barefoot boy pried his way out of the crowd. Running at full speed, he latched onto Buck's Levi pants leg. The scrawny youth pinched tight his eyes hugging the faded denim.

Buck with a lump in his throat rubbed the top of the boys head. "Looks like Corky found us," Looking down, he said, "Howdy lil' pardner."

Loc crouched down beside the boy and asked, *"Where is your family* Corky?"

Not relinquishing his firm grasp on the cowboy, Corky pointed up the trail.

Buck hoisted his small admirer on his shoulder. Perched atop the wiry Texan, Corky pointed the way to a long shed. The front of the thatch and bamboo structure opened to the elements. Partitioned off by canvas tarps, small ten by twelve foot units housed twenty people. At the feet of the standing inhabitants, Va-Meng squatted beside his wife. May La plucked the feathers off a small gray sparrow. The young warrior Hip-shot stood proudly, slingshot in hand.

"Hello brother," Loc said as the entourage approached.

To the cackling of neighbors, Va-Meng stood and bowed.

"Tell him on behalf of the United States of America, we are here to honor his agreement," Roche announced. Looking at Hip-shot, Roche winked. The boy nodded.

As Loc conversed with his countryman, Max asked Roche, *"Ami* now that we found them what's the plan?"

"I'll tell you what the plan is," Buck blurted out. "We walk out of here with our friends get in the car and catch that mid-night flight. If anyone opposes us, they have a problem."

Roche shrugged. "That may work if we do it discreetly."

Loc stuck his head into the conversations. With downcast eyes, he said with a growl, "Thai soldiers have taken Angel."

"She's just a child?" Buck questioned.

Looking at the cowboy, Loc informed. "The apprehending officers are known rapist. They pluck the flowering new arrivals, detain them for a few days and release them bruised and broken." Glancing over at the distraught parents, he added, "Beauty and youth is a curse in this camp. They will not leave without her."

"And neither are we!" Buck exclaimed. "I say we go up there and blow away those fuckers now."

Slowly nodding, Max said softly, "I appreciate your sentiment, but discipline and control is the key to success and survival; lose your temper, lose your life." Looking at Roche, he offered, "Let's get the family out of here before dark and then we can probe the barracks to formulate a rescue."

Loc interjected, "Va-Meng told me the weekly meat ration arrives this afternoon. His neighbor says there is always a lot of commotion. The men scramble for the limited supply. The guards are kept busy keeping order. Obtaining meat for the family is a man's job. We can dress May La as a man and scoot out of here in the confusion." Discreetly he handed a wad of greenbacks to Roche.

"What is this?" Roche questioned stuffing the currency in a front pants pocket.

"It's the money you gave Va-Meng on the plane to hold for you." Loc answered.

"This may come in handy," Roche said.

"Spot me a few bucks *Ami*," Max said rubbing his thumb across fingers.

"What for?" Roche questioned handing a random fistful of crinkled bills to the German.

"Loc and I will buy the tapestry and spread some of the wealth around," Max responded. "Don't worry Roche we won't cause a scene. The same skill in tipping a *maître d'* at a fine restaurant will be used in our discreet contributions to the less fortunate."

Max and Loc wandered deeper into the bowels of the densely populated labyrinth.

"*Pa'ndau?*" Loc called soliciting the Hmong needlework.

His request invoked gnarled fingers pointing down a tight path under a rusty corrugated tin overhang. Following Loc, Max slouched down under the low ceiling.

All around refugees stood, sat, or reclined. Staring into space the lifeless survivors of a march to freedom endured another long day with empty stomachs.

"Mack!" a voice called out above the whining children.

Max's head jerked. Did someone call my name? He wondered.

Loc stopped. Looking at the German, he asked, "Did you hear that?"

Max nodded.

A grated voice shouted, "Loc, Mack!"

Max stared into an overcrowded tin shack.

The women and children parted. An old one-legged man sat on an upturned wooden bucket. A gnarled callused stump poked out of a short raggedy pant leg. A tree limb crutch lay across the cripple's lap. Scraggly long silver hair poured out of a black skullcap.

Max examined the man's leather face and sharp cheekbones. His eyes Max thought, there is something familiar about the eyes.

The cripple flashed a toothless smile.

Visualizing the ridge-running Meo warrior from twenty-five years ago, Max grinned. My god its Chue, he realized. I thought him long dead, "Chue!" Max exclaimed entering the dirt floored hovel. Reaching down Max attempted to shake Chue's hand. The German settled for affectionately squeezing the Hmong's missing fingered paw. Looking at Loc, Max asked, "Tell my brother it is always a good thing when are paths cross."

Chue chuckled, "No need Loc. I speak American." Looking at Max, he asked, "Do you still carry that Vietminh pistol that kills communist?"

Reaching for the small of his back, Max retrieved his Tokarev. Holding his trophy, Max said, "It seems like yesterday, I claimed this as you and I cleared a battlefield."

Chue barked at the standing women and children. A middle-aged woman hastily retrieved a wicker-encased bottle from a box of pots and pans. She pulled out a crumbling cork and handed it to the slouching Chue's good hand. He took a healthy swig, pointed the bottle at his guest and said the tribal greeting to get drunk, "*Nam lu.*"

Loc squatted down and took a cautious sip. "Wow," he commented exhaling toxic fumes.

Max took the bottle and a shallow gulp of potent white whisky. My days of heavy drinking are long gone, he realized. "We can help get you out of here," Max said. "We can vouch that you fought for the Americans as a veteran..."

Holding up his mangled hand, Chue interrupted, "I know. I could have left two years ago if I abandoned all but one of my wives." He informed. "I've seen it before; husbands taking all their children and leaving all but one of their wives. The unwanted women wail. It is very sad. They said

I could go to a place called Detroit. Why would I want to live amongst the Americans that abandoned the Hmong? They are not a noble race." Tossing back the bottle, he took a healthy swig. After wiping his moist lips with a soiled forearm, he continued, "I have five wives and twenty children. Two of my wives belonged to my brother who gave his life rescuing an American flyer. So here I sit, and wait for the day we can cross the river and go home. I'm too old to hope for anything less." Looking around, he said, "For an old cripple it is not so bad. The guards leave me alone. Two of my sons work for the relief agency. My wives sell *pa'nda*. The little money we receive allows us to eat." Holding up the wicker bottle, he added, "And get drunk."

Max grabbed the bottle and tipping the neck in Chue's direction said, "To going home." To make the toast official, he swallowed a large shot. Reaching into his pocket, he grabbed the handful of cash and handed it to Chue. A resonating sigh erupted from the surrounding women and children. "For your wives best needle work," he said.

Chue snorted almost falling off the bucket. Flashing his signature toothless grin, he said, "It is always good when our paths cross."

CHAPTER FOURTY FIVE

The late afternoon sun hung in the sky. Billowing clouds collected on the horizon. In front of the refugee camp, a sheet of plywood lay across sawhorse legs. Around the rough wood tabletop, Hmong teenagers waited with hatchets in hand. The young butchers focused on the billowing red dust cloud heading towards the camp. Out of the crimson haze, a wood paneled lorry skidded to an abrupt termination. Rancid boney meat filled the truck bed. Buzzing flies feasted on the putrid animal flesh. An orderly queue of Hmong men armed with sticks and twine snaked out of the razor wire compound. A young butcher slapped a scrawny carcass on the plywood table. The other boys hacked it into small portions. A refugee scrambled to tie a rotten ration of bone and cartilage to a stick. Slinging the foul smelling meat over his shoulder, he shuffled back into the wire wrapped city. The line of hungry men surged forward. In the comforting shade of a large tree, four Thai guards casually observed the festivities.

At the back of the line, Va-Meng and his family lingered. May La dressed in the black tunic and pants of a man. Her scraggly black hair tucked under an oversized skullcap.

Just inside the compound, Roche turned to Loc and said, "Tell Va-Meng we'll put him and the boys in the car's trunk, his wife on the floor of the back seat." Loc nodded. Roche turned to Max, "Give me the tapestry." The German handed him the folded *story cloth* blanket. "When I distract the guards with my purchase, load the passengers."

Max nodded.

"Now," Roche said. The Hmong family plunged into the flow of meat toting traffic. With the folded tapestry under arm, Roche strutted towards the lounging Thai guards.

From his seated repose the five-thousand baht greased guard asked, "Find what you were looking for?"

"You tell me," Roche answered with a smile. Unfolding the cotton fabric, he held it high with outstretched arms. The intricately embroidered fabric depicted Communist soldiers pursing Hmong across the Mekong River. Roche heard the faint sound of a car door shutting. Peering over the cloth canvas, he asked, "What do you think?"

With indifferent expressions the guards shrugged. The blast of a car horn caused Roche to turn. Behind the wheel of the idling Toyota, an impatient Buck raced the engine.

"I better get going," Roche said to his apathetic audience.

Kicking up dust, Roche held back the urgency to quicken his pace. We are out of here, he thought. Grabbing the passenger door handle, he glanced down. May La was crouching in the back seat.

"Halt," shouted a Thai guard.

Roche scowled over the white vehicles roof. An armed soldier approached. "What is it?" Roche asked.

"I told you no needle work depicting war," the guard said with a commanding tone.

From the back seat, Max scowled at the prancing uniformed feline closing in. Enough already, he thought reflecting on the squalor forced upon his *kameraden*. Carefully screening the tiny Hmong woman, he exited the vehicle. Flexing broad shoulders, he intercepted the little man playing soldier. Standing in front of the guard, he presented the mask of death. The pint-sized bully wilted.

Looking past the hostile German, the guard said to Roche, "I hope your wife enjoys her gift."

Max and Roche climbed into the vehicle. It rolled forward.

Looking at the dust trail reflected in the rearview mirror Buck said, "Jesus Max, I got nervous watching you stare down that punk."

"After what we saw today, I was willing to back it up," Max responded.

"You bought a tapestry depicting war?" Roche questioned.

Max looked at Loc.

The tribesman shrugged and offered, "It was the biggest one they had."

"Well we got out of there," Roche conceded. Patting Buck on the knee, he said, "Not too far cowboy, we have to return at dusk."

After crossing the railroad-tie bridge, Buck pulled over under a large tree. Jumping out the vehicle, he rushed to the car's trunk. Gravel crunched under his boots as he fumbled with the keys. The turn of a wrist popped open the trunk. A sweaty Va-Meng blinked at the sunlight. His son's lay curled around the spare tire. The cowboy grabbed Corky and easily hoisted him onto the ground. Hip-shot waived off assistance and climbed out. His father followed. Va-Meng hugged his wife and sadly looked back in the direction of the camp.

Approaching the distraught parents, Loc said softly, *"Don't worry my friends, we won't leave without your daughter."*

Va-Meng nodded. His wife looked up at Loc with watery eyes. Burying her face in the comfort of her husband's shoulder, she wept.

Max and Loc checked their side-arms. Buck pulled a tire iron out of the open truck before slamming it shut.

Seeing the cowboy testing the weight of the metal baton, Roche took a deep breath and approached the cowboy. "I want you to stay with the family," he said firmly.

Flexing his grasp on the heavy steel rod, Buck barked, "Look here Major..."

"It's not negotiable," Roche interrupted. "We can't take the family with us and we can't leave them exposed outside of the barbwire without an escort." Placing a consoling hand on the cowboy's shoulder, he said, "Don't worry, a hefty portion of vigilantly justice will be served tonight."

CHAPTER FOURTY SIX

I t was a dark night. Ominous storm clouds prowled overhead. In the distance random lighting flashed. Dust swirled about the refugee camp's administrative complex. Lighting attached to the barracks, office buildings and atop several waste-wood utility poles illuminated the hilltop compound. At the hills base tall weeds flanking the sewage canal swayed. The wind scented with approaching rain. Peering through the fertilized vegetation, Max studied the hillside.

"Do you see him?" Roche whispered.

Max shook his head and continued to squint at the dark scars and creases of the rolling hill.

"He should be back by now?" Roche commented.

Never underestimate a Meo warrior, Max thought focused on the rippling grass moving against the wind. That must be him, he assumed. He grinned as Loc slithered into view.

Shielded by the deep growth, Loc slid in between Max and Roche. Rolling onto his back the tribesman's chest jumped up and down.

"Did you find her?" Roche inquired.

Loc nodded gasping for air.

"Is she alive?" Max asked.

"Unfortunately," Loc sighed. Rolling onto his belly, he took a few deep breaths. Softly he informed, "Four soldiers in the end unit have her lashed to a bed for their pleasure."

"Bastards," Roche growled between gritted teeth.

Max held up a calming palm. "Focus *Ami*," he said softly. Looking at Loc, he asked, "What are our extraction options?"

Loc shrugged and informed. "The compound is bright but quiet. I didn't see any sentries."

"The Thais are guarding the Hmong not their barracks," Roche interjected.

"I don't know how we could go in there and take her without an incident." Loc said shaking his head.

A bolt of lightning shot across the stormy sky. Max's mind raced. A diversion won't work he concluded, there are too many hostiles. Bribe, he pondered. The rapists are not going to sell her and be exposed, he realized. Waiting them out won't work, he rationalized. It would only prolong Angel's ordeal. To the crashing sound of thunder, he grinned.

"What is it?" Roche asked.

"We'll let the Lord provide the covering fire." Max answered. Extending a finger into the stormy sky, he added. "We time our assault with thunder."

"Max," Roche said with hesitation. "I've seen your rapid fire skill. It is truly remarkable how you can make three accurate shots sound as one. But that was over twenty years ago. Do you think you are up to the task?"

Max examined the pistol in his hand. It felt good. There is nothing like a challenge to summon the reflexes of youth. Confidently nodding he said, "It's time to correct the mistakes of our creator. There are four men who should not have been born." Tucking the Soviet pistol in the small of his back, he crawled out of the weeds.

The wind howled. Max clawed his way up the hill. The spot lit objective sparkled. A flash of lightning caused him to pause. Hugging the red powder his heart pounded. He counted the passing seconds. The sharp crack of thunder terminated at the count six. A low rumble faded.

At the edge of the compound's downcast lighting, he waited on his belly. Loc and Roche joined him in the shadows. Max pointed to the row of red roofed plywood barracks. Loc nodded. The three commandos sprang up and raced to the dark side of the end unit. Max held his breath. A flash of lighting captured him and his companions standing exposed. He exhaled under the comforting shroud of subsequent darkness. The predictable thunder growled.

Cautiously Max peered into the lighted window. From a frayed cord, a single light bulb dangled down from the ceiling. On a bed against the wall, a naked Angel laid spread eagle. Leather straps lashed her hands and feet to wrought iron bedpost. The young girl's taut bare skin blemished and bruised. Her bare chest pulsed with shallow breaths. She is still alive, Max thought. Two uniform soldiers casually sat on wooden stools in the center of the room flipping playing cards on a small table. Reclining comfortably on a cot, another assailant thumbed through a magazine. The fourth rapist leaning back in a chair enjoyed a cigarette. His feet propped up on Angel's bed. The smoker blew smoke in the direction of Angel's disconnected gaze. Smoker, magazine, card players, Max thought visualizing his shooting sequence.

Skirting along the wall, Max approached the door. Grasping the door-knob, he felt resistance. Its locked he concluded. A flash in the sky started the countdown. On five, he determined. The seconds clicked by. Three, two, and on one a size eleven combat boot and a clap of thunder burst through the door. Blindly Max fired at the mental images of his targets. A blast hit the smoker in the temple. A spout of blood erupted out of the man's head. The casualty toppled to the plywood floor. The periodical reader's head snapped back from a penetrating projectile that slammed into the bridge of his nose. A bullet through the back of the head terminated one card player. The lifeless body toppled the gaming table. Playing cards went flying. The other player froze with an open mouth. A slug shattered his front teeth on its journey through the back of his throat.

The rippling thunder faded. A missing toothed casualty gulped for life. The rapist gurgled on clotted blood flowing out of his mouth. Max stood over his dying prey. "Patience my friend," he mumbled grinning down at the wide-eyed pedophile.

Roche with pistol in hand peered out a crease in the door. Loc strad-dling a corpse spoke softly to Angel. He untied her restraints. Wrapping the broken child in a blanket, the tribesman cradled the girl in his arms. He tenderly kissed the top of her head.

Waiting for the Lord to provide another blast of thunder, Max flexed. There was no stiffness of age, no bile taste in his mouth. You can still do it, he thought savoring the sense of a young man's accomplishment. A bolt of lightning illuminated the barracks. Displaying a fisted hand, Max began extending fingers. On five, cloaked with a load crack from above, he blew off the top of the gargling man's head.

CHAPTER FOURTY SEVEN

The approaching storm whipped up a pinkish dust. The misty squalls shook the compound's downcast lighting. The air was rank. Between the red roofed plywood barracks, Loc peered out of the shadows. The foul breeze slapped his face. The rain is close; he concluded snorting at the swirling odor. Tenderly he held the broken Angel. Tightly curled up in his arms, she sucked on his shirt collar. With a gentle toss, he secured his grip. Into her sweaty matted hair, he whispered, "We are going home now." Squinting into the irritating wind, he saw Max. At the fading edge of the compound lighting, the German with pistol in hand squatted on the red clay ground. Max flicked confident beckoning fingers. Taking a deep breath, Loc ran out of the shadows. The fluid girl was an awkward load. She began to whimper. Sucking in the soiled air, Loc focused on his partner. The German's head methodically scanned the Thai compound. I got you, Loc thought trying to ignore the growing fatigue running down his spine. A large raindrop struck the back of his head. Large droplets began to stain the surrounding red earth. Twenty yards in front of Loc, Max rose with outstretched arms. A glowing vein of lightening shot across the sky. A blast of thunder exploded. The night sky conceded to the impatient precipitation. In driving rain, Loc attempted to handoff the fragile girl. She resisted, firmly latching her arms around his neck.

"I got her for now," Loc mumbled jogging past Max.

Small streams flowed down the hillside. Wrapped in a soaking wet blanket, the naked Angel shivered. Loc huffed and puffed trying to maintain balance. A steady flow of water ran down his face. The torrential down pour accelerated. The wet night was black. Each challenging slippery step required skill.

"Hold up," Max called out.

At the base of the hill, a wobbly Loc leaned back for balance.

"It will be all right *liebchen,*" Max said softly to the trembling girl. Gingerly he pried her from Loc's grasp. Angel quickly curled up into Max's broad chest.

Loc took a knee in the mud.

There was movement on the hill. At the summit, the lighted compound illuminated sheets of cascading rain. Water splashed in the darkness.

"I hope that's Roche," Loc said brandishing a sidearm.

Flaying his arms, a waterlogged Roche sprinted out of control. Leaning back his legs shot out from under him. His ass hit the ground hard. The slick mud splashed. "Shit," he mumbled sliding by. The momentum carried him another ten-yards. On his back in the muck, Roche surrendered to the falling rain and closed his eyes.

Looking down at the drenched American, Max commented, "I take it we are not being followed?"

Opening one eye, Roche said, "Nope."

"Well if your done playing in the mud," Max said. "Can we get going? I have a flight to catch."

Sitting upright, Roche shook his arms tossing sludge. Water drained out of his shirtsleeves. Slowly he rose. Looking at his friends, he said, "Just catching my breath." Tilting his head back, the storm cleansed his soiled face. After shaking his balding head, he smiled at the package in Max's arms. "It's only a short click before the family is reunited."

The path was dark but flat. The rain continued. A firm step was rare. Mud under boot attracted more mud. The sound of rushing water resonated from the sewage canal.

Plodding beside Max, Roche asked, "Do you want me to take her?"

Max looked down at the trembling bundle in his arms. Shaking his head, he answered, "No."

Rounding a bend the three men froze. A hundred yards down the path, the railroad-tie bridge spanned the canal. A poncho clad silhouette stood in the center of the overpass. Slowly the mercenaries retreated.

"Did you think he saw us?" Loc mumbled.

"I doubt it," Roche responded.

"Can we go around?" Loc asked.

While Roche shook his head, Max said, "We need the bridge to cross." Roche squatted down and untied his bootlace. Standing up, he said in a dark voice, "This one is mine." Shoulders back and head held high, he strutted around the bend. Thick with mud his boots pounded the wet roadway. The ends of the freed leather lace flapped.

On the bridge, a sentry flexed. Pointing an automatic rifle, he barked in Thai. Ignoring the warning, Roche advanced. The soldier repeated the threat. Displaying jazz hands, Roche stood in front of the guard's gun barrel.

"Rough night?" Roche asked calmly.

The sentry poked Roche with his weapon. Looking down at the probe, Roche raised his eyebrows. Squatting down, the American tied his bootlace. In a fluid motion, he drew his Baby Browning pistol from an ankle holster. Ascending Roche popped the guard in the forehead with a small caliber bullet. The sentry's lifeless face conveyed shock. The falling rain diluted the crimson fluid flowing out of the puncture wound. The sentry dropped his weapon and collapsed. Roche's fat muddy boot kicked the rifle off the bridge. The heavy weapon splashed in the churning white water. Roche tucked the small handgun in the small of his back. Grabbing the dead man's boots, he dragged the corpse to the edge of the bridge.

"You were in the wrong place, at the wrong time." Roche mumbled to his victim.

Max and Loc approached. Coddling Angel in his arms, Max asked, "You alright *Ami?*"

Roche nodded. His heart raced. Breathing heavy, he looked at the girl. From her cradled perch, she focused on the dead soldier. A satisfied smile emerged on her stone face. The spark of Angel's emotions justified the termination, Roche realized. "I'm just fine kraut," he exclaimed. Placing a mud clad boot on the carcass, he added. "The Siamese cat must learn that sometimes the mice bite back." Flexing his leg, he pushed the body into the violent water. The poncho shrouded remains plunged deep into the murky current. Downstream it surfaced and peacefully drifted into the darkness.

The rain softened. Penetrating moonlight reflected off the wet terrain. The pace was slow but steady. Walking into a pocket of chilled air, Max's young bundled stirred. He flexed his arms and whispered, "Stay strong little-one."

Out of the surrounding brush, Va-Meng popped up. The tribesman was soaking wet. Wading through the waist high growth, his face showed delight, his eyes concern. Seeing her father, Angel twisted to escape the German's tender grasp. Max set her down on the cold ground. The soupy soil engulfed her bare feet. She hugged her father. Max adjusted the heavy wet blanket wrapped around her naked body. Quietly she wept.

Va-Meng scooped up his distraught daughter. She buried her face into his shoulder. Her muddy feet dangled in the night air. The muffled sound of Angel's pain resonated from her father's bosom. The tribesman turned and gave a grateful nod to the mercenaries.

"Greener pastures," Roche mumbled softly to the father. "That is our destination."

Loc looked at Roche. Roche shook his head. No translation was necessary.

CHAPTER FOURTY EIGHT

A pair of bouncing headlights reflected off approaching ponds of carroty mud. Raindrops falling through the twin beams sparkled. Following the piercing illumination, a soiled white Toyota splashed down the waterlogged country road. A wave of murky orange water erupted along the driver's side. Hugging the steering wheel in the crowded compact car, Buck grimaced. The vehicle skidded sideways. The passengers grunted and groaned. Easing off the gas pedal, Buck cranked the wheel regaining control. In the passenger seat, Max lifted up the boy encroaching on the stick shift. Hip-shot bent down below the automobile's headliner. The cowboy downshifted.

"Thanks," Buck mumbled.

"Just don't get us stuck again," Max replied craning his neck to glance into the backseat. Crammed next to window, Roche sat with Corky across his lap. The glow of the dashboard lights illuminated the crusty mud covering the American's face. Recalling Roche's mud bath during the last successful dislodging of the vehicle, Max grinned. Beside Roche wrapped in the Hmong tapestry trembled the broken Angel. Is her chill from the damp cold, Max wondered or the ordeal. Looking over his other shoulder, he smiled into the grateful eyes of May La. The Hmong woman with rounded shoulders nodded at the German. Turning back around, he asked Buck, "I wonder how our trunk passengers are enjoying the ride?"

"Hell," Buck exclaimed. "After tossing the spare tire and the jack, Loc and Va-Meng got the best seats in the house. Knowing Loc, he is probably curled up in a comfortable ball fast asleep."

Fishtailing up a steep grade the vehicle gained traction. The surface changed to gravel. A riveting burst of pebbles ricocheted of the wheel wells.

The crackling faded. Buck slowed down towards the summit. The shimmying vehicle's tires spit mud as the country road flowed onto the asphalt highway.

"Thank god," Roche mumbled from his cramped quarters. "How are we doing for time cowboy?"

Buck checked his watch. "Let's see," he responded focused on the deserted glistening paved road. "Traffic is not an issue," he mumbled to the steady beat of wiper blades. "We should make the ten-o-clock airport rendezvous...it'll be close...but we'll make it."

"I never like being late for a flight, but let's make a quick stop before the airport," Roche said. "Do you remember the Udon night market?"

"The one by the train station?" Buck asked.

"That's the one," Roche delightfully replied. "I have five large in very wet US greenbacks burning a hole in my pocket. I want to buy Angel some clothes."

Down the long dark wet road, a pair of red taillights appeared. Buck tapped the cars horn. To the pulsing high-pitched beep, an overloaded lorry migrated towards the shoulder. The Toyota blew by the transport. The truck acknowledged the passing with a single aooga honk. Max chuckled. Corky's eyes lit up. Angel lifted her head from the comfort of her mother's shoulder to investigate.

"Socks!" Roche exclaimed. "We should get some dry socks. I need to get out of these wet boots. I feel my toes are starting to web."

"I sure could use a cigarette," Buck offered. "Let's pick up a carton of Marlboros at the night market."

"I wouldn't mind getting something to eat," Max chimed in, "Something quick."

"Satay," Buck interjected licking his lips. "Both chicken and beef with lots of peanut sauce."

The car accelerated. It passed a sprinkling of residences flanking the highway. The Hmong passenger's heads pivoted back and forth attempting to comprehend the English dialogue.

"We should pick up some beer," Max said with a convincing nod. "Nothing washes down that broiled marinated meat better than a cold brew."

Looking at the puzzled expression of his backseat companions, Roche said, "Coca Cola?"

The brand name broke the language barrier. Corky nodded with a wide grin. Even Angel mustered up a smile.

"Have a Coke and a smile," sang an off key Roche.

The rain stopped. The Toyota's wiper blades now cleansed the windscreen of the spray from passing motor scooters. The provincial capital of Udon Thani glowed in the distance. Stopping at a traffic light, Buck with impatient fingers drummed a beat across the top of the steering wheel. Motor bikes crowded around the delayed vehicle. Next to the driver side window, a family of five balanced across the gas tank and banana seat of a small Honda motorcycle. Buck glanced over at the capacity crowd and chuckled. The light turned green. The traffic flowed.

Buck commented, "When I was very young the circus came to Denton, Texas. It was not one of the big productions but a cheap knock-off. My family sat in the bleachers...the cheap seats. The only thing I remember was that somewhere during the show a Volkswagen beetle drives into the center ring."

"The people's car," Max interjected.

Buck nodded and continued, "Well out of this Nazi box, clown after clown slowly emerges." Laughing, he adds, "I'm not talking midgets but lots of big tall clowns in large shoes."

"What's your point cowboy?" Roche asked.

"I always wondered how they got some many clowns into a compact car," Buck responded. "Now with nine people in this Toyota, and seeing a family of five traveling on a Honda-Fifty, I figured it out. There is no gimmick. You just cram a bunch of circus performers into a small car and have them get out." After a reflective pause, he added, "I don't think that gag would play very well in Southeast Asia."

"Nazi box?" Max questioned.

CHAPTER FOURTY NINE

In front of the Udon Thani train depot a sea of neatly rowed compact cars reflected distant light. At the far end of the parking lot, Buck shut off the soiled Toyota's engine and extinguished the vehicles headlamps. The cowboy jingling keys exited quickly. The other passengers slowly unpacked themselves. Fried food odors circulated in the moist air. The pulse of popular music faded in and out. Standing over the trunk, Buck fumbled with the cars keys. Standing on the wet asphalt, Roche leaning forward attempted to touch his muddy boots. Reaching over his head, Max interlocked his fingers and twisted in search of comfort. The curious Hmong boys stared across the parked cars at the glowing commotion of commerce.

As the trunk lid popped open, Max asked, "How did our boot passengers fare?"

Out of the small compartment crawled Loc and Va-Meng. Slowly turning around Loc questioned, "Is this the airport?"

"Nah," Buck answered, "Just a quick pit-stop to buy Angel some travel clothes."

Loc nodded and squinted through the vehicle's rear window at the Hmong mother comforting the naked child. Va-Meng bowed in Buck's direction before joining his wife and daughter.

"How we holding up partner?" Max asked.

"I'm fine Max," Loc replied quietly. Still focused on the Hmong family, he added, "My heart goes out to that girl. In my culture a raped woman is considered damaged property, no longer worthy of marriage. What is she twelve? Maybe thirteen years old? She was coming of age and now her life is over." Looking at Max, he said, "During our Indochina days I would boast that you could fix anything. I wish we could fix this."

Roche called for a huddle. The mercenaries clustered behind the vehicle. Roche checked his watch, "Alright it's twenty-to-ten. Let's try to keep our shopping spree to twenty-minutes. We'll divide up the list and meet back here at ten."

"I don't think you're going anywhere *Ami*," Max said pointing at the American's chest.

Roche looked down. Blood splatter adorned the front of his damp muddy shirt. "Shit," he mumbled. "It's probably from the guard I popped on the bridge." Reaching into his pants pocket, he pulled out a crinkled wad of moist greenbacks. Handing a chunk of money to Loc, he instructed, "Get some hot food...satay...some beer...and some Coke-a-cola for the kids."

Loc turned and jogged in the direction of the pungent aroma.

"Buck," Roche said handing the cowboy wet wrinkled bills. "Get us something dry to wear...T-shirts, sweat pants and socks." Raising his brow, he emphasized, "Dry warm socks."

"What about Angel?" Buck asked.

"I got that covered," Max interjected.

The cowboy winked and headed off toward the glimmering glow of the night market.

Giving the healthy balance of the money to Max, Roche said, "Ok kraut get the girl something nice."

"You got that right *Ami*," Max replied walking away.

"And don't forget the smokes!" Roche called out to the departing German.

Dragging his jungle boots on the asphalt, Max scraped off mud. Under the bright lighting, a silhouetted mass flowed in and out of the night market. Plunging into the stream, Max shuffled forward. Food stalls flanked the narrow walkway. Shirtless sweaty Thai cooks fried and steamed cheap cuisine. Patrons on wooden, plastic and folding metal chairs encircled carts and stalls. At close range, diners shoveled down street delicacies. Over the gorging locals, Max got a glimpse of Loc enjoying a refreshing bottle of cola. At Loc's feet, a squatting boney man used a palm fan to stoke the coals of a hibachi. Bamboo strips of chicken and pork sizzled on the grill. Jesus that looks good, Max thought swallowing in anticipation. Do I have time to get something eat, he pondered? Spotting a beverage vendor, he tossed a dollar bill on the counter. I have time for a beer; he surmised pointing at a can of Singha. From a galvanized ice filled tub, the hawker pulled out a dripping cold can. Max waived off the change as he chugged down the fresh carbonated brew. Placing the empty can on the counter, he winked at the vendor. Wiping moist satisfied lips, he concluded that beer still is one of the finer pleasures of life.

The heat and odors of the mobile cafeterias faded. Dry goods dominated the narrow thoroughfares. Roving herds migrated past sunglasses, wristwatches and record albums displayed under lighted tarps. Shoppers picked through bins of loose clothing. Radios blared Thai covers of western tunes. Behind a Thai teenage couple holding hands, Max plodded along. They past a headless mannequin draped in a simple gown. The young girl shook out of her date's tender grasp to race into the clothing stall. Pausing next to the figurine, Max glanced at the idle teenage boy. Get use to it, he thought reflecting on his wife's shopping addiction. I never understood Elaine's insatiable pleasure to acquire clothing, he reflected. I suspect most males never will.

In muddy boots and wet fatigues, Max flipped through racks of female garments. Something simple and modest, he thought. The curious young female customers distanced themselves from his quest. A few hastily exited.

"What you want?" barked a pudgy Thai woman. The middle-aged proprietor scowled from the loss of patrons.

Handing her two moist twenty-dollar bills, Max said, "I'm in a hurry too mama. Give me a couple full length knit dresses for my daughter. She is about..." he looked around the clothing stall and pointed at a young shopper, "about that size."

Totting a plastic bag, Max was pleased with his purchase. Weaving his way through the labyrinth, he sought an exit. Along the journey, he acquired a carton of Marlboros, a couple of local cigars and a petite pair of sneakers. Congestion forced him to alter his course. He checked his watch. I got a good five-minutes left, he realized. Passing the repetitive stalls of T-shirts, sandals and airline travel bags, he paused in front of a small kiosk. I don't know if I can fix everything, he thought grinning down at the glimmering merchandise. Nevertheless, I can try. Laid out on a linen tablecloth, engraved silver looped earrings, bracelets and traditional Hmong torque ringed necklaces sparkled. The centerpiece of the display was a heavy necklace of three half loops enclosed by silver chain links. The vendor through thick black framed spectacles suspiciously studied the scraggly German. Max pointed at the prize neck ornament. The curious jeweler grinned. The hawker scratched out a number on a small pad of paper and displayed the price in baht. Max nodded at the offer and then pointed at a bar of silver. The dealer picked up the engraved bullion brick. After examining the underside, he wrote down the price.

"How many silver bars do you have?" Max asked.

The uncomprehending hawker shook his head.

Max pointed at the silver brick and with a fisted hand began extending digits.

The enlightened vendor reached behind the counter. Methodically he began setting silver bullion on the linen cover.

Max tested the weight in an extended hand. Setting the hawker's stock of seven bars and two necklaces in a pile, he flashed a crinkled hundred-dollar bill and asked, "How much in US currency?"

The vendor flinched with delight. Trying to suppress escaping enthusiasm, he reached for an abacus. After flipping the black beads on the manual wood framed calculator, he jotted down a dollar sign and the price.

Examining the scratch pad, Max shook his head. Flicking a finger, he solicited the pencil. Crossing out the offer, he countered at half price.

The dealer snorted and began flipping beads. Pausing he cleared the manual calculator and started over. With a wrinkled brow, he adjusted the offer.

Max studied the counter. Grinning the German added two pair of silver earrings to the pile and shrugged.

The nodding hawker extended his hand to finalize negotiations.

In a plastic bag, Max carried the dresses and sundry items. Slung over his shoulder, a Thai Airlines vinyl travel bag housed his silver acquisitions. Strutting through the parking lot with the calming euphoria of a single beer on an empty stomach, he puffed on a fresh cigar. Mission accomplished, he reflected. I'm heading home.

Greasy bamboo skewers, empty beer cans, coke bottles and cigarette butts littered the periphery of the white Toyota. In the back seat, Angel assisted by her mother slowly put on a western gown. To give the young girl privacy, the males in the late night dinner party looked the other way.

Max tossed the smoldering remnants of a cigar onto the damp asphalt. Seeking comfort, he tugged on the tight neckline of a bright yellow t-shirt. Displayed across his chest was the slogan, *I Love Thailand*. A red heart symbol substituted for the word love. Examining Roche in a pink knit shirt displaying the flag of Thailand and Loc in a light blue pullover adorned with an elephant, he chuckled. "Jesus cowboy," he exclaimed. "Couldn't you find clothes a little less...touristy?"

"What do you mean?" Laughed Buck, "You guys look great."

"I appreciate the dry socks," Roche said sucking on a cigarette. "But to complete the colorful ensemble you should have picked up some large clown shoes."

Snickering laughter faded as Angel stepped out of the car. Dressed in a full-length navy blue knit dress, the petite victim's hair hung down shielding her face. White canvas tennis shoes peeked out from under the long hem line. Her parents shadowed her as she approached the men. With a grateful finger, Angel stroked the large silver loops of a necklace.

"How you doing lil' darlin," Buck said softly.

Patting the vinyl travel bag resting on the trunk, Max said to Loc, "You do the honors partner."

Loc nodded. Addressing the girl in Hmong, he said, *"Chai when you begin your new life, you are allowed to leave the past behind. To ensure a prosperous future in a new land your uncles want to provide you with your wedding dowry."* Zipping open the satchel, he graciously presented seven bricks of silver bullion.

Chai's wide eyes welled up. Flowing tears rolled down her soft cheeks into the creases of a sprouting grin.

"Nicely done Fritz," Roche whispered to Max.

Va-Meng and his wife with palms pressed together in prayer bowed in gratitude. Va-Meng turned and hugged his wife. He added a passionate kiss.

CHAPTER FIFTY

C learing customs at the Los Angeles International airport was a breeze. Especially with a first class express pass, Elaine concluded. Max's wife pushed the overloaded three-wheeled luggage cart through opaque automatic glass doors. Designer stiletto heels clicked on the terrazzo flooring. Greeting masses stood behind a metal railing. Posing she studied the assembly. Trying to get her attention, limo drivers waived name cards. Amongst the tan California crowd a familiar Asian face smiled. "Mei," Elaine whispered with delight.

Max's little Vietnamese sister vigorously waved.

Pushing the cart, Elaine felt a pang of remorse. I never understood Max's bond with these people, she reflected. It's because I never tried. I was young and shallow during my Saigon tenure, she realized. A pompous ass who viewed Max's adopted family as hillbilly in-laws. I thought them beneath me. How wrong I was. Seeing the joy on Mei's face, Elaine bit her bottom lip fighting back tears. The tears won.

Dipping under the dividing handrail, the petite Mei hugged Max's wife. "It'll be alright Missy," Mei consoled. "Are men are coming home."

Sniffling Elaine responded, "Please *em gái*, (little sister), call me Elaine."

Beaming Mei said, "You remember your Vietnamese very well... Elaine."

"Just the phases expressing affection for family," Elaine responded wiping her nose. "And Mei, thank you for picking me up, that is very kind."

"It's what family does," Mei said taking charge of the luggage.

Mei navigated the push cart through the airport chaos. Car horns barked. Cabs and limousines wove in and out along the curbside. The swoosh of automatic glass doors released waves of new arrivals into the

761

California sun. In high heels, Elaine fell behind Mei's brisk pace. Mei's destination a light blue Datsun hatchback imposing on a zone designated for shuttle buses. One of L.A.'s finest bickered with an Asian couple. Under the protective charade of language, the middle-aged Vietnamese bowed with dumbfound expressions. The officer stood fast with an impatient pen and citation pad.

"Is there a problem officer?" Elaine asked as Mei pushed the luggage cart beside the car.

The traffic enforcer paused and glanced at Mei and then back to Elaine. Lowering his gaze, he took a pleasant visual journey up the long legs and silk gown of the sultry Misses Kohl. Looking into her deep brown eyes, his used the cocked pen to raise his visor. With a playful smirk, he questioned, "Do you know these people?"

Elaine smiled at the chubby Lan and answered with a soft, "Yes."

"No problem then," he responded. "Just don't delay your exit."

Elaine reached out and flirtatiously grabbed his dark blue sleeve. She felt him flex. I still got it she reasoned. There is a limit to my persuasive powers, she realized. However short waits at restaurants, jumping the queue and of course avoiding parking tickets are still fair game. "Thank you for understanding," she whispered. "We will not be long."

As the officer strutted away, Mei shot Elaine a mischief grin. She understands, Elaine thought acknowledging the Asian beauties smirk with a wink.

Open mouthed, Lan's husband admired Elaine. The short portly man's thinning hair pasted across a balding head with a greasy comb over. In black slacks and short sleeve cotton shirt showing the repairs of mismatching thread, he stood transfixed.

Lan smacked the back of his greasy noggin. "Don't stare," she growled. "It is very rude."

After rubbing his head, he began to load the vehicle.

"Hello Lan," Elaine said apprehensively hugging the tubby Asian.

Lan squeezed her tight. "I sorry I was mean to you," she whispered.

Elaine closed her eyes and returned the affection. Memories of the catty Lan faded. There is a special bond for those who passed through

Saigon in the late fifties. Poor Lan, Elaine reflected. Her crush on Max was obvious. We all wanted to bathe in his protective shadow. I was selfish in those days, she realized. "I'm the one who's sorry," Elaine responded.

Looking over Lan's cotton candy hair, Elaine smiled at Mei. The solicitation prompted Mei to hug her sisters.

As the women broke the group embrace, Lan scowled at a cluster of gawking businessmen. Waving a threatening finger at the voyeurs, Lan barked, "You want to watch show? You need to buy ticket." The dissuaded shuttle passengers hastily refocused their gaze.

Elaine chuckled, the little firecracker still packs a punch, she thought.

CHAPTER FIFTY ONE

A deep blue California sky hung over the Valhalla subdivision. In back of a modest three-bedroom tract home, a six foot tall wood panel fence enclosed a rough yard. The freshly mowed dark green turf infested with cropped weeds. Patches of brown earth peered through flat growth. In a sun-baked corner, a three-foot high chicken-wire enclosure protected Mei's vegetable garden. The neatly furrowed rows of the rectangular plot yielded lettuce, onions, tomatoes and bok choy. On an uncovered slab of concrete, Max, Roche and Buck sat on folding aluminum lawn chairs. Before the arced seating arrangement of webbed furniture, Loc and Va-Meng stood guard over a kettle shaped barbeque grill. Flames danced in and out of a pile of smolder briquettes.

"I'll work hard to repay your kindness brother," Va-Meng said sipping on a cold bottle of Budweiser.

With a pair of long tongs, Loc rearranged the cubes of glowing charcoal. "You and your family are part of the clan. The foul winds of war have drawn us together as one." Loc said to his new employee. "We look out for each other." Glancing over at the white members of the tribe, he added, "Max and Roche helped Mei and I get started in the ice-cream parlor business in Saigon. Roche assisted with our evacuation from Vietnam. That's what family does."

As the tribesmen conversed in their native tongue, Max holding up a long-necked bottle of watered down American beer said to his compadres, "To our friends we left behind."

Roche nodded.

"Yep," Buck answered raising a Styrofoam cup of club soda garnished with lime. "To Mister Jim."

"To Dugan," the three veterans toasted.

"What do you think happened to that thick spectacled hombre?" Buck pondered.

Max shrugged.

Roche leaned back in the patio chair. The webbing creaked. Looking into the summer sky, he smiled and answered softly, "I suspect he's added a few more communist ears to his jewelry collection. But unfortunately do to his age; his highland tenure will not be long."

"It's the path he chose," Max responded.

"He chose death?" Buck questioned.

"No," Max answered. "He chose a glorious death."

The sliding open arcadia glass door interrupted the solemn moment. Angel exited the modest residence. She smiled as she approached her rescuers. Dressed in a pair of blue jeans, flip-flops and simple peasant blouse, she looked like any other blossoming American teen. Standing in front of the men, she looked down. Over her shoulder, Loc and her father observed. Her hand went to her lips to shield a nervous smile. Taking a deep breath, she said slowly in English, "Auntie want to know," she paused and frowned. Looking at Buck, she saw him wink. Grinning she found the word, "Auntie want to know y'all want beer...more beer?"

"Well said lil' darlin," Buck responded. "No thank you."

"You welcome," she responded quickly.

Max handed her an empty amber bottle and said, "Thank you."

"You're welcome," she answered proudly.

Roche handed her an empty container and winked. Giggling she skipped back into the house.

Leaning forward Max frowned and inquired, "Y'all? Ok which one of you Southerners is teaching my niece bad English?"

Buck shrugged, "She sounded find to me." He looked at Roche for clarification.

"She'll be just fine," Roche said, "Va-Meng and his families' transition to the American way of life will be smoother than most refugees."

"Now let me get this straight," Max chuckled. "To welcome our Hmong family to the U.S., we are going to grill meat on an open fire."

"Yep," Buck responded. "The backyard barbeque is a sacred tradition that was perfected in Texas."

"Texas?" Roche questioned. "I'll give you that the slow and low brisket, sausage and ribs of your people are a delicacy, but it falls short of perfection. It lacks Cajun seasoning. For a real open air celebration nothing comes close to a crawfish boil." Licking his lips, he mumbled, "Ah that spicy mixture of crawfish, potatoes, onions and corn."

"*Schweinshaxe!*" Max blurted out. To answer Roche and Buck's bewildered expressions, he translated, "Bavarian roasted pork knuckle." Running his tongue over his teeth, he added, "Cooked until the skin is extra crisp and served with mustard and sauerkraut. Now that gentlemen is one of the finer pleasures of life."

"Hey Loc!" Buck called out interrupting the tribesmen's conversation. "What is on the menu tonight?"

"Chicken," Loc responded. "We are grilling chicken."

The salivating memory of favorite dishes faded.

"Sounds good," Roche politely responded.

"It could have been worse," Max mumbled. "We could be having Spam again."

The comment invoked laughter. The levity faded as Angel served up two ice-cold bottles of brew.

Displaying his Styrofoam cup, Buck said, "It's been ten days. Ten days of sobriety. I've tried before, but this time I'm hopeful." Looking at his colleagues, he nodded. "Thanks to your generous fee for my transportation services. I will be able to eliminate my debts and focus on a clean start. I'm planning to drive back to Texas and pay my daughter a visit." Smiling he added, "She and I used to have a special relationship."

"Good for you cowboy," Roche said. Leaning back in his chair, he pulled on his belt buckle. Displaying a flat stomach, he informed, "As for me, I lost fifteen pounds crossing the fence. Over the years I tried many fad diets. I'm determined to keep it off this time." Chuckling he added, "If you really want to get into shape, all you need to do is smuggle arms into Laos." Looking at the German, he asked, "What does tomorrow look like for you kraut?"

"Our flight is Tuesday," Max answered. "Elaine and I will spend the rest of the weekend with the family and then..." He paused looking skyward. "I will slowly crawl back into the rhythm of middle age." Middle age? He thought, it sounds depressing. It should be viewed as the passage in time that many in my chosen profession will never know. The taste for a soldier growing old needed to be savored and celebrated. He spotted his wife strutting through the arcadia doorway. She was shadowed by Lan. Elaine in a tight pair of designer blue-jeans had surrendered to the Americans' casual taste for fashion. "Let me rephrase that *Ami,*" Max said admiring his spouse's timeless beauty. "Tomorrow looks pretty fucking good."

Elaine stood on the rough concrete deck. Glancing over a cackling Lan, she lifted a Styrofoam cup of chilled white wine and smiled at Max. He winked. There is still hope for this planet, Max thought observing Lan and Elaine reminiscing like long lost friends. Elaine stepped aside as the Hmong boys in white t-shirts and fresh dark blue denim jeans sprinted into the backyard. Corky's pants cuffed high over canvas sneakers. Both boys sporting large Texas belt buckles. The glass barrier was left open. On the balls of bare feet, Mei came prancing out. Her man had returned safely and she beamed with delight. In black pageboy pants and sleeveless cotton blouse, she held a heaping tray of raw marinated chicken. Specks of black and red pepper adorned the fresh poultry. With wide eyes the two Hmong boys studied the mountain of meat.

Jumping to his feet, Max took the tray from the hostess and said, "I got this little sister."

"*Danke,*" she answered mischievously. Turning she solicited the assistance of Buck and Roche to relocate a large wooden picnic table. They centered the blistered wood table on the slab of barren cracked concrete. Va-Meng's wife May La came out with a folded tablecloth. The shy May La seemed confused about the back yard ritual. Angel assisted her timid mother in draping the hard wood. Mei, Lan and Elaine placed turquoise web chairs around the picnic table. The men and boys huddled around the fire.

Loc toppled the charcoal pyramid with the long tongs. Sparks and escaping heat rose above the whitened black cubes. Buck assisted Loc in placing a round grill over the glowing coals. Utilizing the grasping utensil, Loc spun the metal grate. The simple rotation invoked an impressive sigh from Va-Meng and his sons. Initiating the male cooking ritual, Loc slapped a large chicken breast on the parallel metal bars. The meat sizzled. Puzzle pieces of chicken parts slowly filled the cooking surface. Fat dripped and splattered. The aroma of smoked chicken floated into the cloudless sky. Roche placed a hand on Hip-shot's shoulder. Corky looked down to examine for the umpteenth time his belt buckle shaped like the state of Texas. Grinning wide, the boy hooked a finger through one of Buck's belt loops. Nodding slowly, the cowboy playfully rubbed the top of the boy's head. The circle of men and boys stood focused. The grate branded the meat a golden brown. Max took a puff on his cigar. Stepping out of the circle, he looked into the cloudless sky and exhaled a plume of smoke. Elaine approached. He lifted an arm. She accepted the invitation and melted under his protective wing. Affectionately she patted his chest. Behind the wood fenced property divider, a lawnmower coughed to life. To the erratic drone of the neighbor cutting grass, Max realized there are few moments in time when all is right with the world. This is one of them.

CHAPTER FIFTY TWO

The lonely night was cold and quiet. Dugan walked with a limp. Each step a shard of pain tormented his hip. His ears burned. Festered sores and jungle rot nibbled on his tender flesh. A swollen ankle joined in the irritating eroding chorus. I can't blame them, he reasoned stumbling through dense growth. To slow down your predator, you throw out bait. I could not keep up with my Hmong brothers and became sixty-year-old chum. In the decomposing foliage of the dark jungle, he shuffled forward. A starry night sparkled above a small clearing. A fat dry tongue explored cracked parched lips. He stopped. Swaying on wobbly legs, he pulled out his canteen. Sticking out his dry tongue, he hoped for a hidden drop to roll out of the empty container. There was nothing. Releasing his grasp, the hollow metal flask clinked on the moist ground. After a deep breath, he surged forward. Dipping a shoulder, he released the AK-47 slung across his back. Shuffling through the brush, he dropped a cartridge belt. A pistol and combat knife followed. Morning he thought. That is my objective. I don't want to expire in the dark. He staggered in search of the rising sun. His load reduced to a necklace of communist ears dangling over a chest rigging holding three grenades.

"It's over," whispered a firm cold voice.

Dugan ignored the advice. If I'm not going to listen to my own body, why would I accept your counsel, he rationalized.

"Lay down Mister Jim," consoled the soothing advisor.

Dugan paused. A pocket of cold air engulfed him.

"I want to thank you for all your past contributions Mister Jim," The chilled air informed in reference to the trophies around Dugan's neck. "Lay down, your time has come."

"Go to hell," Dugan shouted with a thirsty throat. His blistered lips smiled. Probably not the best insult to sling at the Grim Reaper, he chuckled. Morning he thought. I will shake the specter of death in the sunlight.

The horizon glowed in anticipation of the new day. Dugan exited the forest. He welcomed the lack of cover. His journey was less strenuous. The air was crisp and cool. As it had for the last two-thousand years, the rising sun illuminated thousands of megalithic pots sprinkled across the grass-covered hills. The hollowed out boulders varied in height and diameter from three to ten feet. "The Plain of Jars," a light headed Dugan mumbled admiring the lipped urns of solid rock chiseled by an ancient civilization. Looking down at his shadow, he sighed. The silhouette before him included the Grim Reaper's skeletal presence. Lying down beside a two-ton stone pot, he conceded to death's suggestion. An appropriate tombstone, he thought.

The warming rays felt good. He closed his eyes. The pain faded. Summer sand, he envisioned. Moist cool sand kissed by rolling waves. Feeling tiny cool grains between his toes, he walked along the isolated shoreline. Soft waves lapped at his feet. Shallow breaths filled his nostrils with a salty sea breeze. The beach was bleach white. A luminous blue ocean rippled under a red morning sky.

A sharp poke in the side disrupted Dugan's seaside journey. Blurred yellow faces wearing bulbous communist caps bobbed in and out of his purview. A khaki uniformed thief removed his boots. The gun barrel of an AK-47 lifted up the cartilage necklace around his neck.

Dugan grinned at the rabid barking pack. "Can I interest you in Pepsi and a line of Pepsi products?" he mumbled to the irate faces floating before him.

A hard slap across his face answered the query.

Casually Dugan reached inside his chest rigging. His numb hand grasped for hope. Victoriously he felt metal rings sliding down his dancing fingers. It was meant to be, he thought.

"Fuck me?" he questioned with a low growl. Pulling the pins on three grenades, he smiled wide and mumbled to the harsh audience, "Fuck you."

***

Acknowledgments

I am most grateful to my wife, Sharon. Her belief in the cigar smoking Max from the initial outline sparked the epic endeavor. Her assistance as editor, researcher and ally gave much-needed support to an unpublished husband.

Many thanks to Mark Nobile, Jamie Marshall, Jan Ghelfi, Jeff Erhart, Catherine Ivy, and Diane Bertrand, all who treaded through very rough initial drafts. Their observations, encouragement, and some of their criticisms assisted in shaping the final text. An acknowledgment goes to Kurt Lefteroff for his insights into the German language and culture.

Lastly, I'd like to thank my mother, Mary for her unbiased praise.

CPSIA information can be obtained at www.ICGtesting.com
Printed in the USA
LVOW11s1412110414

381353LV00010B/105/P